ANNE SCHMIDT

The *Women* of *Pinecraft*

Three Florida Mennonite Romances

BARBOUR
PUBLISHING

A Stranger's Gift © 2011 by Anna Schmidt
A Sister's Forgiveness © 2012 by Anna Schmidt
A Mother's Promise © 2012 by Anna Schmidt

Print ISBN 978-1-62836-211-4

eBook Editions:
Adobe Digital Edition (.epub) 978-1-63058-109-1
Kindle and MobiPocket Edition (.prc) 978-1-63058-110-7

All scripture quotations are taken from the King James Version of the Bible.

Additional scripture quotations are from The Holy Bible, English Standard Version®, copyright © 2001 by Crossway Bibles, a publishing ministry of Good News Publishers. Used by permission. All rights reserved.

This book is a work of fiction. Names, characters, places, and incidents are either products of the author's imagination or used fictitiously. Any similarity to actual people, organizations, and/or events is purely coincidental.

For more information about Anna Schmidt, please access the author's website at the following Internet address: www.booksbyanna.com

Published by Barbour Publishing, Inc., P.O. Box 719, Uhrichsville, OH 44683, www.barbourbooks.com

Our mission is to publish and distribute inspirational products offering exceptional value and biblical encouragement to the masses.

 Member of the
Evangelical Christian
Publishers Association

Printed in the United States of America.

A Stranger's Gift

Dedication

Blessed are the poor in spirit:
for theirs is the kingdom of heaven.
MATTHEW 5:3

For Ella & Grace.
For Ivan & Merle.
And with special gratitude,
this book is also dedicated to
Doris, Rosanna & Tanya.

Part One

*When your fear cometh as desolation, and
your destruction cometh as a whirlwind. . .*
PROVERBS 1:27

*I went to the woods because I wished to live
deliberately. . .and see if I could not learn
what [life] had to teach us.*
HENRY DAVID THOREAU, *WALDEN: LIFE IN THE WOODS*

Hurricane Hester
Headed for Sarasota

*Monster hurricane expected to smash Gulf Coast
Florida within forty-eight hours.*

*Hurricane Hester is expected to make landfall
by late Friday afternoon. The dangerous storm is
predicted to bring potentially devastating storm
surges and dangerous high winds well in excess of
one hundred miles per hour. Home and business
owners are urged to secure all property and prepare
to move inland as soon as possible. Once the
hurricane makes landfall, the storm is expected to
weaken, but there remains the strong potential for
heavy flooding and tornadoes. As a precaution,
those residents living inland near any body of
water including creeks and canals are advised to be
prepared to evacuate and stay alert.*

Chapter 1

Wisps of Hester Detlef's ebony hair escaped her stiff mesh prayer covering, tickling her face as she unloaded boxes of canned goods from the back of a van. In the Mennonite and Amish community of Pinecraft, within the greater borders of Sarasota, several women had formed a kind of bucket line to pass the boxes to other women waiting at a line of tables set end to end along the protected walkway of the shopping mall. The increasingly strong wind whipped at the ankle-length skirts the women wore, reminding them that in spite of the blue skies, a hurricane lurked just a few miles offshore. Hester had just received news that the entire Gulf Coast, from Fort Myers north to Tampa–St. Petersburg, was under a hurricane watch—meaning that within the next thirty-six hours, it was entirely possible that the storm could move into their area. But with the predicted storm stalled several miles offshore, things could go either way. The hurricane might simply have paused to gather strength before moving east. Or it could weaken to a tropical storm that would bring heavy rains and some wind but nothing like the devastation that a category three or four hurricane might deliver.

"Hester? Shouldn't you let someone else handle this and see

to more pressing matters?" Olive Crowder was a large-boned woman of indeterminate age with a permanent expression of disapproval etched into her face. She had never married, and her constant companion was her younger sister, Agnes, a gentle soul who seemed immune to Olive's generally sour demeanor. The sisters were dedicated members of the conservative Mennonite congregation where Hester's father, Arlen, served as senior minister. While women did not usually assume roles of appointed or elected leadership in their church, Olive came as close as any woman ever could to having declared herself an elder of the congregation—the gatekeeper for all things traditional.

Often when Hester was in grade school and other girls were busy learning homemaking skills, she had tested her teachers with her questions about why certain things happened the way they did.

"But why?" she would ask when the answer she got was dismissive or unsatisfactory.

It was that insatiable curiosity coupled with her stubborn determination to explore as much of God's world as possible that made her stand out in a community where sameness was not only preferred but also expected. It was that same insatiable curiosity that had brought her under the microscope of Olive Crowder's concern.

"Getting these food goods sorted and packed is a priority right now, Olive," Hester said, forcing herself to smile.

"Well, you know best, I suppose. After all, you are the lead volunteer for MCC in this area."

The Mennonite Central Committee—or MCC—was a national organization dedicated to offering disaster relief, community development, and international aid with no concern for whether or not those who received that aid were Mennonite. The mission of the organization was to build a worldwide community of people connected by their love and respect for God, each other, and all of God's creation. Following her mother's death, Hester had put her career as a registered nurse on hold indefinitely and volunteered to manage the agency's work in and around Pinecraft.

"After all," Olive continued, "Emma has gone straight to the shelters to oversee the work there."

Emma Keller had once been Hester's closest friend, but the two of them had grown apart after Hester decided to attend nursing school in Illinois. Emma now held the position of local leader of the more conservative Christian Aid Ministries. CAM was the agency that Olive—not to mention several other members of Arlen Detlef's congregation—had suggested might be a more appropriate venue from which a conservative minister's daughter might pursue her desire to serve.

"I understand your concern, Olive, and believe me, I would really love to be able to be in more than one place at the same time. So I am truly grateful that Emma and others have taken on other projects like preparing the shelters." Hester turned back to her work. "With everyone doing their part, we should have things pretty well covered."

Olive stood rooted to her spot in the line of volunteers scowling down at Hester until Hester noticed that others were beginning to wonder what was going on. "Besides, Emma and I will both be attending the volunteer organizational meeting at command central later this morning, so I'll be sure to check in with her then. In the meantime, if you wouldn't mind. . ." She handed a box of canned goods to Olive and nodded toward the woman waiting to receive them and pass them on. Olive's lips thinned into a sharp straight line. "Just because you see this as your little hurricane, Hester, it would behoove—"

"My little hurricane?"

"*Ja*. Hurricane Hester," Olive replied and then turned back to her work.

Certainly Hester could see the irony of a hurricane with her name. Even before she'd learned that this season's eighth hurricane was to bear her name, others had compared her can-do personality to the massive fury of a hurricane. She certainly did not aspire to be linked to something so destructive, but she had to admit that once she latched on to a cause that she believed in, there was no stopping her.

As soon as the van was unloaded and the women began filling smaller cartons with a selection of canned goods, Hester retrieved her bicycle from behind the distribution center. Promising to return as soon as possible, she pedaled off toward downtown Sarasota. At the corner of Highway 41 and Bahia Vista, she waited for the light to change, tapping one foot on the ground as she balanced her bike. Her foot tapping was not an indication of impatience. She was simply filled with energy, ready to face whatever Mother Nature might bring in the hours and days ahead. Hester Detlef was like a warrior prepared to go into combat.

She couldn't help but smile at that thought. Her Mennonite faith had taught her to be peace loving and to avoid conflict, but there was indeed a battle coming in the form of a hurricane that bore her name. The only question was where the storm would focus the brunt of its attack.

Hester had lived her entire life in this area, and she knew that the city of Sarasota with Pinecraft in its midst was an unlikely target. Protected by a line of barrier islands, the mainland rarely suffered a direct hit. Most hurricanes weakened over land so that by the time the storm passed over the islands and reached the mainland, it would likely be demoted to a tropical storm. And because the Amish/Mennonite community lay another five miles inland, it was even less likely that her friends and neighbors would suffer direct damage. But Pinecraft's position on Philippi Creek always carried the threat of flooding. If the hurricane hit shore from a certain direction, it could push waters inland, and she and her neighbors living along the creek would be forced to move to shelters. Whatever the storm's path, it was due to make its move within the next thirty-six hours.

The light changed, and she pedaled on. Down Bahia Vista to Orange Avenue, past the beautiful Selby Botanical Gardens and around the curve where the road ran parallel to the bay. How she loved this part of the city. As a girl, when her friends were busy tending kitchen gardens or joining their mothers for quilting bees, Hester would slip away to wade in the calm clear waters of the bay.

She never tired of observing the wonders of sea life she saw there—jellyfish and sea anemones that looked like transparent floating flowers and the occasional and rare live horse conch, its outer shell black and almost indistinguishable from the beds of oyster shells that at low tide clacked like castanets. Sometimes as she waded through ankle-deep clear water, she would spot a flash of orange as vivid as the skin of a tangerine and would carefully turn the blackened conch shell over to reveal the strikingly colorful animal coiled inside. To this day, seeing a seashell that still housed a crab or sea animal made her smile and, as the old adage stated, was all the assurance she needed that God was in His heaven and all was right with the world. But she had no time for wading this day. She was already late for her meeting.

John Steiner leaned in closer to the battery-powered radio on the kitchen counter as it crackled and wheezed out the latest weather update. ". . .Hurricane watch. . . Prepare for evacuation of barrier islands and bay-front homes and businesses. . . ."

Reports from early that morning had the hurricane stalled offshore and unlikely to make landfall for another day or so. He had time. Time to board up the last of the windows. Time to double-check his emergency supplies. Time to cage the chickens and get them to safety. He would ride out the storm right here on the property into which he had sunk two years of his life and most of his money renovating.

He ignored the warnings to move to higher ground. He wasn't going anywhere. Since he'd moved to Florida, there had been other orders to evacuate, and they had all come to nothing. On one such occasion shortly after he'd moved in, John had complied only to find himself crowded into some shelter with hundreds of others. For his trouble, he had spent a miserable night among crying babies, unruly children allowed to roam free, and adults who did nothing but complain. He would not leave again.

After nailing a piece of plywood over the last of the windows, he walked down to his pier and closed his eyes as the hot August wind buffeted his shirt and ruffled the red-blond hair on his forearms. It might have been any Florida summer day—hot, gusty winds from the west, humidity so thick it was like being draped in a towel soaked in hot bathwater, and a blinding sun set high in a relentlessly blue sky. It was hard to believe that in just a matter of hours this could all change to blackness and pounding waves and water walls that could topple trees and power lines, rip off roofs, and set mobile homes as well as cars and trucks afloat or flying through the air.

John was surprised that what he was feeling wasn't apprehension but rather anticipation. He was excited. He opened his eyes and saw his neighbor Margery Barker puttering his way in her small fishing boat.

"Came to see if you're ready," she called, throwing him the rope to tie her boat up at his pier.

The woman had a voice like a foghorn and the leathered skin of a native Floridian. She ran a fishing charter business about a quarter mile up Philippi Creek around the point from John's place on Little Sarasota Bay. She'd taken it over from her husband after his death thirteen years earlier, and she'd been the first person John had met when he came to Florida. Without the slightest encouragement from John, she had designated herself his surrogate mother from that day to this. She meant well, but like him, she could be stubborn and refused to back down from her zealous campaign to get him involved in "community," as she liked to call it.

"All secured," John replied, catching his end of the rope and looping it around a post. He jerked his head toward the house, its windows now shuttered with plywood.

Margery had scrambled out of the boat and was standing on the pier surveying his house and the old packinghouse, her hands on her hips. "Looks good," she said. "Where you gonna ride this thing out?"

16

Her question annoyed John. The two of them had discussed this when the hurricane had first started to form. "Here," he replied with a wave toward the house.

Margery hooted. "Are you nuts or just plain naive?"

Neither, John wanted to snap, but instead he bit his lip and glanced out across the bay to the inland shore of Siesta Key. He had learned quickly enough that it did no good to argue with Margery.

"I guess that it's unlikely you'll take a direct hit," she reasoned, more to herself than to him. "And I suppose if you've never been in one of these things, you can't help but wonder what it'll be like."

"I've been here through two hurricane seasons, Margery. That first year I even left for the shelter. I am not leaving again."

She frowned and then turned back to her boat and knelt down to retrieve two large containers of water. "I figured as much, so I brought you some extra supplies."

"I've got five jugs of drinking water," John protested.

"Well, you might just want to wash up a bit." She sniffed the air around him. "Truth be told, you could do with a shower *now.*"

"I've been working," he protested, resisting the urge to tell her she didn't smell like lavender water herself.

Margery sighed. "You are a serious one, aren't you, Johnny? After this storm blows through, we are going to have to find some way to get you to loosen up, son." She shook her head as if he were a lost cause and climbed back into her boat and unleashed it from the post. "I baked you some of those chocolate chip cookies you seem to like." She tossed him a cookie tin and eased her boat away from his pier. "Stay high and dry," she called as she rounded the point.

John used the stubs of his fingernails to pry open the tin box and took out one cookie. He bit into it, savoring the taste— and with it the childhood memory of his mother's baking. He hadn't thought to ask where Margery planned to stay during the hurricane. The houseboat where she lived would not be much protection against the winds, and her bait shack was no sturdier than a beach shack. She'd probably head for one of the shelters. He suddenly felt guilty that she had wasted precious time coming to check on him. He stepped farther out onto the pier and shouted her name. "Be safe," he yelled.

Margery just waved and kept going.

Hester arrived fifteen minutes late for the meeting. This was the county's effort to coordinate response activities for all emergency response volunteer leaders from across the entire Sarasota County area. She was there to represent the two largest Mennonite organizations—the Mennonite Central Committee or MCC, for which she was the local representative, and the Mennonite Disaster Service, better known in the community as MDS. Her father was the local director of that agency, and with the hurricane predicted to scythe a wide swath across the Gulf Coast of Florida, both agencies would have their work cut out for them in the days following the storm. Emma would represent CAM, the third arm of a trio of Mennonite agencies.

She parked her bike in a rack and mentally rehearsed the report she was prepared to give. MCC was ready to supply food, water, and shelter for those hundreds of volunteers sure to come once the storm passed over, not to mention those poor souls who might be directly affected by the storm. She had a mobile clinic ready to go into action as a backup to the one the Red Cross was already setting up. There were three large shelters in and around Pinecraft outfitted with cots and generators and other necessities to care for those who had no place to go. Along with MDS teams, her volunteers were fully prepared to go into action helping victims of the storm recover and rebuild in the weeks and months ahead should the storm be as disastrous as was predicted. She stepped into the small foyer of the county's administrative building and took a moment to allow her eyes to adjust to the change from the blistering late-August sun to the cooler shadows inside, then followed the sound of voices down the hall.

But when she opened the door, prepared to make her

apologies as she took her place at the long table at the front of the room, she stopped. Emma Keller stood at the lectern delivering the report for all three Mennonite agencies. Hester squeezed her eyes closed and silently prayed for God to take away the pang of jealousy she felt toward the woman. After all, she and Emma were working toward the same goal. What was the matter with her? Emma was not her competition. There had been a time when they had been the best of friends. But God must have been busy elsewhere, for when she opened her eyes, she still felt a prickle of rivalry as she listened to Emma deliver her report. Hester slipped into a vacant seat at the back of the room and waited her turn to fill in anything Emma might have left out—a scenario so unlikely as to be laughable, knowing how thorough Emma was in tackling any project.

Reports from other local volunteer groups followed, and then the professional hurricane experts and meteorologists got up to give their reports. Hester shook off her jealousy and focused on taking notes to share with her father and other volunteers. Emma slid into the seat next to her.

"*Es tut mir leid*," she apologized, her voice a whisper. "They called for the report from Pinecraft first thing."

"*Ich verstehe*," Hester murmured and glanced at Emma, who was looking at her with genuine concern. "Really, it's fine," Hester assured her and grasped Emma's hand.

Emma's smile was radiant with relief. Hester had to ask herself if she had become so territorial when it came to where her volunteer efforts and Emma's overlapped that her good friend felt she had to tiptoe around Hester's feelings.

"*Kaffee?*" Hester whispered conspiratorially in an attempt to break the tension that stretched between them.

As teenagers, the two of them had often saved their money and slipped away to share a cup of cappuccino at one of the sidewalk cafés that dotted Main Street in downtown Sarasota. There they would sit for hours, gossiping and giggling and dreaming about their futures as they ignored the gawkers who stopped to stare at their prayer coverings and distinctive Mennonite style of dressing. It had been far too long since they had shared such a moment—years had gone by. Emma had married Lars, her childhood sweetheart, and they had two wonderful children. Hester had gone to nursing school and then come home to find her mother dying the slow, horrible death that followed a diagnosis of Lou Gehrig's disease.

To Hester's surprise, Emma's large blue eyes filled with tears. She smiled and nodded. "Ja, once this storm passes, coffee would be *wunderbar*," she replied, her voice breaking.

Hester couldn't help wondering if perhaps she'd become so wrapped up in herself that she had failed to appreciate that her friend might miss her as much as she had been missing Emma. "Hey," she whispered, gripping Emma's hand tighter. "It's okay. We're okay." To her relief, Emma smiled.

A lively discussion followed the reports, and the room was electric with anticipation and not a little fear for what the hurricane might leave in its wake. The news was not good. All the experts agreed that the watch status would change to a warning before the day was out. A warning meant the hurricane would be expected to hit within twenty-four hours. According to their best indicators, the only good news was that the storm might yet continue to stall offshore, buying them more time. One meteorologist had confirmed that once the storm came across the islands, it could weaken significantly before it hit Sarasota, but those barrier islands—Siesta, Lido, and Longboat Key— were in the storm's direct path.

Following the meeting, as members of the group broke out into clusters to compare notes, Emma went to the side table where coffee and tea had been set up and got Hester a paper cup filled with two-thirds coffee and one-third cream, just the way she liked it.

"Thanks." Hester took a sip and grinned. "This will do for now, but once this is all over, I'm going to hold you to the promise of a latte on Main Street."

"Just name the time and place," Emma said, sipping her own black coffee. "I've missed you, my friend."

"Ja. Me, too."

The two of them sat knee to knee on the hard metal folding chairs of the county meeting room as they made lists of what each agency would be responsible for so there would be no duplication of services and everything could be covered. They had to prepare for the worst. If necessary, Emma's group would take charge at the three shelters, while Hester's volunteers would feed the army of volunteers from Mennonite churches in surrounding states and as far away as the upper Midwest. Once the initial needs were met, everyone would pitch in to manage the long-term work of cleaning up and rebuilding.

"Sounds like a plan," Emma said as she put away her notebook and finished her coffee.

"How are the kids?" Hester asked.

"They are growing up so fast. Matt is completely wrapped up in soccer. Can you believe that Sadie is going to be sixteen years old? She and her cousin, Tessa, are as inseparable as Jeannie and I were at that age," she said, referring to her younger sister.

"Okay, now you're making me feel ancient. I mean, it seems like just yesterday they were babies."

Emma crumpled her empty cup and nodded. "I know. Can you believe it? Jeannie says that her Tessa is sweet and so reliable just like me, and I tell her just wait. Sadie was a sweetheart at that age as well."

"They'll be fine," Hester said. "Look at who they got for mothers."

"And what about you?" Emma asked as the two of them headed down the corridor.

Hester shrugged. "Not much to tell."

"Really?" Emma's eyebrows arched.

"Oh, you mean Samuel Brubaker?" It was like old times the way she had read Emma's question without her friend needing to explain.

"Oh, you mean Samuel Brubaker," Emma said, mimicking her too-casual tone. Samuel was a young carpenter who had come to Florida for a visit and been recruited by Hester's father to stay and work with him in his carpentry business. And there wasn't a person in Pinecraft who didn't think that Arlen's real motive in hiring the Pennsylvania carpenter was to promote a potential romance with Hester.

"Come on. Tell me the truth. Do you like him?"

"He's nice," Hester said as she drained the last of her coffee and let it burn its way down her throat.

"I see. Well, take some advice from an old friend and don't settle, Hester. He might be a fine man, a good provider and all, but if you don't feel. . ."

"Oh, Emma, I don't know what I feel. It's all come about so suddenly, and I know Papa has the best of intentions and only wants my happiness, but. . ."

"And are you happy as you are?"

Hester shrugged. "I love my work. . . ." She sighed as a realization dawned on her. "So much so that when I saw you up there giving our report today, I felt threatened, like something could be taken away from me. It was the strangest feeling."

"You have no reason to feel that way, Hester. You're one of those people who truly cares for others, who thinks nothing of putting her own life on hold to help someone in trouble or pain. You have a rare gift, my friend."

Embarrassed yet touched by Emma's praise, Hester held the door for her friend as they stepped out into weather that had already begun to change. The traffic was bumper to bumper, and all headed east away from the shore and the sky that was beginning to change from brilliant blue to ominous gray.

"I have the car," Emma said. "We could put your bike in the trunk."

"*Nein, danke*. I'll be fine. I want to go by the bay once more, you know, in case things change." As she pedaled off, she silently thanked God that she and Emma had found their way back to the friendship they had treasured for so many years.

Chapter 2

If Hester thought traffic had been bad on her way to the meeting, it was nothing compared to the jammed streets and impatient drivers she saw on her way back to Pinecraft. Clearly people had taken the evacuation order to heart in spite of the fact that in the past such evacuations had often been an exercise in futility when the hurricanes missed them completely. As a light changed and Hester eased her bike into the crosswalk, a pickup truck hurtled within inches of her as the driver rushed to make an illegal left turn. Car horns blared a belated warning, and she hesitated. Hester could see panic eroding what she could only assume were the normally pleasant features of the driver.

"Move it or lose it, honey," another driver yelled from the open window of her car as she edged forward to make a right turn. The woman glanced up at the sky, her eyes wide as if she thought the hurricane might well appear full-blown at any second and wash them all out to sea.

The crossing lights were with Hester the rest of the way, although the parade of traffic headed east did not slacken in the least. She was faster on her bicycle than any of the motorized vehicles she passed. Just as she slid her bike to a stop at the small prefabricated building that served as the local MCC headquarters for collecting donations and distributing supplies, she heard a car horn and someone calling her name.

"Hey, Hester, your hurricane looks like it might be pretty impressive!" She turned to see Grady Forrest, the director of the county's disaster-relief program, leaning out the window of his Jeep and grinning. He pulled into the gas station lot across the street from the center and got out. It had been Grady who'd suggested that she volunteer to serve as the area representative to MCC.

"Guess I'll have to treat you with a little more respect," he added as he dodged traffic and jaywalked across the busy street. "I wanted to touch base with you at the meeting, but you were out of there before I could break away. How are things coming here?" He nodded toward the open door of the MCC building.

"I expect we'll see the first volunteer teams from up north start to arrive within hours after the storm hits," Hester said. "We got word that there are groups on their way from Ohio, Indiana, and—"

"That's great, Hester." Grady glanced at his shoes and then up at the sky, clearly gathering his thoughts—or was it his nerve? "Actually, I have a request. . . ." He paused. "There's this. . .thing. After I missed you at the meeting, I drove over here to ask you to help me with what could be a delicate situation."

"How can I help?" The volunteers from all three Mennonite groups would be expected to focus first on the elderly, the infirm, and the underinsured—regardless of their faith or politics. For the county's coordinator of disaster relief to ask for their help was evidence that their agencies were every bit as well regarded as the Red Cross or other more well-known relief agencies. She looked at him curiously. "Our volunteer cup runneth over," she teased, but Grady did not smile at the pun. "Hey, just tell us what we can do."

"Not 'we'—you. I want to do this quietly if possible."

Hester felt a tingle of alarm. "I don't understand."

"There's this one guy out on the point just down from the mouth of the creek where it empties into Little Sarasota Bay."

The creek was Philippi Creek, the meandering stream that wound its way from the intercoastal waters that separated the mainland from Siesta Key eastward through the very heart of Pinecraft and beyond. It was that very creek that posed the greatest threat to the residents of Pinecraft. If it flooded, dozens of people right in her own community could be displaced. "You mean Tucker's Point?"

Grady nodded. "His name's John Steiner. Came here a couple of years ago from the Midwest, as I understand it, and bought the old Tucker place. He's been renovating the property. Word has it that he plans to revive the old packinghouse."

"Okay," Hester said, wondering where this conversation was going and wishing Grady would come to the point.

"Apparently he's also done a fair amount of planting—fruit trees, veggies, and the like. Somebody mentioned that he'd just started keeping chickens." He shook his head. "You'd think the man was living out in the country miles from any neighbor instead of just across the creek from a large condominium complex."

Hester studied her friend for a long moment. "Who is this man, Grady?"

"Well, now there's the interesting part. Seems that he's the grandson of the late Thomas E. Carter. Remember? He was the speaker of the house, and this guy's aunt took the old man's seat in Congress after he retired. She just happens to serve on the House Subcommittee on Homeland Security and is a close friend of my boss, who is planning a run for Congress himself, which is why this landed on my plate."

Hester nodded, although the convoluted government bureaucracy of the outside world remained a mystery to her. "So this congresswoman called you?"

"Worse. She called my boss and his boss, and, well, the message is pretty clear that we need to make sure this guy Steiner knows what he's in for if he stays. Ideally we need to persuade him to head for the nearest shelter."

"That's not our mission," she reminded Grady.

"I know. That's why I'm asking for a special favor. If he

decides to stay and then gets hit, I really can't put everything on hold to rescue him, or we'll be labeled another Katrina by the media. Could you just go out there and quietly check it out?"

"I guess. . ." she said reluctantly. "Why me?"

Grady ducked his head. "Steiner is Amish—or was. I didn't get the whole story yet." He grinned. "So, a woman's touch?"

"I'm Mennonite, not Amish."

"Close enough."

She fingered one of the ties of her prayer covering. Perhaps doing this for Grady was one way of atoning for her bout of green-eyed envy at the meeting earlier. "All right."

Obviously relieved, Grady took out a map of the area where Philippi Creek flowed into Little Sarasota Bay. He tapped the point that jutted out into the bay across from Siesta Key. "Word has it that he's left the road in pretty overgrown, so it might be best to go down the creek from here. Margery Barker can help with that. She's already tried to get the guy to leave but to no avail."

So much for a woman's touch.

As a prelude to the storm, the rain had started to fall in a steady downpour while John was having his supper. He was just finishing when there was a loud pounding on his front door. He knew what this was. No doubt the authorities had come to order him to evacuate. According to the latest data, the beast that had been lurking offshore for days had awakened and was stretching its tentacles toward the west coast of Florida. Throughout the day he'd been aware of the ceaseless stream of traffic crossing over the Stickney Point Bridge as the residents of Siesta Key fled to safety. It was past time to go if he was going, which he wasn't.

Fueled by his determination to stand his ground, John pulled open the door, prepared to state his case, but found himself speechless. Instead of the uniformed muscleman he'd been expecting, there was a young Mennonite woman clinging to her skirt and trying without much success to hold the hood of her raincoat over her stiff white *kapp*. "John Steiner?" she shouted above the wind.

Dumbly he nodded, and the woman strode right past him into his house.

"I'm Hester Detlef with the Mennonite Central Committee," she said as the wind slammed the door. With most of the remaining daylight blocked out by the plywood covering the windows and only the battery-powered lamp on the kitchen table for illumination, it was hard to gauge her expression, but certainly her posture even in silhouette as well as that bossy tone spoke volumes. The irony that a woman named Hester had appeared on his doorstep at the same time that a hurricane by the same name was headed his way had not escaped him. "You really need to leave now," she added.

"No, ma'am. *You* need to leave now," John replied, forcing his voice to remain calm as he retraced his steps and prepared to open the door for her.

"Apparently your aunt is worried about you," she continued. "So worried that she has contacted the local head of county government, who in turn has directed the director of the county's emergency management program to make sure that you get to safety."

John made a show of glancing around. "Well, I don't see anybody from the county or my aunt, and I am not leaving."

To his surprise, she began rummaging through the pockets of her rain jacket until she unearthed a notepad and pencil. "That's your decision?"

"It is, and. . ."

She thrust the paper and pencil at him. "Then please write that down and date and sign it."

She was giving up? Just like that? What had happened to the do-gooder Mennonites he'd known back in Indiana? The ones who quietly went about the work of helping others and did not leave until the work was finished? This woman had been sent to get him to evacuate, and yet. . .

She pushed the paper and pencil toward him again. "Either

write the statement or come with me right now," she said. "Those are your choices, and I don't have time to debate the merits of one over the other."

He grabbed the paper from her and scrawled out a one-sentence message. *I'm staying on my property.* Then he signed it with a flourish and handed it back to her.

"Date it," she said. Only after he complied did she accept the paper. She folded it carefully and headed for the door. "Last chance," she said quietly, her hand on the doorknob.

He reached around her to open the door, bracing it with his shoulder against the force of the wind, taking note that the rain had stopped and there was some light in the western sky. The storm might well swing to the north or south and miss them entirely. "Good day, Hester."

She glanced up at him, and in the fading but yet stronger daylight after the dark of the barricaded house, he was stunned to see genuine concern in her expression. "You really should leave," she said. "This is the real thing."

In the bay behind her, John saw Margery idling her boat near his pier. Irritated that his neighbor had interfered in his life once more, he stepped back inside his house and closed the door. Then he stood next to the door, listening. A moment later he heard the throttle of Margery's boat, and then he was alone. He went back to his radio and, despite the static, received the news that the watch had changed to a warning.

In all the time that John had occupied the point of land that jutted out from the mainland into the mouth of Little Sarasota Bay, there had been only two other times when a hurricane watch had turned to a warning. Both storms had missed Sarasota and its protective barrier islands, but neither had come close to the power that this one was predicted to be. John felt a surge of adrenaline as he digested the storm's change in status and mentally went over his checklist. Every window was securely covered. He'd gathered ample supplies—drinking water, first-aid kit, a change of clothes, and nonperishable food. He had enough to cover his needs even if he got stuck here for several days.

That was a distinct possibility. His property had stood abandoned for years before he'd bought it and started renovating the main house, the packinghouse, and a variety of other outbuildings. The work had gone slowly because he was determined to do it all himself. He had deliberately ignored the overgrown lane that led to the house from the road, preferring to access his land by kayak so as to discourage visitors until he had the place ready for business. But getting in or out by water might prove impossible depending on the path of the storm.

Still, John had come to this place to prove to himself—and to others—that it was possible to live a strict Amish life in the midst of the outside world. Even the battery-powered radio was stretching the boundaries, but it was the one concession he had made to Margery after the last hurricane. He picked up his Bible and his dog-eared copy of Henry David Thoreau's *Walden: Life in the Woods*. The book had been a favorite of his mother's, and other than his Bible, it was the only book he had brought with him to Florida. It had also been at the root of his break with his Amish community—or theirs with him.

After his father died, John's interest in Thoreau's ideas of living a completely self-sustaining and separate life had increased. Thoreau's experiment seemed to John to go beyond even the strict traditions of separateness practiced by those of his faith. His zeal for Thoreau's idea had been his undoing in the tightly knit Amish community where he had grown up. Stubborn like his mother, John had stood his ground, and she alone had stood with him. And then his mother had died, and he found himself standing utterly alone.

He washed his supper dishes. Then he made a final survey of his emergency supplies. Satisfied that he had everything within his reach that he might need to ride out the storm, he picked up his Bible and let it fall open one last time. He closed his eyes, praying for guidance, and let his finger run down the page to whatever passage of scripture God might choose for him.

"And seek the peace of the city whither I have caused you to be

carried away captives, and pray unto the LORD for it: for in the peace thereof shall ye have peace."

His Bible had fallen open to the book of Jeremiah, the twenty-ninth chapter. His finger had stopped on verse 7. It seemed an odd message—in some ways appropriate yet in others a mystery. He was hardly a captive. John considered finding another random passage, but that would be like saying God had not guided him to this one. He marked the page with the red ribbon bookmark, and then placed his Bible and Thoreau's book into a plastic bag that had once held nuts delivered by Margery the previous spring and zipped it shut. Whatever the meaning of the verse, he was prepared to face whatever came.

He checked the clock and saw that he had a couple of hours yet before dark. Outside, he stood on his porch and let the wind and rain take their licks at him. He surveyed his property—perhaps some of it for the last time, depending on which way the storm hit. In between remodeling the house and cleaning up what remained of the abandoned orange groves, he'd started planting what he would need to sustain himself. Near the house he'd put in a large garden of herbs and vegetables in the Japanese raised-bed style that he'd read about. He'd also added to Tucker's groves, planting a variety of kiwi, orange, lemon, lime, and mango trees, carefully orchestrated to give him a harvest during most of the year. More recently he'd bought a couple of laying hens to supplement the steady diet of fish he'd been living on since arriving in Florida.

The chickens! He'd forgotten all about them. The rain had let up some, but the sky had a sickly yellowish-green cast to it, and the air was heavy with moisture. The winds were already gathering strength. *It's coming too fast,* John thought as he took precious seconds to pause and consider the rapidly rising level of the intercoastal waterway and creek. This storm was definitely on the move.

Oversized raindrops plopped onto his head and shoulders, and within seconds the intermittent drops turned once again into an opaque curtain of pelting rain that had accompanied the

Mennonite woman's arrival earlier. Visibility beyond his hand in front of him was nearly impossible. Too late he covered his head with the hood of his slicker and stumbled on toward the chicken coop. In spite of his muscular six-foot frame, he had to fight to maintain his balance in the wind that had every tree on the property swaying in a ghoulish dance.

On the far side of the house he spotted one piece of plywood that had come loose from a window. Grabbing a large rock, he tried without success to hammer it back into place. Repeatedly the weight of the wood in tandem with the power of the wind threw him against the house, and when he heard the glass shatter, he dropped the board and focused on making it across the yard to the chicken coop.

The chickens were in full panic as John tried to corral them into a wire cage. They squawked in protest and pecked at his hands. He'd been stupid to wait so long to take them to shelter, but he'd gotten caught up in trying to protect the house and dealing with Margery and the Mennonite woman. He'd been sure that he had time, that he would know when the storm was about to hit.

"Come on, ladies," he muttered as he tried in vain to catch the hens. Just then he heard the ear-splitting shriek of metal torn from the roof of the coop. John heard more glass shatter as the metallic missile apparently found its target. He looked up in time to see a giant royal palm sway drunkenly for a moment. "Tucker's folly," the realtor had called this place, noting that this specific breed of palm was not made to withstand the winds of a strong tropical storm, much less a hurricane, but Tucker had planted them anyway, wanting to mark the location of his citrus business with something uniquely tropical. Now, decades later, a double row of the giant palms lined each side of the lane that ran from the house out to the main road.

As John watched, the tree seemed to find its balance, and then, as if in slow motion, it started to fall right toward the open roof of the coop.

"You're on your own," he shouted at the squawking hens as he raced out of the coop and tripped over his kayak. The vessel had apparently come loose from its bonds and flown halfway across the yard. So much for properly securing everything. He stumbled for several feet and then fell. And as he covered his head with both hands, the falling tree missed him by inches. Entreating God to keep him safe, John scrambled the rest of the way back to the main house, half crawling and half running for what he hoped would be safety.

It took him what seemed an hour but was probably no more than a couple of minutes to force the door closed and block it with the vintage desk he'd inherited with the house. Breathless and battered, soaked through with perspiration and rain, he sank to the floor, hugging his knees to his chest like he had as a boy whenever he was frightened. From outside he could hear the wail of the wind. The thunder rumbled an apocalyptic chorus in concert with the rain, which seemed to offer its own brand of percussionist accompaniment. It felt as if the house were shifting on its foundation as the walls groaned in protest. Florida homes did not have basements, and John had foolishly thought the heavy oak table would be enough to protect him. As he huddled against the wall, John had to admit that his decision to stay had been born of sheer stubbornness. Perhaps Margery and the Mennonite woman had been messengers, messengers he had ignored. He took out his Bible from its protective plastic and clutched it to his chest as he awaited his fate.

Hour after hour on through the night, the wind howled like a banshee, and the rain stoned the house relentlessly. And just when John would doze off from sheer exhaustion or when he thought he would go mad from the ceaseless pounding, he would hear the sound of another tree ripped from its roots and crashing against an outbuilding, followed by a swell of water breaking over the land. There were times when he imagined that he could hear the sea itself—that it had already wiped out Siesta Key. If that were the case, what chance did the rookeries—the small islands of mangroves that provided roosting and nesting havens for the flocks of pelicans, ibis, and egrets that inhabited the area—have of standing between him and the full fury of Hurricane Hester?

The house continued to sway and moan under the beating it was taking, but it held. After what seemed like forever, John stopped trying to figure out the source of the various convulsions and quakes that threatened to tear the place apart. His mind raced with the need to do something, anything to stop the chaos.

Then he saw water creeping across the floor toward him and knew he had to get to higher ground. He grabbed what supplies he could carry and ran for the stairway, hoping the surge of water would recede before it could reach the second floor. But just as he reached the landing, he realized that the winds had in fact abated significantly, and the rain was no more than a steady late-summer shower. Through the small round window at the top of the stairs, which he had decided to sacrifice rather than climb up and cover, he saw the black sky lighten slightly. He stood frozen for one long moment until the only other sound he was hearing was that of his own ragged breathing. And then he started to laugh.

It was over and he had survived.

He sat down on the step, his feet on the landing where he had stacked his supplies and his elbows resting on his knees. His breathing came in heaves as if he had just run a marathon, but he was smiling. He had made it through his first real hurricane. He threw back his head and let the release of laughter and relief roll through him. He had done it and his house had held. For the first time in hours, his breathing became normal, and as he savored the blessed calm, he felt the tension that had hog-tied his entire body for hours drain away. He opened a jug of water and drank a long swig, then pried the cover off Margery's tin of cookies and pulled one out.

But after he'd given himself permission to celebrate by devouring two more cookies, he heard the wind start to build again. His body and mind went on immediate alert as he listened. He was confused by the exact replay of the ominous sounds he had spent the last several hours enduring. Only now they seemed to come from the opposite direction. Once again the house sang out in protest as rain and wind blasted away at the stucco of the outer walls until it succeeded in working its way in around the plywood window coverings and moldings.

John stood up, unsure of his next move. The calm had been the eye of the storm. How could he not have known that? He berated himself for his stupidity, his arrogance in thinking that he had won. Then he saw the water rising rapidly on the main floor. It was pouring in now, inching its way up the sturdy legs of his kitchen table. He turned to complete his journey to the second story, praying as he went that it would be high enough.

But just as he turned to clamor his way up the last of the stairs, the ceiling above him collapsed, and the stairs dropped away beneath him as the house surrendered to the storm.

Chapter 3

On the night the hurricane was predicted to strike, Hester prepared supper for her grandmother and her father. The three of them held hands as Arlen asked God to bless the food and keep them safe through the night.

"Amen," Hester's grandmother, Nelly, pronounced as she passed the plate of sliced rye bread to her son. Arlen took two slices and slathered each with the dark spicy mustard he liked before stacking on slices of ham and cheese.

"*Und das Gemuse,* Arlen," Nelly instructed, handing him the bowl of green beans. "I never could get you to eat your vegetables. It's a wonder Hester and the boys are as healthy as they are, given the way you eat."

"Sarah made sure they ate right," Hester's father replied as he bit into his sandwich. "That was her department."

Nelly rolled her eyes and looked at Hester's plate. "This one eats like *der Vogel*—reminds me of one of those little birds on the beach as well. All nervous energy, always ready to just fly off somewhere."

"I'm home tonight, Gramma," Hester assured her. "We've done everything we can to make sure as many people as possible are secure, and Grady tells us there's plenty of time to get you and the others to shelters if the creek floods after the hurricane passes."

"We'll be fine," Nelly assured her. "*Gott ist gut*. Now eat. Wherever that hurricane lands, I know you and your father are going to be out there in the thick of things trying to help folks recover and rebuild. You need your strength."

Hester smiled and heaped another spoonful of Nelly's famous potato salad onto her plate.

"There's a good girl."

Shortly after they had finished supper and washed and dried the last of the dishes, her grandmother yawned and announced her intention to get into bed and read her Bible for a bit before going to sleep. Arlen had insisted that his mother spend the night with them. Hester kissed Nelly's cheek, knowing that she would need to gently remove the Bible from her grandmother's hands before getting into bed and turning out the light.

All through the night she and her father sat together inside their secure house miles from the Gulf or even the bay. Unless the creek flooded, they would suffer little damage so far inland. Some trees down and roof tiles blown off but generally no real damage. They listened as the edge of the storm passed over them on its way inland. Her father read aloud from his much-worn Bible as the winds weakened and her grandmother slept through it all.

Before going to bed, she told her father about going to see John Steiner the day before. "I abandoned him, Dad. I let my irritation at being asked to go there get the better of me."

Her father handed her his Bible. "Seek guidance, *liebchen*, and remember, God forgives us. You pray on the matter and I'm sure you will find your answer."

As always she found comfort in her father's lack of censure when it came to her actions. But then her father placed his arm around her shoulder as they walked down the hall together. "You know, Hester, sometimes even I lose sight of my role as pastor to others. Being someone others look up to can be heady stuff." He did not have to remind her that in their faith, such pride was unacceptable. "Your post with MCC is not unlike mine as pastor—we have both been chosen to show others the way, but we are no different than those who follow our leadership."

"I can't help it if I've been given a good deal of responsibility," she replied defensively.

"And if God saw fit to relieve you of that leadership role, to have you simply follow, do you believe in your heart that you could do that?"

"Of course," she replied. But as she drifted off to sleep, she had to admit that a good part of her annoyance with John Steiner had been that he was keeping her from her responsibilities as director of MCC's efforts back in Pinecraft. "I'll work on that," she promised herself—and God.

"How soon can we get started?" Hester asked Grady early the following morning as she dashed across a parking lot, dodging puddles and hoping the light drizzle falling was the last of the rain. Grady was making his rounds, checking in person with the various relief groups around the county, all of them anxious to get to work.

"We've got some serious damage," Grady told her. "Turtle Beach is basically gone, and the entire coastline of Siesta has been devastated. There's probably not a home or business over there that hasn't suffered irreparable damage at least in the short term."

Hester knew what this meant. People were going to need food, water, shelter, and a comforting presence to assure them that everything was going to be all right. This time of year most of the condominiums and homes on Siesta were vacant. A big part of Grady's job would be to work with owners to get the properties repaired in time for the onslaught of snowbirds—the part-time winter residents. Those folks would begin arriving around Thanksgiving, and that meant there was less than three months to get ready. The annual return of the snowbirds was a mainstay of the economy in the area. If they decided to go elsewhere, that could be catastrophic on a whole different level.

"Unfortunately, Siesta Key is not the entire story, although they certainly took the hardest hit."

Hester thought of the sugar-white beaches that were Siesta Key's trademark and wondered what they might look like now. News reports she'd heard left no doubt, though, that all up and down the Gulf Coast, scores of homes and businesses had been totally wiped out by the storm. Those who had waited too long to leave and couldn't make it to a hotel or friend's safe haven were now crowded into shelters, including the ones set up in two schools and a large church just on the outskirts of Pinecraft. She tried not to think about what might have happened to John Steiner's place, or the man himself. "So, back to my question—when can we get started?"

"I should be hearing from the local search-and-rescue teams soon," Grady said, shielding her from the drizzle with a large golf umbrella decorated with comic strip characters. "Crews from gas and power have been out since before dawn. But there is some positive news—a few minor injuries, but no fatalities that we know of."

Hester nodded. "That's better than we might have expected given the power of the storm." She knew the drill. The representatives from the Federal Emergency Management Agency, or FEMA, had arrived on the scene, but they would wait for the local authorities to take the lead. County and state rescue teams would be the first out checking those places that they knew had not been evacuated. Soon the gas and power crews would be roaming the barrier islands as well as the mainland looking for downed wires and other telltale signs of problems, repairing them so that the real process of cleaning up and securing property affected by the storm could begin in earnest.

Grady removed a battered, sweat-streaked baseball cap and mopped his forehead with his forearm. He was wearing a worn T-shirt that looked as if it had seen dozens of trips to the washing machine, faded jeans, and running shoes. The thing Hester liked most about Grady was that he was not the typical government employee. He dressed in shorts or jeans instead of the more formal business attire that FEMA contacts arriving from Washington seemed to prefer. And he always looked like he was ready to get his hands dirty and get the work done. Those qualities above anything he might say gave people confidence. Since Katrina and the oil spill, folks in the Gulf area had had their fill of politicians flying down from Washington, looking around and shaking their heads, and then heading back to their plush homes and offices, leaving people like Grady to take the brunt of people's frustrations and anger.

"Still, this is a biggie, Hester." Grady shook his head. "It's beyond bad. We've got power outages from Fort Myers all the way to Tampa and no word on when power—not to mention water—might be restored. With this heat. . ." He swiped his forearm over his brow.

"Well, we're ready with meals and water for the workers, and we've got generators at the shelters and in other strategic locations to keep the air-conditioning and refrigeration up and running."

Pinecraft had suffered only minor wind and water damage. The streets were a mess, but already volunteers were out, moving branches and cutting downed trees so that the main roads were open. That morning a truck loaded with clothing, food, and other supplies had arrived from MCC's national headquarters in Pennsylvania. In calmer times most donations that Hester received in Pinecraft were shipped north, where there were warehouses set up to sort, store, and distribute the goods wherever they might be needed around the world. This time the donations would be distributed right here in Sarasota—not just to the residents of Pinecraft, but to anyone who might need their help. Hester already had a team of women working to sort through the goods and get them distributed to the shelters.

In fact, the entire Mennonite and Amish communities of Pinecraft had come out to offer their help. She glanced across the street to the assembly line of women in plain cotton dresses and head coverings that ranged from pioneer sunbonnets to small black lace headpieces to the starched mesh caps so familiar to outsiders. They stood shoulder to shoulder filling empty produce boxes with canned goods and other nonperishables, while men in their brown, navy, or black trousers, collarless shirts, and trademark straw hats were handling the work of clearing the debris. Of course, it wasn't just the residents of Pinecraft who had stepped up to meet the challenge. Hester knew that a similar scene was being repeated at churches all over the city.

She also knew that her father had called out the community's full complement of MDS team leaders, who in turn each had six to twelve volunteers they could call upon when needed. Every available crew had gotten the word, and now they were just waiting for the signal that they could get to work. They would begin the weeks of cleanup and ultimately months of rebuilding homes and businesses for those without insurance who had been hardest hit by the hurricane.

"I did a fly-by this morning, past Tucker's Point," Grady said quietly.

Hester knew that Grady had been disappointed when she handed him the signed note and told him that John Steiner had refused to evacuate.

"And?" she asked, curious in spite of her annoyance at the man for wasting time and valuable resources by his stubborn refusal to follow protocol.

Grady shook his head. "I saw no signs of anyone, and the road into the place is even more blocked with downed trees and power lines. The only way in is by boat, and that's tricky as well."

Hester was still wondering how anyone could be so arrogant as to believe that a mere mortal could withstand nature's fury and simply walk away unscathed. "Do you think he survived?"

Grady actually shuddered in spite of the oppressive August heat. "From what I could see on the fly-over, everything on his place is pretty much kindling except for the packinghouse—one wall down and the roof gone but otherwise standing. The main house might be okay, hard to say. The upper branches of a large banyan tree had fallen onto it and hidden most of it from view."

Hester bowed her head. She hadn't done enough. She had

allowed her irritation at John Steiner's arrogance to color her actions. She should have insisted, but the more Margery had talked about the man on the quick bumpy boat ride from her marina to Tucker's Point, the more upset Hester had become. By the time she had knocked on the man's front door, she had been seething with righteous indignation.

Now John Steiner might be dead. A casualty of the hurricane that carried her name.

"I am so sorry," she murmured and swallowed back tears of shame and regret. "I should have. . ."

"Hey, easy there," Grady said, patting her shoulder. "We don't know what happened. Maybe the guy thought better of his decision and moved out. Maybe he was able to ride out the storm—like I said, the house didn't seem to be a total loss. A good part of it was still standing."

"You said 'kindling,' " Hester reminded him.

"I embellish. You know that."

"Well, I hope you're right and he made it."

Grady tapped his pen on the clipboard in a drumbeat. "One way to find out," he muttered, not looking at her.

"You can't seriously be thinking of going out there with everything else you have to do," Hester said.

"Not me. I asked your father if he might go. Maybe take Samuel Brubaker along in case there's any heavy lifting to be done."

Her father had been up and out before Hester was dressed that morning. "And he said?"

"He'd go as long as you came along as front porch sitter."

"You want me to. . ." Hester could barely get the words out. A "front porch sitter" was usually one of her Dad's volunteers who was designated to sit with the home owner in those first moments after the crew arrived. That was the time when the home owner was likely to be most emotional and not thinking clearly. The sitter would listen and offer comfort until the home owner calmed down enough to give written permission for the MDS team to start clearing away the worst of the debris.

Presumably in this case, her job was to get the guy to let them escort him off the property, assuming he was alive.

"You're joking, right?"

"Not so much," Grady replied. "Look, his aunt doesn't want any publicity about this. She's called in some favors, I take it. Arlen's agreed to go, but he says he'll make the time only if you agree to take the hand-holding part of this."

Hester saw the situation for what it was. This was exactly what she and her father had been talking about the night before. This was what she had prayed about.

"If the guy's alive but injured," Grady pressed, "we need to get him out of there, Hester. You're a trained nurse." He waited a beat. "Please?"

Hester closed her eyes, reminding herself that God had given her the mission to serve Him by helping others. Whether she was leading or following was hardly the issue. And even though this man had defied logic to ride out a hurricane, he was a human being in need. It wasn't the first time she'd heard of such stubbornness. Plus, if she helped Grady with this, then Grady would be free to help those who had played by the rules and still lost everything. "I'll take care of it." She took the map from him and folded it up. "How's Amy doing?"

Grady grinned. His wife was eight months pregnant with their first child, and he was already a very proud father. "She's ticked off because this hurricane wasn't a male name. She was all set to name the baby after the storm. I do not even begin to understand why we would wish that on a kid."

"It's a boy, then?"

"Yep. You know what she told me this morning? She said there's still a month before the baby is supposed to come, and even if the little guy is late, hurricane season goes through October." He shook his head, but his smile told the real story of his abiding love for his wife. Hester couldn't help feeling a twinge of envy. Over the years she'd pretty much given up on the idea that she would ever know the kind of deep commitment and love that bound Grady to Amy. The two had so much in common, and in many ways it was hard to imagine one without the other.

Hester had always thought that she had more in common with males like her brothers and the boys she'd gone to school with than she did with the girls she'd known. Guys all seemed to like her, like having her around. But when it came to one of them considering her as spouse material, things changed—fast. She was thirty-three years old now, well past the age when most women of her faith had settled down to the business of making a home and raising a family. Many people thought she had missed her chance at marital happiness when she had insisted on going to college and getting her nursing degree. Others thought that it was her devotion to caring for her sick mother that had made her miss out on the opportunity to meet a suitable young man.

There had been one young man, a farmer from Indiana she'd met after she'd completed her nurse's training and had returned to Pinecraft. He had even proposed. But just a week before their wedding, he had made it clear that while he had found her unorthodox behavior appealing when they first met, it simply would not do to continue along that path once she became his wife and the mother of his children. Hester had called off the wedding, once again setting tongues to wagging throughout the little community. But shortly after that, her mother's battle with Lou Gehrig's disease had begun its downward spiral, and the tide of sympathy had turned in Hester's favor. Many had seen it as part of God's plan that Hester should be free to care for her beloved mother.

"I'd go myself," Grady was saying. "But there are still dozens of people unaccounted for, and. . ."

"It's your job to account for them."

Grady puffed out his cheeks and then blew out a breath of frustration. "Yeah. I have to admit that at times like these I sometimes question my career choice, but this is the path I chose."

And I chose my path, Hester reminded herself sternly. *Just as staying put in a hurricane was the choice of John Steiner. Judge not, Hester Detlef.*

"Okay. Tell Dad I'll meet him at the shop. I need to let Emma know she needs to take full charge of things here for a while."

"Be careful out there, okay?" Grady said. "The area is still unstable with all those downed trees, and, of course, there's no power or water. Don't go poking around. Just see if you see any sign of Steiner. If you find him, do what you can to get him stabilized, and then call in the evacuation chopper."

"Unless he's okay," Hester corrected.

"Either way," Grady said, "call the chopper and get him to a hospital. I'm not taking any chances."

"Got it," she said. "Do you have any further information about him? Anything else that might help in case he's—you know—confused or delirious?"

"Not really. Word has it that his mother—the congresswoman's sister—was some sort of hippie who abandoned the high-society life for a simpler style. She married this Amish farmer and moved out to his place in Indiana."

"So John Steiner's father is Amish?"

"And so was Steiner until a few years ago. I think he was shunned or whatever they call it when he's gotten himself kicked out of the community."

"Banned," Hester corrected quietly. "If he cannot go back, then he has been banned or ex-communicated."

"Whatever. He left, came here, and bought the old Tucker place." Grady let out a sigh. Both of them knew that he might very well be the first fatality of the storm. "Do your best, okay. Just be careful. I warn you, Hester, from the air the place looked pretty unstable."

"We've probably seen worse," Hester assured him.

But an hour later as she and her father and her father's newly hired cabinetmaker, Samuel Brubaker, beached the sturdy fishing boat they'd borrowed from Margery and worked their way over uprooted trees and dunes of wet sand that had not existed the day before, Hester was not so sure.

"How could anyone survive this?" she murmured. In spite of her annoyance that John Steiner was somehow entitled to special attention, her heart went out to the guy. If he was still alive, he had lost everything.

Chapter 4

It had taken John most of the morning to claw his way out from under the rubble that had once been his bedroom above the kitchen and the heavy cypress beam that had proved his salvation. Oblivious to the pain that racked his body, he'd just broken through the last barrier into the gray and ominous aftermath of the hurricane when he got his first look at the fury and devastation the storm had wrought. It looked like Hurricane Hester had roared straight through his property on her way to who-knew-where. His once-pristine cluster of faded candy-colored outbuildings that tourists liked to associate with "old" Florida looked more like an oversized game of pick-up sticks.

The chicken coop was flattened. He hated to think of what he might find beneath the rubble. The cage he'd left behind when the roof blew off the coop was now embedded in the trunk of a palm tree like a spike. The concrete walls of his toolshed had collapsed in on each other, and the corrugated metal roof was missing. He turned toward the old packinghouse and saw that one section of its tin roof now balanced precariously in the branches of the large banyan tree that dominated the yard; one half of that tree was leaning against the house. The second floor of the main house was gone with the exception of the door frame that once had led to his bedroom. On the first floor all of the doors and windows were missing, and one of the four walls had fallen as well. The only recognizable furnishings were the kitchen table, mired in at least a foot of sludge, the stove, and half of the fireplace chimney. He was able to identify his kitchen cabinets and countertops only by the splintered pieces of wood that littered the landscape.

His life had been spared when he was able to crawl onto a fallen ceiling beam and cling to it until the storm finally abated sometime just before dawn. The angle of the beam had protected him as the second floor of the house collapsed and had kept him from drowning in the waters that filled the first floor as he lapsed in and out of consciousness. He tightened his grip on the Bible he'd managed to rescue from the rubble and thanked God for saving his life. He turned to the old citrus groves and to where he had planted his kitchen garden and additional fruit trees.

Muck and sand covered the entire property where just the morning before he had walked through the rows of evenly spaced trees. Over there was where he'd planned to add green beans, and over there, pea pods. This larger bed was to house large heads of cabbage and lettuce in alternate rows alongside tomato plants. But now what little he could see of the remains of the carefully plotted garden was buried under several inches of muck and water. He set his Bible on a window ledge, and then walked farther into the orchard, where he bent to scoop wet silt and sand from the ground. He could find nothing that was salvageable of the work he had poured his heart and soul into for the last two years. Here and there the recycled cypress boards he had used to build the planters stuck up from the sand like grave markers. The branches on the fruit trees that had managed to survive the storm's rage were gray with sea salt. Other trees had been snapped off at the base.

Slowly he took stock of his losses, trying without success to comprehend the fury of a storm that had robbed him of everything he'd worked so hard to build. When he'd settled on the Tucker property in spite of the naysayers who had thought him mad, he had seen not an abandoned homestead and business but a place where at last he could pursue his Walden experiment unencumbered by the disapproval of others. Here he could prove to those who had banned him that he was a man of faith and tradition—perhaps far more so than the neighbors he'd left behind had been. Here he could honor the memory of his mother and the way that she had encouraged him even with her dying breath.

Still stunned by the extent of the storm's damage, he finally registered the steady throttle of a fishing boat puttering close to what had once been his pier. It was now no more than a twisted aluminum sculpture sticking up from the muddy water. "What now?" John muttered as he watched a trio of Mennonites—conservative judging by their dress—beach the boat on a nearby sandbar and wade through the uncommonly high waters of the bay to shore. John bit his lip hard and silently prayed for strength and patience. Like he didn't have enough to deal with.

"Plain people" as the various sects of Anabaptists were often called. Amish, Mennonite, Hutterites—all linked under the yoke of plain dress and a simple separatist lifestyle despite their differences. In particular, the Mennonites seemed to have this thing about needing to help people—whether anyone asked for their help or not.

So here they came—two men and that woman—the one who'd demanded he leave the night before. The men could have been father and son. The elder sported a full white beard, while the younger was clean-shaven, indicating that he was single. Both wore the somber uniform of their faith. Dark loose trousers with suspenders, solid blue cotton shirts with no collar, and the telltale stiff-brimmed straw hat. John had abandoned the dress code when he came to Florida because he believed it would be easier to maintain his anonymity if he did not call attention to himself.

He turned his attention to the woman. She was wearing sneakers that were stained with the brown muck of the creek. Her dress was a pale blue floral print covered with a black apron.

She carried a cloth satchel. Her skirt was wet and muddy for a good foot above her ankle where she'd waded in to shore. Her hair was parted in the middle, then pinned up and back and crowned by the traditional starched white mesh prayer *kapp*. And while the men were both fair, the woman was not. Her hair was as black as the night that had engulfed his property just before the storm struck.

In no mood for company and especially not for the woman's right to gloat, John glanced around, seeking escape. But other than the boat they'd arrived in, he had no other options. Where once there had been a winding lane out to the main road in the days when Tucker had owned the property, there was now a jungle of downed palm trees and uprooted shrubs to add to the maze that had been the overgrown path he'd so carefully avoided clearing. On top of that he sported a long bloody gash on one arm along with a variety of throbbing bruises and possibly a broken wrist given the pulsating pain he was feeling there. His shorts and shirt were both ripped, and his signature planter's straw hat was probably halfway to New York by now—along with most of his other possessions that had not been nailed down against winds that must have topped well over a hundred miles an hour. Three uprooted Norfolk pines that the nursery owner had advised him not to plant now formed a kind of bizarre natural obstacle course for the trio of do-gooders to navigate.

Seeing that there was no way to avoid them, he waited with arms folded across his chest and his feet planted firmly in the soft sandy soil. "Can I help you?" he called out when they were less than ten feet away. Where had they come from? It was as if the storm had dropped them off on its way inland.

"Ah, *mein bruder*, it is we who should be asking that of you," the older man replied with a sympathetic nod toward the chaos that lay all around John. He pulled a brochure from the pocket of his trousers and tapped it lightly against his thigh as he made the introductions. "I am Arlen Detlef. This is my friend Samuel Brubaker and my daughter, Hester."

"Hester." John was unaware he had spoken aloud until he

saw the widening of her eyes at the sound of her name. "Like the storm," he added. He had failed to fully appreciate the significance of the connection the night before, but now it made sense, for certainly she had roared in and out like the hurricane itself.

The older man chuckled. "In many ways, yes, my friend."

"Dad," the woman said. Her tone held the rebuke that her smile disarmed. John studied that smile, but she had offered it to only her father—not to him. She had barely glanced at him. The woman clearly did not like him. So much for Christian charity.

She doesn't even know me, he thought. Not that it mattered whether the woman liked him or not. It just irritated him that she had apparently decided to disapprove of him on sight.

"May we know your name, sir?" Arlen asked, and John saw Hester nod at her father.

"John Steiner." The innate good manners of his upbringing clicked in, and he thrust out his hand for a handshake. The male Mennonites seemed inordinately relieved to accept it. The old man gave him the traditional single pump as if priming a well, while the younger man wrapped both his hands around John's and murmured, "We are so thankful that you are safe."

"But apparently not without a cost. We have come to offer help," the ever-cheerful Arlen assured John, handing him the pamphlet. "I have the honor of serving as the local director of this relief agency. My daughter here holds a similar position with the Mennonite Central Committee, and the two agencies work together in times like these to bring assistance to people like you who have suffered loss."

Mennonite Disaster Service was imprinted in blue on a circular emblem that featured two people shaking hands and—of course—a cross. *Staying Safe after a Natural Disaster: Hints* was the title of the piece.

"Thanks, but I've been through stuff like this before. Not a hurricane of this magnitude, but smaller ones down here and tornadoes back. . ." He'd almost said *back home.* "A few years back," he amended and handed the pamphlet back to Arlen.

"Understood," Arlen replied. Undaunted, he folded the pamphlet in thirds and placed it in the ripped breast pocket of John's shirt. "You'll find this useful later, then. For now let's concentrate on your physical well-being. My daughter is a nurse. Why don't you sit a moment while she tends your wounds and Samuel and I have a look around?"

John wiped sweat from his forehead with the back of one hand and almost cried out at the shot of pain he felt with that simple motion. "Look, folks," he gasped. "It's really decent of you to want to help, but. . ." He looked up at the sky, gathering his thoughts, then felt the extraordinary heat and overwhelming humidity more oppressive than ever press in on him until it was difficult to breathe. He realized that he was on the verge of passing out. His wrist and bloodied arm were both throbbing. It was as if having finally accepted that he'd survived, he had no strength left with which to go on.

"You should sit," the woman said as she wrapped her fingers around his good arm and guided him to a spot shaded by a cypress that had survived the storm unscathed. She spoke to him as a nurse instructing a patient, and so he followed her direction. The younger man—Samuel, was it?—fanned John with his hat.

"Drink this." Hester-like-the-hurricane handed him a pint of bottled water after removing the bottle cap and tucking it in the pocket of her dress. "Slowly," she coached when he would have chugged it. While he drank, her father picked up John's Bible and handed it to Hester. She tucked it into her satchel. "I'll make sure you have it once we get you to safety," she assured him.

The older man had removed a two-way radio from his pocket. John could only hope that he was calling for backup in the form of a medical helicopter to get him to a doctor. He truly did not think he could make it to the boat they'd brought. Meanwhile, the younger man kept fanning, all the while looking around as if sizing up the ways he might be able to contribute to their mission. "Do you have battery-powered communication equipment, John?"

"I did," John replied as he drained the last of the water. He tossed the empty bottle onto a pile of rubble. After removing a first-aid kit from the cloth bag she wore bandoleer style across her chest, Hester retrieved the bottle, recapped it, and slid it into the bag. "It's all pretty much garbage," he said, glancing around at the devastation surrounding them.

"And yet there is no point in adding to it," she replied as she splashed alcohol over her hands before pulling on a pair of latex gloves and preparing to treat the open cut on his forearm.

John couldn't help it. He laughed. The Mennonites no doubt took his laughter for hysteria, but he really didn't care. "Have you folks taken a good hard look at this place? There is nothing left."

The two Mennonite men made a visual inspection of their surroundings. John had pretty much seen all he needed to in order to know he was done for, at least financially. "Look, folks, I appreciate your concern, but the Red Cross and FEMA will be getting here before too long. As you can see, there's not much you can do for me now." He waited for Hester to finish bandaging his arm and then stood up, forcing a steadiness he didn't feel into his legs as he stepped forward to extend a handshake of dismissal. "I'm fine. Really."

"Sit," Hester ordered. John was beginning to think that barking out orders was one of the woman's finer skills. "MDS works with FEMA as well as all the other agencies involved in cleaning up the mess that comes after a storm. Furthermore, my father has called for evacuation," she continued. "You need to see a doctor and get that wrist set. In the meantime. . ." She took out a length of cloth and tied it into a makeshift sling. "Let's keep this arm elevated."

John looked past her to what was left of his house and released a long, shuddering sigh.

"It looks dire, but sometimes it may not be as bad as it seems," Hester said, following his gaze. "Of course you'll need to wait for the assessment of the engineers, but overall, I would say you were blessed, John Steiner."

She had to be kidding, right? As of an hour ago, every element of his life boiled down to two eras—before the storm and after the storm. Before the storm there had been a house, a packinghouse, and half a dozen other outbuildings. The remains of most of the outbuildings now lay scattered across the property in no particular order. The interior of the main house that he had worked so hard to renovate before the storm had now collapsed in on itself like a house of cards. The packinghouse was missing an entire wall, not to mention its roof. And that didn't begin to address the devastation his garden and the citrus grove had suffered. Before the storm, those plantings had been the very foundation of his dream of living a self-sustaining life without the need to rely on the outside world. Before the storm, the citrus from his restored groves had been the root of his plan to raise extra funds when needed by reestablishing Tucker's original business. Before the storm, his life had been on track, and now it was a train wreck of disastrous proportions.

"I'm blessed? Do you. . ." he began, then closed his mouth. *I don't know where to begin to tell you the magnitude of stupidity contained in that statement,* he thought, gritting his teeth. These people were just trying to help, he reminded himself.

"Johnny Steiner!"

He was rarely happy to see Margery Barker. But at the moment anything that might interrupt the missionary zeal of these do-gooders was more than welcome. Besides, her chocolate chip cookies had given him unexpected comfort when the tin had floated by his position on the beam and he'd snagged it.

"We tried to warn you, but no," she bellowed, "stubborn as the day is long. That's you, mister." She expertly guided her boat through the murky but mostly calm waters of the bay.

She anchored the boat, then splashed her way ashore through knee-deep water before turning her attention to the Mennonite trio. "I see you found him, Arlen." She grinned at the older man.

"We did and God has blessed us all to have found him little the worse for wear," Arlen replied.

John rolled his eyes heavenward. He was lost. Of course, Margery had been with Hester the evening before. She was in cahoots with them. In fact, she'd probably sent them.

"Well, I see little Hester here has managed to tend your wounds, John," she commented as she wrapped one arm around Hester's waist.

John did not see the need to comment that *little* Hester was actually a good six inches taller than Margery was. Still, he could not help taking note of the change in the Mennonite woman when the older woman embraced her. She actually smiled. A smile that stretched all the way to her eyes. It was the most positive expression she'd managed since arriving on his property.

"Sarah would be so proud of you, sweetie." Margery turned to include John and both of the Mennonite men in her monologue. "Oh, many's the time that dear woman was the first person to come calling when help was needed." Then in a voice so soft that John thought someone new had joined the group, Margery murmured, "We grieved with you over her loss. No finer woman than your Sarah, Arlen."

"Thank you for that," Arlen replied.

"You know that I would have been at the funeral," Margery continued, "but I had charters, and it was the height of the season, and after last year's hard times. . ."

Arlen covered her weathered hand with his. "You were with us in spirit. We felt that."

Absolved of her guilt, Margery turned her attention back to John. "Hopefully you have learned your lesson and will pay attention to these people. They know what they're doing, and trust me, they're a sight more qualified to help you get back to renovating this place if that's still your mind-set than those dandies from DC are. By the time they tie you up in all that red tape they're so fond of, you won't know if you're coming or going."

John cast about for any possible way to turn her focus away from him. "How did you come out?"

She shrugged. "Four or five seriously damaged boats, but they're insured. Blew the roof off the bait shop." She shrugged. "Nothing that time and the right materials can't fix. Who are you again?" she asked, turning her attention to Samuel.

"Samuel Brubaker. I've just moved here from Pennsylvania."

"And what do you do, Samuel?"

"I make furniture with Pastor Detlef."

Margery glanced from Hester to Samuel and then back to Arlen. "Is he son-in-law material?" She winked, and Arlen laughed.

"Now, Margery, don't make trouble where there's none."

But John found himself considering the couple in this new light. Samuel was tall with large strong hands, and his short-sleeved shirt revealed the roped forearm muscles of a man used to hard work. He also sported the pasty skin of someone who had not been in Florida that long. Hester was not tanned exactly, but her cheeks were sprinkled with freckles, and she had the look of a woman who enjoyed the out-of-doors. She was also well past the age when most conservative Mennonite girls married and started families of their own. He found himself intrigued. She certainly had yet to demur to her father—or to young Samuel Brubaker, as most women of her faith would.

Actually, he couldn't help but feel a little sorry for both men. One thing about being of the Anabaptist faith that had always made a lot of sense to John was the idea that there was a clear division between women's work and men's work. He had thought the same was true among these Florida Mennonites, especially the more conservative ones. A woman's place was at home, not out running around taking charge of things as Hester Detlef seemed prone to do.

"Have you got someplace to stay tonight, Johnny?" Margery asked. "I'd have you stay on the houseboat with me, but it's listing badly, and. . ."

"You can both stay with us," Arlen interrupted. "It would be our honor."

Put that way it was going to be hard to refuse, but John was sure going to give it his best shot. "I appreciate that, but I'll just get a hotel room—"

Margery let out her characteristic howl of a laugh. "Did you get conked on the head while you were riding out this monster storm? There isn't a hotel or inn within miles that's got a room to spare—that's if they've got any rooms at all." She turned her attention to the older man. "Johnny is stubborn as they come, Arlen. He's got this bug about going through life alone—no help, no dependence on anyone but himself." She wheeled around to face John again. "Stop being so blasted mulish. Take the man up on his offer. You look like you've been run over by a truck, and that wrist is not going to set itself."

"I've called for medical evacuation," Arlen said.

John had trouble concealing his relief. A muttered "Thank you" was all he could manage.

Margery scanned the sky, and the others followed her lead. "There's the chopper," she shouted, waving wildly as she marched out into calf-deep water with Arlen following.

"Somebody please just shoot me now," John muttered.

"That would be against our traditions and yours," Hester said as she and Samuel helped him to his feet. "You are Amish, are you not?"

"How do you know I'm. . ."

She handed him his Bible, which he tucked into the sleeve of his sling. "Perhaps later you would like to speak with my father about the events that brought you here to Florida," she said, her expression one of pity. It made his stomach roil.

"I came here to live, to make a life for *myself*," he replied tersely. "Now if you and your father. . ."

She scowled up at him. "You know something? Margery is right. It's time for you to stop giving orders and pay attention to those who only want to help you. In short, please do not cause any further trouble than you already have."

Chapter 5

When John stumbled and nearly fell on his way to the shore, Hester and Samuel were there, prepared to assist him into the helicopter's rescue basket once it was dropped. But he shrugged them off and stood his ground. Given his apparently minor injuries, Hester thought that he probably could have made the trip with them in the boat, but Grady had made it clear that they were to airlift him to the hospital. He had come very close to passing out, and if—as she suspected—he was dehydrated, the team on the helicopter would be better equipped to treat him.

As for him staying with her and her father, she was quite certain that John could not possibly be any more reluctant to return to Pinecraft with them than she was to have to cater to him while the real work of disaster relief was being handled by others. She knew these thoughts were unworthy of her. Why should it bother her one way or the other where he stayed? He was simply one more human being in need. Yet there was something about him that she found unsettling.

"I can walk," he growled when Samuel reached once again for his arm.

He shot her a warning look to keep her distance as well, and she realized that it was those eyes that unnerved her. Their sea-green depths seemed to question everyone and everything. No, he was not a man who would go along with them willingly. She sighed and indicated the route her father and Margery had already taken to the shore, knowing that the chopper could not land amid all the debris and John would need to be airlifted from the open water. Well, let him protest and find his way around her father. That would be quite something to see.

"Look, Pastor. . ." John had to shout to be heard above the beating of the chopper's blades.

"Arlen."

"Okay, here's the thing, Arlen. I'm not about to leave my property to looters and vandals."

Arlen surveyed the wreckage behind them. "I see your point," he said. Hester saw John's eyes widen in surprise and then narrow with suspicion.

"You do?"

"Ja," her father continued. "You are not a trusting man, are you, John? And without trust—whether in the Lord or our fellow man—we cannot see the full range of possibilities."

"I see them quite well," John protested. "I see the possibility that those clouds there on the horizon could develop into another storm or a tornado, and I have at best a few hours to secure whatever might be left of my property. I also see that even if there aren't more storms, there's open water leading straight to my property that could be most tempting to my fellow man living not half a mile away who may have lost everything and decided to rummage through this rubble to find. . ."

The chopper pilot had headed off to make another circle over the property, and in the sudden silence that followed, Arlen's question filled the void. "Do you not see the good, John?"

"The good?" John's mouth worked, but no other sound came out. Finally he shook his head and released a bark that might have been a laugh. "I'm afraid you've got me there, sir."

"Could this not be God's way of suggesting a change for you—a change in the way you live your life, the things you hold in esteem, the lives you touch?"

"Seems to me if God wanted to get my attention, He didn't need to send a hurricane to do it."

Hester heard Samuel suck in a shocked breath at such blasphemy, but her father only smiled.

"Perhaps the Lord has made many attempts, John. Could it be you weren't listening? It's a common fault among young people." He glanced at Hester, and she knew he was thinking of their conversation of the night before.

"I'm thirty-six years old, Arlen, hardly a teenager out to test my wings before I decide to join up."

Again Arlen smiled. "Ja, I had forgotten. You are one of us after all." Hester saw her father glance at John's bright yellow shirt smudged with filth and his cargo shorts ripped in several places. "Perhaps *die Kleidung*," he mused more to himself than to John. "You choose not to dress in the plain fashion of your ancestors?"

"I choose not to draw attention to myself. Look, Arlen, the point is. . ." John prepared to state his case as the chopper moved closer.

"The point is, John Steiner, you cannot stay here. At least not for tonight." Arlen removed his straw hat and fanned himself as he watched the helicopter make its final approach just as it started to rain again. "In a few days the Lord may see fit to bless us with a steady sun that will start to dry things out," he shouted. "In the meantime those clouds out there promise a full day of rain, and we must go and offer our help to others who are as devastated as you."

The chopper hovered, its blades whipping what trees were left in a weak imitation of the hurricane's gale-force winds, as the rescue basket emerged from its belly. Arlen strode back down the path they had taken over fallen trees and smashed shrubbery, waving to the pilot. Samuel fell into step behind him, but Hester waited to see what the Amish man would choose.

"Stubborn old. . ." John muttered under his breath as he watched her father navigate the debris as nimbly as someone half his age.

"He is a respected man of God," Hester said. "And whether you like it or not, John Steiner, he is right."

His answer was a feral growl as he gave up the fight. And when he headed for the beach—albeit by a different route—Hester found that she could not suppress her smile. She watched as Samuel and her father assisted him into the basket. Once he was safely on board the chopper, the pilot dropped the basket again.

"Go with him, Hester," her father shouted above the din. "Samuel and I will meet you at the hospital after we return the boat."

"Why me?" Hester shouted, but her father and Samuel were already on their way out to where Margery had climbed into her boat and pulled it closer to theirs.

"How is he?" Grady asked later as he and Hester stood several yards away from where a Red Cross medic was applying a splint to John's wrist and forearm. He was being treated at the temporary quarters the agency had set up in back of her father's church. The doctor they'd seen at the hospital had sent them away, citing the need to attend to a host of people with far greater needs than a broken wrist.

Stubborn. Rude. Arrogant. Hester rejected the litany of adjectives that sprang to mind as she recalled the short flight to the hospital, where they had landed on the roof and been met by a harried-looking team of medics. "I believe he will survive," she said.

"He looks like he could spit nails," Grady observed.

"Like many *English*, he's taking the storm personally." Hester deliberately used the term commonly applied to those from outside the Amish or Mennonite community.

"But he's Amish."

Hester shrugged. "And yet he shows none of the acceptance of God's will that would be common to his faith. So what's in a name? You can contact your boss and let him know that Mr.

Steiner is fine. His property is probably a total loss, although I didn't tell him that, but he's alive." She gestured to the man now sporting a more traditional and substantial sling on his left arm as he stood and looked around. "He's all yours, Grady."

"I don't have time. . ." Grady sputtered.

Hester narrowed her eyes as she studied her friend. "And I do? We're swamped now, and Dad tells me there are at least three more church teams on their way here from surrounding areas. They'll be here by suppertime. I need to make sure they're fed and have a place to stay. There are the food boxes that must be delivered, Grady, and John Steiner—"

Grady grimaced. "Remains a priority."

"Why?" Hester could not disguise the childish petulance that flavored her response.

"It's politics," Grady replied with a long-suffering sigh. Hester knew that Grady was familiar with her lack of patience when it came to the political gamesmanship so common in his world. "Come on, Hester, help me out here. Put the guy to work on one of your teams just until I can get things fully organized at my end."

"He only has one good arm," Hester pointed out.

"So let him serve meals or hand out bottled water. That only takes one good arm."

As if he would agree to such menial labor, Hester thought. He was clearly a man used to being in charge, although she doubted very much that he inspired others to work for him. But then suddenly she thought of something Arlen had said to John: *"Perhaps you weren't listening."*

Was it possible that God had deliberately set this cantankerous man squarely in her path to test her while obstructing her ability to relieve the suffering of more deserving souls? Was it possible that John Steiner was some sort of challenge the Lord had placed before her? Perhaps to show her that He was in charge, not her? To test her willingness to take direction—God's direction— rather than go her own way as her father had noted earlier?

Certainly in all the time she had been volunteering with

MCC, this wasn't the first time she'd seen a person respond with anger and affront at loss or tragedy. Instead of accepting the outstretched hands of those who wanted to help, such people would push past their rescuers determined to go it alone. More often than not they would fail and only add to their loss and misery. With God's help they would sometimes return, emotional hat in hand so to speak, and ask for the help they had rejected in the first place. Hester studied John as he stood outside the Red Cross tent now with his legs widespread as if balancing on a ship's deck. He appeared to be surveying the activity around him. Everything about his posture commanded others to stay out of his way. But when she looked at his face, she saw uncertainty and just the slightest touch of defeat.

All right, Lord, I will see him through this, for now. I don't understand why You have chosen this path for me to follow, but follow it I will.

"Lend me your cell phone," she said, holding her hand out to Grady.

"Not great service," he warned. "Who are you calling?"

"Not me," Hester said as she started across the parking lot. "He should call his aunt and let her know he's alive."

John felt disoriented. It wasn't just the pain medication the Red Cross medic had given him. It was as if he had stepped into a nightmare. The wreckage of his property haunted him, coming back to him in such vivid detail that it took his breath away. As the helicopter had turned north toward the hospital farther up the coast, John had sat speechless staring down at the surreal scene below. He'd spotted bits and pieces of his life cast away among the downed trees and crushed shrubs. In one stripped tree hung a shirt of his, whipped by the breeze until it resembled a flag. And was that his red metal toolbox half buried in the muck of the bay? The packinghouse was useless until he could get the wall and roof repaired, and his own home was equally uninhabitable.

The evacuation chopper had airlifted him to the hospital, where Hester had filled the emergency room personnel in on the situation. Arlen and Samuel had met them there after returning the boat to Margery's marina. But after examining him for injuries beyond a broken wrist and a variety of abrasions and bruises, the resident told Hester that with the more seriously injured people waiting to be treated—three who had suffered possible heart attacks—it would be hours before they could treat John. The doctor suggested that she would be better off to take him with her back to Pinecraft. The first-aid station there could splint his wrist and tend his other wounds. It did not escape his notice that the doctor spoke to Hester and her father, rather than to him.

By that point he'd been overcome by a wave of pure exhaustion, feeling every inch the refugee he'd become so that when his rescuers had led him from the ER to Arlen's car, he had not questioned their destination. He'd heard of Pinecraft, hard not to know something about the Amish/Mennonite haven that attracted tourists in droves in high season. But he had no interest in sightseeing. Instead, he slumped down in the backseat and stared out the window, vaguely aware of palm trees with their crown of fanlike foliage sheared off by the raging winds and water-covered streets through which Arlen navigated his thirty-year-old car. While they were in the emergency room, it had continued to rain, as Arlen had predicted. The usually jammed Highway 41 that cut right through downtown Sarasota was eerily deserted. Only a few cars and the occasional ambulance or patrol vehicle roamed the four-lane road.

Businesses were boarded up and closed. Parking lots were empty of cars and covered in water. Once they turned onto Bahia Vista, the surroundings changed from commercial to more residential, but the homes and condominium complexes were also shuttered and deserted. It was like driving through an abandoned city littered with huge palm fronds and downed power lines tangled in uprooted trees that had been partially pushed to the side of the road. Bits of broken asphalt tiles from roofs and other debris floated on the water that had overflowed from the clogged drains and gullies so that in places the streets were more like canals than roadways.

Then almost as soon as they crossed a main thoroughfare and entered the Pinecraft area, it was as if they had left the worst of the storm behind. The east/west street that bisected the community was filled with people and activity, while side streets bustled with bicycle and foot traffic. The scene had all the attributes of a church meeting, but John was well aware that it wasn't celebration that had brought these people out in force. It was the need to help and to care for others.

In the faces of those he passed, he saw worry and anxiety and concern for a neighbor who might have suffered. Through the rolled-down windows of Arlen's car, John heard a man call out to a neighbor inquiring about damage the second man had suffered from the gale force winds. At long tables on the covered walkway of a shopping mall, women in traditional Mennonite garb worked in unison filling heavy cardboard boxes with clothing, canned goods, and bottled water. As soon as a box was filled, a boy would load it onto a three-wheeled bicycle, and when the bike's rear basket was filled, the youth would pedal away toward another area where a fleet of small trucks and vans waited. At the same time another boy would pedal forward and hop off to help. Their industry was impressive. Their cheerfulness to be doing God's work and helping others was merely annoying.

Arlen had pulled his sedan into a parking lot near a building marked PALM BAY MENNONITE CHURCH, and Samuel escorted John to the first-aid tent set up by the Red Cross at one end of the lot. There he had turned him over to a jovial young medic who had cracked stupid jokes with a nearby nurse while attending to John's wrist. They'd given him some pain medication to get him through the next twenty-four hours plus a regulation sling to replace Hester's temporary fix. "You want to keep it elevated," the medic had instructed. Then he'd patted John on the shoulder and turned to address the next problem.

"Now what?" John said aloud to himself as he looked around

for some idea of how he might get back to his place.

"How are you feeling, *Herr* Steiner?"

John turned to find Hester standing next to him. She shielded herself from the steady drizzle with an umbrella, so it was hard to see her features. Still, he could not help but take note of the fact that she was tall enough to meet him nearly eye-to-eye. Memory told him those eyes were blue, although he had no idea why that detail had registered with him. Certainly with everything else he'd had to deal with, the color of a plain woman's eyes should be the least of his concerns. "I'll be fine," he muttered and turned his attention back to his surroundings as he tried to figure out his next move.

"I thought you might want to call your aunt in Washington." Hester lifted the umbrella higher to cover both of them and handed him a cell phone. "Or I could do it for you if you like. I mean, I appreciate that your people. . ."

"Look, let's get one thing straight. I am no longer Amish, okay?"

"You may have chosen to leave the community, Herr Steiner, but. . ."

"I did not *choose* anything, starting with being born into an Amish community. That was my mother's choice."

"And your father's," she said, clearly unruffled by his attitude. "I'll leave you to make your call, then." She crossed the street and slipped under the canopy that protected the tables where the other women were working.

"Hold on a minute." John hated asking anyone for anything, especially a woman, especially *this* woman.

She tilted the umbrella to one side and waited for him to catch up to her. But just before he reached her, he faltered and for one awful moment feared once again that he might pass out. "Let me get you something to drink," she said, steadying him by placing her arm around his shoulders and shielding him with the umbrella. "When was the last time you ate an actual meal?"

"Yesterday sometime. Maybe the day before," he admitted, trying to remember the meal. Supper, he thought. He recalled a plate of cheese and fruit. Last night. It seemed like forever ago.

"Come with me," Hester said and steered him across the shopping center's parking lot. A few yards away she pointed to an empty rocking chair in a row of similar Amish-made bentwood rockers that lined the porch of a restaurant touting HOMEMADE PIE on the large sign that was now listing to one side. "Sit. I'll be right back."

She handed him a bottle of water and went inside the restaurant. John guzzled and once it was gone wished he had more. His hand started to shake uncontrollably, and he felt suddenly light-headed.

"Here."

She was back and handing him a paper plate stacked with bread, slices of sandwich meat, cheese, a banana, and chips. "Start with the banana," she urged, even as John crammed chips into his mouth. She pulled a bottled sports drink from the ever-present cloth satchel. "Drink this. You need the potassium, and I expect your system needs some electrolytes as well."

"Arlen mentioned that you're a nurse. What kind?"

"A trained one," she snapped, then seemed to mentally count to ten, softened her voice, and added, "Although there are some things you just pick up along the way." She handed him the sports drink, then sank down in the chair next to him. "As soon as you've eaten, if you could make that call. . . I need to return the phone."

"To?"

She nodded toward a man in a T-shirt and jeans and a battered Boston Red Sox baseball cap. "That's Grady Forrest. He's with the county and pretty much the main man throughout the entire region when stuff like this happens."

"Stuff like this being a mere category-four hurricane?"

"Amazingly, it didn't quite hit a four—made a good effort though." She pushed the rocker into motion with one foot.

"Felt like it when I was clinging to that cypress beam." He took a swallow of the sports drink. He couldn't help noticing that her canvas shoes were still soaked and caked with mud.

"Which allows me to politely raise the obvious question," she said softly.

He arched an eyebrow and waited.

"Why were you clinging to a beam that might just as easily have crushed you as saved your life? Why didn't you leave when you were warned—repeatedly, from what Margery told me—to do so?"

John shrugged. "I don't like other people deciding what I should and should not do." He noticed that she had stopped rocking and was gripping the arms of the chair.

"You know something?" She got to her feet and glared down at him.

"What?"

She bit her lower lip and shook her head as if shaking off whatever it was that she'd been about to say. "I'd appreciate it if you could return the phone to Grady as soon as possible. I have to go." She looked both ways, checking for traffic on the street, which was congested with people and bicycles, and then headed left.

"Hey," he called.

She stopped walking but did not come back. He wondered if she had any idea what it was costing him to be dependent on her, a woman.

"When can I go back to my place?"

"Check with Grady," she called, and then she was gone, lost among the hordes of women similarly dressed in plain cotton dresses, their heads now covered by umbrellas or hoods extinguishing the telltale prayer coverings.

Hester knew the answer to John's question. It would likely be days, if not weeks, before he could return to his property for good. For certain that first look-and-leave visit would be in the company of some trained disaster volunteers who would help him retrieve whatever could be safely taken before bringing him back into town. Although her father had invited John to stay with them, she couldn't help hoping that Grady would find him a place at one of the three shelters that had been set up in the area.

"Surely Dad will understand that we have a lot of work to do and a lot of volunteers depending on us for guidance," she muttered aloud as she made her way toward the church. "John Steiner will be perfectly fine at the shelter. In fact, a night spent sleeping on an old cot might be just what he needs."

"Are you talking to yourself or to God, Hester?" Samuel asked as he fell into step beside her and offered her the shared shelter of a rain slicker he'd picked up somewhere. She'd left John her umbrella, surely a sign that she made no distinction between caring for him and caring for anyone else who might need protection from the elements.

"Myself," she admitted. She was glad of Samuel's company. He was a gifted craftsman and certainly a nice-looking and gentle man. Hester had little doubt that he would make a fine partner to spend the rest of her life with. He was mild-mannered enough that he might not even insist that she abandon her volunteer work in order to devote herself exclusively to keeping house and raising a family. But Hester wanted more from a marriage than a fine partnership. She had always fought against wanting more. It was her greatest failing, that longing for something beyond the norm. She loved her work with MCC, and it was that very idea of being expected to focus on her own household and raising a family to the exclusion of anything else that terrified her. Hester was well aware that her father had been pleased by her agreement to volunteer rather than seek a paid position in a hospital. But he'd made no bones about his preference that after her mother died, Hester should transfer her loyalties to the more conservative Christian Aid Ministries where Emma was the local leader. But neither Hester nor her mother believed that God distinguished between the work she did with MCC and the work that Emma did with CAM. Her mother had not only supported her decision to work with MCC but also encouraged it.

Then Sarah's illness had worsened. The end had not come quickly, and the suffering her mother had bravely endured had inspired Hester as she sat with her day after week after month. Hester's guilt that perhaps her mother's suffering was somehow her punishment for not more closely following the traditions of her faith had been staggering. And even in her pain, Sarah Detlef had seen that. In spite of her loss of physical capacity, Sarah had found a way to communicate to her daughter that she had made the right choice in going for her degree and that she was very proud of her for her decision to come home to Pinecraft to serve others.

After Sarah died, Hester had convinced herself that her volunteer work with MCC was her way of honoring her mother's memory and Sarah's own deep dedication to service. The greater truth was that she enjoyed the diversity and demands of the work involved in the variety of projects for which she could volunteer within the committee. Already she had traveled to Central America to help rebuild communities that had suffered the effects of a rebel uprising that had left thousands huddled in makeshift camps. She looked forward to more opportunities to serve overseas. Yes, this was her calling, and John Steiner was only an obstacle, testing her determination to stay on course and help those truly in need.

"Hester?"

She had been so lost in thought and there were such crowds of people about that she had nearly forgotten Samuel was walking alongside her.

"Yes, Samuel?" She did not miss the way he glanced at her and then immediately looked down at his work boots, soaked now and heavy with mud. There had been many times since his arrival that Samuel had made awkward attempts at engaging her in conversation that she assumed was his way of trying to bring them closer.

"I was thinking about John Steiner's place."

Oh, the sin of pride, Hester Detlef. She had expected Samuel's comment to be something more personal. Perhaps an expression of his concern for her working so hard and not eating properly. He was that kind of man, always thinking of others—in this case a complete stranger. "What about it?" she asked.

"Perhaps it's not nearly as bad as it appeared at first glance," he said, his words coming in a rush. "If we could salvage the first level of the house, then Herr Steiner could move back there in a matter of days."

"And just how would you accomplish that?"

"Arlen mentioned a volunteer crew that is expected to arrive later today from Georgia, experienced builders and even a plumber and electrician. If Grady agrees, I could go with that crew and an engineer from the county to assess Herr Steiner's property."

"And you would do this because. . . ?"

Samuel smiled. "Because I overheard you and Grady talking, and, well, if helping him helps you and Grady attend to those who may be in more dire straits, then why not?"

Hester stared at him as if truly seeing him for the first time. "You are a gut man, Samuel."

"Ja, I am," he replied without the slightest trace of arrogance.

"I appreciate your thoughtfulness, but as each volunteer crew arrives, they must first go where the need is greatest. It's only fair. Herr Steiner will be fine."

Samuel's smile widened. "Nein. Herr Steiner would disagree." He pointed to where the man himself was berating poor Grady.

Hester couldn't help it. In spite of the chaos all around her, she started to laugh. "I would say in addition to being a good man, Samuel Brubaker, you are an excellent judge of character."

"Ja, Ich *bin*," Samuel replied, and he looked at her so intently that Hester stopped in her tracks and gave him her full attention. "I am also well aware that others have their ideas of why your father brought me into his business, Hester, and I know that those are not necessarily ideas that you agree with. But perhaps in time. . ."

He smiled at her, then left the thought hanging as he walked away. Hester watched him go, wondering if she had misjudged him. It had never occurred to her that Samuel might have his own doubts about a future for the two of them. The thought gave her an unexpected sense of relief.

"You should perhaps go," Samuel called out over his shoulder. "Your friend Grady might need your help."

But Arlen was already there ahead of her. Seemingly from out of nowhere he appeared, stepped between Grady and John, and murmured a few quiet words that had the potential combatants eyeing each other warily and then shaking hands. Hester saw her father beam with his usual delight; then he took hold of John's good arm and started across the parking lot, taking shelter under Hester's umbrella. Little good it did either of them as the wind had started to pick up again and the rain seemed to come at them sideways.

"Ah, Hester," Arlen called out when he spotted his daughter. His hand remained on John's elbow. "Our friend here has had quite an ordeal. Show him the way to our house so that he may shower and rest."

"I really need to. . ."

Her father's impressive white eyebrows shot up, and his blue eyes narrowed as he handed her the umbrella. Hester knew that look, and she knew it was useless to defy it. "But that can wait," she amended. Her father's gaze softened with approval. "Come along, Herr Steiner. It isn't far."

Chapter 6

In spite of her polite smile, everything about Hester Detlef told John that she would prefer to be anywhere other than escorting him down the lane bordered on either side by what just a day earlier had to have been pristine white cottages set in well-maintained yards. Now the streets and yards were pocked with pools of muddy water and littered with debris. Every house had some degree of damage from the storm.

She stepped around a neatly stacked pile of flattened picket fencing and into a yard that held the remnants of what must have been a lush tropical garden. She bent and rescued an orchid plant and carefully hung it back in the sheltering branches of a tree.

"I thought I had gotten them all," she murmured more to herself than to him, and seeing that Hester and her father had suffered their own losses, John turned his attention to her.

"It was obviously a lovely garden," he said as he followed her, taking care not to step on any other plant that might have survived.

"Danke." She led the way up a shell-lined path through an obstacle course of puddles to a front porch that stretched across the width of the cottage. "Normally when a storm's on the way, we move the orchids inside. I must have missed that one."

"Are you the gardener?" He was determined to somehow make a dent in that prim facade that she wore like armor.

"My father and I take our turn," she replied.

He couldn't help but notice that she simply turned the knob of the front door. The house was not locked. If they were on a farm in Indiana, he might not think anything of it. But Pinecraft was located right on the borders of Sarasota, a growing and changing city with its fair share of petty crime. More than once he'd had to chase would-be vandals from his property.

She slipped off her shoes and stood aside to allow him to enter. The foyer, if one could call it that, was made darker by the absence of sunlight from outside. He took a minute to get his bearings. A cozy living room to his left furnished with a plain but comfortable-looking sofa and two upholstered chairs. Rag rugs brightened the polished hardwood floors. Next to one chair—hers he assumed—was a basket of sewing. A side table next to the other chair was loaded with books and papers. Both chairs faced the fireplace.

Across the hall was a small room that must be Arlen's study. An old-fashioned wooden desk took up most of the space. John caught a glimpse of a small television set and a telephone on a side table next to a leather recliner. He noticed a hallway that he assumed led to the bedrooms and a shorter hallway leading straight back from the front door, where he was certain that he would find the kitchen. He turned his attention back to the living room, where one wall was lined with bookcases, every shelf crammed with volumes of every size and description. He felt immediately at home. His mother had loved books.

"If you'll wait here," Hester said, starting down the hall toward the bedrooms, "I'll make up your bed and put out fresh towels for you. You can use my brothers' room, and Margery will stay with me."

"You have a brother?"

"Four of them. All married with families of their own and living in Ohio now. We see them often; they come here or we go there. They have a better opportunity to build a good life for their families there. Work is limited here. Of course it's not the same as being all together, but we make it work." She paused briefly to deliver this bit of information.

"Let me help you," he said, starting down the hall after her.

She stopped so suddenly that he almost ran into her. When she turned, her cheeks were flushed, and she seemed to focus on some point just past his left shoulder.

"Or not," he said, retreating back toward the foyer. "I'll just. . ." He glanced around for a place to sit. "I'll just wait here," he said, indicating the living room.

She nodded once and continued on her way.

As John scanned the titles that lined the bookshelves, he could hear her moving around, making the necessary preparations for hosting overnight guests. A dresser drawer was opened and then closed. He heard the snap of fresh sheets as she made up the bed. He heard her move across the hall, where she opened a closet or cabinet for some new purpose. She poured water from one container to another. His mind followed the sounds of her actions as surely as if he had followed her all the way down that hall.

He'd been in the *English* world for far too long, he realized. He should have known that even for a woman who seemed as sophisticated and streetwise as Hester Detlef, she was clearly dedicated to the conservative ways of her faith. The idea that she might find herself alone in any bedroom with a man she barely knew was unthinkable. He pulled a thin volume from a shelf and absently read the title without really seeing it, all the while wondering if he should apologize or just let the matter drop.

"My mother wrote poetry." She pointed to the book he was holding.

As attuned as he'd been to her movements, he had failed to notice that she had finished her work and come back to the living room. He ran his fingers over the cloth cover of the book, trying to decide if opening it would be an invasion of privacy.

"The garden was hers," she added, inclining her head toward the front door. "My father and I try to keep it in order to honor her memory."

He recalled Margery offering her sympathies to Arlen earlier and nodded. "May I?" John asked, indicating the book of poetry.

"Yes." She waited while he opened the book to a page about a third of the way through. He scanned the contents and could not disguise his surprise. "She was quite. . ."

"She was a plain woman," Hester interrupted, and he knew that she was reminding him that in her world as in his, compliments were unnecessary and unwanted. "She recorded her observations of God's handiwork as a way of showing her appreciation and gratitude."

John nodded and replaced the book on the shelf. "She died recently?"

"Yes."

"I'm sorry for your loss."

She accepted his condolences without comment and turned her attention back to the business at hand. "I left towels for you in the bathroom. Your room is the second one to your left. There are dry clothes in the closet and bureau. You're thinner and taller than my brothers, but the clothing there should do for now." She delivered these bits of information as if she were reading from a prepared list as she edged toward the open front door. "I should go and find Margery and see that she gets some rest as well. My father would want you to make yourself at home, so please refresh yourself, and, of course, if you are hungry or thirsty. . ." She waved her hand in the general direction of the kitchen.

She was halfway out the door and clearly anxious to be rid of him when he called out to her. "I still need to know when I might be able to return home."

She stood on the path and made no move to return to the shelter of the porch away from the steady drizzle. "That depends."

"On?"

She let out a soft sigh that he surmised was about as close to an expression of exasperation as she was likely to display. "Many things, Herr Steiner. Surely you're aware. . ."

He felt more certain than ever that it was important to get on this woman's good side. He gave her his most engaging smile.

"Could we make that *John*? Calling me Herr Steiner makes me want to turn around and look for my late father."

"Your father died?"

"When I was thirteen, farming accident."

"And your mother?"

"Couple of years ago." He took a step closer. "It seems we have that in common, the loss of our mothers."

"Yes. Please accept my condolences. Both parents gone." She shook her head. "That must be especially difficult."

"Thank you, Hester—like the hurricane."

She stared at him for a long moment. "I don't mean to be rude, Herr. . .*John*, but I have responsibilities that go beyond. . ." He guessed that she had come very close to saying something like *babysitting you*. But she caught herself, took a deep breath, and said, "The short answer to your question about returning to your home is that it will surely not be today."

She was backing her way toward the missing picket fence, but he was determined to make his point. "I am going back, Hester. I'll stay the night here, but. . ."

"I understand that you are anxious to return to your property, John. What you need to understand is that going back is not the same as going home to stay. Once you accept that, then the day you can return may come sooner than you think."

"Meaning?"

"It's possible that Samuel Brubaker along with an engineer from the county and a crew of MDS volunteers could make a visit to your property as soon as tomorrow to assess the damage and give you a better idea of when you might—"

"MDS?"

"Mennonite Disaster Service." She pointed toward his shirt pocket, where the pamphlet her father had given him lay damp and limp.

"Yeah, well, understand this—nobody's going to my place without me, Hester."

She had taken two determined steps back toward him when a red-haired woman about Hester's age but not in plain dress came rushing down the street. "Hester! Zeke's gone missing."

Jeannie Messner was Emma Keller's younger sister. Hester had known her since the three of them had played hopscotch and jacks together in Pinecraft Park as kids. Emma and Hester were the same age, but Jeannine—better known as Jeannie—had always tagged along. Emma and her family still lived in the same house where the sisters had grown up just across from the park. But Jeannie, ever the rebel, had left the Palm Bay church that her family preferred after marrying a man from the more liberal congregation. Her husband, Geoff, worked as the athletic director at the Christian school, and Jeannie had taken a job as the activities director at a local senior center. Generally she was a happy-go-lucky sprite with her curly red hair that framed a heart-shaped face featuring an impish smile. But Jeannie was not smiling now. Her brow was deeply furrowed with worry, and her lips were pencil thin and pale.

"Jeannie, calm down and tell me what's happened." Hester led her friend to the shelter of the porch, her heart hammering with this fresh evidence that while she had been tending to John Steiner, people with real problems were being neglected.

"It's Zeke. He's missing."

"Who's Zeke?" John asked with a hint of irritation.

"Zeke Shepherd. He lives on the beach down near the bridge," Jeannie explained. It was a clear measure of her distress that she showed not the slightest curiosity about who John was or why he was standing on Hester's front porch.

John's eyebrows lifted slightly as he focused his attention on Hester, waiting, she assumed, for her to dispense with this interruption and get back to the subject of his property.

"He's homeless," Hester added, hoping to elicit a drop of sympathy from the man. "He camps on a seawall concealed by several mangrove and sea grape trees along the bay downtown." She motioned toward the porch swing, but Jeannie shook her head and kept pacing. "Surely when the storm hit. . ."

"He left," Jeannie finished her sentence. "But he went back. He'd left his guitar there, and. . ." Her huge hazel eyes filled with tears. "No one has seen him since," she whispered.

Hester wrapped her arm around the smaller woman. "Now you know Zeke. He probably found some place to ride out the storm."

"Geoff and I have already checked every place he usually hangs out," Jeannie protested. "What if he got washed away? The surge that came with the back side of the storm was enormous, and the wind. . ." She shuddered. "I just. . .I pray he's all right, and I know you can't spare anyone to join a search party. But could you make sure all the volunteers know to keep an eye out for him?"

"I. . ." Hester understood that for Jeannie, Zeke would always be the brother she never had. *We made special arrangements for John Steiner,* she thought and smiled at Jeannie. "Sure. I'll tell them to be on the lookout. And you should talk to Grady so he can spread the word, okay?"

"Thank you." Jeannie sucked in air and glanced at John as if seeing him for the first time. "Hello," she said, her usual smile restored. She thrust out her hand. "I'm Jeannie Messner, and you are?"

"John Steiner," he replied, accepting her handshake.

"Herr Steiner has suffered the loss of his home. His property was destroyed—with him inside—and as you can see, Jeannie, he's fine. Well, not fine but certainly well enough," she stammered as she considered John's arm and the many cuts and bruises evident on his face and hands.

"Your friend probably just found higher ground until the hurricane passed," John said. "He'll turn up eventually." Hester couldn't help noticing that his words seemed to carry more weight in consoling Jeannie than hers had.

"You're staying with Hester?" Jeannie gave Hester a curious look.

"He's staying with my father, as is Margery Barker. I'll be working, and by tomorrow morning we'll all be packing up to move to a shelter in case the creek floods," Hester said firmly. She stopped short of physically steering her friend down the lane.

"Nice meeting you," Jeannie called as she waved at John.

"Well," Hester said, turning her attention back to John, "do you have everything you need, John? If so, I'll just. . ."

"What's the connection?" he asked, returning Jeannie's wave halfheartedly.

"Jeannie and her sister and I have been friends since childhood, and—"

"I mean with the homeless guy."

"Zeke? He and Jeannie have been friends for years. Zeke introduced her to her husband, Geoff. Then Zeke enlisted, and, well, after he returned from overseas, things weren't the same for him. He fell on hard times and started living on the beach. Jeannie is a social worker at heart. She and Geoff have tried everything to get Zeke to accept help from his family, but he refuses."

"Zeke's not Amish or Mennonite, then?"

"No."

"Maybe she ought to leave him alone," John muttered.

"That's not in our nature," Hester replied. "Now, then, I really must be going. My father should be back in an hour or so."

"And my place?"

The man was like a dog with a bone.

She surveyed her mother's destroyed garden, giving herself a moment to gather strength. Then she took a long, steadying breath and raised her face to look directly at him. "Your property is not in imminent danger. Likewise, you are safe. You have shelter, food, and water. You even have dry clothing available. Do I really need to remind you that there are hundreds—perhaps thousands—of others who are not nearly so blessed?" She closed her eyes again and murmured, "Sorry." Whether John heard this last as directed at him or some higher being she could not have said. She really didn't care. She knew that it was a prayer, not an apology.

"And what I need for you to understand is this. That property is my life. If I lose it, then I have lost everything."

"And still God saw fit to let you walk away from the devastation of your property," she reminded him softly. "Perhaps my father was right. Perhaps you are supposed to start over, take a different path."

"I don't need sermons, Miss Detlef," he growled. It started to rain harder, and the heat and humidity seemed as tangible as the rain.

"Look," she said, forcing a bedside manner that she didn't feel.

"You look," he snapped. "Just don't even think of going out there without me."

"Believe me, *John*, nothing would make me happier than to get you back to tending your business so that I can tend to mine. I suggest you take advantage of the blessings before you," she continued. "The water is still off, but I left you fresh water in the basin so you can wash yourself, put on dry clothing, and get some rest." And with that she walked away from him, her spine rigid, her shoulders back, and her stride determined.

Chapter 7

Hester could practically feel John glaring at her retreating back. Well, they were even, because he definitely tried her patience, too. Still, she was not going to give in to the temptation to tell him what she really thought of his selfishness and arrogance. Let her father deal with him. There were people who needed her far more than John did, people who might actually appreciate what she could offer them in the way of comfort and assistance without asking for, no, without demanding more.

She spotted Jeannie pouring out her tale of Zeke's disappearance to Grady when she returned to the center. He listened intently and then patted Jeannie's shoulder, obviously assuring her that since Zeke was well known and liked, everyone would be looking for him. Hester knew that all Jeannie really needed was some guarantee that Zeke would be on their radar screen as they carried out the rescue efforts. Jeannie gave Grady a brilliant smile and then hurried off, calling out to Emma and then no doubt repeating her story to her sister. Hester couldn't help wondering if Jeannie's charm could soothe the ruffled feathers of John Steiner.

John Steiner is well taken care of, she silently reminded herself. *Surely now I can concentrate on the work I have been led to do.*

"Grady," she called out as he climbed into his Jeep and prepared to drive away.

Perhaps if she got Grady thinking about sending the team where they could do the most good, then by the time Samuel spoke to him, it would be too late to reassign them to the old Tucker place. *Now that just seems vindictive,* she chided herself. What was it about this man that brought out the worst in her?

Besides, if John's place hadn't even been cleared by search and rescue yet or by the gas and power crews and there were all those downed power lines on the main road leading past his place, an MDS crew could hardly go there. "Samuel tells me we can expect a crew from Georgia by suppertime."

"I know. I'm asking them to go check out Tucker Point." Grady drummed his fingertips on the steering wheel. Hester's heart sank.

"Surely. . ." she began, but Grady just shook his head and turned the key to start the engine. "Look, Hester, I have to go. Believe me, I know there are more urgent needs, and I have tried hard to make that clear, but you know how this works."

Actually, she didn't, because in her world attending to those most in need took precedence over political considerations. On the one hand she felt sorry for Grady, because he was a good man and he truly wanted to do the right thing. But on the other, it made her so angry that some bureaucrat in Washington who had no idea of the situation could make decisions for them. She forced a smile. "Politics," she murmured.

"You got that right," Grady replied, and he finally looked directly at her. "I'm really sorry, Hester. But if we get the Steiner thing assessed once and for all, then we can focus on the real need."

"All right, I see your point. And you're only talking about a small crew, right? Just to assess the damage and report back?"

"That's the plan."

"Well then, I suppose there are enough volunteers to focus on the real need *and* address Mr. Steiner's problems."

"That's my girl," Grady said. "Thanks."

"For?"

Grady grinned. "Relieving me of my guilt." Then he sobered. "We've got a long road ahead of us, Hester."

Hester nodded. They both knew that making it through a hurricane without massive physical injuries or deaths was only the first tiny step in the process of truly surviving such a disaster. At the moment everyone was driven by adrenaline and the sheer will to be sure people were accounted for, fed, and had shelter. The news would bring enough shock and awe with it that the media and help from around the country would arrive in droves, at least during those first couple of weeks. After that the residents would face the true test of survival—finding ways to keep going weeks and months from now after the media had turned their cameras to some other story and the relief money had dried up to a mere trickle. By then most of the volunteers would have gone home because they had families and jobs that needed their attention, leaving half-rebuilt homes and businesses under a sea of blue plastic tarps and the residents of the area to make it on their own.

She scanned the sky. The rain had fallen steadily all night and through the morning. Was it her imagination that it was getting worse?

"Wind's picking up," she noted. "Maybe we need to step up the timeline for getting folks moved away from the creek here." The weather reports had predicted steady rain for the foreseeable future, but there had been no mention of the rising winds. Anyone who had lived on the coast for any length of time knew that rain accompanied by high winds would push the already-deluged Philippi Creek over its banks even this far inland.

Grady nodded. "My best info tells me that we've still got at least until noon tomorrow. In the meantime there are other more pressing needs. For starters, we're going to need more cots, blankets, and food at all three shelters. They're already nearly full, and we need to stretch their capacity to handle the overflow." He must have taken note of Hester's expression of doubt. "Hey, if you and Emma can have your people alert everyone to get ready to move tomorrow, that should be time enough to get everyone to a shelter."

"Got it covered." Hester paused as she and Grady watched a large eighteen-wheeler navigate the turn on its way to the donation center run by MCC. "That'll be another load of supplies from national," Hester said. "See you later?"

"I'll be back tomorrow, got to check on some reports of tornado damage further east." Grady shifted the vehicle into reverse and let it roll backward before making the turn out of the parking space. "With any luck at all I'll be able to sleep in my own bed tonight."

"Give my best to Amy," Hester called.

It was after midnight before Hester could be convinced to go home and get some rest. Throughout the long day and well into the night she had been on her feet, sorting through the massive volume of canned goods, bedding, clothing, and other supplies sent from national MCC headquarters in Pennsylvania as she organized everything for distribution to the shelters. She took a break around supper time to meet with her father and Emma and other volunteer leaders in Pinecraft. After that she had insisted that her father go home and get some rest. Once he agreed, she had put in another six hours working in the kitchen of one of the local restaurants that had offered their facility for volunteers to cook and box up meals. She was bone-weary, but her spirits were high. They always were after such a day, a day when people came together to do God's work.

As she walked down the lane, a light glowed in the front window of the small white house where Hester had lived all her life. She smiled. Her father always left a light on for her. He would have retired hours ago—both her parents had always been of the "early to bed and early to rise" persuasion. She opened the front door and was momentarily confused when she heard the low murmur of voices. Then she saw her father sitting at the kitchen table.

"Ah, here she is now," he said, pushing himself away from the table and coming to the doorway.

"Dad? It's so late."

"Is it? We got talking and I suppose we lost track of the hour. Did you eat?"

She nodded just as Margery Barker eased past Arlen and yawned audibly. "Way past my bedtime," she said as she started down the hall toward the room she and Hester would share. "Don't worry about disturbing me when you come to bed, Hester. I'll be asleep before my head touches the pillow. I expect nothing will wake me for the next eight hours."

Hester saw John rinsing out his cup at the kitchen sink before coming to stand next to her father. He was dressed in one of the outfits that her brothers kept in the house for their annual visits, his straight red-gold hair freshly washed. "You look plain," she blurted without thinking.

Margery laughed. "I told him the same thing. But why shouldn't he? After all, our friend here was raised Amish."

"Ja. So he was." Hester half expected John to protest the label, but he said nothing.

"John is most anxious to return to his place," Arlen reported as if this were news to any of them. "Margery told him that it would be unwise to return so soon. I agreed, but he's determined. Maybe you can talk some sense into him."

"Actually, Grady is planning to send a crew there tomorrow." Still addressing her comments to her father and avoiding any eye contact with John, she delivered the news of the volunteer team from Georgia that had gotten delayed and had finally arrived just before she'd left for home. "He'll take care of it, assuming there are no other more pressing emergencies."

"Really? One of our RV teams."

Hester nodded. She was glad to see doubt cloud her father's eyes. Apparently she wasn't the only one troubled by this preferential treatment.

"What exactly is this RV team?" John asked.

This time she met his gaze directly. "In circumstances like these where there has been devastation following a hurricane or tornado, or other natural disasters, members of our fellow churches throughout the region and up into the Midwest mobilize teams of volunteers to come and help. They drive their recreational vehicles—RVs—to the site so there's no need for

MCC or MDS to lose valuable time seeking appropriate housing for them. They bring their own tools and supply of food so that they can go right where there's the most need, park their vehicles, and get to work."

"Sounds like a barn-raising," John murmured.

"Yes. I suppose that would be an appropriate analogy."

"And Grady has assigned this first team to John's place?" Arlen asked.

"To assess the damage," she stressed. "Apparently John has friends in the government who are determined to look out for him."

"I didn't ask them to," John protested.

"Still, Grady's under a lot of pressure, and even though most would agree that our mission is to serve where the demand is greatest, apparently he who makes the most fuss. . ." Her father placed his hand on her arm, a warning to calm herself. In the silence that followed, she covered her embarrassment by setting the cloth satchel down near the front door. It would be the last thing she grabbed as she headed out at dawn.

"Well, good night, all," Margery said quietly, breaking the uncomfortable silence as she stepped into the bathroom and closed the door.

"You look exhausted, Hester." Her father stroked her cheek. "Come have a glass of milk."

"It's been a long day," she admitted. "I'll just have a little something to eat and then get some sleep." They could all hear Margery moving into the bedroom and settling in for the night.

"How about you, John? Will you join us for a late snack?"

"Thank you, no. I'll say good night as well." He took two steps toward his room and paused. "I do appreciate everything you've both done for me today."

"It's our pleasure to be of service," Arlen assured him, but Hester seemed incapable of finding a single shred of graciousness to offer the man. She bowed her head, entreating God to give her more patience.

"Sleep well," she finally managed as she squeezed past her father and headed for the kitchen.

"And you," she heard John murmur, but neither of them looked at the other.

When John woke the following morning, sunlight streamed through the open window. The rain had stopped for the time being, but it was going to be another steamy day. He reached for the sling he'd abandoned during the night and nearly cried out with the pain that shot through his body from head to foot. Overnight his muscles had stiffened significantly, and minor movements that most people took for granted were suddenly monumental. Slowly he lifted the covers and stretched out his legs, then swung them over the side of the bed, resting his bare feet on a small cotton rug on the wooden floor between the two sets of bunk beds.

He sat for a minute, sorting out the hum of activity. It didn't take long to grasp the fact that all sounds came from outside the window. The rooms next to and across the hall from his were silent. Cradling his broken wrist, he pushed himself off the bed and padded barefoot to the window. In the yard that backed up to Arlen's property, a woman was clearing away fallen palm fronds and other debris while several small children played nearby. He couldn't help but notice that the cleanup had already been taken care of in the Detlefs' yard. Hester? Arlen? They must have been up well before dawn to accomplish that particular chore. When he'd looked out the kitchen window the evening before, the yard had been littered with debris, except for the front garden. He recalled the neatly stacked sections of picket fence and the way the space had been raked and set to rights in spite of the obvious loss of most of the plantings.

John checked the old-fashioned wind-up clock on the dresser. *Seven thirty.* A jolt of panic rushed through him. He knew the routine. Amish or Mennonite—they were up with first light and by seven thirty had already put in what for some people would be considered a full day's work. So the others had left without him. He headed for the bathroom and awkwardly splashed water onto his face with his one good hand. He didn't miss the fact that the washbasin had been filled with fresh water or that the towels he'd used the day before had been replaced with clean ones. *If she thinks she's going to get around me by letting me sleep in while she and the county guy decide the fate of my place,* he thought, *she doesn't know John Steiner.*

On the bathroom counter he noticed an unopened toothbrush and a partially used tube of toothpaste. He scrubbed his teeth with all the vigor of his irritation at the woman and then limped back to the bedroom to dress.

His regular clothes were missing from the hook where he'd hung them to dry the day before. Meanwhile, neatly folded over the back of the room's single chair were the clothes he'd left when he went to bed—Hester's brother's plain clothes. He dressed quickly as his mind raced with alternatives he might put into action to get him out to Tucker's Point. There was always Margery, though there was no sign of her. When he started down the hallway, he noticed that the doors to both Hester's room as well as Arlen's were open and the beds were made.

"Hello?" he called out as he rounded the corner and headed for the kitchen. A single place was set with a foil-covered plate at the small table, and near the stove sat a thermos that, when he opened it, released the aroma of hot coffee. On the counter next to the cookstove were half a dozen shoofly pies still warm from the oven, their crumb crusts glistening with sugar. And spread over a clothes rack were his still-damp but freshly washed shirt and shorts.

There was also a note taped to the kitchen table. He ripped it free and moved to the open back door for better light.

We hope you rested well. Please enjoy your breakfast. The juice and milk are in the refrigerator. Blessedly the generator continues to function. I will be at the church, and my daughter is helping her grandmother and others move to a shelter before the creek overflows. To reach my mother's house, go to the end of the lane, then left and three lanes over. I'm sure they would be happy to have your help.

Blessings on you, John Steiner, and may you have a good day.

P.S. Please close the doors as you leave; no need to lock up.

John's instinct was to find Hester as quickly as possible. He didn't want to take a chance on missing her, but the smell of the coffee combined with something cinnamon hiding beneath that foil-covered plate made his stomach growl. He supposed he should eat. After all, who knew when he might have his next meal? Surely he would be able to catch up with her at her grandmother's house.

He poured himself a cup of coffee and took his first bite of the cinnamon concoction that clung to his fingers. The woman was multitalented—John would give her that. The minute he uncovered the pan and released the aroma of the cinnamon roll plus eggs scrambled with fried potatoes, onions, and sausages, he knew that Hester Detlef was a first-class cook. He imagined the pies cooling on the counter would be equally impressive and had to stop himself from cutting into one even after he had downed the feast she'd left for him.

Hester was a conundrum all right. It was barely eight o'clock, and she had already cleared the yard of debris, washed the filth from his clothes, made breakfast, baked pies, and who knew what else. And she wasn't that bad looking either. So the question was why weren't Mennonite bachelors lined up around the block to take her out walking or to a church function or out for dinner in one of Sarasota's many restaurants? Why had Arlen thought it necessary to bring in a suitor from the outside?

John was pretty sure he knew the answer to that one. The woman did not know her place—had never accepted her role in either the community or a relationship. She had a college education, still quite rare among the conservative Mennonite population, and she had taken on a job, albeit an unpaid one, that put her in a position of authority. Being the daughter of the senior minister would only buy her so much in the realm of amnesty and respect. He had the feeling that she just kept pushing the boundaries, and he felt sorry for poor Samuel Brubaker. From the way Brubaker looked at Hester and followed her around like a lost puppy, the guy was probably doomed to. . .

"Johnny? Come quick!"

There was no arguing with the alarm in Margery Barker's voice. She rushed up to the screened door, banged on it, and bellowed at him. Then she turned and took off at a run. By the time John gathered his wits enough to follow, she was already several yards from the house. "Well, come on," she yelled. "You didn't break your legs, did you?" She didn't wait for an answer as she turned the corner at the end of the lane. John had been so engrossed in his thoughts that he'd failed to notice that the sun had disappeared behind a solid cover of gray clouds. *So much for a break in the weather,* he thought as he felt the first drops of rain and followed Margery down the lane.

Chapter 8

Hester dragged another sandbag into place and then stared at the floor of her grandmother's carport. In addition to several puddles that were spreading across the concrete slab, water was shooting like a small geyser out of the drain that normally handled any runoff.

"It'll settle down in a bit," her grandmother assured her as she sipped her second cup of morning tea. "It always does."

But Hester had her doubts. Those other times Grandma Nelly was remembering followed a heavy rain when the water had gurgled up through the drain like a bubbling fountain. This was something far more dramatic. This was a really good imitation of Old Faithful. According to revised weather reports Hester had heard that morning, the creek was rising faster than anyone had predicted. There was no way they had until noon to get Nelly and her neighbors out of here. They had to go now.

We should have gone yesterday, she thought. *I should have insisted.*

"Where's Samuel?" she asked, noticing that his small camper was gone from its usual place in Nelly's driveway. He'd been staying with Nelly since arriving in Pinecraft. Nelly clearly thought the sun rose and set in the young carpenter. Hester had hoped to herd the less agile residents living along the creek into Samuel's camper and have him drive them to the nearest shelter and then come back for another group until everyone was safe.

"He left before dawn." Nelly took another swallow of her tea. "Did I tell you that Lizzie Gingrich's generator went out last night? Samuel went over there to check on it and get it going again, and—"

"Margery went to get help," Hester interrupted as she dropped the last of the sandbags into place. "We need to get going here, Gramma. Are you all packed?" She didn't mention what her father had told her that morning—that another tropical storm was forming over the Gulf, a storm that had the potential to blossom into another hurricane. "Come on. We need to hurry."

As if a switch had been turned on, it seemed that Nelly finally recognized the need for panic. "And who's going to help Ivan and Jane next door? And what about Lizzie? She's alone, you know, and just had surgery on her hip. What's she supposed to do?" Nelly pointed to houses in every direction as she continued her roll call of neighbors who were going to need extra help. "At least I can walk and carry my load," she muttered as she headed back inside the house. "*Gott in Himmel*, Hester, come now! The sink's about to explode."

Sure enough. Water was gurgling up through the enamel basin in the kitchen. If it was coming up there, then. . .

Hester raced down the hall to the bathroom, where the toilet bowl was rapidly filling with water and sewage.

"Gram, get your pocketbook and get in the car," she ordered as she ran into her grandmother's bedroom and started grabbing precious items that Nelly had laid out on her bed. The photo of Hester's grandfather, the Bible Nelly had received when she was baptized and still read several times a day, the basket of quilt squares and the quilt of scraps from family members' cast-off clothing that had covered Nelly's bed for decades. On her way out, she grabbed the small suitcase filled with clothing and toiletries that Nelly kept packed and ready for just such emergencies.

In the hallway, water was already spreading across the planked floor. As she passed the kitchen, she set Nelly's suitcase on the counter and scooped the bottles of medications her grandmother took into her cloth satchel and then ran outside, where her worst fears were realized.

Up and down the street people were racing around, their arms filled with whatever they thought they might most need. These goods they deposited in the baskets of three-wheeled bicycles or the backseats of cars as they urged family members to hurry, then sent someone back for something they had forgotten. Next door Ivan Miller assisted his wife to their car as if the two of them were going out for a Sunday picnic; then slowly he walked back up the front sidewalk to lock the door to his house.

"Head straight to Lakeview Elementary, Herr Miller," Hester called. "It's the shelter where we reserved spaces for everyone." Hester shoved the last of Nelly's things into the car and got behind the wheel. "We'll be there. We're going to pick up Lizzie first," she added.

"We'll do all right," Ivan assured her with a wave. But his voice quavered with uncertainty, and she saw him look around as if he couldn't quite believe what was happening.

"Follow me," she called.

Ivan Miller hesitated briefly, and Hester could see his wife pleading with him from inside the car. Just then Margery Barker came running down the lane, and not three steps behind her was John Steiner.

"Where do you need us?" Margery huffed, leaning against the car as she tried to catch her breath.

"Here," Hester instructed as she got out of the car and held the door open for Margery. "Take our car and go get Lizzie and then drive her and Gramma to the Lakeview School while I make sure the others follow. You'll also want to pick up anyone trying to go on foot."

Margery had the motor running and the car backed out of the driveway before Hester got the car door closed. When she took a step back to avoid getting run over by Ivan Miller, who was driving inches away from Margery's rear bumper, she nearly tripped over John.

"I can't take you to your place today," she said, her defenses on instant alert and her mind already assuming the reason he'd come. "Not now. The creek is overflowing its banks. . . ."

"I can see that, Hester," he said irritably. He stood watching as she directed the line of cars and bicycles that formed a surreal parade headed away from the creek for a moment, then muttered, "How can I help?"

It annoyed her that he made it sound like something he was loath to do. She had to bite her lip to refrain from telling him he should go back to her father's house and try getting up on the sunnier side of the bed. Of course their house would also soon be flooded, although it was farther from the creek. And then it started to rain in earnest. Not a drizzle or a gentle summer shower. This time they were deluged as if the clouds had grown weary of their burden and simply burst open.

Anxiously Hester looked down the road and saw Lizzie Gingrich climb into Nelly's car. A moment later the red rear lights of the caravan of cars inched forward. But to reach the school, they would have turned the other way. Margery must have decided that the water was rising too fast to head in that direction and decided on an alternate route. "I should go," she said, but as she looked around for some vehicle to speed her on her way, she understood that with the water already creeping across the road, obliterating its boundaries, the only conveyance that could help was a boat or canoe.

"Come on," John shouted over the lashing rain as he took hold of her arm and started slogging through the mounting water. "Now," he commanded when she hesitated.

Together they splashed their way toward the main road, dodging floating debris and trying hard to maintain their balance as they moved with the swift current. By the time they crossed Bahia Vista, the water was ankle-deep and rising fast. All Hester could think about was that drowning because of inland flooding was the primary cause of death after a hurricane. How could she not have made sure everyone was moved last night? If it hadn't been for John Steiner's stubborn refusal to move to a shelter. . .

"The church?" John shouted, pointing to a large modern structure as the rain formed rivulets down his hair and face.

"Yes," Hester called back as she realized that Margery must have turned in this direction so that she could lead everyone to the church rather than try to make the longer trek to the school. She squeezed her eyes closed against the sting of the downpour as they made their way to the impressive campus of the community's more liberal Mennonite church. It sat on higher ground and had been built with a specially designed drainage system to handle just such emergencies as these. Hester could only hope it would be enough to hold back the floodwaters.

The downpour in combination with the wind made visibility impossible, and Hester had almost bumped into one of the cars from Margery's procession before she grasped the fact that they had stalled out less than fifty feet from the church parking lot after trying to drive through deeper water. Most of the people were still sitting in their cars looking frightened and bewildered. Margery was up ahead, trying to force the door of Nelly's car open against the water that was swirling around her feet and legs.

Before Hester could form the words, John yelled for her to stay put, and then on his way to Nelly's car, he pulled open the doors of the four other cars stalled behind. "Give us a hand here," he shouted to some unseen person he'd spotted. Seconds later Hester had to smile as Zeke Shepherd emerged from behind one of the cars carrying Lizzie Gingrich, with Ivan and Jane Miller on either side of him. They hung on to each other and the dangling ends of Zeke's rope belt. She had never been so glad to see him.

"This way," she shouted and motioned toward the church. Her voice sounded like a whisper thrown against the pounding of the rain. Zeke staggered past her while volunteers from the church ran toward them. They took Lizzie and assisted the Millers, freeing Zeke to go back to help Olive and Agnes Crowder. Hester was relieved to see that with each step Zeke took closer to the church, the water was shallower. "John!" she shouted when she had assured herself that everyone was accounted for except her grandmother and Margery.

"Right here," he huffed from no more than a foot away. He was carrying Nelly, his sling dangling uselessly from his neck.

"Where's Margery?" She tried not to let her panic seep through.

John jerked his head in the direction of the car. "She went back for your grandmother's stuff."

"Go," Hester ordered even as she fought her way against the rushing current to where she could just make out the flashing hazard lights of her grandmother's car. Margery was on her knees in the backseat, bundling Nelly's things into the already-soaked quilt. "Leave those and come on," Hester shouted as Margery emerged from the car and was almost swept away by the rushing water.

"Got everything," the fisherwoman shouted back with a smile of triumph lighting her face as she clung to the open car door. Finally she regained her footing, but then the car started to float and drift.

"The car! Let go, Margery," Hester shouted, swiping at her hair that had come free and was covering her eyes. She wrapped one arm around a lamppost and reached out toward Margery, catching one end of the quilt. Slowly she pulled the fisherwoman toward her until she was able to grab the lamppost as well.

"We can make it," Margery yelled. "Come on." Swinging the quilt and its cargo like a cradle between them, the two women struck out through murky water, carefully measuring the depth before taking each step until the water became shallower.

"Will you look at that?" Margery shouted, her tone filled with surprise as water ran off the pavement of the parking lot back toward the street-turned-canal that they'd just escaped. "Never would have imagined it could drain like that. Just wait 'til those government engineers have a look at this! Might teach them a thing or two." She was out of breath and clearly exhausted, but Hester knew that Margery's running commentary on the world around her was what got her through the day.

"You okay?" Hester asked as she relieved Margery of her half of their burden and slung the sodden quilt with its precious contents over her shoulder. The older woman was out of breath and holding her side.

"I'm fine," Margery protested, but she sat down on the first of several concrete benches lining the covered courtyard of the church and fanned herself with her hat. "You go on and check on Nelly and the others. I'll be okay. Just need a minute to catch my breath."

Hester signaled to a teenage girl who was passing out oversized beach towels that had been among the donated goods to bring one to Margery. "I'll be back soon," she promised as she scanned the throngs of refugees for any sign of her grandmother. When she heard her father's distinct full-throttle laughter, she followed the sound, knowing he would be attending his beloved mother. She took a quick tally to make sure everyone was accounted for and thanked God that they were all safe, soaked to the bone but safe.

For a man who prized his solitude, the mass of people huddled under the eaves and cypress arbor that covered the church courtyard was John Steiner's worst nightmare. He'd spent so much of the last two years living alone that finding himself in the midst of so many people who were all talking excitedly made him feel as if he might be physically ill if he could not find a way out. There was a lot of milling about as plans for making it the rest of the way to the shelter were suggested and rejected. Everyone was trying to come up with the best alternative for getting people settled until it was safe to move on to a shelter. Chaos reigned in a world where John craved only peace and quiet and order. "At least the rain's let up," he muttered to himself.

"Not for long," a male voice to his left replied.

He glanced over to see the man he'd called to for help in rescuing the stranded senior citizens from their cars. He had straight black shoulder-length hair that hung in wet clumps, and he was dressed in a long-sleeved cotton shirt and cotton work pants—both a couple of sizes too small for his lanky frame. He was sitting with his back against a wall of the courtyard, his knees bent and his chin resting on his crossed hands as he watched the crowd.

"Still, the letup is a relief after what we went through back there," John replied. He was in no mood to be debating the matter or to hear more bad news.

The man shrugged. "God just must have decided to press the PAUSE button. Give us time to get those old folks to a safer place."

Whatever, John thought and turned his attention to his arm, throbbing now from having cast off his sling in order to transport Hester's grandmother to higher ground.

"You get that broke in the hurricane?" the man next to him asked, nodding toward the cast.

"Yeah." John didn't want to be rude, but he couldn't help glancing around, searching for any means of escape.

"Wanna get outta here?" the man asked as if reading John's mind.

"Yeah," John admitted.

"Follow me." And the man stood and moved like a cat along the fringes of the crowd until he reached a small opening between two steel columns that supported the covering of the church atrium. "This way," he instructed as he sloshed through water that covered his shoes and started out toward an overgrown vacant lot. "Get us some water," he added with a nod toward a box loaded with bottles of water.

John hesitated. But then he spotted Hester. She was headed his way. He grabbed two bottles and took off after the stranger before she could spot him.

"Name's Zeke," the long-haired man said after they had plodded their way across a field and finally climbed onto a loading dock at an abandoned warehouse. Zeke settled in with his back against the concrete wall under a torn awning that would protect them if the rain started up again. After he'd screwed the top off his water, he drank half of it in one gulp and then wiped his mouth with the back of one hand. "And you are?"

"John Steiner."

To his astonishment Zeke grinned. "And a legend in your own time, my friend." He patted the place beside him. "No joke. Among folks like me you are the man. Setting yourself up in the old Tucker place with nobody bothering you or telling you where to be and when to be there." He shook his head in amazement. "How'd you manage it?"

"I bought the property," John said.

"Well, I *know* that," Zeke replied, clearly offended.

Something clicked with John. "Zeke? You're a friend of Jeannie Messner's?"

"Ah, little Jeannie with the flaming red hair," Zeke said, and the softening of his features said more than words about the special place the young woman held in his life. "Like my little sister," he added.

"She was worried about you," John told him.

Zeke grinned. "Jeannie's a people person. Doesn't understand folks like you and me."

John was more than a little uncomfortable with the assumption of some kind of bond. He wasn't homeless after all. Well, he was for the time being, but that would change for him once he got back to his place. The night before at the Detlef house, he'd fallen asleep planning what he would do first, where he could stay while he rebuilt, how he would revive the citrus groves and garden.

"I could help you get back there if you like," Zeke said. "You wait around for permission, and you'll be sitting here for a couple of weeks."

John was tempted to laugh. Surely the man was joking. Zeke didn't appear to have any means of transportation beyond his two feet, which at the moment were clad in combat boots with soles that needed replacing. Still, the man deserved some respect.

"How would you do that?"

Zeke shrugged. "There's always a boat around, down at the bay."

"Look, I think you've got the wrong idea about me. I mean, I appreciate your interest and the offer to help, but. . ."

"Relax, dude. We're not talking about stealing a boat. Sarasota's a friendly town. I know people who know people, and, well, from time to time we do favors for each other. You know Margery Barker?"

"We've met," John replied cautiously.

"Thought so. Margie knows everything there is to know about anyone and anything having to do with the bay." He polished off the rest of his water and then stuck the bottle out into the rain to let it refill with the runoff from the awning. "She'd help us with getting a boat."

"Thanks. I'll think about it." John found the entire discussion uncomfortable and decided to change the subject. "Are you Mennonite or Amish, Zeke?"

To his surprise, Zeke seemed to accept the abrupt shift in topics as normal. "Neither," he replied. "Used to be Catholic." He laughed at some private joke and then added, "Can you see me as an altar boy?"

John could not help smiling. "Not really," he admitted.

The two men sat together in the silence of comrades for several minutes. They watched the rain dripping off the awning and studied the restless sky.

"Looks like Ma Nature's not done with us yet," Zeke commented with a nod toward the west.

"Maybe we should get back," John suggested. "There are people who worry about you."

Zeke turned his gaze to John. "And you?"

John shrugged and got to his feet. "You coming?" He jumped down from the loading dock and started back across the vacant lot.

Zeke drained his water bottle, then once again refilled it under a rivulet of rain running off the awning before heading in the opposite direction. "Got to go get my guitar—music soothes the restless and the terrified," he said with a wink. "You let me know if you change your mind about that boat."

John nodded. "Thanks," he called out as the homeless man

headed around the side of the deserted warehouse. "How will I contact you?" he added, realizing that Zeke hardly seemed the sort to carry around a cell phone.

"I'll find you and check in." He slid past a barricade intended to keep people from trespassing inside the deserted building and disappeared into the shadows. "No worries," he called out, the words echoing in the empty structure.

John wished he could agree with that statement.

Chapter 9

Samuel Brubaker liked Hester well enough. She was a hardworking woman who clearly took to heart her devotion to serving others. She was also a good homemaker. The house she shared with her father was spotless. She was an excellent cook. She certainly was an attractive woman. And yet the truth of the matter was that she made him uneasy. She had a gravity about her that should have impressed him, he supposed, and he respected that side of her. But what seemed to him to be missing was some semblance of softness, of lightheartedness. Some evidence that she found joy in her life.

He was younger than she was by two years, and somehow he always felt as if he should defer to her greater wisdom and maturity. She seemed more like a teacher he'd had in elementary school than a woman he might consider a friend, or a wife. He'd tried to convince himself that it was because she was the daughter of a minister, but back home in Pennsylvania, he'd been friends with the daughters of his minister, and they had been nothing like Hester.

On the other hand, she would make an excellent mother for his children. She would know exactly how to instill the respect for others and the love of God that he had always hoped to find in a mate. Samuel himself tended toward softheartedness when it came to children. His nieces and nephews adored him because—to the consternation of his sisters and brothers—he almost always sided with the youngsters. That would not do when he had children of his own. Discipline was key to living the plain life.

He watched Hester as she moved among the crowds of people driven from their homes by the flooding creek, now waiting for permission to take one of the cots that had been brought to the church in case of an overflow at the shelters. She offered them a kind of quiet comfort that she rarely displayed when she was handing out assignments in her volunteer role. She cradled a baby and placed a caressing palm on the tangled hair of a toddler crying over some missing toy. And all the while she knelt next to a woman who looked ready to pass out from fear and exhaustion.

"She's a wonder—our Hester," a woman's voice commented from behind him. When he turned, the young woman he'd seen in church and around Pinecraft was passing out bottles of drinking water. She thrust a bottle of water into his hand. "Here, you look like you could use some." She wore a captivating smile, a white prayer covering gone limp in the rain and humidity, and the unmistakable scars of having been badly burned in a fire.

She pulled an overturned milk crate next to him and plopped down as she opened a second bottle of water and took a long drink. "Hester was the first person I saw after the fire," she continued as if she and Samuel had been engaged in conversation for hours. She absently fingered the purplish stains on her neck. He saw that they also covered her forearms, the backs of her hands, and what he could see of her ankles. "She was the one who had to tell me my parents and siblings had all died, and that I was the only survivor."

It occurred to him that she had simply assumed, perhaps from long experience, that his first questions would be about the burns. "I'm sorry for your loss," he murmured, then quickly corrected himself, "Losses."

The young woman glanced down. "God's will. Hester says

there's a lesson to be learned from whatever happens, and just because we can't figure it out right away doesn't mean there's no good reason."

She turned to face him squarely and smiled. That smile in combination with the deep violet of her eyes took his breath away. "I'm Rosalyn, by the way. Can I get you something to eat?"

Samuel shook his head, still dumbfounded by the unexpected beauty of her smile. "Samuel Brubaker," he said, "from Pennsylvania."

She laughed and the sound was like music. "Well, Samuel Brubaker from Pennsylvania, glad to make your acquaintance." She pushed herself to her feet. "How about giving me a hand over here? We've got about a bazillion cans of tuna we need to open and pass out to people—before they pass out from hunger," she added and laughed again. "Get it? Pass out before they pass out?"

Hester heard Rosalyn's laughter and glanced up. Her friend was talking to Samuel, and he was grinning down at her, his eyes fairly dancing with interest, even attraction. Hester wondered at her own lack of jealousy. After all, in the weeks since Samuel's decision to stay on in Pinecraft, they had spent many evenings together in the company of her father or her grandmother. The four of them had played board games and worked in her mother's garden. And more often than not, Samuel came by to share breakfast with Hester and Arlen each morning before the two men headed off to Arlen's furniture store and workshop. Yes, over the short time he'd been in Pinecraft, Samuel had become like a member of the family, and yet. . .

He was handsome in a perennially boyish way, and he was kind and had a wonderful sense of humor. He complimented her cooking and admired her needlework even though Hester was well aware that in that arena she was not as gifted as most despite her mother's and grandmother's efforts to teach her. Surely when she saw him talking to another woman—flirting with her even—Hester should feel some twinge of alarm. Wasn't it normal to become somewhat territorial under such circumstances? So how come all she felt when she glanced up at the sound of Rosalyn's merry laughter was pleasure at seeing her friend so obviously enjoying herself?

"It's too soon," she muttered. "Feelings will grow. . .in time."

"I need to talk to you."

Hester turned to find John Steiner standing across the table that was loaded with cases of canned tuna. He was scowling at her, which seemed to be his usual demeanor. She couldn't help but pity the poor woman who would one day end up married to this cantankerous, not to mention irritating, man.

"Herr Steiner," she began.

"John," he corrected automatically. "Look, what do you know about this Zeke character?"

Okay, she hadn't seen that coming. "Zeke? He's. . ." She narrowed her eyes and studied John. "Why?"

"Why what?"

"Why do you want to know my opinion of Zeke Shepherd?"

"All I want to know is whether or not I can trust the guy or if he's all talk."

"Why?" she repeated, refusing to back down.

John let out a sigh of frustration. "It's a simple question, Hester. Can I trust the guy or not?"

Hester looked over to where Zeke had just made his way through the throngs of people and was now sitting cross-legged on the ground strumming his guitar and singing to a group of toddlers. "You tell me," she said, nodding toward the scene.

She didn't miss the surprise in John's expression. "I thought he was still. . ." he muttered, then shook his head and turned his attention back to Hester. "Looks can be deceiving. Anyone can pull off an act when they've got kids around."

"Even you, John Steiner?" She couldn't help it. There was something about the man that brought out a disturbing streak of impishness in her.

He frowned down at her. "Okay, so he's one of the good guys. Thanks." He started toward Zeke, then turned back to her.

"When do you think this rain might let up?"

"It's not raining at the moment," Hester said.

"You know what I mean—clear skies?"

She shrugged. "Only God can answer that."

"Best guess?"

Hester stepped out from under the arbor that protected a portion of the courtyard and scanned the sky. "There's some clearing there to the west. That's a good sign. Probably by morning we'll start to see the waters recede and the skies clear." She let him take two steps before adding, "Why?"

"Just curious," he said, his voice far too casual. After all, in the short time she'd known the man, he'd done little other than bark out demands or object to the instructions of others. This was not a man who casually asked about anything. He had a plan, and Hester was going to figure it out before he placed himself—and possibly Zeke—in more danger.

"We could use a hand passing out this food," she called as he walked quickly away.

"Can't," was his curt reply.

"Can't or won't?" Hester seethed through gritted teeth as she watched him disappear into the crowd.

By late the following day, the rain had stopped, and the skies had indeed started to clear. True to his word, Zeke managed to get a small fishing boat and meet John at the city's main marina. He fired up the motor, and the two men headed south through the mostly deserted waters of Sarasota Bay.

"I bunked on that boat for a while before I got set up in my place near the bridge," Zeke said, nodding toward a battered old sailboat that was listing badly and had been marked with a neon orange tag warning the owners to move it or lose it. "Does no good to tag these things," Zeke added. "They've been abandoned. Folks think having a boat is romantic. It's work is what it is, a lot of work."

John let the man continue his monologue without comment.

He was thinking about his property, about the last view he'd had of it from the air. Was it really as bad as it had seemed? Maybe not, given the scenery they were passing. The botanical gardens, for example, seemed to be in pretty good shape. Some wind damage to the structures and greenhouses plus flooding near the bay, but overall, the gardens looked to be reasonably intact. He allowed himself to hope.

Zeke guided the boat around a rookery where pelicans roosted by the dozen as if trying—like John—to decide their next move. Zeke steered on past the mouth of Philippi Creek. "Tricky here," he muttered as he maneuvered the boat carefully around trees that had fallen into the water where the rush of water had eroded the shoreline. "You got a pier?"

"I had one, until a couple days ago," John replied, remembering now how Hester and the others had had to wade in to shore that first day after the hurricane hit.

"No worries." Zeke guided the boat toward a fallen tree and expertly looped the rope around a branch stripped bare of its foliage.

Awkwardly John climbed out using his good arm for leverage and reminding himself that his ability to do anything useful in the next six weeks was limited. Not only had an X-ray taken at the hospital that morning confirmed that his wrist was broken, but it was his left wrist, and he was left-handed. Daily activities he had taken for granted had become all-consuming. Already he'd had to teach himself the rudiments of eating and brushing his teeth again. Wielding a hammer, never mind a saw or screwdriver, would be monumental.

"Geezle Pete," Zeke said. The expression came out like a long-drawn-out whisper. He had made it up the bank and over the fallen pine trees and was staring at his surroundings.

John picked his way carefully over the rubble of the trees until he was standing next to Zeke. Speechless, he forced himself to scan the land. His memory of how it had looked when he'd left didn't do the scene justice. He jumped slightly when Zeke clutched his shoulder and squeezed it. Anything Zeke might have said was expressed in that single gesture of sympathy. Grateful for the man's instinct to stay silent, John did not shrug away from the contact. Instead, he drew strength from this stranger's gift of understanding. He was very glad that he had not come here alone.

"Thanks for bringing me here," he muttered and reached down to unearth a dented teakettle that had found its resting place some fifty yards from the main house.

Zeke took a couple of tentative steps toward the house and almost tripped over a kitchen chair buried under a pile of broken palm fronds. He dug it out and examined its metal legs and vinyl seat before setting it next to the kettle that John had carefully placed on a patch of reasonably dry ground.

John watched as Zeke tested the chair for sturdiness, and again he felt a surge of gratitude toward the man. Zeke continued to prowl through the debris for other salvageable pieces to add to the chair and teakettle. "What's your plan?" Zeke asked.

"Not sure," John replied.

That was the last the two men spoke for the next hour as they wandered the property. Collecting the bits and pieces that had once been the makings of John's life seemed as good a first step as any.

Only when they heard the rumble of heavy equipment and the whine of gas-powered saws in the distance did the two men look up from their scavenging. The noise was coming toward them from the overgrown and now completely impassable lane that led from John's house out to the main road.

"Company," Zeke shouted above the din and added a plastic dish rack filled with a couple of unbroken glasses and cups and one plate to the growing pile of goods.

John finished digging out a No Trespassing sign, grasped it with his good arm, and stood at the end of the lane waiting. He couldn't help noticing that Zeke took this opportunity to roost on top of what was left of one wall of the packinghouse as if settling in to watch a baseball game.

The din of the heavy road equipment roared ever closer, although the foliage was so thick that John could not yet see the actual vehicles. He heard the whine of the saw and then the crackle of breaking wood, punctuated by a heavy thud as a large tree branch hit the ground. John tightened his grip on the sign and waited. Zeke leaned back on one elbow and watched.

When the bulldozer broke through the last tangle of pepper vines, scrub oak, and royal palms that had fallen like dominoes during the hurricane, the driver set the engine on idle and stared at John through mirrored sunglasses. Then he glanced back as if looking for reinforcements.

"You're on private property," John yelled.

The bulldozer driver held up one finger and continued to look behind him.

A battered four-wheel-drive open-air Jeep rumbled over broken branches and sand dunes until it came to a stop next to the bulldozer. A man John recognized as Grady Forrest emerged from the passenger side, and then Arlen Detlef and Samuel Brubaker climbed out of the backseat. The Jeep's driver cut the engine and waited.

While Grady consulted with the bulldozer driver, Arlen and Samuel started toward John. Arlen was smiling broadly as if he had simply stopped by for a visit.

"John! *Wie geht's?*" he shouted above the low sustained drumbeat of the motorized vehicles lining the lane now.

"Pastor Detlef," John replied respectfully, but he did not lower the sign. "Samuel."

Undaunted, the two men continued walking toward him. "I see Zeke was able to borrow a boat so you could get here," Arlen continued, glancing at Zeke, who raised two fingers in the peace sign but made no move to leave his position. "We looked for you at the church, but. . ."

John ignored this observation. "What do you want?" he asked. "More to the point, what do they want?" He jerked his arm toward the entourage of men wearing bright yellow hard hats now gathering around the bulldozer.

"Now, John, I explained all this. Samuel and I are with the Mennonite Disaster Service. Those men are with the local utility company, and Grady there is with the county. It is our job to—"

"I know who everybody is. I don't want you here."

"We only wish to help," Samuel said. His voice was soft, conciliatory, but his stance was every bit as unyielding as John's.

"I see you have been able to rescue several items from your home," Arlen observed, moving closer to the pile that Zeke and John had created over the last hour. He held up a ceramic mug. "Not so much as a chip," he observed. "And yet it flew from all the way over there."

"Mr. Steiner?" Grady and the man who'd been driving the Jeep were picking their way across the rubble. "Do you have a few minutes?"

Perhaps because he had been expecting the county's man to dish out orders instead of asking permission, John nodded and relaxed his grip on the sign slightly.

"Great." Grady waved a clipboard in the air. "This is Dennis Jenkins. He's an engineer with the county. I thought maybe we could make a survey of your property and see what might be the best plan for going forward."

"What's your plan?" Zeke had asked, and after over an hour of digging through rubble to salvage bits and pieces of his life, John had to admit to himself that he didn't have one. Surveying the damage made sense. Grady was now close enough that John could see that the paper on the clipboard was a sort of checklist. It couldn't hurt to let the engineer have a look around.

"I thought you were bringing in a team of volunteers, an RV team," John said to Arlen.

"Ja, well, we could hardly drive RVs in here with the lane impassable," Arlen reasoned. "Let the engineer do his job, John."

"Very well," John said, "but those guys stay put. And cut off those motors," he added, glaring at the cluster of workers in hard hats.

"Done." Grady gave a signal, and the rumble of machinery wheezed to silence.

As he walked the property with Grady and the engineer, John noticed that Arlen and Samuel followed along. Every once in a while Arlen would murmur something to Samuel, and the younger man would nod and make a notation on a folded sheet of paper with a stub of a pencil. In spite of his fluency in the German dialect common to both the Amish and Mennonite faiths, John could not decipher these exchanges, but he could certainly appreciate that it was far more important to give his full attention to Grady and the engineer. For in the midst of what appeared to be casual and sympathetic comments about the outbuildings, the house and the plantings, Grady was eliciting other information.

"Do you have insurance?" he asked.

The question stopped John cold in his tracks. Of course he didn't have insurance. In his world, neighbors took care of neighbors. There was a fund within the church congregation for helping people in his situation. But he was no longer part of that community, the one that had rebuilt his neighbor's house after a fire. The one that had provided a young mother and her seven children with the funds to keep going after her husband was badly injured in a farming accident.

"I have money," he growled even as he mentally calculated just how little money was left from the sale of his farm after he had paid for the property, the renovations, and the plants he'd had to buy here in Florida. Even before the hurricane, he'd been grudgingly considering the prospect that he would need to find ways to supplement his meager funds by fall. "I have tools," he added. "I can rebuild."

"In time perhaps," Grady said with a barely concealed glance at John's injured arm. "Why don't you wait here while we poke around the foundation of the house?"

The suggestion didn't deserve an answer, and John doggedly followed Grady and the engineer over a mound of wet sand and rubble to what had been the front door of his house.

"Arlen?" Grady shouted, and the minister turned away from the chicken coop that he and Samuel had been inspecting. "Wanna come have a look at this?" John waited while the three men slowly worked their way to the interior of the house. He was aware that Zeke had come to stand with him. The two of them watched as Samuel scrambled up a pile of broken bricks and chunks of concrete to get a closer look at the chimney. He turned to Arlen and shook his head, and Grady made a note on his clipboard. This pantomime was repeated at least three other times before Grady came back to where John waited.

"The good news is that there's no reason you can't rebuild," Grady said slowly, not meeting John's eyes.

"And the bad news?"

"You'll have to start from scratch. This stuff—" Grady waved a hand over the remains of the packinghouse and outbuildings and shook his head. "You'll need permits. I can help you get the survey and flood certification documents, but you're going to need permits for the building, plumbing, electrical—if you decide to put that in—and when it's all up again, you'll need a final inspection and occupancy permit before you can move in."

"It's my land," John argued. "I don't need anyone's permission to live on my own land."

"You're right," Grady agreed. "But unless you plan to live in a tent here, you're going to need those permits."

"And if I refuse?"

"There will be fines, hefty fines that will make the cost of the permit look like peanuts. And you could go to jail."

John felt a sense of overwhelming grief rise up into his throat. He had worked so very hard, and he had come so close. Why would God test him in such a way?

"I'll start over," he said and only realized he had spoken aloud when Zeke grinned.

"That's the spirit," the homeless man said as he clapped John on the back.

John couldn't help noticing that neither Grady, Arlen, nor Samuel seemed to share Zeke's enthusiasm. And their obvious doubt only strengthened John's will to succeed.

"You'll still need those permits," Grady warned.

John did not acknowledge this comment. Instead, he held out his right hand to Grady. "Thanks for coming," he said as in turn he shook hands with Grady, Arlen, and Samuel. He even shook hands with the engineer. "Now, if you don't mind, I've got work to do."

"As long as they're here," Arlen said with a nod toward the men in hard hats and the bulldozer, "why don't we clear away those fallen trees by your beach?"

John weighed his answer against what was most likely to get these people to leave as soon as possible and decided that since the bulldozer and other equipment had to turn around, they might as well move the fallen trees. "I'd appreciate that," he told Arlen and could not deny that it felt good to see the older man's smile. It was not a smile of victory. Rather, it was one of appreciation. Arlen was grateful for John's willingness to allow him to do at least a part of the work he no doubt believed that he had been sent by God to accomplish.

True to their word, Grady, Arlen, and Samuel climbed back into the Jeep driven by the engineer and followed the heavy machinery back down the lane as soon as the trees were moved out of the way and the path from the house to where the pier had once stood had been cleared.

"You're going to need some help," Zeke commented as he watched them go. "Those MDS crews can get a lot done in a short time if you give them half a chance."

"I expect you're right," John replied, "but I just need time to think it all through. Can you understand that?"

"Yep." Zeke headed back to where he'd left the boat. "You ready?"

It was just past noon, and there was so much to do. Surely Zeke wasn't planning to—

"I gotta get the boat back," Zeke called as he unleashed the boat from the tree and waited. "You coming?"

John wasn't ready to go. Not yet. But then, the boat was the only way in or out. He let out a sigh. "Be right there," he called and turned to take one more look around, memorizing every detail. And that was when he remembered that the lane was open. He could stay and walk out to the road.

"You go on," he shouted. "I'm going to stay awhile longer."

"No worries," Zeke replied as he pulled the starter rope and eased the boat back out into the calm waters of the bay.

Part Two

O thou afflicted, tossed with tempest, and not comforted,
behold, I will lay thy stones with fair colours,
and lay thy foundations with sapphires.
ISAIAH 54:11

A single gentle rain makes the grass many shades greener.
HENRY DAVID THOREAU, *WALDEN: LIFE IN THE WOODS*

Chapter 10

Hester and her family had spent over a week at the church shelter before Jeannie Messner insisted they come and stay with her. By that time, power and water had been restored to Jeannie's neighborhood as well as much of Pinecraft, although there were still outages in the homes along the creek.

Jeannie and her husband, Geoff, lived with their daughter, Tessa, in a large house on Slipper Street just outside the Pinecraft area. Given that there was no word when they might be able to move back to the houses ruined by the flooding, Hester and her father gratefully accepted Jeannie's invitation.

"Emma and her brood are in here," Jeannie told Hester as she led her down an upstairs hallway past three inviting-looking bedrooms. "My sister insisted on taking only one room for her entire family." She rolled her eyes. "Do not ask me to understand the sense of that when Sadie and Tessa could easily share. They've always been more like sisters than cousins, and we could put a cot in my sewing room for Matt."

"Gramma and I can share a room," Hester suggested.

"Actually, I thought Nelly could stay in Geoff's study on the ground floor. It's close to the powder room and no stairs for her to manage," Jeannie continued. "And the hide-a-bed is fairly comfortable, short-term."

"This is very kind of you, Jeannie. I mean, after all, with school about to start, you and Geoff must have your hands full."

The perky red-haired woman's large eyes sparkled. "Hey, I didn't completely lose my way when I came over to the 'dark' side." She laughed at her own joke about making the leap from the conservative to the more liberal branch of the faith. "I thought you and Margery could share this room, and then your dad and. . .what's his name? The guy from Tucker's Point?"

"John?" Hester's step slowed. Surely Jeannie wasn't thinking of inviting John Steiner to stay with her as well.

"John Steiner," Jeannie repeated, committing the name to memory. "He can bunk in with Zeke and your dad—if I can get Zeke to come in out of the rain."

"Unlikely," Hester said, although her mind was still on the idea of John Steiner in this bustling house.

Jeannie laughed. "Yeah, I know, but I do keep trying. The man is a gifted musician. One of these days he's going to be discovered, and, well, I want to be sure he doesn't forget me when he's rich and famous."

Hester smiled. "You are such a good person, Jeannie."

"Aw shucks, ma'am," Jeannie replied, mimicking a shy cowboy digging the toe of a boot into the carpet. "Just like this friend of mine who will hopefully be getting married to a certain young carpenter from Pennsylvania soon, I just can't stand seeing folks in need."

But Jeannie's brand of service was different. While Hester and Emma were constrained by the rules and protocol set forth by their respective agencies, Jeannie simply went out and did good in the world. She walked down a street, saw someone in need, and took action. No questions asked about should I or could I— just action. Once, when Hester had mentioned Jeannie's gift for helping others, Jeannie had grinned. "Like the ad on TV says, 'Just do it.' Works for me."

This certainly wasn't the first time that Hester had felt confused by Jeannie's references to popular media. Hester and her father owned a small television, but it was used for information like weather updates, not entertainment. But she understood that like any Mennonite woman would, Jeannie was simply deflecting the compliment she'd been given.

"And speaking of good-looking carpenters from Pennsylvania, I forgot about a place for Samuel," Jeannie said, frowning. "Well, Geoff can just bring in another rollaway. How about some lemonade?"

"Samuel has his camper. He had taken it to pick up more cots for the church the morning the creek flooded, so it was unharmed," Hester reminded her.

Jeannie grinned and clapped her hands. "Perfect. We can park it on the drive, and Matt can bunk out there with him." She started down the curved stairway with Hester following. "I mean, my sister is pure salt of the earth when it comes to being good people, but can you imagine expecting two teenagers to bunk in with their parents even for a couple of nights, and this will be a lot longer than a couple nights." She shook her curly hair. "She has got to loosen those apron strings."

Jeannie filled tall slender glasses with ice and then covered the cubes with lemonade. "Tessa cannot wait to have what she likes to call 'our' lemonade," she said, nodding toward a tree that was heavy with fruit not yet ready for picking outside the kitchen window. "And how blessed are we Floridians to be able to walk outside our back door and right there hanging from branches are lemons and limes and oranges and grapefruit? I've lived here my whole life, but I still can't get over how fortunate we are to be living in such beauty." She seemed not to notice the destruction the winds and rain had caused to the variety of fruit trees in her yard. Instead, she boosted herself onto one of the high stools that lined the serving counter separating her kitchen from a large family room and took a long swallow of her store-bought lemonade.

"Speaking of Samuel," she said as she set the glass on the counter and gave Hester her full attention. "What's the deal?"

Hester felt the familiar prickle of irritation that had lately begun to accompany anyone's question regarding Samuel's place in her life. *I don't know,* she sometimes wanted to scream. *And besides, it's none of your business.*

But there was something about Jeannie that invited sharing, and before she could censor herself, Hester was telling Jeannie all about her exasperation with her father's clumsy attempt at matchmaking. "He means well," she said, trying hard to walk the fine line between criticizing her father and expressing her own frustration. "He just wants me to be happy."

"Aren't you?"

The question stunned Hester. For so long she had been going about her life, her daily routine, under the assumption that she was doing what she needed to do to care for others and at the same time find some personal happiness for herself.

"Of course," she replied too quickly.

Jeannie lifted an eyebrow and got up to refill their glasses. "I mean 'happy' as in over the moon, can't wait to get up in the morning to see what the new day might bring," she said. "I mean having someone or something in your life that just thinking about it, or him, makes you glow." She set the glasses down and looked at Hester. "Samuel," she whispered and leaned forward to study Hester more closely. "Nope. Not even a twinkle, much less a glow."

"It doesn't always happen that way. I barely know the man," Hester protested.

Jeannie shrugged. "I met Geoff on a Friday morning down at the bay. He was fishing and I was looking for conch shells. He asked me out. I said yes and three days later he proposed, and I said yes." She glanced around. "And fifteen years later, here we are. . .happy as clams."

"But everyone knows that both you and Geoff are incurable romantics," Hester reminded her. "Some of us are more—"

"Take the word of a romantic, then. Samuel is not for you, and, for that matter, you aren't for him. The two of you might make a go of it, but for all the wrong reasons. Life on this planet is way too short to settle." It was the same advice that Emma had offered her.

Hester took a moment to drink her lemonade and let Jeannie's advice sink in. Emma's sister had always had a reputation for being spontaneous and even a little capricious at times, but she was making perfect sense now, and that alone made Hester uneasy. A clock chimed in the family room. "I have to get back," she said. "Thanks so much for taking us in. We've got crews ready to start scrubbing down the homes that got flooded as soon as MDS gets the go-ahead to go in and take care of the major stuff. I expect we'll be able to move everyone back in by mid-September—that's only a week and a half away, but if having us here becomes too much. . ."

"Hey, stay as long as you need to. We thrive on the ruckus," Jeannie assured her as the two of them walked to the front door. She stood on tiptoe and kissed Hester's cheek. "I'll take care of getting Nelly from the shelter. She'll be all settled in by the time you and Arlen get here later tonight."

"Thanks. We really appreciate it."

Hester was already on her bike when Jeannie crossed the yard to stand next to her. "And don't forget to let John know he's welcome."

Hester felt her cheeks grow pink, and she missed her footing on the bike's pedal and almost fell.

Jeannie laughed. "Hey, is that a twinkle I see?" she called as she headed back to the house.

"Twinkle, my foot," Hester muttered as she pedaled hard down the street. The man had been nothing but trouble from the moment she'd met him.

When Hester got back to Pinecraft, she saw Samuel loading his camper with a variety of tools, gallon jugs of bleach, and boxes of rubber gloves, along with dust masks and protective goggles. Assuming that he was preparing to muck out the houses in the neighborhood by the creek, she pulled her bike up next to him.

"Hi," she said, slightly winded from having ridden away from Jeannie's so fast.

"I was just thinking about you," Samuel said. "Do you have some spare clothes and canned goods I could have? Maybe a sleeping bag or some blankets?"

Hester couldn't help smiling. "Oh, Samuel, you aren't going to have to work all night. The ladies from MCC and CAM will make sure you and your crew have plenty to eat and drink. Just be careful that you—"

"It isn't for me. I mean, it's not meant for cleaning up the houses." He nodded toward the deserted lane where the floodwaters had finally receded and after days of waiting the men could finally start their work. "Arlen's got that covered. I'm taking this stuff out to the Tucker place."

"Why?"

It occurred to Hester that she had seen John Steiner only twice in all the time since he'd helped rescue her grandmother and the others. The first time had been that same day after he and Zeke had taken off together. The second had been earlier that very morning when she was on her way to Jeannie's and she had seen John arguing with Grady. More than a week had passed in between. Where had he been all that time?

"John Steiner has moved back out to his place, and he's refusing to leave," Samuel explained. "I'd really like to help him."

"I saw him in town this morning. He'd traded the splint for a cast and certainly seemed fine."

"Well, yeah, he comes and goes, but he's staying out there and I don't know. There's just something about the guy, Hester. He seems so determined and at the same time so lost."

"What's he doing out there?" Hester had a sudden image of the wreckage of the place the day they had gone to rescue him. It couldn't be much better now. "And how in the world is he managing a boat with one arm in a sling?"

Samuel shrugged. "The utility company cleared the lane to his place, so he gets back and forth by foot, or he hitches a ride. And Zeke and Margery help him out some when he lets them."

"Dad told me that he and Grady surveyed the place and it's pretty much a total loss."

Samuel nodded and continued loading the supplies. "He's got his work cut out for him, that's for sure. So I thought maybe he'd accept the loan of my camper. I mean, he needs a place to sleep and get out of the sun."

"But where will you stay? We're all moving in with Jeannie Messner and her husband, and she's counting on you bringing your camper for extra sleeping space for you and her nephew." She couldn't believe what she was saying. Here was Samuel making a real sacrifice to help a fellow man, and all she could think of was how it was going to be an inconvenience for Jeannie. What was it about John Steiner that made her go against the very mission she had set for her life? Helping others was her calling. She had never questioned the worthiness of a person's cry for help before.

But John wasn't asking for help. In fact, he was doing everything he could to go it alone. And maybe that was her problem. She rarely had faced someone so desperately in need who had neither wanted nor asked for her help.

Samuel pushed back his wide-brimmed straw hat so that he could look at her more directly. "Look, Hester," Samuel said. "I can't explain why I want to help this guy, and I do understand that this may be a fool's errand, but I feel like it's the right thing to do. Spending a night or two in the shelter isn't going to be a hardship for me, but spending another night or two out in the elements with mosquitoes and no-see-ums feasting on his unprotected skin could be a real hardship for John, not to mention a health hazard."

Hester couldn't argue the point. "Stop by the center and tell Rosalyn what you need." She got off her bicycle and leaned it against the back of the RV. "And take this with you so you don't have to walk back to town," she said. "Don't even think of going back to the shelter. Jeannie would never forgive me if I let you do that. There's plenty of room at her house."

Samuel lifted the bike into the camper, then climbed into the driver's seat and smiled down at her. "I won't be gone long, and when I get back I'll get to work helping Arlen and the others get those houses fit for living in again."

John had run out of food. The canned goods he'd put into his emergency kit and unearthed the first day he and Zeke had returned to his property had lasted only a couple of days. The food Margery had dropped off had taken him through the rest of the week. He still had water because he'd rationed that by using water from the creek and boiling it to clean himself up and wash out his clothes and dishes. The first-aid kit had come in handy, especially the sunscreen and bug spray, but both were almost gone. He was well aware that sleeping outside without any protection other than the makeshift lean-to that Zeke had helped him build was just asking for trouble.

On top of everything else, he'd overdone it trying to use his left hand and probably cracked his wrist again. Then he had stepped in a sinkhole while trying to net fish in the bay and sunk in up to his knee, wrenching it badly as he struggled to get out. In short, he was a mess. He knew he should give up, but then what?

He ran his fingers through his hair and swallowed back a lump of sheer panic and frustration. He had put everything he had into this place, and now it was in shambles. He was close to running out of money, and it went against everything he believed to accept any of the help Grady had suggested was available from the government. Back on the farm he would have turned to his neighbors for help. Check that. He wouldn't have had to turn for help because they would have just been there.

Here, by his own stubborn choice, he had deliberately estranged himself from any semblance of community. And although he had out of sheer necessity allowed himself to be helped by Samuel and Zeke, his suspicions had been on high alert whenever anyone representing any official agency— including those run by the Mennonites—offered help. What was in it for them? How much of their concern came from the fact that his aunt held a position of power in the outside world? Hadn't Hester made it clear that there were others who were more in need and more grateful than he was?

He heard the muffled sound of an engine coming down his lane. He waited, knowing he was out of sight on the banks of the bay, well hidden by a cluster of mangroves. Zeke had talked about how he often used the shelter of the mangroves that surrounded his hiding place on the bay as a way of observing without being observed. Stealthily John crawled to a position that would allow him to identify his visitor without being seen.

Samuel Brubaker pulled his camper to a stop under the shade of the split banyan tree closest to what was left of the house. He cut the engine and got out.

"John?"

He glanced around and called out twice more. He walked around the property, picked up a couple of odds and ends, and added them to the pile that Zeke and John had started days earlier. Then on his way back to his vehicle, he paused and studied the ground. After a moment, he bent down, dug into the mud with a stick, and unearthed something that John couldn't quite make out. Instead of adding it to the pile of retrieved objects, he cleaned it off with his handkerchief before carrying it back to the camper. Opening the back hatch, he laid the object inside, removed a bike, and then closed the hatch before taking one last look around.

He balanced the bike against the wall of the toolshed and leaned in through the driver side window of the camper to get pencil and paper. After some thought, he scrawled a note and placed it under the windshield wiper. Then he mounted the bicycle and rode off back toward town, leaving the camper parked there in the shade.

John stayed put for several minutes, making sure that the cabinetmaker was truly gone; then he limped back across the yard and retrieved the note.

John,

Please make use of my camper while you work on your property. I have stocked it as best I could, but if I've forgotten anything, let me know, and I'll see that you get it.

Arlen wants you to know that our offer to send a crew from MDS to help you stands. He's staying at Jeannie Messner's house with Hester and her grandmother if you need to reach him. By tomorrow we should be able to get started shoveling mud from the houses that got flooded there in Pinecraft so hopefully everybody can be back home soon. Power and water are still off by the creek, but in the meantime generators are working. Know that you are welcome anytime to come into town for a meal or a place to rest and refresh yourself. You are in our prayers.

Samuel

John folded the note and placed it back under the windshield wiper. He opened the driver-side door and looked around the cab. Up close he saw that Samuel had basically taken an old pickup truck and mounted the camper top over the bed. The thing looked as if it had seen better days. But John couldn't help but be impressed with how organized and clean everything was inside the cab. Samuel had left the keys in the ignition, and John was unexpectedly touched by that. Samuel had to know that John, being Amish, didn't drive—wouldn't drive. He also had to know that even if he were willing to drive, it was unlikely that he had ever driven a motorized vehicle, at least not in real traffic. The keys were a message of trust. This small camper was probably all that Samuel Brubaker owned other than the clothes he wore. And yet he had entrusted it to John. He considered for a moment whether or not he would have been as charitable had the shoe been on the other foot.

Unlikely, he thought as he walked around to the back of the camper and opened the entrance to the sleeping and storage space. Again, everything was organized and pristine. The area was loaded with supplies. In addition to the cleaning supplies that John would need to get started with reclaiming what he could of the buildings, there were canned goods, bottled drinking water, sunscreen, insect repellant, a battery-powered lantern, and mosquito netting. And lying there in plain sight was his copy of

Walden, still in the plastic bag he had packed it in the night of the hurricane.

John had been looking for this precious book without even being conscious that finding it had driven his search. And here Samuel Brubaker had plucked it from the muck as if it had been right there in plain sight the whole time. John removed the book from the bag. The pages were waterlogged and flattened together, but it was intact. He cautiously turned to the first page. For perhaps the hundredth time he read the words that had started him on this path. Words that had helped him through numerous times when he had grieved for his mother and for all that he had left behind in Indiana, words that led him to this moment.

"*When I wrote the following pages, or rather the bulk of them,*" Thoreau had written, "*I lived alone, in the woods, a mile from any neighbor, in a house which I had built myself, on the shore of Walden Pond, in Concord, Massachusetts, and earned my living by the labor of my hands only.*"

Always he had stopped there, skimming over Thoreau's next words, but now that last sentence of the opening paragraph that he had ignored for so long seemed to be the one that resonated. "*I lived there two years and two months. At present I am a sojourner in civilized life again.*"

"As am I," John whispered, his voice cracking with emotion.

Chapter 11

In spite of the cooler nights that came with the turning of the calendar from August to September, the days could still heat up to a high in the low nineties. So the volunteers from MDS and MCC took full advantage of the cooler early-morning hours to work inside the small houses along the creek.

The men worked tirelessly from dawn until well after dark to clear out any standing water from the Pinecraft dwellings, using portable generators to power the equipment necessary to get the job done. The neighborhood that had been silent and deserted for days vibrated with the sound of power washers, pumps, dehumidifiers, and fans. Every window and door that could be opened was. Some members of the work crews spent their time outside, making sure that drains and gutters were properly attached so that any additional rain would be directed away from houses.

Once the MDS crews had done their work on a cottage, it was time for Hester's volunteers to do their part. Arlen's crews had taken care of removing larger items such as soaked drywall, as well as mattresses, large furniture, and carpeting that were sure to be fertile ground for mold. Hester's volunteers would take the next step, scrubbing down undamaged walls and floors and washing smaller items that could be salvaged.

Olive Crowder was the first person to show up for work on the morning Hester finally got the green light to begin cleaning the cottages along the creek. She acknowledged Hester with her usual scowl of suspicion as if she were already anticipating a problem. Vivid memories of times when Hester had faced Olive's censure were never far from the surface whenever she had to deal with the woman.

In her youth, if Hester ran up the aisle of her father's church to deliver a message from home, Olive would abandon her work stuffing envelopes in the church office or cleaning the sanctuary to glare at Hester. If Hester failed to take note of this condemnation, then Olive would clear her throat loudly, sounding for all the world like a foghorn warning an errant ship.

Later when Hester was in her teens, she had developed a habit of constantly questioning the ways of her faith. "Why?" she would ask, and her parents would patiently explain the tradition and the history. But Olive Crowder saw her curiosity as doubt, and she would warn Hester's parents that the child was becoming far too interested in the *English* lifestyle or ways of outsiders. When Olive heard the news that Hester was headed off to nursing school, she had been—for once—speechless. Not that it was so unusual for Mennonites to seek higher education. The problem for Olive, and others, was that Hester had insisted on pursuing her nursing degree at an institution that had no ties to the church.

The day Hester boarded the bus for college, there in the midst of her family, friends, and neighbors stood Olive. Her arms had been folded around her chest like a straitjacket, and she had stared at Hester through the wide window of the bus as Hester leaned out to touch her family's hands and shout her good-byes. No, Olive Crowder did not approve of the way her pastor's only daughter had turned out one little bit. But Hester knew that out of respect for her parents, the woman would do her part even if that meant taking direction from Hester.

"Thank you for coming," Hester said as other women arrived.

They all donned galoshes and brought rubber gloves, goggles, and masks in preparation for the work. "Due to the power outage and limited availability of generators, it has taken the men longer than we expected to get the standing water cleaned up in these houses, but finally it's our turn to get to work. And look how the Lord has blessed us with the perfect September day to begin."

She had turned to lead them inside when she heard the unmistakable clearing of Olive's throat. "Yes, Olive," she said, turning to smile at her nemesis.

"You know best, of course, but it seems important to me to review the procedure. . .in case there are those among us who have not done this work before."

"Of course," Hester agreed, deciding in an instant that acquiescence was going to get them to work a lot faster than pointing out that every woman there was experienced in cleanup. "First we need to go room by room, removing any wet materials and personal belongings. . ."

"Wet or damp," Olive corrected.

"This includes any throw rugs, bedding, clothing, stuffed toys, books, and the like," she continued. "If you uncover significant mold or mildew on a wall or other surface that you cannot easily remove, please mark it and call it to my attention. A crew will come back and address those larger projects that may have escaped their notice earlier."

"Ja, leave that to the men and the professionals," Olive chimed in.

Hester bit her lower lip hard and continued, "Once we have everything cleared out, then we can start the process of scrubbing down walls and other surfaces such as countertops, cabinets, and floors. Questions?" She looked directly at Olive, who said nothing. "Excellent. Let's get to work."

She had reached the doorway of the Millers' house when she heard Olive mutter. "A prayer would be nice."

Hester stopped in her tracks. "Ja," she said, "it would." She bowed her head and the others followed her lead. She didn't know what the others were praying for, but in her case it was, as always, patience. "Amen," she murmured after a moment of silence.

Once inside the first of a dozen homes that would need their services, the women paired off and went their separate ways—one pair to tackle the kitchen while another headed down the hall toward the bedrooms. Hester smiled when she saw Olive's sister, Agnes, scurry off to join another woman in the kitchen, leaving Hester and Olive standing in the living room.

"Well," Hester said, "those books and boxes of papers are soaked through." She quickly loaded a box, determined it was too heavy to lift, and started to slide it toward the open front door.

"You'll scar the floor," Olive huffed as she lifted one side of the box and waited for Hester to take hold of the other.

Hester stared at the water-stained floor—a floor that would have to be replaced—and then back at Olive. "I've got this."

"Suit yourself," Olive said and dropped her end of the box. "You always do," she added as she turned her attention to removing books from the shelves and stacking them in piles on the floor.

Hester had had enough. She was past thirty years old and a trained nurse, not to mention an experienced community organizer. She pushed the box out onto the front porch and then returned to face Olive.

"Olive, I am doing the best I can in a situation that is beyond what anyone might have imagined. And yet I sense that you don't agree with my approach to this project." *Or any project I am involved with.*

Olive continued removing books one by one, flipping through the pages of each before setting it in one of the piles. "If you must know, Hester, there are several people who don't think that you are doing your best."

Hester took a moment to listen to the sounds coming from other areas of the house. The rest of her crew was occupied. She and Olive were alone and unlikely to be overheard or disturbed. The time had come. "Please explain that statement," she said quietly.

Olive turned and looked at her. Hester met her gaze directly and lifted one eyebrow to emphasize her determination to get their differences out in the open once and for all.

"Very well. You have an unfortunate tendency to give your attention to outsiders when many in your own community are suffering."

Hester opened her mouth to respond, but Olive held up a restraining finger. "For example, it has been noticed and commented upon that you put the welfare of that man, John Steiner, before the welfare of your own grandmother, never mind others in this neighborhood who should have been evacuated hours before it flooded—"

"The county command center gave specific instructions about—"

"And since when do we take our direction from some outside government agency?" Olive demanded. "That is your problem, Hester Detlef. You have always put far too much stock in what outsiders want."

Hester waited a beat, fighting to quell the tide of her own anger and resentment toward this woman's constant judging of her. "That's really what this is about, isn't it?"

Olive sucked in her cheeks. "I don't know what you mean. You asked—"

"Oh, Olive, I truly believe that you have my best interests at heart. Your respect for my father and the years of friendship you shared with my mother make that clear. But just because I have friends in the outside world and I sometimes—"

"Sometimes? Do you not see the sin that is your ego and pride, Hester? I know you think you are merely following in your dear mother's path, but you are not. And I must warn you. . ." Olive raised one gloved hand, stained now with the ink from the wet newsprint she'd begun collecting once she'd gone through the books. She shook her finger in Hester's face. "I feel compelled to warn you that neither your father's position in the community nor the memory of your dear mother can protect you should you continue down this path of pride and conceit."

In the silence that followed this announcement, Hester was aware of a light tapping on the open door, and then Rosalyn stepped inside. "Sorry I'm late," she said, glancing from Hester to Olive and back again. "I—is everything all right?"

"Fine," Hester said. "I'm just going to check on the others." She brushed past Olive, who had returned to her work as soon as Rosalyn entered the room.

But she stopped halfway to the bedrooms and forced herself to take several deep breaths to regain her composure. Olive's words had struck closer to home than Hester was willing to admit aloud. She had chosen to help Grady with the situation at Tucker's Point when she should have focused on getting her grandmother and the others packed up and moved to shelters. Due to her negligence, they had barely avoided disaster. She twisted the tie of her prayer covering around her finger. Pinecraft was her community, not the world beyond that and certainly not Tucker's Point.

Olive had hit another nerve, too. Ever since her mother's death, Hester had felt this urgency to fill her days with work. It was almost as if by running from one task to the next she might be able to suppress the discontent and restlessness that dogged her even when she tried to sleep.

Hester retraced her steps down the hall. "Olive, do you have a minute?" she asked.

The older woman eyed her suspiciously but put down the cloth soaked in beach solution that she was using to wipe down a painted built-in bookcase and waited.

Rosalyn looked from one woman to the other. "I'll just go see if I can be of help in the kitchen," she murmured as she hurried off.

"I'd like to apologize," Hester said. "Both for my behavior earlier and for my actions over the last days and weeks. You were right."

Olive released a self-righteous huff but said nothing.

"Actually, you have done me a great favor," Hester continued, picking up the cleaning rag that Rosalyn had left behind and starting to wash the wall next to where Olive returned to her scrubbing. "I was feeling such guilt about how long I waited before helping my grandmother and others get moved to the shelters. I am so thankful that nothing happened to any of you. If someone had been injured or suffered a heart attack from the stress. . ."

"Fortunately for you, God was with us that day. Perhaps He was using the situation to teach you a valuable lesson—one you have refused to heed despite numerous warnings from others."

Hester did not like thinking of God placing others in harm's way simply to teach her a lesson, but she held her tongue. This was no time for a theological debate. She had come back to apologize and confess that there was an element of truth in Olive's concern.

"Yes, well, I wanted you to know that my rudeness before was born of that sense of guilt."

Olive sloshed her rag in the bucket of sudsy water and twisted it into a skein to squeeze out every extra drop before she returned to wiping down the top of the bookcase and then started on the wall above it. The two of them worked in silence for several minutes until every inch of the wall had been scrubbed clean. All the while Hester was aware that Olive's lips were pressed into that thin line that was a sure sign that she was about to make a pronouncement.

"Am I to understand that you are telling me that you have seen the error of your ways at long last and that you will be resigning your position with MCC?"

Hester could not have been more shocked if the woman had asked if she planned to cut off her right arm as retribution for her transgressions. "I. . . Why would. . . ?"

Olive ignored her sputtering. "Because if you are truly sorry for what you admit is a fault brought on by your decision to volunteer for that agency, then perhaps. . ."

"MCC is a Mennonite agency," Hester reminded her.

"Do not lecture me, *bitte*. I am well aware of who and what they are. I am also well aware that over time the people who have been given responsibility for running that agency have fallen prey to the ways of outsiders. MCC is barely distinguishable from—"

"They do good work—*we* do good work," Hester said quietly as she tried in vain to stem the anger rising inside her.

"That may be, but as the daughter of a minister, you would do well to reconsider your allegiance to that group. CAM is a far more appropriate group, as your friend Emma Keller has been quick to appreciate."

"Appropriate?"

"For us. For you, the only daughter of our pastor."

Hester bit her lower lip and closed her eyes, silently praying for God's guidance. Aware that Rosalyn had returned and was standing in the doorway, Hester forced herself to remain calm. "My work—"

"*Your* work? What about God's work? Oh, Hester, sometimes I despair for you," Olive moaned. "Against all tradition you decided to pursue a career, and, unpaid though it may be, you clearly see yourself as a working woman."

Hester had opened her mouth to deliver a retort that she was sure to regret when Rosalyn stepped the rest of the way into the room and saved her. "Seems to me, ma'am, that we are all working women, at least until we get these houses cleaned up and folks moved back in."

She did not give Olive a chance to respond, but turned instead to Hester. "Kitchen's almost done, so I thought I'd get started on Lizzie's house. If you'll come show me what you want done over there, Hester, I'll round up some warm bodies and get to work."

Gratefully, Hester dropped her rag back into the bucket and followed Rosalyn outside.

———

John was having trouble focusing, literally. His eyes constantly clouded over from the sweat that dripped off his face like raindrops, making it next to impossible to see what he was doing. Between his broken wrist and the ankle he'd twisted, he was already severely limited in what he could accomplish on any given day.

Still, he had made some progress. With Zeke's help he'd

managed to get a tarp over the exposed rafters of the house where the roof had blown off. He'd also scrubbed down the kitchen walls and removed anything that had already produced mold or that might if left untended. It would be some time before he could afford the repairs that would be necessary to restore the second story of the main house, so he had decided to focus his energy on the packinghouse and smaller outbuildings instead. To that end his plan was to make use of the plywood sheets that he'd nailed over the windows before the hurricane came ashore to put down a base for the roof of the packinghouse and work from there.

He had leaned the boards against the walls of the packinghouse that had remained standing after the storm and turned them daily to allow them to dry. Of course they had warped, but not so much that they wouldn't do until he could afford something better. With his one good arm, turning the boards took several hours all by itself, and there was no way that he alone could wrangle them up and into place on the rafters without help. So he would wait until Zeke decided to stop by and they could do it together. He had learned that Zeke's schedule was unpredictable to say the least.

Samuel was more reliable. He had biked out to John's property several times in the days that had passed since leaving the camper with him. He always came alone and after dark when his work in town was finished for the day. John understood that his impromptu visits were the young carpenter's way of building trust. And it was working. He never stayed long, just walked around looking at what John had been able to accomplish since his last visit. Every once in a while he would comment on the progress in Pinecraft.

"MDS has cleared out all of the houses along the creek," he'd told John on his latest visit. "The women from MCC and CAM are scrubbing everything down, and Pastor Detlef expects some folks will be able to start moving back in as early as next week."

"That's good." It occurred to John that Samuel never mentioned Hester. Not that he had any reason to talk about her to John. Besides, why should he care?

"Everybody doing okay otherwise?"

"*Sehr* gut. Jeannie Messner and her husband took in a bunch of people, and others did the same. The shelters aren't nearly so filled as they were right after the storm."

John waited for more explanation of Samuel's definition of *very good* as applied to the situation at hand, but apparently Samuel had nothing more to report. "Well, I'll go back now." He paused and studied John for a long moment. "You look thinner, John. Are you eating?"

"I am. Margery shows up regularly to check on that, and to just in general be sure I'm still breathing."

Samuel nodded. "That's good. She's a good person, perhaps too concerned at times about the welfare of others. She probably told you that she suffered some real damage during the storm, but far more afterward when the floods came. Now that we've cleared out the houses in Pinecraft, Pastor Detlef plans to take a team over to help her get her repairs done so that her business can open again." He mounted the bicycle and began pedaling slowly toward the lane out to the main road. "God bless you, John," he called.

As John watched him go, he had the sudden urge to call him back, to suggest a cup of coffee or a game of checkers—not that he owned a checker set. But he wanted to know more about Margery. He'd been so wrapped up in his own problems that he'd failed to consider that Margery had to have suffered such serious losses as well. It struck him that watching Samuel pedal into the darkness and not knowing for sure when he might see him—or anyone—again, he felt something he hadn't felt in a very long time. John felt loneliness.

That night he had trouble sleeping. Usually at the end of the day he was so thoroughly exhausted that he had barely closed his Bible from his nightly reading before he was asleep. But on this night that wasn't the case. Long after the white noise of the traffic that ran along Highway 41 in the distance had subsided, John lay on his sleeping bag in the back of the camper, his eyes wide open as he stared up through the mosquito netting and listened to an owl calling to its mate.

Margery had said nothing about further damage to her place from the floods. He'd asked her how she was recovering after the storm, and she'd brushed him off as she always did.

"You just get yourself back in shape," she'd barked. "I'll be just fine."

And why would she confide in you? he thought. She could hardly count on him to offer any real help or, for that matter, common sympathy for her plight. Margery knew very well that he cringed every time she showed up and that everything he said or did was with one intention—to get her to leave as soon as possible.

He hadn't always been like this. Back in Indiana he had been known as a man who could be counted on to help a neighbor, help a total stranger for that matter. But he had changed. Instead of his move to Florida being the start of a new life healing the wounds he'd suffered, it seemed those wounds had festered. His anger at the unfairness of life had infected his ability to trust. His ability to care.

True, back home, people he had thought he could count on had turned away from him. People who had expressed love for him had sided with those who accused him of becoming too prideful. John closed his eyes and allowed himself to think about Alice Yoder for the first time in two long years. Just as he had been banned by the church, he had banned the woman he'd been ready to marry from his thoughts, refusing to allow anything about her to color his mind. And in time he had succeeded. Once he'd gotten settled in Florida, the work to get the garden planted, the groves back to producing, and the house habitable had exhausted him to the point where at night it was all he could do to prepare a simple supper, read his Bible, and fall into bed.

Every morning seemed to bring with it some fresh challenge that had to be faced and dealt with, and in time, the image of Alice had faded. But it came to him now that in banning her from his thoughts, he had banned anyone who showed the slightest interest in him, regardless of their age or gender. He had trusted Alice because he'd had no reason not to believe that she would stand with him no matter what. But at the first sign of conflict she had chosen the safety of the community over him. That had been the final straw.

Then when he'd moved into the old farmhouse that had sat unoccupied and abandoned for over a decade, Margery had shown up offering him food and friendship, but he had sent her away. His distrust of others and their hidden motives had been too fresh, too painful, and he had quickly decided that what Thoreau had gotten right was the idea of depending solely on one's self. And over the two years that followed, he had thought the plan was working. He kept so busy that his need for human companionship became secondary to his need to prove himself.

But now he found himself wondering if he had ever intended that his self-imposed isolation would go on indefinitely. It had begun for him as it had for Thoreau, as an experiment. Nothing more. But with each passing day, each challenge met and conquered, the idea that it was possible to live a life of near-self-sufficiency had become the ultimate challenge.

The truth was that he had not allowed himself to think beyond getting through each day. Every victory was something he celebrated alone. No, not alone. With God. For when he'd seen the first vegetables thriving in the raised planter boxes or the blossoms on the trees in Tucker's abandoned grove, he had raised his eyes to the heavens, thanking God. He had needed nothing more than that as evidence that he had made the right choice in coming to Florida.

Back then he had told himself that his community had deserted him, resulting in the loss of his farm, his future wife, and the life they would share. But it was long past time for him to admit that he and he alone had made the decision to leave. He had come to Florida to prove a point. Now he had to wonder if he had really intended to stay forever.

He opened the door to the camper and stepped outside. Above him a full moon sat low in the western sky, casting a beam like a path straight onto the waters of the bay. It would be light soon. Tied up at the pier—one of the first things he and Zeke had restored on the property—was a small boat. Margery had towed it over one day, insisting she had no place for it until her pier could be repaired.

"You'd be doing me a favor keeping it here, Johnny. Not that you're inclined to handing out favors, but I'd appreciate it."

"Fine," he'd told her and gone back to working on clearing out the remains of the chicken coop.

"I'll leave the keys in the ON position–that way you just need to pull the cord to get her started. You know, in case you want to use it or have to move it or something."

"Fine," he'd repeated. He had waited for the sound of her boat fading before going down to the pier and having a look at the craft.

Now with his one good arm, he released the rope from the post and climbed in. Awkwardly he managed to get the boat started, back it away from his pier, and turn it toward the mouth of the creek. By the time he was on his way, he was drenched in sweat. The sky had started to lighten. He headed up Philippi Creek, and just ahead he could see what was left of Margery's marina.

Margery Barker had watched over him for two long years. She had never asked for or seemed to expect anything in return. Indeed, she had endured his barely concealed annoyance at her visits with humor and grace. And his bad temper had not deterred her from coming back again and again. How many times had he shown genuine interest in her business, her health, her happiness? What did he really know of her? That she was a widow and that she ran a fishing charter business. That was pretty much it.

Something his aunt Liz had said the last time they spoke by phone—a phone call that had ended with John hanging up on her—came back to him now.

"You were never a selfish man, John. In fact, you have always been one of the most giving people I have ever known. Rachel was always so proud of the way you turned out."

His aunt had been taking a risk. She knew that any mention

of his mother opened floodgates of remorse and guilt for John.

"Sorry," Liz had murmured, realizing too late her mistake. "But really, John, I am worried about you. You've changed so much."

"I'm fine," he'd managed before hanging up the pay phone. And as he'd stood there in the middle of a nearly deserted bus station where he had gone to use the phone, he had felt a lump of grief fill the cavity of his chest like unset concrete until he'd been forced to sit down to catch his breath.

That conversation had taken place six months ago. Since then Liz had contacted him by mail as often as not delivered by Margery without comment.

His aunt was right. He had changed, and not for the better. He had allowed his bitterness to color everything he did, every interaction with others. He looked into every face these days with distrust, expecting the person to have some agenda other than simple kindness. Margery had proved him wrong, and she deserved more from him than the disdain he'd dished out for two years. For that matter, so did his aunt Liz, but one step at a time.

Chapter 12

As the sun painted the sky in streaks of vermilion and orange, John idled the boat, taking stock of Margery Barker's marina. In spite of catastrophic damage to the bait shop and pier, John could see that a lot of work had already been done. Of course Margery would have gratefully accepted the help of neighbors and friends. She was well known and deeply respected, at least among those who lived and worked along the bay.

Margery's houseboat was tied up at one end of the pier, a pier that he was surprised to see had been fully rebuilt. To either side, small boats in various stages of repair bobbed in the calm water of the creek, the pulleys used to raise their sails clanking against metal poles as if someone were picking out a tune on a row of glass bottles. A tarp covered what had been the roof of the bait shop, but the place appeared deserted, abandoned even. The creek waters smelled faintly of dead fish and the fuel that had obviously leaked out of the damaged boats. In addition to the bait shop, Margery made her living running fishing trips and renting boats to tourists. From the looks of things, the bait shop was closed, and other than the small boat Margery used to get around, there wasn't a vessel worth chartering among the half dozen tied up at the pier.

He eased his craft closer to the houseboat. Margery had once told him that the day she buried her husband she had returned to the marina, boarded the houseboat, and stayed. After a year she had found the strength to return to the house they had shared and clear it out before putting it up for sale. All of this came back to him now as the boat she'd loaned him rocked gently and he tried to decide on his next move.

His heart was beating so hard it was as if he could hear each thud. It had been a very long time since he had reached out to anyone. It came back to him that Samuel had mentioned the fisherwoman was staying with Jeannie Messner. But there were definite sounds of occupancy coming from the houseboat.

"Margery?" He sniffed the air as he brought his boat closer to the side of the houseboat. Coffee. Bacon frying. If vandals had taken over the place, they were surely making themselves at home.

"Margery?" This time he shouted the name.

"What?" Margery barked, coming onto the deck, waving away an unseen bug with a spatula. Then she saw him, and her eyes widened, as did her smile. "Well, now, will you look at what the tide brought in! Praise God and pass the cranberry sauce—I never ever thought I would see this day."

He threw her the rope. "You gonna help me tie this thing up and invite me in for breakfast or stand there yapping all morning?" he grumbled.

True to form, Margery made no further comment about his unexpected visit. Instead, she guided him the rest of the way into her pier and looped the rope over a post. Then she gave him a hand as he made the short leap from boat to pier and led the way into the galley kitchen, where she turned on the gas under the skillet and cracked four large eggs into the bacon grease.

"Moved back here four days ago," she announced. "Jeannie's place was nice, too nice for the likes of me. Lots of pretties in that house, and you know me, clumsy as the day is long. I kept worrying I might break something. And with school starting they were all busy with that. Truth be told, I could not wait to get this old bucket in good enough shape so I could bunk here again."

John attacked the food as soon as she set the plate in front of him. He'd been eating little other than prepackaged meals or canned goods for days now, and he couldn't remember the last time that he'd had a hot meal. "Good," he muttered with his mouth full of scrambled eggs and biscuit. He glanced up when he realized Margery had stopped talking and was leaning against the sink, arms folded as she watched him eat.

"Didn't you forget something?"

John felt color rise to his cheeks and was grateful for the sun-scorched skin that he assumed hid his embarrassment. "Sorry," he muttered and put down his fork. He leaned back and waited for Margery to fill her plate and join him.

"I'm touched," she said as she set her plate down and took the chair across from him, "but I was talking about saying grace. I thought a good Amish man like you—"

"I. . ." John decided not to debate the point. Instead, he closed his eyes and bowed his head. After a moment he resumed eating.

"Arlen's sending me some help today," Margery said.

"MDS team?"

"Not officially. Just neighbors helping neighbors, as Arlen likes to put it."

He drank a full glass of orange juice before he found the nerve to make his next statement. "I have some time if you can use an extra hand."

John was pretty sure it was his unsolicited offer to help that had struck Margery speechless for once. But when he glanced at her, he saw that she was fighting the urge to burst into laughter. "What?"

"An extra hand and maybe one good leg," she managed, her laughter escaping as she pointed to his cast and wrapped ankle, "is about all you're in a position to offer."

John couldn't help himself. The situation was so ridiculous that laughter seemed the only response. And once he got his own good humor rolling, it seemed as if he had unleashed a wellspring that had for far too long been capped.

Hester and Arlen exchanged curious glances as they walked the length of Margery's pier and heard her hearty laughter rolling out the open windows of the houseboat. Then they heard the unmistakable raspy growl of John Steiner's voice. "All right already," he was saying, but he was laughing as well.

"Hello," Arlen called as he stepped onto the deck and then offered his hand to Hester.

Margery stuck her head out the missing door. She was wiping tears of merriment from her eyes with the hem of her oversized T-shirt. "Come on in and have some breakfast," she invited. "You are not going to believe who has offered to lend us a hand." This last seemed to set her off all over again, and when Arlen and Hester stepped into Margery's cramped living space, Hester was stunned to see John apparently still recovering from whatever joke Margery had told. The effect that his smile had on her was unsettling, and she looked away.

"Well, now, this is a nice surprise," Arlen boomed as he grasped John's shoulder and gave it a squeeze. "How are you faring over at Tucker's Point, John?"

All traces of humor disappeared. When Hester glanced his way, she saw that John's deep-set eyes had darkened like storm clouds over the Gulf. "Well enough. I should thank you for sending Samuel to check in on me from time to time. The loan of his camper has been a special blessing."

Hester and her father exchanged a look. Neither of them had had any idea that Samuel had continued to visit John after he had gone out there to leave his camper.

"Samuel makes his own choices," Arlen replied.

The tiny space was suddenly filled with silence until Margery came to the rescue. "Well, we'll get nothing done standing around here jabbering. Go on out there on the deck where there's more room. Find some shade and have something to eat. Whoo-ee! Guess this is what folks up north call Indian summer. Cool nights and scorching days. Welcome to autumn in Florida."

"We ate at home," Arlen told her, "but I always leave room for at least one of your biscuits, Margery."

"Let me help you," Hester offered, taking down two more

plates from the open shelving above the sink and holding them while Margery dished up bacon with one hand while scrambling more eggs with the other. Hester was glad to see John take his almost-empty plate and coffee mug and follow her father outside. "When did he get here?" she asked Margery in a near whisper.

"John?" She glanced at the clock and shrugged. "Half hour ago. You could've knocked me over with a feather when I saw him out there, steering that old piece of junk of mine with one hand." She chuckled. "I'll bet it took him near quarter of an hour just to get her fired up and backed away from his pier, but the man is stubborn."

"What does he want?"

"Want?" Margery looked at Hester as if she had suddenly started speaking in tongues. "He says he's come to help."

"After two years?"

"Oh, honey, it may seem like two years, but that storm blew here only just over a month ago." She topped off the plates Hester was holding with two hot biscuits each. "Oh, I get it. You mean why come now when he's never made the move before?"

Hester nodded and waited for Margery to pour coffee in two chipped, mismatched mugs.

"People change all the time," Margery said. "Admittedly some take longer than others, but he's here, and that's the main thing." She led the way out to the deck, where John and Arlen had found shelter in the shade. John was pointing to something above them, and Arlen was nodding.

"You want a refill?" Margery asked John. He held out his coffee mug.

"Get it yourself," Margery barked. "This cook's done her thing for the morning."

Hester watched as John got up and made his way back to the galley. He was limping.

"What happened to your ankle?" she asked.

"Stepped in a sinkhole and twisted it," he replied and disappeared inside.

"One good leg and one good arm?" Margery called after him.

"You're a real bargain, John Steiner." She turned her attention to her breakfast but gave Arlen a conspiratorial wink. "I think the boy might be coming around finally."

"He looks terrible," Hester whispered back.

"I expect he's not sleeping much. He was pretty bitten up before Samuel brought the camper and mosquito netting and such." Margery glanced up as John started back toward them, his plate loaded with the rest of the bacon and biscuits. "You're gonna eat me out of house and home," she growled.

"I figured we'd all save energy if I just brought out what was left."

"Yeah, everybody knows you're a real sweetheart," Margery said as she helped herself to another biscuit from the plate and plopped one onto Arlen's plate.

Hester was sure she wasn't seeing right. Had John Steiner almost smiled as he took his seat again? Somehow Margery had gotten to the man, won him over.

The crunch of car tires on packed sand and gravel followed by the slamming of car doors and voices told Hester that the rest of the crew had arrived. Arlen and Margery went to meet them and help with the unloading of supplies. Hester started to clear away the breakfast dishes.

"I can do this," John said. "You go on and help Arlen and the others."

She glanced at the cast that looked as if it had been through its own hurricane. "Let me look at that," she said, taking his arm before he could refuse. "What have you done to yourself?" she muttered as she examined the fiberglass cast that in places was worn down to his bare skin.

"I'm fine," he grumbled, pulling his arm away and ducking his head to clear the galley doorway.

"You are not fine, John. Your wrist probably needs resetting, and then there's the matter of that ankle. You're wearing a compression bandage?"

"I do what I need to do to get around."

"And you're wearing flip-flops? When you're working in

areas hard hit by a hurricane, that is just plain stupid. With all the debris, you could easily trip or step on a nail." She followed him inside and set down the stack of plates she was carrying. "As long as I'm here, you might as well let me take a look."

"Don't do me any favors, lady."

Hester released a weary sigh. "Could we call a truce here and agree that you might actually benefit from my examining you?"

He eyed her suspiciously.

"If you want to help Margery, then you're doing her no favors by not taking care of yourself." She took down Margery's first-aid kit from the shelf above the door.

She decided to maintain her professional demeanor in spite of the fact that what she really wanted to do was to lecture the man that his refusal to accept help when it was offered had endangered his health.

"Did you ice it?" she asked as she removed the filthy compression bandage and dropped it in the trash.

His answer was a snort of derision that she suspected just might be covering a grimace of pain as she probed the bruised skin. "Sure. I used the icemaker on my refrigerator. You know, the one that got thrown halfway to Siesta when the hurricane blew through?"

She glanced up at him. "A simple 'no' would suffice." She continued to examine him, her fingers working their way over the arch of his foot and up and around his ankle.

"You're going to bite the tip of your tongue off," he said.

From her kneeling position on the floor next to his chair, she looked up to find him studying her closely. His eyes roamed over her features, her hair, her prayer covering. "Why are you always so angry, Hester Detlef?" he asked when she quirked an eyebrow at him.

"If you take my seriousness about my work for anger, then maybe that's because you're the one who walks through your days with barely concealed hostility."

"Maybe I've got my reasons."

"I'm sure you believe that you do, but I would remind you that the people you have been fortunate enough to meet here have nothing but your best interests in mind. They—we—do not deserve to be treated with such—"

"Got it. And so we come back to you."

She decided to ignore him. "Point your toe," she instructed and was amazed when he complied. "Now trace the letters of the alphabet using your toe like a pencil."

"Why?" He eyed her with suspicion.

"Because my goal in life is to make you look as ridiculous as possible," she snapped. Then she forced herself to swallow her annoyance. "It's a rehabilitation exercise, one you can practice on your own while your ankle heals. Try the vowels."

He slowly traced the letter *a* and then an *e*.

"Good," she said. "Try that later with the entire alphabet and repeat it three to five times a day. It will help improve your range of motion."

"What else?"

She checked to see if he was baiting her, but he was continuing the exercise on his own. "Okay, here's one more. Put your foot flat on the floor. You need to be sitting in a chair for this one."

"I am sitting in a chair," he pointed out.

"I mean when you do it on your own. Foot flat on the floor. Now move your knee from side to side slowly while keeping your foot pressed flat."

He tried it.

"Slower," she instructed. "Good. Do both of those three to five times a day, and it should help." She took out a tube of ointment and started applying it to the insect bites on his good arm. Then she stood up and bent over him to treat the bites on his face. She paused. It was her turn to study his features. His skin was scorched a deep russet. The beginnings of a beard had sprouted on his chin, golden-red like his hair. His eyes were deep-set under a strong forehead accented by thick eyebrows that had been bleached almost white by the sun. His eyes, fixed on hers, were the verdant green of a tropical forest. And yet his overall appearance was that of a man who was deeply troubled, who had known great sadness in his life. Hester felt a twinge of empathy for him.

"We, my father and Samuel and the others included, do not wish to cause you further pain, John," she said as she continued to apply the salve to his cheekbones and temples. "I don't know why it seems important to say this to you, but you are safe here."

She stepped back, recapping the tube of ointment as she checked to be sure she hadn't missed any bites. "Better," she said more to herself than to him. "As for that wrist," she went on, "we'll have to go into town for that to be looked at. It may need to be reset."

"Now?"

"What's to be gained by waiting?"

"I came here to help Margery."

"There'll be plenty left to do once we go and come back." She took a fresh compression bandage from the first-aid kit and knelt to wrap his ankle.

"I thought you said this wasn't a good idea."

"I'm just covering it loosely. It will serve as a reminder to you to take care as you move around on it, at least until we can get you a proper pair of shoes."

She put away the first-aid kit and poured water over the dishes to let them soak while they were gone. "Coming?" She waited by the doorway.

"Coming," he said as he grudgingly got to his feet.

Hester took visual stock of the room until she spotted a walking stick leaning against the wall. "Use this," she said. "We'll stop by the distribution center as long as we're in town and find you some work boots and a hat that properly covers your ears, neck, and face."

"Don't push it," he muttered as he followed her onto the pier and walked on toward the car while she collected car keys from her father and explained why they were leaving. To her surprise, when she got to the car, he was holding the door open for her.

"Thank you," she said as she slid in and pushed the key into the ignition. She watched him walk around the front of the car and with some satisfaction noticed that he was not limping nearly as badly as he had before she'd treated him. She also couldn't seem to stop noticing that John Steiner was one good-looking man.

Chapter 13

Predictably the wait in the emergency room promised to be a long one, and they hadn't been there half an hour when John suddenly stood up.

"This is a waste of time."

"That depends on how you choose to look at the situation," Hester replied. "Your wrist needs a new cast. Without it you will likely do further damage and set back your efforts to restore your own property and help Margery."

He sat back down and Hester slid a bench closer to him. "You should keep that ankle elevated when you're sitting."

"Steiner," the attendant called.

"Do you want me to come with you?" Hester asked as John struggled to his feet.

"I'm not twelve, Hester," he grumbled and hobbled off.

Down the hall a cheery aide greeted him with, "And how are we doing today?"

John answered her with a nearly inaudible, "How do you think?"

Hester sighed. Whatever common ground John may have found with Margery earlier that morning, it certainly had not carried over to others.

But when John emerged from the examining room, he was wearing a smaller cast that left his fingers free to move, as well as what Hester had come to understand was for him a pleasant expression. He crossed the room wiggling his fingers, and that was when she noticed that the ER doctor had also outfitted him with a boot to support his ankle.

"Ready?" she asked, realizing instinctively that it would not do to make a fuss about this change in his attitude.

John nodded, his focus still on experimenting with how he might use his hand and fingers.

"That's quite an improvement," Hester ventured as she drove back to Pinecraft so John could get some sturdier shoes and perhaps some clothing.

"Yeah."

She turned onto Bahia Vista and followed a stream of traffic east. "You know, now that the cottages in Pinecraft have been restored, I'm sure Dad would be willing to send a team of workers out to help you, once they've finished with Margery's bait shop, of course."

"I'll be okay," he said.

"Yeah, we can all see that you're managing just fine," she said. And then on a whim she pulled her father's car into the parking lot of Big Olaf's Creamery. "I need ice cream," she announced as she cut the engine and got out of the car.

When John gave no sign of moving, she turned and called back to him. "Chocolate or vanilla?"

"Vanilla," he replied after a moment.

"Figures," Hester muttered to herself. As she waited in line to order their cones, she considered why she was prolonging her time with John Steiner. Didn't it make more sense to take him over to the distribution center and let Rosalyn help him find shoes and clothing there? But no, she had stopped for ice cream. Like they were on a date or something.

She shook off that thought and stepped up to order. The man behind the counter was a member of her father's congregation. By the time he had chatted with her about the storm, the cones he'd handed her were beginning to melt.

"Sorry about that," he said as he placed two plastic sundae dishes under the cones so she could invert them into the cups. "A new invention," he teased. "You've heard of upside-down cake? Well, these are upside-down cones."

Hester couldn't help laughing, and by the time she returned to the car, her mood had lightened considerably. "Let's sit out here in the shade," she invited, holding up the dishes and leading the way to a bench that was shaded by the eave of the building.

John joined her a moment later and accepted the dish she offered him.

"Earl is a talker," she offered by way of explanation. "These started out as regular cones, but then. . ."

"It's fine," John said, filling his spoon and then his mouth with the ice cream. "Thank you."

"I had an ulterior motive," Hester admitted.

John cocked one eyebrow but kept eating his ice cream.

"Look, we kind of got off on the wrong foot, you and me. It was my fault. I'd like to rectify that since it looks like we might be traveling in the same circles now and again." She saw a hint of mistrust flitter across his face and sighed. "Whatever happened to you back in Indiana, John, I assure you that my father and I and Samuel and Margery and anyone else you might meet around here are exactly who and what we appear to be."

"What you see is what you get?"

"Something like that."

He scraped a spoonful of ice cream from the dish and then picked up the cone and took a bite.

"So what did happen back there?" Hester asked, her gaze fixed on the passing parade of cars and bicycles. It was none of her business, and she wasn't sure why she should care. The question had just popped out as if it had been lodged there in her throat for days.

To her surprise John did not rebuff her. Instead, he leaned back on the bench, propping his injured foot on top of his good foot as he licked ice cream.

"Did you ever read the book *Walden* by Henry David Thoreau?"

"A long time ago. My mother had a copy, and then it was on the required reading list in college. Why?"

"Tucker's Point is—was—my Walden."

"It was your dream," Hester murmured. She understood all about dreams, all about wanting things you weren't supposed to want but believing that—for you—they were the only path.

John nodded and took the last bite of his ice cream. He savored the taste of it. Hester had already finished hers, including the cone.

"But why here? Why not back in Indiana?"

"It started there actually, a few years ago. That's when I first read the book. It was at a time in my life when things were changing, and I was looking for some direction. I had prayed on the matter for weeks, but nothing seemed right to me. Thoreau wrote about men living lives of 'quiet desperation.' That certainly was a fit way to describe how I was feeling at the time."

"You were a grown man."

John shrugged. "I had just turned thirty, but what's in an age? I had lived my whole life on that farm, in that community. Even when other teens went off to try their wings before being baptized, I stayed. My dad had died and Mom would have been alone. Maybe that's where the desire came from," he mused, more to himself than to her.

"So you decided to leave everything and come here?"

"That may be oversimplifying it, but yeah."

"You just picked up and left? Your family and friends? Your community? The woman you were to marry?"

He frowned at her, and his eyes narrowed as if what he was revealing about himself had just dawned on him. "I didn't desert anyone or anything, if that's what you think. If anything, that shoe was on the other foot."

"Meaning they deserted you."

"They weren't bad people," he said defensively.

"I didn't say they were." She waited until he had bitten into the last of the cone as if he were chomping down on something far tougher than a sugar cone.

"What about your family? Siblings?"

"I told you, my father died of a heart attack when I was thirteen. My parents never had other children."

"I'm sorry for your loss. Your mother has never remarried?"

He was quiet for such a long moment that Hester thought perhaps he hadn't heard her question. And then very quietly he said, "My mother died the year I decided to come here. That was. . ."

Hester watched as an expression of abject sadness crossed his features. She was so taken aback by the pain and fragility she saw in that expression that she felt compelled to change the subject and spoke aloud the first thought that popped into her mind.

"Grady Forrest told me you had left your community," she ventured, uncertain of what could possibly drive her to want to explore such a painful topic.

"I was banned," he said quietly, his eyes daring her to pursue the topic any further. When she said no more, he stood up and threw the empty dish into a nearby trash bin. "Are we getting those shoes today or not?" He limped to the car and got in, slamming the car door like an exclamation point to his silent announcement that this conversation was over.

Meddling little do-gooder, John thought as he waited for Hester to dispose of her ice cream dish and climb behind the wheel of the car. She had gotten to him, and he'd almost told her about his mother's tragic death, about his part in that tragedy. He'd almost trusted her.

"Sorry," she said finally. "Look, I. . ." She sat for a moment with both hands in her lap, working the car keys like worry beads.

"Let's just go," he said and fastened his gaze on a spot on the windshield where a small insect had met its end.

With a sigh, she turned the key and eased the sedan into traffic, pausing to let a three-wheeled bicycle pass and returning the rider's greeting with a prepackaged smile.

When they reached the thrift shop and donation center where clothing and other goods were stored, Hester led the way inside. A young woman looked up from her sorting work and smiled. In spite of a face marred with burn scars, she had the most strikingly beautiful smile, and her eyes were so guileless that John felt his annoyance with Hester ease slightly.

"Rosalyn, this is John Steiner," Hester said in a monotone. "He needs shoes and some clothing and a decent hat. I'll be in the office." Without another word she stepped inside a small office and closed the door.

"Well, John Steiner," Rosalyn said, sizing him up with a glance, "I would say you need some jeans for starters. Thirty-four waist, I'm guessing?"

"Right, but in this heat. . ."

"Aren't you the Amish guy living out there on Tucker's Point?"

"Right again, but. . ."

She took hold of his good arm and steered him toward a line of shelving. "Trust me, you want some long pants if you're tramping around out there among all those downed trees and weeds and such." She pulled out three pairs of jeans and handed them to him. "Okay, moving on. Shirts." She plucked three of those from the well-organized stock. "Oh, and how about these cargo shorts?"

"I thought you said. . ."

Rosalyn gave him an exasperated smile. "Well, not all the time. Now and again a pair of shorts comes in handy." Then her eyes widened in horror and she grabbed the Hawaiian print shirts she'd handed him back. "I almost forgot. I mean about you being plain like us. The jeans will work, but. . ."

Gently he relieved her of the shirts. "These are fine," he said. "Now how about those shoes?"

On their way down a second aisle, she tossed him an unopened package of tube socks and then nodded toward a second bin that held brand-new packages of underwear. "Help yourself," she said. "Target's finest, bless them." She gave the store's name a

French pronunciation that made John smile. By the time he had rummaged through the bin and found a package in his size and followed her to the back of the storeroom, Rosalyn had pulled out three pairs of work boots for him to try.

"Sit," she instructed as she worked the lace loose on one boot. "Socks?" she added, nodding toward the unopened package.

John took out a fresh pair and gathered one onto his good foot. Then Rosalyn handed him the boot. He pulled it on and tied the laces then stood up. "Feels fine," he said.

Rosalyn smiled and uttered a soft, "And the kid does it again." She boxed up the other shoe and then glanced around. "So, a hat—and then our work here is done." She held out a traditional Mennonite straw hat with a stiff wide brim and black band. When he hesitated, she grinned at him. "I thought you were Amish," she teased.

"He is. . .was," Hester said softly. She turned her attention to John. "It's a hat," she rationalized. "It's what we have in stock, and it will serve the purpose of protecting you from the sun while you work."

John took the hat from Rosalyn and put it on.

"And once again, folks, we have a perfect fit," Rosalyn said, her naturally vibrant spirit restored.

John couldn't help smiling, and when he glanced at Hester, he saw that the burn-scarred woman had disarmed not only him of his bad temper but Hester as well. "How do I look?" he asked, directing his question to both women.

"Ah, John Steiner, the sin of pride," Hester warned, shaking a finger at him, but she was smiling. She had the loveliest smile. It was a pity she didn't use it more often.

The door opened at the far end of the storeroom, and a Mennonite man stood for a moment silhouetted in the entrance.

"Samuel Brubaker from Pennsylvania," Rosalyn called out before either Hester or John recognized the carpenter.

Samuel hesitated. "*Guten tag,*" he said when he finally met them halfway up the aisle. "Hester, I saw your father's car, and I thought perhaps. . .Ah, John."

"We went out to help Margery this morning," Hester explained, "and John was already there. He needed medical attention, so. . ."

"You do not need to explain," Samuel said gently. "Are you not well, John?"

"My ankle," John replied, pointing to the boot. "And the cast on my wrist had to be replaced."

Samuel examined the cast with interest. "I see they've given you more freedom for your fingers. *Das ist* gut."

John did not miss the fact that the vivacious Rosalyn had turned uncustomarily quiet and that Samuel had yet to look at the young woman. "Then Hester decided I needed clothes."

"You do," Samuel agreed. "You have worn your own clothing to tatters." He glanced up at John. "The hat is good."

"It'll get the job done," John replied.

The four of them fell into an uncomfortable silence.

"So, you were working, Samuel?" Hester said finally as she relieved John of the stack of clothing he'd collected and started up the aisle toward the front desk.

"Ja. In spite of the hurricane, your father had orders to fill. One cabinet needed to be stained and prepared for shipping by the end of the week."

"But you've finished that?"

"Ja. I could come with you and John to help Margery."

"Dad would appreciate that," Hester said as she bagged the clothing.

John reached for his wallet, far thinner these days than it had once been. "How much?"

Hester thrust the last of the clothing into the bag with unnecessary vigor. He was mystified by her sudden change in attitude until Rosalyn helped him understand his mistake. "Now, John Steiner, you know very well we won't take your money. Mennonite or Amish, we are alike in this. Neighbor tends to neighbor. Put your wallet away."

"Thank you," he said as he stuffed his wallet back into his pocket and accepted the bag Hester held out to him. "Thank you all for. . .everything," he added, taking Rosalyn and Samuel into the circle of his gratitude.

Samuel nodded. Rosalyn grinned. Hester looked down and then announced, "We should be getting back."

At the car, Hester handed Samuel the keys. "I'll sit in back," she said.

They rode along without a word passing between them for several minutes until John found he could not stand the silence a moment longer. Ironic, he knew, but it wasn't really lack of conversation that bothered him. It was more that the car was filled with things unspoken.

"How did Rosalyn receive those burns?" he asked, and saw Samuel glance in the rearview mirror, deferring to Hester.

"It was a house fire," she said. "The rest of her family died in the fire. She was the only one we were able to rescue."

John half turned in his seat to look back at her. "You were there?"

"Among others," she said softly. "It was my father who saved her."

"Not only Arlen," Samuel corrected her. "She says that while your father pulled her from the fire, you were the one who treated her and held her until the paramedics arrived."

"I'm a nurse," Hester replied with a slight shrug.

"And you have been her good friend," Samuel added. "She tells me that without your support she could not have endured the recovery she had to go through, and she would not have found her way past all the stares of pity."

It struck John that Samuel seemed to know quite a bit about Rosalyn. He thought about the way Samuel and Rosalyn had both seemed reticent in the other's company back in the thrift center. The way Samuel looked at Rosalyn, stealing glances when he thought she was otherwise occupied, was the look of a man who found that particular woman fascinating. It was the way his parents had looked at each other years into their marriage. It occurred to John that he could not recall a single time when Samuel had looked at Hester that way. For that matter, had John looked at Alice Yoder, the woman he'd been about to marry, that way?

He couldn't help wondering if Hester had noticed, or if she cared. She certainly seemed indifferent to Samuel, at least romantically speaking. On the few occasions when John had seen them together, she had interacted with Samuel more as a colleague, the way she was with Grady Forrest.

Well, it was hardly his concern. Why should he care if Hester's intended fell for another woman? Why should he care about her happiness at all? Not that she didn't deserve to be happy, he thought, as Samuel turned onto the cracked and broken asphalt road that led to the parking lot for the marina. She was clearly a good and caring person, a little too bossy for his taste, but her sincerity when it came to her concern for others could not be questioned.

The marina parking lot was filled with cars and trucks. John could see men shingling the roof of the bait shop as Arlen directed progress from the ground. The combination of the medical boot and closed shoe gave John more confidence in his movement, and he was out of the car and walking down to the pier before Samuel and Hester.

"You're looking more like a human being than a lagoon monster," Margery commented. "The hat's a nice touch."

John grimaced as he fingered the brim of the straw hat. "It does the job," he repeated. "And speaking of jobs, looks like you'll be back in business within a couple of days."

"Yep. Amazing what friends and neighbors can accomplish when they work together," she said. "And when you let them help," she added dryly. "You ought to try it sometime, Johnny." She didn't give him a chance to respond. Instead, she walked away, calling out encouragement to the roofing crew.

John stared up at the crew, watching as the men worked on the roof and a group of women scraped peeling paint from the exterior walls of the marina, chattering and laughing together as they worked. Suddenly he was a boy again back on the farm, working alongside his father as they rebuilt a neighbor's barn after a tornado had roared through their valley. In the laughter of the women, he heard his mother's laughter, deep and rich, and he remembered how his father would stop what he was doing just to look at her for a moment. It was as if he wanted to memorize every detail of her.

"John?"

Coming back to the situation at hand, John blinked and turned his attention to Hester. She was standing next to him, looking up at him with a puzzled frown. "Are you all right?"

"Ich bin gut," he said softly and realized it was the first time since leaving Indiana that he had used his German. "Fine," he added, clearing his throat. "I came here to help, and so far I've done nothing. Time to get to work." He picked up a hammer with his left hand and began pulling nails from the discarded boards that had been replaced by new wood.

A moment later, Hester was working alongside him. John sighed. The woman was as bad as Margery, always hovering around.

Chapter 14

Samuel had taken his place on the roof, helping the other men finish the shingling. When the last nail had been pounded in, the men stood for a moment checking their work. Then Samuel waited his turn to come down the ladder and saw Hester working alongside John. She was unaware that he was watching her, and so he took the time to study her, consider his feelings for her.

Hester was by anyone's measure an incredible woman. The care she had devoted to her mother for five long years was in and of itself an act of such astonishing selflessness, but she had not stopped there.

Rosalyn had told him that in the months that followed Sarah Detlef's death, Hester had thrown herself into her work. She had stayed nights with sick children, and with elderly people whose main affliction was loneliness. And then the fire had come, and when Rosalyn had regained consciousness, it was Hester who had broken the news that her family had not survived. It was Hester who had stayed with Rosalyn and worked with her day in and night out until she recovered.

And yet in all the conversations they had shared, Samuel had not once heard any of this from Hester herself. She was a plain woman in the larger sense of that word, taking none of the credit for the things she accomplished. And Samuel admired her greatly.

He simply did not love her.

He had come to Pinecraft in the spring. He had seen Hester every day, spent numerous hours sharing meals with her and her father and grandmother, attended services and other church and community functions with her. Yet when he examined his feelings for her over that time, he had to admit that they had not changed. He respected her enormously, and in the beginning he had told himself that was a good start. They could build on that.

He also understood that she liked him. He had seen it in the way she would run her palm over some furniture he had finished for a customer. He saw it in the way she smiled at him when he teamed with Arlen on the shuffleboard court in the evenings after they had closed the shop. And he had told himself that in time they would find their way.

And then he had met Rosalyn.

In the weeks since the hurricane had passed, he had tried hard to tell himself that Rosalyn was merely a good friend to him, as she was to Hester. But when he found himself looking for her and at the same time trying to avoid her, he knew that his feelings had already blossomed beyond the point of simple friendship.

The fact that Rosalyn seemed oblivious to his attraction only made matters worse. For because of her work for MCC and her close connection with Hester, Rosalyn was often with Hester, and whenever Samuel was with them, Rosalyn did not treat him any differently than she did anyone else. He knew that he should have found that reassuring, but the fact that she clearly did not see him as someone special was downright depressing.

He could hardly avoid Rosalyn without raising questions about why he was avoiding Hester. So he buried himself in the work at the carpentry shop, insisting to Arlen that he could fulfill the back orders while Arlen attended to his work with MDS. And as he worked on a china hutch or desk that would find its way north to some snowbird's home, he silently prayed for God's guidance.

For Samuel was deeply troubled by the state he found himself in—falling in love with a woman he'd barely exchanged more than four true conversations with while having in theory agreed to a union with the pastor's daughter. If he turned his back on Hester, then what right did he have to continue to work for Arlen? He loved his work and had found his true calling in the crowded shop where sawdust and wood shavings littered the floor throughout the day.

And his sense of loyalty was not just to Arlen. It extended to Hester as well, for it had been clear to Samuel from their first meeting that she had surrendered to the idea that one day they would marry and make a home and raise a family. She had accepted the life her father had planned for her in spite of the fact that Hester Detlef rarely acceded to the plans and wishes of others. And given her innate willfulness, Samuel could not help but wonder why Hester would acquiesce to her father's wish.

Samuel paused at the top of the ladder to watch Hester and John pull nails from discarded wood. It was true. In her way Hester was every bit as determined and stubborn when it came to doing things her way as—say—John Steiner was. More than once Arlen had alluded to the comparison. Arlen had always counseled patience, meaning Samuel's need to practice patience with Hester, of course. And perhaps that was why Samuel had taken to visiting John Steiner more often. Perhaps in getting to know the Amish man who was in many ways like Hester, he was hoping to come to a better understanding of the woman who seemed destined to become his wife.

Once Margery's place had been restored and she was back in business, John was anxious to get his place to the point where he could move into the packinghouse and start planning how best to revive the groves of citrus trees that had been wiped out in the hurricane. During the three days it had taken Arlen's crew to repair the damage to the marina, John had faced the reality that even without his fractured wrist and badly sprained ankle, he might eventually have to accept more help than Zeke could provide.

"But no government people," he told Margery one night as the two of them sat on the deck of her houseboat sharing supper.

She rolled her eyes. "Did you see any so-called government people working here?" she asked. "No, you did not. If I had waited for them to show up, I'd be out of business 'til a month from next year."

"I'm just saying," he grumbled and turned his attention back to his food.

"I suppose it's too much to hope that your sudden epiphany or whatever it was that brought you over here to lend a hand might extend to accepting Arlen's help."

John frowned. He had neither the physical strength nor the cash to rebuild the second story of the house. In the meantime, he had continued to focus his efforts on what he could repair—the planting beds, the packinghouse, the chicken coop. And yet. . .

"Thought not," Margery said as she stood up to clear away their plates. "You want pie, or is that against your principles?"

"Got any ice cream to go with it?" he replied.

"No, but you'll never have a better-tasting pie than this one." She ducked inside and emerged a few minutes later with two large pieces of shoofly pie on paper plates. "Hester made it," she said, setting a piece in front of him.

John recalled the pies cooling on the counter in the Detlef kitchen the morning the creek flooded. "They're back home now?"

"Not quite. Drywall is up and the paint's drying in most of the properties from what Arlen told me. They'll wait to work on their place last, get everybody else home and settled before they take care of themselves. That's their way."

"What about the garden? Arlen's wife's garden?"

Margery shrugged. "I expect that'll be even further down the list, although I know it must be killing Hester not to be tending it. She planted it, you know. Called it therapy. Only question is who was it therapy for."

"I don't understand."

"She thought of it as therapy for her mother. Toward the end there when Sarah could no longer do anything but sit in that wheelchair and just blink her eyes to show yes or no, Hester got this idea of turning the front yard into a garden."

"You think the therapy was for her—Hester," John said. It wasn't a question.

"Well, of course it was for Sarah. But long after Sarah passed, you'd see Hester out there tending those orchids, ferns, and bromeliads like they were precious babies."

John took another bite of the pie. He had to admit that it was the most delicious thing he'd tasted in weeks. "She bakes. She raises orchids. She runs a charity. She's a nurse. What doesn't this woman do?"

Margery grinned. "Interested, are you?"

"Not the way you mean it. Besides, she and Samuel—"

"Are beyond wrong for each other." Margery sighed. "I don't know what Arlen was thinking. Sarah must be rolling over in her grave thinking that her spitfire daughter might end up with that mild-mannered man. Not that he's not a perfectly good man—kind and generous to a fault, but not for our Hester."

John fought to disguise his interest. "You think so?"

"You think so?" Margery mimicked in a high falsetto before taking a bite of her pie and washing it down with a long drink of iced tea. "You sound like some high school boy. Get to know the woman. Come to think of it, the two of you. . ."

She eyed John, sizing up the possibility. He raised both hands, palms out as if stopping traffic. "Get that idea out of your head, Margery." He was willing to tolerate Margery's attempts to get him involved in the larger community, but allowing the woman to get any idea of matchmaking would be disastrous.

She shrugged and turned her chair so that she could prop her feet up on the railing of the houseboat and look out toward the sunset. "Suit yourself, but methinks the man doth protest—"

"I have to get back," John interrupted. "Thanks for supper, and if you see Zeke, ask him to stop by, okay?"

"Yep." Margery sounded half asleep.

He made the short leap from the deck to the pier and then into the boat Margery had lent him, thankful that she had loaned him the boat when she probably could have rented it out. "And don't go spreading it around that I'm looking for help," he said.

"Got it, you stubborn blockhead."

The following morning Zeke was there, sitting on the stump of a cypress tree when John crawled out of bed. "Morning," he called. "Margery said you could use a hand."

John glanced around, saw no boat other than his own and no other visible means of transportation.

"Did Margery bring you?" he asked, hoping the fisherwoman hadn't talked about him in front of others.

"Nope. Caught a ride." Zeke nodded toward the lane. "Want some coffee?" He held up two large cups from one of several fancy coffee vendors John had noticed on Main Street.

"Thought you were broke and homeless," John commented as he gratefully accepted the hot liquid.

Zeke grinned. "Can still sing for my coffee," he said. "Had to give 'em two songs this morning, so you owe me." He glanced around and released a long, appreciative whistle. "You've made some real progress here."

"Getting there," John admitted.

"Got yourself a small generator, I see."

"Samuel Brubaker brought it out one afternoon."

"Good man."

"Yeah."

"So what's on tap for today, boss?" Zeke drained the last of his coffee and crushed the cup in one fist.

"I'd like to finish closing in the kitchen and get it covered."

"No worries," Zeke replied and set to work.

For the next several days he came every morning, bringing John coffee and then getting to work. After a week, though, John noticed that Zeke didn't look well, and he took frequent breaks either to relieve himself or simply to sit for a long moment, his head bent low to his knees.

"You feeling okay?"

"Picked up some kind of bug," Zeke replied. "It'll pass," he added and grinned. "Hotter today, though, so I'm knocking off. See you tomorrow?"

"Take a couple of days and rest up," John said. "We've made good progress here. Take care of yourself, okay?"

When Zeke did not return the following day or for two days after that, John figured he'd taken the advice to get some rest. But when he hadn't come back after a week, John began to worry. He was well aware that Zeke marched to his own drummer on his own unique time schedule, but he also knew that if Zeke had committed to doing something, he was there until the job was complete.

Something was wrong. He fired up Margery's boat and sped under the Stickney Point Bridge then past the mouth of the creek, leaving a wake that earned him a warning blast from the shore patrol.

How could he not have seen that Zeke was getting worse? The man had switched to tea the last day he arrived, telling John that he needed something to settle his stomach. And he was thinner than usual. He kept hitching up his pants, the same ones John had seen him wear every day for a week, and knotting the rope belt a little tighter.

But John's focus had been on the incredible progress they were making. The night before, he had slept in the packinghouse under an actual roof for the first time since the storm. He'd still slept on the sleeping bag that Samuel had provided and covered himself in the netting, but he had been inside, not in the cramped camper.

As he navigated, he scanned the shore for any sign of Zeke. He passed under the Siesta Bridge. Nothing. Zeke was the kind of person who stood out with his long hair and his guitar slung across his back. As John passed the botanical gardens, he spotted the abandoned boat Zeke had shown him. Slowly he circled it, calling Zeke's name but getting no answer. He pulled into a vacant slip at the far north end of the city's main marina. Remembering Zeke's description of where he had set up his "crib" as he called it, John ran down the sidewalk, dodging runners and dog walkers until he reached a small patch of exposed mud flats. He was very near the Ringling Bridge that carried traffic from the mainland over to Lido and Longboat Key and the fancy shopping area known as St. Armand's Circle.

Glancing around, he saw a cluster of mangroves and sea grape bushes where the seawall curved. He ran toward them, seeing a man lying there. "Zeke!" His heart hammering, he touched the inert shoulder of a body folded in on itself and was relieved when he heard a low moan. "Zeke? It's John."

"Oh, sorry, man. I. . ." Zeke sat up suddenly and wretched in dry heaves. "Pretty sick," he said with a weary smile, his voice husky.

"Let's get you to a doctor," John said.

"Hester," Zeke protested. "Get Hester. Hospital takes forever."

"All right. Hester, then. But I'm not leaving you here. Can you walk?"

"No worries, man." But when he tried to sit fully upright, a wave of dizziness overtook him.

In spite of the stench of his clothing and body, John scooped his friend into a fireman's carry and headed back toward the marina.

"Guitar," Zeke moaned.

"I'll come back for it," John promised.

"Tide coming in," Zeke managed.

"Then I'll buy you a new one if it gets ruined." He could barely afford groceries, much less a guitar, but the important thing was to get Zeke some medical attention—and fast.

As Hester had predicted, once the sun came out and the floodwaters receded, the public's attention moved on to other matters. No longer did she turn around while restoring the houses along the creek to find a television reporter and cameraperson carefully picking their way across a soggy lawn, hoping for a story. And after it became clear that there had been massive property damage but little human loss, the media packed up and moved on for good. The National Guard, too, had moved on, as had other disaster-relief groups that had set up temporary headquarters in Sarasota.

Even the out-of-state volunteer teams from Mennonite and Amish congregations that had appeared in droves during the first seventy-two hours following the storm had headed back home after a few weeks. The difference there was that they sent replacements, crews of teenagers or college students who were eager to spend a few days rebuilding someone's house and rejoicing in the reward of seeing a family moved from one of the cramped FEMA trailers back into their own place.

It was a pattern that Hester was well used to and one that she saw as a natural part of the rhythm of life on Florida's Gulf Coast. When another storm struck their shores—and it would—if not this season then next, or the one after that, these wonderful caring people would be back, ready to once again help the residents of Pinecraft and the surrounding area rebuild.

She was putting the final touches on her father's house when the phone in Arlen's study rang. "Pastor Detlef's residence," she said as she cradled the phone on her shoulder and wiped her paint-stained hands on a rag.

"Hester?"

John Steiner sounded as if he'd run a marathon and called her straight from the finish line. "It's Zeke Shepherd," he said. "Can you come?"

"What's happened?" Hester asked, already setting the rag aside and reaching for her bag. "Where are you?"

"He's really sick. We're at the city marina, north end. I'm illegally parked."

"You drove?"

"I've got Margery's boat. I'm in one of the vacant slips. When Zeke didn't show up at my place for over a week, I went looking for him. I mean, it wasn't like him to disappear for over a week without at least stopping by."

Hester didn't see the need to tell John that it was exactly

like Zeke to disappear for long periods of time without letting anyone know where or how he was. Eventually he would show up, his impish smile all Jeannie needed to forgive him for giving her such a fright.

"I'm on my way."

She wrote a quick note to her father, grabbed the car keys, and prayed the traffic lights would be with her.

They were. She reached the marina in record time and saw John standing at the end of one of the piers near a pay phone. He was looking far healthier than he had the last time she'd seen him. In the days that had passed since they'd worked together on Margery's place, the ankle boot was gone, and his bruises and insect bites had healed. Only the wrist cast remained, and the way he was waving his hands around, it didn't look as if that was much of a concern.

She followed him out to the boat. Zeke was lying on the deck curled into a fetal position. He moaned and rolled onto his side, clutching his stomach. The stench from his clothing and lack of proper hygiene almost overpowered her, but she sucked in a deep breath and knelt next to him. "Tell me what's going on, Zeke," she said softly as she began taking his vitals—pulse, temperature, pupils.

"Hurts," he moaned.

"Where?"

"Head. Stomach. Everywhere."

"John, could you get Zeke some water?" For once John did as she asked without questioning her.

"No!" Zeke protested weakly but firmly. "Goes straight through me," he added as he pulled his knees up to his chest and rocked from side to side.

"You're dehydrated, Zeke. We have to get some fluids in you. How long has this been going on?"

"Couple of days like this, maybe a week in all. Seems like forever."

Hester was beginning to have her suspicions as to a diagnosis. "Anybody else sick?"

169

"He lives alone," John reminded her.

She ignored him. "Zeke?"

"Yeah. A couple of others that I know of."

"Okay, let's get you to the ER, and then I'll go check on the others." She turned her attention to John. "Can you carry Zeke?"

Once again he lifted Zeke in a fireman's carry. Hester held the door of her car open as John laid the man across the backseat. Then he got into the passenger seat while she took the wheel.

"What others, Zeke?" she asked as she navigated traffic between the marina and the hospital.

"Danny, for one." He paused. "I can't think."

"Okay, well then, let's get you to the emergency room, and then I'll go see what I can find out."

"I can stay with Zeke," John volunteered.

"No worries, man," Zeke mumbled. "Go help Hester."

It was clear that the ER staff was less than thrilled to see this disheveled man who reeked of sweat and the aftermath of severe diarrhea come through the door. But Hester ignored their displeasure and gave them her credentials as a registered nurse. "He's showing all the symptoms of crypto," she said curtly. "I suspect there are more cases among those of the homeless community that hang out around the library. We're going there to check on them. You got this?"

The admissions person and a burly aide who had brought a wheelchair out to the car to help Zeke inside both nodded.

"Good. We'll be back as soon as possible." She squeezed Zeke's hand and then headed back to the car.

"What's crypto?" John asked as she started the engine and eased into traffic.

"Cryptosporidium—a parasite. Causes a pretty awful gastro-intestinal illness called cryptosporidiosis. Mostly it comes from consuming contaminated food or water." She leaned forward as if willing the light they were stopped at to turn green. "People like Zeke are at risk because they tend to get their food and water from unorthodox sources—trash bins behind restaurants, and water from streams or other places."

She waited for a car to pull out of a parking space across from the library, a large white concrete structure surrounded by pineapple-shaped columns. "Uh-oh," she murmured.

"What?"

"Nobody around. Normally there would be clusters of two or three people sitting up there on the steps or over there in the park." She pointed.

"It's close to ninety degrees," John reminded her. "Maybe they went inside to take advantage of the air-conditioning."

"Maybe." She hoped John was right. She started across the street and was surprised when John took her arm to stop her from stepping out in front of a car speeding up the short side street.

"Careful," he said, releasing her arm before crossing.

She caught up to him. "You don't have to come," she said. "I mean, you can wait in the car or out here if you'd rather. I know this really isn't—"

"I'm here, aren't I?" For reasons Hester couldn't fathom, his characteristic gruffness gave her comfort. "That's better," she said as they climbed the steps together. "For a moment there I thought you'd gone all soft on me."

"Not a chance," he said, but he was smiling.

Inside she sent John upstairs to walk through the stacks and see if there were any likely candidates while she did the same on the first floor. She even checked out the children's library with its popular arched aquarium entrance as well as the used bookstore operated by the Friends of the Library.

"Bathrooms," she said when John came down the stairs, shaking his head. She led the way to the corridor where the public restrooms were located. Again nothing.

She was considering where else they might go to look when she spotted the library's security person. "Excuse me," she said.

She watched as the security guard took in her plain garb and John's traditional straw hat before smiling politely. "Yes, ma'am?"

"The men and women who are. . .*regulars* here," she said, and the guard's eyes narrowed.

"The homeless people?"

"Yes. Do you have any idea where they are?"

"Try Rainbow House," he said and prepared to turn away.

"It's closed down," Hester continued, fighting to maintain her patience. "The county never reopened it after the hurricane. Someone I know in the county government tells me it's unlikely it will ever reopen."

"Well, they aren't here," the man replied curtly.

"We can see that," John said, his terse tone forcing the guard to meet the intensity of his stare. "And since this is where they are normally, what happened?"

The guard sighed and looked at something beyond their heads. "Look. You didn't hear it from me, but there were complaints from our, you know, other patrons. Some of those people were coming in here and stinking up the place and throwing up in the restrooms and just in general making it—"

"*Those people* are ill," Hester said. "Some of them may be dangerously ill, and if we don't find them, one or more of them could die. At the very least they could spread a parasite that might infect a great many others. Including your other patrons. Now where did they go?"

"I really don't know. We called the cops, and they moved them away from here. That's all I know about it."

Hester dismissed the man with a look and turned her attention to John. "Any ideas?"

"We could try the bay front, near the public restrooms there."

Hester nodded, and she did not miss the fact that as she and John headed out the door, the security guard was already squirting disinfectant from the dispenser near the front doors onto his palms and rubbing them vigorously together.

Chapter 15

W hat made you think of the bay front?" Hester asked as she pulled into the parking lot near a popular tiki-style restaurant and found one of several open spaces.

"It's where Zeke lives, so I figured maybe. . ."

He was not about to admit to her that Zeke had taken him to these same restrooms one day and suggested he wash up.

"You stink, man," Zeke had told him in that 'no worries' tone he used to address every topic. "And until they get the water back on out your way, this may be your best bet."

"Do you think maybe that's where he got the infected food or water?" Hester asked.

"Could be. From what I've observed, Zeke is pretty resourceful and tends to take what he needs wherever it's available."

John recalled the day he and Zeke had first met. The way Zeke had drunk the bottled water and then refilled the plastic container with the runoff from the awning at the abandoned warehouse.

"They need a safe haven," Hester muttered as she headed for the women's restroom.

"Can I ask a question?" John said, stopping her before she could enter the open door.

"Okay."

"What are we going to do if we find half a dozen or more sick people in these restrooms?"

"Get them some help," she said and handed him a pair of latex gloves she'd pulled from her bag. "Wear these." She pulled on a pair of her own. "And this," she added, handing him a mask.

"And after you get them help, then what?" John wondered aloud as he took a deep breath and went in to check the men's room.

Moments later, he emerged supporting a rail-thin man who stumbled along beside him. Hester was sitting with two women—one who had to be in her sixties and the other a decade or so younger. They seemed to be in far better shape than either Zeke or the man John was supporting.

"Best diet I was ever on," the older woman crowed. "Look at this." She stood up and pulled out the waistband of her trousers to show how big they were on her. "Need a belt just to hold them up."

"Dangerous diet," Hester corrected her. "We need to get your friend there to the hospital. Will you two wait here until I can get back with some medicine?"

"Got nothing but time," the younger woman grumbled, fanning herself with an old magazine.

"You get Danny there the help he needs," the older woman urged. "He's been sicker than a dog for days now."

"Have you got any cash with you?" Hester asked John.

"Some."

"Could you get these ladies each a bottle of water from the stand there?"

"Sure." John headed off.

"Could we make that a nice cup of coffee?" the older woman shouted.

"Water," Hester said firmly. The woman grinned a wide, toothless grin and shrugged. "Anybody else sick?" she asked the women as she waited for John to return with the water. The one thing she knew was that the homeless community was almost as tight as her own Mennonite community was. They all knew each other, knew who was a newcomer and who had been on the streets long enough to know their way around. And as was true of any group, not everyone got along. There were petty jealousies, turf wars, and cliques. But if there was a threat from outside forces, these people would stand together. The two women exchanged a look but remained silent. "Okay. If anyone starts to show signs of running a fever or especially diarrhea or throwing up, make sure they drink lots of water, *clean* water. You have to boil it if you don't get it from a reliable source, okay?"

"Drink boiling water? In this heat?" The younger woman shuddered as John returned with two bottles of water and handed one to each woman.

"You let it cool down first," the older woman said. "Right, Doc?"

"She's a missionary, dope."

"Who you calling—?"

"I'm a nurse," Hester interrupted. "Yes, let the water cool to room temperature before drinking it, and stay away from anything with caffeine like soda or tea or coffee. That will just cause the dehydration to worsen."

"Yeah. Yeah. Got it. Any medicine to clear this thing up?"

"There are some over-the-counter anti-diarrheal medicines that I can bring you." She sighed in frustration. "Look, it just has to run its course. If anyone is really suffering, take them to one of the walk-in clinics or to the emergency room."

"Yeah, that'll work," the younger woman said sarcastically.

"Try it," Hester said, "and please spread the word." She took her place to one side of Danny while John supported him from the other and they led him toward the car. "I'll stop back later," she called, but both women were already gone.

With her help, John got the semi-conscious Danny into the backseat and they headed back to the hospital.

"After we pick Zeke up, I want you, Zeke, and Danny there—if he's not admitted—to come back to our house and take a long, hot shower. You've been exposed to this thing now, and you need to take precautions."

But when they reached the emergency room, Jeannie was there. "I was visiting a neighbor," she explained. "And on my way out, I saw an aide wheeling Zeke out from the ER. He looks terrible. Don't you think he should be admitted?"

"I'm okay, Jeannie," Zeke said weakly.

"Well, at the very least you're coming home with me and having yourself a nice hot shower and changing out of those clothes. You stink to high heaven."

Zeke managed a grin and put up no resistance as Jeannie led him across the driveway to her car, chattering all the way. Hester saw her open the trunk and remove an old quilt that she placed on the front seat before letting Zeke get in. Meanwhile, the aide had helped Danny into the wheelchair vacated by Zeke and taken him inside.

"Jeannie, wait," Hester called. "John needs a ride back to the marina."

Jeannie nodded. "Tell him to come on," she said.

Back inside, Hester saw John conferring with the doctor.

"Danny passed out while the admissions person was taking his information," John explained.

"Are you the family?" the doctor asked.

"Close enough," John said before Hester could go into an explanation of the situation.

The doctor studied the chart the desk clerk had handed him. "Looks like he's been here several times before in the last couple of months. Whether or not this is an outbreak of crypto, he is dangerously dehydrated, and we're going to have to admit him at least overnight."

"Surely he has family we could contact," John said.

"I'll stay with him," Hester said.

The doctor was clearly relieved. "Okay, then. We'll get him stabilized and then contact social services here in the hospital."

After he'd left, Hester turned to John. "You go on to our house and take that shower and change into clean clothes. Jeannie's waiting for you, and I'll call Rosalyn at the center and have her bring you some things so you don't have to take time to go home first. There are clean towels in the—"

"I'll find them," John told her. "I need to call Margery. I'm sure she knows somebody who can get the boat back or at least get the okay for it to stay there until I can come back for it."

"Good thinking."

He started for the exit and she walked with him. "You'll be all right?" he added.

"Yes. I just want to go and wash up, and then I'll stay with Danny—make sure he's settled."

"You don't even know this guy," John reminded her.

"I know that he's a child of God, as are you and everyone else on this planet. He's alone and probably a little scared. If I can ease that some, then I will."

She waited for more argument, but John just nodded. "I'll be back after I get cleaned up."

"That's okay. Go on back to the marina and take care of the boat. I can. . ."

"I'll be back," he repeated firmly. This time she saw from the look he gave her that arguing would be useless.

"Fine."

John asked Jeannie to drop him off at Arlen's shop instead of the Detlef house. He wanted to let Arlen know he would be there in case he came in and heard the shower running.

"You saved me a trip," Arlen replied jovially as he held up a stack of clothing. "Rosalyn just came by to leave these for you."

"Thanks." John accepted the clothing. "Must be a relief to be back in your house."

Arlen beamed. "Yes. We've been back in residence for a few days now. Others, like my mother's place, were a bit of a challenge, but with God's blessing everyone is back home safe and sound."

"That's good," John said.

"And you? Samuel tells me progress is slow."

John shrugged. "I do what I can." He nodded toward the cast on his wrist. "The ankle's much better, which helps a lot."

Arlen frowned. "It is not only your physical injuries that hinder your progress, my friend. I think you know that." He lightly tapped his own chest over his heart. "But this, the hurt that is here. . ."

John looked away. "I'd better get going," he said. "I told Hester I'd meet her back at the hospital."

"No need," Arlen told him. "Samuel and Rosalyn have gone to sit with her and bring her home. You go and get that shower and some rest. And don't forget to drink plenty of fluids," he added as John headed for the door.

The Detlef house smelled of fresh paint mingled with the faint odor of bleach and other cleaning substances. Everything was as pristine and organized as it had been on his first visit.

The first thing he did was call Margery, but there was no answer, and he decided not to leave a message. Knowing that Samuel and Rosalyn were going to the hospital to be with Hester, he decided he could handle things at the marina.

John took the clothes Arlen had handed him down the hall to the small bathroom and set them on the counter. He undressed and then let the shower run over him for several long minutes, relishing the coolness of the water after he had soaped and scrubbed himself with hot water. As he dried himself and dressed, it occurred to him that he felt physically lighter, as if pounds of dirt compacted by sweat over the last several days had flowed down the drain with the soapy water.

Once dressed, he made sure to leave the bathroom as clean as it had been when he entered it. He dropped the towel into the hamper and then bundled his soiled clothing. On his way out, he walked down the front path that had once guided visitors through the garden—Hester's garden. Her therapy while her mother moved daily closer to dying.

He stood on the porch and saw that the garden looked exactly the same as it had weeks earlier when he'd first stayed the night. There wasn't a shred of evidence that Hester had spent any time replanting. Even the orchids that she had told him had been taken inside to avoid being damaged by the hurricane had not been brought outside again. He didn't know much about growing orchids, but surely by now. . .

She's been a little busy, he reminded himself, thinking of all the different things that Hester was managing. The distribution center, getting the houses along the creek fit for occupancy again, working on Margery's place, cooking and cleaning and caring for her father, and presumably finding some time in there to spend with Samuel. It would be nice if someone might notice that maybe Hester could use a little help, that restoring the garden might be just the ticket to ease those lines of worry and exhaustion that so often marred her face. Maybe he should mention it to Samuel. It would be a way that Samuel could show his affection for her. It might even move things along for the two of them.

John frowned. Try as he might, he could not see Samuel and Hester together long term. Friends, yes. Married and facing a lifetime of evenings across the supper table from each other— nope. Still, from everything Margery had told him and everything he'd observed on his own, that was the plan. Hardly his business, he thought as he tucked the bundle of soiled clothing into the basket of Hester's bicycle and headed for the marina. The last thing Margery needed was to have her boat towed.

Later that evening after he'd retrieved Zeke's guitar and returned to his place, he built a fire and set a large kettle filled with water to boil. Then he walked his property and came across a patch of ferns growing wild near the packinghouse. He had no use for the things himself, but it occurred to him that they would make a nice lush addition to the garden. She could set the orchid pots on the ground and let the dark green lacy foliage of the ferns hide the pot and highlight the blossom. He'd point them out to Samuel when he stopped by to pick up Hester's bike and suggest he dig them and take them to Hester. Or maybe he would do it himself. After all, the plants were likely to get trampled over the next couple of days while he was working on rebuilding the damaged wall of the packinghouse. Besides, why was he troubling himself with matchmaking? Wasn't the match between Hester and Samuel already made?

Even a few days later when Jeannie assured her that Zeke was on the mend and eating like a horse, Hester couldn't seem to get Danny and the other homeless people out of her mind. Before the suspected crypto outbreak, her interactions with that sector of the local population had come either through Zeke or through her work distributing clothing and food for MCC. Zeke was homeless by choice mostly. He had family in the area, family he was in touch with from time to time, and, of course, he had Jeannie and her husband looking out for him.

Besides, Zeke was always well groomed, and his clothes were always clean, if ill-fitting. He made some money by playing his guitar at the city's downtown farmers' market during the high tourist season, and at other times of the year he could be found strumming his guitar on Main Street outside one of the vacant storefronts. He never actually panhandled. He simply left his guitar case open on the sidewalk next to him, and people dropped money in as they passed by.

But most of the others clearly had no such connections. Their hair was matted, and their clothes reeked of the need for a good washing. She recalled the two women at the bay front with their battered grocery cart, rusted and piled high with a variety of black plastic garbage bags filled with who-knew-what. Both the women and their cart had disappeared without a trace, and Hester couldn't help wondering what had happened to them. Without the safety net of Rainbow House—a place where homeless people could get a hot shower, a decent meal, and a cot—where would people like those two women go? She hadn't even gotten their names.

Something needed to be done about getting the shelter back in operation. She had no direct association with Rainbow House, but she knew people who did—Grady, for one. She would call him and let him know about the women.

"There are still some of those trailers FEMA sent down parked over near the park," her father told her when she raised her concerns for the homeless population that night at supper.

The house trailers had arrived after a story about the flooding in Pinecraft and other Sarasota neighborhoods that sat along the creek hit the national news. Grady had tried to assure the FEMA reps that the community was well prepared to care for their own, but those in charge of the agency in Washington had insisted. They had also insisted that Grady make sure the delivery was well documented by local media, and he had orchestrated the move of half a dozen families from the shelters to the trailers.

"It's a temporary fix at best," Hester said, "but they're not doing anybody else any good, and the homeless folks could sure use them."

After supper Hester and Samuel drove to Grady's house and explained the problem.

"I'd like to help. I really would," Grady told them. "But we've got a bunch of Homeland Security bigwigs on their way down here to tour the area. Some talk show host did a sensational piece focused on what hasn't been done, so the folks in DC are nervous. They sent those trailers for people wiped out by the hurricane, and if we use them to house folks who were homeless before the hurricane. . . Well, you know how these things go."

"But no one is using them, and until Rainbow House can be reopened—"

"Rainbow House is closed, Hester."

"I know, but maybe some local charity could—"

"There are dozens of local charities, and at times like this we definitely count on their support. But starting up something new?" Grady shook his head. "Money is tight, and I hate to say it, but that's not going to happen."

Hester sighed. "I understand. I just hoped that maybe there was something we could do."

Grady's wife, Amy, offered dessert, but both Hester and Samuel turned her down. "Thanks, but we should be getting back." Not wanting to leave her friends to think that she was upset with them, she smiled at Amy. "Hey, I'm a nurse, and you should be off your feet."

Amy patted her very pregnant midsection. "This little guy doesn't like sitting around. I think he's going to be a football player the way he kicks."

Grady wrapped his arm around her shoulders. "It won't be much longer now," he promised.

Amy laughed. "Then we probably won't get any sleep at all—either of us." But in spite of her complaints, Amy seemed so very happy and content that Hester found it hard not to envy her.

"If either of you get any ideas about helping these folks, let us know, okay?"

"Tell you what," Grady said as he and Amy walked them down the driveway, "I'll introduce you to our visitors from DC if I get a chance. I mean, it would be a long shot, but you never know."

"I'd appreciate that," Hester said as Samuel opened the car door for her. "And don't worry, Grady. We'll figure something out."

"You always do," Grady said.

Hester sighed heavily, and after Samuel pulled away from the curb, he glanced at Hester. "He's right, you know. You will find a solution for this."

"I wish I had your confidence."

Samuel laughed. It was a good laugh, hearty and filled with the pure joy of being alive. "Oh, Hester, the one thing you do not need is any more confidence. You are perhaps the most self-confident person I have ever known, man or woman." But then he sobered and focused on his driving. "You take on too much, Hester. You cannot save the world."

Why not? she thought. Not that she was so egotistical as to think she could, but wasn't the world, and more to the point the people in it, worth doing everything possible to save? Hadn't God entrusted His creation to their stewardship? Wasn't that the whole point of life on this planet? "I know, but if we don't do our best, then don't you think we'll regret not at least trying?"

"So we'll do our best," he said. "We just have to figure out what that might be."

Reassured, Hester leaned back and closed her eyes. There

was comfort in his words. She wasn't in this alone.

"There is one regret that I have," he said after several minutes.

His tone was so solemn that Hester's eyes flew open, and she turned in her seat to face him. "What?"

He grinned. "That we turned down Amy's offer of dessert. I find that I suddenly have a real craving for a chocolate sundae."

"With pecans?" Hester asked, falling so easily into the rhythm of his teasing that it might have been something they had shared for years. She couldn't help thinking how different this ice cream date with Samuel was from the one she had shared with John, not that the cone she'd shared with John had been a date. Far from it.

"And whipped cream?" Samuel was smiling at her, a twinkle in his eye. Nothing like the glowering John Steiner.

"Of course," she said. "And a cherry on top."

"Two," Samuel assured her.

Later that night as she lay awake and relived the hour that she and Samuel had spent sitting outside the ice cream shop, she realized that in many ways it had been their first real date. Always before whenever they were together, other people were there as well— at family meals, at church functions, even working together after the hurricane, they had always been in the company of others. Not tonight though. Tonight it had been just the two of them, and she had to admit that she had enjoyed herself immensely.

For one thing she had never fully appreciated Samuel's dry sense of humor before. But as they shared a huge sundae with all the trimmings and even one made with the chocolate ice cream that he knew she preferred, he had kept her laughing with his wry take on various people in the community.

"And then there's Olive Crowder," he said with an exaggerated sigh. "I owe her a huge debt of gratitude."

"Why?"

"She warned me."

"About me?"

"About Arlen."

"Dad? She's always spoken so highly of him."

Samuel grinned. "And nothing about that has changed. She told me he would treat me like a son, trying to replace your four brothers according to her. She indicated that I would have a great deal to live up to in that department. Olive seemed to think that might be a problem. She's been most vigilant in offering me advice."

"She means well," Hester said. "It's just that sometimes she. . ."

"Oversteps?"

"That's one way of looking at it."

Samuel scraped the last of the hot fudge from the side of the dish and offered it to her.

"No more," she protested with a laugh.

He shrugged and licked the spoon. But then he sobered. "I think you might want to watch yourself when she's around."

"Oh, she's harmless. She's been on my case practically my whole life. I fear I have been a bitter disappointment to her with a few exceptions."

"Such as?"

"She was surprised, I think, when I cared for my mother for the last five years of her life. In all that time I don't think she could find one single fault with me."

"Must have driven her crazy," Samuel said with a grin.

"She's making up for it these days."

"I kind of heard that the two of you had some words when you were working on the houses by the creek."

"Kind of heard? How do you kind of hear something?"

He actually blushed. "Rosalyn mentioned it. She wasn't gossiping," he added hastily. "She was concerned about you, and so am I. . . . I mean, what if Olive decides to find some concern about you to bring before the congregation?"

"Oh, it's nothing so dire. She's just determined to get me to quit MCC and go to work for CAM. Rosalyn worries about me," Hester said with a smile.

"So do I." Samuel stared at her for a long moment, his eyes

flitting across her features. "I want you to be happy."

"I am happy."

He gave her a skeptical look. "Really?"

"Well, I mean, lately there's been a lot for me to do, and—"

"And yet you keep adding to that pile—now you're trying to make the world better for homeless people. It's like you're always running from one project to the next. Where in all of that is there time for you?"

"That *is* me," she replied, hating the defensive edge that crept into her voice. She stood up and threw their trash into the container near the car. "We should get back. Dad will worry."

In the silence that cloaked their drive back to her father's house, Hester had thought about Samuel's comment about wanting her to be happy. And lying awake now, she thought about the lie she had told in declaring that she was.

Chapter 16

In the week after John rescued Zeke, a few other homeless men whom Zeke had brought with him from time to time showed up to help John get the first floor of the house back in good enough shape that he could move from the packinghouse to the main house. He could hardly believe that he was finally able to enjoy breakfast at his own table in his restored kitchen after his first night back in the main house. The first floor had been scoured of mold and silt, and the space was protected by one of the signature blue tarps that dotted the landscape where roofs had been ripped away all up and down the coast. Margery had given him a single bed complete with mattress and linens that she claimed to have no use for, and Rosalyn had sent him dishes and pots and pans from the thrift shop.

"Housewarming present," Samuel had told him when he protested.

For the first time in weeks he felt something like hope that things just might work out for him. And not wanting anything to disturb this idyllic moment, he decided to ignore the approach of a car, the slam of a door, and the muffled voices followed by the sound of the car leaving, and the rhythmic click of hard-soled shoes climbing the steps to his door.

There was a knock. A pause. A repeated knock. And then a pounding. "I know you're in there, John Steiner. Now open up."

The last person John thought he would see standing at his makeshift front door was his aunt. Congresswoman Elizabeth Carter-Thompson from the great state of Virginia was dressed in a hot pink designer suit and four-inch stiletto heels. She also wore a ridiculously floppy straw hat that matched her suit and completely hid her platinum hair except for the wisps of bangs.

"How did you get here?" John asked as soon as he recovered from the initial shock of seeing her. The real question he'd meant to ask was, "What are you doing here?"

"I came by covered wagon," she quipped as she glanced back at the cab already headed back to town. "Now please tell me you have air-conditioning, or failing that, a bucket of ice and a gallon of sweet tea."

"No air-conditioning," he said, stepping aside so she could enter what there was of the house. "No ice. But there is tea, and I have sugar."

She pulled off the hat and glanced at her surroundings. "Primitive," she said in the same polite tone she might have told someone else that their home was charming.

"We had this little storm pass through," John replied, falling easily into the banter that he had shared with her throughout their lives. "Perhaps you heard about it?"

"Thus my visit. I'm here on what we politicians laughingly call a fact-finding tour. Seems to me the facts are pretty straightforward and we could have read all about them in the reports sent by the FEMA reps." She fanned herself with his copy of *Walden*, then glanced at the cover. "Oh, please do not tell me you are still on this mission." She was almost pleading with him as she continued fanning herself. He set a glass of tea in front of her and pushed the sugar bowl across the scarred table.

"It's hardly a mission. It's an experiment. It was for Thoreau, and it is for me."

"How about a life?" She shoveled three heaping teaspoons of

sugar into the tea and stirred. "Ever consider going after one of those?"

He gestured to the space around them as if to say, *For the time being, this is my life.* Liz's answer was to laugh, snorting tea out her nose in the process. "I don't know who you think you're fooling, John, but this is me. I know you, and I know why you are doing this." She stood up and strolled around the kitchen. "This is your version of sackcloth and ashes. This is not a life. This is penance, and I am here to tell you that my dear sister, your beloved mother, would be downright horrified."

John opened his mouth to say something, anything, to forestall the lecture he knew she'd been working on through all the weeks that he had not been in contact. But she was not to be denied.

"You want to honor Rachel's memory? Good for you, but this is not the way to go about that. You know it and I know it. Holing up here like some hermit. . ." she muttered.

"My mother chose a plain life," he reminded her.

"In a community surrounded by dear friends and family, shared way too briefly with a husband who adored her and a son who gave her more joy than most of us know in a lifetime." She ticked off each item with her long manicured nails. "For you to abandon that community, those people, that life, to hide away here like some wounded puppy, borders on blasphemy."

All he needed to do was lift one eyebrow at her to remind her of the circumstances under which he had come to Florida.

"Oh, right. Rachel died and then you got yourself banned or shunned or excommunicated, whatever the term is. Well, so what? Life on this planet is tough, thus the promise of a better afterlife. The key is to make something of this life while you have time. My sister ran out of time to do all the good she set out to do, but I would be willing to bet my next election that she died thinking that you would carry on where she'd left off."

John had had enough. "She died because of me," he reminded her.

Liz placed her hand on his back and abandoned her soapbox

voice. "She died in your arms. You were the last person she saw, the last voice she heard, the last conscious thought she had."

The silence between them was punctuated by the slow, steady drip of the faucet. Liz took a long swallow of her tea, and John pushed himself onto a countertop.

"Why do you think she stayed?" he asked. "I mean after Dad died. She could have just walked away. After all, she wasn't born Amish. It would have been so much easier for her to return east to the life she had known as a child, the life she shared with you and your parents."

"But she fell in love with Jacob. She chose to live his life, and she was so very happy living that life, John. It suited her. That's why she stayed. Thinking back on it, she was never comfortable in the life of a politician's granddaughter. She used to ask Grandpa Tom, 'Why are those men taking our picture, Papa?' Me? I was always wondering why they *weren't* taking our picture more."

John smiled as a memory flashed through his mind like the midday sun. "She used to tease Dad that she'd only married him and become plain to avoid the camera."

Liz walked over to the door and then out into the yard. John followed her. He stood on the porch Zeke had helped him rebuild, watching her. Both of them were lost in the memory of a very special woman—her sister, his mother.

Then he heard the buzz of a motorboat approaching and prepared to introduce his aunt to Margery. It occurred to him that the two women would get along famously. Margery was something of a politician herself, not that she had ever seen her name on a ballot, but she certainly knew how to work the system when it suited her.

"Look who's back among the living," Margery shouted as she pointed to the back of the boat where Zeke stood, poised to help her dock the boat. "He insisted on coming out here to give you a hand. Do not ask me to understand why he would turn down a—" When she spotted Liz in her pink suit, her mouth remained open, but no sound came out.

Liz had removed her shoes and now walked barefoot along

the makeshift boardwalk that John had laid over the mud and silt down to the pier. "Hello," she called. "I'm John's aunt Liz. I'm sure he's been singing my praises." And as John had mentally predicted, Margery was immediately captivated. As apparently was Zeke. He gave her a mumbled greeting as he combed his hair back from his face with his fingers and then made his way toward the house, casting furtive glances back at her.

"You're looking better than you did the last time I saw you," John said. He could not hide the relief he felt at seeing Zeke doing so well.

"And you're still the same scruffy guy I've been having to look at for weeks now," Zeke replied as he perched on the edge of the porch and watched the two women. "That's your aunt, huh?"

"My mother's sister," John said.

"She's definitely not *plain*, is she?"

"She's a congresswoman."

"Well, I suppose that explains some of it," Zeke said. "She staying long?"

John caught the drift of Zeke's question and laughed. "She's not staying here at all. She and her so-called 'fact-finding committee' are probably booked at the Ritz-Carlton."

"The people's tax dollars at work," Zeke murmured.

"*Your* tax dollars maybe. Anyway, since my mom died, Liz has taken it upon herself to watch over me."

"She doesn't look old enough to be your mom."

"No, Liz is closer in age to a cousin or big sister. Big gap between my mother and her, in years, not to mention personality."

Zeke studied Liz for a long moment. "She's hot," he said finally in a tone that declared an assessment had been made and this was the final verdict. Then he took a deep breath and surveyed the property. "Well, I can see you've been able to make some progress without me." He glanced around. "So what's our plan?"

John had heard this question every time he'd been with Zeke. At first it had been "What's *your* plan?" But in the time they had worked together, it had become "What's *our* plan?"

"First we need to get my aunt back to town. Margery is already filling her head with her version of what I should and should not be doing." He nodded toward the pier where the two women were deep in conversation, or rather Margery was talking nonstop, and Liz was nodding as she listened intently. Liz kept flicking a glance over to where John was sitting with Zeke and giving him her tight campaign smile. This was not a good thing. It meant that she was agreeing with Margery's assessment of how he should be conducting his life, and the last thing John needed was two women trying to mother him.

"Dad? I'll see you later. Grady and Amy are here," Hester called out as she gathered her things and glanced out the window.

Her father lifted his bifocals to the top of his head and leaned back in his chair. "This meeting, Hester. What is it again?"

"It's not a meeting exactly," she hedged, unwilling to admit that she was about to attend a reception for the visiting congressional committee at Sarasota's fanciest hotel. "It's more of a gathering."

Arlen said nothing, just lifted one eyebrow skeptically.

"They just want to know how FEMA works with the various volunteer agencies, Dad. Since the oil spill and Katrina, they are looking at ways the agency might be more proactive."

"Will Emma Keller be there?"

"I don't know for sure."

Arlen caught her hand and held on. "Meaning you think probably not?"

She shrugged. "I'm doing this for Grady," she said as if that explained everything.

"I should not need to remind you that it is not our way to get involved in these outside politics, Hester."

"But it is our way to help a friend in need, and Grady can use our support to show those in authority that we respect the work he does here. With the baby coming and all, he really shouldn't have to worry unnecessarily about how others are judging his work."

"Still, you don't have to go to this event. You could write a letter to these government people praising Grady's work. In fact, we could all sign it."

"He's done a lot for Pinecraft, Dad. I think this is the least I can do," Hester told him as she heard Grady lightly toot the horn of his car a second time. She flicked the porch light switch off and on to signal that she had heard him. "Besides, this committee is interested in hearing ideas for how to improve the coordination of disaster relief efforts. The president himself appointed them to this commission."

"Impressive, but nevertheless, none of our business." He squeezed Hester's fingers, then released them.

"Are you asking me not to go?"

"I am asking you to remember who you are, who *we* are." He gently touched the ties of her prayer covering.

"I know all that, Dad."

"I am asking you to think about how this might raise questions among people in our community, our congregation."

"Olive Crowder?"

"*Liebchen*, surely you know that if Olive should ever become so concerned that she actually files a formal complaint against you, there is nothing I can do except to follow the protocol of our faith."

"I know," Hester admitted. "But I cannot let Grady down, Dad. He's been a good friend. I will go tonight to support Grady, and that will be the end of it. I give you my word that I will turn all of my efforts toward helping others through the church, starting first thing tomorrow. No more meetings with outsiders, no more—"

Her father stood and embraced her. "I am asking no such thing of you, Hester. I would never ask you to be other than the woman God has led you to be. The only thing I ask of you is that you be certain in your heart and mind that the choices you are making are those that God has led you to make and not those of your own choosing."

Hester hugged her father harder. "Even if those choices go against—?"

Arlen held her by her shoulders so that they were face-to-face, his blue eyes piercing as they held hers. "If you have prayed on these matters and listened for God's answer, then I will stand with you, and together we will see what plan God has in mind for you."

"Danke, Papa," she whispered as she kissed his cheek.

He chuckled. "You have not called me 'Papa' since you were seven or eight, and as I recall, you always did so when you had gotten your way." He gave her a little push toward the door. "Now go—before I change my mind."

At the reception, Hester was relieved to see that everyone attending was dressed in regular daytime attire. Only Jeannie and a woman whom Grady pointed out as a member of the committee as well as John Steiner's aunt arrived wearing something that could be called fancy. Jeannie was dressed in a flowing ankle-length caftan-style dress, and John's aunt was wearing a silk pantsuit in peacock blue.

Likewise the food was basic—cheese and crackers, vegetables and dip, and no alcohol. Instead, they served fresh-squeezed orange juice.

"Are we having fun yet?" Margery murmured as she came alongside Hester and bit down on a cracker. "Bunch of politicians trying to act like they might actually make something happen," she huffed. "Although that one there"—she pointed toward John's aunt—"she has potential." She chewed her cracker and continued her monologue as if Hester had raised the question of how she might know that. "I had a chance to spend some time with her this afternoon when she was out visiting Johnny. Oh, she knows how to push his buttons." She cackled with delight. "Got him so riled up that he actually agreed to show up here tonight."

In spite of herself, Hester made a quick scan of the crowded room.

"He's over there," Margery said with a nod toward a marble pillar at the far end of the room where, sure enough, John Steiner was leaning with arms crossed, his signature scowl firmly in place.

"So that's his aunt," Hester said, swinging her attention back to the woman in blue as John's eyes met hers. "She looks young enough to be his sister."

She nodded. "She gave me the whole family history. After Johnny's father died, his mom would have Liz come and spend summers on the farm with them. She told me she would have come here right after the storm passed, but duty had to take precedence. That's why she called the mayor here, who called Grady. . .who called you."

It was definitely hard to picture the anything-but-plain woman on a farm at all, much less one in the midst of an Amish community. Still, she had a way about her that made her seem downright approachable. Perhaps it was that she focused all of her attention on the person speaking to her at any given moment. Her eyes met theirs, and her features registered genuine concern and sympathy. Now and then she would place one manicured hand on the person's arm, give them a few words of what appeared to be reassurance or appreciation, and then move on to the next person.

Hester focused her attention on a man who Grady had told her was also on the Homeland Security Committee. In sharp contrast to John's aunt, the man appeared to be lecturing those gathered around him when he should have been listening.

"Hester?"

She turned to find Grady approaching her with the congress-woman close at his side.

"I'd like you to meet Congresswoman Elizabeth Carter-Thompson," he said. "This is Hester Detlef, the woman I was telling you about."

"It's a pleasure to meet you in person, Hester. May I call you Hester?" She had taken Hester's hand between both of hers and lasered her with eyes that were the same color as John's.

"Yes," Hester replied.

"And I am Liz. Margery Barker told me about the work you've been doing through your agency—MCC, is it? And your father as well with MDS, I believe. Both groups were so key to our efforts after Katrina. Walk the talk, we like to say, but so few of us really ever do."

Hester felt herself caught up in the whirlwind that she understood was Liz's way of drawing total strangers into her circle of supporters. Instinctively she pulled her hand free and took a small step away. She saw something pass across Liz's eyes that she would not have expected. She saw a hint of embarrassment.

"I'm sorry," Liz said in a tone that sounded far more sincere than the bright chatter she'd delivered before. "Give me a second to retire my politician hat." She pantomimed removing a hat and casting it to the wind; then she turned back to Hester. "I really want to hear any ideas you might have about how best to help those affected by this hurricane," she said. "Can we go sit somewhere that's a little quieter and have a real conversation?"

Realizing that Grady had moved on to another group after making the introductions, Hester hesitated.

"It's not a trap," Liz assured her. "I really want to talk."

"All right." She would take the congresswoman at her word, for now. But remembering the stories that Grady had told her about how government worked, she would also be cautious.

"Shall we ask my nephew to join us?"

But it was a moot question since Liz was already signaling to John. Hester glanced over at him, fully expecting him to ignore his aunt and walk away, but to her amazement, he started working his way through the crowd toward them.

"I know he can be a pill of major proportions," Liz confided, "but he does have a way of thinking outside the box. That's what got him in trouble in the first place." She sighed, then plastered on her brightest smile as John reached them. "John, I believe you and Hester know each other?"

He nodded and then focused his attention on his aunt. "You summoned?"

"Oh, stop being so contentious," Liz replied as she reached up and straightened his shirt collar. John let her without shrugging away. He was wearing jeans and one of the tropical print shirts Rosalyn had pulled for him from the supplies at the center. He was clean-shaven instead of sporting the stubble that she'd gotten used to seeing on him. It surprised her that this pleased her. She had always found the stubble slightly pretentious.

"Now, then," Liz said, pointing to a cluster of three upholstered chairs in the atrium outside the crowded ballroom. "Let's talk. Rather, you talk. I'll listen." She nodded to a young man who had trailed them from the ballroom. "This is Alan. He's a member of my staff. If you don't object, he'll sit quietly and take notes."

John shrugged and Hester nodded.

"Excellent," Liz said as Alan moved a straight chair behind and to her left and pulled out a notebook and pen. "Where shall we begin?" she asked. "Tell me about the efforts MCC and MDS have already made, Hester."

It got easier after that. Once Hester started to list the various projects coordinated by MCC and MDS and describe how the two groups worked together with the better-known secular agencies, she was in her element. Now and then John would interject a comment or Liz would ask a question that would lead them into the discussion of something else. They told her about the distribution center, the RV teams, and the work that had been done to get Margery back in business.

"Tell me about the flooding in Pinecraft," Liz asked.

"That wasn't Grady Forrest's fault," Hester said, and then she blushed at her uncensored remarks.

"Why would anyone think that it was?" Liz said quietly. "Are you saying there was a problem there?"

"They were busy with me," John told her. "It's what happens when people try to pull strings from a thousand miles away."

Hester watched as John and his aunt locked eyes. "I was concerned," she said through a tight smile even as she quietly placed one hand on Alan's to stop his moving pen.

"And with good reason." Hester could not help her instinct to try to smooth things over between them. Now their gazes shifted to her. "I mean, at times like that, it's hard to know where to put your resources first. The human tendency is to protect those you know and love. You don't think much about how it affects others."

"I was the one at fault," John said quietly. "If I had left when

Hester told me to, then. . ."

Liz's eyes widened with interest. "I wasn't aware that the two of you knew each other before the hurricane."

"We didn't," Hester said.

"Then why send. . ."

"Drop it, Lizzie," John growled. "It's over and done with. Let's move on." He did not look directly at Hester, but she understood that John had come as close as he would ever come to admitting that he had been wrong to stay.

"All right, then, let's talk about plans for the future and the resources available to help." Liz signaled Alan that his note-taking could resume.

"Whose?" John asked.

"Yours makes for an interesting case study. How are things coming out there at your version of *Walden*?"

Hester's heart went out to John as she watched his features collapse into an expression of such utter defeat that she had to stop herself from reaching over to comfort him. He had done as much as he could to repair the damage to his property. Did his aunt have any idea what it had been like that first day after the hurricane passed through?

"I have the first floor of the house fairly livable." He held up his left hand, cast removed. "I have the use of both hands for the first time in weeks." He hesitated as if searching for words.

"But?" Liz asked, her voice gentle.

"But the undeniable fact is that the orange trees that Tucker planted and I worked at reviving for the last two years are gone." His voice trailed off as if he had just realized this, when Hester knew that he must have known it all along. The rows of trees had for the most part been snapped off in the high winds, and those few trees not totally wiped out by the hurricane were half buried in the salty muck left behind when the waters of the bay finally receded. They were as good as dead.

"So how will you support yourself and your work on that place?" Liz pressed, her tone that of a mother nurturing a small child.

John blinked as if he were just awakening from a nightmare. "I have no idea," he admitted. "I put everything I had into that property."

"You still have the packinghouse," Hester reminded him.

"And exactly what would we pack there?" he asked her, but this time he was the one who had assumed a tone that one might use in speaking to an overly optimistic child. He turned his attention back to his aunt. "So there you have one of what must be hundreds of sad stories, Lizzie. What are you and your fact-finding team going to do about it?"

A commotion just inside the ballroom drew their attention away from the tension that radiated between John and his aunt.

"Somebody call 911," a voice yelled. "This lady's having her baby."

Hester was on her feet instantly. With John and Liz not far behind, she worked her way through the throng surrounding Amy and Grady. Amy was sitting on one of the small straight-backed and gilded chairs at a white-cloth-covered table, a pool of water at her feet. Grady was on his knees next to her.

"Hang in there, honey," he coached. "They've called for an ambulance."

Amy's response was a prolonged keening of pain that sent everyone into retreat as she gripped Grady's hand. "Can't." She gritted out the word. "Now."

"Get back," Hester heard John order the onlookers, and to her amazement everyone complied.

"People," Liz shouted, clapping her hands. "Please follow Alan here out into the atrium while we wait for the ambulance." The crowd shifted only a little. "That's the way," she said, encouraging them to keep moving. "Let's give these folks some privacy," she said as the others headed reluctantly toward the doors.

"When did the pains start?" Hester asked.

Amy was between contractions and breathing heavily. "This afternoon," she said.

"This afternoon?" Grady shouted. "And you didn't say anything? We should have—"

"You needed to be here," she replied, panting in preparation for the next round of pain. "Job," she managed, as the pain gripped her once more.

Grady glanced at Liz then back at his wife. "You don't worry about that. We're going to be fine," he murmured.

Liz waited for the contraction to pass and then knelt next to Grady, taking Amy's free hand. "Now you listen to me, both of you," she said. "There is nothing so precious—or important—in this world than the beginning of a new life. That child could change the world."

Amy's eyes brimmed with tears.

Hester saw John clasp Grady's shoulder. "Your job's not on the line," he said. "Right, Liz?"

"Oh, for goodness' sake," she grumbled as she got to her feet. "We aren't monsters. We didn't come down here to check up on or make anyone our scapegoat, Grady. We came here because. . .it's what we do when the media pushes our buttons and we don't know what else to do," she finished lamely. "I'll speak with your boss, okay?"

"Thank you." Grady squeezed Amy's hand. "See, honey? It's all going to be fine." In the quiet that followed, they could hear the siren of the arriving ambulance. In seconds the room was a beehive of activity as Amy was checked, then placed on a gurney and rolled away with Grady clinging to her hand and running alongside.

"You coming?" he shouted to Hester.

"Sure."

Grady dug into his pocket and tossed his car keys in the air. John caught them with one hand, then passed them to Hester.

"I could have caught them," she said.

"No doubt."

When he started walking with her toward the exit, Hester hesitated.

"Lead the way," he said, holding the door open for her. "It's not like I know what Grady's car looks like."

Chapter 17

It took Hester a minute to familiarize herself with the mechanics of Grady's hybrid car. John seemed to instinctively know that it would be best to remain silent and let her work things out for herself. Still, she could practically feel him wanting to offer his ideas about how to start the thing. Finally, she got it started, and they were on their way to the hospital.

"You don't have to do this," she repeated. "Come to the hospital, I mean."

"I'd do pretty much anything not to have to stay another minute at that party," he said and grinned.

"Reception," she corrected. "And I don't know why you were there, but I was there for Grady."

"Sure you were."

Was that a smile? Hester clamped her mouth shut and concentrated on driving. "I take it your sarcasm means you think I was there for other reasons?"

"I think you like being where the action is. I think you really struggle when it comes to being in the background."

"I. . ." She absolutely could not find the words to refute that, but he was wrong. Wasn't he? "And you know this because. . . ?"

"An observation. Nothing more. And it's not like it's a bad

thing." Out of the corner of her eye, she saw him study her for a long moment, but she refused to take her eyes from the road. "Anyway, let's talk about something else."

"Such as?"

"I don't know. We're on our way to the hospital, where in a few hours Grady and Amy will bring a new life into this world. Did you ever wonder what it might be like to be a parent?" he asked as they stopped for a light that was notorious for taking forever to change.

She felt herself relax as she thought about Amy and Grady and all the ways this night was going to change their lives forever. "Sure. I think everyone must wonder about that."

"Maybe you and Samuel—"

"What about you?" she interrupted before he could pursue that thought, a thought that she had not really wanted to consider in all the time she'd spent imagining a future with Samuel.

The light changed to green, and a car behind them honked impatiently. Hester eased the car forward much as she might have coaxed a horse and buggy into motion, deliberately taking her time. "You never married?"

"I came close, I guess," he said as the impatient driver passed them on the right, horn blasting.

"You guess? How do you guess at a thing like that?"

"Same way you think maybe you and Samuel might marry one day," he shot back. "It seemed like it was going to happen and it didn't, in my case."

"Fair enough," she murmured as she turned onto a side street.

"The sign says the entrance to the emergency room is that way." He pointed.

"But the parking lot is down this side street."

She pulled into the first available space and had barely turned off the engine before she was out of the car and walking quickly toward the hospital entrance. *"It seemed like it was going to happen."* His words beat a cadence that matched her steps as together they hurried along long deserted corridors to the main lobby.

"Mrs. Forrest has been taken to our obstetrics unit," the

person at the desk told them. "Take these elevators to three, and the waiting room is on your left as you exit."

As soon as they stepped off the elevator, a nurse whom Hester knew assured them that Amy was doing fine and Grady was with her. "The contractions have stopped for now," she said. "It could be a while." She turned her attention to John. "Are you the family?"

"We're friends," John replied before Hester could.

"I'll let Mr. Forrest know you're out here. There's coffee and tea," she said, motioning toward a machine in the corner, "and our vintage selection of three- to five-year-old magazines." She offered an apologetic smile, and then continued on her way through a pair of swinging doors that whooshed shut behind her.

"You don't need to stay," Hester said.

"If you keep saying that every time we end up in the same place, I'm going to think you don't like my company," John said and sat down on a chair facing away from the television that was on but muted. He picked up a magazine and started flipping through it. The cover featured a colorful summer fruit salad and a bold headline about weight loss. The picture of the fruit salad reminded Hester of rainbows.

"Do you think there's any chance your aunt and her group will help get Rainbow House reopened?" she asked.

"I doubt it. It's not what they do."

"I've been checking up on some of the people who were so sick. They seem to be okay physically, but it's hard for them and the others. . .all the others. . . ." Her voice trailed off.

"How's the guy we left here that day? Dan?"

"Danny. His brother came and took him back to his home in Georgia. That's pretty much all I know about him, but at least he had family."

"Margery tells me that Zeke also has family, locally."

Hester nodded. "Zeke comes from a fairly prominent family in this area. They give him money regularly, but he just gives it away, takes care of the others, especially his fellow veterans. Some of them take advantage." She paced the room, ending up finally in front of the coffee machine. "Do you want something?"

John shook his head and continued paging through the magazine, stopping now and then to skim an article.

"If we could just find a place," Hester continued as if there had been no pause in the conversation. She pushed the button for tea and, once it was ready, cradled the Styrofoam cup between her palms instead of drinking from it.

"Isn't finding homes for homeless people a little out of your jurisdiction?"

"I don't have a jurisdiction. When people are in need, then it's our mission to try to help them."

"And what about the people devastated by the hurricane—property and job loss and such as you must have mentioned to me at least five hundred times. . . ."

"Don't exaggerate." She fought against a smile. "It wasn't more than two hundred tops. There are systems in place to help them."

"Systems that don't work much of the time," John reminded her.

"I know, but when we were helping Zeke and Dan and the others, it struck me that for these folks—people who live on the street and have to rely on public facilities for their basic needs and eat out of trash cans and—"

"Some would say they should get a job."

"How? Where? Everything's against them—their hygiene or lack thereof, their age in many cases, their mental health. They are invisible and lost, and no one really notices them until they interrupt the tourist season by hanging out down at the bay or get businesses all nervous or in some cases cross paths with the police and. . ." In spite of her determination not to, Hester started to cry. She'd been repressing her concerns and worries for so long that there seemed to be no place to put anything more. "Don't mind me. It's just been an emotional few weeks, and I'm worried about Grady and Amy and. . ."

John laid his magazine aside and moved to the chair next to hers. He put his hand on her back and leaned in closer. "Hey, you're doing the best you can, okay? You can't save the world, although Samuel tells me you are stubborn enough to try."

She glanced up, swiping at tears with the back of her hand. "Samuel said I was stubborn?"

"I said you were stubborn. Samuel seems to think you can do whatever you set your mind to."

"Takes one to know one—stubborn, I mean," she said, far too aware of John's face close to hers, his large palm resting on her back. His eyes with their fan of golden lashes held the promise of understanding and acceptance. And in that moment she fully comprehended that she and John Steiner had a lot more in common than she might ever have imagined. For, like her, he was a person who looked at the world and saw possibilities and challenges that required going beyond the norm to solve. She had never talked like this with Samuel, and even when she raised these issues with her father, more often than not he looked mystified and counseled her that there were many in her own community in need of her help.

John leaned in closer and wiped one tear from her cheek with his thumb. She thought for one incredible moment that he might kiss her, but instead he rested his forehead on hers. "Ah, Hester Detlef, we might be a formidable team if we stopped fighting each other," he said softly.

"You would help me?"

"I would help Zeke," he corrected. "You don't need help."

Yes, I do, she thought, and for the first time since her mother had died, she admitted to herself that she had been running on empty for months now, lost in her desperate need to find some way that she could save *someone,* because she couldn't save her mother.

It was well past midnight when Samuel closed up the workshop and saw Rosalyn walking along Bahia Vista. He cut across a parking lot behind the cabinetry shop to catch up to her and was just about to call out to her when a convertible filled with teenagers roared past her going at least twenty miles over the posted speed limit. One of the occupants shouted at her, and then Samuel saw something fly out of the car and strike Rosalyn in the face. Glass shattered as the object hit the ground, and before he knew it, the car was making an illegal U-turn. Rosalyn was holding her hand to her forehead. As the driver and another young man got out of the car, he started to run toward Rosalyn.

From their unsteady gait, he was pretty sure that the two young men were drunk, and instinct told him they had not come back to help Rosalyn.

"Hey, honey," he heard one of them croon. "You shouldn't be out walking alone at this hour. How about a ride with me and my friends here?"

The second young man snickered as one of the two who had remained in the car called for his friends to come back so they could be on their way.

"Why, you're bleeding, sweetheart," the driver continued, a wide smirk of a smile contradicting his words of concern. "We'd better get you to a hospital and get that looked at right away." He took hold of Rosalyn's arm and started pulling her toward the car, while his friend stumbled back to open the passenger door for her.

"Let her go, man," the man in the backseat said. "Let's get out of here."

"Shut up," the driver growled. "What happened to your face, honey? It's all purple and stuff."

When he was within a couple of yards of the group, Samuel slowed to a walk and forced his breathing to calm. "Is there a problem?" he asked as he emerged from the shadows, deliberately startling the young man who was holding Rosalyn's arm.

"What do you want, Amish boy?" the guy holding the car door snarled.

Now that he was closer, Samuel saw that all of the men in the car were barely out of their teens, if that, and the car they were driving was an expensive one. Everything about them screamed money and entitlement. Samuel had encountered guys like these before when he was attending public school. They truly seemed to believe that their family money could buy them anything they wanted, or in the case of Rosalyn, anything they decided to take.

He took a few seconds to gauge the situation. He was pretty sure that at least the two guys in the backseat were not a threat. One was nearly passed out, and the other looked like he wished he were anywhere else but on this street corner.

Samuel memorized the license number of the car as he moved closer to the man holding Rosalyn's arm.

"We got this, man," the one standing by the open car door said.

"Let her go," Samuel said calmly.

The driver released Rosalyn's arm as he took a step toward Samuel. Rosalyn seized the moment and ran to Samuel's side. He wrapped his arm around her shoulder and faced the young man who was swaying unsteadily.

"There are four of us," he pointed out. "And I've heard that you Amish boys don't believe in fighting."

Samuel glanced at each of the other three, relieved that the two in the backseat had made no move to join their friend, and the one standing next to the open door of the car would do whatever this guy told him to do. The person he needed to deal with was standing not three feet in front of him, his eyes glazed and his smile cocky.

"Actually, we are Mennonites, but you are right," he said, and the driver's grin widened as he once again reached for Rosalyn.

Samuel pressed her closer to his side as he smiled at the man and at the same time looked him directly in the eye without blinking. "So here is my suggestion," he said quietly. "You and your friends leave now, and my friend and I will not report the matter."

"Yeah. Right. Do I look like a complete fool?"

Actually, yes, Samuel thought, but he forced an expression of contrition. "You seem to know something of our ways, and therefore you probably know that when a man of my faith gives his word then you can count on it."

From the corner of his eye he saw that one of the group who'd been sitting in the backseat had moved to the front, into the driver's seat. "Come on, Robbie," he called. "We got places to go and beer to drink. Time's not on our side."

Samuel stepped back, creating more distance between the drunken young man and Rosalyn. He nodded to the man behind the wheel. "You okay to drive?"

"Yes, sir," he said. "I've only had one. Sorry about that." He nodded toward Rosalyn. "Is she okay?"

"She'll be fine," Samuel assured him as he watched Rosalyn's attacker sway slightly as he made his decision. Finally, he climbed into the backseat and slumped down. Samuel felt his fist clench and wondered at the power of his instinct to rip the guy to shreds. He closed his eyes and silently prayed for the strength he needed to see this through. "Just go," he said quietly, and to his relief he heard the last car door slam and the car roared away.

Rosalyn slumped against him and broke down sobbing.

"Come on, now. It's all over," he said, gently leading her to a streetlamp so he could assess the extent of her injury. "It doesn't seem to be that bad."

"It's fine," she said, accepting the handkerchief he offered her and pressing it to her forehead. "It was just that I was so scared, and if you hadn't come along, and what if. . ."

"Shhh. . ."

Samuel pulled her into his arms and held her, rocking her gently from side to side as they stood together under the amber glow of the old-fashioned streetlamp. "I'm right here and I'm not going anywhere," he promised, and he knew in that moment that where Rosalyn was concerned—and Hester—he had made his decision.

By the time Amy had her baby, both her parents and Grady's had arrived to greet their first grandchild. The waiting room had become a beehive of activity as other family members were called with the good news. Amy had delivered a seven-pound boy at 4:12 in the morning. Both mother and child were doing fine.

"We're naming him Harley," Grady announced, his eyes sparkling with new-dad wonder in spite of his exhaustion.

Hester congratulated him as well as each set of grandparents and then realized that John was no longer in the room. While everyone else headed in to see Amy and Harley, Hester went into the hallway and found it empty. She checked at the nurses' station, and a weary night nurse pointed down a connecting hall. "I saw him head to the nursery," she said.

And there he was standing outside the nursery window, his hands twisting the rolled magazine as he stared at a row of newborns tucked into their bassinets.

Hester stood next to him, gazing at the new babies. She couldn't help wondering if she would ever know the special joy of motherhood. "John?"

"You have to wonder," he said without preamble, "how it will all turn out for them. I mean, I sure never thought. . ." He shook his head and turned to her. "Ready to go?"

"We came in Grady's car," she reminded him.

"Right. Well, let's give him the keys, and then if you're up to it we can walk back to Pinecraft."

"That's pretty far out of your way."

He shrugged and then smiled. "I thought you might be in the mood to celebrate."

Hester must have looked at him as if he had suddenly grown another head, because he explained, "The truth is, I'm famished, and breakfast at Yoder's sounds pretty good to me right now."

"But first a five-mile hike," she said, pointing out the obvious.

"Unless you've got another idea of how we might get there."

She was beyond tired but knew that the fresh air would do them both good, and at this hour of the morning it was unlikely to be as hot as it would become later in the day. "Okay. Just let me give Grady his keys and say good-bye."

John was waiting by the stairway when Hester left Amy's room. She was smiling, but he sensed it was a private smile, not meant for him. He expected it had to do with the baby. It occurred to him that she would make a good mother, and he tried to imagine the kids she and Samuel Brubaker might have someday. It surprised him that not only could he not imagine such a thing, but he also really didn't like imagining her having a family with Samuel.

Whoa! he thought as she came toward him, her eyes still with that dreamy dazed look women tended to get after being exposed to babies. *You barely know this woman.* But he wanted to know her. He didn't know when his attitude toward her had changed, but it had. He wanted to know everything about her.

He held the door for her, and she started down the stairs ahead of him, never once questioning why they hadn't used the elevator. Outside, they walked along without speaking, the noisy traffic whizzing past them on the busy four-lane road, until they crossed onto Bahia Vista and started walking toward Pinecraft.

"You were an only child, right?" she asked.

"Yeah."

She didn't seem inclined to pursue the matter, and John was relieved to let the subject drop.

"You're still carrying that magazine," she said when they'd walked half a block in silence.

He hesitated and glanced back toward the main street. "I forgot. I should return it. . . ."

"I can do it when I go to visit Amy and the baby later today."

"You're going back? Today?" *Do you ever sleep?*

"Well, she'll probably go home tomorrow, and they live some distance away, so, yes, today would be best. I made a crib quilt for the baby." She held out her hand for the magazine, and he gave it to her.

"Thanks. I expect it won't be missed, but still. . ."

"As Zeke would say, 'No worries.' " They passed the local branch of the YMCA, where childlike chalk pictures decorated the running track that surrounded the main building. "You know what you said before about wondering how they'll all turn out? Those newborns?"

"Yeah."

"I think about that sometimes myself. I mean, how did I get this far in life without really having a plan?"

"You? Seems to me you've always had a plan. You went to nursing school. You took care of your mother while she was so ill. You take care of others now." He avoided mentioning the possibility that within the coming year she would probably marry Samuel. *Would not saying it aloud help to keep it from happening?* he wondered. And more to the point, why shouldn't it happen? She deserved to be happy, after all. "I'd say you not only found your calling, but you've followed it to the letter."

"I certainly didn't plan to spend five years caring for a terminally ill parent," she said in a tone that was so filled with sadness that John felt guilty for having brought up the subject at all.

"I expect that Grady and his wife will make good parents," he said, trying to find some other path for their conversation. It worked. When he looked over at her, she was smiling.

"They are so excited and the baby is beautiful. Harley Forrest is one fortunate child."

They waited for a light to change even though there was no traffic on the cross street. The green seemed to signal yet another shift in conversation.

"I like your aunt," Hester said. "She's not at all what I would have expected a politician to be like, or anyone related to you," she added with a teasing smile.

"Meaning?"

"I don't know. You strike me as someone who is constantly carrying around a heavy burden, one that you refuse to allow others to help you lighten."

Her guess was closer to the truth than John would have expected, and he was tempted to confide in her. He was so tired of the exhausting weight of his past. But would a woman who had tenderly nursed her mother for five long years and fought every day to bring joy and beauty to a life that was surely slipping away understand a son who had been the cause of his mother's death?

Hester waited for some response, but John said nothing. They had reached the restaurant, and he held the door for her without comment.

The restaurant was already busy with locals who made a habit of starting their day there. The counter was completely occupied. The patrons there barely glanced up as the hostess led John and Hester to a booth and placed menus in front of them. "Coffee?"

"Please," they chorused as each of them opened the menu—one Hester practically knew by heart—and studied the list of breakfast items.

"How's the garden coming?" John asked, setting his menu aside and adding cream to the coffee the waitress had brought.

So they were going back to safer topics of conversation. "I haven't had much time to work on it," she said.

"I have some ferns you can have. They might work in the shady spots under the arbor."

"That would be nice. Thank you."

He shrugged. "They'll just end up trampled now that I'm ready to paint the packinghouse."

Hester sighed. "Why do you do that?"

"What?"

"Turn a nice gesture into something else—like I'd be the one doing you a favor."

"Well, you would and it's our way, yours as well."

She shook her head. "No. This is different. It's like you don't think you deserve the gratitude of others. I noticed it last night when Grady tried to thank you for coming to the hospital."

"I—"

"And then there was that day we went searching for Zeke's friends. You didn't have to do that, and yet you were as concerned for them as I was, but when they tried to thank you—especially Danny—"

The waitress appeared at their booth and hesitated. "Should I come back?"

"No. Two eggs over easy on whole wheat toast with a side of fruit," Hester said.

"Pancakes—triple stack," John muttered.

"Well?" Hester said when the waitress had left them alone again. "I mean, what is it with you, John Steiner?" She knew that her exhaustion only added to her exasperation with the man. "Ignore that," she added before he could respond. "I'm just tired. I'll come out and dig the ferns next week if that's all right."

"Fine."

If Hester had learned one thing about John, it was that he was anything but fine. She rearranged the condiments on the table and refrained from starting any further conversation.

A few minutes later, the waitress set their plates in front of them, steam rising from both, as Hester folded her hands in her lap and bowed her head.

And it came to her that the burden John was carrying had something to do with his mother's death and that the birth of Grady's child had somehow brought all of that back to him.

"You don't have to answer this, of course—after all, it's certainly none of my business."

He continued pouring syrup on his pancakes, but she saw his hand twitch slightly.

"How did you mother die?"

With more care than necessary he set the syrup pitcher down. "I killed her."

Part Three

And a man shall be as an hiding place
from the wind, and a covert from the tempest;
as rivers of water in a dry place,
as the shadow of a great rock in a weary land.

ISAIAH 32:2

There is more day to dawn. . . . The sun is but a morning star.
HENRY DAVID THOREAU, *WALDEN: LIFE IN THE WOODS*

Chapter 18

Hester was searching for words to respond to John's astounding admission when they were interrupted.

"Hester? Is that you?" Olive Crowder brushed past the hostess with Agnes trailing behind her. "What on earth are you doing out at this hour?"

A question that Hester understood wasn't complete without the unspoken "with a strange man." Olive focused all of her attention on John.

"I might ask you the same thing," Hester said, fighting to keep her tone light. "It's early even for the two of you. Olive and Agnes Crowder, this is John Steiner." Hester's mind raced with how she might quickly get rid of the spinster sisters and get back to addressing the astounding confession John had just made to her.

But Olive's eyes flickered with interest when she heard John's name, even as she bristled at the idea that he was having breakfast with Hester.

"Hello," Agnes said with a smile.

Olive stepped between her sister and John as if she needed to protect Agnes. "You're that man—the one who bought land at Tucker's Point. The one who got wiped out by the storm. The Amish man."

"Guilty on all counts," John said. He had stood up when Hester made the introductions, and he now met Olive Crowder eye-to-eye. "And you are. . ."

He glanced at Hester, who was holding her breath, silently praying that he would not say something to set Olive off.

"You are the lady of whom Hester speaks so often," he said.

Olive looked past John to Hester. "What are you doing here?" she demanded again.

"We're having breakfast," John replied as if she had addressed her question to him. "Perhaps you know Grady Forrest and his wife, Amy?"

"Oh, they are the loveliest couple," Agnes chirped.

"They had their baby last night," John explained. "Hester and I happened to be with them, so we went to the hospital to be sure everything was all right."

"And stayed the night?"

"Yes, Olive, we were at the hospital," Hester said quietly. "The child was born a little after four this morning. Now if you'll excuse us, our breakfast is getting cold, and both Mr. Steiner and I have a busy day ahead."

"Well," Olive huffed and turned on her heel. "Come, Agnes. Let's find another place to have our meal. We know when we're not welcome."

"But, Olive," Agnes said, pointing to a row of empty tables. Then, seeing the futility of arguing, she smiled apologetically. "It was so nice to meet you," she said in a near whisper as she scurried after her sister, who was already out the door and striding toward the larger restaurant across the street.

"Well, that can't be good," John said. "Will you be all right?"

The question confused her. "Oh, you mean Olive? That's just her way. No doubt she will stop by the house later to have a word with my father. He'll assure her that he'll look into the matter, and that will be the end of it." He was still standing next to the booth. "Let's just finish our breakfast." *And our conversation.* "You were about to tell—"

"I should go." He folded his napkin and left it next to his

half-eaten pancakes; then he reached into his pocket and pulled out a slim fold of money. "Think this will cover it?" he asked, placing a five and four singles on the table.

Hester saw that this left him with a single bill, a twenty. She wondered how long that had to last him. "It's fine, but, John. . ." She didn't want to make a scene, but surely he was aware that he'd made an incredible admission to her, and she could hardly just let him walk away without an explanation.

"I didn't murder her," he said, "but I was responsible for her death." He took a long swallow of his water and then left. Outside he ran to a bus stop, where a westbound bus was just pulling away. He flagged it down and jumped on board.

"Anything else, miss?" The waitress hovered uncertainly, holding a carafe of coffee in one hand and their check in the other. She was new at working here, and that comforted Hester some. At least whatever she might have witnessed, she wouldn't be telling it to others who knew she was the preacher's daughter having breakfast with a man who was not her father—and not Samuel Brubaker. But why worry about a gossiping waitress when Olive already had a head start?

"No, thank you. I have to. . ." She picked up the money and handed it to the waitress, then practically ran from the restaurant as if she might be able to flag the bus and stop John from leaving. He was the most exasperating man.

"Miss?" The waitress had followed her out to the parking lot. "You forgot your magazine."

Hester turned back to meet her halfway. "Thanks." She rolled the magazine and looked up and down the street. Pinecraft was already bustling with business owners out sweeping their entrances or unloading stock for their shops. Her days had begun to run into one another, but she might as well head for the MCC office—the haven she had gone to every day since her mother's funeral. It was where her mother had done so much good, and the constant work made the hours fly by.

She was surprised to find the door locked. Rosalyn almost always arrived ahead of her, her bright smile something Hester had been especially looking forward to seeing today. Of course it was early yet, just past seven.

But Rosalyn still had not come by nine. . .or eleven. By that time, Hester was seriously worried. She had called several friends and neighbors. No one had seen her. She'd even stopped by Rosalyn's house. Out of ideas of where she might be and beginning to worry, Hester decided to stop at her father's shop. He would know what to do.

"She's with Samuel," Arlen told her as he concentrated on sanding the double doors that would attach to a large china cabinet that had already been stained and polished. "There was a bit of trouble last night. Fortunately, Samuel was nearby when the bottle hit Rosalyn—"

"What bottle, Dad? Is Rosalyn all right? Who—"

"Some rowdies had been drinking. They were driving in the area and spotted Rosalyn on her way home. According to Samuel, one of them threw away his beer bottle, and it hit Rosalyn in the forehead. She has quite a nasty cut. You weren't here, so Samuel took her to the walk-in clinic, and they stitched it up fine."

"She had to have stitches?" Hester was appalled at the calmness with which her father was relating this news. "Where is she now?"

"You just missed her. This morning Samuel stopped to check on her and was worried that she seemed to have a fever, so he brought her to the house for you to have a look. When you weren't there, he took her back to the doctor just to be sure she was all right. Samuel stopped by to let me know he was taking her home so she can rest. The doctor says she should be fine in a couple of days but that she's had not only a physical trauma but an emotional one as well."

"I would say so." Hester decided to ignore her father's inference that it was odd she wouldn't be at home first thing in the morning. Instead, she perched on a stool and watched him work. "What about the men who did this?"

"Samuel said they were barely men, more like boys trying to play at being grown up. He spoke with them and they left."

"I should go see if she's all right."

"Yes, perhaps later." He put down his paintbrush and pulled a stool next to hers. "Olive Crowder brought cookies," he said, nodding toward a tin on his workbench. "Oatmeal with chocolate chips."

"No thanks."

Olive Crowder had been bringing her father baked goods and sometimes huge casseroles since the day after Sarah died. The casseroles always came with the implied message that Hester was far too busy with her nursing and volunteer activities to take proper care of her father.

Come to think of it, she had been bringing him baked goods for most of Hester's life. Her mother had marveled at what a gifted baker Olive was, which only encouraged her. As girls, Olive and Hester's mother had been the best of friends and rivals for Arlen's affection. And while there had been some distance between the two women once Sarah and Arlen married, Hester could not deny that Olive had been a devoted friend to both her parents all through the long years of Sarah's illness. She had often suspected that once Sarah died, Olive had permitted herself to think that maybe in time Arlen would turn to her, that one day they might even marry. Of course, her father seemed oblivious to any underlying motive that might accompany Olive's baked gifts.

"Olive has a concern," her father said as he bit down on a cookie and took his time chewing.

"Dad, I know that she has become more and more upset about my work with MCC. She believes that CAM is—"

"Her concern is about you being seen walking with John Steiner before dawn and then having breakfast with him. Her concern is that there was no reason you needed to stay the night once Grady and Amy arrived at the hospital, and I have to say that I agree."

"Papa. . ."

He held up a finger and continued speaking. "I began to think more about this after our conversation last evening, liebchen. Since your mother died, you have run from one project to the next, and in between you have taken on the running of our household, something you had been doing more and more as Sarah's health failed. I have to admit that I allowed this, even encouraged it once your brothers moved away and your mother was gone—"

"Oh, Papa." Hester stood and wrapped her arms around her father's shoulders.

His eyes filled with tears, but he pulled a handkerchief from his pocket and wiped them away. "You have fallen into the habit of caring for everyone but yourself. Olive has made me see that I have been selfish, Hester, and that the time has come for us to consider your future and happiness, not mine."

"She said that?"

"No, I am saying that. Olive chastised me for allowing you too much freedom."

"I am a grown woman," Hester protested.

"And a good Mennonite woman. But Olive has a point. You know my concerns. You have become so involved in matters of the world outside Pinecraft. Not that the people you have befriended aren't perfectly wonderful, and in most cases God-loving people, but you cannot find happiness out there, Hester."

"I'm happy. I'm busy with so many things because that is the work God has called me to do." She hesitated, wondering where this was all coming from. It wasn't like her father to become so emotionally invested when a member of his congregation came to him with a concern. Of course, this concern did involve her, but still. . . "What exactly did Olive say?" she asked, taking her seat across from him so that they were knee to knee.

"Oh, you know Olive. She was quite upset seeing you this morning. She said that you and John seemed to be having quite a serious conversation. I told her that you had been trying to help that young man get back on his feet, but she was adamant that this conversation appeared to be of a more personal nature and, given the circumstances, was totally inappropriate. She raised the question of whether or not she should report her observations to Samuel."

"She can report her observations to anyone she pleases, and she no doubt will. John Steiner and I were indeed having a serious and personal conversation. The man had just told me that he killed his mother when Olive interrupted. I really can't imagine things could get much more serious or personal than that." She clasped her fingers over her mouth, horrified that she had revealed such incriminating information when she had no idea what it meant.

"He killed his own mother?" Arlen closed his eyes for a moment, and Hester knew that he was sending up a prayer for John.

"He didn't murder her," she hastened to assure him. "He was just somehow involved in her death."

"In what way?"

Hester blinked. "I don't know," she admitted. "Olive started in, and then once she left John left without elaborating. I think he regretted saying anything at all."

"I knew the man was deeply troubled, but this. . ." Arlen began to pace, wringing his hands as he considered this news. "I think it best if you stay away from him."

"You would judge him?"

"The man has admitted a crime to you, Hester."

"And what if his only crime is guilt, Dad? I would stake everything on that being the case. It explains so much about the way he is, his lack of trust, his running away from the only home and community he's ever known. His determination not to make connections here." The more she talked, the more she saw parallels between John's actions and her own.

"You can't know that until we know the whole story."

"But that was what I felt, what I have felt every day since Mom died. I am a trained nurse, and still. . ."

"There's no cure for ALS, Hester. You know that. You did everything you possibly could have done to see that her last days and months were the best they could be, and it took its toll on you. I should have seen what it was doing to you. I should have recognized it when you spent so many hours in the garden after her death—the garden you had created for her. I thought once Samuel came to work here and became our friend. . . I hoped. . ."

She took his hand between both of hers. "I know. I know."

Father and daughter sat that way for a long moment.

"I will go and speak with John," Arlen said, finally getting down from his stool and turning to his workbench.

"No, Dad. Let me go. He almost told me this morning, and if Olive hadn't interrupted, I'm certain that he would have told me the entire story."

"I think it best if you keep your distance for now. Give Olive a few days to calm herself."

Hester glanced down at the tin of cookies. "She's in love with you, you know."

Arlen shrugged. "I know. Your mother even suggested that if I remarried, Olive would be a good match."

This was news that Hester had never imagined. "Mom said that?"

"Yep. Badgered me for a promise that I would do just that almost right up to the end. Even when she could no longer speak, it was there in her eyes every time Olive stopped by."

"But you didn't. Why?"

"Because Olive may love me or think she does, but I don't love her."

"But if you promised. . ."

"I promised only that I would find peace in God's will for Sarah and that I would move forward with my life. I have done that," he said, gesturing to the shop, where partially completed pieces of hand-crafted furniture lined the walls.

"But if you didn't like it that Mom chose Olive as the most likely candidate, why would you do the same by bringing Samuel. . ."

"I know that you and Samuel have not yet found your way, but I am convinced that his coming here was God's will. You and Samuel are young, Hester, and with time all things are possible, even falling in love. Just give him a chance, all right?"

She wrestled with the double standard that lay behind his

words. There was some truth to the idea that two young people just starting out might find love after years of companionship, but something about the idea did not seem right to Hester. "And what about John Steiner? I truly believe that he has begun to trust me, to reach out for help."

Arlen sighed. "Ja. The man is in danger of becoming a lost soul. I can't order you to stay away from him, but I would prefer that you give me time to speak with him before you get involved with him any further."

"And if he won't talk to you?"

"Then you must let this go, Hester. Clearly his community and church have dealt with the matter in their own way. It is out of our hands, and I am asking you to stay away from the man."

"Are we to shun him as well, then?"

"Hester, can you not understand that my concern must be first for you? John Steiner—whatever his sins may or may not be—has made it clear that he does not seek or want our help. You said it yourself when Grady first asked you to go see the man—there are others in greater need who need you."

"But he seems so lost."

"Only God can find him and lead him back into the fold, child. You can do much good, but only God can truly rescue a soul in peril."

Hester reluctantly agreed, but the saga of John Steiner still troubled her after she had stopped by to take Rosalyn some lunch. And then later as she pedaled her way across town to deliver the crib quilt she'd made to Amy and Grady, she silently prayed for guidance, for some sign that she was to either let the matter rest or pursue it. She believed God had given His answer when she entered Amy's hospital room and found John's aunt Liz cooing over the baby. Here was the one person who might tell her the whole story without her having to disrespect her father's wish that she stay away from John.

Samuel was deeply troubled. He had always thought of himself as an honorable man, and he was well aware that in coming to work for Arlen Detlef, he had not only agreed to apply his skills as a carpenter and furniture maker; he had also agreed to consider asking Hester to be his wife. Arlen had made little secret of his wish for that.

"I know that you can only do what God leads you to do," Arlen had told him. "Only God can guide your heart, and Hester's, but I do pray that a union between you two will be His will."

It couldn't get any plainer than that. Now that he'd gotten to know Hester and watched the interaction between her and her father, he had decided that Arlen probably had not been quite so direct with his only daughter. Hester had a strong will and a streak of independence. It was those two characteristics that made her the community leader whom she had become. It was also those two traits that had made Samuel question whether or not he could ever make her truly happy. And in the meantime, he had fallen deeply in love with Rosalyn.

After taking Rosalyn back to the doctor and then seeing her home to the small cottage he'd helped restore following the hurricane and flooding, he had gone to the park and walked along the banks of the creek, sorting through his feelings and trying to decide what to do. After an hour and with no real answers, he headed back to work. Arlen was bent over his workbench, carving the molding for a china cabinet.

"Is Rosalyn all right?" Arlen asked.

"She will be once she has a few days to rest and heal," Samuel said as he hung his wide-brimmed straw hat on a hook near the door and put on a carpenter's apron.

"Hester stopped by."

"Ah," Samuel replied and gathered the tools he would need to attach the hinges for the cabinet doors that Arlen had finished staining.

"She was at the hospital overnight with the Forrest couple. They had a baby boy."

"That's good news." Samuel barely heard Arlen's conversation, his mind was so troubled.

"John Steiner was there as well."

"Ah," Samuel murmured as he measured once and then again and thought about the fact that he loved working here with Arlen.

"You may expect a visit from Olive Crowder," Arlen added. "Apparently she saw Hester and John having breakfast after they'd stayed all night at the hospital with Grady and his wife. It upset her." When Samuel said nothing, Arlen asked, "Does it not upset you?"

Samuel looked up from his work and saw that the older man had turned away from his workbench and was watching him closely. "Rosalyn says that Olive is often upset with Hester," he replied evenly.

The shop was silent for a long moment. Samuel laid down his screwdriver and the hinge and turned to face Arlen. "I have something to discuss with you."

Arlen folded his hands in front of him and waited.

"I do not think that Hester and I. . . I am in love with another woman." There, it was said. Samuel pictured himself packing up his camper and heading back to Pennsylvania. Rosalyn would be loyal to Hester, he knew that—loyalty would win every time.

"I see. And this other woman returns your feelings for her?"

"I believe she does, but I also believe that she would deny her feelings as I have—until now."

"Have you spoken to Hester of this matter?"

"Not yet."

Arlen closed his eyes, a habit that Samuel had noticed whenever the minister was faced with a dilemma. "How do you think my daughter will take this news?"

"I believe that she will be relieved," Samuel replied without a moment's hesitation, and because he hadn't so much as considered the possibilities, he was certain that he had spoken the truth.

Arlen nodded. Then he opened his eyes and smiled. "You are probably right," he said and turned back to his workbench and resumed carving a piece of trim for the cabinet.

"I will stay until the end of the week, if that's all right. We can finish the orders by then—"

The carving knife that Arlen was holding clattered into a pile of wood shavings that littered the floor around him. "You are leaving?" He clutched the now-ruined piece of wood.

"I thought that you would. . . I cannot marry your daughter, Arlen."

"One thing has nothing to do with the other. We work well together, and. . ." Arlen fumbled for words. It was the closest that Samuel had ever seen his employer and friend come to being concerned for himself instead of others. "I am asking you to reconsider and stay on here with me as my partner. I'm hoping that one day this business will be yours."

Samuel felt his heart swell with the possibilities Arlen had just offered. If Rosalyn would agree to marry him, they would have a secure future.

"I would like that," he said, "but I cannot give you my answer until I've spoken with Hester. She has a right to be part of any decision I might make to stay on here."

"Of course," Arlen said. "She's gone to the hospital to visit the Forrests and their new baby. Perhaps this evening? Come for supper."

"I'll stop by," Samuel promised, and as he took the damaged molding from Arlen and went to find a matching piece, he couldn't seem to stop smiling.

Chapter 19

"Well, Johnny," Margery said as she leaned the kitchen chair she'd carried out to John's porch back on two legs and braced her feet against the porch railing, "what are you going to do with this place? I mean, you've got the main floor here and the packinghouse pretty well back in shape, at least until the next storm comes by. But the grove there?" She shook her head. "That'll take years, if you can get anything to grow."

John knew she was right. In fact, he'd been thinking the same thing before she'd stopped by with a cooler filled with her southern fried chicken, potato salad, and fresh sliced tomatoes. She'd been stopping by a couple of times a week ever since he'd helped out with the refurbishing of the marina. Sometimes she read his mood and simply left him the food and headed back to her place. Other times, like tonight, she seemed to instinctively understand that he would welcome her company. On those occasions, she did not hold back, but said whatever was on her mind.

"Maybe the experiment has run its course," he said.

Margery snorted. "This is life, Johnny, not some lab research. Are you saying you're giving up after everything you've put into this place?"

"I'm open to suggestions."

"Well, there's a first," Margery muttered.

John ignored her sarcasm. "I don't want to give up, but what choice do I have?"

"What choice did you have when you packed up and left Indiana? What choice did I have when I walked down to the marina and found it in ruins? What choice did those folks over in Pinecraft have when the creek washed through their homes? Start over or give up. You've got your quirks, but I never figured you for a quitter, Johnny."

"I could sell the place, I suppose."

"And then what? What are you going to do with your life? You're neither here nor there—not Amish but not one of my world either. Who are you, John Steiner, and what are you planning to do—not just with this place but with the rest of your life?"

"I don't know—on either count," he admitted.

Margery pushed herself to her feet and slapped at a mosquito on her arm. "Well, the clock's ticking, son."

She could have been saying that it was getting late and time for her to head home, but he understood that she was issuing a warning. John walked with her down to her boat and helped her in.

"Careful there," she said with a teasing grin. "You're coming mighty close to becoming a real gentleman. Next thing I know you'll be out courting the ladies." She gave the pull cord on the motor a brisk yank and it fired to life. "Hester Detlef might be a good start since you two seem to be getting along so well these days," she called out as she putt-putted her way back toward the mouth of Philippi Creek.

Instantly he regretted telling Margery about the previous night's reception and the trip to the hospital. He groaned. How many times over the course of the evening had he uttered the words "Hester and I," or "Hester thinks," or just plain "Hester." Margery was a romantic and would take such things as a sign. But he could not deny that his opinion of Hester Detlef had changed. He stood on the shore where he had stood weeks earlier and watched her wade through the murky waters with her father and Samuel. He remembered how her manner had been brittle, but her touch when she tended to his cuts and other injuries was gentle, even tender. He also remembered how she had tried to reassure him. He wished she were here now. There was something about her, a unique combination of practicality mixed with just a pinch of the whimsical. Somehow it made him think that she would see possibilities for this place that he no longer could.

He started back toward his house, although he wasn't ready to settle in for the night. He was restless, his mind racing with the details of the work yet to be done and the costs still ahead of him. Costs he could not afford.

True, he wasn't homeless, and he was a far sight better off now than he had been right after the hurricane. Despite the dire predictions of others, he had been able to move back into his house and so far no one from the government had come around to ask if he'd filed the required paperwork. He hadn't and had no intention of doing so. This was his land, his home. He did his cooking—what little he did—over a camp stove that Zeke had rescued from a Dumpster; the two of them had managed to rig the stove to the propane gas line that ran to the house. He had water and a bathroom, although no shower or tub. Those were in the full bath on the second floor, or at least they had been. All in all he had what he needed. But he lived under a makeshift roof, and the second floor of the house was still a disaster.

He wandered between what had been a grove of orange trees—several dozen of them that he had salvaged from the grove Tucker had originally planted. There had also been a grove of lemon and key lime trees that he had planted and nursed as if they were his children. They weren't his children, but they had been his future—the source of income he would need if he hoped to keep this place running. That ship had sailed, as his aunt Liz was fond of saying. The soil was completely ruined by the salt water. Even if he could afford to replant, there was no way anything would grow.

He considered the ruined beds of celery, tomatoes, beans,

and other vegetables he had planted. In spite of the fact that the salvaged cypress beams he'd used as borders had been ripped free and scattered across the property during the hurricane, Zeke had worked for days gathering them and putting them back into place. The problem was that the rich, fertile soil that had filled them, along with the plants themselves, had washed away. It would take several truckloads of soil to refill them, and that would cost a lot of money. On the positive side, the toolshed and chicken coop were restored and ready for use. The problem was use for what?

Depressed and defeated, John walked back to the house. The sun had set, and the last rays of light were waning. Wearily he climbed the porch steps, picked up his and Margery's glasses, and went inside. He lit the battery-powered lantern and pulled a chair up to the kitchen table that was littered with drawings he had created when he first bought the Tucker place and kept stored in a metal box. Dreams he had allowed himself to entertain as if they were fact.

He swept them off the table with his forearm, in the process uncovering the two books he'd managed to salvage after the hurricane. *Walden* lay next to his Bible. He picked up the paperback volume and paged through it; then he tossed it onto the pile of papers littering the floor. He had walked with Thoreau for two long years, and where had it gotten him?

He pulled his Bible closer, cradling it with his folded arms as he rested his forehead on its crackled leather cover and prayed. From this night forward, he would walk with God, listening for His still, small voice and opening himself to the kinds of messages delivered by couriers like Margery and Zeke—and perhaps even Hester. No, not Hester. He thought of how he had left her sitting there in the restaurant earlier that morning. He had told her the truth that his mother's death had been his fault. And then true to form, he had run away, hopped a city bus without explaining the details. He had assumed that she would judge him, as others had and as he had judged himself. And who would blame her?

And yet he missed her, missed talking to her, missed her

no-nonsense ways, her wisdom. He realized that for most of the day he'd been watching for her, listening for the crunch of her bicycle or Arlen's car tires coming up his lane. But she hadn't come.

"She's to marry Samuel," he reminded himself. Samuel was a good man, a far better man than he was—and besides, the carpenter could offer Hester a secure future. What did he have to offer her? He was broke and living in a half-finished house on land that would not yield even so much as a kitchen garden for some time to come. Perhaps once she and Samuel had married, the three of them could be friends.

"Perhaps you ought to stop daydreaming and face reality," he growled. He had few choices. He could stubbornly refuse to change and end up like some of the people whom Zeke had introduced him to at the bay front. Or he could face facts, sell the property, and use the money to start over once more. He thought about the farm he'd sold in Indiana, the land where his father had worked such long hours. The place where for so many years he and his mother had lived. The place he had planned to bring his bride and raise his family. Could he go back there and start again, asking forgiveness, admitting the error of his prideful ways to the congregation in which he'd been raised?

He closed his eyes and silently prayed for guidance. When he opened them minutes later, he knew that he had made his plan. Tomorrow he would go to Arlen and ask for help getting the rest of this place restored, and then he would put it up for sale.

Hester stayed at the hospital longer than she'd meant to. But when she'd seen Liz Carter-Thompson handing Amy and Grady a huge gift basket that was filled to overflowing with items for baby and mother, she had seen her opportunity to find out once and for all how John had been involved in his mother's death. It took close to half an hour for the new parents to properly exclaim over each item and hold it up for Hester as well as Harley's two sets of grandparents to admire. But Hester was determined to stay, hoping that she and Liz might take their leave at the same time and that she could perhaps suggest they share a cup of coffee before the congresswoman hurried off to pack for her flight home.

After the grand finale of the gift basket was unveiled, a cashmere shawl for Amy to wrap herself in while she nursed, Hester waited for Grady to place all the items back in the basket and set it on a side table already filled with vases of flowers. Then she handed him her package.

"Congratulations," she said.

"Oh, Hester, you made this yourself, didn't you?" Amy exclaimed as Grady spread the crib quilt over Amy's bed. "It's lovely. His room is blue and it will be just perfect. Thank you."

Hester fought against a swell of pride. "You're welcome. Nelly helped with the actual quilting," she added.

"Hester's grandmother," Amy explained to the others as she lifted a corner of the quilt to show her mother the tiny stitches.

Hester saw that Liz was watching her closely as if trying to figure her out. "You are a most remarkable young woman," Liz said with such genuine admiration that Hester felt herself blush. "The reports about the work you and your community have been doing in helping others to get back to normal are impressive."

"My father and the Mennonite Disaster Relief teams have done most of the work," Hester said.

"You know, ever since I joined the Homeland Security committee, I've been hearing more and more about the work people from the Mennonite community do whenever there's a natural disaster. You certainly don't get the credit you deserve, and I think it might be high time we did something about that. Why, you and your volunteers are every bit as much of a national treasure as any federal or state agency. They just have better marketing."

Hester glanced pleadingly at Grady, hoping that he would intervene. To her relief, he nodded.

"The Mennonites don't really believe in blowing their own horn," he said. "They prefer to perform their good deeds without fanfare."

"I'm not suggesting they hire a public relations firm," Liz said. "But. . ."

"Our reward comes in having served others," Hester said quietly. She could see that this was in many ways a foreign concept to the congresswoman, as it was to others in the outside world, where award ceremonies were common and highly anticipated.

"You remind me a great deal of my sister," Liz said. "Rachel was always doing things for others, and never once did she receive the recognition she deserved."

"Your sister lived in an Amish community. It was not their way to offer or accept praise either."

"Tell me about it," Liz said, and then she smiled. "I'm afraid my big sister struggled mightily with our family's lack of understanding when it came to the lifestyle she chose. And yet," she said almost wistfully, "I don't think I have ever known a person more at peace with herself and her life."

"Then she had her reward," Hester said, fairly itching to pursue the topic of John's mother now that Liz had brought it up. But this was neither the time nor the place.

"Oh my, if you're not careful, I'll sit here babbling on all afternoon—occupational habit." Liz gathered her oversized leather purse and swung it onto her shoulder, then glanced at her watch. "I have a flight to catch in two hours. Can I give you a lift back to Pinecraft, Hester?"

"I have my bike, but I'll walk out with you."

They said their good-byes, cooed over the sleeping baby, and tiptoed from the room.

"Ah, babies," Liz sighed as soon as the door closed behind them. "If ever I need a refresher on why I put up with all the political mumbo-jumbo it takes to get anything done in this job, I go visit a hospital nursery and right there is my answer. Harley's generation will someday inherit the work I do now. Makes a person think."

"You have no children of your own?" Hester asked as they stepped onto the elevator together.

"Nope. My sister, Rachel, was the earth mother in our family.

She should have had a dozen kids."

"But John has no siblings."

"Unfortunately, no. Maybe if Rachel had remarried. . . She certainly had offers."

The elevator doors slid open, and Hester found that her heart was hammering. It seemed as if God might be giving her the opening she needed to find out what John had meant in saying he had killed his mother.

"I'm over here in the parking structure," Liz said as they exited the building.

"The bike rack is there as well," Hester replied, and the two women continued walking together. "John told me his mother died shortly before he moved here. Was she ill?"

"Not a day in her life," Liz said. "One January evening at dusk, she'd set out in the buggy for some church meeting. Something spooked the horse and it took off. Rachel was a fighter, and she was not about to let that horse have the upper hand, but she didn't count on a patch of black ice. The horse slid, and she was thrown from the buggy, hit her head on a field rock, and died before the ambulance could get there."

Okay, so now she had the circumstances, but for the life of her, Hester could not find anything in any of it that would even hint that John had had anything to do with his mother's unfortunate accident.

Liz looked both ways and jaywalked across the street as Hester hurried to keep up with her. "Was John with her?"

Liz paused by the bike rack. "He found her, and that's part of his grief. I don't think he's ever forgiven himself for not being the one driving that night." She got the kind of faraway look a person had when lost in memories. Then she shook it off and offered Hester a handshake. "It's been a real pleasure to meet you, Hester. I know you and your people don't take to compliments, but know that on behalf of a government that is deeply overextended, you have our deepest gratitude."

"You're welcome," Hester replied, still trying to reconcile what Liz had just told her with the conversation she'd had with

John. John had lost his mother just a short time before her own mother had finally succumbed to her illness. In her case she had known death was coming. John had had no such warning.

"Be patient with that nephew of mine, Hester. Rachel's death hit him pretty hard."

"I can understand that. My mother died of Lou Gehrig's disease a couple of years ago."

Liz pressed Hester's hand. "Then you know all too well. I'm so sorry for your loss. Still, it's a blessing that John has landed here, where he can hopefully find the kind of peace and contentment Rachel would have wanted for him. Rachel would say it was no mistake, his being here. It's God's will." Impulsively she bent and kissed Hester's cheek. "Have to run. Stay in touch," she added as she waved and headed off past a row of cars, her stiletto heels clicking on the pavement long after she was out of sight.

Hester unlocked her bike. She thought about going to Tucker's Point. It wasn't that much farther, but then, it was also close to suppertime, and her father would be wondering where she was. Besides, she had agreed not to seek John out. Mentally she checked the contents of the refrigerator and decided on a cold supper of chicken salad, fresh fruit, and whole grain bread. After all, it might be late September and the humidity had noticeably lessened, but it was still Florida, and it was still hot.

She pedaled fast, enjoying the wind cooling her face and whipping at the hem of her dress. The hurricane and its aftermath seemed light-years away, and yet each day they faced more work to be done. At the center they were still seeing a steady stream of people in need of clothing, bedding, and household goods. Food goods were still pouring in, although not nearly as strongly as they had right after the storm hit.

She thought about Rainbow House. Grady had told her that there was no way the agency would be able to start over. They'd need a building, a couple of them. Before the hurricane, the agency had offered shelter for the homeless, a food and clothing bank, and an educational center. There, people with no other options could come to learn job skills and hopefully find their way out of the ranks of the nameless, faceless men and women who gathered outside the library or along the bay front. Bundled all together, Rainbow House had offered hope to the hopeless. Without those services, where would these men and women— more and more of them in these hard times—go?

You're a nurse and Mennonite, Hester. These outsiders have their government to care for them. That is their way, not ours, she could practically hear her father reminding her. But hurt was hurt, and these people were in pain. It sure didn't seem like their government would come to their rescue anytime soon, so where better to focus her skills? Maybe she could organize a walk-in clinic to serve the homeless population. She would speak to Grady about it as soon as he came back to earth and got through his first week of sleepless nights. Maybe there were federal funds available. Maybe John could talk to Liz. Maybe. . .

Maybe her Dad was right. Her habit of running from one project to the next had escalated in the years since her mother's death. Surely her grief should have begun to abate in all that time. But it hadn't. Her work had become her life, her way of escaping things that confused her, like falling in love and marriage and raising a family. Like managing a household instead of a community center. Perhaps in her zeal to save others she was really avoiding the obvious—the need to save herself.

"I was beginning to worry," her father said when she wheeled her bike to a stop just outside the front gate. The fence had been repaired along with the house. Only the garden still showed signs of the flooding and wind damage that had accompanied the hurricane.

Arlen was sitting on the front porch, his wire-rimmed glasses pushed onto his forehead, a book in his lap. "How's the Forrest family?"

"Still a bit dazed but fine. Amy has both her mother and Grady's mom just chomping at the bit to help, and who can blame them? That baby is so precious." She tucked a piece of hair that had worked its way free back under her prayer covering, and then cleared her throat. "I spoke with John's aunt. She was there visiting as well, and we walked out together. She told me the circumstances of his mother's death."

"How did that subject come up?"

"We were talking about babies, and she mentioned that John's mother, Rachel, should have had more than just John."

"I see."

"It was an accident, Dad. John was nowhere near her when it happened." She repeated the details that Liz had told her. "So I think I was right about John feeling guilty that he wasn't there and couldn't save her."

Arlen took several minutes to consider this. "Still, he is a troubled soul, Hester. Perhaps we need to respect his need to work this all out himself."

"Are you still asking me to stay away from him?"

"I think it best if we let John come to us when he's ready. Samuel tells me that he is a man of strong faith, and we have to trust that God will guide him through this dark period in his life, as He did you." Arlen stroked her cheek. "As I recall, after Sarah died you needed your solitude."

Solomon himself could not have found a more effective way to frame his decision. Arlen had found the one argument for letting John determine who he saw and when that Hester could not debate. For it was true that it had been months after her mother's death before Hester had opened herself to others. "You're right," she said as she began taking ingredients for their meal out of the refrigerator. "I'll have supper ready in just a few minutes. I thought we'd have cold chicken and—"

"I'm having supper at your grandmother's," Arlen said as he followed her into the kitchen. "But you go ahead and fix two plates. I invited Samuel to come by."

Hester stopped.

"And you won't be here?"

"No, I told you—"

"Why not have Grandma come here?"

"Because you and Samuel need some time."

"Dad, I really don't need you orchestrating my social life."

"That's a matter of opinion, liebchen," he said and tweaked her cheek. "But Samuel's purpose in coming here this evening is not. . ." He faltered, clearly trying to find the right words without giving too much away.

"Is not what?"

"Just keep an open mind, Hester." He took his hat down from the hook next to the door and walked down the front walk. "You know where I'll be should you need to talk," he said.

Samuel is going to propose. Hester had never been more sure of anything in her life, nor had she ever been less prepared. She had thought she would have more time. But here it was. The moment of truth, as Jeannie would say. And why not? Perhaps this was the first step on the path to finding her true place in this community. She would still be able to volunteer. Samuel would never ask her to sacrifice that. And she had always dreamed of having children. Yes, perhaps the time had come.

Hester closed her eyes and tried to imagine herself standing next to Samuel as her father pronounced them man and wife. But the man she saw in her imagination was not Samuel Brubaker. It was John Steiner.

She shook off the image. Of course she would think of John. She'd been focused on him ever since he'd made his shocking confession to her that morning. Even the conversation she'd had with his aunt had done little to clear up the mystery, so naturally he would be the man on her mind, she reasoned. It meant nothing.

She set the table and prepared the food, then returned the serving dishes to the refrigerator as she waited for Samuel. The clock her grandfather had built chimed six. Maybe Samuel had gotten cold feet. *Please, God, let him get cold feet.*

The telephone jangled, startling her.

"Oh, Hester, hi," Samuel said, his voice unsteady.

"Hi. Dad said you were coming for supper, but maybe he. . ."

"I'll be there. I just. . . Six thirty, okay? We can go out if you'd rather."

"No. It's just cold chicken and such. It'll keep. Samuel, are you all right?"

There was a pause. "I am. I'm out at John Steiner's place. We got to talking, and I lost track of time. I'm really sorry, Hester."

"It's fine," she assured him.

"John's sending you some ferns for the garden," he added. "See you soon."

"Sure." As she hung up the phone, she spotted the magazine she'd meant to return to the hospital waiting room. Now she'd have to make a special trip. It was lying on the table next to the phone where she'd placed it so she would remember to take it with her. She picked it up and went out to the porch to wait for Samuel.

Chapter 20

When Samuel stopped by, John was surprised that he was inordinately glad to see the man. He had come to a decision, and he respected Samuel as someone with a level head and as someone who was good at listening before he jumped in with an opinion of his own.

"I've decided to sell this place and go home to Indiana," he said. When Samuel made no comment, he went on, laying out the facts that he'd already gone over dozens of times in the last hour. "The trees won't come back, and the vegetable beds need to be completely rebuilt. It'll take several truckloads of good dirt to fill them, and who knows what that'll cost. I'm pretty close to being broke, and I'm going to need to find work. So even if I could afford to keep working on the place, when would I do it?"

Samuel tipped his hat back with his thumb and looked around. "You truly think of Indiana—the life you left behind—as your home?"

In his calm, quiet way Samuel had identified the one sticking point of John's plan. For he did not think of Indiana as home. This was his home. This was the place where he had invested everything, where he had formed friendships that he hadn't even recognized as such until now.

"In time," he said, "I will. I grew up there, after all." Wanting to change the direction of the conversation, he looked around. "Of course, before this place can be put on the market, I've got a lot of work to do."

"You could let us help," Samuel said. "Arlen and me and the others. Zeke and some of his friends. With so many hands, you would have things back together in no time, and you could stay here. . .if your mind isn't made up, that is."

"I was thinking about that. . . ." John conceded. "Still, there's the matter of money."

"Ja. There is that."

"And even if I get the place back in shape, it'll still take time before any new crops start to come in."

"Ja."

"Selling solves my problem."

Samuel frowned and set his hat back on his head as he looked directly at John. "Selling will be hard in this economy. Besides, I think you know as well as I do that your lack of income is not the source of your poverty, my friend."

"I can't eat or keep a roof over my head without money, Samuel."

"True. But if you leave this place, give it up as you did your farm and the life you once knew, how will you feed your soul, John? Your spirit?" He climbed into the cab of his camper. "I'll speak with Arlen about organizing a crew to help you."

John had never before accepted charity on such a scale. It still went against all he'd set out to do. "No. Let me take care of it," he said, his throat closing around the words.

"Das ist gut." Samuel turned the key. "I'm late for an appointment, but I'll come back tomorrow, and we can speak about this some more if you'd like."

John nodded. "I'd appreciate that."

"Do you mind if I bring Rosalyn with me?"

The question surprised John. "Why?"

"Because she is someone like you who has been terribly wounded both physically and spiritually, and yet she has found her way through it. I just thought that perhaps she might be someone who could listen and understand."

John moved away, stepping back from the camper, putting distance between himself and Samuel. "I'd really rather just. . . Could we just keep this between us for now?"

"Of course." Samuel shifted the camper into gear.

"Wait," John called as he ran to get a bucket filled with ferns. "Could you drop these off at Hester's? For her mother's garden."

Samuel reached across and opened the passenger side door so John could set the bucket on the floor. "I'm on my way there now," Samuel said. "We're having supper together." He waved and drove the camper down the rutted lane.

John stood watching him go and thinking that it was odd the way he'd spoken of being late for an appointment when clearly he had a date with Hester. And then he thought how unusual it was that he had suggested bringing Rosalyn out to Tucker's Point when surely Hester had suffered the aftermath of nursing her mother through all those years, watching her grow more frail and dependent day by day, unable to do anything to stop the downward spiral. It seemed to John that in many ways his situation had far more in common with what Hester had experienced than what Rosalyn had gone through. And why would Samuel suggest allowing Arlen to help, and Zeke, and even Rosalyn—but not Hester?

After stopping at a gas station to call Hester, Samuel used the rest of the drive to practice how to tell her that he had fallen in love with Rosalyn. Perhaps he shouldn't mention Rosalyn at all. Perhaps he should just state the obvious, that he and Hester did not love each other and were unlikely ever to share such feelings. Perhaps he could phrase things in such a way that she would be the one to break off with him.

But that would be dishonest and manipulative. The gossips in Pinecraft would forever lay the blame for their failed relationship at her door. No, he was the one who wanted to end things, and he should be the one to say so.

"Dear God, may the words of my mouth and the meditations of my heart be acceptable in Thy sight," he murmured as he turned down Hester's street. "And hers," he added when he saw her sitting on the porch.

He parked his camper and got out. "Good evening, Hester. I'm sorry to be so late."

She was engrossed in reading a magazine. When she looked up at him, he understood that as usual something in that magazine had caught her attention so completely that she'd been unaware of his arrival until he spoke to her.

He thought about the way Rosalyn had looked at him after the doctor had stitched her forehead and she'd returned to the waiting room to find him standing there. Her eyes had widened with pure joy as she moved toward him, as if the distance was too great and she couldn't wait to be closer. There was the essential difference between the two women. One of them now openly looked forward to seeing him, having him near, sharing her day with him. The other gave him a distracted smile and waved her hand in dismissal at his apology for being late.

"It's okay," Hester said. "Come on inside. It will only take me a moment to put everything on the table." She walked ahead of him into the kitchen and started pulling dishes from the refrigerator. "How was John?" She pointed to the place he normally took whenever he shared meals with her and Arlen.

"He has decided to sell his place and return to Indiana for a fresh start." He watched her scurry around the large kitchen, slicing bread and placing a plate of it on the table, then hurrying back to the refrigerator for butter and applesauce. She seemed distracted, and he wondered if she had heard him. She stood in front of the open refrigerator door for a moment, a jar of orange marmalade in her hand. "The applesauce is fine," he said, "unless *you* prefer the marmalade."

Again she gave him a distracted smile. "No. I was just. . ." She removed a pitcher of lemonade and then shut the refrigerator with her foot. "John's giving up?"

"That's one way of looking at it, I suppose. But he seems genuinely relieved to have made the decision. I think he has some unfinished business in Indiana that he needs to address, but he seems prepared to do that."

"I see. He's leaving soon?"

"Not so soon. He can't put his place up for sale until the house is finished and everything is in order." He stood up and pulled out a chair for her. "Come and sit, Hester," he said. "We have everything we need."

She glanced at her father's empty chair and then sat down at her usual place. When she poured lemonade into the two tall glasses on the table, her hand shook, and Samuel realized that she was nervous. "Dad said you wanted to talk to me," she said, offering him the chicken salad first and then helping herself. "I think I know what this is about, and before—"

Samuel relieved her of the pitcher and set it on the table. She did not protest. Instead, she kept her gaze focused on her plate. "I just—"

"Shhh," he whispered when she glanced up, looking ready to speak. "Pray with me, Hester."

She nodded and closed her eyes, and they prayed in silence. After a moment Samuel murmured, "Amen."

She looked directly at him for the first time since he had arrived. Samuel drew in a long, resolute breath and uttered the words he'd come to say. "I can't marry you, Hester."

He didn't know what he had expected. Perhaps tears, anger, those fathomless blue eyes filled with hurt. He had even prepared himself for her eyes to widen in surprise, perhaps even shock. What he had never considered for one moment was the reaction he got.

"Really?" she said. "That's what you came to say?" She leaned toward him, her expression one not of hurt but of hope.

He nodded, half afraid to utter any sound until he could be sure of her reaction. She sank back in her chair, a half-smile twitching the corners of her mouth. She pressed her fist to her lips as her eyes filled with tears, and then she burst out laughing.

Soundless, shoulder-shaking laughter that she seemed incapable of controlling.

It was worse than anything he could have imagined. The woman who had always seemed stronger than any person—male or female—he had ever known was now clearly hysterical. "In time," he began, but the words only seemed to set her off again. "Hester, please," he pleaded, wishing Arlen were there.

She shook her head and used her napkin to blot away the tears. "Oh, Samuel, I thought. . ." A fresh wave of laughter threatened, but she controlled it and continued, "I thought you were coming here tonight to propose, and I was trying to find a way to tell you that I couldn't marry you."

It was Samuel's turn to feel the flood of relief that led to a smile that matched hers and then shared laughter as the two of them rocked back in their chairs. It was the closest he'd ever felt to Hester, and whatever the future might bring for each of them, they had found tonight something even more precious than they could have imagined, given that they both had understood that theirs most likely would have been a marriage of companionship. They had each found a friend for life.

When Arlen came home an hour later, Hester and Samuel were still sitting at the kitchen table, their heads close together, the dishes still on the table along with a legal pad, pens, and the magazine Hester had meant to return to the hospital.

"Dad, read this," Hester said, tapping her forefinger on the magazine. She waited while her father scanned the article that she had practically committed to memory. A decade earlier a woman in California working with a group of teenagers had come up with the idea of collecting the unwanted fruit from her neighbors' backyard orchards and turning it into jam to donate to food banks.

"I don't understand," Arlen said, handing her back the magazine. "Now you are thinking of working with young people to collect fruit? I thought we had discussed this, daughter. I thought you had agreed that you need to concentrate on your volunteer work here in Pinecraft."

"But this is about our people, Dad. Our young people will be an enormous part of this. I'm counting on the women of Pinecraft to make the marmalade and jam that the young people will sell at the markets."

"But you also plan to include others from outside. . . ."

"Yes, homeless people and maybe senior citizens looking for something to do, some way to make a contribution. But, Papa, that is what we do. Think of the auctions we held these last several years to raise money for the people of Haiti. Are we saying that those funds can be used only for Haitians who are Mennonite? No."

Arlen pulled out the remaining kitchen chair and sat down. "I'm listening."

But Hester knew from the furrowing of his brow and the way he glanced at Samuel that he remained unconvinced.

"The process that they used in California might not work exactly for us here, but there's a similar program in Tampa that we could follow. The point is that we can make this work, Dad, and we can use it to rebuild Rainbow House, and after that. . ."

Arlen folded his hands over his stomach and waited.

Hester took a deep breath. "This woman in California got the word out that these teenagers were willing to clean up unwanted fruit in private yards for free as long as they could take the usable fruit for their jam-making project."

"That was the start of it," Samuel explained. "But then they received so many requests, and there was so much fruit, that it was impossible to keep up with making it all into jam."

"So they went to the local food banks," Hester said, taking up the story, "and offered to give them the best of the whole fruit. Dad, they collected as much as twelve hundred pounds of citrus, all of it from private residences each with just a few trees."

Samuel searched the article and then showed Arlen a passage. "Right here it says that just two years ago they collected nearly one hundred and seventy-five *thousand* pounds of fruit from just five hundred homes, and they now have nearly a thousand volunteers of all ages."

"I still don't see—"

"Dad, think about it. Grandma has at least half a dozen citrus trees in her yard, and Jeannie Messner? She must have six lemon trees and another four key lime trees."

"Slow down and help me to understand this. I can see where you might gather the fruit. I don't see how this raises funds for Rainbow House."

"We make marmalade and jam and sell it at the local farmers' markets. Perhaps even some of the specialty stores would stock it, as well as the shops right here in Pinecraft." She made another note on the legal pad. "We need to speak with Grandma," she said to Samuel. "She has a wonderful recipe for marmalade."

"And I've tasted some jam made by the Crowder sisters that was quite tasty as well," Samuel said. "It might be good to get them involved."

"I suppose," Hester said reluctantly; then she brightened and made an addition to her list. "And Emma. I must speak with Emma first thing tomorrow. She always has such wonderful ideas when it comes to organizing these kinds of projects, and it will be great to work with her on something like this." She sat back and looked across the table to her father. "Wouldn't Mom just love the whole idea?"

"She would indeed," Arlen murmured thoughtfully, and Hester could see that he was beginning to warm to the concept. He pushed back his chair and began gathering the dirty dishes and taking them to the sink. "So the two of you have been planning this. . .all evening," he asked.

Hester shot Samuel a smile and then went to her father. She placed her hands on Arlen's shoulders. "Not all evening," she admitted. "There was a little matter of deciding we were not right for marrying each other that came first." She felt the tension drain from his shoulders as easily as the soapy water circled the sink and disappeared. He rinsed a plate and set it in the dish rack.

"And you are all right?" he asked, turning so that he could

read Hester's expression.

"It seems that Samuel and I were thinking along the same lines," she told him. "He came to say he wouldn't be proposing, while I had sat here since you left trying to figure out how to turn him down if he did. Grady always talks about that as a win-win situation."

Arlen was not completely convinced. "But you must be. . ."

"Hurt?" Hester asked. "Oh, Dad, how could I be when I had been agonizing for days now over how best not to hurt Samuel?" She smiled. "Now all we have to do is figure out how best to get Samuel and Rosalyn together."

She heard Samuel suck in a surprised breath. She turned to face him. "Oh, come on now. I'm not blind, you know. Half of Pinecraft knows the two of you are perfect for each other."

"You might try telling her how you feel," Arlen suggested. "In my limited experience that always seems to work best."

"Ja, Samuel, look how much time we wasted not speaking our true feelings."

Instead of relieved, Samuel looked worried. "Rosalyn is very loyal, especially when it comes to you, Hester. She would set her feelings aside if she thought being with me might hurt you."

Hester sighed. "All right, I'll talk to her for you. Coward," she teased, and Samuel grinned. "In the meantime, Dad, what do you think of our idea? We could have a shelter, a food bank, even a free clinic."

"You could certainly do all of that," Arlen agreed as he dried his hands on a dish towel. "The question, of course, becomes where you would do all of this plus set up a kitchen to make the jam with a space for collecting and packaging the fruit for delivery to the food banks."

"Okay. I know we have some things we have to work out, but the idea is a sound one, don't you think? I mean, it worked for this group in California."

"It has merit," Arlen admitted.

"And if anyone can make it a reality," Samuel added, "it's you, Hester."

"But it is a huge undertaking," her father warned her, his expression leaving no doubt that he was concerned that this was yet another of her grand projects that would distract her from the need to focus on herself and her future.

"I don't know how I know this, Papa, but I feel in my heart that God is leading me to do this. I have never felt anything so strongly in my life."

"Then His will be done." Arlen held out his arms to embrace her.

But in spite of her relief, Hester could not repress a feeling of panic. When she had thought she would marry Samuel, there had been a certain security in that. She could clearly see her future laid out in front of her. Now that was gone. She found herself thinking about the Crowder sisters. Neither had ever married. Hester couldn't help wondering if either of them had ever come close. Would her future be like theirs, caring for others through her volunteer work? And as the years passed, would she reflect the giving, joyful spirit of Agnes or the bitter, controlling personality of Olive?

She shuddered at the thought and firmly reminded herself that her calling had always been that of service to others. Tomorrow she would begin the process of devoting all of her energy to the new project. She would turn her work for MCC over to Rosalyn and focus all of her waking hours on making sure that the faceless, nameless, and homeless souls she had seen on the streets of Sarasota would have a chance to start fresh, to make a life, to find their purpose. And if some people in her father's congregation took exception to that calling, then too bad.

She fingered the magazine that had followed her for days now—from the hospital to the restaurant to her father's house. The article had caught her attention at the very moment when she knew that her life was about to reach a crossroads. If God was not showing her His plan for her life, then what was all that about?

No, Samuel would marry Rosalyn; Rosalyn would take over Hester's position as the local MCC representative; Hester would join forces with Emma and Jeannie and others and create a new, bigger, and better Rainbow House. And John would go back to Indiana and, God willing, find happiness and peace.

The following morning as she sat with her father having breakfast, Hester studied her to-do list.

> Get Grandma's recipe for marmalade
> Have coffee with Emma
> Talk to Rosalyn
> Set up meetings with:
> Grady
> Emma
> Jeannie
> Samuel
> Olive and Agnes
> Zeke
> John (???)

She was not at all sure why she had added John's name to the list, but there it was. She had hesitated far less time over including the Crowder sisters than she had adding his name to the list. In the end she crossed it off.

But when Samuel had mentioned that John had decided to put his place up for sale, she had felt a jolt go through her that she could only equate with panic. *What was that about?* she wondered. Why should it matter to her one way or another if John Steiner sold his place, moved back to Indiana, and she never saw him again?

And there it was. What if she never saw him again? It wasn't so much that she might never know what he'd meant by saying he had killed his mother—in terms of the facts, Liz had cleared that up. It was more that she would never know if he found what he'd come to Florida searching for.

She went to sleep and awakened the next morning thinking

about him. It had come to her that she and John shared many of the same personality quirks. They were both stubborn and determined. They both looked at difficult situations as challenges to be overcome. They both wanted something more than the normal that seemed to satisfy others. And in the predawn as she finally gave up on getting any more sleep, she realized that the reason she and John Steiner had so often knocked heads was because they were missing the obvious. Working together instead of alone or against one another, they could accomplish a great deal. The problem, of course, was going to be convincing John of that.

Chapter 21

Samuel might have a point," Zeke said as he stood up from repairing a gutter at one end of the packinghouse and stretched the muscles of his back. "We're going to finish this up by the weekend, and then the only thing not restored is the top floor of the house. You know, if you had a whole crew working on the place. . ."

John continued to roll paint onto the cinder block wall without comment. It had been ten days since Samuel had suggested the same thing. It had been only yesterday that John's aunt Liz had gone home to Washington after she'd stopped by his place one last time.

"John," she'd said, "I'm only going to say this once, and then I am off to the airport and out of your hair, for a while anyway."

John had steeled himself for the lecture he knew was coming, but instead Liz had cupped his cheek, forcing him to meet her gaze. "I know that you loved your parents deeply, John, but is this suppressed rage at the world any way for you to honor their memory?"

"This has nothing to do with them."

"It has everything to do with them. Look, I have tried and tried to understand this crusade you seem to be on, this life of absolute isolation. But then ask yourself why you chose this place? Why would you buy property near the heart of a bustling community where avoiding others is next to impossible? Why would you tolerate Margery Barker and that homeless man and, for that matter, Hester Detlef and her father and Samuel?"

He started to answer, but she just squeezed his jaw a little tighter the way his mother had when he was a boy. "Wake up," she whispered. "Life is short, and even if you think life on this planet is only a stopping-off place, God expects you to make the best of it, and so would my sister." She released him. "You have allowed your pride to get the better of you, John. Rachel would be disappointed. Frankly, I am disappointed. You are better than this." She waved her hand around the room with its tarp roof and a stairway that led nowhere.

Outside, a car horn honked.

"That's my ride to the airport." She held out her arms to him, and he accepted her embrace. "I just want you to be happy."

"I know."

The horn sounded again, and together they walked out to where the sleek steel-gray town car was waiting. The driver took Liz's suitcase and put it in the trunk while John opened the back door for her.

"Get a life," she advised John from the backseat as the driver got behind the wheel. "I'm serious," she shouted as the car moved slowly back down the lane.

John had stood watching it go, his hand raised in a wave until the car was out of sight, and then he had walked slowly back up the steps to his unfinished house, knowing that his aunt was right.

"Hey"—Zeke called him back from his revelry—"did you hear what I said?"

"Sorry." John shook off the memory of his aunt's farewell words.

"I said that October will bring the snowbirds. Some retiree who is looking for a place to call home just might be interested. Or barring that, some developer. It's prime land, and you know what they say in the real estate business."

John glanced over at him and waited for the answer.

"Location, location, location."

"How do you know that?"

Zeke shrugged and went back to work. "I hear things. I read. It's a sound byte like pretty much everything else people say that makes the world turn these days."

A west wind carried the sound of reconstruction at the south end of Siesta Key across the bay. That area had been even more devastated than John's property had been when Hurricane Hester roared through, but property owners and developers over there had insurance to rebuild without having to rely on Zeke scrounging for materials.

Or on the charity of others.

"You could repay Arlen's crew out of the money you make selling the place," Zeke said as if John had spoken aloud.

"They wouldn't accept payment," John said. "It's not their way."

"Then you make a donation to one of those committees Hester and the others are on—MDS or MCC or whatever the alphabet soup of the hour might be."

"With the economy the way it is, it could take years to sell this place," John said.

"Or it might sell in a week."

John fought the grin that threatened to ruin his foul mood. Zeke was a glass-half-full guy. Hester was like that, too, he thought, and then he wondered for maybe the hundredth time why he hadn't seen or heard from her.

"Margery tells me that Samuel and Hester are no longer. . .together," he said, unable to keep himself from probing to see what Zeke might know. "Do you think that Samuel will go back to Pennsylvania?"

"Not likely, unless he can persuade Rosalyn to go along with him. Why would he leave a partnership that could secure his future?"

"You're saying that Samuel and Rosalyn. . ."

". . .are an item, and it's about time, from what Jeannie tells me. According to her, the two of them have been making moon eyes at each other practically since the day they met." He tipped a bucket of water up and over his face and neck. Then he shook himself off like a dog coming out of the surf and grinned. "Arlen took him into his furniture business as a full partner. My guess is that there will be wedding bells before Christmas."

"Arlen made him a partner?"

Zeke sighed. "You really need to get out more, my friend. This is week-old news."

John ignored that. "How's Hester taking all of this?"

"Haven't talked to her personally, but from what Jeannie tells me, she's taking it with a huge sigh of relief. She never loved Samuel, not that you need love to make a good marriage, but it helps. Besides, that whole arranged marriage thing. . . That ship sailed a long time ago, especially for someone as independent as Hester. Don't know what Arlen was thinking."

"He's okay with all of this? Arlen?"

"Yeah. I expect he just wants Hester to be happy, and he finally figured out that he couldn't make that happen. She'll find her way—a survivor, that one. Of course, I expect she's a little surprised." He shrugged. "She might be relieved, but her future just got a little murky, if you ask me."

"How so?"

"Think about it. You have this life all laid out for you; marry this guy, start a family, set up a household. Then—*poof*—all of that's gone."

"Samuel's not the only man available."

Zeke glanced at him and grinned. "You offering to step up?"

"Don't be ridiculous," John growled.

Undaunted, Zeke continued to talk. "On the other hand, Samuel sure came out of it all right. He's in love with Rosalyn, and now he's got a solid future with Arlen's business."

Still, John couldn't help feeling sympathy for Hester. After all, she might not have wanted to marry Samuel, but now she was back at square one—starting over—and he knew how that felt.

"She's working on some new project," Zeke continued as he climbed back up the ladder to paint the trim. "Got most of

Pinecraft all excited about it, from what I hear."

"What's the project?"

"She's set up a meeting with a bunch of us to work out the details. She's pretty determined to get a program like Rainbow House back up and running."

"But that's not part of a Mennonite agency, is it?"

"Nope. The county ran it and then, once it was destroyed in the hurricane, decided to shut it down. Hester has this idea about getting it going again as some kind of nonprofit community thing."

John frowned. It seemed to him that Hester was moving way too fast in reacting to her breakup with Samuel. She was casting off pieces of her life like the years of work she'd devoted to MCC, as if they were of no importance. He'd done that once. Back in Indiana when the elders of his community had opposed his ideas, he'd been so determined to prove them wrong, to show them that he could make a life for himself without them. That had been a mistake, and he couldn't help but think that Hester was making a similar mistake now. "A nonprofit still needs funding," he muttered.

"Yep. That's one stumbling block. If she does raise the cash, the trick is going to be to find a place to do all that work, and trust me, there are very few people who want a bunch of homeless people hanging out anywhere near them or their businesses, so good luck to her on that one."

They worked for another hour before Zeke put away his tools in the restored shed and left, promising to return the following day. "Weather permitting and the creek don't rise," he called as he gunned the motor of Margery's boat and took off. John had finally understood that the translation of that last statement was really "If nothing comes up that's higher priority." He had learned never to directly ask anything of Zeke, and for accepting the man the way he was, John had been repaid a hundred times over in friendship and free labor.

Under threat of showing up to watch over him herself, Margery had gotten John to promise that unless either Zeke or

Samuel were around, he would not try any work that involved climbing or hauling or lifting. "I don't want to be responsible for coming out here one day to find you lying flat on your back after falling off a ladder," she'd groused.

"I wouldn't hold you responsible," he said.

"Well, I would, so don't do it."

Having gotten used to Margery's unique style of mothering, he'd stuck to her rule. Once Zeke left, he used up the rest of the paint in the tray, then cleaned up the roller and brushes and left them ready to start again the following day, assuming Zeke returned. With at least three hours of daylight left, he turned his attention to working on the planting beds. He'd found a stretch of his property that ran along the main road where the soil had been left undamaged by the surge that came with the hurricane. It was decent growing soil probably hauled in years earlier by Tucker, and having been left to its own devices for a decade or more, it was rich enough to form a solid base for planting vegetables once he separated it from the grass and wildflowers that had taken root. Every day since he'd made the discovery, John had taken a shovel, pickax, and wheelbarrow out there and worked at gathering the usable soil and hauling it back to fill in the planting beds.

The discovery had been a double blessing, because in digging out the soil, he had begun to create a drainage ditch where the water would run away from the house and outbuildings instead of turning the yard into a swamp. On top of that he now had enough of a soil base to fill the beds without having to spend a fortune on topsoil from a nursery. Now that the weather had started to cool off some, he could try planting some seeds. Surely the place would have a better chance of selling if he could show that the land was viable for growing things. Besides, it might be months before he could find a buyer for the place. If he could raise a few vegetables, he could save himself some money and not have to rely so much on Margery stopping by with food.

As he worked, he thought about the news Zeke had told him. So Hester and Samuel would not marry. The idea gave him unexpected pleasure. Most of all he was happy for Samuel. The man had talked a lot about Rosalyn whenever he stopped by, and it had been pretty clear that he was falling for her. He liked thinking that Samuel and Rosalyn would end up together.

He thought about Alice, the woman he'd come so close to marrying, and tried to imagine what their life might have been like had she stood by him instead of siding with the rest of the community. He'd been drawn to her physical beauty. She was seven years younger than he was, and maybe that had accounted for her reaction when he'd begun talking to her about his fascination with the Walden experiment. Alice had listened politely but shown no enthusiasm for the idea. Indeed, she had seemed mystified by his interest in the book. Why, she had asked, would he even bother to think of trying anything other than what others in their community had done for generations?

His mother had counseled patience, but he'd seen in the reserve with which she treated Alice that she thought he was making a mistake. "Just because you've waited this long before settling down doesn't mean you can't take some time to find the perfect partner. It's for life, you know," she'd told him once.

Instinctively, he knew that she would not have reacted that way to Hester. No, something told him that she would have loved Hester's independent streak and her can-do personality. Like his mother, Hester was a person who looked for ways to help others, whether they wanted her assistance or not, he thought wryly and smiled at the thought. Between Zeke and thoughts of Hester, his earlier bad mood had completely disappeared.

He leaned on his shovel after spreading the last load of dirt for the day and looked out toward the bay. The waters were calm and clear. They had long since receded to normal levels. Nothing like that day when she and her father and Samuel had come wading ashore. And certainly nothing like they must have been the night before the hurricane hit when she and Margery had come to get him to leave.

"She gave up pretty easy," he muttered aloud. But he could not ignore the fact that she had come back the following day.

And over the weeks that had passed since that day, she had stayed in touch in some way or another—or he had. In spite of his best efforts to annoy her into leaving him alone in those early days, not to mention that she clearly wanted nothing to do with him, the two of them had found themselves cast together time and again. He missed her, even her sometimes-irascible personality.

Was it possible that having some kind of relationship with Hester Detlef was part of God's plan for him? Perhaps he should take some time to examine that more closely. Why would God bring this feisty, my-way-or-the-highway woman into his life and keep bringing her back even when John was certain that they were on two very different paths and there was no reason for them to see each other again?

And yet, it was to Hester that he had spoken the single thing that he had carried with him all the way from Indiana to Florida. The guilt that he had buried so deep under long days of work and endless nights of loneliness and isolation that he had thought he finally had overcome it. It was to her that he had spoken the words he had never said aloud. *"I killed her."*

Hester could not seem to stop thinking about John. She was so sure that he was going to regret selling his place, and she couldn't see such a proud and independent man going back to Indiana and begging forgiveness from the very elders he had opposed. She itched to talk to him, but she had promised her father that she would not initiate contact, and she had never gone back on a promise. Still, it certainly seemed as if God was guiding her down a new path, given the way the silliest thing seemed to bring John to mind.

For instance, she was having ice cream with Emma one day, and it struck her that every time she had ice cream she thought about the time she and John had sat in that same spot. It occurred to her that sitting outside Big Olaf's that day, they had formed a kind of truce, fragile as it was. Of course, it hadn't been anything so formal as all that, but looking back on it now, she realized that on that day she and John had changed from being natural adversaries to. . .what?

"Okay, you are a thousand miles away," Emma said.

"I was just thinking about another time I was here recently."

"With Samuel?" Emma guessed and gave Hester a sympathetic smile.

The date she'd shared with Samuel had not even entered her mind. "Okay, stop looking at me as if you think I might burst into tears at any moment. I am fine, really. And so is Samuel."

Emma raised a skeptical eyebrow. "Still. . ."

"It's the best for everyone. Samuel and Rosalyn were meant for each other, and Dad still gets a gifted partner for his furniture business."

"Everyone just wants you to be happy," Emma told her.

"I am happy. The Rainbow House project—"

"Not with work or projects, Hester."

"My work and new projects give me a great deal of pleasure."

"Not the same thing as having that special person to share it all with. You deserve that kind of happiness, Hester. Don't surrender yourself to a life of service to the exclusion of everything else." Emma stood up. "I'm not finished with probing what this all means for you and your future, Hester, but I really have to go. Jeannie and her family are coming over for supper."

"Tell Jeannie I have some more names for her, people who will have fruit ready beginning in October." Emma waved and headed across the street. But as she watched her friend leave, Hester could not deny that Emma's words had rung true. Her decision to place all of her energies in the Rainbow House project had been made at least partly because she did not want to face the fact that she was unlikely ever to marry now that Samuel was out of the picture. Who was she kidding? If her father hadn't brought Samuel to Pinecraft, her chances of ever marrying had already been slim to none.

Hester and Rosalyn spent the rest of the afternoon sorting through donated goods, and all the while Hester kept trying to figure out the best way to break the tension between them. Ever since her breakup with Samuel, things with Rosalyn had been uncomfortable, despite her talk with the younger woman.

"Samuel told me that you've made good progress recruiting neighbors to donate fruit for the Rainbow House project," Rosalyn ventured. As had become her habit, she did not look directly at Hester when she mentioned Samuel's name. But at the same time she couldn't seem to hide the shy smile that lit up her face. Hester recalled the day that Jeannie had talked about not seeing such a glow on her face, at least not when Samuel's name came up.

"Have you and Samuel decided on a wedding date yet?" Hester asked. At least Rosalyn wasn't trying to pretend there was no courtship going on.

"Oh no, it's much too soon," Rosalyn protested.

"For what? You're in love. You're of age."

"Past age," Rosalyn murmured.

"Aren't we all? Which is exactly my point. Why wait?"

Rosalyn fingered a donated blouse that was embroidered with tiny blue flowers. Carefully she clipped a couple of loose threads before placing the blouse on a hanger. "I just have to be sure," she said.

"About Samuel?"

Rosalyn turned and looked directly at Hester. "About you." When Hester started to protest, Rosalyn held up her hands. "I know what you say, Hester, but are you sure?"

"Sure that I admire Samuel enormously? Yes. Sure that there are moments when I wish he might have been the one? Yes. Sure that I don't love him and that we would have bored each other to tears? Absolutely."

Rosalyn's eyes flickered with hope but also caution. So Hester put her hands on Rosalyn's shoulders and leaned in close. "He loves you. You love him. Marry him already. I may not be ready to be a bride, but I am hoping to be a godmother before this time next year."

"Hester!" Rosalyn's cheeks darkened with embarrassment.

"Oh, don't sound so shocked. You get married. You have

kids—at least that's the way it's supposed to work."

"So if your father were to include our names among the list of couples to be married next month. . . ?"

"Let me put it this way: if he doesn't include your names on that list, the gossips of Pinecraft are going to be buzzing like you've never heard before. And knowing Olive Crowder, I will get the blame. Frankly, I don't have time for that. So do everyone a huge favor and get on that list, okay?"

Rosalyn hugged Hester hard. "You are the kindest person I know, Hester Detlef," she exclaimed. "I am so glad that God sent you to care for me after the fire. I don't know what I would have done without you."

Hester couldn't help but think that it was Rosalyn who had been *her* salvation. With her positive attitude and determination to go on with her life in spite of her injuries and the loss of her entire family, she had brought Hester through her own period of grief. Hester's mother could not recover, but Rosalyn could—and did. With Hester working beside her every day, she had grown physically stronger, not weaker, and in the process, Hester had found at least some peace with her mother's passing.

"Well, I'm glad that's settled," Hester said as she returned Rosalyn's hug. "Now let's get this stuff put away and go shopping for fabric for your wedding dress."

"Oh, I have that already," Rosalyn said and then blushed again. "I mean. . ."

"I am shocked," Hester announced, and then she grinned. "Pretty confident that I was going to give you my blessing, weren't you?"

"Hope is a powerful thing," Rosalyn admitted.

The two of them went back to sorting through the boxes of clothing, working in easy silence for several minutes until Rosalyn said, "How are things going with John Steiner?"

Hester swallowed as she considered her answer. "Samuel would know more about that than I do."

"And why is that?"

"Well, I haven't seen much of—"

"So Samuel has mentioned. And why is that?" she repeated.

"It seemed for a time there that the two of you were getting closer. I mean, at least you weren't coming in here all irritated and such after being with him."

"Are you trying to play matchmaker?" Hester said, keeping her tone light and teasing.

"I am trying to figure out why the woman I admire probably more than anyone I know and the man that Samuel thinks very highly of have suddenly gone their separate ways. Samuel thinks that John has come to some kind of spiritual crossroads. You could help him, you know. You *should* help him."

Hester could hardly tell Rosalyn about her promise to her father, mostly because Rosalyn would want to know what had made her promise such a thing, and she certainly wasn't about to say, *Well, John told me that he killed his mother, and Dad thought . . .*

"And how do you suggest I go about helping a man who has repeatedly made it crystal clear that he doesn't want or need help, from me or anyone else?"

"Well, what if you asked him to be part of the planning committee for Rainbow House?"

Hester opened her mouth to refute that ridiculous suggestion, but Rosalyn rushed in. "I mean, the man is a farmer. He knows stuff."

"He has enough to do right now," Hester said in a tone intended to end this thread of conversation once and for all. "Samuel tells me that he plans to sell and move back to Indiana."

But Rosalyn was not on that particular wavelength. "That could take months. I mean, I know the two of you are like oil and water sometimes, but that's the very reason he would be good for the project. He looks at things from a different perspective."

"He does at that." Hester pictured John's expression whenever he was mulling over a new idea.

"So you'll think about asking him to help?"

"I'll think about it," Hester agreed. It looked like agreeing with Rosalyn was going to be the only way to get her off the subject of John Steiner.

"Good. Now I have to run. I promised Samuel that I would

meet him at the park. He's playing shuffleboard with your father. Come join us."

"Maybe later," Hester said. "I have some things to do first."

"Why doesn't that surprise me?" Rosalyn asked with a wry smile as she hurried off.

John helping on the Rainbow House project. John serving with her—and Emma, Jeannie, Grady, and the others—on the planning committee. It might work on a number of different levels, she thought.

But how to convince her father of that?

On Saturday evening as Hester and Arlen shared the task of washing and wiping the supper dishes, she decided the time had come to address the matter of John Steiner. "Dad?"

Obviously distracted, Arlen said, "Samuel brought me a letter from John today."

"A letter?" She tried to contain her excitement at news that John had been in contact. Perhaps this was a good sign. She had certainly prayed long and hard for God to show them the way. And she couldn't deny that underlying every prayer was her hope that God's will would include the opportunity for her to see John again. The more she thought about the pain he must have suffered after his mother's tragic and sudden death, the more she felt that they shared something in common and could possibly provide the understanding and comfort that others could not. After all, each of them understood at least some of what the other had been through. She could help him.

"Hester?"

She'd been so lost in thought that she'd failed to pay attention as her father talked on. Now Arlen was holding a sheet of yellow paper ripped from a pad and folded several times.

"Read it, and see what you think. You know John as well as any of us."

She dried her hands and unfolded the paper.

Dear Pastor Detlef,
    This is my formal request for you and your disaster
committee to consider whether or not your offer to help in
restoring the second story of my home is still valid. If so,
I would be grateful for a meeting to discuss terms.

                                Yours in the Lord,
                                John Steiner

Hester felt a smile tug at her mouth. This was so like him. Blunt and to the point and yet leaving the reader somewhat mystified. She could almost see him struggling over the choice of each word.

"What do you think it means?" Arlen asked.

"Well, it seems pretty clear that John is finally ready to accept the help you've offered," she said as she carefully folded the letter and handed it back to him. "On the other hand, he's determined to maintain control of the process."

"But why now?" Arlen scratched his head. "We have made numerous offers and all have been rejected. Samuel tells me that Grady also made attempts to provide assistance and was turned away. And just what does he mean about 'discussing terms'? What terms?"

Hester shrugged. "Samuel did mention that John was thinking of selling the place. Perhaps he's come to accept that he'll have more success with that if the property is fully repaired, especially the house."

"It's certainly prime real estate," Arlen agreed. "And now that the hurricane has ruined the soil for growing anything, I suppose the most likely buyer might be some developer. But a developer wouldn't care about the house, and with the economy still uncertain. . ."

"Will you help him?"

Arlen was clearly surprised by her question. "Of course we'll help him. We judge not, Hester. You know that."

And yet in a way he had judged John, she thought. When he had asked her to promise to stay away at a time when the man clearly needed every friend he could turn to, wasn't that the same as judging him?

"I don't think you can just show up there with a crew, Dad," she said as she dried and put away the last pot. "He asked for a meeting."

Arlen unfolded the letter and read through it again. "I could send word by Samuel on Monday. In the meantime, after church tomorrow, I'll speak with some of our volunteers and see when they might be available."

"You could drive out there after church," Hester suggested. "That would give you time to see exactly what the work might be before you put a crew together."

"That's a good idea," Arlen said, kissing her lightly on her temple. He headed for his study, where he would spend the rest of the evening going over his sermon for the following day. "And, Hester? If you have no other plans, perhaps you could ride along? It occurs to me that you, as well as John, have had some major changes in your life's journey these last days. Perhaps it would help him to talk to you, and vice versa."

She tried without success to quell the sudden leap of pleasure she felt at his invitation. "That would be fine," she said, turning away so that he would not see that she was smiling.

Chapter 22

Sunday morning held all of the promise of a day that would yield many blessings. A blue sky sprinkled with marshmallow clouds greeted those arriving for services at the Palm Bay Mennonite Church. There was an aura of excitement. In the Mennonite tradition, this was the day Arlen would announce the planned nuptials for four happy couples, among them Samuel and Rosalyn. Even Olive Crowder was smiling, at least until she spotted Hester outside the church.

"I understand that you have abandoned your duties as our representative to MCC," she said.

"I would hardly say abandoned," Hester replied, trying to smile through gritted teeth. "I have asked Rosalyn to assume those responsibilities while I—"

Olive sighed and raised her eyes to the blue skies above as if praying for patience. "Ja. Ja. We have heard of your new *project*. And I would ask you how the gathering of fruit from the yards of outsiders can possibly measure up to the work you have performed for MCC since your dear mother's death. Work that you took on in order to honor Sarah."

"My mother," Hester began and then found she had to gulp in a deep breath of fresh air before continuing. "I believe that my mother would be proud of all the work I do for others. She made no distinction between helping those outside the community and those within."

Olive pursed her lips, and Hester could see that she was considering her next words very carefully. Just then her sister Agnes came rushing over. "Oh, Hester, so glad to catch you before the service. I wanted to tell you that yesterday at our quilting session, everyone was just buzzing about your plan to collect fruit and rebuild the shelter. Oh, there are a few who cannot yet see the brilliance of your idea. . . ." She paused for a breath and cast a sidelong glance at Olive, who huffed and left to find her seat. Then Agnes squeezed Hester's arm. "May God bless this wonderful work you are undertaking to help those less fortunate, Hester."

"Danke, Agnes."

"Whatever I can do to help, you just let me know," she pledged and hurried off after her sister.

Inside the small frame church building, the women sat apart from the men on wooden pews. Several ladies fanned themselves with cardboard fans mounted on sticks. The building was not air conditioned, and although the weather outside was mild, inside the packed church, the air was close. Hester slid in next to her grandmother, Nelly, and a minute later, Emma and her daughter, Sadie, squeezed in next to them as Rosalyn took the seat on the aisle.

"Exciting day," Emma whispered to Rosalyn.

"Ja," Rosalyn replied as she cast an adoring glance at Samuel, who had just entered the building. "Ja," she repeated, folding her hands and closing her eyes tightly as she bowed her head in what Hester guessed was a prayer of thanksgiving.

As everyone settled in and grew still, Emma Keller's husband, Lars, stepped to the front of the crowded room to deliver the call to worship.

For I was an hungred, and ye gave me meat: I was thirsty, and ye gave me drink: I was a stranger, and ye took me in.

"Matthew, chapter 25, verse 35," Lars said and then took his seat as everyone found the first hymn and stood as one to sing.

Their voices rose in the a cappella harmony that in their faith left no room for the organ or piano accompaniment common in churches of other faiths.

It always made Hester smile that those members of the congregation who seemed the most reserved outside the church were the very ones who sang out with the greatest enthusiasm and gusto. Agnes Crowder's powerful alto, for example, could be heard above all the rest of the women combined.

At the close of the hymn, her father stepped forward to lead them in prayer. Several years earlier he had persuaded the congregation that this opening prayer should be a silent one with each member of the congregation setting aside whatever joys and sorrows he or she might have carried to church with them that morning. "It is a time to open our hearts and minds to consider God's concerns and how you might best serve Him in addressing those concerns."

From outside the open windows came the sounds of traffic, the occasional distant siren, voices of those on the street. But inside the crowded sanctuary, everything and everyone was absolutely still.

Next to Hester, Nelly put down her fan and took in a deep breath then silently moved her lips in prayer. On the other side of her, Emma folded her hands in her lap and closed her eyes. But Hester's mind was clogged with everything she had to do in the coming week. Even now, nearly two months after the hurricane, the work went on. And on top of everything else, the Rainbow House project was moving forward almost with a will of its own.

Jeannie had called a reporter she knew at the local Sarasota newspaper and provided him with information about the project. Since that article had appeared, Jeannie's telephone had been ringing constantly with people across the entire city offering to donate fruit that would be ready to pick in just a matter of weeks. Jeannie's daughter, Tessa, had come up with the idea of recruiting her friends and their grandmothers to prepare the jars and labels they would need for making the marmalade they would sell. Emma's daughter, Sadie, who was far more outgoing than her cousin, had gone from store to store on both Main Street and around St. Armand's Circle collecting cash donations. And Jeannie had persuaded the manager of the city's largest farmers' market to give them a space for the coming season at no charge. So whether Hester was ready or not, the Rainbow House project was on the march.

The problem was that they had no place to store and sort the fruit or make the marmalade. No means to distribute their goods. They had no viable building that they could say was the future location for the shelter. The homeless population was still out there, wandering the bay front and downtown, being harassed by local police if they stayed too long in any one place, eating their meals in the dwindling number of open shelters. Those shelters had been set up to provide a haven for victims of the hurricane. But with school in session and most of those affected by the storm having found other accommodations or moved back home, the need for such community resources had ended.

Be still and listen, Hester could almost hear her father counseling her. Instead, Arlen began reciting the Lord's Prayer, the signal that the time for silent prayer had ended, and everyone joined in. Hester squeezed her eyes closed, knitted her fingers together, and prayed the familiar words, pleading with God to show her the way.

". . .is the kingdom and the power and the glory forever and ever. Amen."

She opened her eyes and blinked against the light that followed the darkness. She glanced toward an open window. Just outside the church she saw John Steiner pacing back and forth, his hands clenched behind his back, his head bowed.

John had come into Pinecraft for two purposes. He was fairly certain that Arlen would take his change of heart about letting the MDS volunteers come out and help him rebuild the second story of the house as good news. He was not nearly so certain that Hester would be willing to listen as he explained his part in his mother's tragic death. For he had been the one to sever the fragile thread of friendship they had begun to forge all through the long night when they had waited together at the hospital.

The truth was that he felt a unique connection to Hester. He had seen a side of her that made him want to confide in her. On the other hand, he owed her an apology. As had become his habit, he'd run off that morning and holed up at his place, licking his wounds like an injured animal, waiting for her to come and find him. But she had made no effort to contact him, and why should she?

As a peace offering, he had brought her a wild orchid that he'd found growing along his lane. He had gone to the Detlef house and only realized that it was Sunday and she would be in church when he saw a cluster of bicycles gathered around a house across the street. Several Amish boys were standing around in the yard. John well remembered how he and his friends had lingered outside, always the last to go inside whatever home the service was being held in that week. The Amish held services in private homes, while the Mennonites had a separate church building—in Sarasota, John had learned, there were several of them.

He set the plant down among the ferns he had sent earlier, ferns that were still sitting in the bucket of water they'd arrived in, although they had clearly been tended with fresh water and kept out of direct sunlight. For reasons he didn't examine too closely, it was disturbing to him that she had not found the time to plant them in the garden that had been her solace after her mother died.

Unsure of his next move, he had wandered over to the restaurant where they had shared breakfast and then noticed the church on the opposite corner. Its plain white exterior gleamed in the morning sun, and through the open windows he heard voices raised in song. He moved closer and heard Arlen's familiar voice as he invited those in attendance to pray with him.

After a few minutes of silence, Arlen began reciting the Lord's Prayer and everyone joined in. Even John found himself mouthing the familiar words around the lump that had formed in his throat.

Although he was dedicated in his routine of morning devotions and evening prayer and often read the Bible—especially these days when his future was so uncertain—he missed the ritual of the worship. He missed hearing scripture read by others and silent meditation shared and feeling the press of a neighbor's shoulder against his own. He missed what Margery had been telling him he needed for over two years now—he missed community, the comfort and commiseration that were part of living with others, sharing happy as well as sad times.

He'd been thinking a lot about those newborns he'd seen in the hospital nursery. He'd thought about Grady Forrest being a father, about his own father, who in their too-short time together had taught John so much, and he thought about Samuel Brubaker, who was clearly looking forward to the day when he and Rosalyn would have a family of their own. He'd envied Samuel and Grady. He had thought that he would be the one raising a family by now.

The congregation had finished singing another hymn, and Arlen had opened the part of the service where any member of the congregation could stand up and share with the others. He heard a man announce that he and his wife would be leaving Florida to move back north where they could be closer to their children and grandchildren. He heard another man request prayers for the diagnosis he had received of diabetes. He heard a woman thanking the members who had been so kind in taking her in and bringing food and clothing after her home had flooded. And when the woman seemed inclined to ramble on, naming every person and how he or she had supported the family, John tuned her out.

Instead, he thought about the passage he'd stumbled across in Thoreau's book the night before. Once he was able to at least occupy the first floor of the house, he'd decided to build a bookcase in the living room and celebrate the addition to his meager furnishings by giving *Walden* a shelf all its own, at least until he could afford more books. Then as he'd positioned the book on the shelf, he'd noticed a piece of loose paper sticking up from the top. He'd turned to the page and read a passage he must have marked the first time he read the book.

". . .*things do not change; we change.*"

"John?" Samuel Brubaker stood at the door of the church with an elderly man who had apparently been overcome by the closeness inside. Two women followed him and took charge of getting the man a drink of water and finding him a chair so that he could sit in the shade of the church vestibule and take advantage of the light breeze.

"Hello, Samuel."

"Are you. . . ? Would you like to come inside?"

And without hesitation John nodded and followed Samuel into the crowded church, removing his hat and clutching its stiff, sturdy brim like a lifeline. Samuel indicated the seat that he had vacated on the end of one pew and then went back outside to attend to the man. John was aware of a gentle flutter of whispered comments and the rustle of bodies shifting as people turned to look at him.

Arlen had begun his sermon and paused only a second to glance John's way before continuing. "We have made a covenant with God to love Him with all our hearts, minds, and beings. That is the first commandment. But how are we to do that? Ah, it's right there in the second commandment—we are to love our neighbor. But that raises a new question. What is the manifestation of such love?"

Arlen went on to mention four couples, including Samuel and Rosalyn, whose betrothals had been made known to the congregation during the period of announcements. He talked about other couples in the church who had been long married. He talked about parents loving children and sisters loving brothers and neighbors caring for neighbors. Then he broadened the scope to make it citywide and then statewide and national and international. He talked about love for the land and the sea and the heavens. He spoke of love for other creatures, animals domesticated and wild, and of love for all things growing on this planet that God had created. "And so we see that our love for God is made visible in our love for all humankind and all of God's creation."

He was on a roll, and still he had not provided the answer to the question he had originally raised, a question that John had wrestled with in so many ways.

"Which brings us back to our original question: What is the manifestation of this love in all its forms?" Arlen repeated. "It is sacrifice. It is putting aside our personal comfort and wants and desires anytime we know that there is someone out there who is in need, even strangers we have never met. For they are our neighbors as much as the person who lives next door."

John examined this under the light of his actions over the last several months. When had he put aside his needs for the greater good? Certainly not when he had foolishly insisted on remaining at Tucker's Point instead of going to a shelter. Not even that time when he had gone to help Margery, for he had not had to sacrifice anything for that. And most definitely not anywhere near the number of times that Hester had risked censure by others or put aside her own needs to tend to him or others.

"Brothers and sisters," Arlen said, "I close with the words of the prophet Isaiah, chapter 58, verse 12: 'And they that shall be of thee shall build the old waste places: thou shalt raise up the foundations of many generations; and thou shalt be called, The repairer of the breach, The restorer of paths to dwell in.'

"Shall we pray?"

Every head bowed as Arlen beseeched God to hear those prayers, silent and spoken, that had come from this gathering. And as John prayed with him, he felt more certain than ever that God was leading him to take a new path and change his ways. His experiment had failed because he had thought only of himself. He had spent more than two long years feeling sorry for himself, wallowing in grief and guilt. And while he had opened himself to the friendship of Margery and Samuel and Zeke, he had continued to keep anyone else, including Hester and her father, who had tried to help him at arm's length.

"*. . .things do not change; we change.*"

Once the service ended, there was the usual crush of people at the door, some wanting to talk to Arlen at length and others just wanting to have their presence acknowledged before leaving. Hester deliberately hung back, visiting with Emma and Sadie for longer than usual until Emma caught Lars's eye. "My husband is ready to go," she said. "I'll see you tomorrow for coffee?"

"Yes," Hester said. Lately she and Emma had gotten into the habit of meeting for coffee every Monday morning. It was a good way to begin the week, and it had done wonders for reaffirming their friendship. "Bye, Sadie," she said, but the girl was already halfway to the door, waving to a friend and chatting with two others.

"Hester, do you have a minute?"

She turned to find John standing in the row of pews behind her. He was dressed in the clothes he'd gotten from the distribution center weeks earlier and holding the Amish straw hat that Rosalyn had found for him. He was clutching it actually, and it surprised her to realize that he was nervous. "Hello, John," she said. "How are you doing?" She kept her tone impersonal and just the slightest bit suspicious.

"Do you have time to take a walk with me? Maybe to the park?"

Hester was well aware that setting off after church with any man for a walk in the park would set tongues to wagging. Taking that walk with John would likely draw curiosity even from those who usually avoided gossip. "Why?"

He smiled. She had forgotten what that smile of his did to her. The way his eyes crinkled. The way his entire face seemed to soften. The way her heart suddenly beat in staccato rhythms.

"Direct and to the point as usual, I see," he said. "Well, because the last time we talked I was rude, and I'd like to apologize. Would that be all right?"

"Apology accepted," she said as she picked up her grandmother's forgotten fan and prepared to leave.

He stopped her by gently touching her arm. "And," he added, his expression completely serious now, "I'd like to explain."

"You've apologized," she said breezily. "No explanations

necessary. It was good to see you in church today, John. And I understand that you and my father—"

"Stop it," he grumbled. "You know what I mean. Will you let me explain or not?"

She sighed. "Come home with Dad and me for Sunday dinner and you can tell both of us."

John frowned. "I prefer—"

"Final offer, John. Take it or leave it."

His frown deepened, but she stood her ground, cocking one eyebrow as she waited for his answer. And then he did the one thing she never would have expected. He fingered a dangling tie of her prayer kapp. "You drive a hard bargain, Hester."

For one incredible moment Hester lost herself in the depths of his eyes. For one incredible moment she felt the kind of shared attraction she had only imagined as she watched her parents or Emma and Lars. And then she heard someone clearing her throat, reminding her that she and John were not alone, and looked over John's shoulder to find Olive Crowder scowling at them. The older woman turned on her heel and headed up the aisle to the exit.

John cleared his throat as well. "What's for dinner?"

"Chicken, potato salad, tomatoes, and my grandmother's chocolate cake."

From the look on his face, Hester suspected that John was about as close to having his mouth water as anyone could come without actually drooling. She couldn't help herself—she laughed. "If you could see your face," she said, pointing with one hand while she used the other to cover her laughter. "Come on. Dad looks like he's about ready to leave. Maybe the two of you can talk about how MDS can help you while we walk."

It was unusual for Arlen and Hester to eat their Sunday dinner at home. Usually Arlen was invited to dine with one of the families that attended the church, and since her mother's death Hester was usually included in the invitation. If they did eat at home, her grandmother joined them. But on this Sunday, Arlen had made sure that Nelly had an invitation to eat with friends and that he had turned down any invitations he and Hester might receive.

"We'll have our dinner and then drive out to Tucker's Point," he'd told her that morning at breakfast. "Or we could make it a picnic and include John." He had seemed so pleased with the idea that Hester had fried several pieces of chicken and put potatoes on to boil for potato salad while her father was eating his breakfast. All she had left to do was to mix the potato salad and slice the tomatoes.

"Dad? John has agreed to join us for our dinner," she said when her father had sent the last church member on his way.

"Excellent. We had planned to bring a picnic out to your place, John, so that you and I could talk about how MDS might be of service to you."

"Now we can eat at home," Hester said.

"No picnic? On a glorious day like this one?" Arlen faked a frown.

"A picnic would be nice," John said politely. "I understand that it means more work for you, Hester, but I'd be glad to help."

Her mouth dropped open and then closed again without a sound. Had this man—this Amish man of the women-have-their-place variety—just offered to help out in the kitchen?

"No. A picnic is fine. Besides, Dad, you wanted to see what progress John has already made before deciding how best to help, right?" She had carefully avoided eye contact with John since they'd joined her father for the walk home.

"So a picnic it is," Arlen announced.

The phone was ringing when they reached the house, and Hester hurried ahead of the men to answer it. There was only one reason someone would disturb their Sunday, and that was if there had been some misfortune that required Arlen's help. Mentally Hester took stock of who had not been in church that morning as well as who in the community had recently been ill.

"Pastor Detlef's home," she said.

"Oh good, Hester, it's you." Jeannie Messner's normal voice was always so filled with excitement that it was hard to know why she might be calling, especially because Arlen was not her pastor.

"Is it Emma?" Hester asked, her mind racing with possibilities. Emma had mentioned that she and Lars and the children were having Sunday dinner at Jeannie's house. "Zeke Shepherd's brother, Malcolm, and his family will be there as well," Emma had said and then smiled. "You know Jeannie. It has to be a party." Of that guest list only Emma and her family were members of Arlen's church.

"Emma? She's fine." Jeanne seemed momentarily mystified at the question. "Oh, you thought. . . I guess I shouldn't be calling on a Sunday, but this is such wonderful news that it can't wait."

But Hester did have to wait while Jeannie turned from the phone. "Go ask your parents," she said, her hand apparently muffling the sound. "I'll do it if they say it's okay." There was a teenage moan, and then Jeannie's voice was clear once again. "Sorry about that. Sadie wants to get her learner's permit, and you know how Emma and Lars are."

Arlen was standing in the doorway, obviously expecting the call to be for him.

"It's Jeannie Messner," Hester mouthed. "Jeannie? Dad and I were just on our way to—"

"Okay, I'll make this quick," Jeannie said. "Zeke's brother, Malcolm? He might be interested in setting up a foundation for the Rainbow House project."

"Why are you whispering?" was all Hester could come up with as a response to such startling and admittedly thrilling news.

"Well, it's not a done deal yet. I mean, he said that giving the money to Zeke is like trying to bail out a sinking boat with chopsticks. You know how Zeke does things, just gives everything away to this one or that, no questions asked."

"Jeannie, what exactly did Malcolm offer?" She hated to dampen Jeannie's excitement with a strong dose of reality, but in this case it was important.

"I told you. He said giving Zeke the money was a waste and that he really liked what I was telling him about the project and. . ."

. . .*from there you just naturally assumed the rest,* Hester thought, disappointment taming her initial excitement. "Jeannie, did he actually mention setting up a foundation?"

"No, that was my Geoff, but Malcolm certainly agreed that it was a way to go. I mean, there would be conditions, I'm sure, before he'd be ready to fully commit. He is a businessman, after all, and you know how they are—bottom line and measures of success and all—but I'll just assure him that you and Emma could get that all figured out."

"What does Emma think?"

There was the slightest pause. "Well, I could tell that she was thinking about it. She probably plans to talk to you about it at your coffee tomorrow. Oh shoot, I'll bet she wanted to tell you the good news herself. Well, just pretend I didn't say anything, okay? Gotta run." And the line went dead.

"Is everyone all right at the Messner home?" Arlen asked when Hester came into the kitchen. He and John were seated at the kitchen table drinking iced tea.

"Yes, fine," she replied as she started pulling containers from the refrigerator to pack their picnic. "You know Jeannie. She gets something on her mind and can't wait to share it."

Arlen smiled. "Yes. She's a delightfully positive person, always has been."

John took the knife and the tomato that Hester was slicing and nodded toward the bowl of cold potatoes. "I can do this while you mix the potato salad."

She tried to concentrate on listening to her father singing the praises of Jeannie and her husband, Geoff, but it was hard to do with John working alongside of her as if this was something they did all the time. Before long, images of the two of them working together became visions of them laughing together and then sharing meals and. . .

Stop it.

She finished mixing the salad, then wrapped the chicken and packed the picnic basket. She was about to close the lid after John handed her the plastic bag filled with more sliced tomatoes than three people could possibly eat when he stopped her by holding the basket lid.

"I thought you said something about chocolate cake, but I don't see any sign of it in here. Frankly, I was really looking forward to that."

Arlen laughed. "So am I," he agreed as he retrieved the dessert from the counter and handed it to John. "Hester, your mind is too much on other things today."

She could not argue the point, for between John Steiner's sudden reentry into her life and Jeannie's idea that Zeke's brother might actually help fund the Rainbow House project, she was definitely having trouble concentrating on anything.

"Okay, are we ready to go?" she asked and knew by the look that John and Arlen exchanged that she had sounded anything but cheerful. The truth was that Jeannie's news had been unsettling, even threatening.

Chapter 23

Neither Hester nor her father was prepared for how much work John had actually been able to accomplish. "If you did most of this work with a broken wrist, it would be quite interesting to see what you could do with two good hands," Arlen said.

Uncomfortable with compliments—even subtle ones—John directed their attention to the packinghouse. "Zeke was able to finish the trim and gutters when he was here yesterday. This building is in better shape than it was before the hurricane hit, thanks to Zeke and Samuel."

"And so we can concentrate on the house," Arlen said as the three of them sat on a blanket that Hester had spread on the ground and shared the picnic dinner. Arlen poured lemonade from the thermos and passed the cups around. John laid a two-by-four across the center of the blanket to keep it from blowing in the cooling breeze.

"Instant table," he said, setting his cup of lemonade on it. Arlen followed suit, and then John picked up Hester's cup from its unsteady resting place on the ground and added it to the lineup.

For reasons she didn't want to explore, Hester found herself studying John's hand. It was large with long fingers. His nails were clipped short, and calluses had hardened the skin on his palms. The backs of his hands were sunburnt to a permanent russet, and the coarse hair that covered his forearm glinted golden in the afternoon sun. His hands, like the rest of him, were strong and solid. And yet she felt certain that his touch would be gentle, even tender.

Now where did that thought come from? "Another piece of chicken, Dad?" She forced her thoughts away from the man who was suddenly sitting far too close to her and who seemed to be watching her every move.

"Not for me." Arlen patted his stomach and grinned. "I need to save some room for that cake."

"John?" she offered without meeting his gaze.

"No, thank you." The words came out as if she'd startled him, as if he hadn't really been following the conversation at all. He got to his feet and offered a helping hand to Arlen. "How about we take a walk through the house, and then maybe we can discuss those terms I mentioned in my letter," he said.

"MDS does not place restrictions on our work, John. We give of our talents freely to those in need."

"I'm afraid I can't accept that," John said. "I insist on paying."

The two men stood at an impasse for one long tense moment, and then Arlen smiled. "Why don't you give us the tour and then we can talk more over a piece of Nelly's chocolate cake."

Hester could not help but be impressed with the tidiness of the downstairs rooms where John was currently living. The kitchen was sparsely furnished with a single chair and the heavy oak table that Hester remembered from the night she'd come to get him to leave. An assortment of mismatched dishes lined the shelves on each side of the porcelain sink. The countertops were bare of the usual assortment of small appliances and such that cluttered the counters in Jeannie's large kitchen. Hester suspected that if she opened any of the three drawers, she would find the utensils lined up perfectly inside.

In one narrow room that they passed on their way from the kitchen to the living and dining rooms, he had placed a single bed and small dresser. Hooks on the wall across from the window held the clothes that he wasn't currently wearing. The single window was unadorned. The bed was made up with spotless white sheets, a single flat pillow, and a blanket folded across the foot. It was the bedroom of a plain man, an Amish man. It was the room of a man who was no longer fighting against his roots.

Hester forced her attention to the living and dining rooms. The dining room was bare of any furnishings at all save an ornate chandelier that hung from the center of the ceiling and seemed incredibly out of place. Across the hall, the living room was almost as devoid of furnishings. A bookcase next to the old woodstove caught her eye because the wood was new and there was only one book on the otherwise-empty shelves. She moved closer, unable to suppress her curiosity.

Walden: Life in the Woods.

John and her father were still standing in the front hallway while John pointed out the carving on the banister that led up to the second floor. There was another far less ornate stairway in the kitchen, John was telling Arlen, or there had been until it had collapsed under John's feet the night of the storm.

Hester picked up the book. As she had told John, she had read it when she attended college, but for her it had been little more than another assignment to be completed. Clearly for John it held a great deal more significance. There was a small yellow paper marking a page. She let the book fall open and moved the bookmark in order to scan the two facing pages, trying to guess which passage had resonated with him. And the words that caught her attention just before her father called out to her and she closed the book and replaced it on the shelf were "we change."

"Hester, did you ever see such fine workmanship?" her father was saying as he examined the front door. "Even warped as it is," he added as he ran his fingers over the wood. Her dad had always admired the talent of other carpenters, especially those who had lived well before his time.

"It is beautiful," she agreed.

"Was," John corrected.

"And will be again," Arlen added. He turned his attention back to the stairway. "Is it safe to go up?"

For an answer John led the way. The treads of the stairs were bare wood, and his heavy work boots echoed on each step. When they reached the top, Hester understood why the sound had been so pronounced. An entire wall of the second story was gone, exposing what had been a large bedroom and bathroom to the elements. Wallpaper hung in tatters from the walls that remained intact, and they would need to be stripped, then scrubbed down and whitewashed. The wood floor was gouged and scarred in places.

John entered the first bedroom and pointed to the large banyan tree outside. "A third of the tree broke off and landed inside here. It took Zeke and me an entire day to get it cut up, but it left its mark on the floor, I'm afraid."

Arlen examined the damage and said nothing.

"There are two other small bedrooms on this floor. They suffered water damage, and the storm blew out the doors and windows, but at least the walls are there."

"Excellent," Arlen said, more to himself than to either of them. Hester knew that he was already making a mental list of what would be needed, muttering to himself as he moved around the space, "Electric, water, plaster, paint. First the exterior wall. . . Is there an attic?"

"There was." John pointed to the opening where the roof had been ripped free of the rafters.

"Das ist gut," Arlen said as he removed a small notepad and the stub of a pencil from his pocket and made some entries. "This is the extent of it?" he asked, looking up at John.

"Pretty much."

Arlen smiled and touched the sleeve of John's shirt. "Then you are blessed." He started back down the stairs while Hester and John exchanged a look that shouted, *Blessed? Is he kidding?*

"Let's have some cake, and you and Dad can talk," Hester suggested as she followed her father back to the first floor.

John offered Arlen the only kitchen chair, then brought in

two folding chairs from the porch. Hester cut slices of the cake and placed them on the three plates that she found on John's kitchen shelf. He took forks from a drawer, and she saw that she was right in thinking the utensils would be lined up precisely inside.

Then over large pieces of that chocolate cake washed down with the last of the lemonade, the two men talked over the details of what would be needed to renovate the house. Hester had sat in on dozens of such conversations with her father over the last several weeks, and knowing she would have little to add to the discussion, she finished her smaller slice of cake and then wandered back outside.

We change, she thought as she walked along the property, remembering how it had looked the first time she had come here after the hurricane. All around her was evidence of how that fierce storm had changed the landscape, open spaces where before there had been lush tropical plantings, barren land where there were now stubs of the grove of fruit trees that had flourished there. The pier that had been indefinable that morning had been replaced, using reclaimed materials that she assumed either Samuel or Zeke had provided.

The sun was high, so she sought the cooler shade of the old packinghouse. Outside, the walls had been painted a deep forest green and the flat roof was marked by three ventilation fans housed in metal cupolas. She walked up a short ramp to see the inside where the original conveyer belt made up of a series of rusted metal rollers had remained intact, along with the rough-hewn work counters where once Tucker's employees had sorted fruit for distribution throughout the region.

She walked the length of the long building, her fingers skimming along the equipment as an idea began to take shape. A major piece of the puzzle that was the Rainbow House project that no one had yet solved was that of where to sort and wash the fruit once it was collected. It would need to be packaged or processed, and the resulting products would need to be stored until they could be distributed.

As she walked through the packinghouse, she was barely aware that along the way she was mentally designating the very spots where each step in the sequence could take place. And when she stood in the doorway at the far end of the building and closed her eyes, she could see it all—volunteers working at various stations, their chatter and laughter echoing as they worked. Crates of fruit stacked up and sorted and ready to be turned into marmalade or delivered whole to food banks around the city. Over there a large cookstove and the supplies necessary to make and bottle the marmalade.

"It's perfect," she murmured aloud as she rummaged in her pocket for a piece of paper and pencil. "We'd have to replace the conveyer belt, but otherwise it's exactly what's needed." Now all she had to do was to convince John of that and stop him from selling the place.

John wasn't really listening to Arlen. He was thinking about Hester and how he might find some time to be alone with her. He was as surprised as she would no doubt be to realize that his intentions were romantic. But then he had seen her wandering around his property as he stood at the sink washing the plates and glasses that she'd used to serve the dessert. She walked slowly with her hands clasped behind her back, her head shifting to take in everything around her. He saw her pause near one of the garden beds long enough to pick up a handful of soil and let it sift through her fingers. Moving on, she had touched the shattered trunk of an orange tree destroyed by the hurricane winds and then glanced around as if realizing that something was missing. Finally she had patted the trunk of the tree and then slowly walked past the repaired toolshed and empty chicken coop to the packinghouse. Shielding her eyes from the sun, she had stood looking up at the roof and finally disappeared inside.

". . .like to get Samuel out here to have a look," Arlen was saying. "Maybe tomorrow if that works for you?"

"Sure," John replied, wondering what Hester was finding so

fascinating in the empty packinghouse.

"You know, John, if you're planning on selling the place. . ."

"I am," John said, giving Arlen his full attention. *I don't really have a choice.*

Arlen nodded. "Well then, we'll figure that into the work we do. We can keep things pretty simple. After all, your most likely buyer for such a prime piece of property would be a developer who will no doubt tear everything down anyway."

It wasn't that John hadn't thought of that himself. It just hurt to hear the words spoken aloud. "As long as the developer can pay the price," he said. "I won't be able to repay MDS until the place sells. You understand that, right?"

Arlen took a moment. "And you understand that, as I've already told you, we do not accept payment." He actually sounded insulted and seemed dangerously close to losing what little temper he had.

"But. . ."

"No." Arlen pushed himself away from the table and stood up. "But since it seems so important to you to keep a balance sheet on this project, I have a suggestion."

"I'm listening."

"Open your eyes and your heart, son. God has blessed you in many ways, but He also expects those He has blessed to be a blessing to others."

The concept that he had been blessed was debatable, given his complete failure, but the old man meant well and so he nodded. "I'll give that some consideration," he said.

"Excellent. Now where do you think that daughter of mine has gotten to?" He glanced around as if just realizing that Hester had left them alone.

"She's outside."

"Well, we're going to need some measurements. Do you have a carpenter's tape?"

John opened a drawer and handed him the measuring device. "What else?"

Arlen took paper and the pencil from his pocket. "Nothing I

can think of. Do you mind if I. . ." He nodded toward the front hallway.

"Not at all. I'll help," John said.

"No. If it's all right, I like to do this part alone. I seem to think better in silence and solitude. Go find Hester. Do you have some more of those ferns you gave her for Sarah's garden?"

"I do," John said.

"Good. Go help her dig them. Perhaps it will inspire her. The garden has been sadly neglected for weeks now."

John got a pitchfork and shovel and large bucket from the toolshed and then headed for the packinghouse. Inside, he found Hester perched on one of the long sorting tables that had gone through the hurricane untouched. She was writing furiously on a small pad of paper and muttering to herself.

"Arlen thought you could use some more ferns for the garden," he said. He leaned the gardening tools against the worktable. "What are you working on there?"

"Nothing, a sketch. . .idea."

"May I see it?" She handed him the rough sketch, and he saw at once that it was the packinghouse. "And may I ask why?"

"Remember that magazine you picked up at the hospital and asked me to return for you?"

John nodded.

"Well, there was this article about people around the country—ordinary people—who have put together programs to help others. A woman in California who had gotten the idea to have teenagers collect unwanted fruit from private yards was featured."

"And you thought why not here in Sarasota?"

"Well, yeah. Since then we've discovered that there's a similar program in Tampa and they've been very helpful." She took the sketch from him and put it in her apron pocket. "It just helps to see the layout of a building that was once used for similar work." She motioned around the large, cavernous building, then shrugged. "Ready to dig those ferns?"

"You sure you've got time to get them back in the ground?" he teased.

"Guilty. How did you know I hadn't gotten around to that yet?"

"I found a wild orchid growing along my lane that I thought you might be able to save. So this morning, before I figured out that everyone would be at services, I stopped by your house and saw the ferns still sitting in the bucket." He held up the empty bucket he was carrying. "At this rate I'm going to run out of buckets pretty soon."

Her smile was both beautiful and sad. "I never seem to get around to the things that really matter."

"Right. Like saving an entire homeless population or making sure the survivors of the hurricane get the clothing and household goods they need to start over, like—"

"Honoring my mother's memory," she said quietly. She had not moved from her perch on the sorting table, and her gaze met his directly. "How do you honor the memory of your parents, John?"

So here it is, he thought. She had given him the opening he'd been looking for earlier, but it had come so unexpectedly that he suddenly found that he did not have the words. "I know I owe you an explanation," he said as he put down the garden tools and pushed himself up onto the table beside her.

"You don't owe me anything, but if you're inclined to finish the conversation you started that morning at breakfast, I'm listening."

He glanced at her, expecting to see judgment or at the very least skepticism in her eyes, but instead he lost himself in their sapphire depths. "It's hard to know. . ."

"Start with how she died."

He stared down for a minute, gathering his thoughts, or maybe he was just fighting the memories, reluctant to go back to that horrible time.

"It was winter. There was snow, a lot of it, and it was bitterly cold. Worst winter in a decade, the weather people kept saying. But she insisted on going out."

"Why?"

"It was my fault." He felt tears well and willed himself to contain them. "I had started on this Walden thing that fall, and at first everyone seemed to think the idea might have merit. It's not unheard of even for an Amish community to find itself caught up in more worldly ways."

"So when you read Thoreau's book, you thought that here was a guide for getting back to the old ways?"

John nodded and cleared his throat. "But the more I talked about how the community might apply certain elements of Thoreau's experiment to our lifestyle, the more people seemed to be alarmed by it, and by me."

"Your mother was concerned?"

"Not *with* me, for me. She had heard from a friend that things were getting out of hand. What had begun as trivial was quickly escalating into something much more serious, but I was too stubborn to see that. Mom insisted that we needed to make sure the leadership of the congregation had my side of the story. She hated gossip in any form." He paused and shut his eyes to block out the memory. "She had learned that the bishop would be meeting with the elders that night, and she was determined that I be there."

"So you and she. . . ?"

"No. I refused to go. We had had this really terrible argument, and I had stormed off to take care of the evening milking. Mom and I could knock heads now and then. I come by my stubbornness honestly." He stared up at the light filtering in around the roof vents. "Next thing I know she's got our horse hitched up to the buggy and is climbing into the driver's seat. She hadn't driven that buggy once since my father had died. Either I drove or we didn't go anywhere."

He sucked in a breath and let it out with a shudder. Hester placed the flat of her palm against his back and remained perfectly still, waiting for him to continue.

"But that was Mom. In some ways she had always felt like the outsider in the community, especially after Dad died. She was determined to make my case to the powers that be, even if

I wasn't. I started after her, yelling at her to stop, but she was so strong-willed, nothing was going to stop her from going."

A bird flew through the open door and settled on a crossbeam in the ceiling.

"What happened, John?"

"The driveway was covered in ice. I could see that the horse was nervous. I kept yelling for her to stop, but then a passing car backfired and. . ."

"The horse bolted?"

John nodded and tried to swallow around the lump that filled his throat. "He slipped and the buggy turned over, and Mom. . ." He swiped at the tears he could no longer hold back.

"But you weren't in the buggy with her," Hester said softly. "There was nothing you could have done to prevent this, so why did you say that you killed her?"

"Because afterward I knew what others were saying. I knew full well that I was on the brink of being called before the congregation. I mean, any fool understands that once the bishop gets involved, things have gone to a whole new level. And I should have known that when I stubbornly refused to back down, she would take matters into her own hands. She was fierce that way."

"The old saying applies—hindsight is twenty-twenty. But John, if this is the whole story—"

"It is. . ."

"Then the fact remains that you had nothing to do with her death. It was her choice to go out that night, John. You did everything you could to stop her."

He continued the story as if she hadn't spoken. "A passing car saw the overturned buggy and stopped. The woman had a cell phone and called for help, then stayed with us until the ambulance arrived. But it was already too late."

"She died in your arms?"

John nodded. "She put her hand on my cheek and said three words: 'Find the balance.' "

"I don't understand."

"It was an old joke that we shared. Whenever things got

overwhelming and she had trouble adapting to the Amish life, Dad would always tell her to find the balance. After he died, and I would come home after getting into some argument with another kid or in a bad mood, she would remind me that if Dad were there, he would tell me to 'find the balance.' And as she got older and became frustrated with knees that hurt and eyes that needed glasses for fine needlework, I would throw it back to her: 'Find the balance, Ma.' " He savored this sweeter memory for a long moment, and then looked around. "Haven't exactly done that, have I?"

"I suppose that depends on how you define *balance*," Hester said. "But I do know that for you to go around saying you killed your mother is just one more tactic you've developed to keep people at arm's length."

"It's not something I go around saying to folks," he protested.

"You said it to me," she challenged. "And you don't even like me."

"What gives you that idea?"

"Oh, I don't know. Could be the way we're always on guard around each other. Could be—"

Without taking time to consider what the possible consequences might be, John pulled her against him and kissed her. "I like you, okay?" he whispered, and when she did not fight him, he kissed her again. Then he released her and hopped down from the table. "Are you going to help me dig these ferns or not?"

Hester could not move, much less find the energy to dig ferns. Her body felt like water, and her mind was racing like a speedboat. And she wasn't sure she could handle thinking about the somersaults her heart seemed to be attempting.

John Steiner had kissed her. Twice. Without any warning at all. Without for one second stopping to consider what *her* feelings might be. *Typical.* The man was so. . . She realized she was running her forefinger over her lips. "Oh, get over yourself," she muttered and picked up the shovel he'd left for her.

Outside, John was stabbing the pitchfork into the hard soil.

For all the rain they had had earlier in the season, it had been dry for weeks now.

"Be careful," she said. "You'll break them off without getting the roots."

"We do grow ferns up north," he said, and she could hear frustration in his voice. It didn't help that he refused to look at her.

They dug in silence for several minutes, nothing passing between them other than the sound of metal hitting hard-packed earth. "Maybe if we soak the soil," John said, but it was evident that he wasn't asking for her opinion.

Hester leaned on her shovel. "Look, we cannot just ignore what you did back there."

"You don't have to make it sound like—"

"I'm not trying to make it sound like anything. I just think we need to talk about it."

"Look, it was a kiss, all right? Okay, two kisses."

"Yes, I know. The question is, why?"

"Why? You want me to analyze something that was completely—"

She straightened to her full height, which was still several inches shorter than he was. "I am going to assume that it was a spontaneous reaction."

"Do you always have to make more of a situation than it really is?" Without giving her a chance to respond, he jammed his pitchfork into the suddenly yielding soil and headed back to the house. "I'll tell Arlen you're ready to go," he called over his shoulder.

"Fine," she snapped. "I'll be in the car."

Chapter 24

It took the MDS team only ten days to complete the work on John's house, and by the first week in October, the property was ready to be listed on the market. Hester couldn't help but marvel at the crew her father had put together—a small army of experienced carpenters along with an electrician and a plumber. At her father's subtle insistence and with his promise that he would make sure that John was busy elsewhere, she had asked Emma and Jeannie and their daughters as well as Rosalyn to help her paint the restored rooms and clean the entire house after the workers were finished. Margery had shown up to help as well.

"It's a beautiful house," Jeannie exclaimed. "Wouldn't it make a perfect Rainbow House?"

"Not really," Emma said. "It's too far from town. How are the homeless men and women supposed to get here? Besides, there's only one bathroom."

As usual, Jeannie was undaunted by her sister's practical streak. "Well, it would make a great something. I hate seeing it torn down and yet another multistoried monstrosity going up in its place."

"The packinghouse would be a good place to sort the donated fruit once we start collecting it, and we could even make the marmalade there if we got the right equipment." Hester had been thinking about how perfect the space was for their project practically nonstop since she'd gotten the idea, but she only grasped that she'd spoken aloud when Jeannie squealed.

"It *is* perfect, and we have to find a place soon. I'm already getting calls from people wanting to schedule a date to have the volunteers come get their fruit."

"Same problem," Emma said as she stood back to check her daughter, Sadie's, work on the trim. "I thought we decided that because of people's discomfort with having homeless people in their homes, we were going to have them do the sorting and distribution and we were going to recruit young people to do the collecting. Again, how will people without any means of transportation get here?"

"I know, but. . ." Jeannie got no further.

"Emma's right," Hester admitted. "Even if the place were available—and it isn't—how are we going to transport the volunteers out here to sort and pack?"

Margery snorted. "Well, now, it's going to be a while before John can sell this place. I don't care what that fast-talking realtor says. In the meantime, how about I run a little ferry service? Collect folks down at the marina in town and bring them here by boat on the days you need them to work?"

"Samuel could bring people in his camper," Rosalyn volunteered.

Hester felt a prickle of excitement, but then she looked out the window and saw the realtor's FOR SALE sign prominently posted near the water. There was a mate to the sign posted by the road and another pointing the way from Highway 41. Besides, John would never agree to let them use the packinghouse even on a short-term basis now that the property was on the market. *Would he?*

"Hester could ask him," Rosalyn suggested.

"Ask who what?"

"Ask John if we can use the packinghouse until he sells. It would buy us some time before we had to put the whole project on hold for lack of a proper space to handle the sorting and such," Jeannie explained.

"He might just agree," Margery mused. "He's changed some these last weeks, actually shown some indication that he's begun to realize this going-it-alone thing may not be his best move."

"Do you want me to ask him?" Emma said softly. Emma was the only person who knew that John had kissed her. Her reaction had not been the shock that Hester had been expecting. Instead, she had asked, "Did you kiss him back?" And Hester had nodded.

"Thought so," Emma had said with a smug little smile. But when there had been no further contact with John, Emma had adopted the pitying look that was now on her face whenever his name came up.

"I can ask him," Hester said as she put the finishing touches on the wall she'd been painting. "But be prepared for him to say no."

"Where is he, anyway?" Margery asked. "I haven't seen him all day."

"I asked Dad to—"

"He went off with that realtor," Jeannie said. "I don't like that guy. He's so. . .slick."

"He's just doing his job," Emma said. "And speaking of jobs, it looks like we have finished here." She wet her finger with spit and scrubbed a speck of paint off Sadie's cheek.

"Ah, Mom," Sadie protested, and all the women laughed. Then they heard male voices downstairs.

"Looks like here's your chance, Hester," Emma said. "John's back."

"Hey, John, come see what a woman's touch can do for this place," Jeannie called.

John looked up the restored stairway, its carved wooden banister now gleaming with fresh polish, and saw the women gathered at the top. *All but her,* he thought. And then Hester stepped out of the large bedroom and joined the others. She was not smiling, but she met his eyes for the first time since the day he'd kissed her. On the other hand, she was wearing that expression that he'd come to know so well, the one she seemed to reserve just for him.

The one that shouted, *Let's get one thing straight, mister.*

He forced a smile and climbed the stairs. "Looks great," he said, glancing around. "Thank you. I—"

"Oh, you can't see anything from there," Jeannie said, taking his arm and leading him into the bedroom that had been his sleeping quarters before the hurricane. "Check this out."

The walls had been painted a pale blue, a softer version of the color of Hester's eyes, he thought, and he glanced at her. The woodwork and ceiling were white, and the wood floor that Samuel and Zeke had sanded and restored was a soft blond. The whole effect was one of "Come on in and rest for a while."

"This room alone would sell the place," Margery said. "Some young couple looking to start life together." She nudged his arm with hers. "Wait 'til you see the nursery down the hall." Subtlety had never been Margery's strong point.

"We should find you one of those old-fashioned white iron beds," Jeannie said. "And a wicker rocking chair over there to look out over the garden and—"

"He's selling the place," Emma reminded her. "He doesn't need to spend extra money on furnishings."

"Well, I've always heard that a house shows better when it's staged properly with furniture and all."

"Let's see the rest," John said, heading down the hall to the other two bedrooms. The larger one had been painted a melon color with the same accents on woodwork and floor. "Nice," he murmured and moved on to the smallest bedroom—a cramped, dark space that Tucker had used for storage and John had done little to change in the time he had lived on the property.

He stopped at the door, speechless. The women had transformed the space into a bright and welcoming oasis. Sunny yellow walls made the room look larger than he'd remembered. Simple lace curtains hung on either side of the single open window. It would indeed make a perfect nursery. The house that he had thought of only as a place to eat and sleep now had the feeling of *home.*

"I don't know what to say," he murmured. "I can't thank you

enough or think of how I will ever repay you for your kindness."

"Oh, we'll think of something," Jeannie said. He noticed how she directed this not at him but at Hester.

"Is anyone else starving?" Sadie moaned, and the women all agreed it was time to eat and headed back down the hall.

On the way they passed the tiled bathroom, where every inch had been scrubbed to a high sheen. A stairway led up to the attic, a cavernous space that could be converted to more living space, John thought. But as he followed the women downstairs and into the kitchen, he shook off any ideas he'd started to have about a real family buying the place. As the realtor had pointed out to him, vacant land on water was rare, and that rarity made it valuable, if he was willing to sell to a developer. He wondered if he could insist that the buyer name the development Walden. Or maybe a better name would be Steiner's Folly.

The women set to work preparing sandwiches for themselves and Arlen's team of workers, who were completing the landscaping outside. John had eaten his lunch in town with the realtor. He wandered outside and down to the packinghouse, where he knew he could have a moment to himself.

But he'd barely been there five minutes when he heard the side door open and turned to see Hester standing there in a shaft of sunlight. "John? Do you have a minute?"

"Returning to the scene of my crime, Hester? Could be dangerous."

She stepped inside the building and let the door swing closed behind her. "I don't think kissing a person has yet risen to the level of criminal activity," she said primly. But he couldn't help noticing that she kept her distance. Indeed, she moved away from him along the long worktable that ran the length of the opposite wall. He stayed where he was until she had circled the room and come back to stand near him. "I. . .we, that is, the planning committee for Rainbow House—"

He let out a relieved but disappointed breath. "It's always business first with you, isn't it, Hester?"

Her eyes flickered with irritation. "That's not. . .This is. . ."

"Just spit it out," he said wearily. "I'll do what I can."

Her eyes widened with what he could only describe as hope. "We would like your permission to use this space until you sell the property. The calls for our volunteers to go out and gather fruit are starting to come in, and we have no place to store and sort it, or make up the marmalade that we plan to sell—"

"Breathe," he said, placing his hands lightly on her shoulders as she sucked in air. "Okay, now start from the beginning."

Over the next hour Hester laid out the entire plan for how the program would work and how the packinghouse figured into the equation. As always, they debated various points and even argued over some of her ideas, but in the end he saw how it could work. Specifically he saw how it would benefit Zeke and the other homeless men and women he had met. But more than that, he began to see it as the perfect way to repay everyone who had given so freely of their time and talent to get his property restored and on the market.

"Okay," he said.

But Hester thought he was only giving in, so she continued making her case. "Look, I know this can't be a permanent solution, but. . ."

"I said okay, Hester. You can use the packinghouse."

It was such a delight to see the woman speechless for once that he couldn't help grinning at her. "Anything else?"

She turned to face him, studying his features for a long moment. She placed her hand on his cheek. "Thank you," she whispered. And then she did the one thing he was totally unprepared for—she wrapped her arms around him and rested her cheek against his chest. "Oh, thank you so much."

Tentatively he completed the circle of their embrace and rested his chin on the top of her head where her prayer covering met the center part of her hair. "My pleasure," he said.

The realtor was anything but pleased to arrive the following week for a showing of the property to find it buzzing with activity. John was in the kitchen watching Nelly and Agnes instruct a crew of homeless women in the process of turning baskets of whole fruit into jars of homemade marmalade. He'd suggested they set up this part of the program in the house since the kitchen easily provided everything they needed.

He'd heard the approach of what sounded like an entire motorcade and glanced out the window. The realtor had practically leapt from the lead car before it came to a full stop, ran back to say something to the occupants of the cars behind him, and then headed up to the house.

"John, I thought we had an appointment," Peter York said, his smile revealing overly white teeth and not quite reaching the hard glints of his steel-gray eyes. "What's going on?"

John ignored the question by asking one of his own. "Developers?" He nodded toward the two other cars, where men in suits had gotten out and were beginning to look around in the proprietary way that John hated, as if they already owned the place.

"From Tampa," York replied. "I told you that they were driving down today and that we would be here at eleven and that after they—"

"Okay. Show them around. I'll open the front door so you can come in that way to show the house, although I doubt they care what it's like. I'll be in the kitchen if you need me." He started back inside and heard York following him.

"Look, you cannot have these people around when I'm trying to show the property," he seethed.

"*These people* happen to be friends of mine, and as long as I own the place, I'll have anyone I like around, okay?"

"But John. . ."

Suddenly John remembered how the young man's eyes had fairly danced with excitement the day that John had chosen him to represent the property. At the price he had suggested, the young realtor stood to make a hefty commission. Clearly, at the moment he saw that commission going up in smoke.

"Look," John said, feeling a little sorry for him, "you said this place would sell itself, so why should it matter who is here or what they are doing?" He sniffed the air, catching the aroma of fruit mixed with spices cooking, and smiled. "Take your time, Pete, and there might be a jar of homemade marmalade as a bonus."

York winced, and then he noticed Zeke sauntering across the yard toward his clients and he took off to intercept him. John saw Hester standing outside the packinghouse, watching the scene unfold. He caught her eye and signaled that everything was all right. She smiled and headed back inside.

John stood for a moment staring at the spot where she had been. Ever since he'd agreed to let her use his place for the project, they had worked together in a kind of easy camaraderie. There had been no repeat of the embrace they'd shared, an embrace that had been interrupted by the sound of workers seeking the shade outside the building to enjoy their lunch. Shyly she had pushed away from him and thanked him again before running to the house to tell the others the news.

After that, she had come every day bringing others with her as they worked to set up the packinghouse. With nothing else to do, John had fallen into the habit of working alongside them and become part of the group that bantered back and forth in easy friendship as they worked together to install a new conveyor belt and build more counter space for the sorting and packing processes. More and more Hester would turn to him with some new idea and seek his opinion. More and more when she left at the end of the day, she would take a moment to find him and thank him again for loaning them the space. And more and more as he watched her pedal off, he felt the need to call her back, keep her close.

"You're not making this easy on the kid," Margery observed when John came back inside. She had taken to calling Peter York "the kid," and the way she said it John understood that it was not a compliment.

"He stands to make a boatload of money," John replied. "Making that kind of money shouldn't come easy." He picked up a dish towel and started to dry some of the marmalade jars that she'd been washing.

Margery grinned. "Some would say you're starting to have second thoughts about selling this place."

"And some would be wrong."

"You planning to stay around here after the sale?"

"I'll probably head back to Indiana."

To his surprise Margery burst out laughing. "And do what? Go back with your tail between your legs to those folks that shunned you? That's not you, John. Amish or not, that is not who you are, and that place is no longer your home."

"If I stayed I'd have to find work." He hadn't allowed himself to think about staying. It was what he wanted, but he hadn't seen any option other than to go back to Indiana.

"I'll hire you," she said.

John laughed. "Yeah, that'll work. I know so much about boats and running fishing charters, and I'm such a people person."

"You're improving on that last score, and the rest can be learned, but you've got a point." She put her wrinkled hand on his. "It's a serious offer, John. Give it some thought, and if not, then something's bound to turn up." And then she turned her attention to one of the homeless women standing just inside the door smoking a cigarette. "Get that poison out of this kitchen," she barked and shooed the woman out the door and followed her down the porch steps, passing Hester along the way.

"Hi," she said, wiping her brow with the back of her hand. "How are things going in here?"

"Coming along," John said.

"Do you have time for a walk?" she asked.

"Sure." He folded the towel and followed her outside.

Down near the pier they could see Peter York gesturing and pointing out something that had the businessmen looking anywhere but up to the house and yard, where John had to admit the scene was not exactly enticing to a prospective buyer. Zeke lounged under a tree, strumming his guitar, his long hair falling over his face. Nearby two men dressed in cast-off and out-of-season clothing unloaded baskets filled with oranges and set them on the conveyer belt that carried them into the packinghouse. Rosalyn in her traditional Mennonite garb and the toothless woman and her friend carried empty baskets out of the packinghouse and stacked them in the back of Samuel's beat-up camper.

"Not exactly good advertising for this place," Hester said.

John shrugged. "They aren't buying the people, or the buildings for that matter. What those guys want is the land and the location."

"Still, we're not doing you any favors here. Maybe if you know someone is coming to look at the place, we could shut down for that time period."

"And what? Hide in the attic?"

She smiled and ducked her head. "I was thinking more that we simply wouldn't come out to work that day. I mean, you know in advance, right?"

John shrugged. "Most of the time, not always. It's going to be fine, Hester." He cast about for a change in topic. "Did you get those ferns planted?"

"Not yet," she admitted. "I actually don't think there's much hope for them. I'm really sorry."

He shrugged. "As long as you kept them in water and shade, they should be fine. Besides, I have plenty more. How about I come over tonight after we close things down here and we get them in the ground?"

"Come for supper," she said. "I'll invite Rosalyn and Samuel."

He took her hand. "Does it always have to be a group, Hester?"

She looked up at him but did not pull away. "No, but if you are asking for a date, John Steiner, then ask."

"Okay. I'd like to come by and help you plant those ferns, and after that I thought maybe we could go for ice cream, chocolate."

She ducked her head, surprised that he had called her bluff. "Now you're talking my language," she murmured.

Hester felt like a silly teenager the way she was worrying over her hair and touching her cheeks and lips and wondering if John might kiss her again. *Grow up*, she silently chastised herself. She should be grateful that God had seen fit to let them become friends. Who would have thought that might ever happen given the way they had met?

But when she'd challenged him to call the evening a date, he hadn't backed down. Of course, he never backed down when challenged. She sighed. That was his way, and his way was going to make it impossible for him to sell his property if she didn't do something. After all, using his packinghouse had always been intended as a temporary fix so that they could get the project up and running. But it had worked out so well and John had been so accommodating that little thought had been given to finding a more permanent solution.

"Well, that will stop right here and now," she murmured as she gave her hair a final pat and went to her father's study to use the telephone.

"Jeannie?" she said when her friend answered. "Sorry to bother you, but I was thinking that we really need to be looking for another place to sort and store the fruit. I remembered that you had said Zeke's brother, Malcolm, showed an interest in the project. Do you think he might know of a space we could use?"

"But John's place is so perfect," Jeannie protested. "The season is upon us, and we have to act or wait until next year."

Hester told her about the realtor's visit that day. "When those men got back in their cars, it was clear that they had lost interest. They looked like they couldn't wait to get away. Like it or not, Jeannie, we are hurting John's chances."

Jeannie sighed. "I know. Okay, here's the number for Malcolm's office."

"Thanks," Hester said, jotting down the information. As she hung up the phone, she heard John coming up the front path. He was whistling and sounded like he didn't have a care in the world. Somehow that made Hester think that things might just work out after all—for everyone—and she closed her eyes in a silent prayer of thanksgiving before going out to meet him.

To her surprise he had arrived on a bicycle. He leaned it against the fence and made his way to her. "Ever tasted gelato?" he asked.

"No."

"Me neither, but I hear it's something pretty special, and I thought we might celebrate the restoration of the garden by taking a ride to town. There are a couple of places on Main Street that sell it."

"Where did you get the bike?"

"Zeke brought it by this afternoon." He picked up one of the buckets of ferns. "So where do you want these?"

They worked together in an easy silence until all the ferns had been planted and watered and he had helped her place the orchids so that they received the proper light and showed off their beauty to perfection. "My mom used to say she had a black thumb," John told her. "Couldn't grow a thing."

"But you lived on a farm. Surely she had a kitchen garden."

"She did. My dad planted it for her and tended it until he died; then I took over."

"My mom could get anything to flourish," Hester said. "She used to have a little herb garden out back and her orchids, of course. We'd hear her out there in the yard talking to them." She took on the singsong cadence of her mother's voice. "Now, look at you hiding there. Come on out here where you can get some sunshine, baby." She chuckled at the memory.

"You do know that you were doing the same thing when you were placing that last orchid," he said.

"I wasn't," she protested, but she saw in his smile that she had been talking to the plant.

"You like to keep that soft side of yourself hidden, don't you? Why is that?"

"I don't know what you mean." She felt a familiar defensiveness tighten her throat.

"Yes, you do," he said, stopping to lean on the shovel and meet her eyes directly. "When you think no one's looking, you let go a little. Like that day when the creek flooded and we got everybody to the church. I saw you with the children and your grandmother's neighbors. And out at my place when you're working with the volunteers from the homeless community, there's a kind of tenderness to you that doesn't always come out."

She stiffened. "Well, I'm sorry to disappoint you."

John sighed and set the shovel aside. "I'm trying to pay you a compliment, Hester. I guess I've been living like a hermit for too long, but I'm trying to tell you that when I see you in situations like that, like this, I realize why I can't seem to stay away from you." He held out his arms to her.

Silenced by the feeling of joy that seemed sure to overwhelm her, she walked into his open arms and rested her cheek against his chest. And for the first time in a very long time, she felt as if she had found the safe harbor that she had always thought she would find only in her work. "Thank you, John," she whispered. His answer was to tighten his hold on her. Then as she lifted her face to his, she heard Agnes Crowder calling her name.

"Hester, come quick. Sister has taken a terrible fall."

Chapter 25

Together Hester and John followed Agnes back to the Crowder house at the end of the cul-de-sac. They found Olive lying in the middle of the kitchen floor surrounded by shards of broken glass and an overturned stepstool. Her arm and hand were covered in blood, and her coloring was almost ghostly.

"Olive," Hester said as she grabbed two kitchen towels and folded them into a compress then knelt next to the injured woman.

"Stupid," Olive murmured, her eyes rolling back until only the whites were visible.

"Stay with us now, Olive." She was relieved to see that John was already on the phone, giving the ambulance directions. Agnes stood in the far corner of the kitchen, twisting her apron into a knot as tears streamed down her cheeks. "Agnes, do you have a first-aid kit?"

Agnes looked to Olive as she always did.

"Under the bathroom sink," Olive instructed, and Agnes scurried off to fetch it.

John hung up the phone and found a broom. He was sweeping the pieces of glass away from Olive when they heard the distant wail of sirens. Olive struggled to sit up.

"Stay where you are, Olive. We need to get this bleeding stopped and make sure you have no other injuries."

"Bossy as always," Olive snapped, but she did as Hester ordered.

By the time the EMTs rushed into the house, Agnes had brought the first-aid kit and Hester had the bleeding under control. She moved away and let the medics do their work, hiding a smile when they started shouting questions at Olive.

"Please lower your voices," Olive demanded. "We are not at a sporting event, and I do have neighbors that I do not wish to know my business."

The fact that there was an ambulance outside her house with its red lights whirling like a lighthouse beacon did not seem to enter her mind. But when the paramedics tried to help her to her feet and into a chair, it was Olive who cried out in pain. In the end it was decided that Olive should be taken to the hospital for X-rays to determine whether or not she might have fractured her hip.

"I'll come with you," Hester said.

"Don't be ridiculous," Olive said. "These young people are perfectly capable of handling the situation, Hester. Agnes, bring my purse and come along." But just as the medics were preparing to load the gurney into the ambulance, Olive grabbed Hester's hand. "Thank you for coming," she whispered. "Agnes was so very frightened."

Hester saw the fear that she had chosen to attribute to Agnes in Olive's eyes and knew that this was as close as she might ever get to receiving Olive's approval. She squeezed her hand. "I'm just glad I was able to help."

As they watched the ambulance drive away, John put his arm around Hester's shoulders. "You okay?" he asked.

She stepped away, suddenly aware that anyone observing them might take his comforting gesture for a sign of courtship, and in their society, that was not the way things were done. "I'm fine, but do you mind, though, if we skip the gelato tonight?"

"Not at all. I'll walk you home."

"Actually, I thought I would stay here and clean up the mess so they don't have to come home to it later." In spite of her concerns about the prying eyes of neighbors, she stood on tiptoe and kissed his cheek. "Thanks for helping with the garden," she said, "and this." She waved a hand to indicate the Crowder house, its back door still wide open and every light blazing.

"How about I help?" John said as he followed her back inside.

John was falling in love with Hester Detlef. The admission hit him like a thunderbolt as he peddled back to Tucker's Point later that evening. "Great timing," he muttered. "You finally find the perfect woman, and you have nothing to offer her. No visible means of support. No home, or at least not for long. No prospects for the future."

Of course once he sold the property, his prospects for a financial future would be decidedly better, but he had never stopped to look beyond the day when Peter York would present him with a buyer. If he and Hester were to marry, where would they live? What would he do to earn a living? He could work for Margery, but what did he know about fixing boats or running fishing charters? He knew how to work the land and make things grow, but this wasn't exactly farm country, and the idea that Hester might be willing to leave her father and the community of friends she had built in Pinecraft was ludicrous.

Marry? Talk about a ridiculous idea. Where did he get the arrogance to believe that she would even consider such a thing? That she returned his feelings at all? A couple of kisses? Some tender moments in her garden and later tonight when they'd gone to help the Crowder sisters?

"You are seriously losing it, dude," he said, quoting one of Zeke's favorite lines as he trudged up the steps to his house and went inside. He drank a glass of cold water and then headed for the small room off the kitchen that he had set up as his bedroom until the second floor could be restored. His Bible now rested on the small nightstand next to his single bed. He picked it up, but instead of opening it, he held it to his chest and closed his eyes.

"Lord, I have come to a crossroads and don't know which way to turn. In my life I have turned away from others so many times—and maybe in doing that I was also turning away from You in spite of my daily prayers and devotions. I am asking now that You show me the way." He found himself thinking of a joke that Margery had told him one evening as they sat together after sharing one of her suppers.

"There's a hurricane and this guy's house is totally flooded out," she'd said. "He's on the roof, and the water is still rising. A neighbor comes by in a rowboat and urges him to get in. 'No, God will rescue me,' he assures the neighbor. Then a FEMA crew comes by in a pontoon. Same thing. Finally a helicopter hovers overhead, and he sends that away as well."

"Not funny so far," John had muttered.

"So the guy drowns and gets to heaven. When he goes before God, he's really upset. 'Why didn't you save me?' he demands. And God says, 'I sent you a rowboat, a pontoon, and a helicopter— what were you waiting for?' "

He could still hear Margery's laughter as she slapped her knee and announced, "That one cracks me up every time."

John opened his eyes and thought about how God had sent him Margery and then Hester and her father and then Zeke. Each of them had changed his life over the last several weeks. He thought about Samuel showing up that day and leaving him the camper. He thought about Grady Forrest and his aunt Liz. "What were you waiting for?" he wondered aloud, truly getting Margery's message for the first time.

That night he slept better than he had in weeks. He had no solutions to his problems, just a new confidence that things would work out if he was wise enough to heed God's signs. He was up with the sun and had coffee brewing by the time Margery brought the workers to start their shift in the packinghouse and the Mennonite women began arriving to take over his kitchen to stir up more jars of marmalade.

But Hester was not with them.

"She had a meeting, and then she was going to the hospital to check on Olive," Rosalyn told him. "Her hip was broken after all. She's going to need surgery and then a lot of rehab therapy. She is not a happy person, and Hester is trying to do some damage control."

John was on his way to the packinghouse to see if he could be of help there when he saw a car coming up the lane. He waited for the vehicle to come to a stop and for the driver to emerge, a man who looked to be in his late forties and whose car and clothes left no doubt that he was a man of means. But when he saw John, he smiled and moved toward him with an outstretched hand. "Mr. Steiner? Malcolm Shepherd—Zeke's brother."

The resemblance was startling. This man embodied what Zeke would look like if he cut his hair and put on twenty pounds. "Hello." John accepted the handshake. "I'm not sure if Zeke's here yet."

"I didn't come to see my brother, John. May I call you John?"

John nodded and waited.

"I understand your property is for sale."

"That's right."

"How about showing me around?"

"You're interested?"

Malcolm laughed. "I'm a businessman, John. I hear about a prime piece of land on water and I'm curious."

"You called Peter York, the listing agent?"

"Nope. Thought I'd deal with you directly. If you and I work something out, then we can get York involved." All the time he was talking, he was looking around. "So do I get that tour or not?"

Over the next hour John walked his property with Zeke's brother. Malcolm asked a lot of questions and showed little interest in the house itself. But instead of being turned off by the presence of homeless people sorting fruit in the packinghouse or a bunch of Mennonite women cooking up marmalade in the kitchen, he seemed to find both processes fascinating.

"What's the marketing plan?" he asked Rosalyn as he watched her funnel warm marmalade into jars and then set them aside to cool.

"We've got orders from several businesses in Pinecraft, and we've secured a space at the farmers' market, just in time for the snowbird migration," she said with a smile.

"You might want to think about mail order—a website," he said, more to himself than to Rosalyn. Then he smiled and nodded toward the coffeepot. "John, could I trouble you for a cup of that coffee—black?"

"Sure." By the time John had poured the coffee, Malcolm was sitting out on the porch.

"You do know that you're sitting on a gold mine here in terms of land values," he said as he sipped the hot coffee.

"That's what Peter York tells me."

"So if you find a buyer, and you will—it's only a matter of price—what happens to all of this?" He gestured toward the packinghouse and then back toward the kitchen.

"They understand it's temporary," John said.

Malcolm was quiet for a long moment. And then he said the words that John knew could change everything. "What if it didn't have to be?"

"I don't understand."

"I don't know what my brother has told you about our family, John, but we've done all right for ourselves over the last several generations. Of course, you wouldn't know that looking at Zeke. Believe me, I've tried to help him out, but he takes the money and just gives it away."

"Zeke's a good man," John said and couldn't help the note of warning that crept into his voice as he defended his friend.

"He's salt of the earth," Malcolm agreed. "I wish. . ." He stared off toward the water for a long moment. Then he set the coffee cup on the porch railing and gave John his full attention. "Hester Detlef came to see me this morning. She can be quite persuasive, not to mention single-minded when it comes to something she's passionate about."

"Yes, that's true," John agreed. "She means well."

Malcolm stood up suddenly and walked to the edge of the porch, looking over the land. "Here's what I'd like to do. I'd like to buy your place and set up a foundation for Rainbow House right here. The house could function as the headquarters for the organization, and in time we can find a decent place in town for a shelter and soup kitchen, maybe a clinic. What do you think?"

It was Hester's dream come true, so what did it matter what he thought? If he could help make this happen for Hester—for Zeke. . .

"I think you've got a deal," he said, and this time he was the one offering his hand to Malcolm to seal the bargain.

"Okay then, I'll get in touch with this York fella so he can draw up the paperwork," Malcolm said as he shook John's hand firmly.

"Don't you want to know the price first?"

Malcolm grinned. "Already checked all that out on the Internet. Nice meeting you, John. Zeke's told me a lot about you. I want to thank you for watching out for him."

"He's done far more for me than I ever could have done for him," John said. He was thinking more about the hours of conversation and companionship that Zeke had provided than any physical labor his friend had contributed to restoring the place.

"We're going to need a director to oversee the whole project," Malcolm said. "Somebody with experience in running things, managing budgets and such."

Hester, John thought.

"Ms. Detlef suggested that you might want to apply for the job," Malcolm added as he walked to his car. He glanced back at the house. "No reason you couldn't turn that upstairs into living quarters and have the foundation offices and kitchen and such on the first floor." He got in and took one more look around and then grinned at John. "Thanks, John. I'll be in touch."

John watched the convertible drive back down the lane and disappear. Had he imagined what had just happened?

"What was my brother doing here?" Zeke asked, coming up beside him.

"You were here all the time?" John asked.

Zeke shrugged. "Sometimes Malcolm can be a little much to take," he said. "I like to keep a low profile until I know what's on his mind."

"He just bought this place."

Zeke's expression reflected disappointment, anger, and sadness in rapid order. "Sorry, man," he said softly as he clutched John's shoulder. "I know it's what you need, but I always felt it wasn't what you wanted."

"He's buying it for you, and the others. He's going to set up a foundation for Rainbow House. Hester talked him into it."

"You mean, he's not going to shut us down and rip the place apart?" Zeke was incredulous.

"It's all staying just the way it is," John told him. Almost before the last word was out of his mouth, Zeke had taken off, running toward the packinghouse. A moment later, John heard shouts of joy echoing across the yard.

He thought about going back up to the house to tell Rosalyn and the others the good news, but he knew that Zeke would take care of that. There was only one other person who deserved to know what had happened as soon as possible. John mounted his bike and headed for the hospital.

Hester had finally succeeded in persuading Agnes to leave her sister's bedside and go home to get some much-needed rest by promising that she would stay with Olive until Agnes returned. Since Olive was dozing, she busied herself searching the classifieds for possible alternate locations for Rainbow House. Malcolm Shepherd had finally agreed to drive out and look at John's place, but that was as much of a commitment as he was willing to make. And as her father had reminded her, he was an outsider and a businessman. What was in this for him?

She circled one property on the north end of the city, but then saw the asking price per square foot and knew that the rent alone would eat up any profits they might acquire. She sighed and refolded the paper to show the next column.

"What are you doing?" Olive demanded, although her voice was little more than a croak.

"We need to find a new space for the Rainbow House project, someplace we can sort and store the collected fruit at the very least."

"I thought John Steiner was letting you use his place."

"He is, but he's trying to sell his property, and, well, not everyone is as accepting of. . .some people as others are."

Olive received this news with a snort. When she fell silent, Hester assumed she had dozed off again.

"You've been spending quite a bit of time with that young man," Olive said after a moment.

"I—"

"Has he kissed you yet?"

Hester was so surprised at the question coming from this woman that she automatically gave the answer. "Yes."

Another snort. "Thought as much. I saw the two of you out there in the garden the night I fell. So where is this going?"

"Going?"

A long, dramatic sigh. "Are you in love with the man or not?"

"Really, Olive. . ."

"I thought as much." Her lips thinned into the familiar judgmental line Hester knew so well. "Do not let this opportunity pass you by, Hester Detlef. You are not a young woman anymore. Your prospects are limited. Trust me, I know. If you love the man and there's any possibility at all that he has feelings for you, then you must take the initiative."

Okay. This has to be the anesthetic from the surgery talking. "Olive, would you like a little water to—"

"Oh, don't patronize me, Hester. I promised Sarah that I would make sure that you didn't give your entire life over to caring for others to the detriment of your own happiness. Well, I have failed miserably at that vow until now. But seeing you with John the other night, I accepted that God had sent this young man to you and that it was my responsibility to see that you didn't miss the only opportunity you may have to marry and have a family of your own."

"I'm not quite that desperate," Hester said tightly. "I mean, I do have male friends, and I do go out now and again."

"For work, always for some project you've dreamed up," Olive said with a dismissive wave of her hand. "We are speaking of love here, and either you speak up now or forever hold your peace, as the saying goes."

Hester had the sudden thought that they were not really talking about her but perhaps about Olive's unrequited love for Arlen. "Olive, once John sells his property, there's no telling what he will do. He might even decide to go back to Indiana."

"Then it is up to you to see that he doesn't. If you love him, and he returns that love—"

"And that is the question, isn't it?" Hester said.

Olive's mouth worked to find a retort and came up empty. She closed her eyes and feigned sleep.

Hester smiled and got up to stretch her back. She walked out into the hallway and heard the ding of the elevator bell and then the whisper of the sliding doors and looked up to see John coming her way. Without hesitation she went to meet him, not caring whether he returned her feelings or not but wanting only to bask a moment in the warmth of his smile.

"What are you doing here?" she asked.

"I came to find you. I have some news."

"You sold the property," she guessed. He nodded and her heart fell. "That's—"

"To Zeke's brother, Malcolm."

"Malcolm Shepherd bought Tucker's Point."

"Not to develop. He's going to fund Rainbow House."

"But when I met with him, he seemed so underwhelmed with the whole idea. He asked me a lot of questions, and not once did he show the slightest enthusiasm for the project."

"Well, you must have said something right. He's going to establish the Rainbow House Foundation and use the house as the headquarters. You can stay, Hester. Everything can go on just as it is now."

She could hardly believe what he was telling her. She had prayed so hard for God to find a way for them to make the project a success, and now her prayers had been heard and answered. With no regard for the bustling throngs of medical personnel and patients and visitors moving up and down the corridor, she let out a squeal and leapt up to wrap her arms around John's neck. He spun her around.

"Stop that," Olive ordered.

But as soon as John set her back on her feet, Hester grabbed his hand and pulled him into Olive's room. She just had to share the news. Then Agnes appeared at the door, so they had to repeat the story again. "And John's been asked to be the director of the foundation. You can have an office right there in the house and live upstairs," she told him. "And maybe there would even be room for me to set up a free clinic," she said. "And in time—"

"So that inappropriate display of affection just now was because of the sale of your land, John Steiner?" Olive demanded. "Not because you proposed to this young woman?"

Hester's face felt as if it might melt under the sudden heat of her embarrassment.

"I was getting to that, Miss Crowder," John said. "Although I had thought to make the occasion something a little more inviting than a hospital room."

Olive snorted derisively while Agnes clapped her hands together and beamed.

"On the other hand, there's no time like the present, right?" John dropped to one knee as he held both of Hester's hands in his own. "Marry me, Hester Detlef."

"Oh, for goodness' sake," Olive groaned.

John ignored her. "I love you, Hester," he continued. "And with God's blessing, perhaps someday you will come to care for me in that way as well. But for now. . ."

Hester pulled one hand free and stroked his hair away from his forehead. "Get up, John," she said softly.

"First answer the question. Will you marry me?" he asked again.

She felt tears leak down her cheeks. "No," she whispered and fled the room.

Outside the hospital, Hester stopped, uncertain of where to go or what to do or how to think of the incredible string of events she'd just experienced. Her elation over the eleventh-hour rescue of the Rainbow House had been short-lived when John had suddenly announced his intention to propose marriage and then had actually done so. Was he making fun of her?

Of course, he had no idea what her feelings were—but still. Surely in his giddiness over the sale and the possibility that he might be offered a position that would support him, he had only thought to make Olive and Agnes laugh with his silly antics. His social skills had never been fine-tuned, especially after he'd spent over two years living as a near hermit. Maybe he'd thought she would join in the joke. But it was a cruel joke, and she had never thought him to be a cruel man. Stubborn, immovable on certain issues, but never intentionally cruel.

For she knew—had known but not admitted—that she loved him. She fled through the hospital lobby and out to the street. In minutes she found herself at the corner of Highway 41 and Bahia Vista. To her right was Pinecraft. She considered going home and letting her father console her, but her unhappiness would only make him feel bad as well. So she turned left and walked to Orange Avenue and then past the parking entrance to the botanical gardens and around the corner to the little beach that led into the bay.

Without bothering to remove her shoes, she waded into the calm shallow waters, uncaring of the way her skirt was getting soaked with salt water and would show the stains once it dried. Far more important was the fact that it was low tide and the exposed mud flats stretched out all around her. She could walk all the way out to the clam beds in water that never rose higher than her ankles. And she had the place to herself. There were a few boats anchored offshore, but the only sounds she heard once she moved downshore from the beach were the clinking of metal riggings against masts and the call of shorebirds as they strutted about collecting their afternoon meal.

"How can you possibly love him, Hester Detlef? You have known this man for a matter of maybe three months, and for much of that time you thought he was the most. . ."

And yet, presented with even the suggestion that they might make a life together, she had begun to think that it might actually become a reality. When she had seen him coming down the hospital corridor, his smile meant only for her, how her heart had sung with joy at the sight of him. She had practically run to him.

"Fool." She bit off the word and splashed on toward the clam beds, hoping that at least one of her favorite horse conches would be feeding there. Their sunset-colored bodies always made her smile, and right now she needed anything that might take away the bitterness she was feeling toward men in general and John Steiner in particular. At least here she didn't have to encounter the man, didn't have to think about what she might say to him the next time they—

"Hester!"

She turned long enough to see John leaning the bicycle that Zeke had brought him against a stretch of wire fencing and kicking off his shoes before he splashed into the bay and tried to cover the distance between them.

"Go away," she shouted and pressed on toward the clam beds.

"We need to talk," he replied and then grunted as he almost lost his balance and then righted himself and kept coming.

"You're going to cut your feet, and I am not in the mood to patch you up. Just go away, please."

"No."

"You are without a doubt the single most obstinate human being I have ever known," she grumbled.

"Well, at last we have something in common, Hester, because that goes double for you." He had come even with her now and dogged her steps as she moved on. "Why won't you marry me?"

"Because you don't really want to marry me. It was sweet

of you to want to entertain Olive and Agnes, but I get it that you proposed on a whim. Olive embarrassed you into it, and I certainly won't hold you to it."

"And maybe—just maybe—I meant it when I told you I love you." His tone was gentle so that the words came at her not as another jab of their argument but as more of a caress.

"How do you know?" She fought against the flutter of fresh hope that stirred within and bent to pick up a small, perfectly striped banded tulip shell.

"Because when I look to the future, I can't imagine meeting the challenges ahead without you there with me. Because, other than my mother, you are the only woman I've known who is strong enough to admit that she had dreams of her own."

"I'm not your mother."

"I'm not looking for a mother. I had the best. I'm looking for a wife, Hester, a partner I can share life with."

"Sounds like starting up a business," she grumbled, but inside she was holding his words close to her heart.

"It's a marriage, Hester, a sacred union."

They waded through the water side by side for another ten yards until they reached the clam beds. "Careful here. The edges of the shells are sharp."

He stayed where he was as she picked her way to an open spot and bent to pick up a large shell. "Hi there," she said softly as she turned the blackened shell over and was surprised when the coiled resident of the shell did not snake back inside and close its aperture to keep danger out. Instead, the creature stretched its sunrise-orange body outward, as if welcoming her. "Look," she murmured, holding the shell up so that John could share in this rare display of God's wondrous creation.

"It's beautiful," he said, and then as she bent to replace the shell on its feeding ground, he added, "But not half as beautiful as you are, Hester."

It was not the way of her people or his to offer such compliments. They came from plain stock, simple people who found beauty in serving God. And yet she could not help but rejoice that this man whom she had come to love found her pretty.

"We should get back," she said softly as she picked her way around the sharp edges of the clams until she was standing with him on a sandbar. "By now no doubt Olive has spread the word of the debacle she witnessed."

She turned to go, but he stopped her by taking her hand and weaving his fingers between hers. Then he lifted both their hands to his lips and kissed hers. "Hester, I believe that everything that has happened for me these last two years has been leading me to this moment, to you. I believe that God has brought us to each other. I know that separately we can each do good, but together just think what we might accomplish." He touched her cheek. "I love you."

She looked up at him and saw in his gaze what she knew she could not hide in her own. She loved him, and in that moment she saw as clearly as if she were gazing into a mirror that he did indeed return that love. "Marry me," he whispered.

"Yes," she answered.

And when he kissed her, she knew that he had been right, that this was right and that God had indeed led two strangers to find each other so that they might travel the rest of the way together.

DISCUSSION QUESTIONS

1. Which character(s) would you say were the strangers and which were the recipient's of gifts? What was the gift offered and received?

2. Hester Detlef seems to be quite self-assured and comfortable in her role as a community leader, but inside, is she really so confident about who she is and how she views her future?

3. In the early chapters of the story, John is a man who has turned away from many aspects of his life—name them and discuss why and how he turned from them.

4. It often happens that a secondary character will be one that the author feels a special affection for. For me in this story that character was Zeke Shepherd. In what ways do you think that Zeke had a positive impact on John?

5. All too often people hide behind masks—their jobs, their role in the family or the community, etc. Which characters in this story were masking their true hopes and desires? How did they finally remove the mask?

6. This story starts with a terrible hurricane that leaves a great deal of destruction in its path, and it is the aftermath of that hurricane that forms the backdrop to the story and the decisions the characters make along the way. Have you ever had a "hurricane" in your life when it seemed as if all was lost? How did you find your way out?

7. Faith is a theme that flows throughout the story—but is illustrated in many different ways. Give some examples of how faith influenced the decisions characters made as the story progressed.

8. In many ways, Hester and her friend Emma had become strangers. How do you think that happened? How did they find their way back to the friendship they had once treasured?

9. Have you ever had a friendship that faltered and perhaps even died? What are the things you miss about no longer having that friend in your life? Are there steps you might take to rekindle the friendship as Hester and Emma did?

10. Hester and Olive seem to be anything but friends, and yet by the end of the book, they have resolved their differences—or at least decided to accept each other for who she is. How did that come about?

A Sister's Forgiveness

Dedication/Acknowledgments

For my wonderful new friends in Sarasota:
You know who you are,
and you know that I could not have done this without you.

Contrary to the Hollywood image, writers rarely work alone. Stories evolve, and for fiction to come alive there must be a foundation in fact. As the saying goes, it takes a village. Here are the generous and supportive and inspiring "villagers" who walked with me every step of the way as this story unfolded:

My agent, Natasha Kern—every story that sees the light of publishing begins with her. She keeps me moving forward by her belief in me and her sometimes very necessary cheerleading to keep me going.

Editor Rebecca Germany gave me the wings to try something I had never tried before, and I will always be grateful to her for that generous gift. I am also indebted to Traci DePree, who in editing the manuscript found ways—large and small—to make it better.

My writing critique group—Donna, Katie, Karen, and Kathleen—read first (and second and possibly third) drafts and were honest enough to say what they thought and suggest solutions to the problems they uncovered. And when they saw the result, they made me smile all over with their enthusiasm for the story.

Members of the Florida Mennonite community located in the unincorporated community of Pinecraft in the heart of Sarasota continue to offer their support and wise counsel. Rosanna and Tanya read the pages and corrected me when I went astray from what people of their Mennonite faith would say and do. Doris and Grace shared breakfasts and lunches with me where we talked about the story and how best to bring it to life.

And for this story, I was so very blessed that the guy who cuts my hair knew an attorney who knew others in the justice system of Sarasota who each generously gave of their time, expertise, experience, and support for the project. They have all requested anonymity, but there are no words adequate enough to thank them.

Prologue

Tessa

Trapped.

Her mind reeled with the possible solutions. She could remain where she was until someone came along, but she was in a lot of pain. And maybe like the guy who fell into the canyon and had to cut off his own arm, she would be better off getting out of this mess herself.

Vaguely she remembered hearing a lot of shouting—both before and after the fact. After all, by the time the shouting started, there was pretty much nothing it could change about the reality that the car was going to hit her.

No, that wasn't exactly true. On this day after their annual family picnic, on her first day of high school, she'd come out of the house to wait for her cousin Sadie. Down the block a car had turned the corner going fast. Too fast. It hit a patch of water and started to skid, and then it righted itself, although it was still on the wrong side of the street. Then her dad came outside fooling with the umbrella, and she'd started toward him, assuming the erratic driver would continue on down the street. She was smiling because her dad never could figure out how to open an automatic umbrella.

But then he had shouted at her and pushed her away. She'd

first thought he was just irritated about the umbrella and getting wet, but then she realized that the crazy driver had turned into their driveway.

The car had suddenly fishtailed—an image that oddly worked under the circumstances—the car as big as a whale flipping its back end to find balance in the pouring rain. And in an instant, Tessa saw the reason for the erratic driving. Sadie was at the wheel, but her hands were in the air, and Tessa thought she could hear her cousin screaming along with her dad.

"The brake," she mentally shouted now, but words failed her as she saw the car coming at her. It struck her, lifted her, and then dropped her hard to the ground.

For reasons she didn't understand, she had put out her hands as if to stop the car. Foolish, pointless gesture. She heard her dad yell her name, and that was when everything went silent—and dark—and she felt herself sinking, fighting to stay afloat but being dragged under.

It was only yesterday they had all gathered for the family picnic. . . .

. . .the day had been sunny and beautiful

. . .but in the night had come the rain

. . .and it was still raining so hard

. . .and Sadie was screaming

. . .and her dad was yelling at someone to call 911

. . .and the bulk of the car was there, silenced at last, but the heat from its engine warmed her

. . .and she could feel her father's strong arms cradling her and hear his voice intermittently soothing her and urging her to stay with him

. . .and then her mother was there, too

. . .and a lot of other people—people she didn't know

. . .and everyone was so very upset

. . .and she wished she had her journal and Grandpa's pen so she could write to them—especially her mom and dad—and tell them it would be all right.

Part One

"Blessed are those who mourn,
for they shall be comforted."
Matthew 5:4

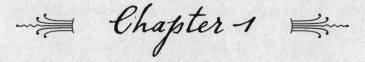

Chapter 1

Emma

Emma Keller had lived in Pinecraft, Florida, her whole life. And from the time that she entered her first year of school, her large extended family had gathered at the beach to bid farewell to the summer and gear up for the busy school year and tourist season that lay ahead. It was in many ways her favorite time of the year. Now, as mothers themselves, she and her younger sister, Jeannie, had assumed responsibility for organizing the day. There was just one problem—Jeannie was nowhere to be found.

Typical, Emma thought, but she was smiling. Her younger sister was such a treasure in the lives she touched, and Emma was certain that wherever Jeannie was, she was making someone's day a bit brighter.

"Mom will be late," Jeannie's fifteen-year-old daughter, Tessa, announced as she helped Emma lay out the food for the noon meal. Around them a dozen other cousins, aunts, and uncles were all pitching in to cover the tables, tend the smaller children, and start fires for grilling the chicken and hamburgers. Emma took a mental roll call and realized that her daughter, Sadie, was also nowhere to be found.

"And have you seen Sadie this morning?" she asked her niece.

Tessa hesitated. "She went somewhere with Mom."

"Wearing her clothes or yours?"

Tessa grinned. "Hers." It was no secret that Sadie often longed for the more liberal traditions of the Mennonite faith practiced by her cousin's family. To that end, she had been caught more than once borrowing Tessa's clothes. The girls were a year apart in age but close in size. And it only made matters worse that Jeannie condoned this behavior.

"Give Sadie a break, Emma," Jeannie would say. "She's got to try her wings a little, test herself. Have a little faith in the way you and Lars have raised her. She'll be fine."

For generations, Emma and the rest of her family had dressed in the traditional garb of their conservative faith. The females wore small-print dresses with long or three-quarter sleeves and a skirt that reached at least midcalf. For males, it was a collarless shirt and black trousers held up by suspenders, sometimes with a jacket or vest.

As a girl, Jeannie had dressed as plain as Emma. Then she married Geoff Messner, a high school coach from Sarasota. When Geoff agreed to convert, the couple had joined a more liberal branch of the faith. Now Jeannie dressed in the same clothes worn by any respectable non-Mennonite woman seen shopping on Main Street. And Jeannie did love to shop. Just last spring she had given Sadie a denim jacket with colorful stitching that she'd only worn maybe half a dozen times. It had quickly become Sadie's favorite item, and she rejoiced in any day or evening cool enough to wear it. Emma would not be surprised to see her daughter wearing it to the picnic despite predicted temperatures in the mideighties.

Emma and Tessa worked in tandem organizing the food into categories—salads, casseroles, meat dishes, and desserts— and Emma couldn't help but reflect on the differences between her daughter and Jeannie's. Tessa was quiet, reserved, and—in Emma's son, Matt's, words—a brainiac. A sweet girl and an honor student with a maturity that made others—including sixteen-year-old Sadie—turn to her for advice. It was impossible not to marvel at Tessa's genuine selflessness and attention to others. She had inherited that from Jeannie, of course, but on a whole different level.

"Here they come," Tessa said, nodding toward her mother and Sadie as the two of them crossed the park, arm in arm, whispering to each other like schoolgirls. "Looks like they have a secret," she added without an ounce of envy. "Did you bring the pies, Mom?" she called, and Emma knew by the way Jeannie clapped a hand over her mouth that she had completely forgotten her one job—to pick up the pies their eighty-two-year-old grandmother had baked.

"I'll go get them," Emma said.

"On your bike? No, you stay," Jeannie said. "Geoff can go." She waved to her husband and headed across the park to where he was helping the other men rearrange heavy wooden picnic tables.

"Geoff's busy," Emma said as Jeannie came closer.

"Em, it will be hours before we serve the pies, so stop being such a worrywart and let me handle this, okay?"

"Okay." It was true. Emma was given to worrying. Once when she had been especially concerned about Sadie's admiration for a group of teens that she had met at a non-Mennonite gathering, she had turned to Jeannie in frustration. "Don't you ever worry about Tessa? I mean, right now she's okay, but as she gets older and has more contact with outsiders. . . ?" she'd asked.

"You worry enough for both of us," Jeannie had assured her, and then she had tweaked Emma's cheek. "Thanks for that," she'd added with a grin.

But Emma was all too aware that life could be hard, especially for children growing up in a society that was estranged from the outside world. And especially when they lived in a community on the very outskirts of that world, crossing its boundaries many times a day as they went about their business. She and Lars had decided to allow both Sadie and her fourteen-year-old brother, Matt, to attend the nearby Christian Academy for their high school years as a way of exposing them to the ways of others without losing the focus on their faith in the process. But she still worried. How would her children fare as adults? Would they be content to follow the stricter faith that she and Lars had raised them in, or would they—like Jeannie—want more freedom, more assimilation with the outside world?

"Hi, Mama," Sadie said, giving Emma a sidelong glance meant to gauge just how much trouble she might be in for being so late.

Where were you? were the words that sprang to Emma's lips, but she swallowed them, heeding her husband's advice to temper her first impulse in favor of a more diplomatic approach. "Oh Sadie, there you are. I was looking for you," she said as if she'd hardly noticed her daughter's tardiness. "Could you please slice those loaves of bread and set them in baskets—one on each table?"

Sadie blew out a soft sigh of relief and sat down on one of the benches to slice the bread. "Sorry I was late," she murmured.

Emma understood that Sadie wanted her to ask what had kept her—clearly her daughter was anxious to tell her something. She was fairly glowing with the excitement of whatever adventure she had shared with her aunt. But then Sadie could just as easily take affront to Emma's inquiry and refuse to tell her what was going on. Patience was the answer, as it so often was when raising teenagers, or so Emma had discovered. "You're here now," she said and tucked a wisp of Sadie's long hair back into place. "When you've finished slicing the bread, go find your brother and make sure he's set up the play area for the little ones; then you can take charge of watching them."

There was no doubt in Emma's mind that her son, Matthew, had already completed the list of tasks she'd given him. He—like his cousin Tessa—was very dependable when it came to such things. In some ways, Matt at fourteen was the more mature of her two children. It was Sadie she worried about despite Lars's assurances that both their children would turn out just fine.

"Can't Tessa do that?" Sadie begged. "She's so much better with the kiddies than I am."

"The children love you and you know it. You'll make a wonderful teacher one day, Sadie."

Sadie's face twisted into an expression of pain. "What if I don't want to be a teacher, Mama?"

"I thought—"

"What if I want to do something else—something more. . . exciting."

"Such as?" This sudden change in her daughter's outlook for the future gave Emma pause. From the time she was four, Sadie had talked of nothing else but someday being a teacher. "A nurse?"

Sadie's frown tightened. "There's more to life than teaching school or being a nurse or housewife," she protested.

"All noble callings," Emma reminded her.

"Sure, and for some people—like Tessa, for example—probably the very best thing. But for somebody like me. . ."

"You're sixteen, Sadie. You've got time."

"I want to go places, Mama," she replied as she filled baskets with bread and covered them with dish towels. "There's so much beyond Pinecraft."

Emma looked at her daughter. To Sadie the world outside the boundaries of their lifestyle was exciting and mysterious. To Emma it was frightening, a place where innocence could be crushed in a heartbeat. And yet she understood that to try to dissuade Sadie from her dreams would only make her cling to them more vehemently. "You've got time," she repeated. "Now please go check on your brother." Clearly weighing the pros and cons of the mundane task of slicing bread in favor of something that at least gave her the freedom to move around the park, Sadie took off at a run. As Emma watched her go, she couldn't help thinking that Sadie would make a wonderful teacher—and someday a wonderful mother, for she had inherited the best traits of Emma and her sister along with her father's wry sense of humor and easygoing manner. Lars was right. She was young. In a couple of years, she would sort everything out.

"What's up?" her husband asked, coming alongside her and nodding toward Sadie. "Why were she and Jeannie late?" His tone held no censure, just simple curiosity.

"Not sure yet, but the two of them have been up to something."

Lars shook his head and chuckled. "I assume we'll be the last to know."

"As usual," Emma said. She smiled up at the man she had

known since she was a young girl. The tall, thin boy who had lived across the road from her parents—an Amish boy then. His grandparents on his mother's side had been Swedish, and he had inherited the white-blond hair of that side of the family. But his eyes were the deep blue of the sea. Emma had fallen for him the minute she saw him.

He was the eldest of eight brothers and sisters, all of them gathering now in the park, surrounded by spouses and children of their own. When she and Lars were teenagers themselves, she had assumed that he would be drawn to the livelier—and prettier—Jeannie, but it was Emma whom he had courted, announcing to her his intention to marry her as soon as they were of age.

And in spite of her delight that he had chosen her over her sister, she had fired back that she would never marry an Amish man—especially one of Swedish heritage. She had told him that such a combination did not bode well for his ability to be flexible and open-minded like her father and brothers were. The very next Sunday he had started attending services at the conservative Mennonite church her family attended, and he converted just before their wedding.

"Our girl is coming into her *Rumspringa*," he said now of Sadie.

"That business of running-around time is from your ways," Emma reminded him. The Amish tradition was to permit children in their teens to have a time when it was considered all right to explore the more liberal ways of the outside world. The idea was that this would help them understand the serious commitment they were making when they decided to be baptized and become full members of the faith.

Lars shrugged. "Still, whether you believe in Rumspringa or not, she's got all the signs—restless, curious about the outside ways. It won't do to try to stop her exploring, Emmie."

"*Ja.* I know. It's just. . ."

"The kids will be fine," he assured her, smoothing the lines of her forehead with his thumb. "Both of them—look who they got for a mother." He waved to someone across the park. "Your folks are here—looks like your mama brought enough food to feed the whole group single-handedly."

"She always worries there won't be enough," Emma said, shaking her head as the two of them headed for the parking lot to help her parents unload the car.

"*Die Mutter und die Tochtor,*" Lars said with a chuckle.

Like mother, like daughter. Emma only wished that the same could be said of Sadie and her.

Chapter 2

Jeannie

The sun was setting by the time most of the extended family and their guests headed back to their homes scattered across the area. Some went by bicycle—the elders and single cousins—while those with children crowded into older model cars and drove away, leaving a trail of fine sandy dust in their wake.

Jeannie watched as her husband, Geoff, helped Lars and Matt reposition the picnic tables and fold the cloths covering them for Emma to wash. Tessa and Sadie were given the job of policing the area for any trash that might have been left, while Emma and Jeannie packed up the last of the food.

"All right," Emma said, drawing Jeannie's attention away from Geoff, "where did you and Sadie go this morning?"

Jeannie had been having second thoughts about her impulsive act all day. What had she been thinking to go behind her sister's back that way?

"Sadie didn't tell you?" she hedged.

"Don't dodge the question. You know she didn't, or I would have said something and she wouldn't be finding ways to avoid her father and me. So just tell me." Emma's eyes widened. "Did you buy her that skirt she's been admiring in that shop on Main Street?"

"It's her news. Just keep an open mind, okay?" Jeannie turned away without waiting for Emma to agree. She called out to the others, "Hey, everybody, sun's setting."

It was a tradition the two young families had adopted years earlier when they had become the unofficial organizers of the annual picnic. They were always the last to leave, staying to watch the sun slip beyond the horizon, marking the end of summer and the beginning of the school year for the children and in many ways a change of seasons for the adults as well.

In the coming week, Matt would start his last year at the small Mennonite school that all three children had attended for the first eight years of their educations. Tessa would start her first year of high school at the Christian high school where Sadie would be a sophomore, and where Geoff would take on the role of assistant principal in addition to his responsibilities as athletic director and coach. He was nervous about that, although he had applied for the position, citing their need for the extra income. He had also joked that maybe they ought to think about going back to the old, simpler—meaning less expensive—lifestyle that Emma and Lars followed.

Jeannie had tried not to take offense at that. After all, she and Geoff had agreed that she would be a stay-at-home mom when Tessa was born, participating in volunteer activities when there was time while focusing primarily on being a homemaker and parent. But over the years, they had gotten caught up in "stuff," as Geoff called it whenever he looked over the monthly bills.

Jeannie held her tongue, although she wanted to remind him that hosting the entire football team for meals several times a season did not exactly come cheap. And he was the one who had insisted they buy a four-bedroom house when it was just the three of them—and they knew it always would be.

She watched as Emma waited for Lars and their children and then saw her sister's family join hands as together they walked out to the beach. Although she would never admit it—not even to Emma—the truth was that Jeannie had always seen the ritual of the sunset as a bittersweet moment—sweet in the way that she and Geoff were so blessed with family and friends, bitter in the passing of time—Tessa growing up and moving closer to the day when she would head off to pursue interests of her own. The day when it would just be Geoff and Jeannie alone in that big empty house. She shuddered at the thought.

Tessa came alongside her, taking her hand as they headed down the narrow sandy path. Geoff was already on the beach, and when they stopped beside him, he wrapped his arms around Tessa's shoulders as he rested his chin on top of her head. Lars had his arm around Emma's waist and his free hand on Sadie's shoulder while Emma pulled Matt to her. Jeannie tried not to think about the fact that only she stood alone—unconnected to anyone by touch.

The two families waited in respectful silence as the orb of sun sank lower and lower, streaking the sky around it in vermilion and orange. And just as the sun disappeared, they all closed their eyes and silently prayed. It was part of the tradition, and usually it was a moment that brought Jeannie comfort, a sense of peace.

Not this time, she thought. She was too consumed with guilt over her impulsive act of earlier that day. Perhaps if she talked to Sadie. Perhaps she should forewarn Emma. *Perhaps I should have minded my own business.*

After the moment of silent prayer, they stayed awhile longer, reluctant to let the day go. Sadie, Matt, and Tessa strolled along the low tide line looking for sand dollars that might have washed ashore, while their parents scanned the horizon for any sign of dolphins. As dusk settled over the beach, they all walked in silence back toward the parking lot.

"Okay, Sadie-girl," Lars said. "Time's up. What's the big news?"

Jeannie saw Sadie glance at Tessa, who nodded encouragingly. Clearly she had already shared her news with her cousin. Of course she would. Despite the year difference in their ages, Sadie often turned to Tessa for support. But then Sadie looked pleadingly at Jeannie. "You tell them," she said.

"It's your news," Jeannie reminded her.

"Well," Sadie said, drawing out the word as she studied the ground, "how about I drive us home?"

"Oh Sadie, stop stalling and just. . ." Emma began; then she stopped and looked from her sister to her daughter and back again. "*Nein*. You didn't," she said softly.

"*Ja*," Jeannie admitted and knew from the way Geoff shoved his hands into his pockets and kicked at a stone in the parking lot that she had been right to regret her actions.

"Did what?" Matt demanded.

"I got my learner's permit today," Sadie told him. "Auntie Jeannie took me." She faced her parents with a hint of defiance. "I'm of age, and you said that I could get it this year. Dad even signed the form and got it notarized so it would be ready once you agreed, and. . ."

Jeannie found it hard to meet Emma's gaze. Her sister was speechless. For much of the summer, Sadie had begged her parents to let her get the permit, but Emma had put her off. She had never actually refused her, but she had found excuses for postponing the inevitable. Jeannie had pleaded Sadie's case to no avail.

"I thought maybe if," Jeannie said softly as she edged closer to Emma. "I mean, I know how hard this is for you and. . ."

You didn't think at all, she could almost hear Emma wanting to yell, but Emma would never start an argument and spoil the day for everyone. Instead her sister cleared her throat and turned her attention to Sadie.

"There will be ground rules," she began.

Sadie grabbed her hand and held on. "I know, Mama, and you don't have to worry a bit. I'll do anything—extra chores—anything."

Jeannie saw Emma glance over her daughter's head at Lars, seeking his counsel on what to do, begging him with her eyes to say something. He nodded and began listing the terms.

"If ever I see or hear from others that you were not wearing your seat belt. . . ," he said, leaving the possible punishment to Sadie's imagination. "And there is absolutely no using a cell phone for any reason when the car is in motion."

"Okay, Dad. I get it."

"I'm not finished. One scratch on person or vehicle, and if ever you get behind the wheel without either your mother or me. . ."

"Or Aunt Jeannie or Uncle Geoff?" Sadie interrupted hopefully.

Geoff held up his hands in the sign of calling time out in a basketball game. "Leave me out of this," he said laughing, but he was looking at Jeannie, his eyes questioning why she would do such a thing.

"You can leave me out of this, too," Matt declared, standing a little closer to his uncle, coach, and mentor.

"You're fourteen," Sadie reminded him. "Not an issue." She turned back to her parents. "So no driving without an adult in the car. . . ."

"A licensed and responsible driver," her father corrected.

Emma closed her eyes for a long moment. "All right, it's done, but you heard what your father said. One infraction, and you forfeit your permit and we do not have this discussion again until you are eighteen years old, understood?"

Sadie nodded solemnly then burst into a grin and hugged Tessa. "Oh, we are going to have so much fun," she squealed. Then catching the mood of the adults surrounding her, she hastened to add, "I mean, once I learn to drive properly. Just think, Tessa, I can pick you up for school, and we can—"

"Time enough for you to daydream later," Lars said gently. "It's getting dark, and the no-see-ums are out in force tonight. Let's get home before they eat us alive."

"Have their own picnic," Matt chortled, nudging his uncle with his elbow as Geoff put his arm around Matt's shoulders.

The two families gathered up the last of their belongings and walked across the park to their cars, the men in the lead with Matt, the two girls, their heads bent close whispering excitedly, and Emma with Jeannie.

"I know I overstepped," Jeannie said. "I just thought—I guess I didn't think. It's just that Sadie is like my own daughter just as Tessa is like yours, and. . ."

"Sadie is not Tessa," Emma replied, her voice tight.

"Meaning she's not my daughter?" Jeannie said defensively.

"Meaning she's not the *same as* your daughter." Even in the dark, Jeannie knew that Emma was struggling to remain calm.

"In spite of the fact that she's younger, in many ways Tessa shows more maturity and responsibility than Sadie did at her age—than Sadie does now. Sadie is like you, Jeannie—she lives in the moment, and sometimes that's a wonderful trait. You, for example, have moved mountains with that attitude."

"And the problem is?"

"Sadie is not only not your daughter—she is also not you. Don't get me wrong. I love that she has your free spirit and ability to reach out to others. In time I hope all of that will be tempered with a certain wisdom that comes with experience and age, but right now. . ."

"Okay, I see your point," Jeannie said as the full tsunami of guilt at her impulsive act washed over her, spoiling the day. "Geoff is always saying that I need to think things out more carefully." Jeannie glanced over to where her husband was talking to Lars. She tried to gauge Geoff's mood, but he had his back to her. "I seem to disappoint him a lot these days."

"How are things?" Emma asked, following her gaze. Emma's tone had gone from tight to sympathetic in a heartbeat. "I mean with you and Geoff."

Emma was the only person Jeannie had talked to about the recent problems in her marriage. For the last several months, she and Geoff had struggled to find their way. He had spent long hours at the academy, and she had gotten more involved in her volunteer work. Emma had noticed—and asked.

"We're. . . Things are a little. . . It's better," she said, but her response sounded unconvincing even to her.

"But?"

Jeannie forced a smile and waved off the question. "It's all the pressure he's under—the new job as vice principal, the start of a new football season. You know how intense he can be when it comes to his work."

But Jeannie understood that her husband was something of a mystery to her family. He had not been raised plain, and while on the surface Geoff was a gregarious and outgoing man, there were times when he could be withdrawn and come across as aloof, even cold. "We just need time," she whispered, wondering who she was trying to convince—Emma or herself.

Emma's strong arms came around her, drawing her close. "You've had a rough road to travel lately. I'm sorry I haven't been there more for you."

"Are you kidding? You're the one constant I know will always be there for me—supporting me—and hopefully forgiving me?"

Emma laughed and released her. "Don't pull that baby sister act on me. You messed up, and you know it."

"Yeah. I did."

"Are you ladies coming?" Geoff called from the parking lot. He was standing near a lamppost, and Jeannie saw that he was smiling, but still a hint of impatience came through the smile.

"On our way," Jeannie called back as she linked arms with Emma. "So, we're okay?" she asked.

Emma pulled her a little closer. "We're fine," she assured her. "Just promise me that when Matt is old enough to drive, you'll. . ."

". . .tell you before I take him to get his learner's permit—got it." She patted Emma's hand. "Wasn't it a wonderful day?"

Emma hugged Jeannie, and in that hug was forgiveness. "It was a very special day—one we'll hold onto for a long time."

Jeannie giggled. "At least until this time next year—just wait and see what surprises I have planned for you then." She took off running, and Emma chased after her as they had so often done as teenagers. They were still laughing breathlessly when they reached the cars where Lars and Geoff and the children stood waiting.

Chapter 3

Tessa

Being an only child had its advantages. It also had its pitfalls. Like when a kid's parents weren't getting along. Lately Tessa's mom and dad had seemed like they were heading down different paths. Her dad was all about his work and was worried about finances more than usual. Mom, on the other hand, seemed to go the other way. She was always inviting hordes of people to the house for suppers or cookouts and such, like she needed to fill the house with any warm body she could find.

While they didn't fight like some parents did—shouting and such—the way they had gotten so quiet around each other was even more disturbing.

While working on a report on the Clinton presidency, Tessa had come across a photograph of Chelsea Clinton walking between her parents when their marriage was pretty much in the tank. Chelsea was holding hands with her father on one side and her mother on the other as if she and she alone were the link keeping their family together.

Tessa was sure that things with her parents weren't anywhere near as bad as they had been with the Clintons, but still. . .

Of course, she wasn't really an only child in the usual sense. Her mom and Aunt Emma were so close that it really was like

347

having two moms plus siblings in the form of her cousins, Sadie and Matt. The two families did practically everything together, and the three kids were back and forth between the two houses so much that they kept clothing and other personal items at each other's houses.

Of course now Aunt Emma was upset with Mom, with good reason as far as Tessa could see. What had given her mom the idea that taking Sadie for her learner's permit behind Aunt Emma's back was anything like a good surprise? Tessa saw it as evidence of her mom's desperation. She had a pattern of going overboard when stuff was going on that she couldn't control, like whatever was happening with Dad. And because Aunt Emma was her mom's best friend as well as older sister, Tessa had to believe that she would understand and eventually everything would be all right. Still, in her humble opinion, it had been a really bad move.

She sat in the backseat of the car, watching her parents for signs of healing. Surely the sunset on the beach, if not the tradition of the annual family gathering, had given them pause for thought. She waited, hoping the silence was a sign of calm rather than indifference. As usual her mom made the first move.

"Nice day," she murmured in a voice Tessa knew was for her dad's ears only. Once upon a time, he would have glanced over at her and grinned, maybe taken her hand in his, even kissed her knuckles. They had always been touchy-feely that way, to the point that sometimes Tessa felt as if they had forgotten she was even in the car. But not tonight.

Tonight he just kept driving.

Her mom turned in her seat, restrained by the seat belt from making full eye contact. But her smile was that fake one that she used when she was nervous. It dawned on Tessa that her mom was as mystified as she was by the chasm that stretched between the occupants of the front seat.

Okay, so she had to do something—anything to break the tension. What would Chelsea do? She tried to imagine what the former president's daughter would have said to her parents. Would she have chattered on about her life? Or would she. . .

Mom was talking—something about being ready for the first

day of school—a topic that Tessa understood was of far greater importance to her parents than it was to her. Even her dad. . .

That's it. I'm starting a new school. Dad's starting a new job there. . . . Instinctively she knew that Chelsea would focus on the obvious connection among the three of them—school.

And lo and behold, it worked—sorta, kinda—at least with her mom.

Chapter 4

Jeannie

Once again she had messed up. And although she truly believed that Emma had forgiven her, Geoff was a different matter. Leaving Jeannie out of the family circle while they all watched the sunset was about as clear a sign as he could have given her that things between them were not good. She didn't think for one second that it was intentional. Geoff was just terrible at hiding his true feelings. If he was upset, she knew it, and if he was upset with her, then he would usually take the easy way out and focus all of his attention on Tessa. The tension in the car was so thick it would take a chef's knife to cut through it.

Jeannie drew in a deep breath, squeezed her eyes shut, and sent up a silent prayer. "It was a nice day," she ventured as Geoff steered the car around the maze that was St. Armand's Circle until they reached the turnoff that would take them across the Ringling Bridge toward home.

He made a sound that could be interpreted either as agreement or indifference.

Silent treatment alert, Jeannie thought and turned in her seat to talk to Tessa. "Have you got everything you need for tomorrow, Tess?"

"Pretty sure I do—at least everything on the list the school put online."

"Excited?"

Tessa shrugged. "You know how it is, Mom. Starting a new school year is always a little exciting."

"Well, it's a blessing that you'll have Sadie there to show you the ropes."

Up to now, Tessa had attended the small Mennonite school that Jeannie and Emma had attended as kids. It was the one piece of her past that Jeannie had insisted on keeping after she and Geoff joined the more liberal branch of the faith. At the little Mennonite school, students of all ages worked at their own pace, moving from level to level as they completed the required work. Jeannie had such wonderful memories of her years there, and when she realized that Tessa was a shy, studious child, she had persuaded Geoff that attending her old school—at least until Tessa was ready for high school—would be an advantage.

"Dad?" Tessa leaned forward so that her face bridged the space between her parents.

"Hmmm?"

"If it's okay for the first day, I'd like to bike to school with Sadie."

Geoff chuckled, and Jeannie felt herself relaxing slightly. Leave it to Tessa to put him in a better frame of mind. "Not cool to arrive with the vice principal?"

Tessa giggled. "Not cool at all, but very cool to arrive with one of the popular kids."

"I'm crushed." He sighed dramatically, and Jeannie and Tessa both laughed.

Suddenly the tension that had held them all captive evaporated like the morning fog as Geoff pulled the car onto their driveway. Together they piled out and started unloading the picnic supplies and lawn chairs and other equipment they had hauled to the park. Tessa ran ahead of them to put away leftover food in the kitchen while Jeannie and Geoff took care of storing the lawn chairs in the garage.

"Looks like rain," Geoff said, checking the western sky that still held a hint of light.

"Smells like it, too," Jeannie agreed as she slipped her hand into his. "Maybe it will cool things off." She felt his fingers tighten on hers.

They stood together looking up through the giant fronds of a cluster of palm trees toward a starless sky. "Is Emma okay?"

Jeannie didn't need to ask what he meant. "She was upset—rightly so. Oh honey, I realize now that I shouldn't have agreed to take Sadie, but I was sure that Lars was trying to find a way to convince Emma. He'd already signed the paperwork. He didn't want to disappoint her, and neither did I." She shrugged. "It just seemed like. . ."

Geoff sighed and wrapped his arm around her, pulling her close and kissing her temple. "Honey, by now you know that how things may seem to you may not always be the way they are for others. I mean, Emma must have had her reasons for delaying this, and even if you don't agree. . ."

"Yeah, I know. It's just that sometimes Emma can be so strict—our folks were that way. You'd think that would make a difference—that she would understand that in this day and age Sadie needs. . ."

"Sadie's not your child, Jeannie. I know that you love her—we all do. What's not to love? She lights up a room, but it's up to Lars and Emma to decide such things. They're her parents."

"You're right." She hugged him, and then trying to cling to the lighter mood, she added, "You're always so wise. I'm sure that's why the school board named you vice principal."

Geoff groaned. "Don't remind me."

"You're going to be great. The kids already love you, and the teachers and staff have great respect for you. You can't lose." She smoothed back his hair and saw the shadow of doubt cross his features. Geoff had always been her rock. "Why do you think Tessa turned out to be such a great kid? It's because of the example you set for her."

"She also has you. . .and Emma."

"But you. . ."

His smile won out over the worried frown as he shrugged off

her compliment. "So, here you are sending the two of us off to conquer new challenges," he said.

"That's right, and frankly I think we'd all better get some sleep. Tomorrow is going to be a busy day." She stood on tiptoe to kiss him, and she couldn't help being a little disappointed when he released her after a quick peck on the lips.

"Coming?" he asked as he started for the house.

"In a minute." She watched him go inside, heard the television come on. Things were better, she thought. Just not what they had been. She felt the first drops of rain and lifted her face to them before going inside.

Tessa had already put everything away in the kitchen, and Jeannie could hear her daughter upstairs in her room. In spite of assuring them she already had what she needed for school on the drive home, Jeannie had no doubt that Tessa was double-checking her backpack. When she was satisfied, she would come downstairs, set the backpack on the straight wooden chair by the back door, and then come to the den that did double duty as Geoff's office and the family's television room to kiss them both good night.

Jeannie took out a gift-wrapped package she'd been saving for this occasion and set it on the chair. Then she went into the den and perched on the arm of Geoff's chair while they watched a sports report together.

As she had predicted, only moments passed before Tessa came downstairs. "What's this?" she asked, coming into the den and blocking the television as she held up the present.

"Well, look at that," Geoff said. "Somebody left me a present."

"Dad, it has my name on the card."

"No kidding. So, are you going to open it or just wave it around all night?"

Grinning, she carefully untied the wide satin ribbon then rolled it around her fingers and laid it aside. She then opened each taped section of the wrapping paper, pressing the paper flat as she laid it on Geoff's desk.

"At this rate, we won't need to set the alarm because you'll still be opening your present when it's time to get up," Jeannie teased.

"The ribbon and paper are part of the gift," Tessa reminded her. "You taught me that." She laid aside the top of the box and then spread the white tissue paper inside. "Oh my," she whispered as she lifted out a handmade journal and an old-fashioned fountain pen. "I love them."

"We thought maybe you might want to start a new journal," Geoff said, clearing his throat as if it had suddenly filled with emotion. "And the fountain pen was your grandfather's."

Geoff's father had owned a small newspaper back in Iowa where Geoff had grown up. After Tessa was born, her grandfather had written her a series of letters with this, his favorite pen. He'd sent a letter to her on every birthday until his death a year earlier, when the pen had been given to Geoff. "Now it's your turn to write," Geoff told her.

"But write what? I have nothing to say."

"How about letters to us?" Jeannie suggested.

"You're kind of right here, Mom."

"I know, but you could write letters to us that we could read later—like when you're off to college or on your wedding day or when you have your first child or. . ."

"Stop it, Mom," Tessa said laughing. "You're going to have me living my whole life before I'm out of high school."

Geoff was laughing as well. He looked at Jeannie the way he used to look at her when they were courting. His eyes twinkled with that same surprise and curiosity that fueled her interest in him from their first meeting. She looked from Geoff to Tessa and grinned. For the first time in weeks, she felt sure that everything was going to be all right for them.

Geoff held out his hand for Tessa's new journal and flipped through the pages. "That's a lot of blank pages," he said. "I figure you'll have it filled up by. . ."

". . .Tuesday," Jeannie said, knowing that when Tessa started any new project, she became single-minded about finishing it.

"I'm going to start tonight," Tessa said when Geoff handed back the book. She clutched it to her chest, her eyes sparkling. "Thank you so much—it's perfect." She started up the stairs then turned back. "And, Mom. No peeking."

"Me?" Jeannie asked, pointing to herself. "Why would that even cross your mind?"

Both Geoff and Tessa rolled their eyes.

"Promise?" Tessa said, and it was clear that she was asking for a serious commitment.

"Promise." Jeannie placed one hand over her heart.

Satisfied, Tessa blew them both a kiss and hurried off to her room.

Jeannie was watching her go when she felt Geoff's arms come around her, his lips close to her ear. "Thank you," he whispered.

"I would never have violated. . ."

"Not for the promise," he said, turning her so they were facing each other. "For raising such a wonderful kid."

Suddenly shy, Jeannie fingered his shirt collar. "I didn't do it alone."

"But you're the one who has given her confidence and your gift for taking care of others."

Jeannie's heart was so full that she circled her arms around his neck and laid her cheek against his chest. "You make me so very happy—you and Tessa are my whole world."

She felt the rumble of his chuckle deep from in his chest as his arms tightened around her. When he spoke, his voice was so soft that she had to stay very still to hear him. "We're going to be all right," he said, and she couldn't help but wonder if he had meant to speak the words aloud.

She looked up at him and stroked his cheek. "I love you, Geoff Messner."

He grinned. "That's Vice Principal Geoff Messner," he teased.

"No. That's Geoff Messner, the best husband and father God ever created."

He kissed her then, and as they walked upstairs together arm in arm, Jeannie silently prayed the prayer she had prayed every night and every morning of her life. *This is the day the Lord did make; let me be glad and rejoice in it.*

Chapter 5

Emma

After weeks of sunny days with cloudless blue skies, the day after the annual picnic dawned with an unexpected and relentless downpour. Emma was making breakfast for the family, although she was well aware that whatever she prepared would probably be eaten on the run. Sadie was already on the phone for the third time that morning, and Matt could be heard banging around in his room, searching no doubt for the supplies that he and Emma had shopped for a week earlier.

She smiled and shook her head. As organized as their parents were—everything in its place—neither child seemed to have inherited that particular trait. Emma could almost imagine the disaster area that Matt's room would be after he left for school. Sadie's room would be no less messy. But in her room, the bed would be covered with rejected items of clothing. For a girl who dressed plain, she could come up with an endless number of combinations of tops and bottoms.

"We can't ride our bikes in this," Sadie moaned. "Dan says he could come by here and pick me up, and then we'd go get Tessa." She delivered this news in a tone that Emma understood was a plea for permission as she covered the receiver with one hand and waited.

Emma exchanged a look with Lars, and he nodded.

"The streets will be slick," Lars told her. "Tell Dan to drive carefully."

Sadie grinned and murmured something into the phone; then she giggled as she hung up and took a long swallow of her orange juice.

Emma turned back to the stove. She had wanted Lars to say that he would drive the girls to school when he took Matt. Dan Kline was a nice boy. He was also a senior and president of the student council as well as the quarterback on Geoff's football team. Emma could see no explanation why he had fastened his attention on Sadie—a mere sophomore. He was older—and by definition more experienced when it came to dating. Of course, that was the real problem—Sadie was dating the boy. Not in groups, spending time with him and his friends or hers, but actual dates—long walks or bike rides and such. Surely Sadie was too young for anything so serious.

At least Lars had stood with her on that one. He had told Sadie that unless they were attending a school or community function with them or Dan's family, she and Dan were to limit their time together to twice a week—during the day.

"Oh Dad," Sadie moaned now as she took a bite of the donut that Emma had gotten up before dawn to make as a special treat for the first day of school, "Dan's eighteen. He knows how to drive in rain."

Lars put down his newspaper. "Ja, und it's because he's eighteen that I worry," he said quietly. "Young men of his age tend to think they are indestructible and that anyone with them is as well."

Emma hoped that maybe Sadie's comment had raised enough of a red flag that Lars would reconsider. In their home, as in most conservative Mennonite homes, the man was the head of the household, and wife and children alike looked to him to make these kinds of decisions. But he picked up his paper again. Sadie rolled her eyes and then turned her attention to Emma. "How do I look?"

"*Sehr gut.*"

Sadie groaned and punched in a number on the phone that under most circumstances was kept in her father's workshop behind the house and used primarily for his business. It was a mark of the importance of this first day of school that Sadie was allowed to use the phone. "Hi, Auntie Jeannie, is Tessa ready?"

Sadie giggled at Jeannie's response. "What's she wearing?"

A beat and her expression turned pained. "Not the black ones. I love those boots."

Emma could hear Jeannie's laugh muted by the phone Sadie clutched to her ear.

"Okay, so tell her Dan is picking me up anytime now, and we'll be by for her in fifteen minutes." She sighed heavily. "I know. I know. Trust me, Dad has already made the point." She listened for a moment then blew her aunt an air kiss and hung up the phone.

Emma knew that she and Jeannie were in agreement when it came to Dan Kline. Although not of their faith, he came from a good family, and his parents were good Christian people. Dan regularly attended church and was an outstanding leader when it came to organizing other young people. But next year he would be off to college while Sadie had two more years of high school to finish. One of the things Emma and Jeannie had discussed more than once was that Sadie would be brokenhearted when Dan left and that they would need to help her mend.

"You mustn't get used to the idea of Dan picking you and Tessa up for school, Sadie." She stopped speaking and took a sip of coffee, hating the way she sounded so like their spinster neighbor, Olive Crowder.

"We won't," Sadie said as she gulped down the last of her orange juice. "But think of it, Mom. This is Tessa's first day at the academy, and think how the other kids will sit up and take notice when she walks into school with Dan."

Emma understood that at least on some level Sadie was sincerely doing this for her cousin. Like Jeannie, Sadie wanted Tessa's first day of high school to be special. It did not occur to either of them that Tessa really did not care about making a first impression socially. She had confided to Emma that she was far more concerned about whether she would be able to keep up academically with the other students.

Sadie looked out the window for the fourth time in ten minutes. Dan was running late, which wasn't unusual, but the last thing Emma wanted was for him to be rushing on a rainy day like this one. Just when Emma was about to suggest that maybe Lars should drive Sadie after all, a car horn beeped and Sadie grabbed her backpack. "That's Dan." Her voice trembled with excitement. She blew Emma and Lars a kiss as she flew out the door.

Emma watched from the kitchen window as Sadie scampered around the front of the car and climbed in. Dan had not gotten out to open the door for her; rather, he had leaned across the front seat and pushed it open. She heard Sadie laughing as the door slammed and Dan shifted into reverse, spinning shell gravel as he peeled out of their driveway.

"They'll be all right," Lars told her as he reached around her to put his cereal bowl in the sink.

"He's too old for her."

"Two years' difference," Lars reminded her. "We have four years between us."

"But that's different. We're adults. She's a child yet, and he's—"

"Sadie is a smart girl. This too shall pass," Lars said as he reached for his hat. "Matt? *Es ist spat*," he called as he passed the hallway that led to the bedrooms. "I'll take Matt to school, and then I'll be in the shop if you need me." He kissed her forehead. "Stop worrying," he advised.

After everyone left, Emma finished washing the breakfast dishes and then poured herself a second cup of coffee. Lars was right. Sadie was very good at sizing up people. And Lars had made an excellent point. He'd just turned fifteen when his family moved in across the street from Emma's. She had been eleven. She certainly did not need to be reminded of a time when she'd developed a crush on a handsome popular older boy—a time when she would have done just about anything he asked of her if he would just walk her home from church.

"Have faith," she murmured as she sat down at the kitchen table and reached for the phone.

Chapter 6

Jeannie

The first day of a new school year was always chaotic around the Messner house. Who was she kidding? Most days were chaotic around their house. But on this day, Geoff was especially anxious. He would never admit it, but Jeannie was well aware that he had hardly slept the night before, and the tension she thought they'd finally laid to rest was back, stretched like a wire between them.

He was running late and that made him even edgier and more impatient. And as was so often the case, it was her fault. It wasn't the first time in their sixteen-year marriage that Jeannie had put something that Geoff or Tessa needed in a place where she was sure to find it and then had promptly forgotten where that was. Only Tessa remained calm in the face of her parents' panicked conversation.

"Look in the bathroom," Jeannie shouted as she searched through the kitchen drawer designated as the catch-all for the bits and pieces of life that had no real home.

"Why on earth would you put the keys to the gym storage shed in the bathroom?" Geoff shouted back.

"Just look, okay?" Jeannie continued rummaging and muttering to herself. "I'd never put anything so important in here, so where are they? Think!"

"Why hide the keys at all?" Tessa asked as she completed her assignment of going through Jeannie's purse.

"Because the shed is new this year, and your father didn't want to add the key to his key ring until he'd had a chance to make copies for the staff. I had the copies made yesterday and then put the original and the copies"—suddenly her face lit in a relieved smile—"in our storage shed. Got 'em," she shouted to Geoff as she grabbed the keys for the small shed behind their house where they kept the gardening tools and other outdoor equipment.

"I'll get them," Tessa said, taking the keys from her and shaking her head at this latest example of her mother's skewed logic. "You make Dad his bagel." She slid her arms into her father's rain slicker, pulled up the hood, and wrapped the sides around her as she dashed across the yard.

By the time the sliced bagel popped up from the toaster and Jeannie was spreading on peanut butter, Tessa was back. She placed the keys on the table next to her father's travel mug and hung the key to their shed back on its hook. Geoff rushed into the kitchen and pocketed the keys as he pulled out a kitchen chair and threw his tie over one shoulder to prevent spilling anything on it. He took a long swallow of his coffee. "You look nice, sweetie," he told Tessa. "Ready for your first day of big-kid school?"

Tessa shrugged. "It's the same as any other first day, Dad—just another step on the ladder."

But Jeannie did not miss the way Tessa nervously smoothed her shoulder-length straight hair, tucking it behind her ears and then immediately flipping it forward again. She placed the bagel in front of Geoff and then brushed Tessa's bangs back from her forehead. "Dad's right," she said. "You look great—no one will guess it's your first day. They'll probably think you're a new kid moved here from some exotic location."

"Sadie's coming with Dan to pick me up," Tessa told Geoff as she slipped the straps of her backpack over her shoulders. "Is that okay?"

"Sure, sweetie." Geoff liked Dan a lot. The boy was Dan's star quarterback, and Geoff had a lot of respect for his talent on and off the playing field. But he couldn't keep a hint of disappointment out of his voice. Jeannie knew that when he'd seen that it was raining, he'd been hoping Tessa would change her mind and ride with him. Tessa wrapped her arms around Geoff's shoulders and kissed his temple. "Ah Dad, if it rains again tomorrow, then I promise to ride with you and all the rainy days after that—it's just that on the very first day. . ."

"Got it," Geoff said with a grin. "Can't start out arriving with the vice principal."

"You're also the coach, and other kids might think that's pretty cool," Tessa teased back. "Maybe when you wear your coaching clothes instead of the button-down shirt and tie. . ."

"Okay, okay, you win. Go ahead and make your entrance with your cool cousin and the quarterback today, but I'm going to hold you to that rainy day promise."

Tessa laughed, and as always the sound of it filled Jeannie with utter joy. This beautiful, intelligent, and incredibly kind girl was their daughter—their only child—and as much as she enjoyed Emma's children and was flattered by how much Sadie shadowed her, Tessa was a gift beyond anything that she and Geoff could have imagined. They didn't even regret the fact that they had not been able to have more children. The house was so often filled with cousins and Geoff's students and Tessa's girlfriends, who loved gathering in Jeannie's large open kitchen while she made them pizzas and homemade cookies and other snacks, that on the rare occasions when it was just the three of them, it felt like such a blessing.

In fact, Jeannie often felt a little sorry for Emma. Whenever Sadie brought friends home, they always went off to Sadie's room. "Young people feel so comfortable in your house—with you," Emma had said more than once.

"I'm sure that it's just the difference in the girls' ages—at their age, one year can make a huge difference," Jeannie had assured her. "Sadie and her friends are just going through that parents-are-not-to-be-trusted phase." But based on the number of times she had heard Sadie bemoan her parents' conservative lifestyle and the number of sentences that began with "I just wish. . . ,"

Jeannie wasn't at all sure that this was just some teenage phase Sadie was working her way through. And the truth was that she couldn't begin to imagine that Tessa would ever deliberately close herself off from her parents.

"The three Messners," Tessa had announced one night, flourishing her arm like a sword. "One for all and all for one." And laughing, Geoff and Jeannie had raised their arms to meet hers.

"Have a wonderful first day," she said now as she hugged Tessa close. She released her, but her hands rested on Tessa's shoulders. "Our baby is growing up, Geoff."

"Mom, I'm not going off to Africa or anything," Tessa protested, but Jeannie noticed how her daughter hung on to her for just a moment longer than she normally did. "Love you both," she called as she hurried out the door.

The cordless phone that Tessa had left on the counter rang. Jeannie glanced at the caller ID information and picked it up on the second ring, even as she straightened Geoff's tie and accepted his kiss good-bye. In all their married lives, the sisters had not missed their morning call to start their day. She glanced at the clock and saw that it was later than she realized.

"Chaos central," she announced, shooing Geoff toward the door and mouthing, "Go. You'll be late."

She handed him an umbrella. "Give this to Tessa. I don't want her catching cold standing out there in the rain." She blew him another kiss then closed the back door after him as he wrestled the umbrella open. "Sorry about that," she said as she settled back in for the daily exchange of schedules with Emma. But before she could say anything more, she heard the squeal of car tires moving too fast and too close followed by Geoff's shout. There was an ominous thud and then silence. With Emma still talking in her ear, Jeannie walked to the open back door and stepped outside.

For an instant she was paralyzed. Surely this was a dream—this surreal scene with an unfamiliar car sideways in front of their closed garage door, the black umbrella Geoff had taken for Tessa open and rolling slowly across the driveway, and Geoff on the pavement cradling Tessa in his arms. She was vaguely aware of Dan Kline standing next to the car holding his side while Sadie sat on the wet ground on the driver's side as if she had simply slid from the car. She was crying hysterically, deep gulping sobs. The only other sound was the annoying beep signaling that the key was still in the ignition.

Jeannie could not seem to make her feet move. So many choices—Tessa, Sadie. . .

"Call 911," Geoff shouted.

Without a word to Emma, Jeannie hung up and dialed 911, all the while standing outside the back door, oblivious to the rain as she stared at her precious child. Tessa's backpack was still attached to her limp shoulders, and her hair fell in wet clumps over her pale face.

"What is your emergency?" the operator asked.

"My daughter," Jeannie began, but words as well as her voice failed her as she fell to her knees next to her husband and child.

A neighbor she hadn't been aware of had run across the yard and now took the phone. Briskly he handled the emergency operator's questions, glancing at Geoff for confirmation when the question was whether or not Tessa was conscious.

"No." He paused. "Breathing?"

Geoff nodded as tears rolled down his cheeks. "Tell them to hurry," he whispered.

"On their way," the neighbor assured him. "Yes operator, I'm still here. . .neighbor. . .looks like a car accident. . .I don't know. Two kids. One of them is a relative of the victim."

Victim. The word echoed so loudly in Jeannie's head that she was unaware that the neighbor had continued to talk, moving closer to the car as he did. She was vaguely aware that she was no longer hearing Sadie's hysterical rantings. She glanced over and saw her niece huddled against the side of the car. She was soaked to the skin, her arms locked around her knees, her eyes riveted on Tessa as she rocked back and forth, mumbling to herself.

Jeannie's mind raced with all the things she should be doing— calling Emma back and telling her to come, asking someone to check on Sadie and stay with her until Emma could arrive. But none of that came close to the urgency she felt to save her beloved child.

"There's no blood," she said softly. Geoff, taking it for a question, shook his head.

It was true. There were no outward signs of injury. No blood. No awkwardly twisted limbs. Tessa was just lying there, her eyes closed, her breathing shallow but steady, her face serene.

Jeannie scooted closer to him, and together they held Tessa between them until they heard the shriek of the siren coming down their street. Someone had picked up the umbrella and was shielding them with it.

"Hang on, sweetie," Geoff murmured. "Just hang on," he begged, his voice choked with sobs.

In what seemed like minutes and at the same time hours, the emergency team arrived and took charge, prying Tessa away from Geoff and Jeannie, turning them over to the waiting arms of concerned neighbors who now filled their driveway and front yard. Three EMTs surrounded Tessa, examining her and reporting their findings even as they started an IV and placed her carefully on a gurney. Through it all, the one thing that struck Jeannie was how very still and calm Tessa seemed.

So like her, she thought, for always in the midst of turmoil, Tessa was the serene one. And to Jeannie, her daughter's stillness seemed a good sign. She took hope from it. She was clutching Geoff's hand when he followed the gurney. She saw Emma running up the street, getting no farther than the front of the ambulance when Dan Kline intercepted her, waving his hands wildly.

Looking past the hysterical Dan, Jeannie could see Emma trying to make eye contact with her. Her expression was full of questions—questions to which Jeannie had no answers. All she knew was that her baby was lying on a gurney that three EMTs were shoving into the back of an ambulance, and Geoff was urging her to ride with Tessa.

"I'll be there," Geoff assured her and backed away so the doors could be shut. Just before they closed, she saw that a police car had also arrived and an officer was talking to one of the EMTs.

He nodded, glancing toward Dan's car and then back to the ambulance just as the doors slammed shut.

"Sadie," she shouted. "Check on Sadie."

"There's another unit on the scene, ma'am," the young man riding with her said.

She nodded and stared blankly around the cramped interior of the ambulance. It was odd how the wail of the siren seemed to come from somewhere far away now that they were inside the vehicle. Jeannie clung to Tessa's fingers, knowing she should be asking questions. The problem was that she didn't know what questions to ask. Besides, the EMT was busy working on Tessa and reporting his findings to the driver up front. She had to assume that he was talking to someone at the hospital, preparing them to care for Tessa the minute they arrived. The EMT in back didn't look old enough to be out of high school, but his actions were performed with a quickness and precision that gave Jeannie confidence in him.

"She'll be all right," she said softly, and when this brought no assurances from the young man, she repeated it as a question. "My daughter is going to be all right?"

"She's hanging on," he replied, and Jeannie wondered why she had added "for now."

Chapter 7

Emma

At first Emma was merely irritated when Jeannie suddenly cut off their morning conversation in midsentence. Her sister was easily distracted and assumed everyone she left waiting would understand. There were times when Emma wanted to remind her that she couldn't just. . .

But the muted sounds that followed Jeannie's abrupt departure triggered an innate warning system, telling Emma that something was seriously wrong. She heard crying and shouting as Jeannie obviously carried the mobile phone closer to the crisis. Then she distinctly heard Geoff say, "Call 911," and the phone went dead.

"Lars!" she shouted out the open back door, thankful that at that exact moment her husband had pulled their car into the short driveway. "Lars, don't get out. Somebody's hurt at Jeannie's. Just wait while I call Hester to meet us there."

Hester Steiner was a registered nurse and—aside from Jeannie—Emma's best friend. The two of them had known each other since elementary school, and Hester was also close to Jeannie and her family. Emma dialed Hester's number, her fingers suddenly clumsy on the phone's keypad.

"Well, good morning," Hester said brightly.

"Hester, can you come to Jeannie's right away? Someone's

been hurt or fallen ill."

"What happened?" In a heartbeat, Hester's voice went from chatty to professional.

"I don't know. Jeannie and I were talking, and all of a sudden she stopped talking and there was a lot of shouting and crying in the background, and then I heard Geoff tell her to call 911."

"On my way. Shall I swing by?"

"No, Lars and I are leaving now. We'll meet you there."

She hung up the phone and ran out to the car without bothering to stop for either an umbrella or her rain jacket. On the short drive to Jeannie's large home less than a mile away, Emma repeated the content of the phone call to Lars.

"Maybe it's a neighbor," Lars said as he patted her knee to still it from shaking. "We don't know that it's one of them."

"Sadie had just left with Dan Kline to pick up Tessa," Emma murmured, "and Matt. . ."

"Is already at his school. I just took him there myself, remember?"

"Right," Emma said. "I imagine that Geoff was on his way when. . ." She could not complete that sentence. What had her brother-in-law seen? Who was in need of emergency medical help? How bad was it? "Maybe it's a fire and everyone got out safely," she said, suddenly preferring that scenario to imagining one that involved people being hurt. "Geoff would tell Jeannie to call 911 for a fire."

"A couple more blocks," Lars assured her as he turned onto Jeannie's street.

Emma leaned forward, willing the car to cover the distance, straining to see—what? Smoke? Flames shooting from a rooftop? Would the pouring rain have already doused a fire? But the fact was that everything looked deceptively ordinary except that there were people gathered in Jeannie's front yard. Emma recognized neighbors that she and Lars had met before. Dan's car was pulled into the driveway, although the driver's side door was standing open. Someone was on the ground next to the car, but because the car was sitting diagonally across the driveway with its front tires resting on the lawn, she couldn't see if it was Tessa or Sadie or someone else. An ambulance blocked the entrance to the driveway.

She broadened her view to encompass the entire yard and entrance to the house. Sadie's bike was leaning against a cluster of palm trees. Sadie had left it there the day before—the day of the picnic—the day she had ridden it over there so that she and Jeannie could go get her learner's permit.

Dan was standing at the foot of the driveway looking lost and scared. He was holding his side, and he had a cut on his cheek. The side door that led from the kitchen out to the driveway was open. Up near the garage door someone was holding a large black umbrella over a group of people kneeling next to someone else on the ground. Suddenly she was certain that one of the two people she couldn't see had to be Sadie. Lars pulled to the curb, and Emma was out of the car before he could come to a full stop.

Sadie? Not Sadie. Please, dear God, not my daughter.

"Where's Sadie?" She shouted to no one and everyone. She was fighting her way through what suddenly seemed like throngs of people but was really only one man on his cell phone pacing back and forth as he talked and a woman peering anxiously down the street toward an oncoming car, waving to the driver as he made the turn onto their street. Emma registered that this was a police car, lights flashing, siren wailing. The car stopped behind the ambulance.

Instinctively, Emma made a wide berth past the back of Dan's car, noticing again that the driver's side door was open and that the quiet chirping of the warning to remove the keys was muffled by the unfurled airbag. And then she saw her daughter, soaked to the skin but alive. Sadie was huddled on the ground, pressed against the side of the car, her arms clasped tight around her knees and her head bowed low as she rocked back and forth. Just when Emma started toward her, the EMTs shouted for people to clear the way as they raised the gurney from ground level onto its rollers so they could get the lifeless form on it to the waiting ambulance. Emma glanced at the gurney and froze.

Tessa.

Everything that happened from the instant that Emma

spotted Sadie seemed to happen in a blur. The team of emergency technical people sped past with Geoff and Jeannie running to keep up. Jeannie looked at her with eyes that seemed like those of a blind person—wide but unseeing—and Emma was momentarily torn between the call to tend to Sadie and the need to comfort her sister. Each of them needed her. Each of them was in such pain—maybe not physically but surely spiritually. She closed her eyes, praying for guidance, and that was when she heard the scream of more sirens arriving. She opened her eyes to find Dan Kline blocking her way.

"Oh Mrs. Keller, I shouldn't have—I mean, we didn't mean to. . ." His eyes were wide with fear, his blond hair plastered against his head. The boy was over six feet tall, but he was crying like a kid half his size, and he was dangerously close to a complete breakdown.

"Dan, calm down. Has someone called your parents?"

"I don't know. I just. . .it was the rain and the streets and the. . ."

"Are you hurt?" She gently touched his cheek where the rain had thinned the blood. But she saw that it was no more than a scratch.

"No, ma'am. I don't know. . .maybe a little. My side hurts."

Then blessedly, Lars came loping toward them, kneeling next to Sadie, who remained completely incoherent in her babblings. She refused to look up when Lars called her name. "She doesn't recognize me," he whispered, his voice choked with panic.

Emma started to turn back to Sadie, but Dan grasped her arm. His eyes were unfocused and wild, and his grip tightened when she tried to move.

"Daniel," she said firmly, and she was relieved when it had the desired effect of making him pay attention. "A second ambulance has just arrived. I need for you to go to them and tell them that Sadie is hurt then get yourself checked over and have them call your parents. Can you do that?"

"Yes, ma'am, but. . ."

"No time for explanations now, Dan. Do as I ask."

She waited until the boy turned away, biting her lip to keep from shouting after him, "Stop. I need to know now. What happened here? What did you do?" Just then she spotted Hester crossing the street, pausing to speak with one of the medics. At the same time, Geoff was helping Jeannie into the back of the first ambulance.

"Go," she heard one of the EMTs yell as he slammed the double doors and raced around to climb into the passenger side of the ambulance. The shriek of the siren drowned out everything else.

"Hester, over here," Emma shouted above the growing noise as people filled the street and yard. In spite of the fact that one of the newly arrived EMTs was attending to Sadie, Emma wanted her friend to reassure them that their child was going to be all right.

"I'm a registered nurse," Hester explained. The young woman nodded and accepted Hester's presence without question. The two of them knelt to either side of Sadie while Lars and Emma stood by and waited.

After what seemed an eternity, Hester looked up at Emma and shook her head. But Emma didn't know how to interpret that. Was Hester telling her that Sadie was not hurt? That she was hurt and it was bad?

"She's most likely in shock," Hester said, standing up so she could talk to both Lars and Emma. "There don't seem to be any other injuries—a couple of bruises and a pretty nasty cut on her lip. She probably bit it on impact. It's pretty deep. She'll need stitches."

The paramedic helped Sadie to her feet. She continued mumbling to herself. "I thought—we were just fooling around—Dan was laughing at me. I glanced away for just a second. . .not even a second. . ." Finally, Sadie looked directly at her parents for the first time, her eyes luminous with disbelief. Then she collapsed against Emma's shoulder, and her words were obliterated by her sobs.

Emma held Sadie and tried to comfort her as she tried to make some sense of what had happened. As if studying a jigsaw puzzle—its pieces scattered across the dining room table, Emma slowly began picking up one piece and then the next as she put together a plausible picture. She replayed every detail of what she'd seen when she and Lars arrived. She remembered first being confused by the odd angle of the car. Sadie had been crouched by the driver's side of the car. Dan stumbling around on the other side—the passenger side.

As the sound of the siren faded, she looked down the street and caught sight of the ambulance carrying her sister and niece as it turned a corner. She closed her eyes, envisioning Jeannie inside that ambulance with Tessa.

The sisters had not exchanged a word, and yet Emma knew everything that Jeannie must have been feeling in that moment. She had seen in her sister's blank stare mirroring the utter disbelief, that her daughter—her only child—could be the person lying on that gurney. Emma tightened her hold on Sadie and rocked her as she had when she was a baby.

"Shhh," she whispered. "One step at a time. Tessa needs all our strength right now, Sadie. She needs our prayers." She stroked Sadie's hair. "Come on now. You've lost your prayer covering, and if ever there was a time. . ."

"It's in the car. In my backpack," Sadie said setting off a fresh wave of tears. "I took it off. I. . .and now God has. . ."

"Shush," Emma said, pulling Sadie closer. "You know better. We'll find your covering, and then we'll all go to the hospital."

"I'll get it for you," Lars said, clearly relieved to have something concrete that he could do.

He went to Dan's car—the passenger side. One of the police officers was standing by the car, and when Lars reached in to take the prayer covering and the backpack, the officer stopped him. The two men had a brief conversation, and finally the officer allowed Lars to take the prayer covering, but he followed him back to where Emma waited with Sadie.

"Evidence," Lars said when Emma raised her eyebrows in silent question. "The car needs to be examined. And Sadie will need to answer some questions."

Of course. It was an accident like any accident. There would be questions. Sadie would be questioned. And Dan. Emma's heart went into overdrive as her instincts to protect her child from any further agony on this morning came to the fore. "She needs medical attention," she told the officer.

Hester was sitting on the curb next to Dan. "They both do," she added with a nod toward Dan.

"We'll see that they get it," the officer assured her. "For now. . ."

Emma took a step that positioned her between the officer and Sadie.

Lars touched her arm. "Emma, their ways may not—"

Without a word, Emma turned and led Sadie toward the second ambulance. She was speaking with the paramedic when the officer caught up with them. But before he could reach them, Geoff grabbed the man's arm.

"I have to get to the hospital, and your partner says I can't take my car because we can't move this one until—"

"You can ride with me," Lars said, indicating his car across the street. "Emma will go with Sadie. The paramedic says that she's going to need stitches and to be completely checked over by a doctor," he continued, addressing the police officer.

The officer glanced toward the second ambulance. Dan was being helped into the passenger seat. "Okay, your daughter can ride along in that ambulance—in the back. My partner will ride with them."

"I want to—" Emma began.

"Ma'am, you and your husband can follow in your car, but your daughter and her boyfriend. . ."

"Let's go," Lars said, taking Emma's arm and guiding her across the street before she could say anything that might further antagonize the police officer. Geoff was already in the car, his head resting against the window as he stared into space.

Chapter 8

Jeannie

At the emergency room, a team of medical personnel came running toward the ambulance as soon as it pulled into the circular drive. In a flurry of activity, the EMTs delivered information about Tessa's status at the same time they lowered the gurney to the ground and started wheeling her inside. Just as they got past the automated doors, someone gently pulled Jeannie aside.

"Ma'am, please step over here," the gray-haired woman said. "We need you to give us some information so the doctors can treat your daughter."

"No." Jeannie dug in her heels.

The woman looked a little shocked. Had no one ever dared to refuse the protocol before? Jeannie couldn't imagine that. "My husband will be here shortly, and then one of us will be glad to give you any information you need. If the doctors need her medical history, then they need me to be nearby."

Logic had never been Jeannie's strong suit, but she felt certain that she was making a good case now. "So either you come with me to wherever they have taken my daughter and ask your questions, or it will just have to wait." Jeannie patted the woman's hand, removing it from her arm and heading down the hall and through the double doors where they had taken Tessa.

Moving quickly she checked every cubicle and room in the emergency ward until she saw a cluster of men and women in white coats and green scrubs at the far end of the U-shaped area. She heard footsteps behind her as she started running toward the doctors.

"Jeannie," Geoff called, catching up to her. "Where is she?"

"Back here, I think." She'd never been so glad to see Geoff in her life. He grabbed hold of her hand, and together they hurried toward the curtained area where someone had set Tessa's backpack on a chair.

"We're her parents," Geoff announced unnecessarily as they pushed their way into the midst of the medical team surrounding Tessa. She was lying on her back, her hair fanned out behind her, her clothing open, exposing her thin upper body. Jeannie felt Geoff's grip tighten. "Can we cover her? She gets cold so easily," he said.

One of the white coats glanced at a woman in scrubs who nodded and turned to Geoff and Jeannie, taking their elbows as she gently ushered them into the area just outside the sliding glass doors of the cubicle. "The doctors need to put in a tube to help her breathe," she said. "We're doing everything we can. Just please wait right here and let the doctors do their job. You're just a few feet away from her. She knows you're here."

Geoff and Jeannie nodded in unison, and the nurse went back inside the cubicle and pulled a curtain closed behind her. Geoff wrapped his arms around Jeannie, and she rested her cheek against his chest, feeling the strong pounding of his heart against her face. Somehow that gave her strength.

"She'll be all right," she murmured. "Tessa is a fighter—quiet, yes, but you always said you'd rather have a strong silent player on your team than one who—" She was babbling, and Geoff quieted her by stroking her hair and tightening his hold on her. The question uppermost in her mind—the question of what happened—could wait. For now all that mattered was that Tessa was getting the medical help that would bring her back to them. Jeannie closed her eyes and silently prayed for her daughter's full recovery as she forced herself to ignore the mental pictures of her beautiful daughter forever crippled or living in a coma or somehow less than her smart self. The idea that Tessa might die was not allowed.

"Mr. and Mrs. Messner?"

They looked up at a short, stocky man with Albert Einstein hair and wire-rimmed glasses. "I am Dr. Morris. Your daughter is bleeding internally. We need to perform surgery immediately. Will you give consent?"

The nurse who had ushered them from the room stood behind the doctor holding a clipboard with some papers. Geoff ripped it from her hand and glanced at it, searching for the blank space to write his name. "Here?"

"And on the next page as well," the nurse said.

Geoff scrawled his name in both spaces and handed the clipboard back to the nurse. "Can we see her before you take her to surgery?"

Dr. Morris pulled back the curtain and with a single glance cleared the small room of medical personnel. "Make it quick. We need to go now," he said, and Geoff nodded.

"Thank you," Jeannie said, her voice choked with fresh tears.

She and Geoff approached the gurney that held their daughter as they had once approached her crib when she was a baby, hesitant and with a certain sense of disbelief. Then it had been because they had been blessed with this beautiful new life and given responsibility for watching over her. Now their disbelief grew out of a surreal sense that everything that had happened to their little family in the last hour had been some kind of horrible nightmare.

"Hey, sweetie," Geoff crooned, taking Tessa's small hand in his large one. Tessa's fingers twitched, and Geoff glanced at Jeannie, his eyes filled with fresh hope.

Jeannie moved to the other side of the gurney and took Tessa's other hand. "We're right here, Tess. Dad and me—right here." Her voice broke, and silent tears dropped onto the sheet the nurse had covered Tessa with. Jeannie found herself fascinated by the polka dot pattern her tears were creating there. She had never felt more helpless in her life.

"You need to fight, Tessa," Geoff said. "That's the way you help the doc get you back to us. You hear me?"

He was using the voice he used in a game when he wanted to inspire his players to keep playing hard against an opponent that was much bigger and stronger than they were. Jeannie felt an inexplicable annoyance. This was their daughter, not his basketball or football team. The doctor cleared his throat, and Jeannie was aware that he had pulled open the curtain and was waiting to take Tessa away.

"How long?" she asked, her voice husky. "The surgery?"

Dr. Morris moved a step into the space. "Difficult to say," he told her. "A couple of hours at least. I'll send someone to give you updates if it goes past that, okay?"

Jeannie felt as if she was bargaining for time on Tessa's behalf—two hours to bring their beautiful laughing child back to them? Or was he talking about two hours just to get her to the point where she could begin the long weeks and maybe months of recovery? Or after two hours would. . . ? She would not allow herself to think beyond those two alternatives. "Two hours," she whispered as she bent to kiss Tessa's cheek and smooth her silken hair away from her face. She tucked a strand behind her daughter's ear as Tessa had done herself that very morning—this very morning—for the large clock on the wall outside the cubicle showed the time as just a minute past nine o'clock.

She stepped away to let the aides unlock the gurney wheels and start down the corridor, but Geoff held on, walking briskly and then trotting to keep pace until they reached an elevator. The nurse gently pulled him away. A second elevator opened, and an aide exited with a young man in a wheelchair followed by an older couple. Dan Kline and his parents. *If Dan is hurt, then what about Sadie?* Jeannie wondered. The Kline family disappeared behind a curtain.

Down the corridor, the light above the elevator carrying Tessa was clicking off floors: 2-3-4. . . . Jeannie stood frozen in the now barren cubicle, her hand outstretched as if to rescue her child from a fall. Then she saw Geoff still facing the elevator. His broad shoulders slumped, and then began to shake uncontrollably.

Relieved to have something to do, Jeannie picked up Tessa's backpack and went to comfort her husband.

"Come on," she said as she saw an aide waiting patiently by another bank of elevators and understood that the young woman was there for them.

"I'll take you to the surgical family waiting room," the aide said as she held the doors of the elevator open.

"There's a chapel just across the hall here," she continued as they exited the elevator after the short, silent ride. She indicated the chapel as if she were leading some kind of tour while Geoff and Jeannie made their way blindly down the corridor after her. "And a café just around that corner and down the hall."

A café? Seriously? How about just a plain old, ordinary hospital coffee shop?

Jeannie couldn't even remember what floor they had come to, but the aide seemed well practiced in her mission, and Jeannie could not help but give herself over to the young woman for the time being.

"There's free coffee and tea in the waiting room," the aide said, continuing her tour. "And vending machines down the hall that way. Oh, and there's also this private room you can use." She opened a wooden door. "It's a good place to sit down with the doctor once the surgery is over." She waited for some response and got none. "The waiting room is just around the corner."

"Bathrooms?" Jeannie asked as they turned a corner.

"Right here and also—"

Jeannie let go of Geoff's hand and practically ran for the door. She locked herself inside the small room with its porcelain sink and single toilet and a mirror that Jeannie found herself staring into as she wrapped her arms tightly around herself.

Who is that? The face staring back at her was nearly unrecognizable—a parody of the woman she had been just hours earlier. The mouth was twisted into a kind of silent scream, and the eyes—always so lively and filled with plans for the day—were lifeless.

Her entire body began to shake and heave as if she were caught in the riptide of a turbulent sea. Wave after wave of sheer terror crashed over her until she thought she could not breathe, and yet she was aware that the tiny bathroom echoed with the sounds of her sobbing. Guttural growling sounds interspersed with the kind of high keening such as she had sometimes heard emanating from women in Middle Eastern countries mourning the loss of a loved one. All the while her eyes remained dry. And in her mind she repeated, *Please, please, please*, as she continued to lock eyes with the stranger in the mirror.

The faith of her childhood had taught Jeannie to turn to God—even for small things, and this surely wasn't small. Surely a loving God would understand her cry for help now. She was a mother, and her only child was even now surrounded by strangers—strangers holding scalpels and attaching machines to keep her breathing.

Please.

Chapter 9

Lars

As Lars and Emma had driven Geoff to the hospital, Lars had resisted the urge to squeeze his brother-in-law's shoulder once he and Emma were in the car. Everything about Geoff's posture showed that he wanted—needed—to be alone, but Lars couldn't resist offering some encouragement. "Tessa will be all right," he said as he kept both hands on the wheel and focused on the road.

To his surprise, Geoff nodded. "There wasn't a scratch on her—no blood at all," he murmured. "I think she hit her head. Just dazed maybe."

"We'll all pray that you're right," Emma said. No one spoke again until they reached the hospital. Lars drove all the way hunched forward, squinting at the road the way he always did, as if operating a motorized vehicle were still foreign to him.

They arrived just behind the second ambulance that carried Dan and Sadie. Geoff leaped from the car and ran into the hospital.

"Where is she?" he demanded of the desk clerk as soon as they were inside the emergency reception area. "My daughter— Tessa Messner—fifteen—just brought in. . . ."

The gray-haired woman glanced toward the double doors

and then back at Geoff. "Your wife is with her. I need to get some information."

Geoff tossed his wallet to Emma. "Take care of this," he said and headed through the doors.

Emma looked from Lars to the paramedic wheeling Sadie through the doors. She was holding an ice pack to her lip. Not ten seconds later, Dan Kline was escorted into the small reception area. His parents arrived a moment later, and Dan's father brushed past Emma, demanding to see the person in charge immediately.

"Dad," Dan moaned, but his mother took his protest for a cry of pain and began to cry as well.

"You need to wait your turn, sir," the receptionist said even as she indicated that Emma should take a seat at her window. "And you are?" the exasperated clerk asked Emma.

"Tessa Messner's aunt and godmother." Emma rifled through Geoff's wallet to produce insurance cards and other identification. "My daughter, Sadie, is—"

"One patient at a time," the woman said. She made copies of Geoff's cards and passed them back to Emma. She typed in bits of information on her computer and finally turned to Emma. "Now, what happened?" she asked, nodding toward Sadie.

Although Lars understood that the receptionist was looking only for information about Sadie's condition and not seeking details of the accident, he also understood that this was a question they were all going to face time and again in the days to come. His wife gave the only answer she knew to be absolutely true.

"I don't know."

The clerk exchanged a look with the police officer who was right behind Dan, and then said something to someone behind her. A man in scrubs came to the door and called Sadie's name.

"Can we go back there with her?" Emma asked. "And can we see our niece—Tessa Messner?"

The man in scrubs deferred to the desk clerk who picked up the phone and repeated the question. "Yes, godmother, I think. Amish, right?" She glanced at Emma.

"Mennonite," Lars corrected automatically, although he could not think how their religious affiliation could possibly matter.

The clerk nodded and then hung up the phone. "Your niece is being taken to surgery. Let's get your daughter treated and then see where things stand." Once again she glanced at the officer. "Next," she called, and Dan's father stepped past Emma and Lars to lean against the desk, his face only inches from the receptionist's.

"Do you know who I am?"

"That's what I'm here to find out," the clerk replied wearily.

"Excuse me," Emma said. "My sister—Tessa's mother. . . ?"

"Will be in the surgical waiting room," the clerk assured her, and Lars did not miss the way the woman looked at her with an expression of abject pity when just ten minutes earlier she had been annoyed with the entire family.

The man in scrubs stepped forward and grasped the handles of Sadie's wheelchair. "This way, folks," he said. The police officer followed close on his heels as he wheeled Sadie into an area with a bed and one straight chair and then pulled a curtain to give her privacy. "The doctor will be right in," he said and disappeared.

"Ma'am," the officer said, indicating that Emma should take the lone chair.

"*Danke.*"

Sadie was staring blankly at the floor. Lars stood next to her, his hand on her shoulder. Sadie showed no reaction, no expression at all.

"Sadie?" Emma said.

Nothing.

Lars exchanged a look with Emma and then glanced at the officer. The man was standing outside the cubicle, his back to them, his hands clasped behind his back.

"She's so still," Emma mouthed.

"*Der Arzt. . . ,*" Lars began, and at that moment a nurse came in, slid the sliding door closed, and softly asked Sadie for her name and birth date, checking to be sure the information matched what was typed on the paper bracelet the receptionist had given Emma to wrap around Sadie's thin wrist. The questions were simple enough. Name. Date of birth. But Sadie remained mute and staring at the floor. Lars answered for her until the nurse came to the tough question, "Can you tell me what happened?"

Sadie looked up for the first time. "We hit Tessa," she whispered, and then she started to shake, her entire body convulsing.

"Are you cold?" Emma asked, edging closer to where the nurse was bent over Sadie.

Sadie said nothing.

The nurse wrapped a blanket around her shoulders, and finally the shaking subsided. "Sadie," she said, her voice now gentle and kind, "we need to check you over for any injuries you may have sustained beyond the cut on your lip. Are you in pain? Can you tell me where it hurts?"

Sadie sat stone still for a second and then pointed to her chest.

"Did you hit your chest on something?"

Sadie shook her head vigorously. "I hurt in my heart. We hit Tessa," she repeated, staring at the nurse as if the woman wasn't very bright. Then she turned to Emma. "We hit Tessa," she repeated and then seemed to fold in on herself as she clutched her arms tightly around her body and once again started to rock back and forth.

"Okay, okay," Lars said, patting Sadie's hand. "That's enough. We need the doctor in here."

The nurse looked over her shoulder at him. "I really need to—"

"Der Arzt," Lars demanded. "Doctor now."

The nurse looked from Lars to Emma.

"Bitte?" Emma pleaded.

With a nod, the nurse put away the blood pressure cuff she had started to attach to Sadie's thin arm and left the room.

Sadie continued her rocking.

"Sadie, let's keep the ice on your lip," Emma said, kneeling next to her and pressing the ice pack against her face. From the corridor outside the exam room, Lars could hear the booming voice of Dan's father. He also heard a calmer male voice say something about running some tests as he assured Mr. Kline that as soon as they knew what they were dealing with, Dan would receive the treatment he needed.

The calmer voice came closer, ticking off instructions to some unseen person as he moved. There was a brief exchange with the police officer, and then a tall young man in his midthirties entered the cubicle. He focused all of his attention on Sadie. Lars liked him immediately.

"Hello, Sadie. I'm Dr. Booker. I need to take a look at you and ask you some questions. Would that be all right?"

Sadie kept rocking.

"Help me get her onto the bed," he said softly, addressing Lars for the first time.

Without a word, Lars scooped Sadie into his arms and set her gently on the narrow hospital bed. She instantly rolled to one side, facing away from them, and curled herself into the fetal position. Dr. Booker was undeterred. He pulled on a pair of latex gloves as he walked to the other side of the bed and bent to examine her lip. "That's going to need some stitches. I could use my special pink thread if you like. My niece likes pink." He continued to probe and examine. "How about you, Sadie? What's your favorite color? I'm partial to blue myself—or green. My mom said that's because I'm the outdoors type. I like nature—water, trees. . . ."

Gradually Lars saw Sadie's arms and legs start to relax.

The nurse had come back to assist Dr. Booker, and the two of them worked in a reassuring rhythm, checking Sadie for any signs of further injury. Apparently satisfied that her split lip was the worst of it, he quietly explained each step of the process for closing the wound. "Okay, Sadie, this is some stuff to freeze the surface so you won't feel anything. I'm thinking no more than half a dozen will do the job, but if you like, I can make tinier stitches and give you more."

Nothing.

Dr. Booker glanced at Emma and Lars, seeming to notice their plain dress for the first time. "I'll bet your mom is pretty good with a needle and thread—maybe I should let her make these stitches."

Sadie stared wide-eyed and unblinking at the ceiling.

As the doctor went about his work, his tone changed slightly and Lars understood that he was addressing them. "I'm going to suggest that Sadie be admitted at least overnight. Right now she's showing all the classic signs of shock, but I'd like to make certain there's nothing else going on."

"The officer. . . ," Lars began, lowering his voice and glancing toward the corridor where the officer had positioned himself just outside Dan's cubicle.

Dr. Booker clipped the thread with a small pair of scissors and then pulled off his gloves. "I doubt it will happen, but don't be surprised if they decide to assign someone to her while she's here." He gave a nod toward the hallway where the policeman was talking quietly to one of the nurses.

"I can stay," Emma volunteered.

"He means the police," Lars explained, and Dr. Booker nodded.

"I'd like to get some X-rays—not that I suspect anything. But since she's not really responding to touch or perhaps pain, we want to be sure. And we should consider a psych consultation."

Lars nodded. "We will wait here," he said.

"Actually, we'll probably take her right to a regular room once we get those pictures taken."

The nurse stepped forward. "It could be some time before we can get her to and from the X-ray department and have a bed for her. I understand that it was your niece who was also in the accident?"

"She's in surgery," Emma said. "My sister's child. . ." Her voice trailed off.

Dr. Booker and the nurse exchanged a look. "Why don't I have someone show you to the surgical waiting room? You can wait there, and we'll come get you as soon as Sadie is settled."

"I can't go with Sadie?"

"You could, but I thought you might want to use this time to check on your niece?"

Lars had never seen Emma look so torn.

"Jeannie will be needing you." He spoke to her in their Dutch-German dialect. "Sadie is in good hands for now."

"Ja," Emma replied, but her eyes were on Sadie.

"All right," Lars said, reverting to English to include Dr. Booker and the nurse in the agreement. "We will wait."

Obviously relieved, the medical duo left the cubicle, the nurse assuring them that someone would be along soon to transport Sadie to radiology.

As soon as they were gone, Emma got up and went to Sadie's bedside, covering her tenderly with the white hospital blanket and leaning in to kiss her forehead and examine her stitches.

"Are they even?" Lars asked. And for the first time since they had left their house, he saw a shadow of a smile play across Emma's beautiful face.

"Perfect," she replied.

As his wife gently fingered Sadie's hair away from her face and the swollen blue area around her mouth that the doctor had repaired, Lars couldn't help but pray that everything that had been ripped open in those few seconds earlier that morning would be so easily restored.

Chapter 10

Emma

"This way," an aide said, motioning for Lars and Emma to join her at the elevator after Sadie had been taken for X-rays. They pressed into the elevator that was already crowded with people in medical garb. Everyone stood facing forward toward the doors, and no one spoke as the elevator stopped at each floor.

A local, Jeannie would have called it with a sigh of impatience. Both Jeannie and Sadie had little time for dawdling. Their days were filled to the minute, and they were always anxious to be on to the next item on their agenda. Tessa, on the other hand, took time to savor life, appreciating the simple details of her daily routine.

Lars stood next to Emma. He kept a strong hold on her, and yet she felt a wave of fear grip her to the point that she thought her knees might actually buckle. She placed her hand in the crook of Lars's elbow and held on.

The elevator doors slid open, and the aide led the way around the corner and into the waiting room. Emma was surprised to see that they were the only ones there. Jeannie and Geoff had not yet arrived, and there were no other families keeping vigil for a loved one in surgery. Lars surveyed the room and chose a cluster of chairs close to the windows. "Over here," he said, and Emma followed him and began dragging additional chairs to the area.

"What are you doing?" Lars asked.

"We need more chairs. Jeannie and Geoff will need a place to wait, and Hester will surely be here, and once the news spreads..."

Lars placed his hand on her arm. "We can add more chairs as needed," he told her. "*Sich hinsetzen* and gather yourself. Jeannie is going to need all your strength."

There was a rustle of movement outside the waiting room entrance, and Emma saw Hester and her husband, John, enter the room. The sight of her good friend was such a relief that Emma went to her and for the first time since arriving at Jeannie's house, squeezed out a few of the tears that she had carefully repressed. Lars was right. Her daughter and sister would look to her for strength and reassurance.

Hester hugged her tight for a long moment. "I'm right here," she murmured. "Hang in there, and we'll all get through this together, okay?"

Emma nodded and gave herself over to that moment of comfort in her friend's embrace—a moment she somehow knew she would need to come back to many times in the days to come. For if they had taken Tessa to surgery, then that had to mean that it was going to take time for her to heal. "Thanks for everything you did for Sadie and for being here," she murmured, and Hester released her. It occurred to Emma that Hester had not once asked her what had happened. She loved her friend all the more for that.

While John talked to Lars, Emma told Hester about Sadie. "There's a policeman waiting to question her as soon as they finish taking X-rays and get her settled into a room," she whispered.

"It's protocol," Hester said with a dismissive wave of her hand. "There's a coffee machine," she added, nodding toward the refreshment area on the other side of the room. "There's bound to be hot water. I could make you a cup of tea."

Tea—green tea, Emma thought, remembering that just a few weeks earlier Sadie had announced that she was on a strict diet to eat healthier. "Green tea," she had told Emma. "It contains antioxidants that are very good for the immune system."

"Iced or hot?" Emma had asked her, and Sadie had been stumped.

"I'm not sure it matters," she had said uncertainly, but then she'd grinned. "But from now on, it's milk or green tea or water. No soda. No coffee. And no juice drinks. Those are so incredibly loaded with sugar." She'd made a face as if disgusted that the beverages that had been her choice for most of her sixteen years had suddenly left a terrible taste in her mouth.

Emma gave Hester a weary smile then shook her head. "Perhaps later," she said. "Thank you." She fixed her gaze on the doorway. "What am I going to say to Jeannie?" she asked.

Hester hesitated and then sat in the chair next to Emma and took her hand. "Jeannie and Geoff will need a little time, Emma. Right now all they can think about is Tessa."

Emma heard the rustle of someone approaching and glanced back toward the door. Geoff was standing in the doorway, looking as if he might shatter into a thousand pieces at any second.

She started toward him, feeling as if the distance between them was far greater than just the width of a small waiting room. And just when she was within two steps of her brother-in-law, Geoff walked past her as if she were an apparition. He went to the far end of the room, where he turned a chair to face the window and literally collapsed into it.

The aide who had accompanied him stood in the doorway, as if unsure of what her next move should be.

"My sister? Mrs. Messner?" Emma asked.

The young woman pointed to a closed door marked with the skirted silhouette used to indicate female. "Shall I check on her?"

"No thank you. The family is here now. We'll be all right." She looked back and saw Hester and John standing next to the chair where Geoff sat slumped forward, his large hands dangling helplessly between his knees.

"We were just fooling around."

That was what Sadie had said, and suddenly Emma understood that they all had to accept the reality that whatever had happened to Tessa, Sadie had played a major part in it.

Out in the hallway, Emma tapped lightly on the restroom

door. From inside she could hear sounds that were heartbreaking and terrifying at the same time. Those sounds were so foreign to her, and yet there was no question that they were coming from her sister—the carefree woman who could bring a smile to anyone's lips.

"Jeannie? It's Emma. Open the door."

The silence that replaced the sobs was almost more distressing than hearing Jeannie wailing. Emma tried the knob and found the door locked.

"Jeannie?"

After what seemed forever but was in fact only seconds, Emma heard the click of the lock. She pushed in on the door at the same time that Jeannie pulled, and the door flew back, banging against the wall as Jeannie stumbled forward and into Emma's arms.

Emma lost her battle to choke back the tears. She let them flow freely now. And the sisters stood locked in each other's arms—one of them dressed plain with her prayer covering knocked sideways by her sister's embrace, the other dressed in jeans and a T-shirt three sizes too large for her, her flaming red curls flattened into clumps against her cheeks by the rain and her tears.

"What happened?" Jeannie sobbed. "I don't understand."

Oh, the questions they must face in the days to come. Even if Tessa made a full recovery, Emma knew that once the relief passed, there were bound to be questions. The truth was that she was beginning to have a pretty good idea about what had happened.

The position of the driver's seat had told its own story—too close for the long legs of Dan Kline. It had been the passenger seat that had been pushed back to its full depth—and reclined. Sadie would never recline a seat. Sadie had once told Lars that she thought that was so dumb. Why wouldn't people want to see where they were going?

Had their impetuous, adventurous daughter persuaded Dan Kline to let her drive them to school? Or was it Dan who had suggested the switch in drivers? The roads were wet and slick with the heavy rain—a rain that followed weeks of drought. Surely the boy would have taken that into consideration. Surely he would have reminded Sadie that he was only eighteen and that Florida law required a driver on a learning permit to be accompanied by another driver over the age of twenty-one. He was a responsible kid—most of the time.

Oh, there was going to be blame enough to go around for all of them, Emma thought. But they would weather that and whatever else came their way as they always had—as a family of strong faith.

"Come on, Jeannie," Emma said as she guided her sister across the tiled hall and into the carpeted waiting room. "Geoff needs you."

Chapter 11

Sadie

"Sadie, my name is Lieutenant Benson. I need to ask you some questions about what happened earlier today."

Sadie kept her gaze fixed on the wall opposite her. She was in a hospital room. She could tell by the whiteboard on the wall that announced: "Your nurse is Marcie."

She had little memory of how she'd gotten here. Her dad was standing by the window while her mom fussed over her, adjusting her pillow and rearranging the covers. They were nervous.

"I'm with the Sarasota police," the man in uniform continued.

"Dad and I will be right here, Sadie," her mom murmured. "There's no reason to be afraid, okay?"

Until that moment, Sadie hadn't really felt much of anything, but now as details of the morning came back to her, she felt heat rush to her face, and her stomach lurched. The clock read 10:25. At night? No. Morning. She could hear the rain beating against the window the way it had been scratching at the car windows when she was driving. She glanced toward the light and saw that it was still daylight outside.

Lieutenant Benson pulled a straight-backed chair closer to the bed and sat down. "Before I begin, there are some things I need to be sure you understand."

Sadie found that the man's voice was not unkind—not bossy like she might have expected. Or angry with her. She had really steeled herself for everyone to be so very angry. It was confusing that her parents weren't upset with her for driving with Dan when they'd been so very clear about the rules.

"You have the right to remain silent. If you give up that right, anything you say can be used against you in a court of law."

Her mom gasped and looked at her dad, but the officer continued, "Tell me what you think that means."

"It means that you—" Emma began speaking to Sadie.

"I need your daughter to tell me, ma'am."

Sadie swallowed, but there was no saliva in her mouth. "It means that I don't have to talk or answer your questions if I don't want to," Sadie said. Her voice sounded like one of those automated message voices. "I don't want to." She did not blink or break her focus on the whiteboard: *Your nurse is Marcie.*

Lieutenant Benson cleared his throat. "Got that. You have the right to have an attorney present now and during any future questioning and—"

"It is not our way," Lars interrupted, but Lieutenant Benson ignored him.

"If you cannot afford an attorney, then one will be appointed for you." He waited for Sadie to respond.

"We're not poor," her mother said. "Just plain. My husband makes a good—"

Sadie saw her father's hand move, and her mother stopped speaking in midsentence.

Lieutenant Benson spoke to her. "Sadie, do you understand that you can have an attorney—a lawyer—if you want one?"

"We don't know any lawyers," Sadie said. She pushed herself a little higher onto the pillows and locked eyes with the lieutenant. "I understand my rights—you just Mirandized me, right? Well, I don't want to answer any questions, and we don't do lawyers." She glanced at her mom. "My stomach hurts."

"Okay. Well, that's your choice," Benson said as he put away the notepad and pencil he'd taken from his shirt pocket. He looked up at her father. "My advice, sir, is that you consider hiring a lawyer to represent your daughter."

Sadie sighed and focused once again on the whiteboard.

Her parents followed the officer into the hall, and she heard him talking to them. ". . .right now culpable negligence but. . ."

Sadie's eyes darted toward the door, and for the first time it dawned on her that she was possibly going to be arrested and charged. She listened harder.

"Dan Kline," she heard her father say.

"He's been ticketed for allowing your daughter to operate his car."

"So you're telling us that Sadie might be arrested while Daniel. . ."

Sadie felt a wave of panic. She didn't want to cause trouble for Dan. He had a full college scholarship. If he was arrested, that could ruin his whole future. She pushed back the covers ready to go to Lieutenant Benson and tell him everything.

"Dan Kline wasn't driving the car, sir," Lieutenant Benson said. "There are witnesses that saw your daughter at the wheel."

Sadie tried to swallow around the lump that suddenly seemed to fill her throat. Uncle Geoff had seen her. So had Tessa. "I was the one," she whispered as once again she saw Tessa's face in the instant before she was struck, her eyes wide and questioning as the car careened toward her. *I was the one*, repeated in Sadie's brain as she climbed back into bed and pulled the covers around her, covering her ears to block out everything that had happened. But even there she heard the drumbeat of the words. *I was the one.*

Seemingly out of nowhere, her mother's arms came around her, holding her, protecting her. "Shhh," she whispered. "Everything will work out."

"Dr. Booker has admitted your daughter for observation," she heard Lieutenant Benson tell her father. "But once she is discharged. . ."

Sadie's choking sobs blocked out the rest of his words.

"And then?" she heard her father ask moments later as her sobs tapered to a whimper. His voice was shaking in a way that Sadie had never heard before.

"She'll be taken downtown for booking. Again, sir, right now the case against her is borderline."

All of the air seemed to go out of her mother as if someone had pierced her with a needle, and Sadie realized that she had been listening to what the officer was saying as well. "No," she whispered and held Sadie tighter.

"Mr. Keller, take my advice and do your daughter a favor. Hire a lawyer," Lieutenant Benson repeated.

"That is not our way," Sadie heard her father reply, and then she heard the quiet click of the door as her father came back inside the room and closed the door, leaving Lieutenant Benson out in the corridor.

She pulled away from her mother and found her voice. "Am I being arrested?"

"No," her father assured her through gritted teeth. Then very softly, he murmured, "Maybe."

"It's what they have to do, apparently, when there's been a serious accident," her mom explained.

"But Tessa's going to be all right?"

"She's in surgery," her mother said. "The doctors are. . ."

There was a tap at the door, and Sadie's dad opened it to Hester Steiner. Her mom's friend looked really awful, as if she had just heard the most horrible news ever.

"Hester? Are you. . . What is it?" her mom asked in a voice that sounded like she couldn't find the breath she needed.

Hester glanced at Sadie and tried a smile that didn't come close to working. She motioned for Sadie's parents to follow her into the hall.

"We'll be right outside the door," her mom said as she gently shut the door.

Sadie strained to hear what Hester was telling her parents. ". . .did everything they could but. . ."

Then she heard her mom moan, "Tessa? Please, God, no."

And in that moment, she knew. Tessa was dead.

And it was her fault.

Part Two

*The beginning of strife is like
letting out water. . .*
PROVERBS 17:14

Chapter 12

Jeannie

Jeannie glanced around the kitchen. She was home, but how was that possible? She had no clear memory of how she'd gotten here. And how could this possibly be the same day? The same house? The same kitchen with its breakfast clutter untouched? And robbed now of the promise of Tessa ever coming through that door again, how could this place ever hope to lay claim to being a home?

Jeannie sat on the edge of the kitchen chair and waited for someone to tell her what to do next. Emma or Geoff, one of them would tell her how she was supposed to go on with her life without her beloved child—her only child—her Tessa.

She thought about Geoff's face when they had heard the news. She had turned to him after Dr. Morris quietly reported that Tessa had died of massive internal injuries. She instinctively knew that Geoff's expression of utter despair had mirrored what he was seeing in her eyes. In that instant, they had both gone from being the parents of a loving, bright, kindhearted, and generous child to being childless. There was a name for children who lost their parents. They were orphans. But for parents who lost their child? There was nothing. No longer a parent, what was she?

As if observing the activity around her from another universe,

Jeannie was vaguely aware of Geoff now in the next room. He was talking to someone on the telephone. She caught snatches of his side of the conversation and understood that he was talking to their pastor. Across the kitchen from where Jeannie sat staring at nothing, Emma was making tea. It was what Emma did whenever something went wrong in Jeannie's life. She came to her house, made tea, and listened while Jeannie poured out all of her frustrations.

How petty those discussions seemed now. Jeannie complaining about Geoff's job and how much time he spent doing it. About how now with extra duties as vice principal he would be home even less, and when he was there, more than likely he would be working. She had even moaned over Tessa and how she spent all of her time studying, and why couldn't she be more social like Sadie?

Sadie.

Suddenly she recalled seeing her niece sitting on the pavement next to the car, her arms wrapped around her knees, her head bowed. She remembered Emma kneeling next to Sadie. What she didn't remember was asking after her niece.

"How's Sadie?"

Emma glanced up, clearly surprised that these were her first words since coming home. "They're keeping her overnight for observation," Emma said. "The doctor ordered something to help calm her and make her sleep."

Jeannie stared at Emma again, trying to make sense of her surroundings. It came back to her that Hester had driven Geoff and her home, where they had been given over to the gentle care of Geoff's mom and her own stalwart parents who were now out on the lanai making phone calls of their own. Meanwhile Hester had returned to the hospital while Lars picked up Matt from school. "Why are you here? You should be with Sadie."

"Lars is there, Jeannie, and Sadie was already sleeping when I left. He was going to sit with Matt and help him understand everything. I'm here with you—where I want to be."

Jeannie went back to staring, this time at the dishes still on the table. Tessa's empty juice glass. The napkin—cloth, she had insisted on for the environment's sake—folded neatly to one side of a plate coated with dried egg yolk and the strawberry jam that she and Emma had made together earlier that year. In fact, they had put up enough jars that they were still being sold at the farmers' market to raise funds for the fruit co-op. Her utensils perfectly aligned on the plate. On the chair near the door sat her backpack exactly as her backpacks had sat every school day morning since Tessa's first day of kindergarten. Jeannie had clutched it to her chest all the way home from the hospital and then placed it there herself.

The very idea that either of them would ever again be able to function normally seemed ludicrous. How could anyone ask Geoff to go back to a job where he was working with children every day—where it would be impossible not to remember that this was the year Tessa was supposed to be there with him?

What was she thinking? This wasn't real. It couldn't be. Surely any minute Tessa would come down the stairs, pick up the backpack by its double straps, and sling it over one shoulder. Just a day earlier she had practiced carrying it that way, noting that kids in high school who wore their backpacks properly were considered dorky, according to Sadie.

Surely Geoff would complete his call and then shout up the stairs for Tessa to hurry or they would be late. Surely none of what had happened over the last few hours was real. Surely she was ill—delusional with fever.

Emma set a steaming mug in front of her and then ran the flat of her hand over Jeannie's back. But she said nothing, just stood there for a long moment as they both listened to Geoff's side of the phone conversation.

"Yes."

"No."

"I don't think that's necessary."

Jeannie realized that he was no longer speaking with their pastor. Every inflection told her that he was talking to a stranger, and the long pauses between his short replies made her curious. She picked up her mug of tea and walked into the den, where just the night before they had gathered as a family while Tessa opened her gift. Behind her she heard Emma start to clear away the breakfast dishes. She heard water running in the sink—Emma never used the dishwasher. She heard the back door open and close. Heard Emma greet someone in the low somber tones that she instinctively knew would become the norm for all conversations in this place over the coming days. And she ignored it all as she moved woodenly toward the den, where her husband was on the phone with a stranger that he really didn't want to be speaking with.

He stood at the window, his broad shoulders blocking the view of the lemon-lime tree that he had planted on Tessa's first birthday. He seemed older somehow, although his sable-colored hair was as thick as ever, and his stance was the same as when he stood on the sidelines of a game coaching his team.

"I'll check with my wife," he said now and turned around, startled to see her there in the doorway but recovering instantly as he slid one hand over the receiver. "Monday afternoon?" he asked.

"For?"

His face crumpled into a series of pockets and wrinkles as if someone had grabbed it like a piece of clean paper and wadded it into a ball and then released it. "The funeral," he croaked.

Jeannie felt the way people did when they dreamed of falling and then woke with a start, as two strong hands clasped her shoulders and pulled her upright and Emma relieved her of the mug of tea now spilling its contents onto the carpet.

"You need to sit down, Jeannie," their good friend Zeke Shepherd said in that calm no-worries voice that was his trademark. He helped her to a chair and then held out his hand for the phone that Geoff was still clutching. "And you need to let somebody else do that."

Geoff willingly handed over the phone and then sat on the hard straight-backed desk chair while Zeke took charge. That in itself had to be an aberration. Zeke was not a take-charge kind of guy. He was a combat veteran who had chosen a life on the streets, the type of person who made his way through life in a live-and-let-live manner. Rules were for people who had no idea of who they were or why they had been put on this earth.

Jeannie was pretty sure that Geoff—like her—had not even realized Zeke was there. But then that was Zeke—he came and went on his own schedule and in his own way.

"Zeke Shepherd here, friend of the family," he said and then listened. "Yeah, well, we'll get back to you on that. Otherwise, have you got what you need to. . .to go get her?"

He listened again.

"Got it," he said and clicked off the phone as he set it on Geoff's desk.

Jeannie looked at the clock that sat on the bookcase. Two thirty. There were hours she couldn't account for—time that had passed in a blur after the doctor left the waiting room. Any minute surely Tessa would walk through the door and calmly report that her first day of high school had been "fine." Her teachers were "fine." Her class schedule was "fine." Her new classmates were "fine."

Jeannie continued staring at the clock for a long moment. It was real, she thought, and nothing Emma or Geoff or anyone else could say would change that. The word *funeral* had been applied to their Tessa. She was to be mourned and buried within a matter of days. That was the way of things. How many times had she been at the homes of neighbors and family for this very purpose? How many times had she been the one uttering the meaningless words meant to bring solace and comfort?

She stood up and walked back toward the kitchen where she picked up Tessa's backpack.

"Jeannie?" Emma's call seemed to come from far away as Jeannie slowly climbed the stairs. The backpack was heavy. How many times had she fussed at Tessa about not overloading the bag? How many times had Tessa rolled her eyes and moaned, "Mom!" How much would she give to have that very conversation right this minute?

She stopped on the landing and stared at the backpack for a long moment, knowing that she wasn't yet ready to go through it. That would be like admitting. . . She retraced her steps and positioned Tessa's backpack on the chair where it belonged.

"Jeannie?" Emma reached out to touch her arm, but Jeannie ignored her, and this time she went all the way up the stairs without hesitating. She walked into her daughter's room and stood there taking in her surroundings. The room was pristine— bed made, everything in its place, clothes hung, drawers and closet door shut. And yet the aura that was Tessa was everywhere. It came from the way she had folded her nightgown and tucked it under her pillow—a bit of the lacy hem peeking out. It was in the very scent of a bowl of fresh fruit that Tessa kept on her desk. It was in the flattened cushion in the small rocking chair where Tessa liked to sit every morning and every evening to read her Bible.

Jeannie stood there taking it all in. Then she closed the door and locked it before crossing the room and sitting down in the rocker to stare out the window at what had to have been what Tessa had seen on her last morning on this earth.

Chapter 13

Geoff

Time had no meaning.

Outside the sun had come out and the skies had cleared, but the sun was low in the sky, and this day that had begun in a deluge of anticipation and excitement would soon be gone.

In the hours that had passed since Zeke handled the call with the funeral director, the house had slowly filled with people—family, friends, neighbors, kids Tessa often invited over, kids Tessa knew from church, kids from Geoff's athletic teams, teachers and other staff that he worked with, people Jeannie worked with in her various volunteer projects. A steady stream of people coming up the front walk, the women carrying some covered dish or basket, the men and young people parking their cars or bicycles wherever they could find a space.

Dan's car was gone now, but no one parked on the driveway as if worried that the space might be needed by someone older or frailer. Or maybe it was just that that space was tainted now—forever stained with Tessa's unshed blood.

Geoff stayed where he had gone when Hester and John had driven them home from the hospital, in the den. It was the room where he had always felt closest to Tessa. It was where she came to study while he graded papers or worked on reports. It was the room where the two of them watched and analyzed college games on the small television in the corner. He would sit in the cracked leather club chair, and Tessa would sit cross-legged on the floor. Jeannie would make them a huge bowl of popcorn then tell them not to ruin their appetites as she headed off to attend to one of what Tessa referred to as her mom's do-gooder projects.

He sat in the chair now, picking absently at the cracked leather as if picking at a scab. He allowed the flow of people to move around him, hearing the hushed tones the women spoke in as they took over the kitchen and set out or stored the food offerings. Once in a while one of the men would enter the den, clear his throat, and offer some condolence. Geoff was amazed at how easily he had fallen into the routine of standing to accept the handshake—or sometimes the hug—before murmuring, "Thank you" when the person stopped speaking and then adding, "I just need some time," releasing the person to go back into the large great room where most people had gathered. He never actually heard the words people spoke to him, but he saw from their faces that it was some form of how sorry they were.

He felt irritation at that. Sorry for what? For him? He didn't want their pity. For the fact that they had not been able to stop this horror from happening? Like he was?

Guilt welled up in him like wet cement, oozing into every crevice of his being. He had been right there when the car raced toward his child. Why hadn't he done something?

"Geoff?"

His sister-in-law set a plate of finger food on the side table next to his chair. "You should eat something," she said. "You haven't eaten since breakfast—"

"Where's Jeannie?" he asked, ignoring the food.

"Still upstairs," Emma replied. "I tried to talk to her. Maybe if you went to her?"

Emma was right. Jeannie needed him—they needed each other. This was their child taken from them too soon. Their home forever stripped of her presence. Their lives forever changed.

"Can you do something about maybe getting folks to move along and give us some time?" he asked.

As if time would help—as if they could somehow get over this.

"Sure." Emma handed him the plate of food. "Try to get her to eat a little something," she said as together they walked into the hall and he started up the stairs.

He was aware that the house packed with people had suddenly gone silent. Only after he had reached the landing at the top of the stairs did conversation resume. He walked woodenly past the bedroom he and Jeannie shared. The bed had not been made. It was something—like the breakfast dishes—that Jeannie would have done once she had seen Tessa and him off to school.

He passed the guest room—the room that Tessa often referred to as her mother's office since it was more often a catchall for whatever project Jeannie was involved in than it was a haven for guests.

The bathroom was still in the disarray he'd left it in that morning after cutting himself shaving and then later scouring the cabinets and drawers for the missing shed keys.

The door at the end of the hall was closed, and hanging from a hook was a cloth angel holding a hand-lettered sign that read: THIS ROOM PROTECTED BY ANGELS.

Not really, Geoff thought as he tried the knob. It was locked. "Jeannie? It's just me." He didn't recognize his own voice. It was so weak. He waited, and then when no sound came from the other side, he cleared his throat and rattled the knob. "Come on, babe. Let me in."

He detected a faint rustling sound as if Jeannie might have been curled up in Tessa's bed. Maybe she had cried herself to sleep. Maybe he should leave well enough alone.

The latch clicked, and he waited, but she did not open the door, so he did and was speechless at the scene. Spread across every possible surface were Tessa's clothes, arranged in outfits, he realized, complete with matching shoes and accessories. They hung on hangers from the curtain rods, on the back of the closet door, and on dresser drawer knobs. There were three outfits laid out on the daybed—like two-dimensional bodies, the tops propped against the back of the bed with the skirt or jeans spread over the quilt and matching shoes set precisely below each outfit on the floor.

"What are you doing, honey?" Geoff asked, fearful that while he was sitting downstairs his wife had quietly gone mad above him.

"We have to decide what she'll wear," Jeannie replied, and he saw that she was dry-eyed and studying each option in the same way she and Tessa had studied the choices of what would be best for Tessa's first day as an upperclassman just twenty-four hours earlier.

"Her favorite outfit is what she wore this morning, of course. Needed to look her best but also be comfortable, but the EMTs had to cut that." She made a face. "This one comes pretty close," she mused, fingering a stretchy lime-green top that looked as if it might fit a doll but certainly not a real person.

She stood transfixed in front of the outfit lying in the center of the bed. "The boots are a nice touch," she murmured as she sat down and picked up a tall tan suede boot. She seemed to lose her train of thought for a moment. Geoff sat next to her and put his arm around her. "The boots," she continued, "she bought with Sadie at the thrift shop." She shook her head. "They were to share them, with Sadie only wearing them when she visited. Tessa made me promise not to breathe a word of it to Emma."

Geoff took the boot from her and set it with its mate on the floor.

"That's why they're here in Tessa's closet," Jeannie continued. "So Emma wouldn't know. . .like the way I took Sadie for her learner's permit. . .so Emma wouldn't know until it was too late. . . ."

Geoff felt tears the size of raindrops fall onto the back of his hand, and he gathered his wife in his arms as she broke down completely. Her soft red hair, like expensive silk, brushed his face, and the scent of her almost blocked out the unique fresh laundry scent of Tessa's clothes surrounding them.

Still holding Jeannie, he leaned back against the pile of pillows at one end of the bed and looked around his daughter's room. He had rarely seen it from this angle. Oh, maybe a couple of times when he had sat with her when she was a little girl and told her bedtime stories or read her one of her favorite books. But now it came to him that this was what his daughter saw every morning when she woke up. She had opened her eyes to this room that very morning and thought. . .what?

He pulled Jeannie closer as he fought back his own tears.

"Geoff, what are we going to do?"

"We're going to go on." What he didn't say was that he had no idea how they would manage that.

Dusk had come by that time, and now Tessa's clothing was cast in shadows, shadows that were somehow comforting.

"Emma sent me up with a plate of food," Geoff said. "I left it on the hall table."

"We should probably go downstairs," Jeannie ventured, and her tone told Geoff that she hoped he would not agree.

"Folks will understand," he said. "Let's just stay here a little longer."

She curled into him, seeking his warmth, his strength, his assurance that somehow they would find a way to get through the next days and weeks. The problem was that Geoff was wishing he had a safe harbor to pull into as well.

"We have to make the arrangements," she whispered after several long moments in which they were both aware of people leaving, car doors closing. Engines started and conversation grew muffled among those left downstairs. "There are people—out of town—that we need to call. . ."

"Emma can make those calls."

Jeannie sat up suddenly, and in the waning light he saw that her eyes had gone wide with shock. "She's still here? She should be with Sadie."

The rage that swept over him in that split second made it hard to breathe. "Lars is there," he managed.

"She must be. . ." She pushed herself off the bed. "Emma said they kept Sadie for observation. Did they tell her? About Tessa?"

He realized for the first time that Jeannie didn't know what he knew—that it had been Sadie behind the wheel when the car struck Tessa. Now was not the time to tell her, he decided. She'd been through enough—too much—already.

"I'm not sure what Sadie's been told, but that's up to Emma and Lars. They'll do what they think best, Jeannie."

Jeannie flicked on a lamp, and Geoff blinked in the sudden brightness. She studied the various outfits for a moment and then took one down from the curtain rod. "This one," she muttered to herself and headed for the door.

"Where are you going?" Geoff asked.

"Sadie needs her mother. And we need to get Tessa's clothes to. . .to. . ." She stopped moving and stared into space, practically catatonic in the doorway. She shook her head, squared her shoulders, and forced herself forward. "To the funeral home," she said, grinding out each word as she walked woodenly down the hall and paused only a fraction of a second before descending the stairs.

Geoff could not help but admire her. Jeannie had always been a just-do-it kind of woman. It was one of the things that had attracted him to her from their first meeting. She was not big on protocol or rules, but with her sunny disposition and features that made her look younger than her thirty-some years, she won hearts and minds without even realizing what she was accomplishing.

"The president should send Mom to the Middle East," Tessa had said one time. "She'd get them all talking to each other in no time."

Geoff took one last look around his daughter's room, taking the time to study the items on her dresser, the stuffed animals that shared shelf space with her books, and the fashion show of outfits that Jeannie had staged. Then he turned off the lamp and left the room, closing the door behind him. When he reached the top of the stairs, he saw his best friend, Zeke, standing at the front door, holding the shoes Jeannie had selected.

Did Tessa even need shoes?

"Jeannie wants to take these clothes over to the funeral home," Zeke said when Geoff reached the bottom step. "I told her I would do it—or maybe Emma could or Hester—but. . ."

"We'll do it tomorrow. Right now I just want to make sure Jeannie eats something and gets some rest." He saw in his friend's eyes that they both knew that the chances of such a thing were slim to none. Zeke handed him the shoes.

"Maybe a doctor could give her something to help her sleep?"

"We'll get through it one hour at a time," Geoff said, not for one second believing they would ever survive this. "Thanks for being here—for both of us."

"No. . ." Zeke shook his head vigorously, and Geoff knew that he had caught himself about to deliver his signature, "No worries, man."

"See you tomorrow," Geoff said, opening the front screen door for Zeke. Emma had done what he'd asked of her—most of the visitors had already left. The street was deserted now as the darkness of night settled over the neighborhood. Zeke headed for the bright orange van he used to deliver produce to markets for the co-op.

Up and down the block, the houses were lit, the golden lamplight spilling out the windows and across the lawns. Those people were counting their blessings, Geoff thought. Those people with children were thanking God that this horrible day had not happened to them. They were holding those children a little tighter tonight. He felt his chest clench as if someone had attached a vise and tightened it until he was having trouble breathing.

For one moment, he thought he might be having a heart attack. For one moment, the idea that he might die along with his only child brought him a measure of comfort. But then he heard Jeannie and Emma coming toward the porch and he remembered that he was the man in this family. He had lost a child, but he still had a wife and others who would look to him for the strength they would all need to get through this. His mom, Jeannie's parents, not to mention his siblings, in-laws, Tessa's cousins, and so many others.

And as he turned to Emma, intending to thank her for all that she had done for them that day, all he could think about was that she still had two children, one of them responsible for the accident that had robbed him of his daughter.

"Where's Matt?" he asked.

"When. . .after. . ." Emma took a breath and cleared her throat before continuing, "Lars picked Matt up from school so he would hear the news from us. Then they went to be with Sadie at the hospital. We thought it best if they had a little time. . . ."

"Yeah. It's good to have time, Emma," Geoff said as he brushed past her on his way back inside.

Chapter 14

Emma

Emma hugged Jeannie and waited until her sister had followed Geoff back inside the house before retrieving Sadie's bicycle. When Hester had driven Emma to Jeannie's house earlier, she had seen Sadie's bicycle still leaning against a cluster of palm trees in the front yard. There was something so poignant about seeing that bicycle where it was so often left whenever Sadie visited the house. It seemed like everything must be all right after all. That the girls were upstairs in Tessa's room, giggling over some silliness or the confidences the two of them so often shared.

"I could load it in the trunk," Hester had offered, following her gaze as she stood at the end of the driveway.

"No, leave it. I'll need a way to get back to the hospital later."

"You'll be okay?"

"I'll stay busy," she promised.

"Be strong," Hester had whispered as the two friends embraced.

On her way into the house, Emma had avoided looking at the closed garage door. It was a relief to see that Dan's car was no longer on the property. In fact, there was no sign of the accident at all.

She had wondered if Dan Kline was being kept overnight for observation like Sadie was. She'd also wondered if the full weight

413

of what Sadie had done—or let her feelings for Dan Kline allow her to do—had hit home yet. What did a sixteen-year-old think in times like these? Was Sadie reliving the accident? What had she seen as she frantically tried to stop the car? Had it even registered in her brain that Tessa was gone forever?

"I've got this," Lars had said as if reading her hesitation to tend to her sister when her child also needed her. "Jeannie's going to need you there to help Geoff and her deal with all the well-meaning people who will be coming to their house once the news gets out."

"Hester could. . ."

"She needs you, Emma."

So before going inside to make the tea that would be the start of comforting her sister, Emma had wheeled Sadie's bike across the driveway and around to the side of the house where it would be out of sight when Jeannie and Geoff got back.

Now, hours later, she pedaled along the usually busy but at this time of night practically deserted main thoroughfare that bisected Pinecraft. With nothing to distract her, she allowed the full horror of the day to wash over her. She saw what they would face separately and alone in the days to come. Geoff's parting remark about time had stalked her every block of the way. Sadie had been reckless in that carefree way that made her so much like Jeannie. It wasn't the first time, but this time everything was different. How would Geoff and Jeannie ever be able to forgive her? How would Sadie ever forgive herself? As Sadie's parents, how should she and Lars react—should they punish her? Surely realizing that her foolish act had caused an accident that had ultimately ended with her beloved cousin dead was punishment enough for anyone.

And Matt? What about Matt?

He was so very attached to Geoff. Lars was not athletic, and having been raised Amish, he had not learned the contact sports like basketball and football that Matt found fascinating. But Geoff had taken Matt under his wing the minute he recognized a gift in their son despite his small stature. Geoff had patiently worked with Matt after school and on weekends. He even allowed Matt to be on the sidelines during the games that Geoff coached. And she couldn't begin to count the times that she had seen her son and her brother-in-law exchange a high five while seated in front of the small television in Geoff's den watching a game together.

Tessa had usually been there as well, Emma thought now. Matt had grudgingly admired his cousin's grasp of the finer points of the various sports.

"She's not bad for a girl," he had muttered.

Emma waited for the light and then pedaled across the nearly deserted highway to the hospital. She parked the bike near the valet parking station and ran inside. The lights had been dimmed in the lobby area—past visiting hours, Emma realized. She followed the maze of corridors to the bank of elevators that would take her to Sadie's floor, and as soon as she arrived, she saw a uniformed woman chatting with staff at the nurse's station. With relief she realized that the uniform was different from the one worn by Lieutenant Benson. The patches on the woman's shirt identified her as part of the hospital's security staff.

She hurried past, wanting nothing more than to have some time with Lars and the children without the presence of others. She felt such a need to gather them into her arms and hold on for a very long time. She wanted to lie next to Lars and pretend this day had never happened. She wanted to feel his strength and know as she had known from the day she met him that everything would be all right, that he would make it all right.

But she shook off such feelings as she passed the small waiting area and saw that it was filled with neighbors and fellow members of their congregation. The first person to come forward was Olive Crowder. Olive was not a hugger, but as she came to meet Emma, she stretched out her arms, and Emma gladly accepted the rare invitation to walk into their circle.

"How's Sadie?" she asked.

"Sleeping," Olive told her. "Lars got both of the children to lie down, and when I checked on them a few minutes ago, they were both sleeping."

"Das ist gut," Emma murmured. "Und Lars?"

Olive glanced back at Lars, who was surrounded by a cluster of men, including Hester's father, Arlen Detlef, who was also their senior pastor. The men were all frowning as if someone had raised a weighty question that needed special consideration. Arlen was stroking his thick white beard.

As she worked her way through the crowded room to Lars, Emma paused to accept the condolences of the other women and thank them for coming. They had brought food—a beautiful cake, a fruit pie, and at least three perfectly formed loaves of bread. The thought of eating anything made her physically ill, so she turned her gaze back to Lars.

"Guten abend," she murmured as she squeezed past several of the men to take her place beside her husband. She was unsure of her role here. Was she expected to play hostess and offer food as she had at Jeannie's house? A foreign house to these people, in that it was not plain in its furnishings, and its other occupants were anything but plain in their dress.

Except Tessa.

It was true that Tessa had not exactly dressed in the conservative small green, blue, or gray prints that Emma had Sadie wear, and she certainly did not use a prayer covering of any sort. Her fiery red hair—so like her mother's in color—was worn straight down, not pulled up in a bun. But even in her modern dress, she had preferred quieter styles than Jeannie did.

Emma suddenly thought of the outfit that Jeannie had brought downstairs to take to the funeral home and knew that it would not have been Tessa's choice at all. Perhaps she should call Jeannie. No, she would go over there in the morning. By then Jeannie likely would have recognized on her own that Tessa would want to be dressed in something quieter.

". . .officer said there would be a full investigation," Lars was saying.

To her. He was telling her something important, and she was thinking about clothing.

"I don't understand the need," she said. "We know what happened. It was a horrible accident, and one child is dead while the other. . ."

"Still, the authorities have questions," Arlen said. Emma realized that some of the people in this very room had already been questioned.

"But they are not our authorities," Lars reminded him. "We are not of their ways." He looked from the minister to Emma. "There will be questions, yes, but nothing so formal as an investigation. It was, as Emma has said, a terrible, terrible accident."

As he spoke, Emma understood that he was looking for assurances. But the other men said nothing.

"Lars," Pastor Detlef said after an uncomfortable silence had fallen over the gathering, "the circumstances here are. . .unusual. The General Assembly has long held that one of ours charged with a violation of the law and summoned to appear in court may indeed make use of the services of an attorney."

"But. . ." Lars started to protest, but Arlen held up one hand and continued. "However, the person accused must not permit the attorney to try to build a case based on denial of what the accused knows to be true."

A hush fell over the room. Several people bowed their heads. Everyone knew what the pastor was telling them. "The attorney's role is only that of establishing the truth, pleading for clemency in the case of guilt, and arguing the supremacy of God's higher law over that of the court."

Emma turned to Lars. "Is Sadie going to jail?"

"Lieutenant Benson intends to take Sadie into custody as soon as the doctor discharges her, Emma. You heard him say that. We have to think about how we can best protect her."

"There is basis in scripture to argue for alternative solutions." Arlen turned the pages of his worn Bible until he found the passage he needed. "Right here in the book of Luke," he said, adjusting his glasses. "As you go with your accuser before the magistrate, make an effort to settle with him on the way, lest he drag you to the judge, and the judge hand you over to the officer, and the officer put you in prison." He closed the Bible and faced Lars. "You must decide the path you will take. Meanwhile we will all pray for your Sadie."

The others nodded.

As the full impact of what lay ahead for Sadie hit her, Emma staggered and reached for Lars's arm to steady herself.

"Emmie"—Lars led her to one of a half dozen identical chairs—"you're exhausted."

"You both are," Olive said. "We'll be going now," she added in that no-nonsense tone she had that made people do her bidding. Everyone moved slowly toward the door, assuring each other as they left that Emma was indeed all right, that it had been a terrible day for the entire family, and that once they had some rest. . .

The voices trailed off as they moved down the hall. Emma couldn't help but wonder, *Once we've had some rest, then what?*

"Emma, can I get you something before I go?" Olive asked.

"I'm fine," Emma assured the older woman. "I'm just suddenly so very tired, and tomorrow. . ."

And the day after that and the week after that. . .

"Get some rest even if you can't sleep," Olive advised. "I'll stop by Jeannie's first thing tomorrow. And you know that Zeke Shepherd will be there for Geoff. You and Lars just take care of Sadie and Matt and yourselves—you've all suffered a terrible loss today."

Emma sat in the chair while Lars thanked Olive and Pastor Detlef and the others for coming. After what seemed a long time, he came back into the small room, and then he just stood there until Emma realized by the heaving of his chest that he was crying. She went to him. No words were necessary as they wrapped their arms around each other and hung on.

"Let's go check on the children," Emma said. She took Lars's hand and led him down the corridor. The security guard glanced at them but continued her conversation with the nurses.

"Mama?" Sadie was standing in the doorway to her room. Emma held out her arms, and Sadie ran to the safety of her mother's embrace. She was wearing a hospital gown and robe that were far too big for her, and Emma could not help thinking about the clothes she'd worn earlier that morning. Clothes so carefully selected from the limited range of choices that any conservative Mennonite teen might have.

"You're so lucky," Sadie had moaned to Tessa two days earlier. "You can wear anything you like."

"And you are so lucky that you're the kind of person that others want to be friends with no matter how you look," Tessa had replied without a touch of jealousy or malice. It was a truth they all recognized, for Sadie drew people to her like hummingbirds to sugar water.

"You'll have lots of friends, too," Sadie had told Tessa. "You'll see. Smart is the in thing these days, and nobody is smarter than my genius cousin."

Emma recalled how later, over glasses of iced tea, she and Jeannie had relived that conversation. "They're like we were at their age," Jeannie had said and then had gone on as only Jeannie could to lay out her plan for the girls' future.

Now Sadie seemed incredibly small and fragile as she pressed close to her parents. How on earth were they going to see her through everything she had yet to face—the funeral, facing Jeannie and Geoff, the full pain of the realization that Tessa was gone? Emma refused even to think about her daughter being arrested.

"Can we all sleep here tonight?" Sadie asked, her voice muffled in the cloth of Emma's dress.

"Oh honey, I'm not sure. . ."

"Matt's already sleeping. The nurse gave him a blanket and everything."

"There's nothing to be scared of," Lars told her, stroking her hair.

"We're not scared," Sadie replied. "Well, maybe we are, but don't we all just need to be close right now?"

Emma and Lars looked at each other. "Yes, that's exactly what we need," Lars said. "I'll just let the nursing staff know that we'll all be here for the night."

"I'll go with you," Sadie said, following her dad down the hall to the nurse's station.

On the one hand, Emma was thrilled to see her daughter acting more like her usual self. On the other, Dr. Booker had already warned them that he had little case for keeping Sadie in the hospital longer than overnight. And if he failed to keep her longer, she would be discharged and immediately taken into custody.

Emma walked into the semidarkness of Sadie's hospital room. It was small but private, and that was something to be glad about. As Sadie had told them, Matt was curled up on a reclining chair, the hospital blanket cast off to one side. Even as a baby he had always curled in protectively as if there were some need to fend off danger. His expression now was not what she would describe as peaceful. His brow was furrowed and his mouth was drawn into a thin straight line.

She knelt next to him and touched his shoulder. "Matt?"

He rolled to his back and blinked up at her. "Mom?"

"Right here," she said. "You okay?"

He pushed himself to a sitting position and rubbed his eyes with his knuckles. "It's true?" His features lit by the hall light begged her to tell him it had all been a mistake.

"Ja," she said.

"But. . ." The logic he was so fond of employing failed him, and his mouth worked though no sound came out of it.

Emma sat on the arm of the chair and put her arm around his thin shoulders. "But there's nothing to be afraid of, Matt. It will take time to get through the sadness and the terrible, terrible loss. You will always miss Tessa, but. . ."

"Is it true that Sadie killed her?"

For an instant, Emma stopped breathing. "Where did you hear such a thing?" she gasped.

"That's what Sadie told me. She said it was all her fault that Tessa died—that she killed her."

"Tessa's death was an accident, Matt. Do you hear me? A horrible accident."

Matt's head bobbed in the affirmative, and Emma realized that she had grasped his shoulders and shaken him. She hugged him to her. "Sorry," she murmured against his hair tousled by sleep. "So sorry. We need to talk about this together—all of us as a family. There's a lot we're going to have to work our way through, okay?" Emma's assurances that they would get through this somehow rang hollow even as she thought the words.

"Yes ma'am." Matt pulled the blanket a little closer, and Emma instinctively gave him some time to collect himself.

"Mom?" He did not look at her, just sat fingering the blanket. "I never really thought about somebody dying so young before—I never really thought it could happen to one of us."

"Me neither," she admitted.

Chapter 15

Lars

How was a man supposed to protect his family? How could he turn back the clock to a time when his wife and daughter and son were happy and safe? When their house rang with laughter and was filled with extended family and friends sharing plans and dreams for the future?

Lars drew the blade of a handsaw across a thick board and began the rhythmic back-and-forth strokes that would change that board into something else—in this case something he sorely wished he were not called upon to craft. He was building a coffin. Tessa's coffin. The large board would be changed by the cutting and sanding and finishing, much the way his family had been changed by the event that led to Tessa's death.

It was Saturday, a day that Lars normally reserved for doing his paperwork and making trips to the lumberyard with Matt to choose the wood he would need for the coming week. But today was different. Today was the day that he would pour everything God had given him in the way of carpentry skill into making a coffin for Tessa.

Although Emma had awakened earlier with the same outward calm with which she had greeted every day of their lives together, she was not the same—none of them were. The morning before, she had tended to the housekeeping chores in Sadie's hospital room, folding up the bedding the nurses had brought for them so the whole family could stay the night and wetting paper towels from the bathroom to wipe down all the surfaces in the room the same way she wiped the countertops and kitchen table and stove every morning at home.

The nursing and hospital housekeeping staff had tried to stop her, but Emma had continued her cleaning alongside them, using the time to get to know each one of them a little better. It occurred to Lars that she was nurturing those strangers the same way she nurtured their neighbors and friends. And when one large maintenance worker had pulled his wallet from his hip pocket and proudly showed Emma photographs of his grandchildren, Lars had thought that there might actually be a chance that Emma would see them all through this the same way she had shepherded their family and Jeannie's through countless other lesser catastrophes in the past.

And yet there was something different about her. Something in her eyes. The kind of furtive wariness of an animal that fears it is about to be trapped. Before, her eyes had always been alive with curiosity in spite of her inclination toward worrying. Now they were clouded by dread and doubt.

Before. . .

All of time now seemed to be divided into before and since—before the accident, since Tessa's death. No one spoke the actual words. Such sentences usually broke off abruptly, but the meaning was clear. Before the accident, his daughter had been a lively, outgoing girl who was enormously popular with her friends and classmates and much beloved by their large extended family. Before the accident, his son's world had revolved around sports—games played, games watched, games analyzed at length usually with his uncle Geoff. Before the accident, there had not seemed to be enough hours in the day to do all that they needed or wanted to accomplish.

But since. . .

The accident had happened on Thursday—odd to begin a school year at the end of a week, but Geoff had explained that the school board had decided that the first three days of the week needed to be given to faculty and staff to do all the things necessary to assure a smooth start for the students. So Emma and Jeannie had set the family picnic for Wednesday afternoon, and on a rainy Thursday morning, their children had headed off to school.

Only one of them—Matt—had made it there.

By that evening, Tessa was dead and Sadie was confined to the hospital. On Friday Lars and Emma had split their time between the hospital and Jeannie and Geoff's home, and they had been thankful when Dr. Booker had announced his intention to keep Sadie in the hospital for the weekend. But he had been overruled by hospital protocol, and late on Friday Sadie had been discharged, taken downtown to be charged and then taken—without them being allowed to go with her—to spend her first night in the juvenile detention center in Bradenton.

In this new and unfamiliar and frankly frightening realm of living, Sadie would be allowed limited visits and phone privileges. She would attend classes during the day and have chores to complete, just as she did at home. She would dress in the faded blue jumpsuit mandated by the county. She would not be allowed to wear the traditional prayer covering or keep her Bible close at hand. On Wednesday of the coming week, she was to appear in court for her arraignment, where she would plead guilty or not.

"Guilty of what?" Emma had protested. "It was an accident."

How can today be only Saturday? Lars wondered as he continued to plane the wood that would form the curved lid to Tessa's coffin. The funeral was scheduled for Monday afternoon. Would the judge hear their pleas and allow Sadie to be there? Lars was not so sure. He was not certain of anything when it came to the ways of the outside world, a world that now held the fate of his beloved daughter in its grasp.

Matt's response to everything happening around him was to become more talkative, filling any lengthy silence with reports on how things were going with the current football season— at his school, in the college ranks, and with the professionals. He continued to pepper his delivery of this information with such things as "Uncle Geoff thinks that. . ." or "Uncle Geoff told me. . ." And he needed only the slightest encouragement to keep talking, a nod of Lars's head or a murmured but distracted "Really?" from Emma.

"I think when I get out of school I want to be a coach," he had announced as the three of them shared their first meal since Sadie's arrest.

"What sport?" Lars had asked, grateful for any distraction.

Matt had shrugged. "All of them."

Lars had looked across the table at Emma and seen the fleeting lift of the corners of her mouth. And that almost-smile had been a lifeline for him. They would get through this somehow, and one day they would be able to do all the things they had done before—smile, laugh, plan a future.

The cut piece of lumber clattered to the concrete floor of the workshop, and Lars put down his saw and blew the excess sawdust off the edge of the board, examining it closely for any possible flaws. He was sanding the board when he heard Emma's bike tires crunch the crushed shell driveway.

By the time he got to the screen door of his shop, she was already on her way into the house. With Sadie confined and their ability to see her limited, Emma filled her hours helping Jeannie prepare for the funeral. Normally this was Emma's day to help out at the thrift shop, and she would come straight to his workshop full of news she'd heard from customers and other volunteers.

But since the accident, their family was the news. He watched as Emma went inside and returned a moment later with a broom and dustpan. "Emma?"

She paused but did not turn.

"Come on out here and give me a hand with this," he said, holding the screen door open.

"I've got housework, Lars," she replied.

"And plenty of time to attend to that." For some reason he felt compelled to break the cycle of her need to be constantly busy—cleaning, cooking, doing laundry. "You can't keep going on like this, Emma." He knew by the way her shoulders tensed that she understood what he was saying.

She swept a small pile of dead leaves into the dustpan and set it with the broom on the back stoop as she started toward him. "Why?" she asked when she was almost there. "Why can't I do what I want? Why do I ever have to do anything again?"

Amazingly her response gave Lars a flicker of hope. She sounded like Sadie, who had always leaned toward the dramatic. "You don't have to do anything," he said handing her a wood block wrapped in sandpaper and indicated the edge that needed work. "We have a choice, Emmie. We can shut out everything and everyone and hide behind chores. Or we can find some way to move forward. Shutting all this out may seem the easier path, but it seems to me that as time goes by, it might be a decision we'd regret."

By the way she ran the sandpaper over the rough edge of the board, he could tell that she was listening, hesitating now and then as she considered his words.

"It's so very hard."

"Ja. Life's like that."

He set up a second board to cut, and the conversation between them was drowned out by the whoosh of the saw moving back and forth.

After they worked in silence for a while, Lars saw her pause and study the rough penciled drawing he'd made, noting the dimensions for the piece. She watched as he cut another board, and then she said, "I know you've made coffins for others in the community, Lars, but what is it like making a coffin for Tessa?"

The directness of the question startled him, and he had to wonder what other unspoken thoughts she might be entertaining. "I don't know. I never really thought about it. Don't misunderstand—I am taking special care—all of the special care that Tessa deserves."

Emma nodded. "She would have liked that. She always thought your furniture pieces were the finest." She actually smiled. "There was this one day when the girls and Jeannie and I were at Yoder's and these women were in the next booth. They were snowbirds, we guessed, from the way they talked and were dressed and all. Anyway, they were going on and on about how they'd always heard that Amish furniture was the best made anywhere."

She was sanding the edge of the board now with smooth regular strokes, as if for a moment everything was as it had been before and she was just relating this incident. Her voice was livelier than Lars had heard it since that moment at the hospital before they'd gotten the news—that moment when there had still been hope.

". . .and Tessa just turned around and said, 'Well, my uncle was raised Amish, and he makes the most beautiful furniture you've ever seen. You should give him a call—his name is Lars Keller.' And remember? They did. That one woman came here with her husband and ordered that dining room set from you."

Lars nodded and kept working, afraid to break the special moment of memory.

"Tessa said she might just have to ask you for a commission."

"What did you say?"

"Nothing, but your daughter told her good luck with that. She said that everybody knew that you're cheap."

"Thrifty," Lars corrected with a smile.

It was so wonderfully normal—this conversation with his wife. This time together in his workshop. This banter. But as quickly as it came, it was gone. Emma sat staring at the sanding block she held in one hand for a long moment. Then she placed the block on Lars's workbench and stood up.

"The kitchen floor needs washing," she said.

Chapter 16

Sadie

Sadie had never been more terrified in her life. The whole day had been a nightmare from which she couldn't wake up, and now it was night and she was in jail—or detention as she'd been corrected by the ginormous, uniformed African-American woman driving the van as she was transported from the police station to the center. "No, miss. That place we just left? That was jail. This is different."

How? she wondered. *Worse? It couldn't be worse, could it?*

The rain had stopped. In fact, it was a beautiful, clear day—a Friday. She should be out on her bike with Tessa sharing stories of what had happened in school. Instead, she had spent the day in her hospital room, and then the social worker lady had come to tell them that she was being discharged. Right behind her had stood Lieutenant Benson.

The ride to the juvenile detention center took forever and at the same time was over way too soon. Sadie glanced at the other girl in the van. She looked a lot younger than Sadie, and she sat curled up as if trying to make herself disappear. When they were first escorted to the van in shackles and handcuffs, Sadie had tried to give the girl an encouraging smile, but the girl had refused to make any eye contact. Sadie had made the same attempt at eye contact with the guard sitting with them with no better results. Finally, she had given up and stared out the window for the remainder of the trip.

Tessa was dead. Dan had disappeared into thin air. No word. No visit. Nothing. And when she'd asked about him, all her mother would tell her was that Dan had been treated for minor injuries and released. "He's with his family," she'd said as if that should end the discussion. And then Sadie had been arrested.

The world had gone insane.

The van driver turned into a driveway between a couple of one-story concrete buildings then waited for another uniformed person to open the gate that led into a wire enclosure before driving in. The uniforms—as she had decided to call them since there seemed to be so many of them and distinguishing one from another took more effort than she could muster—exchanged brief banter while the gate was closed again. Only then were she and the other girl allowed to leave the van.

Sadie was exhausted. Like a sleepwalker, she followed instructions. Whatever the uniforms told her to do, she did without protest.

Once inside the building, she was told to remove all her clothes. She did not protest, nor did she make any comment when a female uniform searched her from head to toe, including looking inside her mouth and examining her even "down there." She was directed into a shower. She was then given a whole new set of clothing—a faded blue jumpsuit, underwear, socks.

Once she was dressed, she was taken to a room where another uniform asked her more questions—not about Tessa or the accident, but things like whether she wanted to harm herself.

"Well, duh," she wanted to say. *"My best friend is gone forever, and it's my fault. What do you think?"* But she said nothing.

"You can call your parents now," another uniform told her.

How could she? How could she ever explain? All the time they'd been with her since the accident, not once had her parents asked her what had happened. But the question had been there in their eyes. She was well aware that her day of reckoning had only been postponed.

She said nothing.

"You know, a kid like you from good people like your folks seem to be. . . All I'm saying is that's not always what we see here. They're probably waiting to hear from you," the uniform said, holding the phone out to her.

Sadie focused on her hands. From somewhere outside the small room, she heard doors slamming.

"Call your folks," the woman urged again.

Sadie took the portable phone from her and punched in the numbers. It rang once and started to ring a second time, and then she heard her father's voice. It was supper time, and he hadn't turned off the phone. That alone gave Sadie a feeling of relief— that whatever happened, her dad would take care of her.

"Hello?"

She collapsed into tears, and the phone slipped from her fingers and clattered to the concrete floor.

Vaguely she was aware that the uniform had rescued it and was talking to her dad. "Yes sir. Well, understandably she's a little. . .she's upset, but she's here and getting settled in. Tomorrow. Thirty minutes. Yes sir. Good night."

Sadie continued to cry. Then she began to shake.

"Your folks will be here to visit tomorrow. How about something to eat?"

Her mother would have wrapped her arms around Sadie and held her until the shaking stopped. The uniform offered food as if the two of them were out shopping or something and the idea of eating had just occurred to her.

Sadie shook her head vehemently. She wanted to go home. She wanted to turn back the clock. She wanted this to be over. "So tired," she managed through sobs and hiccups. That had to be the understatement of the year. The truth was that she was exhausted on every level—physically, mentally, and especially spiritually.

They moved through another series of locked doors into a larger room furnished with molded plastic chairs that looked really uncomfortable. At the opposite end of the room were a series of tables with attached stools similar to the tables in the cafeteria at the academy. Near the door they'd come through was a kind of podium-style desk. Sadie glanced up and saw cameras attached to the ceiling and a series of identical doors around the perimeter of the large room.

The uniform unlocked one of the doors and held it open. Inside Sadie saw two concrete risers the size of her twin bed at home and a metal toilet attached to the wall just inside the door. There was also a small window high on the wall opposite the door. It was still light outside. She glanced at a wall clock imprisoned in a metal cage. Seemed like everyone and everything was in jail around this place.

"Not tonight," another uniform told the woman with Sadie. "She's on watch status until mental health can evaluate her."

The uniform led her back out into the larger room where someone had placed a mattress on the floor. The guard handed her a pillow and thin blanket. "You'll sleep out here tonight."

Did they think she was dangerous? That she might try to escape? What? The one thing that was crystal clear was that her jailers were not inclined to provide her with information beyond the basic. *"Sit here." "Wear these clothes." "Sleep there."*

She took the bedding and curled up on the mattress. The two uniforms talked in low tones that Sadie was too exhausted to interpret, and then one left while the other took up her position at the podium desk. "Just so you know," she said, "I'll be right here all night, and about every thirty minutes I'll be checking on you. Got that?"

Sadie rolled onto her side and pulled the blanket up so that it covered her face. From somewhere outside, she heard a train whistle and thought it must be the most forlorn sound she had ever heard. But she was so wrong

It wasn't the train whistle that made her long for her own bed. It was the slamming of all those doors as they'd led her through this place, especially the one heavy door just outside the room where she lay on a mattress that was nothing like her bed at home, under a blanket that had been through too many washings.

Chapter 17

Lars

In spite of the advice of Arlen Detlef and other leaders of the congregation that he hire a lawyer to defend Sadie, Lars was uncomfortable with the whole idea. But on Monday morning, Lars awakened well before dawn.

Emma was sleeping for once, and he was thankful for that. With the accident, preparing for the funeral, and now with Sadie being held in detention, neither of them had gotten much rest these last several days. He realized that for the foreseeable future, every new day was likely to arrive with a fresh set of challenges to be faced. The night before, he and Emma had come as close to a shouting match as they had ever come in all the years of their marriage.

Oh, they had disagreed in the past—even argued. But they had never lost their tempers with each other to the degree that they had flung angry words around like fists. They had never looked at each other with such repressed fury—such doubt. That had been the most painful blow of all. The way that Emma had looked at him, her mouth working but no words coming out, her eyes wide with distrust. "I'm going to bed," she had finally managed and had gone down the hall to the room they had shared for nearly twenty years, to the bed that she had declared on their wedding night should never be sullied by anger or ill will between them. Clearly time could change everything.

They had argued over the hiring of a lawyer. Emma wanted one, and Lars was not yet ready to give in to the ways of the outside system.

Why couldn't they talk to the judge? he had asked. They could go there with Arlen and others from the church and community and plead Sadie's case themselves. If the judge would only talk to Sadie, he would see for himself how filled she was with remorse and regret for her reckless act. And if he had children of his own, Lars continued, surely the judge would be sympathetic to the pain that Tessa's death had brought to both sides of the family.

"Besides," he'd reminded Emma, "Lieutenant Benson said the case was borderline, remember?"

"Well, Lieutenant Benson apparently has no say in that," Emma had replied. "You heard him, Lars—the state gets to decide these things."

"It is not our way to—" he had begun, but Emma had interrupted, her fists clenched at her sides, her voice tight, strangled with emotion.

"They don't care about our ways, Lars. They will do things *their* way. Sadie has violated *their* law. She is in their hands even as we speak. The news reports quote the attorney for the state as saying that too many teens are dying because other teens are not paying attention when they drive. He wants to make an example of our Sadie."

"Sadie is in God's hands," Lars had replied, and when Emma had rolled her eyes, looking more like Sadie than usual, he had felt his stomach lurch.

"And did you never hear that God helps those who help themselves?" She had practically spat the words at him, and there had been a terrible silence between them following that. Then Emma had touched his arm. "Lars, Arlen has given you the church's permission to hire a lawyer to defend our child. What more do you need?"

"Our ways do not allow for such—"

"Your ways? You mean Amish?" She looked down at her

hands and made an effort to relax them. She drew in a deep breath. "We are Mennonite, Lars. The children have been raised in that way, not your way."

"I realize that, but. . ."

"This is about what is best for Sadie—for our child—our Mennonite child. Pastor Detlef has given us the way we need to move forward. Will you do it for Sadie?"

As was so often the case for Lars, the world was moving far too fast for him to clearly comprehend what God's plan for him and his family might be. He hesitated, wanting so much to reassure Emma, to do what was best for his daughter, to salvage what he could from this horror for their family.

"I will pray on it," he had murmured.

And that was the moment when she had given him that look and announced that she was going to bed. Lars had watched her go. Torn between going after her and knowing that he had nothing more to offer her, he'd waited until the door at the end of the hall had quietly closed, and then he'd taken his Bible from its place on the bookcase by his chair and started to open it to the place where he had last left off reading.

But the book had slipped from his grasp, and rather than allow the precious volume to hit the floor, Lars had grabbed for it and found his thumb resting on the second chapter of Paul's letter to the Philippians. He started to read but stopped when he had reached only the second verse—the verse that read: "Fulfil ye my joy, that ye be likeminded, having the same love, being of one accord, of one mind."

He had looked up, removing his glasses as he stared down the dark hallway to the bedroom where a slim shaft of light peeked out from the bottom of the closed door. Emma was sure that hiring a lawyer was the right thing. She had all the proof she needed. Lars was certain of nothing, and yet the scripture counseled them to be of one mind—surely it was God's intent that they follow the will of the mind that had already resolved the question—in this case Emma's mind.

He had closed the Bible and placed it back on the shelf before turning out the lamp by his chair and then walking through the darkness toward that light. When he'd opened the door, Emma was in her nightgown and sitting on the side of the bed brushing out her hair. Hair that fell in rich auburn waves well past her waist. Hair that only he as her husband saw this way—wild and free.

He'd held out his arms to her, and she'd come to him. "I'm sorry," she'd whispered.

"I'll see to the lawyer first thing tomorrow," he had told her at the same moment.

And now morning had come—or nearly so.

Lars got up, dressed, and made his breakfast. He left coffee for Emma and set places for her and for Matt at the kitchen table. He wrote Emma a note and then he walked to town, leaving the car for Emma, and waited outside a storefront office door that read: Joseph P. Cotter, Attorney at Law, Specializing in Criminal Defense.

He had ample time to consider the small brick building that looked as if by mistake someone had plunked it down not twenty yards from the front lawn of the far more impressive courthouse. The building seemed solid enough and at the same time a little vulnerable. For reasons he couldn't understand, Lars found an element of comfort in that. He tried to imagine what Joseph Cotter himself might be like and envisioned a man, tall and slightly stooped by age, with white hair and alert blue eyes. Dressed in a suit that had cost far too much, he would wear a starched white shirt and a blue silk tie that matched his kind eyes.

"Excuse me," a male voice said, interrupting Lars's daydream. He turned and came face-to-face with a man of about thirty, dressed in a rumpled shirt and tan cotton slacks, with sandy hair that was thick and unruly. He had an apologetic smile, not at all in keeping with the mischievous dimple that punctured his left cheek, and his eyes were the color of coffee with cream. They looked sad and weary as if they had witnessed far too much pain and suffering.

Lars moved aside and watched as the young man produced a set of keys and began unlocking the door.

"Do you work here?" Lars asked. It was, of course, obvious that he did, no doubt a clerk or assistant to Attorney Cotter.

The younger man pointed toward the stenciled lettering on the window and grinned. "Yep. That's me all right." He chuckled and pushed the door open and flipped a switch. A ceiling fan started to slowly revolve. "Would you like to wait inside here? It's going to be a scorcher. I'd say the humidity reading is already somewhere around drenching."

He didn't wait for an answer but entered the office and kept talking. "I have one of those fancy new coffeemakers that makes a cup in a matter of seconds. Gift from the parents when I set up my practice."

He talked too fast and seemed to be in constant motion. He turned on the coffeemaker, opened an overstuffed briefcase, and removed a laptop computer, turned it on, and then set about rinsing out one of several mismatched coffee mugs, all the while continuing to talk about his family. Lars was drawn into the small, cluttered office in spite of his intention, now that he had actually seen Joseph Cotter, to look for Sadie's representation elsewhere.

"Just to make it official, I'm Joe Cotter." He extended his right hand.

"Lars Keller," Lars said, accepting the handshake.

"Mennonite, right?" Cotter was opening and closing a series of small drawers under the counter where the coffeemaker sat. "Thought I had some creamer here somewhere," he muttered. "Or Amish?"

"Both," Lars found himself admitting. "Born Amish. Married and converted to Mennonite." He could not think what it was about this vibrant young man that had him revealing personal details of his life, but he did not stop there. "My daughter, Sadie—perhaps you have heard of her case? She was arrested last week, and on Wednesday. . ."

He saw that he had Cotter's full attention now. "Auto accident last Thursday where another girl died?" He handed Lars a mug of steaming black coffee and then exchanged the small serving container for a fresh one before pushing a lighted button.

"You know the case, then?" Lars felt the easing of the tight lump that he'd carried in the center of his chest from the moment that he and Emma had first arrived at the scene of the accident.

Cotter picked up his coffee and took a sip. "In many ways, Sarasota is a small town, Mr. Keller, and a case like this? Well, it's unusual to say the least."

"My daughter needs a lawyer, Mr. Cotter."

"It's Joe or Joseph, okay? And there are far more experienced defense attorneys, sir."

Lars appreciated the young man's honesty, but he realized that Cotter had not said there were better lawyers—only more experienced ones. "I came here and waited for you."

Cotter grinned as he sipped his coffee again. "Well, I did set up shop in the very shadow of the courthouse, so I guess that old real estate adage is correct."

Lars had no idea what the young man was talking about.

"You know, the bit about location, location, location?"

"I have not heard this saying."

"So, let me be serious here. I could give you the names of some other lawyers to call," Cotter offered. "Of course, they tend to have full caseloads."

Lars considered the unorganized piles of paper and file folders that covered the desk where Joseph had placed his computer. He thought about the young man's age and warning that there were more experienced lawyers, but overriding all of that was a gut feeling that this was the man God wanted him to hire. This was the man who would ultimately bring Sadie home to them.

"So if I wait to see one of those more experienced lawyers, Joseph, I could be waiting far past the nine o'clock hour on Wednesday when my daughter will appear before the judge?"

Joseph shrugged.

"I don't know why you got to your office so early this morning, Joseph Cotter, but you did, and perhaps that is God's way of telling me that if you are willing to take Sadie's case, then I should hire you to represent her."

"Okay, let's get to work," Cotter said, lifting his coffee mug in a kind of toast. He set the mug down, hefted a pile of books from a straight-backed aluminum chair, and indicated that Lars should sit. Meanwhile he sat on the opposite side of the large wooden desk and rolled the black upholstered chair closer as he tapped the mouse on his computer, drained the last of his coffee, and glanced at the clock while he waited for the computer to warm up. "Wednesday at nine?"

"Ja. And our niece's funeral is this afternoon at three, and I was wondering—"

Joseph studied him for a long moment, his youthful features contracting as if he were uncertain of how best to convey all that he was feeling. "You want your daughter to be there. Let me talk to the powers that be and see what I can do, okay?" He picked up a pen and pulled a yellow notepad closer. "Okay, Mr. Keller, tell me what happened. Start from first thing the morning of the accident, and give me every detail."

Chapter 18

Jeannie

She made her way moment by exhausting moment through the days and nights that marked the time from the moment the doctor had given them the news to the funeral that loomed over every minute of their lives. She observed the comings and goings of others as if she were watching a play or television show. She felt no connection to the activity that took place around her other than as a disinterested spectator. People gathered in her house, talking always in hushed tones but always turning the conversation to her well-being the minute she entered the room. Emma ran between the hospital, where Sadie had been kept overnight, and Jeannie's house, making sure everything was being taken care of. Geoff was gone for long hours at a time, and when he returned, his answer to her inquiry of where he had been was always the same.

"There are things that need to be done, Jeannie."

Lars had made the coffin in the shop where he normally crafted pieces of fine furniture. The workshop sat just outside the kitchen door of Emma's house. Tessa had loved to go there, loved the smell of the sawdust. Loved the fact that it was her uncle who created furniture designed specifically for the homes of the tourists who poured into Pinecraft during the winter months.

Jeannie had insisted on going to the funeral home with Geoff to see for herself that the staff there had dressed Tessa in the clothes Emma had convinced Jeannie to substitute for those she had originally chosen. She had stared down at her daughter, lying in the smooth pine box.

. . .*laid Him in a manger.* . . Random thoughts and bits of scripture memorized in childhood, apropos to nothing, flitted across Jeannie's mind from time to time. It was as if she were sleepwalking, her dreams surrounding her in no particular order. Nothing made sense, least of all that Tessa would never be coming home again.

How could that possibly be? The house was so filled with her essence. Her toothbrush lay on the side of the bathroom sink. In spite of the fact that Jeannie's parents and Geoff's mother took turns coming every day performing the usual household chores—making beds, dealing with the endless parade of food people brought, doing dishes, and so on—Jeannie insisted on doing some chores simply to keep herself occupied. In the kitchen she poured Geoff's coffee into the mug Tessa had decorated for him with the words WORLD'S GREATEST DAD, and then she reconsidered and poured the coffee into one of the regular cups from their set of dishes. She washed out the mug that Tessa had painted and placed it in the very back of the cabinet. But later that morning when she went to get something from Geoff's desk, the mug was there, half filled with coffee gone cold.

So many little reminders of her.

Outside were the orchids that Tessa had carefully planted in the trees. On the back screened porch were the shoes she wore to the bay to search for shells, and on the round glass table was the large Florida conch shell she had found only two weeks earlier. She'd spent hours soaking it in bleach and scraping off barnacles, then soaking it again to coax out the true sunset-orange color of the shell. She had been thrilled to find one so large and without flaws, especially one that held no living animal. Tessa would never take a live shell, and she had no problem reprimanding anyone who did.

Every room of the house that Jeannie and Geoff had bought

the year before she was born shouted Tessa's name. How odd was that given that Tessa herself had been such a calm and quiet child? A girl who much preferred the background, who liked observing others rather than being observed. Jeannie was the outgoing one. Jeannie and Sadie. . .

Sadie.

On the morning of the funeral, she overheard her mother and mother-in-law talking. Apparently Sadie had stayed only one night and most of the following day in the hospital, but late on Friday she'd been discharged and taken downtown to the Juvenile Assessment Center after she'd been arrested and charged. From there she had gone directly to a detention center. Surely, Jeannie thought, she had heard that wrong.

"Sadie's in jail?" she asked her mother.

"Oh honey, Emma didn't want to worry you with this."

"Is she or not?" Jeannie asked, her voice shaking.

"Yes," Geoff's mother said. "She's been charged with one count of vehicular homicide and one count of culpable negligence."

Jeannie's head started to spin. "But why?"

Geoff's mother looked at her as if she had just uttered a swear word. Her mother put her arm around her. "It's their way," she said softly. "When an accident like this one ends with someone dying, the authorities have to investigate, and in this case. . ."

"But Sadie? I could understand Dan being arrested, but—"

"Sadie was driving," Geoff's mother said as if stating a fact that everyone already knew.

"No. She couldn't have been." Jeannie turned to her mother-in-law. "Sadie only has a learner's permit, and Dan is only eighteen. Sadie knows full well that—"

"She was behind the wheel, Jeannie," her mother-in-law told her, her voice gentler now, as if realizing that she was breaking more bad news. "I thought you knew. I thought Geoff told you."

Jeannie shook her head. "I need to. . ." she mumbled without finishing the statement as she stumbled from the room and out onto the lanai.

Sadie was under arrest, charged with the ominous-sounding vehicular homicide. Her mother-in-law followed her. "You may as well know the whole story," she said.

"Yes, please," Jeannie agreed and nodded to her mother who had come to her rescue. "It's all right. I need to hear this," she said.

"According to reports in the paper and on television, the attorney for the state hopes to use the case to send a message about the rising fatality count among teenage drivers and their passengers," her mother-in-law said. "On Wednesday morning, Sadie will go before the judge for the first time. Until then she is being held in the juvenile detention center in Bradenton."

Jeannie could not begin to imagine how scared Sadie must be nor how worried Emma and Lars were. "But. . ."

Her mother-in-law patted her arm. "It will all work out, Jeannie. You needn't worry about it, especially not now. The courts will find the right way to handle this matter."

But Emma and Lars did not believe in the courts of the outside world. They did not vote or take part in the systems that governed the world they considered separate from their conservative faith. And yet she had nothing to offer them. It was everything she could do just to get out of bed in the mornings once she realized anew that this was day two—or three or five in this case—since Tessa had died.

"You should get dressed, Jeannie," her mother said. "We need to leave for the church in an hour."

So on that Monday afternoon—a day that by two o'clock had already seemed twice as long as any normal day—she and Geoff arrived at their church to receive mourners before the service. There was Sadie. She was dressed in a gray cotton skirt and a shapeless black sweater. She looked gaunt and hollow-eyed as she stood to one side of the room reserved for family to receive mourners before the service. Standing with her was a uniformed woman and, of course, Emma. Lars was there as well, standing with Matt, who looked lost in his too-big suit jacket bought larger so that it might last more than one season.

"He's growing so fast," Emma had sighed when the sisters had gone shopping for the suit at the Pinecraft thrift store.

Jeannie fastened her attention on Sadie—examining the

rush of feelings that swept through her upon seeing her niece for the first time since that horrible day. Her lively and vivacious niece, who could work a room full of people like any politician, now stood pressed against the wall, her shoulders hunched, her head bowed. In spite of her family around her, she looked so very alone. She looked the way Jeannie felt—as if the world had gone mad and she didn't know how to cope with that. Instinctively Jeannie's heart went out to her. She started toward her, but at that very moment, Geoff appeared at Jeannie's side and restrained her with a gentle touch. He took hold of her hand. "Honey, it's time."

Time. There was no time. Time had run out—for Tessa and now for Jeannie to cling to the hope that there had been some cruel mistake. The events of the last five days raced through her mind in fast-forward: breakfast. . .missing keys. . .the search. . .keys found. . .Tessa out the door with a blown kiss to meet Sadie. . .Jeannie more nervous about this first day of high school than her daughter was. . .Geoff out the door with a similar blown kiss and an umbrella for Tessa. . .Emma on the phone. . .a shout. . .the scream of car brakes. . .a dull thud. . .silence. . .

It occurred to Jeannie now that she had observed everything that happened after that in silence as if she were underwater. There were noises around her but none of them clear. Ambulance sirens, strangers huddled around Tessa, the ride to the hospital, the ER, the race to surgery, the interminable wait. . .

And here's where her recall of that day went from fast-forward to slow motion. Jeannie would never forget the way the doctor walked toward her. She relived every detail of his appearance in that moment. His surgical mask pulled down around his neck, his surgical cap and scrubs sweat-stained, his eyes refusing to meet hers or Geoff's, his long strides covering the distance. And the worst part was that she had known the minute he came through the door what he had come to tell them.

Leaning heavily now on Geoff as he led her into the sanctuary, she started to shake as she relived that moment that had changed their lives forever. Geoff wrapped one arm around her shoulders and pulled her close. So close that she could feel his warmth seeping into her suddenly cold limbs. His lips were so close to her temple that she could actually feel his breath.

She glanced up at him and saw that his jaw was set in that forward thrust that was so familiar to her. His eyes were blazing with the glitter of tears held at bay for far too long now. She grasped his free hand, offering him her warmth and strength in return. He looked down at her, and just as they took their seats in the front pew, his lower lip began to quiver.

The service seemed to go on for an eternity, but Jeannie did not want it to end, knowing what was yet to come. She tried to focus on the words of the minister—words about how death was no more than a passage to the other side, to heaven where Tessa, who had just a year earlier been baptized into the faith and accepted Christ as her Savior, would spend eternity. Words about how those present had best prepare themselves for the day when they would be called. Words about God's plan and how this was just a piece of that grander plan.

This? Jeannie felt like shouting. *This is my child, my only child, my baby, snatched from us before we had a chance to truly know her, before she had a chance to realize all that she could become, before. . .*

She knit her fingers together and then felt every fiber of her being tighten in unspoken protest to the outrage that her daughter was lying there before them in a wooden box. Try as she might, she could not open her heart to the idea that taking her child was something God needed to do for the greater good. She closed her eyes against the bile of anger that threatened to overcome her.

And then behind her, a throng of people rose as one and sang the words that had been a comfort to her all of her life.

> *Amazing grace, how sweet the sound*
> *That saved a wretch like me.*
> *I once was lost but now am found*
> *Was blind but now I see.*

Only Jeannie didn't see. She didn't understand this at all.

She looked sideways at Geoff. His lips were now so tightly pressed together that they had all but disappeared. His cheeks burned a bright red. He was sitting tall and straight, and his gaze was fixed on the wooden coffin that Lars had built especially for Tessa.

For Tessa. A box for Tessa.

Suddenly she imagined the coffin being placed in the ground, covered over with dirt, planted with grass and flowers. Tessa was in that box.

No. That was only the shell of her child. Tessa was in heaven. Tessa was with God. Tessa was not in pain or afraid or sick or frail. Tessa was safe and could never, ever be harmed again.

Jeannie clenched her fists and fought off the wave of nausea that threatened to send her stumbling up the aisle of the church to find a restroom.

The singing went on and on.

Please let this end, she prayed. But she knew in her heart that it was not going to end for them anytime soon. This was only the beginning. Tessa was gone. Sadie was under arrest. She heard a little cry of despair and realized it had come from her.

She felt Emma place a comforting hand on her shoulder. Emma and her family were seated in the pew immediately behind Geoff and Jeannie. Jeannie wondered why they weren't there beside them in the front pew. Tessa had been like another daughter to Emma, as Sadie was to Jeannie. But the grandparents were sitting with them in that front pew—three gray-haired people who had adored this child as Jeannie had. Her parents next to her and Geoff's mother next to him.

She glanced at Geoff. He returned her look with unseeing eyes then turned back to stare at the coffin. He would keep his vigil over Tessa until they lowered her into the ground. The night before, Jeannie had wakened to find Geoff gone. A note on the kitchen table read, *Someone should be with her.*

The words had hit her as an accusation. And as she had failed to keep her daughter safe, she had failed to be there to comfort her husband as he sat alone with their child—their only child.

Chapter 19

Geoff

At the cemetery, Geoff found himself fixated on Sadie. She looked different—more like Emma. Odd, when she had always reminded everyone so much of Jeannie. Tessa was the one who favored Emma. That was Tessa's role—not Sadie's. The thought irritated him, as did the way Sadie was dressed.

She wore the traditional garb of a conservative Mennonite—her skirt down to her ankles, her sleeves to her wrists, her hair wound into a tight, smooth bun under her prayer covering. Sadie had never worn the traditional white prayer cap before that Geoff could recall. She always opted for the black lace doilylike covering because it was less obvious, especially against her dark hair.

He shifted slightly, determined to see Sadie's shoes. Shoes were Sadie's passion—as they were Jeannie's. How many times had they laughed about Sadie in her somber Mennonite garb parading around in Jeannie's high heels? But not today. Today she wore plain black shoes.

Geoff looked at his niece again. From head to toe she was the picture of a devout conservative Mennonite. Was this contrition? Atonement? A ploy to fool others into having sympathy for her? Had Emma and Lars insisted? Or maybe the lawyer they'd hired? And to what end?

Sadie reverting to the traditions of her conservative faith would not bring Tessa back—would not undo what Sadie in her reckless, carefree way had caused. Suddenly Geoff saw the future clearly. He and Jeannie alone—their beloved child ripped from them without any chance to know her potential, to give to the world the gifts she had given them from the day she was born. And Emma and Lars shepherding Sadie through this, sharing the pain and agony of whatever sentence the court might impose, until one day they could wake up and think of Tessa only in passing while they went on with their lives.

He saw his nephew Matt watching him, his puppy-dog eyes large and soulful. Matt had always turned to Geoff whenever life became too much of a challenge. The boy loved his parents but he had built a bond with Geoff that went beyond games won and lost. More than once Geoff had taken Matt's side when Emma worried that playing team sports was too much of a physical danger for the boy. More than once he had listened as the boy agonized over his slim build and small size. "You'll grow," Geoff had assured him. "Just take a look at your mom and dad—both tall and athletic in build. Genes don't lie."

"And then there's Auntie Jeannie," Matt had said with a roll of his eyes. "What if I got those genes?"

It was true. Jeannie was petite and small-boned, almost fragile-looking. It was another of the things that had attracted Geoff to her when they first met. She looked like a porcelain doll with her fair complexion and unreal crown of curly red hair. But he had soon learned that she was anything but petite in personality and anything but fragile in the way she took on the challenges that came her way.

Until now. . .

He had never seen Jeannie so lost. For the last five days while they waited for family and friends from out of town to gather, while they endured day after day of people occupying their house and filling it with their whispered conversations and too much food, she had wandered through her days in a kind of stupor, her facial expression either one of permanent disbelief or unrelenting grief. In spite of the fact that his mom and hers showed up every morning ready to take over the day's mundane chores, Jeannie went through the motions of her routine at home—making beds, preparing meals from the endless parade of covered dishes. She'd even done the laundry. He had found her slumped to the floor of their room next to the bed, her fingers clutching a red sweater of Tessa's that had gotten mixed in with the whites and turned everything pink. He'd known she wasn't crying over the stained laundry, but it had shocked him when she had looked up at him, tears running down both cheeks, as she held up the sweater and said, "It shrunk. It's ruined, and it's her favorite."

Now, after a ride that he could barely remember from the church to the cemetery, he instinctively reached for Jeannie's hand. They were standing next to their child's open grave and waiting for the inevitable conclusion to the service, and for the first time he realized that it was raining, a light misting rain— gentle like Tessa. The sun was out, and somewhere he knew there would be a rainbow. Someone was shielding them with a large black umbrella, and all around them people had opened umbrellas of their own or taken cover under the umbrella-like foliage of an oversized saw palmetto tree.

He had a memory of the umbrella he'd been trying to open to shelter Tessa that morning. He saw her face, her smile, her eyes so alive and mischievous. Inside it felt as if his heart were cracking open.

Their minister had finally come to the end of his part of the service. The casket was lowered into the muddy hole, rivulets of water staining the wood. Tessa's classmates and friends from church filed slowly past the open hole. Several of them carried flowers that they tossed into the grave. Then Zeke, who had been one of the pallbearers, took Geoff's arm and led him to the mound of dirt next to the grave.

He handed Geoff a long-handled shovel. Geoff knew what he was supposed to do. He was supposed to place the first shovelful into the hole—the first step toward filling it—a step that the others would take as part of the ritual before the cemetery staff completed the work. He looked up and saw Sadie, her face buried in her father's shoulder, her thin body shaking.

Geoff fought against the temptation to go to her, drag her over to the grave, place the shovel in her hands, and insist that she—not he—be the first to bury Tessa. He wanted her to see what she had caused.

"You can do it," Zeke said softly, and for one incredible moment, Geoff thought that his friend might be giving him permission to play out his fantasy. But then he glanced around, saw all the expectant faces—some of them perhaps wondering if he would fail in this last duty to his child as he had failed to protect her that day when he stood by and watched helplessly as the car rammed into her and crushed her internally without so much as a scratch on her.

He thrust the tip of the shovel into the pile of damp earth and pushed it to its full depth with one foot. Then he swung around and dropped the load into the hole, closing his ears and mind to the plop of packed clods of gritty dirt onto the wooden box.

Zeke reached for the shovel, but Geoff held on. He loaded it a second time and then a third and then twice more before Zeke wrestled it from him and passed it to Lars. Then Zeke wrapped his arms around Geoff and held him upright as the two of them staggered back to where Jeannie was waiting.

She held her arms out to him, and he realized that he was sobbing uncontrollably—the first time he had cried since that terrible moment when the doctor had walked into the waiting room and the truth of what he was about to tell them had struck them all like a punch to the stomach.

"Somebody is going to pay for this," he gasped as Jeannie and Zeke walked him back to the chairs under the tent provided for the grieving family.

"Shhh," Jeannie whispered, and he could not help wondering if she meant to soothe him or to protect her sister and niece from overhearing.

Chapter 20

Emma

Emma was beginning to accept the fact that Jeannie was avoiding her. Over all of the time that had led up to the funeral, the sisters had been in the same place—the hospital, Jeannie's house, the church, the cemetery. They had often sat or stood within inches of each other. And yet there had been an emotional distance between them brought on by Emma's worry over Sadie and no doubt Jeannie's own dilemma of whether she should pity Sadie or blame her.

So as the days after the funeral passed with no call or contact, she tried on one level to understand her sister's reluctance to spend time with her. But on another it made no sense. The two of them had always been each other's rock when it came to getting through tough times. They were certainly no strangers to tragedy.

Their eldest brother had drowned when the girls were only six and eight. Their mother had battled cancer, and while she had won that fight in the end, for years it had fallen to the sisters to care for their father and siblings while their mother went through operations and rounds of chemotherapy that left her weak and unable to manage the routine of a large family. Through it all, Emma and Jeannie had turned to each other, sharing in the chores even as they shared their grief and worry.

So how was this different? They were both hurting. She thought of how terrified they had been at the arraignment when Joseph Cotter had told them that the state's attorney had actually considered moving the case to adult court. Under other circumstances, Jeannie would understand how frightened Emma had been. She would listen and console and reassure. That was what the two of them had always done for each other.

But as the days following the funeral passed without any contact with Jeannie, Emma began to worry. She moved through the regimen of household chores, getting back to the volunteer work that came as regular as the turning of the calendar—and through it all she sorted through the possibilities. How to make things right again? She came up empty every time.

With the funeral behind them and the counsel of Pastor Detlef as well as Jeannie's minister to try and return to some semblance of a normal routine, Emma had made the first move. She had decided to call Jeannie as she had always done first thing every morning. But she had gotten no answer. Seriously worried, she had ridden the family's three-wheel bike to Jeannie's house and found Geoff painting the garage door. He was dressed in a shirt and tie, and she assumed he was on his way to work. It seemed odd that he had stopped to paint the garage door, but then Emma had come to understand all too well that a person had to find his own way through the pain of grief.

"Is Jeannie inside?"

Geoff's hand had paused midstroke, but he had not turned to look at her. "Go home, Emma. She needs some time—we both do." He started painting again, drawing wide strokes across the surface of the garage door.

"But it's just me. I mean, I know there have been a lot of people. . ."

"Go home and leave us in peace," Geoff said, and although she could not see his face, the tightness of his voice told her that the words had been uttered through clenched teeth.

Emma stared at the kitchen window, trying to decide what to do. If their situations were reversed and Lars told Jeannie to leave, her sister would ignore him and march herself right up to the house. But Emma wasn't Jeannie, and as much as she wanted to go to her sister, she could not help but respect Geoff's pain. She understood how difficult it must be for him especially to distinguish between Emma, the sister of his wife, and Emma, the mother of the girl who had caused the death of his only child.

She got back on the tricycle. "Tell Jeannie that I'll keep calling, and when she's. . ."

Geoff laid the paintbrush carefully on the open can of paint and walked into the house, closing the door behind him with a finality that made Emma's heart thunder with fear for what the future might hold for all of them.

She turned the tricycle around and started slowly back toward Pinecraft, hoping with every push of the pedals that she would hear footsteps running behind her and that Jeannie would call out to her.

"I should have just gone inside," she had told Lars. "Jeannie would have. You know she would."

"Perhaps," Lars said. "Perhaps Geoff is speaking for her. Give her a few days at least, Emmie. This is uncharted territory—for all of us."

Emma had to agree. "Is Matt coming straight home?" Ever since Sadie's arrest, Emma had noticed a need to have her son close, to know that he was in his room or out in the workshop—not out in the world where he might get into a situation he couldn't handle—as Sadie had.

"He said he was going over to the academy to watch football practice." Lars cleaned some wood stain off his fingers. "Geoff's gone back to work then?"

Emma shrugged. "Looked that way. He was dressed for it."

"It might be the best thing for him. Get his mind onto other things at least for part of the day."

"And Jeannie? She'll be totally alone."

Lars frowned.

"What is it?"

"Look, I know how worried you are about Jeannie and Geoff, but, Em, our focus has to be on Sadie—on how we're going to help her find her way through this."

Emma felt a wave of irritation. Didn't Lars think she was as worried about Sadie as she was about Jeannie? Didn't he know that she lay awake at night trying not to imagine how confused and frightened their daughter must be—alone in a strange place with girls who, by some reports, were capable of violent attacks for no reason?

Everything was spinning out of control, and she felt so helpless. Her role had always been the strong one—the one everyone could turn to in times of crisis. Well, she was failing miserably now.

"I'm doing my best," she whispered, ignoring that Lars had reached out to her as she walked quickly back to the house.

Supper that night was a strained affair. Only Matt behaved as if nothing were amiss.

"How did the team look?" Lars asked after a prolonged silence had engulfed the family.

Matt shrugged. "With Dan Kline not playing, they've got problems."

"Don't talk with your mouth full," Emma snapped irritably, annoyed that Dan's name should ever be heard again under their roof. She glanced at Lars, who was looking at her with concern.

No, I am not all right, she wanted to say in response to his unasked question. *I have this horrible feeling that somehow we are waiting for another shoe to fall.*

"Excuse me," Emma murmured instead as she stood up and fled down the hall to the bedroom.

It took Lars less than a minute to follow her. He closed the door and sat down on the side of their bed next to where she had curled onto her side facing the wall. "I don't know what to do," she said. "I don't know how to help—either of them— Jeannie or Sadie." She gulped back the lump that seemed to have permanently taken up residence in her throat. "I have prayed and prayed for guidance, but I am so lost, Lars, and my greatest fear is that we are all lost."

She felt the mattress give as he lay down next to her, spooning himself to her back and wrapping his arms around her. He started to say something and then swallowed back the words. This was his way. He would not speak until he was certain that what he had to offer would make a difference.

"I spoke with Joseph today," he said after a moment. "I wanted to have a better understanding of what may come of this."

"And?" Every muscle in Emma's body went still and stiff.

"There's a strong likelihood that she will receive detention."

"She's in detention now," Emma argued.

"We're talking months—perhaps even a year or more," Lars said after a long silence in which she knew he was struggling to find the words that would cause her the least pain.

She pulled free of his grasp and turned to face him. "No. It was an accident. She didn't mean. . ."

"There are laws. . ."

"Their laws, not ours. Their justice, not ours."

"You've said it yourself, Em. We live in their world at times like these. And we need to prepare Sadie for what she may have to endure."

"Maybe we should consider some of those counseling services the intake worker from the probation department suggested."

Lars shook his head. "Joseph advises against that at least for now. Accepting such services could be viewed as an admission of guilt."

They stared at each other. *She is guilty*, Emma almost said. But they had already had that conversation. When Lars had hired Joseph, he insisted that Sadie must tell the truth about what had happened. "That is our way," he'd told the young lawyer.

"That is my way as well," Joseph had assured Lars, "and I would not expect her to do otherwise. But telling the truth about what happened that morning and pleading guilty to vehicular homicide are two entirely different matters. I'm asking you to trust me."

"Joseph believes that he can get the charge reduced to just 'culpable negligence,' " Lars told Emma.

"I don't understand these terms. Sadie certainly didn't mean to. . ."

"According to Joseph, the prosecution doesn't have to show intent—that she meant to do harm—just that she was driving in such a way that harm could be the result."

Emma's head was spinning with all this legal jargon. "Then explain to me why Dan. . . I mean, what about him and his responsibility in this?"

"We must let his parents deal with that. We will pray for him, of course, but Sadie—"

"Is a child. Surely that will count for a great deal."

Lars frowned, and she knew that she had not heard the worst of it. "What else?" she demanded, half sitting up.

He swallowed once, twice, and then simply stared at her as if trying to decide something.

"Tell me," she growled.

"If I understood what Joseph was saying, if the court agrees with the state, there is a good possibility that she could be sent somewhere across the state."

After her arraignment, Sadie had been taken back to the detention center in nearby Bradenton. She was to be held there while the lawyers built their cases—one for her and one against. Joseph had told them they'd be back in court in just three weeks. He'd made it sound like nothing, but three weeks without their Sadie at home and without the ability to see or talk with her whenever they chose seemed an eternity.

It was a short drive for them to visit her, but the visits were already so limited. Only on certain days and for certain times. If they moved her somewhere far away. . .

Emma began to shake, spasms that jerked her whole body and flung her head from side to side as the lump that had been in her throat ballooned in her chest. Lars pushed himself to a sitting position against the head of the bed and pulled her against him. "We will get through this, Emma," he promised, but the way his voice shook, she understood that he was no surer of such a thing than she was.

And lying there against him, she closed her eyes and gave herself up to the only One who could save their daughter. She prayed to God that somehow He would save Sadie, and them.

Chapter 21

Jeannie

Three weeks after Tessa's death, Jeannie left her house and started her morning run. The bay near the botanical gardens had become Jeannie's refuge. For reasons she didn't quite understand, it was the place where she felt closest to Tessa, so she marked the passing of the days and weeks since her death by going there. Each morning she crawled out of bed before dawn, pulled on sweats, and jogged the five miles from their home near Pinecraft, down Bahia Vista across Highway 41 to Orange Avenue and then around the corner to the place where the road curved near the botanical gardens and the exposed mud flats of the bay stretched out before her.

Depending on the timing of the tides, she could walk on the hard-packed sand all the way out to the point where the mussel beds had formed without ever stepping in water higher than her ankles. Even when the tides weren't with her, she would roll up her sweatpants, anchoring them above her knees. The clusters of shells were razor sharp, but the old pair of running shoes protected her feet as she picked her way carefully over the clumps. This was where Tessa had found her prized Florida conch shell—the one that sat in the center of the glass-topped table that dominated the screened porch at the back of their house. The lanai was

456

where the three of them had so often gathered for supper on balmy nights. The place where she and Emma and Sadie and Tessa had played board games on hot summer afternoons once they had finished their chores and errands and volunteer work.

Jeannie walked on tiptoe across the flats, changing course when her foot sank suddenly into a pocket of soft, mushy sand. Houseboats and sailing boats with their dinghies attached bobbed in the bay, their rigging clanking softly against the metal mast poles like wind chimes. A blue heron scolded her for invading its territory and then lost interest as it speared a small fish and swallowed it down.

Breakfast, Jeannie thought. She had forgotten to set the timer for the coffee. Geoff would be annoyed. But then he often seemed either annoyed with or indifferent to her these days. At a time when the two of them should have drawn closer, they were drifting further and further apart.

Once Geoff started back to work, his entire morning routine had changed. No longer did he come to the table for his usual bagel, fruit, and coffee. Instead, he filled a stainless steel travel mug with black coffee and headed out.

Unable to face eating alone in that big, empty house, Jeannie had begun her routine of running every morning. But she had continued to set the timer for Geoff's coffee. He counted on that coffee being there.

"*Too bad, so sad,*" Jeannie remembered Sadie commenting once. Sadie.

Her beloved niece was being held in juvenile detention, awaiting the hearing—or adjudication, as the newspaper had reported—of her case. According to a voice message that Geoff's sister had left for Jeannie, she'd been fingerprinted and photographed like "any common criminal." Geoff's sister had reported this in a tone that indicated that the news should come as some sort of solace to Jeannie and Geoff. "Maybe there will be some justice for Tessa after all," she had concluded.

But that kind of justice—that eye-for-an-eye vengeance—was not what Jeannie had been raised to believe in. In the faith of generations of her family, finding true justice was about finding the path to forgiveness. And yet she and Geoff had lost their only child. No one involved had meant for that to happen, yet it had, and try as she might, Jeannie could not yet find it in her heart to forgive an act of such pure irresponsibility and selfishness. And neither could Geoff.

From the moment they left the cemetery, she had watched him close himself off more and more. At the house, filled with mourners wanting only to offer support and comfort, Geoff had said something about needing some time and disappeared. People had come and gone all through the long afternoon and well into the evening, but Geoff had stayed away. Jeannie had assured everyone that he would be back any moment, but hours had passed without a sign of him.

It was Zeke who had gone in search of him and finally located him, sitting alone in the bleachers of the athletic field at the school. Using the battered pay phone mounted on the back of the shuttered concession stand, Zeke had called the house to assure Jeannie that Geoff was unharmed.

"He needs some time is all."

The idea of needing time had become the anthem of the entire horrible and unthinkable event. What good was time going to do? Time certainly would not bring Tessa back. Time stretched out in front of them like a life sentence—life without parole. Life without Tessa.

And yet Jeannie was as guilty of using the excuse as anyone. She had heard Geoff send Emma away a few days after the funeral, telling her that Jeannie needed some time. She had avoided answering the door after Geoff returned to work, knowing it was some kind neighbor or fellow church member come to drop off a potted plant or covered dish. She had willingly allowed Geoff to steer her away from Sadie at the funeral, and later as she watched the uniformed guard escort Sadie from the cemetery, she had told herself that right now she needed to focus on Geoff—his needs, his pain.

They needed time.

But time was not working in their favor. The more time that passed, the wider the gap seemed to grow between Geoff and her. Each night he isolated himself in his den, citing the need to catch up on administrative reports or reviewing game tapes of the next football opponent and then coming to bed well after midnight. Even in the days between the funeral and his return to work, he had filled the hours with chores—repairing a shelf in the laundry room, resurfacing the driveway, trimming the shrubs that divided their house from the neighbor's.

They had taken to having their dinner—a meal that Jeannie created from the overflowing larder of food left by others—in front of the television. It had started a few nights after the funeral—after others had stopped filling the house with their whispers and covered dishes. Geoff had been watching the news, and Jeannie had called out that dinner was ready.

"I'll take mine in here," Geoff had called back. "There's a story coming up that I want to see."

Jeannie had prepared him a plate and then one for herself, and they had sat staring wordlessly at the television as they ate.

Now it had been nearly a month since they had sat down for a meal together at their kitchen table. Just yesterday she had put the placemats and cloth napkins in the laundry, and once they were dry, she had put them away in a drawer instead of back on the table. Every action or inaction like that one felt like one step closer to giving up on ever being able to make a life together without Tessa.

"Hey there, pretty lady," a voice called, and Jeannie turned to see Zeke coming toward her in a barnacle-covered dingy powered by a trolling motor. "I brought you something."

He cut the motor and beached the boat, then climbed out and dragged it onto higher ground. He wore ragged jeans rolled to midcalf, a faded T-shirt, and an old baseball cap. He was barefoot and had tied his long black hair back into a ponytail. He greeted her with the kind of sad, how-you-holding-up? smile that Jeannie had come to expect whenever she ran into anyone she knew these days.

"Close your eyes," he said, "and hold out your hands."

It was such an incredibly normal request that Jeannie allowed herself to let go of all the *should's* and *ought to's* of how she was supposed to be feeling and did as he asked.

He laid something in her hands. Small and slender, hard but also, she realized, a little fragile.

"Angel wings," he said softly as she opened her eyes and saw a petite matched pair of pure white ruffled seashells that carried the name so fitting to them.

"Oh Zeke, they're smaller than any I've ever seen and so perfect. Where did you find them?"

He shrugged. "Coming down the creek. They were covered over pretty good, but there's no mistaking that pure white color."

Jeannie ran her finger over the ridges of the shells. Surely this was a sign, a prayer answered. It was unusual enough to find a half of the bivalve. To find a matched pair was rare indeed. "Thank you, Zeke."

"No wor. . ." Zeke's tanned face turned a deeper shade of burnished red. "Sorry," he mumbled.

"No worries," she said. "It's okay, Zeke. I know what you mean."

Most of the time a gesture like this would bring tears to her eyes, but what she felt now was something different. The gift had given her a feeling that had been absent for days now. The perfection of the matched shells gave her a glimmer of hope.

"Would you like to go for a cup of coffee?" she asked Zeke and realized it was the first effort she had made since the funeral to reach out to someone other than Geoff.

Zeke studied her sweats and frowned. "You didn't bring any money, did you?"

He was right, and it was her turn to blush. "You could come to the house. The pot's all set. I just need to turn it on."

Zeke grinned. "You wouldn't have any of those cinnamon rolls you make, would you?"

"Not that I made, but certainly plenty made by some of the best cooks in Pinecraft."

"Emma?"

With one word he had changed the lighter mood he was working so hard to establish. But then that was Zeke's way. Just when she thought she had him figured out, he would surprise her by changing course.

"How is she?" Jeannie asked, knowing that Zeke wouldn't judge her for not knowing the answer herself.

"Sadie's in detention. They dodged a bullet when the state's attorney decided against taking the case into adult court, but the kid's still locked up."

He took Jeannie's elbow as she climbed into the dingy, then pushed the small craft into deeper water before getting in and pulling the cord to start the motor.

"And Dan Kline?"

Zeke shrugged. "His parents know people—you know how that works. He got ticketed and his license was suspended. Then he was sent home, but then I imagine Geoff already told you that."

"Not really," she murmured, thinking about how little she and Geoff shared.

Zeke frowned but made no comment. "You should call Emma."

"I know." But she couldn't bring herself to promise that she would. Besides, there were circumstances beyond what Zeke or others might think that kept her from reconnecting with her sister. As Geoff had reminded her on more than one occasion, things had changed. She still woke up every morning thinking that if she hadn't taken Sadie for her learner's permit, none of this would have happened. Then just as quickly she would repress that thought, unwilling to pile guilt on top of the already staggering load of her grief.

Emma had left numerous phone messages—none of which Jeannie had responded to, all of which she had saved. One morning her sister had even taped a note to their back door. Jeannie had found it when she came back from her run. "I'm here," it had read. "Call when you can."

Jeannie cradled the angel wings in one palm, fingering them as Zeke navigated around the sandbars of the bay. It was an unusual day for September—cooler and less humid. A perfect day for a boat ride. Jeannie was so very tired of the pain and the sadness and the pressing stone of loss she carried with her every minute of every hour. She leaned back and closed her eyes as

461

Zeke guided the boat up the channel to the creek that wound its way to Pinecraft.

"So, about Emma—you'll call her?" Zeke pressed.

"Can we just talk about something else—just for now?"

"Why talk at all?"

Jeannie gave him a half smile. "Sometimes it helps to remind myself that the rest of the world has moved on even though our world. . ."

"Oh, you want normal, do you? Right. Well, the fruit co-op is booming. Hard to keep up with everything, and here we are on the brink of a new growing season. First calls are starting to come in from folks wanting to schedule the volunteers to come pick fruit from their yards."

It had been a little over a year since Hester and others had organized volunteers from the Mennonite community to offer a service of collecting fruit from the yards of private citizens requesting the service. The fruit was then delivered to a packing house on the property that Zeke's brother, Malcolm, had purchased and set up as a foundation for the project. There Zeke and others from the community who were homeless or preferred a more unorthodox lifestyle came to sort and box the fruit and deliver it to the various food pantries in the area.

The project mirrored the work of similar co-ops operating as far west as California and as nearby as Tampa. But the Pinecraft co-op also offered Emma's strawberry jam as well as homemade orange marmalade and pies for sale at local farmers' markets. "Like I said, it's starting to get busy, and we could use some help. Might be good for you to come on back, as well. I mean, now that Geoff's gone back to work and all."

Jeannie and Emma and their daughters had volunteered regularly at the co-op from the day it first opened. Sadie had been a wonder at getting local publicity for the project, and Jeannie's phone had rung constantly with homeowners wanting to schedule a pickup of fruit from their yards. Tessa had been responsible for setting up a schedule that kept everything running smoothly.

Lars used to call them "the Fruit Loops" with that dry sense of humor that was his trademark. How Geoff had laughed at that. He and Matt had picked up on the tag and even made up a song about it.

They had laughed together so often through the years. Jeannie could not imagine laughing over such silliness ever again.

"I'll tie up at the park, and we can walk from there to your house, okay?"

"Sure." Leaving the boat at the park meant walking through Pinecraft to reach her house, which could mean crossing paths with Emma. Jeannie mentally ran through her sister's routine. It was Thursday. On Thursday she joined other women for the weekly cleaning of the church.

"Emma's in court today," Zeke said, reading her mind. "No worries."

But Jeannie did not miss the hint of sarcasm with which he delivered his trademark phrase, and for the rest of the trip, he said nothing more.

Chapter 22

Emma

On the day that Sadie's hearing was to begin—and possibly end—Lars and Emma arrived at the courthouse early. They parked in back and then walked past Joseph Cotter's small office, peering in the window to see if the young lawyer was inside.

"He's probably already left for court," Lars said.

Inside the courthouse lobby, they endured the curious glances of the uniformed staff as they went through the security checkpoint and then took the stairs to the third floor as instructed.

"This way," Lars said, pausing a minute to check room numbers. The corridor was carpeted and there were chairs and benches outside the closed doors that lined the wall opposite a wall of windows. "This one," he said, stopping at one of the doors and then trying the knob. It was not the courtroom where the arraignment had taken place. That courtroom was two doors down the hall. *So many courtrooms*, Emma found herself thinking, and she couldn't help but think that if the system needed more than one courtroom to handle all of the problems coming before the judges, then perhaps the world had far bigger problems than she'd ever imagined.

The door was locked. Through narrow glass windows to either side, Emma could see that the room was identical to the one they had been in three weeks earlier. Chairs like those she and Lars had sat in when Sadie was arraigned were lined up to either side of a center aisle and were separated from the area where the court's business would take place by a low polished wooden wall.

"We're too early," she said and took a seat on one of the benches positioned so that she could continue to monitor the activity in the courtroom. She tried to imagine Sadie riding in the locked van from the detention center in Bradenton. Would she be with other teens or alone? Emma hoped that she was alone, although what did it matter?

"It's not so bad," Sadie had told them every time they visited her. "They keep us busy from the time we get up until we go to bed, so the time passes."

"How's school?" Lars asked her every time, his repetition of the same question only emphasizing the fact that there were topics they would not raise and there was little else to talk about.

Sadie had smiled wistfully. "It reminds me of the Mennonite school. Every girl has her own work to do. You know there are all ages in here. The youngest is only ten," she whispered.

Ten years old, Emma thought as she watched Lars pace down to the elevator where he stood reading some sign. *What could a ten-year-old possibly do that would result in her being locked up?*

A woman dressed in tan slacks, a white shirt, and a brown leather jacket took a seat on the next bench over. Emma glanced at her, but the woman paid no mind. A few minutes later, an older African-American woman came down the hall from the direction of the elevator and joined the first woman.

"I can't have her moving back home," the older woman said. The first woman nodded. "I have the other children I have to consider. Last time she was sent home she got so mad she threw the television across the room. Smashed it to smithereens."

The other woman made a noise of sympathetic understanding, and Emma shuddered. Was this girl being held in the same place Sadie was? She prayed not and then prayed for forgiveness for eavesdropping, but as Lars continued pacing the corridor, she found herself leaning closer to listen to the two women.

"She lied to my face," the younger woman said. "We have the whole thing on video. She knew we did, and yet when I asked her if she hit that girl, she said no."

The woman that Emma had decided was the mother of the girl in question sighed wearily. "She does that all the time—lives in a world of her own, that one. Her mother was the same."

So, she's the grandmother, Emma thought. *So young.*

There was a moment's pause, and then the woman in the leather jacket said, "So you're on board with our sending her away?"

The grandmother nodded. "I don't see any other solution. You've tried everything possible—counseling, medication. None of it works. Maybe if she realizes she's not getting out for a good long time, she'll change."

Emma was incensed. How could any mother—or grandmother for that matter—just give up on a child the way this woman seemed to be doing?

"She's a very angry girl," the younger woman agreed.

Then help her, Emma wanted to tell them. *Hold her. Pray with her. Anything but give up.*

"She doesn't believe for a minute that she's going away," the grandmother said.

Why should she? It's unimaginable that a child. . .

Lars had stopped pacing and had come to sit beside her. He was looking at her with a worried frown. "Emmie? Are you all right?"

"Yes," she lied and immediately sent up a silent prayer for God to forgive her. "No. What if they send Sadie so far away that. . . ?" she whispered.

"One step at a time," Lars said, his voice tight. "You know what Joseph told us. Today the state will present its case, and then Joseph will tell Sadie's side of things. Remember, he said that it's unlikely the judge will decide today."

"And she'll have to go back to that place?"

"Joseph is going to try to argue for her to be released to us. He seems to think that he has a pretty good chance of getting that."

There was a rustling of clothing on the bench next to them as the two women got up and entered the now-open courtroom. Lars and Emma followed them, taking seats in the front row behind what they had learned at the arraignment was the defense table. The other two women sat across the aisle from them, and gradually the chairs behind them filled in with people who had business with the court.

In front of the low banister that separated them from the officials who would soon fill that area, Emma saw the state's attorney talking to his assistant. His last name was Johnson, she recalled. When it was time to begin, the judge would enter the courtroom from a side door behind the high counter where he sat. For now, in addition to Mr. Johnson, she counted the bailiff, the clerk responsible for recording the proceedings, and a couple of uniformed people she had seen when Sadie was arraigned. There was no jury for a juvenile case and no sign of the young man Lars had hired to defend Sadie.

"Joseph is late," Emma whispered then turned when she heard the door to the hallway open and close. A man and a woman entered the courtroom. They glanced briefly at Emma and Lars and then took a seat across the aisle and behind them.

"Dan's parents," Emma murmured, nudging Lars. "Why would they be here?"

Lars shook his head. "Don't know, but here comes Joseph."

The young attorney, looking not quite put together, entered the courtroom from a side door and nodded at them as he placed his brief case on the defense table and then turned to greet the state's attorney.

Emma laced her fingers tightly together as she watched the two men converse. They were both smiling at first, but then she saw how Joseph started to frown and shake his head. The state's attorney moved a step closer to Joseph to make his point. Both men seemed agitated—that could not be good for Sadie.

"Lars," she whispered and almost added, "do something." But what could he do? They had already tried everything they could think of. At Sadie's arraignment, Pastor Detlef and other leaders of the church had sat with them, and Joseph had assured them that the judge had taken note of this.

Even so, she had never felt so powerless. Her unrelenting prayers for God to show Sadie mercy seemed to fall on deaf ears, and yet she knew that there was some plan in all of this. Tessa's death, Sadie's arrest, the destruction of two families that had been so close. What could possibly be accomplished by such tragedies? And why one piled on top of another this way?

Just last night she and Lars had tried to answer Matt's questions—impossible questions about why God would test them this way. At least that was the explanation that Emma had come up with for herself. This was all a test—like Job's faith being tested over and over again. "This is our Job moment," she had told Matt.

Matt had given her a look of pity and frustration. "I have homework," he'd said quietly and gone to his room.

Earlier that morning, he had come to the breakfast table, gobbled down his food without a word, and then headed out the door.

"Do you want me to tell Sadie anything for you?" Emma had asked.

Matt had hesitated but not turned around. "Tell her that...," he began, but then he shook his head and left, closing the back door softly behind him.

Emma had gone after him, but by the time she reached the door, he had already mounted his bike and taken off for school. "Matt," she had called.

"I'll be late," he shouted back as he turned a corner and rode out of sight.

She shook off the memory as a side door opened and a female guard escorted Sadie into the courtroom. She wore the faded blue jumpsuit and shackles on her ankles. Her hair was down and fell across her face as the guard led her to the defense table.

Sadie nervously tucked her hair behind her ear, and Emma sucked in a breath when she saw that Sadie's cheek was bruised and she had a fresh cut over one eye. It took a moment for Emma to realize that Lars had gotten up out of his seat and moved to the railing. The bailiff started toward him just as Sadie said,

"I'm okay, Dad. It's okay."

"Sir, please take your seat, or I'll have to ask you to leave," the bailiff instructed.

"Give us a minute," Joseph said. The bailiff nodded. Joseph opened the swinging gate and took Lars's arm as he escorted him back to his seat. The attorney sat in a chair next to Emma. "They tried calling you, and when they didn't reach you, they called me. Sadie was attacked late yesterday at the center. She was treated in the infirmary. The girl responsible will be removed to another facility."

"We need to take her home," Emma pleaded. "Please, help us."

"I'm working on it. Just promise me that you'll stay calm, okay?" His eyes were on Lars.

"What kind of place is that?" he asked through clenched teeth. "I thought it was a place where children would be safe."

Joseph looked down. "It's a juvenile detention center, Mr. Keller. That means that there are going to be kids there who have problems. Some of them unfortunately believe that the only way to protect themselves is to lash out."

"What happened?" Emma asked.

"I'm not clear on all the details, but the girls were at dinner, and Sadie had bowed her head to pray. For some reason that set another girl off. She grabbed Sadie by her hair, and when she did, I assume Sadie resisted." He shrugged as if Emma should be able to figure out the rest for herself.

"Sadie would not have resisted," Emma told him. "It is not our way. She would have given that girl anything she wanted."

Joseph looked skeptical. "Perhaps you underestimate. . ."

Emma bit her lip. "I know my daughter. Will the other girl be punished?"

"I guarantee it," Joseph replied, and Emma realized that he thought that this was exactly what she wanted to hear.

"Without discussion? Without a chance to explain herself, to apologize?"

"Apparently the whole thing was caught on video camera," Joseph explained. "She hit Sadie in the face and then pinned her down and punched her repeatedly. She'll be here later today and probably be sent to a more secure facility. She definitely won't be back where Sadie is."

Emma wondered if Joseph truly believed that somehow this news would comfort her. He was talking about another child in trouble. Surely there was a better way other than that of moving the girl from one locked facility to another. She glanced across the aisle at the two women she had overheard talking outside the courtroom and locked eyes with the woman she was certain was this girl's grandmother. The two of them exchanged a look that spoke volumes before the other woman looked away.

"What happens now?" Lars was asking Joseph. "I mean, now that the judge knows that Sadie is not safe there."

Emma saw the way that Joseph studied his scuffed loafers for a minute before answering, and she knew that he had no good news to offer them. Their nightmare was going to continue, and their only recourse was prayer.

"Go do your best," she said softly as she touched the sleeve of Joseph's suit jacket.

The bailiff tapped Joseph on the shoulder at the same moment and nodded toward the judge's bench.

"The judge is coming in," Joseph told them. "You'll be all right?" Again he focused on Lars.

Lars took Emma's arm as the two of them sat down and the bailiff called out, "All rise." The judge entered the room and took his place in the high-backed chair that seemed to Emma suddenly to resemble a throne.

The judge studied some papers that the bailiff handed him and then looked at the state's attorney and nodded. It struck Emma that he had not once so much as glanced at Sadie—had not seen her bruised face, had not noticed the way she sat with her hands folded and her head bowed. *Look at her*, Emma silently pleaded as she stared at the judge.

She was a good girl who had made a horrible error in judgment. There was no need to sentence her—she had already been sentenced by her actions. Every day for the rest of her life she would have to live with what she had caused. Wasn't that enough? For this judge, this court? Wasn't that enough for God?

Emma made a strangled sound as she tried to breathe around

the fear that gripped her. The judge glanced her way and frowned, and Lars coughed loudly as he pulled out his handkerchief to blow his nose, drawing the judge's attention to himself. The judge paused for just a moment as he glanced from Lars and Emma to Sadie and back again. A hint of surprise crossed his features as he returned his gaze to Emma, taking in her plain dress and prayer covering. Then he turned to Mr. Johnson and instructed him to present the case for the state.

Unexpectedly, Emma felt a fleeting shadow that she named hope. The man had seen them—had really looked at them and Sadie for the first time. Surely that was a sign—the first positive sign since that terrible rainy morning. Emma closed her eyes and sent up a silent prayer of thanks.

Chapter 23

Matthew

The world had gone crazy as far as Matt was concerned. How was it possible that his life had gone from boring and normal to crazy upside down? Stuff had been coming at him like the rocks hurled at him by a bully when he rode through his neighborhood after taking a shortcut on the way home one day.

Tessa was dead—as in *d-e-a-d*. Grasping that alone was beyond huge.

Then add in the fact that his sister was in jail—had been fingerprinted and everything, according to what a kid at school had told him. He'd actually gone to the main downtown post office one day and studied the wanted posters for any sign of Sadie's face. One of the kids who had once been his friend had insisted he'd seen her mug shot there.

Add to that the fact that his parents barely talked anymore, at least not to him. They talked to each other, usually in whispers that stopped the minute he came into the room. Then they would give him these fake smiles that didn't really reach their eyes, and his dad would ruffle his hair, and one of them would ask some dumb question like how football practice or school had gone that day.

They didn't care about football—his dad didn't even approve of contact sports. And neither one of them knew the first thing about how the game was played or about the plays that his uncle Geoff was truly brilliant at crafting to beat the opposing team.

Uncle Geoff.

Matt rested his chin on his palm and stared out the window of the small schoolhouse. What had he done to make Uncle Geoff so mad? For the umpteenth time, he went over every move he'd made since the funeral. He'd at least been able to pinpoint the timeline to that being when his uncle had started to ignore him or turn away and pretend to be busy with his players or something else whenever Matt was around.

Before then they'd had a routine. After school, Matt rode his bike to the academy where he would stand on the sidelines while Geoff ran the team through their after-school practice. When that ended, the two of them would run laps around the quarter-mile track that surrounded the football field. On Saturdays, Matt always went over to his uncle's house for lunch and to watch college games on TV—either football or basketball, depending on the season. Tessa often joined them, but Sadie never did.

Matt didn't mind having Tessa there. Every once in a while, she would make a comment about a player or play that actually made sense. Sadie, on the other hand, would have wanted to chatter all the way through the game about the uniforms, the school colors, the fact that getting grass stains out of football uniforms had to be a real chore.

He missed Tessa.

He even missed Sadie. The house was too quiet without her. Meals were eaten in silence until he decided to start filling the silence with babble about sports. Never mind that any information that Matt had about how a college team or professional team was doing came from his reading the sports section of the Sarasota *Herald Tribune* instead of from conversations with his uncle.

Every day on his way home from school, Matt would ride his bike past a coffee shop where he knew he would find a used copy of the sports section. He would fold the paper and put it in his backpack and spend the time between finishing his after-school chores and supper reading up on the various teams. It amazed him that his folks never seemed to catch on that he was suddenly able to spout off statistics he'd never shared before. Clearly they either weren't listening or they weren't nearly as smart as he had always thought they were.

But, on the other hand, these were tough times for their family, and maybe his going on and on about sports was the one thing that he could do to help bring things back to normal again. Of course, that wasn't likely to happen as long as Sadie was in jail. What if the judge sent her away for real? Right now she was in a place called a juvenile detention center in a town just a few miles away. His folks were allowed to visit her for half an hour at a time four days a week, and Sadie got one fifteen-minute phone call a week.

But he wasn't allowed to go along for the visits. He was just a kid. It did help some when he'd heard his mom say that she didn't like to think of either one of her children being in "a place like that," and if he never had to see it, all the better. But he wanted to see it. He wanted to see Sadie. He wanted to ask her what it was like in there. And more to the point—now that his uncle Geoff wasn't talking to him—he needed Sadie. She had always been the backup to Uncle Geoff—the one Matt could go to with his questions and problems when his uncle wasn't available. She'd never laughed at him or made him feel dumb. In spite of the way she always seemed to be thinking about herself, Sadie was a good listener. He missed that.

But he was still mad at her. At school everybody—even the teachers—were talking about what Sadie had done. His friends had suddenly decided that they had other things to do whenever he asked about going somewhere with them or having them come to his house. She'd ruined everything for everybody.

Then there was Tessa. It was like after she was buried nobody wanted to talk about her. Were they supposed to pretend she never existed, or what? Is that the way grown-ups handled death? He tried to remember the times somebody old—like his grandparents' age—had died. It seemed to him that people couldn't stop talking about the dead person, telling stories about funny things that person had done or said.

Tessa had made them laugh plenty of times.

"Matt!"

Matt blinked and looked up at his teacher. Miss Kurtz did not look happy, but then she rarely did. "Ma'am?"

"I asked if you had completed your English assignment."

Matt tried to cover his paper—the one he hadn't yet started much less finished. "Almost," he hedged.

Miss Kurtz held out her hand. "Time's up."

Reluctantly, Matt handed her the paper. She scanned it and frowned. "You only answered the first three questions, Matthew," she said, and he didn't think it was his imagination that her voice had gotten softer. "What's going on?"

He shrugged.

"Matthew, please step out into the hallway with me for a minute." The suppressed giggles of a couple of his fellow students followed him to the door. "That'll do, class," Miss Kurtz scolded as she followed him into the hallway.

Matt waited, his mind racing with the excuses he might offer for his poor performance lately.

His teacher sighed. "What's going on? Talk to me, Matt."

"Ma'am?"

Another heavy sigh. "Don't play dumb, Matt Keller. You are an excellent student, as your sister was before you. But these last several days. . ."

"My cousin was killed, and my sister killed her," he reminded her and was as surprised as she obviously was by the sarcasm that colored every word.

"Manners, young man," she scolded, but he could tell that her heart wasn't in it. She was looking at him strangely. "Is there something you need to talk about, Matt?"

"No, ma'am. Sorry, ma'am. Can I go now?"

She opened the door to the classroom and waited for him to return to his desk, but her question stayed with him.

Yeah. I need to talk about why God would let Tessa die and in such a terrible way, and why He would make it so that it's my sister who killed her, and why my mom keeps talking about how this is our "Job time," and why when I need to talk to him more than ever, my uncle Geoff looks at me like I'm somebody he'd like to never see again.

Chapter 24

Sadie

In the surreal state that she had dwelled in ever since the accident, Sadie tried hard to focus on what her lawyer was telling her.

He was semi-cute for someone over thirty. Not as good-looking as Dan by any stretch of the imagination. He was of average height and slim, whereas Dan was tall and muscular. And the lawyer's hair was wavy and light brown while Dan's was the color of sunflower petals.

She had seen Dan's parents glaring at her when she turned around as her dad had practically jumped the barricade. The guard that had ridden with her to court had told her that they had been unable to reach her parents to let them know she'd spent the night in the infirmary.

"They turn the phone off for the day when we have supper," she'd explained.

"We left a message."

"They wouldn't hear it until they turned the phone on this morning, which they probably haven't done because Dad isn't going to work today since he's coming to court."

"You don't have a cell phone?" The woman had seemed stunned at the very idea of being so out of touch.

Sadie had actually laughed. "It's not our way." She quoted

the line her parents had given her and Matt time and again. But laughing made her jaw ache where the other girl had hit her, and she quickly sobered. "You'd be surprised at all the things that are not our way," she added.

Like courtrooms and detention centers and lawyers. For the hundredth time she wondered how Joseph Cotter had managed to persuade her parents that her only chance was a plea of not guilty when she couldn't be guiltier. It was not their way to lie—even about something so horrid.

"All rise," the bailiff announced.

Sadie felt her hands begin to shake, and she clasped them behind her back as she got to her feet and waited for the judge—a small dark-haired man with black-rimmed reading glasses perched on the end of his nose—to take his seat. The high-backed chair seemed way too large for him in exactly the same way that Matt's Sunday clothes seemed too large for him.

In unison everyone else took their seats, and a hush fell over the room. It was a little like being in church the way everybody did stuff at the exact same moment. The bailiff handed the judge some papers, and they exchanged a brief but unintelligible conversation. Then the judge glanced up. He looked first at Sadie, studying her face for a moment, and then she realized that he was looking at her parents behind her. His dark, thin eyebrows lifted slightly, and he cleared his throat and turned his attention to the state's attorney.

"I assume you have an opening statement, Mr. Johnson?"

The prosecutor was on his feet at once, striding to the podium reserved for his side while Joseph Cotter remained seated next to her.

Sadie tried hard to focus on what Mr. Johnson was saying, but her mind wandered. She wondered why Dan's parents were here. She wondered where Dan was and if he was mad at her. She had tried using one of her phone privileges at the detention center to call him, but his cell had been disconnected. And when she tried calling his house, his mother had told her in no uncertain terms that Dan was not available and she should not call their number again.

It had been worse the time she had tried calling Aunt Jeannie. Uncle Geoff had answered the phone, and hearing his voice—so sad and devoid of his usual good humor—she had burst into tears. There had been a long pause on the other end of the line and then a soft click as her uncle hung up on her. She had tried to call a few other times in the three weeks she had spent at the detention center awaiting her hearing, but neither Jeannie nor Geoff had ever picked up, and when the phone had gone to voice mail, Sadie had found that she had no words. On those occasions, she had been the one to hang up, and finally she had stopped calling.

". . .show that she exceeded the speed limit and drove erratically in conditions that were dangerous for her, her passenger, and anyone she might encounter. Further. . ."

Johnson was talking about her. He was making her sound like an irresponsible monster, like someone who had intentionally set out to hurt Tessa. That wasn't the way it was at all. She had tried to be so careful about staying under the speed limit. Then Dan had said that she needed to speed up, and she had remembered that on the way to the picnic when Jeannie let her drive, her aunt had told her that it was sometimes as dangerous to go too slow as it was to drive too fast. "You'll soon get the rhythm of it," Jeannie had told her.

Sadie felt her lawyer staring at her and realized that she was close to smiling at the thought of time spent with her aunt. She was drumming her fingers on the arm of her chair. Joseph nodded toward her fingers and frowned. Sadie folded her hands together to hold them still and tried to concentrate on what the state's attorney was saying.

"Call your first witness," the judge said. He shuffled the papers on his high desk and then looked up as the bailiff escorted Mr. Diehn, Tessa's neighbor, to the stand.

"Please state your occupation and home address, sir," the attorney instructed.

Mr. Diehn—who was a little hard of hearing—did so in the loud voice that was his normal conversational tone.

"And tell us what you were doing just before seven thirty on the morning of August 28th."

"I was leaving for work. It was raining, and I had just pulled out onto the street and driven to the corner."

"What were the road conditions?"

"Well, it hadn't rained for several weeks—most of the summer we were in a drought, don't you know. The rain was coming down in sheets, don't you know, and the roads were covered over in places. And slick," he added as an afterthought.

"Did you see this car that morning?" Mr. Johnson held up a photograph of Dan's car and went through the routine of entering it into evidence. Sadie half expected Joseph to object, but he didn't, just made scribbled notes on his yellow legal pad in a script that was so tiny Sadie couldn't begin to read it.

"Sure did. That car almost ran smack into me. If I hadn't—"

"Who was driving the car?"

"Well now, like I said, there was a torrential rain coming down, and windows were fogged with the humidity and all, so I can't be all that sure." He turned to the judge. "I had the air conditioning turned up, helps make the defrost cycle work better, don't you know."

Joseph was on his feet immediately. "Objection. Calls for legal conclusion."

"Sustained," the judge murmured.

Mr. Johnson started to ask his next question, but Mr. Diehn turned back to him and interrupted. "I do know that there were two people in that car, and I do know that it was going a little too fast for the conditions." He seemed satisfied with his answer, punctuating it with a sharp nod of his head.

Joseph stood up a second time. "Objection."

"Sustained," the judge repeated before Joseph could even say why he'd objected.

Mr. Johnson returned to the prosecutor's table and sat down. Joseph stood up and smiled at Mr. Diehn. "Good morning, sir. Just a few more minutes of your time. Did your car skid or slide on the morning in question?"

"No sir. I'm a cautious driver. My wife says sometimes I'm too cautious."

"Did the car you saw like the one in the photograph slide or skid?"

Mr. Diehn frowned. "Not that I noticed—just came at me a little close, you know? A little too close."

"Then how did you determine that the rain had made the roads slippery?"

"Common sense. No rain for weeks is bound to result in a buildup of oil and other stuff from cars running over the same road time after time. Bound to be."

"And you say your windows were steamed up with humidity, and the pouring rain made for poor visibility?"

"That's right. Those youngsters could barely see their hand in front of them much less—"

"And what about you, Mr. Diehn? I know you said you had your air conditioning and the defroster running, but were the windows on your car steamed over, and did the pouring rain in even a small way hamper your ability to see clearly?"

Mr. Diehn glanced past Joseph at Mr. Johnson, who did not look back at him. "I reckon you've got a point there," he admitted.

"So just to be clear, you saw a car that resembled the one the state's attorney showed you in the photograph turn the corner where you were waiting—"

"At an unsafe speed," Mr. Diehn interrupted.

Joseph smiled. "Ah yes. Thank you for reminding me. And how were you able to determine the speed of this other car?"

Mr. Diehn actually grinned. "Instinct and over forty years of driving, son."

"And did this car hit your vehicle?"

"Came pretty close."

"But no actual contact—no damage? You didn't have to veer out of its way?"

"No. I gave the driver a blast of my horn, and that probably was the reason why that car—" He pointed toward the photo lying on the prosecutor's desk.

"Thank you, sir. No further questions."

Mr. Johnson called his next witness, another neighbor that lived next door to Tessa. She and her husband had heard the crash and come running outside. Her husband had been the one relaying information to the 911 operator. But as far as Sadie could tell, Joseph was able to make it clear that neither this woman nor her husband had seen the actual accident or events that may have led up to it.

There were three other neighbors and one other driver whom Sadie must have passed while making the trip to Tessa's house, but none of them really added much to the state's case. Then a forensics expert as well as the surgeon who had operated on Tessa were called to testify.

Each of them laid out the massive injuries that had led to Tessa's death—a broken collar bone, broken ribs, a torn spleen, injury to her lungs, injury to her liver, brain injuries, and internal bleeding.

One thing that Sadie had noticed was that unlike the dramatic court scenes on television, here the lawyers and judge spoke to each other in normal tones. They didn't seem to worry about whether those in the chairs behind the little wooden fence could hear. Sadie herself had to sit forward and really listen hard to follow what was happening. The list of Tessa's injuries was delivered in a dry, no-nonsense manner that irritated her.

This was Tessa they were talking about. Tessa who had sustained these horrific assaults to her body. Had she felt pain? Had she known she was dying? Had she forgiven Sadie before she died?

She was starting to feel nauseous as the list of injuries was repeated. Every time the doctor named one of the things that had contributed to Tessa's death, it felt as if he were hurling stones at Sadie. Her mind raced with images of her cousin's lifeless body. She tried to concentrate on something else and block out the drone of the testimony. What she wouldn't give for a bowl of her mom's chicken noodle soup. That would settle her stomach.

The doctor finally left the stand, and Sadie took a deep breath, forcing herself to relax. Surely that had been the worst of it. Now the prosecuting attorney would stop and her attorney would begin to make the case for her.

"The state calls Daniel Kline," Mr. Johnson said in a voice that sounded as if he were making a comment on the weather rather than calling Dan to the stand.

Sadie resisted the urge to smooth her hair and bite her lips to give them some color. Dan was here. He would tell them what had happened, how it was an accident, how all she was guilty of was driving with him instead of a real adult.

He looked wonderful. He was dressed in his best Sunday clothes—crisp pressed khaki slacks, a light blue shirt, a chocolate brown tie, and a navy sports jacket. Sadie was embarrassed for him to see her looking so awful. But she needn't have worried. He walked straight to the front of the courtroom without so much as a glance her way and took the oath to tell the truth, the whole truth, and nothing but, and then sat down.

Mr. Johnson stood so that he was between Sadie and Dan as he asked Dan to state his name, age, and occupation for the record. He asked him if the car in the photo was his. He asked if he had operated that car on the day in question. He asked if anyone else had driven that car that morning.

"Yes sir. Sadie Keller."

Johnson stepped aside and pointed to Sadie. "The defendant?"

"Yes sir."

"You knew that she was underage?"

"She has—had—her learner's permit."

"But you at age eighteen did not fill the state's requirement that an adult twenty-one or older be in the vehicle?"

"No sir."

"Was anyone else in the vehicle?"

"No sir."

"Tell the court how it happened that the defendant was illegally driving your vehicle on the morning of August 28th."

Sadie gave Dan an encouraging nod. Tell them. Help this nightmare end. She was certain that this was the moment when Dan was going to make it all right for her. He would tell the court how she had hesitated, how he had insisted, how much he regretted—

"She was all excited about getting her learner's," Dan began, and Sadie fought a smile, knowing that her lawyer wouldn't like it.

"It was only like a mile from her house to her cousin's house," Dan continued, but his expression was all wrong—tight-lipped as if he were fighting to keep his emotions in check. "I didn't see the harm, and she can be pretty persuasive." He slumped forward and bowed his head. "I didn't see the harm," he repeated, and his voice broke as he looked down at his hands.

"Who was at the wheel of your vehicle when it went out of control, striking fifteen-year-old Tessa Messner with such force that she later died on the operating table?"

"Sadie Keller," Dan mumbled. He turned to look at the judge. "I wish I could have done something to make it right, but I was too late."

"No further questions."

Sadie had moved to the edge of her chair, and she was grasping the table. Joseph leaned close and whispered, "Stay calm." Then he stood up and moved toward Dan.

"So just to be sure we're clear here, it is your sworn testimony that my client asked to drive your car from her home to her cousin's house?"

Dan shrugged.

"Words, Mr. Kline," the judge instructed.

Dan sat a little taller and looked directly at Joseph. "That's what I just said." He sounded angry.

"And you gave in to her request because"—Joseph consulted his legal pad then turned back to Dan—"and I quote, 'She can be pretty persuasive'?"

Sadie saw Dan's cheeks flush. "Well, she can."

"What year in school are you, Daniel?"

"I just started my senior year."

"And my client?"

"Sophomore."

"Am I right in stating that you made a plea bargain with the state's attorney's office?"

Dan looked at Mr. Johnson. "Yes sir."

"What were the terms of that plea bargain?"

"I pled guilty to the charge of culpable negligence."

"In exchange for?" Joseph prompted.

Dan hesitated the way he did when he wasn't sure of the right answer. Sadie's heart went out to him. He looked as scared as she felt.

"Mr. Kline?"

"I agreed to testify here today."

"Against my client?"

"To tell what happened."

"And once again, just so we are very clear, you are telling this court—under oath—that it was Sadie Keller's idea to—"

"Objection. Asked and answered," Mr. Johnson said.

"No further questions," Joseph said and sat down.

Sadie couldn't believe it. Dan had lied. More to the point, he had lied after swearing to tell the truth. What kind of Christian was that? Why would he possibly. . .

"The state calls Geoffory Messner to the stand."

Uncle Geoff? Couldn't be. Why would he testify for the prosecution?

Sadie heard a gasp behind her and turned to find her mother half out of her chair and her father standing. The judge was banging his gavel, and the bailiff was taking hold of her father's arm, and other people—like Dan's parents—were also standing. Everyone was talking and shouting, and it was all because of her, because of what she had done. She turned in a slow circle, seeing everyone yelling, but suddenly Sadie could bear it no more. She shut her eyes and opened her mouth to release the screams she'd been swallowing back now for days.

Chapter 25

Jeannie

News traveled fast in a close-knit community like Pinecraft and even though Jeannie and Geoff technically lived in Sarasota, Jeannie heard about Geoff's appearance at Sadie's hearing within half an hour of the event itself.

Although Zeke had stayed for a cup of coffee, Jeannie could see that his heart hadn't been in the visit. Clearly torn between his loyalty to Geoff and Jeannie and his concern for Emma and her family, he'd left as soon as possible. But he'd again challenged Jeannie to get back into the community, and so she'd decided that a good first step would be to resume her habit of shopping at the fresh market in Pinecraft. There were still plenty of casseroles and breads and cakes and pies in her freezer and refrigerator, but she was hungry for the lighter fare of fresh fruit and a green salad.

The news of Geoff being in court had come to her in whispered conversations that abruptly stopped as she moved around the store, nodding to those she knew and receiving in return a quick glance before the person gave her a nod or smile and then pretended interest in the produce. These were Emma's friends and neighbors, and although Jeannie had grown up in this community and among these very people, and even though she was used to people's sympathetic glances by now, the demeanor of the patrons in the fresh market was different. They looked at her with eyes that questioned even as they covered their mouths with their cupped hands and murmured to their companions.

Jeannie's guilt over avoiding Emma almost overwhelmed her, and she was on the verge of making some excuse about why she had not been in touch with her sister when Olive Crowder stepped up next to her and made a show of studying the bananas.

"Hello, Olive," Jeannie said as she selected a large bunch of the fruit and placed it in her basket. "The bananas look especially nice today." She'd almost said that they were Tessa's favorite, but she'd caught herself, swallowing back the now familiar bile of grief that seemed to rise in her throat every time she thought of her daughter. "Geoff loves to slice them over his cereal at breakfast," she forced herself to say instead.

Her mention of Geoff seemed to give Olive the opening she'd been hoping for. "Ja, I'm sure he does." The older woman pursed her lips as if she'd just bitten into an especially tart lemon. "I'll come straight to the point, Jeannine." Olive had always called Jeannie by her full given name. "Everyone appreciates the pain and suffering that you and your husband must endure, but testifying against your own sister's child, your own niece?" She clucked her tongue. "You were raised to walk on the path of forgiveness and reconciliation, Jeannine. What is to be gained if they send that child to prison? It will not bring your Tessa back, and what else might you lose in the bargain?"

"I wouldn't. . .I couldn't," Jeannie protested. The very idea that anyone who knew her might think her capable of such an act was unimaginable. She realized that she had made no effort to keep her voice to a murmur, and the other women apparently saw that as their invitation to join the conversation.

"Maybe she wouldn't, but when it comes to her husband. . . ," she heard one of the women mutter.

"What about my husband?"

Olive studied her for a moment then held up her hand to forestall any further comment from the others. She took hold of Jeannie's elbow and guided her outside. "Please don't try to pretend that you are unaware that Geoffory was in court today to testify against Sadie—to testify for the prosecution," she told her.

They had to be joking.

Geoff?

He had struggled with his emotions to be sure. He had been depressed, morose, and yes, angry. And it was true that since the funeral, conversation between them had been limited to information about where one of them might be going, or whether he needed anything from the store, or a reminder that he would be late because he had a faculty meeting. But this? Sadie was family. He could never. . .

"Sometimes it's hard for one raised outside," Olive said as if Jeannie had spoken the rush of thoughts aloud. Olive's voice was unusually soft, appeasing. "Even after conversion there can be ties to the old ways."

"What old ways, Olive?" Jeannie felt irritated that the woman would say anything against Geoff. He was a pillar of the church, a respected educator and coach. Everyone in Pinecraft—be they old- or new-order Mennonite—admired him.

Olive pursed her lips. "An eye for an eye is not our way, Jeannine. That's all I'm saying here."

"And it's not Geoff's way either. He is not a vengeful man."

"He's a former outsider who has lost his only child to a senseless accident," Olive reminded her. "In his upbringing, forgiveness and reconciliation would have been mixed with Old Testament justice. His parents made it clear at the funeral that they blamed Sadie. Why, they barely acknowledged that child. I suppose others might understand, but. . ."

Jeannie turned back to the gathering inside the store. The customers and clerks were all listening to what Olive was telling her and watching her with such pity. Well, she didn't want or need their pity, and she would stand by her husband. If Geoff had gone to court that day, then he had his reasons. She walked back inside and replaced every item from her basket in its rightful place, and then she left.

But she could not shake the words Olive had spoken. She had said that Geoff had gone to testify—against Sadie. *There had to be some other explanation*, she thought as she walked home.

The prosecutor must have required Geoff to appear in court, and Geoff hadn't told her because he hadn't wanted to worry her. That had to be it. Geoff would never. . .

But later that night as they sat in separate chairs in front of the television eating their supper off of paper plates, Jeannie decided to break the silence between them by telling him about the encounter at the fresh market.

"Can you imagine?" she said as she warmed to her story, throwing in details about who was there and how each reacted and what Olive Crowder said and did. And all the while she waited for him to laugh it off or wave his hand dismissively as he gave her a simple explanation of just how the rumor must have gotten started.

But Geoff said nothing. He just chewed his food and stared at the television.

"It's ridiculous, of course," she said, finally running out of steam in her attempt to present the situation as one worthy of their disdain. She took her plate and his and headed for the kitchen. "I think there's some of that baked peach pie left," she called over her shoulder, aware that her hands were shaking as she walked the short distance from the study to the sink. "Geoff? Do you want peach pie?" She heard the annoyance and fear in her voice.

"I was there, but I didn't testify."

He was standing in the doorway, the television flickering behind him.

Jeannie set the plates on the counter and took a step toward him. "Why were you there at all? I mean, we could have gone together. Emma would have appreciated that—and Lars—and Sadie."

Geoff's features contracted with pain. "I have asked you not to mention that girl's name, Jeannie. Can you do that much for me? For us?"

"That girl? She's part of this family, Geoff."

"She is as dead to me as Tessa is," he replied and turned on his heel and went back to the den. A moment later, Jeannie heard the television volume go louder and become a jumble of channel surfing as Geoff punched the remote repeatedly.

Ignoring the cleanup of their supper, Jeannie walked slowly

back to the den. "Please stop walking away from me," she said as she reached over his shoulder and removed the remote from his hand. She aimed the device at the television and clicked the power off. "Talk to me," she said calmly. "Tell me why you were at the courthouse at all." She knelt next to his chair and took his hands in hers. "Help me understand, Geoff."

"There's nothing to tell. I went there to testify, but when she saw me, she started to scream, and the judge ordered a recess until Monday. . ."

"Sadie started to scream?"

He did not argue with her use of her name this time. "Yeah." He actually shuddered at the memory. "It was like some wild animal howling in pain," he said.

Tears filled Jeannie's eyes. Would this never be over for them? Would the hurt just go on and on? "Emma?"

"She was there, and Lars. I thought he was going to punch me, but then I realized that he never would."

"What did they say? Emma and Lars?"

"Nothing. Emma ran off to a side door where the guard had taken her. . ."

"Taken Sadie?"

Geoff gave her an impatient look and nodded. "The bailiff let Lars and Emma go to be with her and then cleared the room."

"Who else was there?"

Geoff shrugged. "People I didn't know, probably for other cases. Dan's parents." He must have seen the next question coming. "Dan testified."

"So the judge ended it before you had to testify. Then it's over now." Jeannie knew that she was trying to reassure herself, knew that she wanted only to block out the realization that it wasn't over at all. She so badly needed for something about this whole nightmare to turn out to be all right, and if that was that Geoff had been stopped from testifying so that he could reconsider, then she would take that crumb and thank God for it. "I'll speak with Emma. I can simply explain that you've reconsidered, that you didn't realize what testifying could mean. She and Lars will understand that you—"

"I'm going to testify, Jeannie."

"But why?"

"How about asking the real question here, Jeannie? How about asking why not?" His voice was raspy, as if he didn't have the strength to argue but was determined to fight on. "Isn't that the question you should really be asking for Tessa's sake?"

Jeannie stared up at him, this stranger with her husband's face. She didn't understand this side of him, this rage that seemed to build a little every day. "Help me understand why you would do this," she pleaded.

"Because I saw what happened." He ground out each word as if afraid she would miss one. "I was outside there. Your beloved niece almost struck me. Do you understand that you could have lost both of us?"

"But it was an accident, Geoff. A horrible accident. Sadie never intended to hurt anyone."

Geoff looked at her as if she were as much a stranger to him as he had become in these last several days to her. "Do you hear yourself, Jeannie? It's Emma or Sadie you worry about—not Tessa and certainly not me." He stood up and stepped around her. "Well, here's the thing, Jeannie. I know you love your sister and her family, but I'm not wired that way. My only child is gone—forever. . ."

"Stop it," Jeannie hissed, getting to her feet to face him. "Stop talking like you're the only one who has suffered the loss of Tessa—she was my child—my only child, too."

"Then maybe you ought to start acting like it instead of looking for ways to defend her killer." He turned away, grabbed his baseball cap, jammed it on his head, and left the house.

Jeannie waited for the sound of the car starting but instead heard the steady pound of his feet as he ran down the driveway and on down the street. She knew where to find him. He would be at the track at the school, running off his anger and grief. It was hardly the first time their evening had ended this way—with him running off steam and Jeannie at home alone.

Like a robot, she went through the motions of putting the kitchen in order and setting the coffeemaker timer for the following morning. Then she remembered that tomorrow was Friday and a teacher's work day for Geoff. The weekend would start early.

Memories of the plans she and Emma would make to spend such days off with the girls—just the four of them—hit her like an unexpected wave at the seashore. This would be a long weekend, and weekends, she had discovered, were in many ways the worst. It was easier to get through the hours that Tessa would have been in school. But weekends were always a time when they did everything together. On Friday nights, they would all go to the football game and then out for pizza. On Saturdays she and Emma and Tessa and Sadie would spend the day together—working at the fruit co-op, shopping, or going to search for shells in the bay. And on Sunday after each family attended services at their separate churches, they would spend the rest of the day together, going on outings or just sharing an afternoon and evening of board games or shuffleboard followed by a potluck meal filled with chatter and laughter and togetherness.

As lights came on in houses up and down the block, she switched off the kitchen light and started upstairs, but then she turned and retraced her steps to the wall phone in the kitchen. She dialed the number for retrieving their voice mail.

"You have no new messages," the electronic voice reported. "You have eighteen saved messages."

Eighteen saved messages—all of them from Emma. None of them returned. She hadn't known what to say. Aware that Geoff needed time to forgive Sadie, she had kept her distance from Emma and Lars out of respect for Geoff. She had hoped that once the funeral was over and he had gone back to work, he would realize that Emma and Lars and Matt—and yes, Sadie—were family. But it was clear that he was going to need more time, and she would not abandon him when he was in such obvious pain.

Still she needed support as well, and in the absence of Geoff's ability to offer her that, she pressed the key to retrieve the first message and give herself the gift of the comfort and strength that she knew she could find in her sister's voice.

Chapter 26

Geoff

By the time Geoff reached the track, he was already soaked with sweat. He had run full out from the house to the athletic field where he had spent so many good times, celebrated so many victories with his teams, coached and cajoled and parented young boys into the fine young men they had become. This place was the setting for his success. The house he had run from had turned out to be the setting of his greatest failure.

His anger and guilt combined to push him forward in spite of the burning pain in his chest and the heaviness of his legs. He was out of shape. The extra duties as vice principal had cut into the time he usually took to work out at the end of every school day. Work out here with his players, or on off days, run with Matt, who was always hanging around waiting for practice to end and hoping for an invitation to join Geoff in laps around the track.

The kid was an excellent runner, and once he filled out a little, he'd make a good running back. Matt had an instinct for the game of football that was impossible to teach. He had a phenomenal grasp of the intricate plays that often had to be dumbed down for others.

But ever since the funeral, Geoff had avoided any contact with his nephew. After practice if he saw Matt hanging around, he headed back inside the school with his players without so much as a glance at Matt. It wasn't the kid's fault. Geoff knew that, and it certainly wasn't fair to him. But Matt reminded him of Lars and Emma, and that reminded him of Sadie, and that took his mind places that he really didn't want to go.

It was the same at home. It had gotten so that he had to bite his tongue sometimes to keep from reminding Jeannie that none of this would be happening to them if she had thought before she took Sadie for that learner's permit. But that was a line he would not cross. Jeannie would be devastated if she knew for one minute that he harbored this thought. At the same time, Geoff suspected that she already carried the weight of regretting that impulsive act with her every waking hour. Speaking the accusation aloud would take their marriage to a place so dark that they'd have no hope of ever recovering, and it scared him to think how close he'd come to shouting that very accusation at her earlier.

He took another lap and focused on his breathing, steady outbursts of air as he pushed his way around the track, quarter mile by quarter mile. He tried to empty his mind, to focus on nothing more than the uniformity of his stride, the form with which he ran. But each puff of his breath came out sounding like Jeannie's question: *"Why?"*

Because a child has died needlessly. . . .

Because our child was that child. . . .

Because justice demands that Tessa's death come with a cost for the one who caused it. . . .

Because Sadie has always been too free-spirited, too oblivious to consequences, too reckless in the way she treats others. . . .

Because testifying against Sadie gave him back a feeling that he had control over the situation, that he could do something to make things right.

Testifying was the only way he'd come up with to dampen his own overwhelming guilt—the guilt that he'd carried with him from the moment he'd realized that in trying to protect her he had actually sent Tessa to the exact spot where the car had hit her. Every time he relived the force of that blow, he forgot how to breathe.

Why couldn't Jeannie understand that?

Why did she always choose her sister and her sister's family over her own? How many times in all the years of their marriage had he heard her say, "but Emma needs" or "Emma doesn't understand" or "Emma says" or "Emma thinks"? How many times had they changed the plans he had made with others to include Emma and Lars and their kids? And worst of all, how many times had Jeannie turned to Emma for support or comfort or advice instead of to him?

He heard footfalls behind him. Jeannie was a good runner, and if she had decided to come after him, maybe she had begun to understand things from his point of view.

"Hey, man, hold up."

He stopped running and turned to see Zeke Shepherd bent nearly double, his hands on his knees as he tried to catch his breath. Geoff walked slowly back toward his friend.

"You okay?"

"No worries," Zeke gasped, but he took a minute longer to catch his breath.

"Did Jeannie send you?"

Zeke glanced up, and the way he cocked his head suggested that his friend had no idea what he was talking about. "Actually, I was going to camp out here tonight under the bleachers. Forecast said something about rain and. . ." He blinked up at Geoff. "Why would Jeannie send me to find you?" Zeke stood up straight, still massaging his side.

The streetlights outside the ball field were dim enough and distant enough to cast the field and track in shadows. "We had a fight."

Zeke released a long sigh. "Well, I can't say I didn't see that one coming. Okay, I lied. I heard about you being in court today, so I stopped by. Jeannie was on the phone and told me you'd gone for a run, but she didn't send me to get you."

"Probably calling Emma so the two of them could commiserate over what a terrible guy I am."

"Whoa. So it's a pity party we're having. Got it."

Geoff felt a twitch of a smile. Nobody but Zeke had ever

talked so straight to him—he wouldn't allow it from anybody else. But from the time Zeke and his family had moved in across the street from Geoff when both boys were ten years old, Zeke had shown Geoff that he was not especially impressed with Geoff's size or athletic ability.

"You wanna be my friend or not?" he'd asked bluntly one day after the two of them had gotten into a roll-around-in-the-dirt-without-landing-any-punches fight on the playground.

Geoff wasn't used to such a direct question. "I don't know," he'd hedged.

Zeke had gotten up, dusted himself off, and headed for home. "Take a day to think it over," he'd said. "I think it might work out, but it's your call."

The following morning, Geoff had fallen into step with Zeke on their way to school. Neither one of them had ever mentioned the fight again, and they had been fast friends from that day to this. Geoff doubted either of them could even remember what they had fought about. He knew he couldn't. Even a separation of years while Zeke was in the service in the Middle East and Geoff was in college had done nothing to loosen the bond formed in that silent no-need-for-words walk to school.

As they walked in step around the track now, Geoff looked down at Zeke, who was a good three inches shorter and twenty-five pounds lighter than he was. "You think I messed up." It was not a question.

"I think you're hurting just like Jeannie is and Emma is and Lars is and Matt is and, yes, just like Sadie is."

They walked the next half of the oval in silence. "I think I'm losing faith," Geoff murmured.

To his surprise, Zeke chuckled. "You can't lose what you've never really taken hold of, Geoff. You're neither fish nor fowl, as they say. You treated conversion like it was nothing more than moving from one house to another. I'm not saying you don't believe. I'm just raising the question of what it is you do believe."

"I used to believe in a loving God, but what kind of God takes an innocent child's life and leaves everybody that ever knew her or loved her reeling?"

Zeke shrugged. "Have you talked to Jeannie about this?"

"Her faith is unshakable."

"You're sure about that? Even now?"

He wasn't sure of anything when it came to his wife these days. They spent their time in different stratospheres even when they were in the same house—the same room. It was a relief for him to leave for school every morning as he suspected it was for her to see him go. Clearly she didn't want to be with him, because lately she was up and out running before he even crawled out of bed.

"Maybe I made a mistake that day that I turned Emma away. She means well, and she probably could be a comfort to Jeannie. It's for certain that I'm not filling that particular role. It's just that ever since the funeral, I find that I can't handle anyone from that family being around."

"Jeannie's a big girl. If she wants to see Emma, you aren't going to stop her. And the fact is, for everyone involved it's all still so fresh—like an open wound. You'll find your way back to each other in time, and my guess is that Emma and Lars understand."

"And then there's Matt," Geoff said. "How do I explain to him why I've turned away, why the very sight of him makes me remember every second of that morning even though he wasn't there, had no part in it at all?"

"That's a whole other ball game, my friend—no pun intended. Look, Matt comes about as close to hero-worshipping you as his upbringing will allow. But right now you need to focus on Jeannie. Mattie's got his folks. You and Jeannie just have each other." Zeke gave Geoff a not-so-subtle nudge with his elbow. "Come on, man. Go home to your wife."

"First tell me that you understand why I'm still going to testify."

"Make me understand," Zeke challenged.

Geoff ran a hand through his hair. "It's like I'm speaking for Tessa, telling what I saw, because Tess must have seen almost the same thing. Surely that's important—for someone to speak for Tessa?"

"When you put it that way, it makes some sense. You might

want to try that with Jeannie." He picked up the guitar he'd left leaning against one of the scoreboard uprights and slung it over his shoulder. "I got to get my beauty rest," he said with a grin. "Farmers' market on Saturday. Payday." Zeke had regularly played for the tourists crowding the closed-off street at the weekly farmers' market in downtown Sarasota, leaving his guitar case open to receive their tips. It was one of his main sources of income.

Geoff shook his friend's hand. "Thanks for hunting me down. Maybe Jeannie and I will come to the market this week. It would be a nice break for her—for both of us."

"Great idea. And may I suggest that you plan to support your local musician friend by bringing along some cash—as in large bills," Zeke shouted as he trotted off the field.

Feeling better, Geoff took one more lap around the track and then headed for home. Zeke was right. He hadn't explained things so that Jeannie would understand why he was doing what he was doing, why he needed to do things this way. Once he told her that it was for Tessa. . .

But somehow the words that had come so easily and concisely when he was talking to Zeke failed him entirely when he tried to explain his reasoning to Jeannie.

"For Tessa?" she asked incredulously. "You seriously think that our daughter, that sweet, caring child, would want anything to do with contributing to the problems that Sadie already has?"

"I think she can't be here to tell her side of things, and someone—I—can do that for her."

"Her side? What does that even mean?"

They were back to shouting at each other. He didn't want this. He had imagined that he would come back and explain and they would go upstairs to bed where for the first time since the funeral they would curl up together and hold each other through the night.

"Geoff, do you understand that Sadie could be sent away for a very long time?"

"What I can't understand, Jeannie, is why you seem determined to put Sadie's future ahead of your own daughter's complete lack of any future at all."

"I am doing the only thing I know to do. Tessa is gone, and I can't change that, but if we can save Sadie. . ."

Geoff couldn't believe he was hearing her right. "Where is your anger, Jeannie? Where is your fury that this girl you have spoiled rotten for most of her life has repaid you by thoughtlessly taking the life of your only child?"

"That's a solution? An eye for an eye?"

Geoff felt as if he might explode under the tension of his anger and his wife's total lack of understanding. "I'm going to bed," he said. "I told Zeke we'd come to the market this weekend."

"I can't."

"Why not?"

"It's visiting day at the detention center." She did not try to hide the defiant look she gave him.

"You're not going to see her!"

"I listened to Emma's messages while you were out. Almost daily reports about how Sadie was doing in that place. And in all of them the underlying message is that she needs the chance to tell us how sorry she is."

"My heart bleeds for her pain," Geoff said sarcastically.

"I'm going to give her that chance, Geoff. It would be good if you came with me so she can apologize to us both."

"And then what? We all join hands and sing 'Kumbaya' together?"

"Or we could do things your way and destroy another life or two in the bargain," she snapped.

Geoff felt his legs go weak with physical and emotional exhaustion. He sat down on the third step and put his face in his hands. "Jeannie, this is insanity. I'm asking you not to go."

"And I'm asking you not to testify." She edged past him on her way upstairs. "Stalemate," she said softly as she walked down the hall past their bedroom and into Tessa's room. A moment later he heard the door close.

He got up and retraced his steps down to the kitchen and den where he shut off the lights and turned the lock on the back door. Then he unlocked the door and stepped outside the way he had that rainy morning. He stared at the place where Tessa had been standing laughing at him as he wrestled with the umbrella. She had taken a step toward him, prepared to help. If he hadn't stopped her, she might have been safe—the car might have missed her as it did him.

At the end of the block, he heard a car backfire, and he remembered the sound of Dan's car coming up the street. It had caught the pool of water that covered half the street and sent it spraying into the air. He closed his eyes against the memory of the car coming at them, at him.

"Tessa, move!" he'd shouted as he tossed the umbrella aside ready to take the blow for her. She had leaped away, but the car had spun suddenly in the opposite direction entirely. The back end had caught his precious daughter and sent her sailing until she'd landed with a soft thud on the driveway.

Now he stared down at the spot and then up at a sky filled with stars. How could anyone who knew what had happened here ever believe again that God was in His heaven and all was right with the world?

Chapter 27

Jeannie

The door to the bedroom she and Geoff shared was closed when Jeannie came out of Tessa's room after a sleepless night spent crying as she went through her daughter's things for the hundredth time since the funeral. The one thing that she had not found was the journal that she and Geoff had given Tessa the night before the accident.

She thought if she could just find that journal and see what Tessa had written in it, she might be able to show it to Geoff. Perhaps Tessa's own words—whatever they might be—would convince him once and for all that vengeance was not justice. But the journal was nowhere to be found.

Usually Jeannie would have called Emma to come and help her in the hunt. But she would not ask Emma to come now. It would only upset Geoff further. She regretted their argument, and yet she would not back down on this one. If Geoff thought he was speaking for Tessa, then so was she. Tessa would be more concerned for Sadie than for herself. That was the way they had raised her, and that was why it was so hard to understand why Geoff could be so unforgiving when it came to Sadie.

The phone rang, and automatically she glanced at the display to check caller ID.

Hester Steiner's name popped up. Jeannie had promised Zeke that she would return to her volunteer work at the fruit co-op, and no doubt he had passed that message along to Hester. Well, why not? The work there would at least fill some of the hours that stretched before her endlessly each new day. She picked up the phone.

"Okay, okay, I'll be at the co-op on Monday," she said in what she hoped passed for her usual pre-accident teasing tone.

Hester chuckled. "That's good news, but actually I was just calling to see if you have time for coffee this morning. A friend from my college days is in town to start a new job, and I thought the two of you ought to meet."

Ought to meet was an odd way to put the invitation.

"Why?" Jeannie blurted before she could censor herself.

"Just say you'll come," Hester replied further, adding to Jeannie's suspicion. "How about that place on Main Street that you and Emma like?"

"Is Emma coming?"

"No. I wouldn't do that to either of you without first asking. How's half an hour?"

Jeannie checked the clock. It was still early. She certainly had little else to do. Why not enjoy a latte and meet Hester's friend? It would be good for her. "Okay. Sure. See you there."

As she hung up the phone, she heard the shower turn on in their bathroom. Knowing that Geoff was in the shower, Jeannie went back upstairs to their room and changed from the clothes she'd worn the day before into a pair of denim Capri pants and a green cotton blouse.

"I'm going," she called out, standing at the partially closed bathroom door. "Geoff?"

The water running was the only sound.

"Geoff? Did you hear me? I'm taking the car."

"I heard you."

She waited, but he said nothing more, and the water just kept running. "Okay. See you later," she said, fighting hard against the wave of irritation at his stubbornness. Or maybe she was the one who was unwilling to bend. He had brought on their argument of the night before, and it was up to him—

Reconciliation. Forgiveness. Wasn't that what she had said he needed to have for Sadie?

She retraced her steps.

"Geoff?"

No answer, but she had the sense that he was listening.

"I love you," she said and then softly closed the bathroom door all the way—just in case he didn't say anything back.

Jeannie was the first to arrive at the coffee shop. She chose a table outside, away from the street traffic and other customers. She pulled a third chair over from an adjoining table and sat down to watch for Hester and her friend. Moments later she saw Hester's car across the street, and then Hester and a petite woman of about Emma's age got out.

She was dressed plain and wore the simpler white kerchief prayer covering common among the younger conservative Mennonite women. Her caped dress was a light lavender, and the color worked well with her dark hair. Her skin was very pale and completely unblemished. Jeannie couldn't help but think that she would need to invest in some sunblock if she was going to move to Sarasota. Jeannie got up and waved to Hester.

"Over here," she called, and the two women hurried across the street, dodging traffic on their way.

"Jeannie Messner, meet another dear friend, Rachel Kaufmann," Hester said.

"Hester and I were college roommates," Rachel explained. "She used to rave about Pinecraft and everything it had to offer, so I finally decided to come down and see what all the fuss was about."

"You two get acquainted," Hester said. "I'll get the coffee."

"Tea for me," Rachel said.

"Got it. Two coffees and one tea."

Rachel and Jeannie took chairs opposite each other. Rachel leaned back and looked at her surroundings. "It's all so very. . .tropical," she said and then laughed. "Well, duh. But this is certainly what it feels like midsummer in Ohio where I come from." She fanned herself with her hand. "Are you from here originally, Jeannie?"

"Born and raised right in Pinecraft," Jeannie said. She could see Hester standing in line inside the small shop. "It's wonderful that you and Hester have stayed in touch over all this time."

"She's a terrific letter writer," Rachel replied. "Me? Not so much. But I'm good at calling, so between the two, we made it work." She leaned forward. "I met Hester's John. He's wonderful, isn't he? And they are so perfect together."

Jeannie found herself smiling as she recalled the rocky start that Hester and John had had. "Well, now they are. In the beginning. . ."

"Oh, I know. You should read the letters I was getting from Hester back then. But I knew the way it was 'John Steiner this' and 'John Steiner that'—I mean, after the first three dozen times his name came up in a matter of a couple of weeks—she was in love with the guy."

Jeannie laughed, and it felt odd—like something she used to do a lot in the past and then had given up on.

"Coffee for you. Tea for you, and coffee for me," Hester said as she arrived with three mugs of steaming liquid. She doled them out before taking the third chair.

"Hester tells me you just took a job here, Rachel," Jeannie said. "Do you have a family?"

"Yes. My husband was killed a year and a half ago. We have a son, Justin. He's twelve. When I was laid off from my job a few months ago, Hester suggested that I look for work here." She smiled at her friend. "I'm going to be working at the new hospital that just opened out on Cattlemen Road."

It seemed like it had been such a long time since Jeannie had allowed herself to think about the suffering of others. She felt ashamed and selfish. "I'm so very sorry for your loss."

Rachel gave her a grateful smile. "It's been a journey, but every day Justin and I realize that we are a little further along the path of healing. Of course, staying busy helps—work for me and school for Justin."

"Are you a nurse like Hester?"

"I have my degree in nursing but—perpetual student that I am—I went back to school and got my master's in psychology.

I'll be working as a chaplain and spiritual counselor."

Was this the real reason for Hester's call and sudden invitation to meet her friend? She shot Hester a look. "Subtle," she murmured as she took a sip of her coffee.

"Coincidence," Hester corrected, and suddenly the lighter getting-to-know-you environ shifted to one that was filled with questions and suspicion—at least on Jeannie's part.

"What's this really about?"

Hester sighed and set down her mug. "Rachel, tell Jeannie about the program that you and Justin took part in back in Ohio after James was killed." Hester focused all of her attention on Jeannie and added, "Just please keep an open mind, because the minute I heard about it, I wanted you to at least know that such an idea exists in other communities. Seems to me that it's something that could work here."

Jeannie relaxed a little. This was the Hester that everyone knew and admired. She was a woman always looking at her surroundings and thinking about ways to make things better. "Okay, I'm listening. What's the new program?"

"Actually, it isn't all that new," Rachel said. "At least not in some communities."

"It's called VORP," Hester interrupted.

"Which stands for. . . ?"

"Victim Offender Reconciliation Program," Hester replied, her eyes locked on Jeannie's. "Rachel's husband was killed by a drunk driver."

"At first," Rachel said, picking up the story, "I didn't know what to do, how to react. I was so angry and devastated, and our son was really at a loss. He and his father did everything together."

"What happened?" Jeannie's mouth had suddenly gone dry.

"The driver was a young man, out of work, with two small children of his own. He'd hit rock bottom and started drinking early one afternoon and kept it up. Then he got into his truck, and on his way home, he crossed over the median and struck my husband's car."

When tears welled in Rachel's eyes, Jeannie reached over and squeezed her hand. "I know," she whispered. "I understand."

"Sorry," Rachel murmured. "Anyway, we were in the midst of the trial when I read something about VORP, and I thought maybe it could work. Maybe it would be a way for Justin—and me—to find some peace with this senseless loss."

"So, what did you do?"

"I contacted the organization, and they sent out a mediator to talk with me and with Justin. There were several steps along the way, but the upshot was that eventually we sat down with the young man. We met his wife and his children. It's a complex program, but in the end we came up with a contract—things that Justin and I asked the young man to do for us and himself and his family. He still went to jail, but he's following through on his end of things, and I think he's going to be all right."

He's going to be all right? What about you and your son? Jeannie wanted to ask.

And then as if reading Jeannie's mind, Rachel added, "And we're going to be all right as well. We're starting fresh—new job for me, new school for Justin." She looked away for a minute, gathering her memories. "Going through the program allowed us both to talk openly about how much we were hurting to the very person whose action had brought us that pain."

"Think about it, Jeannie," Hester said. "If we could get the justice system here in Sarasota to hear us out, it could be a way to help Sadie."

"Who's Sadie?" Rachel asked. Jeannie knew by her expression that she genuinely was unaware of the circumstances that had taken over her life and the lives of all of her family.

"Jeannie? Is it okay?" Hester asked, seeking permission to tell her friend what had happened. "I'm sorry. Sadie's name just popped out. Is it okay if . . ."

Jeannie shrugged and picked up their mugs. "Sure. Go ahead. I'll get refills for you."

"And you," Hester urged, "you'll come back and sit with us so we can talk, right?"

"I'll come back, but, Hester, I'm making no promises."

"None expected. Hearing us out is huge. I appreciate that. Thanks."

Inside the coffee shop, Jeannie took her time getting the refills. She did not want to be present for any part of the recounting of the accident that had taken Tessa's life and landed Sadie in jail. She could see Rachel and Hester through the window of the shop. Rachel was facing her, and Jeannie knew the exact moment that Hester must have given her the news.

She put her fist to her mouth and just sat there staring at Hester and shaking her head, as if by denying what she was hearing she might change the story. Jeannie recognized that reaction. It was a milder version of the one she had experienced when Dr. Morris told her that Tessa had died on the operating table.

Here was a woman who had experienced firsthand the kind of loss that Jeannie and Geoff had. Jeannie thought about how Geoff was so certain that if he could just testify, things would be better—at least for them. But what if what they both really needed was to speak out for themselves instead of against Sadie? She picked up the refilled mugs and returned to the table outside.

"So now that you know my story, can you honestly tell me that this VORP or any program like it can possibly make any difference at all?" Her words were laced with skepticism.

"It won't bring your daughter back, Jeannie. But I really do believe—in fact, I know from our experience—that if you and others who have been victimized by this horror are willing to try, it could be a new beginning."

"For Sadie?"

"For her," Rachel agreed, "and for you and your sister and your husband if they are willing to take part."

Jeannie released a bitter laugh and stood up, prepared to leave. "Wow, sounds wonderful. Where do I sign up?"

Hester frowned and glanced nervously at her friend, but Rachel just nodded. "I know it sounds like some kind of magic pill, but Jeannie, the program does work." She pulled Jeannie's chair a bit closer to her and patted the empty seat. "Will you let me explain?"

Jeannie hesitated for a moment then perched on the edge of the chair and waited for Rachel to regale her with stories of past successes—victims who had embraced their offenders and forgiven them wholeheartedly. But she was not at all prepared for Rachel's opening question.

"Jeannie, knowing that Tessa can't come back to you, what is the single most important and positive thing that you would want to come of the event that took your child's life?"

Images of Geoff, then Emma, then Sadie flitted across Jeannie's mind. Memories of Geoff and Matt tossing a football back and forth, of making marmalade with Emma and the girls in their large modern kitchen, of shopping with Sadie because both Emma and Tessa detested shopping. Memories of better times—times when they had laughed together and worked toward the same goals together and prayed together.

"Jeannie?" Hester said, covering Jeannie's hand with hers. "Are you all right?"

Jeannie realized that tears were sliding down her cheeks. She swiped them away with the back of her hand and looked at Rachel. "I want our lives back—the way things were before. I know it will be without Tessa, but surely for those of us left behind, we could find our way back to some semblance of the love and caring we shared before."

And having said it aloud, she realized that this was what she had been wrestling with through all the long days and nights since the accident. How could they be a family again?

"I know," Rachel said. "That's exactly what I wanted, for my son and me."

"Do you really think that you can help us?" Jeannie asked.

"I'll do my best," Rachel promised then hesitated a moment before adding, "Hester mentioned that you were thinking of visiting your niece. You might want to postpone that, Jeannie. My guess is that she won't be able to handle your visit—and more to the point, in my experience you're not quite ready for that meeting yet either."

Chapter 28

Emma

On Friday evening the family had just finished saying grace when someone knocked on the front door.

"I'll get it," Matt said and was up from the kitchen table and on his way to the front door before Lars or Emma could stop him. They heard the muffled exchange of male voices, and then Matt was back, followed by Joseph Cotter.

"I'm sorry to interrupt your supper," he said.

"Not at all. Join us," Lars invited at the same moment that Emma got up to set another place.

"We have plenty."

Joseph sat down in the fourth chair at the table—Sadie's chair. There was a heartbeat when Emma, Lars, and Matt all looked at each other, but they said nothing.

"I have sweet tea and lemonade," Emma offered.

"Lemonade is fine," Joseph replied as he waited for her to set his place and bring his beverage. When Emma sat down and Lars began passing him dishes of the shrimp, rice, vegetables, and rolls that Emma had prepared, Joseph filled his plate. Then he smiled. "It's been awhile since I enjoyed a true home-cooked meal," he said. "Thank you."

When the young attorney started eating without first saying

a silent prayer, Emma shot Matt a look that warned him not to make the comment that she could see coming. Matt rolled his eyes and went back to pushing food around his plate.

It occurred to Emma that lately their son had changed. For one thing, ever since he'd heard that Uncle Geoff had been in court to testify against Sadie, he had been quiet at mealtimes, no longer regaling them with sports facts. More often than not, he ate in silence and then excused himself, mumbling something about a quiz or homework. It was understandable, of course, given everything going on with Sadie and the break with Geoff and Jeannie. Still, she and Lars needed to remember that Matt needed them more than ever now. She resolved to speak to Lars about it later after Matt had gone to bed.

"Your friend Hester Steiner stopped by my office earlier today," Joseph said.

Lars looked at Emma but said nothing.

"She has this college friend—Rachel something-or-other. Anyway, her friend is a trained grief counselor, but more to the point, her husband was killed by a drunk driver a little over a year ago. I got to thinking that if you approved, it might be good to have her visit Sadie. After what happened in court yesterday, it's pretty clear that Sadie has reached her breaking point."

"Sadie wasn't a drunk driver, and besides, I don't understand why Hester would come to you before talking to us," Emma said.

Joseph ate another bite of his supper and took his time chewing and swallowing.

"Matt, if you're finished, you may be excused," Lars said.

Joseph cleared his throat. "Actually, you might want Matt to hear about this," he said quietly.

For the first time in days, Matt seemed interested in what was going on around him. He sat up a little straighter and focused his attention on Joseph.

"What is it that you've come to tell us, Joseph?" Lars asked. Emma felt the now-familiar tightening of her chest and throat.

"This friend of Mrs. Steiner's—Kaufmann—that's the name."

"She's Mennonite?"

Joseph nodded. "By her dress, I'd say she's conservative like you. She apparently has moved here from Ohio to take the chaplaincy at that new hospital just east of here."

"What's that?" Matt asked.

"Ministers at the hospital—trained people of various faiths who are there if needed for patients and their families," Lars explained. Then he turned his attention back to Joseph. "Go on."

"So, Ms. Kaufmann's husband died, leaving her to raise their son, Justin, on her own." Joseph glanced at Matt. "I think the boy is a year or so younger than you are."

"Why move here?" Matt asked.

"Good question. Apparently she lost her job a few months after her husband died, and Hester suggested she look for work here. But the key thing is that after her husband was killed, she took part in a program that's had some real success in cases like Sadie's."

Emma's heart beat faster. "She can help keep Sadie from going away?"

Joseph shook his head as he took a long drink of his lemonade. "She can't influence the court proceedings—at least not directly."

"So, what can she do?" Lars asked quietly, his disappointment obvious.

"Back in Ohio, she and her son took part in a program called VORP—Victim Offender Reconciliation Program." Joseph waited a beat to allow that to sink in then continued. "It's a program where the victim of a crime—or in many cases like yours, it would be victims—and the offender meet directly."

"How can there be more than one victim?" Matt asked. "Tessa was the only one who died."

Joseph looked at him for a long moment, and then he said, "You're a victim in this, Matt. So are Tessa's parents and your parents and grandparents and even Sadie."

Matt's face went nearly purple with anger as he shook his head. "Sadie's the one that caused this whole mess—she's the one that—"

"Matt," Emma scolded. Her son looked at her with such fury, such frustration that it took her breath away.

"I'd like to be excused," he mumbled already half out of his chair.

"*Sich hinsetzen,*" Lars said quietly, pointing to Matt's chair. "We have a guest."

"But you said before. . . ," Matt protested, and then he slumped back into his chair and folded his arms across his chest, refusing to look at either parent.

"Go on, Joseph," Lars said.

Emma saw that Joseph was decidedly uncomfortable with the dynamics around the table. "Would you like more shrimp, Joseph? Or perhaps a slice of raisin pie?"

Joseph gave her a grateful and relieved smile. "It's been years since I tasted raisin pie," he admitted. "But let me help you clear."

"Matt will do that," Lars said.

Matt looked at his father and then got up and began clearing the dishes. "This is Sadie's job," Emma heard him mutter as he passed her with the stacked plates. She picked up the serving dishes and followed him to the sink.

"Matt? Has something happened at school that you haven't wanted to tell us?" She kept her voice low, mindful that Joseph was close by, although he and Lars were talking. But company or not, Matt was not himself.

Matt filled the sink with soapy water and laid the plates in it to soak. "I'm okay."

"Because I want you to understand that Dad and I realize that everything going on these last weeks has been hard on you as well as the rest of us. You can talk to us anytime about anything. It's just that right now Mr. Cotter is here, and he might be able to help your sister and—"

"And that's what matters right now," Matt said. "I get it, Mom." He shut off the water while she took down plates for the pie.

"Helping Sadie can help us all," Emma said quietly. Then when Matt made no comment, she handed him the clean plates. "Take these to the table, bitte. Coffee, Joseph?" she called out in what she had intended as a normal tone but realized was too shrill and tight with tension.

"No ma'am. The lemonade is fine," Joseph said.

At the table, Emma cut slices of the pie and passed the first slice to Joseph. He waited for everyone to be served and for her to be seated before taking a bite. He was a well-mannered young man even if he had started his meal without first thanking God.

"Wow," he said after tasting the pie. "That is seriously great pie."

In spite of her faith's caution when it came to accepting compliments, Emma fought back the first genuine smile she'd managed in days. "Danke, Joseph."

"I mean, help me out here, Matt. This whipped cream topping tastes more like. . . ." He frowned as he savored a bite of the topping.

"Marshmallows?" Matt said wearily. It was true that people unfamiliar with their whipped cream often described the flavor that way, but Emma did not like the way Matt was acting.

"That's it exactly," Joseph replied. He watched Matt for a minute, and Emma understood that the attorney had somehow realized that Matt was struggling to find his place in everything that had happened to their family. "Hey, Matt, Mrs. Steiner tells me that you're some kind of statistics genius."

Matt glanced up from eating his pie, his eyes interested but still wary. "She said that?"

"She did. When Rachel started rattling off the statistics about the VORP program's success rate, Hester said you were the one with a head for stats. Is that right?"

Matt shrugged. "Sports stats mostly."

"Stats are stats," Joseph observed and went on eating his pie. "Marshmallows," he repeated, nodding as he took another bite of the whipped cream.

Matt fought to hide his smile, clearly beginning to feel a connection to Joseph.

"I'm not a hundred percent clear on the details, but after Mrs. Kaufmann and her son participated in the program, she trained to become a mediator for other cases."

"She would be there if Sadie sat down with Jeannie and Geoff?" Lars asked, drawing the lawyer's attention back to the adults.

"Actually, that's only the first piece."

"What else?" Emma asked.

"The idea is to personalize the crime for the offender by showing them the human consequences of their actions."

"I think our Sadie is very aware of the human consequences of her action, Joseph. She grieves every hour for this terrible tragedy." Emma tried to keep her voice calm. The last thing she wanted to hear about was one more process that would only add to the suffering Sadie was already enduring.

"Well, the idea is to give the victims—those who often never have a chance to speak their piece in the criminal justice system—the opportunity to talk about their feelings directly to the offender."

"It is not our way to involve ourselves in such things, Joseph," Lars said, glancing at Emma. His tone reflected his doubt and discomfort. He had already gone well beyond what he believed to be the way to handle Sadie's troubles by agreeing to hire Joseph. Now this?

"And yet people of your faith are some of the strongest advocates for the program in communities where it has been used," Joseph said.

Emma saw Matt gauge the mood and decide that once again he needed to break the silence. "You said there were statistics?" Matt prompted, fully engaged now.

Joseph focused his attention back on Matt. "The program in one form or another dates back two decades, and there are now thousands of such programs operating around the world."

"Around the world—you mean in other countries," Emma said unable to disguise her skepticism.

"And here as well. There's more," Joseph said softly. Emma could see that her husband and son were being drawn into Joseph's presentation, but she wasn't interested in what others had done. She was only interested in how she could best protect her daughter. And she had her doubts that some stranger—whether or not she was an old college friend of Hester's—could ever hope to know Sadie or Jeannie or any of them well enough to make this work.

Joseph had continued to talk, and she forced her attention back to him.

". . .about two out of every three cases referred to the program result in a face-to-face mediation meeting."

Matt shook his head. "So they meet, and Sadie says how sorry she is, and Uncle Geoff and Aunt Jeannie get to say how sad they are. Then what?"

"Like I said—the meeting is only the first piece of it. The meat of the program is both sides sitting down together and drafting what's called a 'restitution agreement.'" He anticipated Lars's question. "The victims lay out terms by which the offender could make restitution for the crime. For example," he said, turning his attention back to Matt, "if Matt here had spray-painted my garage, I might make repainting the garage a condition of the agreement."

Matt's mouth fell open. "But Sadie. . ."

Emma was on her feet before her son could finish the sentence she saw coming. "How about another piece of pie, Joseph?"

Joseph hesitated then pushed his plate away and dabbed at his mouth with his napkin. "No thank you, and my apologies for monopolizing the conversation."

"Not at all," Emma said, relieved that he had given in to her need to change the subject.

"How often does it work?" Matt pressed. "How often does the offender actually repaint the garage or do what the victim wants?"

Joseph focused his attention on Emma, getting her permission to return to the discussion. When she nodded, he kept looking at her as he gave Matt his answer. "In over 90 percent of the cases, the offender completes the terms of the agreement—often within one year. Compare that to court-ordered restitution where there's only a 20 to 30 percent success rate."

"That's impressive," Lars said.

Emma sat down again and took a deep breath as they all turned their attention to her. "I realize that you have Sadie's best interests at heart, Joseph, and of course, Hester is a dear friend. She's also a close friend to Jeannie and Geoff."

Joseph nodded. "She told me that when the offender takes personal responsibility—instead of being ordered by a court to take responsibility—statistics show that everyone benefits."

"And in this case? Sadie cannot make this right," Emma quietly reminded him. Surely she did not need to state the obvious—that what Geoff and Jeannie understandably wanted was Tessa back in their lives.

"I asked the same question. Ms. Kaufmann made the point that the terms of any such agreement must fall within the realm of the possible. Restitution may be only symbolic. The key is to find ways to build a sense of justice between the victim and the offender. In her case, the young man is getting his high school diploma and attending weekly meetings of Alcoholics Anonymous, and he's written several articles on the dangers of drinking and driving that have been reprinted in a variety of newspapers."

A silence fell over the gathering. Emma looked at Lars while Matt looked from one parent to the other. "It could be over?" he asked Joseph finally.

Joseph cleared his throat. "Everyone needs to understand that this does not replace whatever the outcome of Sadie's adjudication may be. If the judge orders her to serve time, this won't change that."

"Then what good is it?" Matt asked.

"It gives you—all of you—a chance to practice what you have told me is 'your way.' It gives you the opportunity to forgive Sadie, and perhaps most of all, it will help Sadie to forgive herself. Of course, Sadie would have to—"

"No," Emma said. "I know you mean well, Joseph, and I can see where this sounds appealing, but having to face Geoff and Jeannie—" She could not find the words to describe the suffering that her child had already endured.

"Your sister knows about the program. She met with Ms. Kaufmann yesterday," Joseph said quietly.

"And Geoff?" Lars asked incredulous at this bit of news.

"I'm not sure whether he knows or not."

"I'll go tell him. He'll listen to me. I know just how to explain it," Matt said. He was up and out the door before anyone could react.

"Lars, stop him," Emma pleaded.

Lars nodded and headed out the back door. Emma could hear him calling for Matt to come back, and she could hear Matt's shouted reply. "It's okay, Dad. I know where Uncle Geoff will be."

Lars returned to the kitchen and shook his head. "I'll take the car and catch up to him," he said, picking up the keys.

"No, let me call Jeannie."

Lars looked at her with something that she could only identify as pity. "She won't answer," he reminded her.

"Why don't you and I go after the boy?" Joseph offered. "My car is blocking yours anyway. I could drive while you keep an eye out for Matt."

Lars nodded, and the two men headed out. "He'll be at the ball field," Emma called after them. "Geoff will have just finished football practice."

Lars waved from the open window of Joseph's car, and as Emma watched them go, she felt the need to do something—anything that might help her feel as if she was in control of something—so she picked up the phone and punched in her sister's number.

Chapter 29

Geoff

Practice had not gone well, and Geoff was glad there was no game scheduled for this week. After suspending Dan Kline for a month, Geoff had finally given in to pressure from other parents and alumni and let him come back. But the boy's head had been somewhere else, and he'd fumbled the ball so often that his teammates had begun to grumble. Geoff's work at school—especially his role as coach—was the one thing he counted on for a respite from the constant memory of Tessa's accident and the oppressive silence that had fallen over the house he shared with Jeannie from that day to this.

Shortly after Tessa's death, Jeannie had asked him about his feelings toward Dan. Of course, those had been the days when he and his wife were actually talking to each other. It was a fair question. It was also one that Geoff had not yet been ready to consider. The team needed Dan if they had any hope of repeating as conference champs this season. That might sound shallow to some, but Geoff could not ignore the power that such an accomplishment could have for the entire student body.

"Kline," he barked as he watched the players trudge toward the locker room, "what's your problem?" Stupid question. What did he think his quarterback's problem was?

517

Dan paused but did not turn around, while his teammates continued on their way. Even wearing shoulder pads, Dan walked like a young man defeated. Geoff had the urge to shake him, but he realized that his irritation with Dan was rooted in the fact that the boy had been in the car that day, had agreed to let Sadie get behind the wheel, had been texting his buddies instead of coaching her. Or at least that was the gossip he'd heard around school—gossip that stopped the minute he passed in the hallway or entered a room. The hours he spent at school had been filled with moments like that, but even so, it was better than the isolation and emptiness he felt at home.

For the last day or so though, it was obvious that Jeannie had something on her mind, something she was reluctant to talk about with him. Whatever it was, she'd been working overtime to soften him up. After several nights spent sleeping in Tessa's room or the guest room, she had come back to their bed the night before. And that very morning, instead of being up and out for her run before his alarm went off, she was in the kitchen cooking a regular breakfast for the two of them.

Knowing Jeannie, she had come up with some plan for putting the family back together again—reconciling with Emma and forgiving Sadie. As if he ever could agree to such a thing. If he never saw Sadie again. . .

"Coach?"

He'd completely forgotten that he'd called Dan back. His quarterback was facing him now, his helmet dangling from two fingers as he squinted at him in the setting sun. Apparently he'd muttered some excuse and was waiting for Geoff to accept it.

"Go on, hit the showers," Geoff growled, and Dan hesitated only half a second before trotting off the field. Geoff picked up the small whiteboard that he used to outline plays and acknowledged the wave of the manager across the field. The kid worked hard. He'd just finished putting away the equipment and locking the shed. As he headed for the locker room, he tossed Geoff the keys.

"See you, Coach."

"Good job."

The kid looked surprised but pleased and broke into a trot

as he left the now deserted field. Geoff realized that he couldn't remember the boy's name.

He took off his sweat-stained baseball cap and rubbed his forearm across his forehead. He was already drenched in sweat, so a long run before he showered seemed like a good idea. Besides, it would use up another hour before he had to go home. Before he had to face another evening of a house without Tessa. Another night of not knowing what to say to Jeannie. Another cluster of hours when he had to face his failure as a father and husband.

He put down his whiteboard and started to jog around the track. On the second lap, he heard footsteps behind him, gaining on him. He glanced over his shoulder and saw Matt dogging his steps with shorter but admirable strides for a kid his age. Geoff felt the predictable flicker of irritation that he'd experienced on seeing Matt ever since the funeral. He thought about picking up the pace. How far down had he fallen to run away from a kid?

Not just any kid.

Matt.

"Hey, Matt," Geoff called out as if he'd been expecting his nephew all along. "Just finished an extra practice and thought I'd get in a couple of laps, but it's getting pretty late."

"I've got something to tell you," Matt said as he came alongside Geoff.

The boy was barely breathing hard and certainly hadn't broken a sweat, although he'd been running full out to catch up. "Okay, walk with me." He headed across the playing field toward the school.

"It's about Sadie—well, all of us actually, but—"

"Not interested," Geoff growled. He forced himself to add, "Look, I admit I've been avoiding you lately, and I'm sorry about that. If you want to talk about school or sports or anything like that, I'm here for you, Matt. But your sister is off-limits."

Matt stopped walking. "But. . ."

Geoff wheeled around, his fists clenched at his sides. "Why can't you people get this? I don't—no, make that I *can't* bear to think about what Sadie did to us much less talk about it."

"But this is different."

"Give it up, Matt. You and your mom and your dad and everyone else needs to stop trying to convince me that I need to forgive and forget." He released a laugh that sounded more like a howl. "Do us both a favor and just go away, Matt."

Matt was looking at him with those puppy-dog eyes that so many times in the past had pleaded with him to help with some problem at home or school. Geoff sighed and softened his tone. "You're a good kid, but seeing you makes me think about your sister, and frankly I'm not a big enough man to be able to manage that— not yet. Maybe there will come a day, but this isn't it, so go home. If you care for me at all, don't be coming around here anymore."

He punched in the security code for the school's side door then rested his forehead against the doorjamb. "Look, this isn't about you, Matt. It's just that right now. . ." He shook his head and added, "Maybe in a year when you're enrolled here—maybe then. Okay?" But when he turned around, Matt was running full out again, this time in the opposite direction.

Feeling frustrated by the very idea that Matt would even attempt to bring up Sadie's name and also guilty for taking out his grief and anger on the boy, Geoff showered and changed, stuffing his dirty clothes inside a duffel before turning out the lights and heading home.

The kitchen light was on when he came up the driveway, and he could see Jeannie standing at the sink. She didn't even glance up when he drove the car into the garage. But her movements told him that it was because she was caught up in whatever she was doing rather than that she was deliberately ignoring him.

Inside the laundry room off the kitchen, he dumped his dirty clothes in the washer, added detergent, and turned on the machine. Through the open doorway, he could see that the table was set—for three. Seeing a place setting where Tessa normally sat took his breath away.

Half expecting to find Jeannie in a state of confusion and denial, he steadied himself and then cleared his throat before entering the kitchen. Jeannie was cutting vegetables for a salad at the kitchen sink. "Hey, babe, what's going on?"

"Oh, good, you're home," she said. "Do me a favor and turn

the oven down to three hundred, okay?"

Geoff did as she asked, all the while looking for signs that his wife had finally lost it and gone fully into the dream world of imagining that Tessa was still with them.

"I've invited a friend of Hester's to have supper with us," she said as she tossed the salad and then covered the large wooden bowl with plastic wrap and set it in the refrigerator. "Her name is Rachel Kaufmann. She and Hester were college roommates in nursing school. She's moving to Sarasota to take a position at the hospital. Oh Geoff, her husband was killed by a drunk driver a year or so ago. Now it's just her and her son, Justin."

"Aren't you three places short?" Geoff asked, feeling an odd sense of relief that Jeannie was fine after all. "John and Hester and the boy?"

"It was all so last-minute. John and Hester had a prior engagement, and Rachel had promised her son that he could spend the night with a friend he met at church. She was going to be alone, so I thought. . . You don't mind, do you?"

Geoff almost smiled. This was so typical of Jeannie. She would invite total strangers to join them for a meal, and then when it was a done deal, she would give him those huge green eyes of hers and say, "You don't mind, do you?"

He felt a tenderness toward her that had been sorely missing since the funeral. "And if I did?" He kept his voice light and teasing, like the old days. He tweaked her cheek and then cupped her face in his hands. "It'll do us both good," he said. "Get our minds on someone else."

Jeannie nodded, but Geoff did not miss the way she hesitated as if there was a little more to the story than she was telling him. *Paranoid.* He shook off the feeling.

"What can I do to help?" he asked as he rinsed his hands under the kitchen faucet and dried them on a dish towel. Just then the doorbell rang, and Geoff glanced out the window and saw a bike parked on the driveway. "How about I get the door?"

By her dress and manner, Rachel Kaufmann was of the same branch of the Mennonite faith as Lars and Emma. It made sense, of course, since Hester and John were also conservative in their practice.

He forgot to smile as he opened the door and took in the pale blue dress, the white starched prayer covering, the tightly bound black hair. Seeing her made him think of Emma—and Matt.

"Hello," she said, her smile tentative in the face of his less-than-warm welcome. "I may have the wrong house. I was looking for the Messner home?"

"Rachel, come in," Jeannie called from the kitchen. "That's my husband, Geoff. Geoff, this is Rachel."

Geoff smiled and opened the door wider, inviting the woman inside. "It's nice to meet you," he said, offering her a handshake.

"Likewise. Hester tells me that you're both the athletic director and vice principal at a local high school," she said. "That's quite a lot on your plate."

"Plus he coaches football and basketball," Jeannie added, coming into the front hallway.

Jeannie was nervous. Geoff knew his wife. She had never met a person she didn't immediately bond with. No, if Jeannie had invited this woman to supper, she had already established a connection of some sort. He decided that her nerves came from being out of the habit of entertaining and making the small talk that came with the territory.

"Jeannie tells me that you've taken a job at the hospital. Are you a nurse?" he ventured.

Rachel laughed. "I was. But one day I realized that it was the emotional and spiritual wellness of people that intrigued me, so I went back to school and got my degree in psychology—counseling—"

"Oh my," Jeannie said as she made a dash for the kitchen. "I left the heat on under the rice, and it's boiling over."

Geoff felt his jaw tighten as Rachel followed Jeannie to the kitchen, offering to help. A shrink? Was this a setup? True, he and Jeannie had been anything but close lately. Even before Tessa died, they'd been having problems, but a counselor? They had their minister for that if they needed him.

Still, he wouldn't be rude. He was feeling guilty about the way he'd handled things with Matt. On the drive home, he'd thought about how he might make that right. After all, Matt was an innocent bystander in all of this. It was unfair—not to mention downright immature—to blame him or even connect him to what had happened. But he hadn't been able to bring himself to stop by Matt's house, and the chances of Lars allowing the phone on at this hour were slim. Tomorrow, Geoff had promised himself, he would get a message to Matt to come by practice after school.

Feeling a little less tense for having come up with a plan for reuniting with Matt, Geoff joined the women in the kitchen where Rachel was filling glasses with ice and water and Jeannie was dishing up their supper. After all, if this was Jeannie's attempt to get them both to counseling, all he had to do was politely say no.

"Looks great," Geoff said, relieving her of the platter stacked with pieces of baked chicken. He set it on the table then pulled out Tessa's chair for Rachel.

"Thank you," she murmured.

He waited for Jeannie to sit before taking his own place across from her. He held out his hands for them to take for the silent grace before the meal, and after a minute, he released Rachel's hand and gave Jeannie's an extra squeeze before offering Rachel the platter of chicken.

"Have you found a place to live yet, Rachel?"

"I have. Do you know Malcolm Shepherd? He and his wife, Sharon, have rented me their guesthouse. Justin and I can walk to everything—his school, the market, the post office, even to work if I want to, although that's a bit more of a hike."

"Malcolm's brother, Zeke, and Geoff are best friends," Jeannie said.

"So what will you be doing at the hospital?" Geoff asked.

"I'm to be a spiritual counselor for the children's wing. It's quite a facility they've built there." She cut a piece of her chicken. "Have you always lived in Sarasota, Geoff?"

"My family moved here when I was ten."

Jeannie laughed. "But he's still not considered a Floridian. People who were born and raised here can get pretty picky about that."

"Like your sister?" Geoff said, and then he forced a smile.

Jeannie hesitated, and he understood that she was trying to

determine if his mention of Emma was innocent or intentional. In order to break the uncomfortable silence that followed his comment, she answered Rachel's obvious question, "Emma has always teased Geoff about being a transplant from Iowa even though he barely remembers when his family lived there."

"So, Rachel, what exactly are the duties of a spiritual counselor?" Geoff asked, wanting to move the conversation away from Jeannie's sister and her family. To his relief, Rachel seemed happy to oblige. While they finished their supper, she regaled them with tales of how she had first learned of the job, and they laughed together about Hester's habit of assuming she could find a solution for just about any problem.

"So, how do you like Sarasota?" Geoff asked.

"It's so clean and quiet," she marveled.

"Just wait until the snowbirds arrive," Jeannie warned as she pushed back her chair and began stacking their plates. "It's such a lovely night, why don't we have dessert out on the lanai?"

"Let me help you clear," Rachel offered.

"No thanks. You and Geoff go sit and get better acquainted. Geoff, Rachel was a school nurse and guidance counselor before leaving Ohio." She handed Geoff a tray already stacked with coffee cups, flatware, and dessert plates for him to carry out for her.

"Really?" Geoff took his cue and escorted Rachel out to the lanai while Jeannie turned on the coffeemaker and prepared to slice what looked like his favorite peanut butter pie.

By the time Jeannie arrived, carrying the coffeepot in one hand and balancing the pie in the other, Geoff was beginning to relax. He liked Rachel. She had the kind of no nonsense manner that worked well in dealing with kids—especially teenagers. He couldn't help but think that the decision to cut her job for budget reasons was a great loss for the school where she'd worked before.

It occurred to him that Rachel might be a good person for Jeannie to confide in. Their other friends were too close to everyone involved, but here was someone who was not only trained in counseling, but had also suffered her own terrible and sudden loss. The fact that she was a lot further down the grief path than they were might help Jeannie through the worst of this.

Given the circumstances of her husband's death, Rachel might even understand why it was important for him to tell Tessa's side of things in court.

He leaned back in the rattan chair and accepted the large slice of pie that Jeannie handed him. "My favorite," he said, smiling up at her.

"Duh," she replied with a little laugh.

For one incredible moment, life was normal again. He and Jeannie were spending an evening with a new friend. And while Tessa would have shared the meal with them, by now she would have excused herself to go up to her room or out with her friends. Geoff could imagine that this was just another such evening, and he allowed himself the moment of fantasy.

Rachel and Jeannie were talking about the fruit co-op that Hester and John managed, when Rachel said, "It's so easy to underestimate the impact a program like that can have on the lives of people. It's like that with the VORP program."

Jeannie went suddenly very still and silent, her eyes flicking back and forth between Rachel and him, almost as if she were warning Rachel about something.

"What's a vorp?" he asked.

Rachel set down her pie plate and coffee cup and leaned forward, her eyes riveted on Geoff. "It stands for Victim Offender Reconciliation Program." She waited.

Jeannie took a sudden interest in watching a bird outside the screened lanai. Geoff felt his throat tighten.

He should have gone with his first impression: This was a setup.

He stood up.

"It was nice meeting you, Rachel. I hope you and my wife have a nice visit, but if you'll excuse me, I have some schoolwork that needs my attention." His voice sounded foreign to him—too tight and high.

"Geoff, hear her out, please," Jeannie pleaded.

But Geoff was already back inside the house and walking away from her—away from her plot to get him to forgive Sadie—as if he ever could. As if *she* ever should.

Chapter 30

Matthew

When Matt left the athletic field, he did not go home. He rode his bike up and down streets, turning corners without thought until he found himself in a strange neighborhood with no idea of how to get back to Pinecraft.

It was nearly dark. The houses he passed were small and crowded close to one another, and their yards were filled with stuff—old cars and rusted pieces of metal and tires. The fences—where there were fences—sagged, and a few of them had whole sections missing. The streets were narrow, barely wide enough for two cars to pass, especially in places where cars were parked along the road.

Every once in a while he would ride past a house and hear voices coming from the darkened porches or see the flare of a match followed by the scent of cigarette smoke. A couple of times he heard laughter coming from inside houses with the shades drawn but the windows open. Families gathered together the way his used to.

He kept turning down new blocks, trying to find his way back to a main street, and then he realized that he was riding in circles. A car came down the street fast, nearly hitting him. The driver blared his car horn and yelled something foul at Matt as he roared past.

As dark as it was, it had to be well past his curfew. He wondered if his parents would even notice that he hadn't shown up yet. These days they focused all their attention on Sadie or Sadie's lawyer or Sadie's case. His mom called his aunt Jeannie pretty much every day and left messages that Matt could tell were desperate attempts to break the silence between the two families. As far as he knew, Jeannie had yet to call back.

He'd been giving some serious thought to running away. There were a couple of good reasons why that was a good idea. One, maybe it would make his parents wake up and realize that life couldn't be all about Sadie all the time. And two—what exactly was there for him around here anymore? Uncle Geoff had made it clear that he blamed the whole family, including him, for Tessa's death, even though at the time of the accident he had been at school working on his math, totally unaware that Sadie had stupidly driven Dan's car and hit Tessa.

Of course, running away meant he would need some money. He could take some food with him and his bike, of course, but the food was bound to run out pretty fast. He'd been trying to think of some way he might be able to earn some cash and save it up until he had enough, like maybe twenty dollars.

Then Sadie's lawyer had told them about VORP, and Matt had gotten really excited. Here was something that might actually work, that might get his uncle Geoff to stop ignoring him and talk to him again and let him come back to practice and all. If that happened, he could probably stand the stuff at home. Uncle Geoff would understand. He would listen like he had before. Geoff was always teaching the team—and Matt—that no matter what, there was a way through the other team's line—a way to win. And this VORP thing sure sounded like it had potential.

But Matt had blown it. Why did he have to blurt out Sadie's name the very first thing?

He stopped to get his bearings then decided on a shortcut through a park where he heard voices and laughter. He saw a group of boys, their bikes carelessly abandoned on the ground as they gathered around a picnic table under a streetlamp.

"Three kings," one of the boys crowed triumphantly. "Read 'em and weep."

Matt edged closer. The boy picked up some coins from the table and turned to go. "My ma is gonna kill me," he told the others when they protested that he couldn't leave yet.

He went to pick up his bike when he saw Matt. "Hey, kid, wanna take my place in the game?"

Matt looked around and then realized that the boy was talking to him. "Me?"

"Yeah. Go on. Hey, guys! Fresh blood," he shouted as he pedaled off.

The other three boys turned around. They weren't much older than Matt was. In fact, one of them looked like he was at least a couple of years younger. Two of them were white, and the third boy was black.

"Wanna play or not?"

Matt realized that they didn't know that he was Mennonite. It didn't seem to dawn on them that he was wearing the plain clothes of his faith. For once in his life he could be just another boy. And if this was what boys outside of the faith did and they wanted him to play, then why not? He was already late, and he could probably get these boys to help him find his way home once the game was over.

"Sure." He dropped his bike alongside theirs and sat down in the empty spot the first boy had abandoned.

"Next hand," one of the boys muttered as he dropped two cards on the table and held out his hand to receive two fresh ones. The golden glow of the streetlamp cast just enough light over the table for them to see the cards.

The boy looked at his new hand and groaned. "I fold."

"Me too," the other white kid said.

"Ante up," the black kid said as he scooped up the pile of coins and placed a dime in the center of the table.

Matt stared at the coins as each boy put one in the pile. One of the older boys shuffled the cards. "You got to pay to play, kid," he said.

Matt started to get up. "I don't have any money with me," he told them, hoping they wouldn't get mad at him. "And I don't know how to play this game."

"No worries," one of the kids said with a grin. "I'll spot you."

No worries? Matt wondered if it was possible that they knew Zeke. The kid put another dime on the table and explained the game. It seemed simple enough. Every player got five cards to start. You tried to make the best hand you could, but you could also turn in cards you didn't need in hopes of getting ones that would give you a better hand.

The black kid explained what a good hand was. A pair, two pair, and so on. At school, Matt's best subject was math, and somehow this all seemed to make sense to him. He nodded and checked his cards.

"I'll take two," the boy next to the dealer said.

"Three."

"I'll keep what I have," Matt said, and three pairs of eyes glanced his way.

"Pass," the first boy said.

"I'll bet a nickel," the second boy said and tossed five pennies onto the pile of dimes.

"I'll see that," the third kid said, adding a nickel to the pile. "Up to you."

"I don't. . ."

The dealer slid a nickel his way. "At this point, you either fold—as I'm going to do—or you put the nickel in the pile."

"Then I owe you fifteen cents."

"Yep. If you want to raise the bet, then you'll owe me twenty cents. What's it going to be?"

Matt checked his cards. If he won, then he could pay the boy who'd loaned him the money and still have some left. He picked up the nickel and tossed it onto the pile, enjoying the clink it made as it hit the rest of the coins.

"Pair of sevens," one boy said displaying his cards.

"Beats me," the second boy said. "Let's see what you've got, kid."

Matt laid out his cards—three twos, an eight, and a six.

"And we have a winner," the boy who'd loaned him the money

said as he slid the money toward Matt, taking care to remove his fifteen cents. "Deal," he told the black kid.

"Ante," the black kid replied as he shuffled the cards.

They played several more hands until a car rolled slowly toward them. "Outta here," one of the boys muttered as he divided the money left on the table between them and gathered the cards. "Same time tomorrow?"

He was looking at Matt, but he didn't wait for an answer.

The car stopped, and Matt could hear the crackle of a two-way radio that indicated a police car. He glanced toward the car, and when he turned back, the other three boys and their bikes had disappeared. A police officer was walking toward him, shining his flashlight over the area.

"Hey, kid, it's pretty late to be out here in the park," he said.

"I took a wrong turn and got lost," Matt replied, shielding his eyes from the brightness of the beam.

"Won't your folks be worried?"

"Yes sir."

"Where do you live?"

Matt gave his address, and the police officer released a low whistle. "You did take a wrong turn, half a dozen of them. You're a couple of miles from there." He turned the flashlight toward Matt's bike. "That yours?"

"Yes sir."

"Well, let's load it in the back of the patrol car and call your folks. I expect they'll be pretty worried by now."

"They won't answer. The phone is for my Dad's work. They don't answer it after supper. If you just tell me the way back, I can get there."

"Amish, are you?"

"Mennonite."

The officer reached inside the patrol car and picked up the two-way radio. He turned away while he talked to someone on the other end.

"Okay, come on," he said, lifting Matt's bike into the trunk and then fastening the lid closed with a bungee cord. "We'll give you a lift."

Matt started to back away.

"You're not running away, are you?" the officer said, his tone laced with fresh suspicion. His partner started to get out of the car.

"No sir."

"Then get in the car," the partner said, opening the back door for him.

Matt did as he instructed. He stared out the window as the officer drove, trying his best to get his bearings. He had just made over a dollar playing a game, and he wanted to be sure he could find his way back to play again.

Chapter 31

Lars

When Lars and Joseph had followed Matt to the school, they'd seen Matt talking to Geoff. Since the two of them were walking across the field together and Geoff seemed to be listening, Lars had thought it best to give this possible break in the stalemate a chance. He'd told Joseph that everything seemed okay, and Joseph had driven him back home.

"Jeannie is probably serving them both huge bowls of ice cream right now," Emma said, clearly hoping that was the case. "I would call her, but she's not picking up."

"He'll be along soon," Lars assured her, but it was past eight o'clock, and he saw by Emma's anxious glances at the clock that she was as worried as he was. "You know, maybe I should drive over to Geoff and Jeannie's and pick Matt up. I mean, I don't like the idea of him riding his bike after dark."

"I'll go with you," Emma said.

"Nein, stay here in case he's on his way home and I miss him." He took his hat from the peg by the door and picked up the car keys.

He was outside with Emma standing in the doorway to see him off when the police cruiser pulled up in front of the house. Lars felt the breath rush out of his chest when he saw the official car and the officer getting out of the driver's side.

"Mr. Keller?" His partner had also gotten out and was opening the back door.

"Ja. . .yes?" Lars's heart was in his throat and beating hard as Matt got out. The boy did not look at either of his parents, just walked to the back of the cruiser to get the bike one officer was unloading.

"I've got it," Lars heard Matt say. "Thanks for the ride."

But the officer who'd been driving followed him up the driveway while his partner waited. He tipped his hat to Emma and then focused his attention on Lars. "Your son said he took a wrong turn. He was over in Payne Park."

Payne Park was the opposite direction from their house, Jeannie's house, or the school. Lars looked at Matt for an explanation. "What happened?"

"He. . ." Tears were rolling down Matt's cheeks.

Emma put her arm around their son. "Come inside," she said. "It's time for your shower." She ignored the officer as she ushered Matt past him and into the house.

"Is everything all right, Mr. Keller?" The officer was watching him closely. Then he blinked and looked even closer. "Keller? Any relation to. . ."

"She's my daughter. Our family has had some difficult days."

The policeman nodded. "Your son was awfully quiet on the ride home. I tried to draw him out—you know, in case somebody had. . .approached him. Sometimes a park, especially after dark. . ."

"I'll talk to him. We appreciate your bringing him home to us, officer. And now if there's nothing else?"

The policeman looked toward the lighted window of the kitchen and then back at Lars. "Glad to be of service." He walked back to his cruiser, shut the trunk, and got in. His partner got in on the passenger side, but they did not leave immediately. Instead Lars saw the two of them conferring, looking up toward the house as they talked.

Lars went inside and closed the door and shut off the porch light as well as the kitchen light. A minute later, he heard the police car pull away. They would file a report, and once again his family's name would be part of an official record.

Down the hall, he could hear water running. He followed the sound, and after confirming that Matt was in the shower, he went to find Emma. She was turning down the bed in Matt's room. "Did he say anything?"

She shook her head. "Not really. Whatever happened when he found Geoff, it didn't end up with them having ice cream together." She clutched Matt's pillow to her chest. "How could he have gone so far afield, Lars? Payne Park is all the way. . ."

"Downtown," Lars said. "I know." He sat on the side of the bed and bowed his head. He had never felt so lost, so incapable of doing the right thing for his family, for his children. God had blessed them with these bright and giving children to shepherd through this world, and after years of success, it seemed to him that he was suddenly at a loss about how to guide them. His daughter was in jail. His son had been brought home by the police.

"I suppose we should come up with some punishment," Emma was saying. "He could have called."

"He saw me turn the phone off after Joseph arrived for supper, remember? And we thought he was with Geoff."

"Ah," Emma sighed.

"The policeman recognized that we are—that Sadie is our daughter. I think he remains concerned that there may be more than one of our children in trouble."

Emma's eyes widened. "Surely not. Matt was lost—not causing trouble."

"These are different times for us, Emma," Lars said. "We have to face the fact that Sadie may have to go away for a time. We have to think about how all of this is affecting Matt."

Emma closed her eyes and sucked in a deep breath. "I am worried for him. Geneva Kurtz stopped me the other day. She says that Matt is not himself at school these days. She thinks perhaps the other children are keeping their distance from him. Why would they do that when he's in such pain, Lars?"

Lars had long ago given up believing that things wouldn't

change with each generation. Especially living here in Pinecraft on the very borders of a city like Sarasota where their children were so exposed to the ways of the outsiders. The life his children knew wasn't like the life he had known as a boy when he and his parents had lived on the farm up north. It wasn't even the way it had been for Emma and Jeannie growing up right here in Pinecraft.

More and more the ways of the outside world had made their mark, especially once the tourists had discovered the small community. Their fascination with the ways of the Amish and Mennonites was perhaps understandable, but Lars struggled with the lack of respect these outsiders showed for their customs. Sometimes it felt as if they were on display for the entertainment of others. But of far more concern was the attraction of their own young people to the dress and language and ways of these outsiders.

So many times he and Emma had had to quietly remind Sadie that such expressions as "so cool" or the sarcastic "Ya think?" weren't part of their way of speaking to others. Sadie's fascination with clothing had not come just from being around Jeannie or Tessa. More than once she had described to Emma some item of clothing she had observed on one of the tourists. It was always clear how much she had admired—even longed for—the garments. Lars had often heard Emma remind their daughter that to covet the goods of another was a sin. But Matt had always seemed indifferent to the ways of the outside world.

"Did his teacher say anything else?" he asked.

"His work is fine—when he does it—but more and more often she has to prod him to finish an assignment, and when she does, she told me that he has on occasion snapped at her. He always apologizes immediately," Emma assured Lars, "but still that's not like our son."

"No, that's not Matt at all."

Lars became aware that down the hall the water continued to run. He walked to the small bathroom the family shared and knocked at the door. "Waste not, son," he said, but he made a point of keeping his tone light, hoping that it would not be heard as a reprimand. Emma was right. Little attention had been paid to

535

what Matt must be going through since the accident. It was past time for them to show their son that they were there as much for him as they were for his sister. "Finish up."

There was a beat, and then the water stopped and he heard a soft, "Yes sir."

When Matt came to his room dressed in his pajamas and carrying his clothes, Emma and Lars were sitting side by side on his bed. Emma immediately got to her feet and took the clothing from him, examining each item to see if it was clean enough for the boy to wear the following day before folding it over the single chair.

"So, you got lost," Lars said, patting the bed beside him. "It happens. What Mom and I don't understand is how you got so far from the school or Geoff and Jeannie's house."

Matt seemed to consider the merits of telling them what happened. Then he took a deep breath and poured out his story. "I was never at their house, Dad. I went to the ball field knowing Uncle Geoff had probably just finished practice, and I was right. He was taking laps around the track, so I caught up to him. I wanted to tell him about the program—about that VORP thing that Mr. Cotter was telling us about. I thought if I could show him a way that everything could be settled again, then maybe he wouldn't be so mad at me."

"He's not mad at you," Emma said. "Oh Matt, he's just so filled with sadness and grief. Sometimes in grown-ups that comes across as anger, but. . ."

Matt gave her a pitying look. "Mom, I know how it is, okay? Every time I've gone to watch practice since Tessa died, Uncle Geoff acts like he doesn't see me, and instead of taking a run with me once practice is over like we always did before, he just walks away."

"Mr. Cotter and I followed you to the ball field, son. It looked like you and your uncle were talking," Lars said.

Matt nodded. "Yeah. At first it was like maybe things would be okay. He didn't ignore me—he even waited for me to catch up to him. But I did it all wrong. I started out saying that this program was something that could help Sadie, and well, he's still really mad at her, and my bringing up her name seemed to make him even madder, and he. . ."

Matt drew in a shuddering breath and bit his lip. Lars realized that the boy was fighting back tears. It was obvious that the last thing he wanted to do was to cry twice in the same evening in front of his father. What kind of father had he been to this child that his own son was afraid to show his true feelings in front of him?

"Matt, it was wrong of Geoff to take out his feelings about losing Tessa on you. He's the adult here. He should have realized that you were only trying to help. You did a good thing in trying to offer an idea that could help."

"What happened after Geoff got mad at you?" Emma asked.

"I took off," Matt told them. "I just wanted to get away from there, so I started riding, thinking about what he'd said about not wanting to see me again for a long time, like probably not until I start school there next year." His voice trailed off. "Why did Sadie have to try and show off for Dan Kline? Now he doesn't even seem to care about her at all. It's because she was only thinking about Dan and how much she wanted him to like her. . . ."

Lars was so stunned at the bitterness he heard in the way Matt talked about his sister, the way he said Sadie's name as if it left a bad taste in his mouth, that he felt compelled to defend her. "Matt, Sadie is very sad and sorry for what happened that day. She knows how much hurt she has caused, and she will have to live with the consequences of her actions the rest of her life. Right now she needs—"

"Okay, I'm sorry." He turned to Emma to plead his case. "I just wanted so much for us to be a family again. I know Tessa's gone, but we're all still here. What about that?"

Lars could see that Emma had no answer to that, and truth be told, neither did he. He touched his son's bony shoulder and felt Matt tense.

"Say your prayers and then get some sleep, son. Tomorrow's another day." He moved aside so that Emma could hold back the covers while Matt crawled into bed and curled onto his side. After Emma had tucked him in, Lars sat on the side of the bed again. "Your mother and I have been blessed with you and your sister, Matt. This is a hard time for all of us, but if we place our trust in God's plan, we'll get through this together."

Matt looked at him with skepticism. "It's okay, Dad," he said wearily. "I understand how things are. I'll be fine. You and Mom just worry about Sadie."

"That's enough talk for tonight," Emma said as she switched off the small desk lamp, leaving the room in deep shadows cast by the single light from the front hall. "We can talk more tomorrow."

Recalling the conversation that Matt's teacher had had with Emma about his lack of attention and his growing hostility at school, Lars could only pray that it would also be a better day for their son.

Chapter 32

Emma

Enough was enough. Something had to be done, and for once Emma was not going to be the one waiting for someone else to take action. After yet another night of lying awake while Lars pretended to sleep, Emma was up with the rising sun. She got dressed, left a note for Lars on the kitchen table, and headed for the bay. She was as certain as she had ever been of anything that Jeannie would be there.

Her sister was already at the far point of the mud flats where the mollusk beds jutted up from the clear, calm waters. Jeannie was picking her way over the sharp shells. She looked thinner and, even from a distance, she looked older—as if she had been beaten down by life. Or maybe Emma was simply projecting the way she felt on her sister.

The muck sucked at her shoes as she made her way out to the higher, drier sandbar. She passed several live tulip shells inching their way along and a huge lightning whelk with an interior that shone like pearls. She knew that Jeannie had passed them by as well. Neither of them would ever take a live shell no matter how large, rare, or beautiful it might be.

Jeannie remained oblivious to her presence, bent as she was over a cluster of mollusks as she peered closely at something hidden there.

"Is it a horse conch?" Emma called out, not wanting to startle her.

Jeannie turned slowly, shielded her eyes with one hand, and then nodded. "Ginormous, as the kids would say," she replied.

Emma smiled and felt a twinge of hope that just maybe they could find their way back to each other. "Alive?"

"Beautifully so."

"Did you see the whelk?"

Jeannie nodded and continued exploring the mollusk beds.

The sisters were shy with each other, skirting around each other like the egrets and little blue herons and other water birds around them. As was their usual practice, they came close to show the other a special find and then separated as they went in different directions, their heads bowed, their eyes searching the clear water for some new treasure.

It all reminded Emma of when they had been younger. They would have a falling out over something and promise never to speak to the other one again. Then it would dawn on them that they had just broken all ties with their best friend, and that would ignite the cautious but always predictable move toward making up. Sometimes it took only a matter of hours. Once or twice it had lasted overnight. This time it had gone on for weeks.

"I've missed you," Emma said as the sisters bent to admire a king's crown conch inching its way across the grassy bottom of the bay.

"Me, too," Jeannie admitted. "It's been. . .hard."

Jeannie had always been a master of understatement, and Emma almost chuckled, but this was not their usual disagreement. This time the stakes had been set far higher than either of them could ever have imagined possible.

"I can't possibly know what this has been like for you and Geoff," Emma said.

"But?" She sounded defensive.

"No 'buts,' Jeannie."

Her sister glanced at her skeptically then went back to shelling, moving away from her. Emma hoped that maybe she was thinking about how hard this had been on everyone—even those of them that had not directly suffered the death of a child. And she realized that this had been the most challenging part of the whole event—this kind of unspoken and unacknowledged but deeply felt contest about who among them was suffering most deeply.

Emma decided that if they were going to get anywhere, she had to risk saying aloud what everyone had avoided. "In one way, Jeannie, we've both lost our children. Tessa was not my daughter, but you know what she meant to us, how we loved her as one of our own."

Jeannie had stopped her cursory search for shells and was staring out across the bay to the islands beyond. She stood perfectly still, and Emma wondered if perhaps she hadn't heard her.

And then so quietly that Emma thought she might have imagined it, she heard Jeannie murmur, "How is Sadie?"

"She's pretty lost right now. It's hard to know what to say when we visit or how best to help her get through this. And, Jeannie, she must get through it. We all must. It can do no honor to Tessa's memory if we fail at that."

After a long moment, Jeannie turned around. She removed something from her pocket and held it out for Emma to see. "Zeke found these angel wings. Aren't they just perfect? So petite—like our Tessa was?"

Was it possible that with a simple exchange of observations about seashells the sisters had found their way to the open door that would allow them to talk after all this time? Emma kept walking to where her sister waited to show her the treasure of the sea. They stood side by side admiring the purity of the shell's white color and saying nothing for several long moments.

"Joseph Cotter stopped by last night," Emma said finally. "Lars and I think that the VORP idea is a good one."

Jeannie hesitated. "Geoff doesn't."

Emma let that pass. "What do you think?"

Jeannie breathed out a long-suffering sigh, and when she started to speak, it was as if a flood of all the things she'd been wanting to say for days came tumbling out.

"Oh Emma, what do I think? I think that I want this

nightmare to end. I think that I want my child back. I think that I want our life back. I think that I want to hear myself laughing again and singing again. I think that I want Geoff and me to start being in the same place at the same time with the same need to be with each other. I think that I want to utter a prayer that doesn't beg God to make this all go away but thanks Him for the blessings of our lives."

"Then let's figure out the best way to get there together, because that is exactly what I want as well."

The sisters slowly made their way back to the narrow beach entry to the bay. Along the way, Jeannie came across an empty moon shell and handed it to Emma, who accepted it for the gift and peace offering she knew it to be.

"I heard that the judge called for a continuance in court the other day," Jeannie said.

Emma nodded. "I think the combination of Dan Kline testifying for the state and then seeing Geoff about to get on the stand was too much for Sadie. She had a complete breakdown. The judge took pity on her and sent everyone home. We go back on Monday."

Emma wanted to ask if Geoff had changed his mind about testifying. She wondered if he could do such a thing, having already agreed to appear for the state. There was so much about the ways of these outside laws and courts that confused her. "It seems to me," she said as if she and Jeannie had been having a discussion about that very thing, "that everything to do with their laws and ways has to do with punishment and retribution."

"Maybe they've tried our way in the past," Jeannie suggested.

"It doesn't seem that way. On the other hand, Joseph tells us that the mediation program just might be a way that we could. . ."

"Save Sadie from having to go to jail?"

"She's in jail now," Emma reminded her sister.

They walked along in silence, a reminder that the chasm between them was not so easily bridged.

"Did you know that she was attacked?"

Jeannie stopped walking. "No. Was she badly hurt? What happened?"

Emma told her the story and about the conversation she had overheard in the hallway outside the courtroom. "I'm certain that she was that girl's grandmother. Can you imagine turning your back on a child? I mean, I don't have the right to judge them without a walk in their shoes, but still. . ."

"But you think that's what I've done? Turned my back on Sadie, who has always been like my own child."

"Oh Jeannie, I didn't mean—"

"I know what you meant," Jeannie said through clenched teeth, and Emma was stunned at her sister's bitterness.

They were walking past the gardens, taking a shortcut through the entrance to the parking lot and out to Orange Avenue as they often did in order to get away from the traffic on Mound Street.

"What time do you have to be back in court on Monday?" Jeannie asked after they had walked a couple of blocks in a tense silence. In the past, she had always been the one to find a way to break any tension between them, and Emma was grateful for her willingness to do it now.

"Nine o'clock."

They had walked past the neat lawns of the houses along Orange and crossed over the bridge on their way to Bahia Vista Street—the street that would take them eastward to Pinecraft. This was a walk they had taken together more times than either of them could count. It struck Emma that through the years they had talked about so many things while taking this same journey—boyfriends, parents, their husbands, their children.

"I'd like you to be there," Emma said softly. "In court with Lars and me. I'd like you to be there for Sadie, if you think you could manage."

Jeannie kept her eyes on her feet. "I don't know, Emma. Geoff will still testify, you understand."

Emma hesitated. "Well, maybe not then. I know how hard it's been for the two of you—I mean, even before you lost Tessa, there were. . ."

To her shock, Jeannie turned on her, her face aflame with rage. "You know nothing. For once in your life, Emma, stop

543

assuming that you have the answers, because you don't. You didn't with Sadie, and you don't for me and Geoff." Tears welled in Jeannie's eyes. "You know something, Emma—here's how I'm going to fix this: I am going to stand by my husband before I lose him as well."

Emma was dumbfounded at the change in Jeannie. She barely recognized her anymore. "Jeannie, it's just that Geoff seems to want some kind of revenge. . ."

"Justice, Emma. He wants justice."

"Okay, but his kind of justice is not our way, not your way."

"Don't be so sure about that. Let God take your child—your only child—and we'll see how much forgiveness you can summon up."

"You blame Sadie like Geoff does," Emma whispered.

"Like you once said to me, Emma, there's enough blame to share all around. If you and Lars had put a stop to Sadie seeing Dan, much less getting into a car with him. . ."

Emma thought she might explode from the sudden thrust of pure anger that pierced her like a sword, releasing the venom of her temper. "Maybe if you'd thought for five seconds before going behind our backs—knowing that Lars and I were not ready for Sadie to drive. . ."

As soon as the words spewed forth, Emma covered her mouth with both hands to stop them. The sisters were facing each other on a public street, their anger crystal clear to anyone who happened to be passing. Fortunately, no one was.

"Oh Jeannie, I didn't mean. . ."

"Yes you did." Jeannie let her breath drain out slowly. "I can't do this, Emma. Maybe one day, but for now the only thing that I have left is my marriage. I don't expect you to understand that, but that's really not my problem."

Emma reached out for her, but Jeannie brushed her hands away and then held up both palms defensively. "Go away," she growled. "If you care at all for me, then go away and leave us in peace."

And not knowing what else to do, Emma let her walk away.

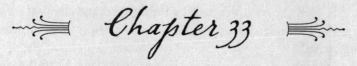

Chapter 33

Geoff

The second time Geoff was called to the stand, he was ready. He did not look either left or right as he walked to the front of the courtroom.

That morning Jeannie had announced her intention to be there with him. She was seated alone in the last row on the side behind the girl who had recklessly taken the life of their only child. On the other hand, he could not suppress his surprise that she was sitting alone—not with Emma and Lars, although there was certainly room in their row. Out of the corner of his eye, he saw that Jeannie was sitting up very straight with her head bowed and her hands folded in her lap as he passed by. Was she praying? For him? For them?

The night before, Geoff had slept in his office at school. After the whole VORP fiasco, things at home had gotten so bad that he had to get away—even if it was just for one night. So, knowing that Jeannie was probably out, he'd left her a voice mail saying he had a meeting that would keep him out late. She had not returned his call but when he'd gone into their voice mail later that night, the message was no longer there, so he knew she'd heard it.

And done nothing.

Well, what had he expected? That she would seek him out, come to the school looking for him? By what means? He had their only car, after all. He'd pulled a childish stunt intended solely to make her come around to his way of thinking. He wanted her to stop thinking so much about Sadie. He wanted her to forget about Rachel and her stupid VORP thing. He wanted his wife back on his side, fighting with him to find their way through this horror show. It wasn't her presence in the courtroom that was confusing; it was her choice to sit alone.

He took the oath the bailiff administered and then sat down in a hard wooden chair as Mr. Johnson, the state's attorney, approached.

Geoff stared straight at the lawyer as he gave his full name, residence, occupation, and relation to the defendant.

"I. . .she is my wife's niece."

"And yours as well by marriage?" Johnson asked.

"Yes," Geoff admitted, aware that Sadie had looked up at him.

"And what is your relationship to the victim, Tessa Messner?" Johnson had softened his tone.

"She's—was—my daughter."

"Sir, tell the court what you were doing on the morning of August 28th."

"Getting ready to go to work," Geoff replied.

Johnson gave him a look that encouraged him to go on.

"I was starting a new position at the school as vice principal, and I was running late." He didn't know what the man wanted him to say. Why didn't he just ask him yes and no questions?

"Go on."

Geoff closed his eyes, forcing himself to remember the day he wanted only to forget. "It was raining. I went outside. My wife had handed me an umbrella." He opened his eyes and glanced at Jeannie, who was watching him intently now.

"I don't. . .Why did I have the umbrella? I was going to drive to school." He realized that he was asking Jeannie.

Johnson glanced at Jeannie and then positioned himself to block Geoff's view of her. "Mr. Messner, you went outside, and then what happened?"

"I was trying to open the stupid umbrella, and Tessa was laughing at me."

"Your daughter was also outside?"

"Yes." He was irritated by the attorney's interruption. "Of course she was. She was waiting for her ride. It was raining. We were both going to be late." Then he remembered. "I was bringing the umbrella out for Tessa."

"Why didn't you drive her to school?"

"She wanted to ride with our niece and Dan Kline."

Johnson picked up the photograph of Dan's car. "This has been identified as Dan Kline's car. Was this the car your daughter was to ride to school in that morning?"

"Yes."

Johnson replaced the photograph on his table. "So, you were opening the umbrella to shelter Tessa from the rain while she waited. Then what?"

"Tessa was teasing me. I can never seem to get those automatic umbrellas to work. She came to help me, and that was when I saw Dan's car coming straight for us."

"And who was behind the wheel of that car, sir?"

"Her." He pointed at Sadie.

"Let the record show that the witness has identified the defendant, Sadie Keller." Next, Johnson held up a kind of floor plan that showed their house and the garage and the driveway and street. "Show us where you were standing," Johnson asked.

Geoff pointed, and Johnson drew a blue circle to indicate the spot. "And Tessa?"

Geoff pointed again. "But I pushed her back—I told her to get out of the way when I saw the car coming toward us." He tried to control the shudder that memory sent coursing through his body but failed.

"Now, Mr. Messner, I know this is difficult, and we're almost finished here, but please tell the court what you saw then."

Geoff closed his eyes again, squeezing them shut against the sight of his wife, his niece, his sister, and his brother-in-law, who in many ways had lost a child of their own that day. He thought about Matt and how when he'd gone to the kid's school to invite him to come back to football practice, Matt had looked away and muttered something about having something else he had to do.

"Mr. Messner?"

"Tessa stumbled away, and the car suddenly changed directions and went into a spin. The back end of it caught Tessa and flung her up and then down again, and then she was just lying there. . .not a mark on her."

"And once again, Mr. Messner, who was operating the vehicle that struck your child?"

"Objection," Sadie's lawyer said in a fairly normal tone. "Asked and answered."

"No further questions," Johnson murmured and sat down.

Sadie's lawyer took his time rising and approaching the stand. He smiled in a polite, friendly way that immediately put Geoff on alert. He sat up a little straighter.

"Sadie Keller is your niece, is that right?"

"By marriage, yes."

"Your wife and Sadie's mother are sisters, is that right?"

"Yes."

"How long have you known your niece?"

"All her life."

"So sixteen years. Your family and hers are close then?"

"We were until. . ."

"Would you say that Sadie is a girl who gets into trouble?"

"No."

"Is she a good student?"

"Yes."

"Were you ever concerned about her influence on Tessa?"

"No."

"Your daughter and Sadie were not only cousins, they were best friends—is that right?"

"Yes."

"In fact, you and your wife had agreed to Sadie's plan to have Tessa arrive for her first day at this new school with Dan Kline and Sadie because they were very popular with the other students, is that right?"

"Yes, but. . ."

"Dan Kline is the quarterback on the football team that you coach, is that right?"

Geoff's head was beginning to ache. The questions were delivered in a completely conversational way, but they were coming so fast. "That's right."

"Would it be fair to say that you've gotten to know Dan Kline fairly well in the four years he's played on your football and basketball teams?"

"Yes."

"Is Dan a good student?"

Geoff relaxed slightly. "Top of his class," he replied.

"Do you consider him to be a responsible young man?"

"Yes."

"And yet on the rainy morning of August 28th, he willingly allowed Sadie to drive his car from her house to yours, is that right?"

"Objection," Johnson snapped. "The witness has no way of knowing. . ."

"Withdrawn," Sadie's lawyer said, and Geoff thought that maybe it was finally over. But the rumpled young attorney only paused to glance at a note on his legal pad. "Mr. Messner, I'm going to ask you to think carefully now. When you saw the car come toward you and then swerve away, you've testified that your niece was behind the wheel."

"That's right."

"And did you see Dan Kline at that same moment?"

"Yes. He was in the passenger seat."

"Go on."

Geoff was confused. The barrage of questions answerable with a simple yes or no had changed.

"I don't understand."

"You've testified that Sadie was driving and that at the last second the car swerved, missing you and hitting your daughter. In that split second, what do you remember about Dan Kline's reaction to the situation?"

It was as if a veil had been lifted and Geoff saw clearly for the first time what had really happened that morning. "He grabbed the steering wheel and turned it hard to the right," Geoff said, his voice almost drowned out by the audible gasp that rippled through the courtroom.

Geoff sat frozen in the witness chair, his mind replaying the detail that had escaped him every time he had allowed himself to think about that morning. Dan had grabbed the wheel.

If he hadn't, would Tessa be alive today?

Chapter 34

Sadie

It felt odd seeing her uncle Geoff and aunt Jeannie in the courtroom—not exactly together, it appeared. Jeannie had come in and sat down alone in the last row, even though there were at least three empty chairs in the row where Sadie's parents were sitting. Then Geoff had come in when called to testify, but he'd barely looked at anyone other than the lawyers the whole time he was on the stand.

She hadn't been sure where Mr. Cotter was going with his questions, but when he'd asked her uncle about her—what kind of kid she was, Uncle Geoff had said she was a good person, a smart student, and Tessa's best friend. She wasn't sure why that gave her some hope, but it did. Surely the opinions of a man of her uncle's position in the community—a coach and vice principal—carried some weight, even if they were related.

"By marriage," she remembered Geoff saying at least twice. It was like he didn't want to admit to being family with her unless he absolutely had to. When she considered that, all hope flew out the window. Geoff was making it clear—under oath—that their relationship as uncle and niece was over.

But then out of the blue Mr. Cotter had asked him about Dan, and Sadie had gone on instant alert. Even though Dan had technically lied about her pleading with him to let her drive, Sadie had decided to forgive him. He'd been under a lot of stress, and maybe he hadn't thought he was lying at all.

Then Mr. Cotter had started to present her defense. He began by entering into evidence the depositions of a string of people who knew her well enough to talk about what a good student and all-around good person she was. Several of those very people were sitting behind her. Pastor Detlef had given her a kind smile as she entered the courtroom. Two of her teachers had also looked at her with sympathy. Sadie noticed that Mr. Johnson did not seem especially interested in what these folks might have said, and she began to have some hope that maybe he—like everyone else—just wanted to get this over with.

"The defense calls Sadie Keller," Mr. Cotter was saying, and Sadie realized that it was her turn to take the stand.

She stood up and went to the place where all the other witnesses had stood when they took the oath. But she couldn't take such an oath. It was against her religion to do so.

Mr. Cotter was explaining this to the judge, and then Mr. Johnson said that the state was all right with Sadie simply affirming her intention to tell the truth as their church traditions had taught them.

"All right," the judge said, turning to speak to Sadie directly. "You understand that you are agreeing to tell the truth here? That this court is relying on you to honor the teachings of your Mennonite faith and tell this court only the truth when you answer these questions?"

"Yes sir." Sadie's mouth had gone dry, and she cleared her throat. "I'll tell the truth," she assured the man in the black robe. "It would be a sin to tell a lie."

"Even if telling the truth may seem to get you into more trouble?"

Sadie swallowed. "I will not lie, sir."

The judge peered at her over the rims of his glasses. "And do you also understand that you do not have to testify at all, and that if you choose to remain silent, that cannot be used against you?"

"Yes, Your Honor. Mr. Cotter explained all of that to me."

"Very well. Get on with it, Counselor."

Joseph asked her to state her name, age, and address for the record. He asked her what school she attended. He asked her why Tessa was only that year starting to attend the academy. He asked her how she knew Dan Kline.

When Mr. Cotter had come to the detention center the day before, he had warned her that the easy questions would be the ones he asked first. The more difficult ones would come later. And then he had gone through the questions, making notes when she gave her answers and sometimes reminding her to answer each question in the simplest way possible without adding any further comment or observation.

When Mr. Cotter approached her, Sadie sat up straight and looked directly at the judge when she gave her answers, as Joseph had instructed. She was a good student normally, and she had caught on quickly to the rhythm of the give-and-take of the process of testifying.

"In your own words, Sadie, begin with the moment you got into the car with Dan Kline at your home, and take us through exactly what happened."

Mr. Cotter had prepared her for this. He had gone over and over the way she would tell what had happened. She wanted to be sure she got it right. She took in a deep breath as Mr. Cotter had instructed and slowly let it out. And then she began, talking only to the judge as Mr. Cotter had coached her. "He is the person trying the case, hearing the facts. In an adult case, there would be a jury and I would tell you to talk to them, but here it's the judge you need to convince." She closed her eyes for a moment, reliving for what seemed the thousandth time every tiny detail of that morning. And then she opened her eyes and told the judge everything she recalled about that day. And even though she was interrupted numerous times by Mr. Johnson's objections and Mr. Cotter's gentle questions, she pressed on. It all came back to her as vividly as if it were happening again, and although she tried to give the judge just the facts, in her mind she couldn't help but go all the way back to that day last spring when Dan Kline had first noticed her.

Dan Kline was undoubtedly the world's best-looking guy. A year earlier, Sadie would have done almost anything to catch his attention. He was tall—just under six feet—with broad shoulders and a slim muscular build. He moved with grace, and when he smiled, he had this dimple that made him appear boyish and almost shy. His eyes were an impossible shade of blue-green, and his blond hair had a way of falling over his forehead that just begged for a girl to brush it back with her fingers.

Sadie could still remember the exact moment when he had focused those eyes and that smile on her. It had been a rainy day much like this one, only it had been last April. Like some dork, she had actually looked behind her to see who the lucky recipient of his attention might be. He had chuckled—a sound that came from somewhere deep in his chest. "Yes, I'm talking to you, Sadie Keller."

He had known her name. She thought she must have misheard him, but he was calling her by name and telling her that he had heard that she was helping out at the fruit co-op that her mom's friend Hester Steiner had started. He wanted to do a term paper on the project, and maybe she could introduce him to some people there whom he could interview for his paper.

Sadie was sure that once she got him to the people he needed to meet, he would forget all about her. But how wrong she had been. Dan had continued to sit with her at lunch, and the day he got an A on his paper, he had caught up with her as she walked home from school and walked the rest of the way with her. That was the day she had introduced him to her father. That was the day that her father had pronounced him a "nice young man."

On the day of the accident, they were starting a new school year—his senior year. Sadie could not help but worry that as a senior he might want to rethink hanging out with a lowly sophomore. There were plenty of girls in his class who were pretty and smart and far more worldly than she was. She had to make sure that she looked her best and that she did nothing that would give him cause to view her as too young or immature for him.

"Do you want to drive?" Dan asked her as soon as they had turned the corner at the end of her street. He was looking at her with that little boy grin that always set her heart racing.

She giggled. When Dan had called her early that morning to suggest that he drive her to school, she had told him about getting her learner's permit. He knew the rules. He had to be teasing her.

"You know I can't. I just got my learner's. . ."

He cocked an eyebrow that turned his question into a dare. "I have a license."

"You have to be twenty-one in this state," she reminded him. "I mean, I have to drive with someone that old in the car."

"Now let's just think about this before you say no. It's what? Less than a mile to your cousin's place?" He pulled to the side of the street and let the engine idle. "Come on. What can happen?"

He was out of the car and coming around to her side before Sadie could protest.

"Come on already," he said, holding the door open for her, his shoulders hunched. "We're going to be late, not to mention that I'm getting soaked."

Her folks would have a cow if they found out. But this was Dan. The last thing she wanted was to start off the year with him thinking she was too chicken to try something just slightly forbidden—well, truly forbidden. But Dan did have a point—it was less than a mile with no really busy streets, and they would switch back once they got to Tessa's. Before they got to Tessa's.

She scrambled out and ran to the driver's side of the car.

"We have to stop and switch back when we get to Tessa's street," she said as she slid into the driver's seat. But then she ran her hands over the steering wheel and felt such a rush of power, of being grown-up. She couldn't help squealing.

"Okay, adjust the seat and the mirrors," Dan instructed as soon as she'd closed the door. "The flashers are on, so turn those off and put on your signal. Then slowly pull out as soon as you see an opportunity."

Sadie concentrated on following everything he said to the letter.

"Good," he said when she had pulled onto the street. He leaned his seat back and took out his cell phone.

"Who are you texting?" Sadie asked as his thumbs flew over the keypad.

"The guys."

The guys were Dan's teammates. Sadie forced herself to concentrate on the driving. There was a lot more traffic than she had expected, and it seemed like all the other vehicles on the road were racing past her at a fast rate of speed. A driver pulled around her, his horn blaring, and she clenched her teeth and tightened her grip on the steering wheel. The side mirrors and rear window were fogged up, so she was having trouble seeing other cars. She glanced at the console. "Where's the rear defroster?"

Dan punched a button. "Come on, Sadie, give it some gas, or we'll be getting to school sometime tomorrow." He continued texting without looking up.

Sadie gripped the steering wheel and pressed down on the accelerator. The car seemed to leap forward, and she immediately fumbled for the brake, sending the car into a slight skid. "What do I do?" she shouted.

"Just stay calm," Dan coached, but she noticed that his voice shook a little and he was sitting forward, the cell phone lying loose in his hand as he watched the road.

As she regained control of the car, she realized that he was laughing.

"It's not funny," she huffed as she bent forward over the steering wheel, as if that position would give her better vision. She looked over at him. "Stop laughing."

Now that she had managed to right the car and get back into the flow of traffic, he was back to texting and fighting a smile. Determined now to show him that she was not some kid, Sadie pressed down on the gas.

The speedometer hovered at just over thirty-five, but it felt as if they were doing at least sixty. It was exhilarating and terrifying but also fun. She hit a patch where the water had covered the road and was thrilled when a high wave shot up on Dan's side.

"Slow down for the turn," he said, and this time there was no humor in his tone. "That's her street ahead, right?"

Tessa's street was coming up fast—too fast—and Sadie

wrenched the steering wheel to the right and prayed that there wouldn't be a car coming out of the lane as she made the wide turn.

Her prayer went unheard. Once again she heard the blare of a car horn as Tessa's neighbor, Mr. Diehn, sped past. All she wanted now was to pull to the side and turn the driving over to Dan. She peered through the windshield, looking for a place where she could park so they could switch.

"Come on, Sadie, we're already running late, and with this rain, nobody's going to notice you driving. Just get to your cousin's," Dan said, his focus back on his texting. Then he started to snicker.

"What?" she asked, her patience with this whole business wearing thin. They were approaching Tessa's block, and the rain was pelting the car so hard that she had to shout to be heard.

Then Dan started to laugh out loud as his fingers flew over the keypad once again. He waited a beat and then laughed even harder. "Oh, that's rich," he muttered.

"What's so funny?" she demanded, only half aware that the more irritated she got the harder she pressed on the accelerator. They were almost at Tessa's driveway. "Are you making fun of me to your friends? Let me see," she said and made a grab for the cell phone with her right hand while turning onto the drive with her left.

"Keep both hands on the wheel," Dan shouted as the car started to skid.

Sadie wrenched the wheel to the left and looked out the window just in time to see that they were headed straight for her uncle Geoff, who had just come outside and was trying to open an umbrella. She slammed down hard on the brake and threw up her hands and screamed as Dan gave the steering wheel a hard wrench to the right.

Unimaginably she looked up, and there was Tessa, her eyes wide like the proverbial deer caught in headlights. Her cousin pressed herself against the garage door. Then there was a thud followed by a whoosh, and suddenly Sadie couldn't see anything but the white pillow of the airbag.

Sadie stopped talking, and Mr. Cotter stopped asking questions, and Mr. Johnson stopped leaping to his feet every twenty seconds with an objection. Everything went quiet—the way it had that morning. Sadie folded her hands, silently praying that her words had been enough to show everyone how truly sorry she was for what she had done. Her aunt was leaning forward as if to catch every word.

Sadie met Jeannie's tear-filled gaze, and for one unbelievable moment, she felt that after everything that had happened there might be a chance. Was there any hope that maybe someday her beloved aunt—Tessa's mom—would find it in her heart to forgive her?

Chapter 35

Emma

Joseph had gently guided Sadie through her testimony in spite of numerous interruptions and objections from the attorney for the prosecution. Step-by-step the story they had never heard—the story of what had actually happened that morning, leading up to and including the moment the car had hit Tessa—unfolded. Emma likened it to watching a ball of yarn slowly unwind as her knitting needles fashioned the thread of wool into socks for Lars or a sweater for Matt. As soon as Sadie repeated Geoff's revelation that at the last minute Dan had grabbed the steering wheel and wrenched it to the right to avoid hitting Geoff, Joseph Cotter thanked her and returned to his place at the table.

And just when Emma was breathing a sigh of pure relief that Sadie had weathered this ordeal without breaking down, Mr. Johnson stood up. "Just a few questions, Miss Keller," he said, looking at his legal pad instead of at Sadie.

Emma mentally went over everything Joseph had explained to them about procedure. The state's attorney would try to unravel the details of Sadie's testimony. "Not with malice," Joseph had assured them. "It's just that what he's been told by others—like Dan Kline—may not match exactly with what Sadie tells the court."

Like that it was Dan's idea for her to drive to Tessa's, Emma thought now. Sadie hadn't pleaded for him to let her drive. Just the opposite.

And yet in the end, she gave in and got behind the wheel.

Emma turned her mind back to what Joseph had told them would happen once the state's attorney completed his cross-examination, willing that part of the process to be over quickly. "If necessary," Joseph had told them, "I'll ask Sadie a few more questions, and then the defense—that's us—will rest."

"Then what?"

"Each lawyer will have the opportunity to make a closing statement, and then the judge will decide whether Sadie is guilty as charged. There are two charges against her, and she could be found not guilty of both, guilty of both, or guilty of one but not the other."

"What do you think he will decide?" Lars asked.

Joseph had looked away. "He's hard to read, and he's new in the system, so I'm not sure. Most judges develop a kind of pattern over time. If he decides against her on either count—or both—then there will be a disposition hearing."

"More time?" Emma moaned.

"Maybe not. It could happen right then, or the judge could schedule it for a later time."

"And Sadie would go back to the detention center?"

"That depends. The judge could choose to release her to home detention."

"He would do that?" Emma's heart had thudded with hope.

"He might—emphasis on *might*," Joseph warned.

With that in mind, Emma folded her hands and leaned forward, her focus on Mr. Johnson.

"Miss Keller, here's what this court needs to know."

Sadie met the lawyer's gaze without blinking.

"Did you or did you not of your own free will and in spite of knowing that it was against the law to do so, choose to get behind the wheel of Daniel Kline's car on the rainy morning of August 28th? And did you then drive eight tenths of a mile to your cousin's house, where you chose to take your attention away from your responsibility for the operation of that vehicle?"

Sadie blinked and glanced first at Joseph and then at the judge.

"Answer the question," the judge said.

"I don't understand—"

"I'll make it simple for you, Miss Keller," Mr. Johnson said. "Did you on the morning of August 28th choose to drive your boyfriend's car and do so in such a manner that you ended up killing your cousin, an innocent bystander?"

Joseph was on his feet immediately. "Objection," he sputtered.

"Withdrawn," Johnson said as he returned to his chair. "No further questions."

Sadie was excused. She hurried to take her place next to Joseph, leaning in to whisper something that Emma didn't hear. Joseph shook his head and squeezed her hand. Joseph stood up and walked to the small podium in front of the judge's high position to deliver his closing statement, but Emma could barely concentrate. Her fury at the way Mr. Johnson had asked Sadie about the accident threatened to overwhelm her. She folded her hands and bowed her head and prayed that God would forgive her for her anger and dislike of that man.

Then, after the state's attorney had made his plea for the judge to find the defendant guilty of the greater charge of vehicular homicide, the courtroom was silent for the second time that morning. The bailiff kept watch, and the clerk's fingers remained poised to record whatever came next. Lars reached over and interlocked his fingers with Emma's.

She knew that he was silently praying for the judge to find their daughter not guilty. The two of them fixed their gaze on the small dark-haired man in the voluminous black robe. He seemed oblivious to the presence of a courtroom filled with people as he studied a file on his desk. Emma realized that he was scanning the documents Joseph had handed him earlier—the depositions from Pastor Detlef and Sadie's teachers and neighbors.

Finally, he cleared his throat, and the bailiff told the defendant to rise. Joseph stood, taking Sadie's arm and coaching her to a standing position as well. The judge focused his attention on

Sadie, but Emma saw that he seemed to be thinking about all that he had heard as he stared at their daughter.

"Sadie Keller, you have been accused of causing the death of another human being through the reckless use of a motor vehicle. It is my decision that under the charge of vehicular homicide you are not guilty."

A collective rush of released breath whooshed through the room, and the judge held up his hand. "On the charge of culpable negligence, I find you guilty."

This time the reaction was an audible but hushed murmur. The judge waited for it to pass.

"I have been impressed by these depositions from others related to the stability of your family and community, and I have taken into consideration the duress that you have had to endure while being held in detention. Therefore, between today and the date set for the disposition hearing, I am releasing you to the custody of your parents."

Emma saw Sadie half turn and smile.

"This is not a get-out-of-jail-free card, young lady. It goes without saying, I should hope, that your learner's permit has been revoked and should be turned over to the clerk of the court as soon as you have retrieved your personal belongings." He leaned even farther forward, his dark eyes pinning Sadie. "I expect you to use the days between today and the disposition hearing to consider how your foolish desire to impress a young man ended in tragedy for a great many people you love."

Sadie nodded and murmured, "Yes sir. Thank you, sir."

Was it over? Emma wondered. But no, Sadie had been found both not guilty and guilty. Still, she was coming home—today. Emma squeezed Lars's hand and then turned to find her sister, wanting so much to share this moment with her, hoping that in spite of everything, Jeannie would share her joy that Sadie was coming home.

But Jeannie was no longer in the room.

It took time to sort out everything once the judge had made his ruling and set the date for the disposition hearing for three weeks later.

Three weeks until the next shoe would fall. Three weeks to have her daughter home and perhaps some semblance of normalcy to their lives, even if only for that brief time.

Emma tried to consider how best to handle this reprieve. It was important not to get their hopes too high. Joseph had explained that the charge of culpable negligence still carried the possibility of commitment plus payment of court costs. Further, it was going to be important that they not put too much emphasis on Sadie being home again. Although she suspected that Matt would see their relief and joy as further evidence that his sister meant more to them than he did, she couldn't help hoping that he would be happy for Sadie.

Lars was certain that Matt's recent habit of leaving the house as soon as possible after supper to meet some friends was nothing more than a combination of his age and the need to find some escape from what was going on around him. She and Lars assumed they would find him at the school playing basketball.

"He's trying to figure out how best to handle Geoff's rejection, and sports seems a healthy way to do that," Lars had told her. "I expect playing a game of pickup basketball—a sport that he knows his uncle Geoff respects—makes him feel a little closer to finding his way back into Geoff's good graces."

But Emma wasn't so sure that they had the entire story. One evening when she had attended a meeting at the church, she had driven past the school on her way home, thinking to offer Matt a ride since it looked like rain. The courts had been deserted, and when she got home, Matt wasn't there.

He'd shown up half an hour later, and when she told him she'd stopped by the school, his cheeks had gone beet-red and he'd looked away. "We were playing in the park," he mumbled.

Later she'd brought up the subject with Lars again.

"Emma, don't we have enough to worry about with Sadie's trial and all without you making up problems?"

She'd been stunned into silence. Lars had never spoken to her in that exasperated tone. He had always listened and comforted and even agreed to do something about whatever situation she was worried about at the moment.

Lars had immediately softened his tone. "Look, he's a good student, and he does his chores without you having to remind him. So if he's out playing basketball with some of Geoff's team, where's the harm?" He'd sighed heavily then. "Sometimes I wish that I could just go play a game of shuffleboard with the men."

"What's stopping you?" Emma had shot back, surprised at the vehemence in her voice. She knew full well why Lars no longer went to the shuffleboard courts. It was the same reason she had stopped working at the thrift shop and going to the fruit co-op unless she knew she would be working alone with Hester.

They didn't want to hear even a whisper of gossip about Sadie and her case, or how Geoff and Jeannie no longer had anything to do with Emma and Lars, or how they had been far too permissive with Sadie all along, and if they weren't careful, that boy of theirs. . .

Oh, she had heard it all. And she knew that Lars had as well.

"It's a pickup game of basketball, Emmie," Lars had said. "You remember how excited Matt was to even be included in their game. You must know how much it meant to him to have Geoff praise his talent on the court before. . ."

She remembered all too well. Geoff had assured them that Matt was "a good little shooter" and that one of these days he would "hold his own with the best of them."

"I know but. . ."

Lars had sighed. "Emma, I'm not sure how much more this family can take. Please just accept that Matt is doing the best he knows how, working his way through all of this—and so am I."

"Well, I'm sorry if my worrying about our son is a burden for you, Lars," she'd snapped.

"It's not my burden, Emma. It's yours, and I can't for the life of me figure out how to get you to set it aside so we can focus on what's really important around here."

"Which is?"

"Right now I'd have to say that keeping our daughter safely at home rather than back in some detention facility is a whole lot more important than whether our son is staying out playing basketball fifteen minutes longer than you think he should be."

It was the second time in just a matter of weeks that they had lost their tempers with each other. After years of marriage with little more than skirmishes, this felt like open warfare.

"I wasn't aware that you found my worrying such a problem," Emma chided, hating the way she sounded—like Sadie when she was at her worst.

Lars gently took hold of her shoulders. "Come on, Emmie. Let's not argue. We've been through so much together. We'll get through this as well."

She fingered the soft fabric of his shirt. "You're right. It's just. . .well, there has been so much attention focused on Sadie these last weeks, and—"

"Matt understands," Lars assured her.

She wished she could be as certain as he seemed to be. She looked up at him and wondered if in fact she had misread him. "You're as worried about Matt as I am," she said, stroking back his hair.

"Ja, but we must have faith, Emma—faith in how we have raised these children—Matt and Sadie."

He had a point. They were good children. Still, Sadie's situation had shaken Emma's faith in their ability to distinguish between right and wrong, especially when they felt backed into a corner. That was how Sadie must have felt that morning when Dan had practically dared her to get behind the wheel of his car. What kinds of pressures were being brought to bear on Matt? If she and Lars were having to deal with the gossip and speculation of others—no matter how well-meaning their friends and neighbors might be—then what was Matt having to endure at school? Children could be much crueler than adults. They often operated without the filter of commonly accepted standards of etiquette.

"Hey," Lars said as he pulled her closer, "Sadie's home, and for however long we have her, let's take this time to be a real family once again."

Emma nestled her cheek against his chest. "Yes," she said softly, but how could they be a real family again when a part of their larger family circle would still be missing?

Chapter 36

Sadie

She was home. For the first time in weeks, she stood before the small dresser mirror in her bedroom. The last time she'd stood in this spot had been that first day of school. August 28th. It was October now. Same year, and yet it seemed as if she had been away for a very long time.

She sat on the side of her bed and looked around at things that should give her a sense of relief and comfort. The stuffed manatee that her uncle Geoff had won for her at a church function. The shelf her dad had built to hold her collection of rag dolls made for her by her grandmother. The closet that held her clothes—skirts and tops in solid colors and small prints that looked foreign to her after weeks of wearing nothing but the required blue jumpsuit.

"Sadie?" Her mother pushed the door open with her toe and entered her small room. She was carrying a tray. "I brought you some tea and a slice of pie." She set the tray on Sadie's dresser, cleared now of the things she had left spread around that day when she was getting ready for school.

"Thanks." But she made no move to sit at her dresser and taste the tea or pie.

Her mother hovered near the door. "If you feel up to it later,

I could use some help in the kitchen. I'm making marmalade for the co-op."

Sadie glanced up. The marmalade for the co-op was usually made at the kitchen on the co-op's property—the big house where Hester and John Steiner lived. "Why here?"

Her mother looked confused and then understood her question. "I just thought—sometimes it's easier just to do it here where I have everything I need."

"We're not under house detention, Mom," Sadie said softly. "Just go on doing what you'd normally do."

"Matt's in school, and your father is out in his workshop, and I—well, like I said, even if you weren't here, I would probably just. . ." Her voice trailed off, and Sadie looked at her, really seeing her for the first time since she'd gotten home.

She had aged. Her skin was sallow. Her eyes darted around as if looking for something she needed to do. Her hands seemed to be in constant motion even though she was just sitting there on the bed with Sadie. She gave off a kind of nervous energy that didn't feel right.

"I'll come down now, Mama," Sadie said.

"No, have your tea." Her mother stood up and glanced around the room. "And rest," she added.

"Mom? I'm not sick. I don't need to rest or have tea brought to soothe my stomach or whatever."

To her shock, her mother's eyes welled with tears. "I know. . . I just. . . It's just so wonderful to have you home." She closed the door behind her, and a moment later Sadie heard the clatter of pans in the kitchen.

Sadie pushed herself off the bed and picked up the mug of tea. Her hand started to shake, and she couldn't seem to stop it, so she set the mug down again without drinking. She turned around and considered her room—the single bed, the dresser, a small desk and chair under the window that looked out onto the backyard and her father's workshop.

She went to the window and pressed close to the screen, breathing in the fresh air. It was one of the things she had missed most about being locked up—the inability to be outside whenever she chose. She saw her bike leaning against the side of the shed and remembered that the last time she'd seen it had been that morning. She'd left it at Tessa's the day of the picnic. When she'd turned too fast into Tessa's driveway, she'd caught sight of rain glistening off the bike's black bumper even as the car spun out of control.

How she wished that she had never gotten into Dan's car. How she wished that she had agreed to have her dad drive her and Tessa or drop her at Tessa's on his way to take Matt to his school so that she and Tessa could catch a ride with Uncle Geoff.

Tessa, she thought and closed her eyes against the memory that came every time she thought of her cousin and best friend. The memory of Tessa's face, her eyes wide with surprise, her hands out as if to somehow stop the car from hitting her as she scrambled directly into the path of the car's rear bumper.

She opened her eyes and wondered if she would ever again be able to think of Tessa as she'd been before that moment. Laughing shyly at Sadie's teasing, listening intently as Sadie poured out her dreams and disappointments to her, and most of all, loving Sadie like a sister—the way their moms loved each other—or had before that day.

She pressed the palms of her hands hard against the window sill. She had ruined everything for everyone. And she could not imagine how it would be possible to fix any part of it. She bowed her head.

Please help me, God. I don't know what to do, and I've hurt so many people. I don't care what happens to me, but please, please, please help them, especially my mom and Aunt Jeannie, find their way back to something that can make them happy again. Make them laugh again and love again. It was all my fault that Tessa died. Please, please, please don't make them suffer, too.

She saw Matt pedaling his bike up the street. It had been weeks since she'd seen him. As a juvenile himself, he had not been permitted to come for visits or to court. Sadie had been glad of that, not wanting to expose him to those places. She had tried to talk to him on the telephone, but their brief conversations had been pretty much one-sided.

"How's school?"

"Okay."

"Are you still going to Uncle Geoff's football practices?"

"Sometimes."

"How's the team?"

A grunt and then Matt would say something like, "Dad wants to talk to you," and pass the phone to him without so much as a "Good-bye" or "Hang in there."

Of course, in those early phone calls, she had really wanted him to tell her about Dan. How he was doing? Had his injuries from the accident healed? Had he asked about her?

That had been before she'd realized that it was not only Dan's parents who were preventing him from being in touch—it was Dan. He was certainly capable of reaching out to her if he wanted to. He couldn't visit her, but he could send a message through her parents. Maybe they were the ones preventing him from having any contact. Still, that day in court he hadn't even looked at her. And she could no longer deny that he had lied about how she'd come to be driving that day.

She fought against the anger that rose up in her like vomit every time she thought about what a fool she'd been. She'd known it was wrong to let him talk her into driving. It was raining, and he wasn't old enough. She should have said no. She shouldn't have worried about what he would think of her. What did that really matter anyway? He was going off to college in a few months and would forget all about her. That wasn't exactly news. In fact, she'd been thinking about that as she'd fallen asleep the night before the accident. She'd been awake a long time after the rest of the house was quiet, thinking how this was going to be her last year with Dan and how she wanted so much to make it the best year of her life.

Instead it had turned out to be the worst. She never could have imagined that she could mess things up so thoroughly for people she truly cared about and loved.

She waited for Matt to put his bike away and then head into the workshop. His after-school chores were to sweep up the shop and make sure the tools were put away properly. Sometimes he was allowed to work on a piece of furniture their father was making.

Sadie watched her brother trudge across the yard. He looked as if he were carrying the weight of the world on his shoulders, and it occurred to her that the trio of boys he usually rode home from school with had not been with him today. Then she realized that the one thing everyone she loved seemed to have in common with her was that they were moving through their day alone.

She thought about Uncle Geoff in court. After he testified, he'd walked out alone without so much as a glance at her or her parents—or Jeannie. Sadie had turned around in her chair to watch him, wanting to make eye contact to let him know that she wasn't mad about him testifying for the prosecution.

And then when she was testifying, her aunt Jeannie had been sitting apart from her parents—isolated in the back of the rows of chairs where spectators sat during court proceedings. She, too, had left alone. And now here was Matt, shuffling across the yard, his head bowed, his shoulders hunched as if walking against a stiff, cold wind.

If only she could have that one day back. . .

From the kitchen, she heard the sound of conversation. Drawn to anything that hinted at a break in the solitude that hung over their house, she opened the door to her bedroom and followed the sound.

A woman she didn't know was sitting at the kitchen table peeling oranges as she talked to Sadie's mom. She was dressed in the simple style that her family followed, and yet Sadie had never seen her before.

"Hello," she said as she entered the kitchen.

Her mom swung around and smiled. "Oh Sadie, did you get some rest?"

"I'm fine, Mom." Sadie focused her attention on the stranger. "I'm Sadie."

"It's good to meet you, Sadie. My name is Rachel Kaufmann."

"Rachel was Hester's roommate in college," Sadie's mom explained. She seemed nervous, and yet the woman—Rachel— seemed really nice. Quiet and watchful, but nice.

"Are you a nurse like Hester?"

"I was."

"Rachel and her son, Justin, have recently moved here. She's going to be working as a chaplain at the new hospital that just opened out on Cattleman Road," her mom said. But she said it in a way that sounded like she was afraid Hester's friend might say something that would upset Sadie.

"That's nice," Sadie replied. "Kind of like nursing, I guess, except in your case, you'll be working on healing the spirit not the body."

She saw a flicker of surprise cross Rachel's features as she smiled. "That's a wonderful way to look at it, Sadie. I hadn't thought of it quite that way. Thank you," she said as if Sadie had just given her a present.

Suddenly shy, Sadie looked away.

"What do you plan to do after you finish school?" Rachel asked.

She had to be kidding, right? Life as she had dreamed it was pretty much over for her, but she really didn't feel like explaining that to this stranger. She shrugged and turned to her mother. "I saw Matt come home. It's okay that I go out to the workshop, right?"

Her mother shook her head. "You know what Dad and I said. In the house unless you're going to school or church. It's for your own good. There have been some photographers and reporters asking questions in the neighborhood, and I don't want you to risk running into one of them. I'm sorry, honey. Let me call him and tell him to come in here."

"That's okay. He's got chores." She turned to head back toward her room. "Nice to meet you," she murmured as she passed Rachel.

To her surprise, Rachel put down the orange she was peeling and stood. She glanced at Sadie's mom, who was twisting a dish towel around her fingers, and nodded. "Sadie, do you have a few minutes? I'd like to talk to you about something."

Sadie's suspicion meter went all the way to panic. "Who are you really?" she whispered.

"I'm Rachel Kaufmann, a friend of Hester and John, and I'd like the chance to become your friend as well, Sadie. If you have some time now, I'd like to tell you about something that might help you to see some light at the end of this dark tunnel that I suspect you find yourself in these days."

All of this she delivered in a voice that was soothing and somehow comforting. But over the time that she'd spent in detention, Sadie had learned one thing for sure—never take anything at face value. The fact was that nobody could change what had happened or how that had permanently damaged everything that Sadie had taken for granted over her short life.

"Just hear her out," her mother was saying. She had put down the towel. Sadie heard the pleading in her voice.

"Sure," she said flippantly. "I've got nowhere to be."

"Sadie!" her mother said, but Rachel seemed unperturbed.

"How about we talk in your room, or would you be more comfortable—"

"My room works," Sadie said and started down the hall. It was true. Ever since she'd gotten home, she'd found that she was most comfortable in her room. Somehow she felt safe there. Outside her door were too many reminders of how much everything had changed. Inside she could still pretend that life was normal—whatever that was.

She stood by her dresser until Rachel sat down on the desk chair. "What I want to talk to you about, Sadie, is a program called VORP."

Sadie curled up on her bed and clutched the stuffed manatee to her chest. "That's a weird name," she noted.

Rachel smiled. "It is, isn't it? Especially for a program that's so intense." She rested her elbows on her knees and explained how the program worked. "It's not just a matter of saying you're sorry, Sadie," she said after going through the process.

"Yeah, well that's going to be a little hard anyway."

"How's that?"

Sadie stared at Rachel as if she had just arrived from another universe then very slowly she spelled it out for her. "In case you haven't heard, my victim is dead."

She announced this without so much as a hitch in her voice. Her tears were all spent. Crying was no longer an option. Tessa was dead, and it was her fault. Crying, as one of the uniforms had commented one night, was just an exercise in self-pity.

"You'd best spend your time figuring out how you're going to go on, girl," the female uniform had counseled. "You might be doing some time when this all shakes out, but that'll be short-term. You got to be thinking about the long term. How are you going to live the rest of your life? How is this thing going to make you better—stronger?"

Sadie had not answered her, seeing her lecture for the I'm-not-asking-you-for-an-answer speech that it was. But after that she had spent a lot of time thinking about what the uniform had told her. Every night she had prayed for guidance. But so far—nothing.

She looked at Rachel Kaufmann now and wondered if just maybe God had sent her a message in the form of this kind stranger. "What do I have to do?" she asked.

"In simplest terms, you have to find a way to forgive yourself."

Sadie laughed. If the woman was making a joke, she was making a really lousy one. "And just how do I go about doing that?"

"By first seeking the forgiveness of those you have hurt," Rachel said softly—"every one of them. And from what little I know of this, Sadie, it's a long list."

Part Three

. . .bearing with one another and. . .forgiving each other,
as the Lord has forgiven you.
COLOSSIANS 3:13

Chapter 37

Jeannie

The mail had begun to pile up on the table in the front hall. Every day Geoff collected it on his way in after school and dropped it there. Neither of them had done more than glance through the envelopes. In the first couple of weeks after Tessa's death, they had received dozens of cards and notes expressing the sympathy and shock of friends and extended family as the news traveled across the country.

At first they had opened those envelopes and read them silently. Jeannie would open the envelope, making some comment about how this person or that must have heard about Tessa. She would scan the verse printed on the card by the manufacturer and sometimes run her thumb over the embossed illustration. Then she would gird herself to read the handwritten message that always accompanied the commercial message.

"That's nice," she would murmur as she passed the card to Geoff and began the process all over again. At first Geoff read the cards as carefully as she did, but after the first three or four, he began taking the card from her, glancing at the illustration, and then without reading them, adding the card to the others they had already opened.

After the first dozen or so, they had stopped even opening

the envelopes. The messages brought them little comfort, just reminded them repeatedly of what they had lost, especially the personal notes sharing memories of Tessa. Jeannie knew that she should write back, thanking these dear, kind people for their expressions of sympathy, but she just couldn't bring herself to do it.

Bills that were mixed in with the cards were noted. "The electric bill came," she would say to Geoff as they sat in front of the television eating their supper.

"I saw it," he might reply.

But day after day, the stack of unopened mail continued to grow until one day after returning from her run, Jeannie was on her way through the front hall and brushed against the table, sending the whole pile scattering onto the tile floor.

"Okay, God," she muttered as she had so often done in the days before Tessa's death, "I'll do it now."

She sat cross-legged on the floor, the coolness of the tiles a relief after her run, and began sorting the mail into three piles—personal cards and notes, bills and other business, and throwaway mail.

The throwaway pile was the largest, the cards came in a distant second, and the bills a close third to the cards. *How long has Geoff let things slide?* she thought and felt the annoyance and irritation with him that had become far more common than the feelings of love and respect she'd always held for him before. It wasn't entirely his fault. She was the one who usually sorted through the daily mail and placed bills and such on his desk. Then he would attend to them at night when he did his schoolwork or worked on a new play for the team.

She began opening the bills. The more recent ones were within due dates, but their failure to pay the preceding month added late fees. Their credit card bill was over a month old and by now would carry a hefty finance charge on top of the balance. What on earth had she bought?

She ran down the list of charges, and in almost every case the charge brought a memory of Tessa. Tessa with her at the grocery store as she searched her purse for enough cash to pay and then pulled out her credit card. Tessa with her at the gas station, washing the windows while she pumped the gas, whatever conversation they had started in the car continuing. Tessa and Sadie and her at the discount store buying the supplies the girls would need for the start of the new school year.

Tessa. Tessa. Tessa.

She crumpled the bill then smoothed it and laid it with the other open bills before picking up the next envelope. The return address marked it as being from the billing department of the hospital. Jeannie breathed a sigh of relief. At least this one should be no more than a receipt showing that Geoff's school insurance had paid the charges. She decided that she would put that one on the bottom of the pile. It would be as much a relief for Geoff to see that at least one bill had been paid as it had been to her.

But as she scanned the page, shaking her head at the itemized list of charges, her heart beat a little faster and her brain shouted, *No!*

The number in the balance-owed column was five figures. Impossible. She had to be reading this wrong. She studied the information. Here was the line that showed the total of the entire itemized list. Below that was the line showing what Geoff's insurance company had paid. And below that was the ominous balance-owed line.

Stuck to the inside of the envelope was a yellow sticky note that suggested they contact the finance department to set up a payment schedule as soon as possible.

Jeannie fingered the stack of bills she'd already opened—with more to come—and mentally calculated the total. She included everything—the regular charge plus extra finance charges and late fees—and then she added the staggering sum to the bill from the hospital. For a moment she felt as if she couldn't breathe. How were they ever going to come up with so much money?

Geoff was already bringing in extra money from coaching just so they could meet their monthly bills and continue to live the way they did. On top of that, ever since the funeral, he had been so close to the edge. His anger and bitterness were eating him alive. This new burden would destroy him—destroy *them*. Somehow she had to find a solution to this. It was up to her. She got to her feet still clutching the stack of unpaid bills in one hand and the hospital bill in the other.

She placed the other bills on Geoff's desk, including the credit card bill that was sure to upset him all by itself. He would notice that the stack of mail was gone, and he would be furious if she tried to hide bills from him and the penalties continued to add up. But she took the hospital bill with her to the kitchen and picked up the phone. There was only one person she could trust to tell about this. Only one person who would know what to do.

Her fingers faltered over the keypad. She and that one person were once again not on speaking terms thanks to the way things had been left that day at the bay. Emma would know what to do, but Emma blamed Jeannie for the fact that Sadie had even thought about driving that morning. And because deep down Jeannie could not allow herself to admit that there was a grain of truth in her sister's accusation, she refused to turn to her.

She had to handle this alone. Find her way through one crisis in her life for once without leaning on Emma. She replaced the portable phone in its cradle then got down on her knees, resting her elbows on the hard wooden seat of a kitchen chair, and closed her eyes. "God, I need help. Please, show me what to do. You know that Geoff won't accept charity even if our church and the community are willing to. . ."

It was the way of their faith to see each other through hard times. If someone's house burned, it would be rebuilt—no charge. If someone lost a job and had bills to cover, the money would be raised. And Jeannie knew that it would be no different for them. But if she went to their pastor with the bill, Geoff would be upset. He was so very proud and so very stubborn.

The phone rang, and she shut her eyes tightly, ignoring the shrill sound. At that moment, a memory of Tessa suddenly came back to her as vividly as if it had happened yesterday instead of years earlier. Tessa had been only five, and the three of them had been at supper, their hands joined as Geoff led them in prayer. The phone had rung, and Tessa had half turned to jump down and get it.

"Not now," Geoff had said softly. "We're busy right now

talking to God, honey."

Tessa had considered that for a second, and finally the phone had stopped ringing. Then she had looked at Jeannie and said, "But, Mommy, what if that was God wanting to talk to us?"

Jeannie pushed herself to her feet and clicked the phone to see who had just called. "Rachel," she murmured. "Not exactly God."

To her surprise, she heard Geoff's car on the driveway. He was home early. Still holding the hospital bill, she went to the kitchen window. He was coming up the walk carrying his playbook and duffel bag. Then she remembered that he had a game tonight. Normally she went with him, sitting in the stands with Sadie and Tessa and Matt, but not lately.

"I'm going for a shower," he said, barely looking at her as they passed in the kitchen. After twenty minutes, she heard the water stop running, and a minute later she heard Geoff in their bedroom opening drawers as he dressed. Game night meant an early supper so he could be at the school early. She laid the hospital bill on the counter as she hurriedly searched the refrigerator for the makings of a cold supper. She cut up fresh fruit and put that out with potato chips and turkey and cheese sandwiches for him. She was just about to pour him a tall glass of lemonade when she remembered the bill.

She reached for it just as he came into the kitchen carrying the stack of bills she'd left on his desk. She hadn't heard him come downstairs, and his sudden presence startled her so much that she dropped the hospital bill and nearly dropped the pitcher of lemonade in the process.

"Easy there," he said as he bent to retrieve the bill. He glanced at the masthead as he pulled out his chair ready to sit down for his supper. "Another bill?"

Jeannie held her breath as he opened it. It seemed as if it took him a long time to read it—far longer than it had taken her to grasp the contents.

"It's high," she said. "I had no idea that—"

Geoff scraped back his chair and picked up the phone and punched in a number. "Roger? Yeah. Something's come up. Can you handle the team tonight? Okay. Yeah. Appreciate that."

He hung up and without a word headed for the door, taking the car keys as he went.

"Geoff?"

He stopped but did not turn around. "Do not try to stop me, Jeannie," he growled.

"Where are you—?"

"It's pretty clear to me that at least this is one bill we don't have to be responsible for. It clearly was sent to the wrong address," he said waving the bill in the air. "I'm going to make sure it gets delivered to the person responsible."

"Geoff, no. Please wait."

He kept walking and got in the car. "Jeannie, you have to face facts and choose already. Me or your sister and her family. You can no longer have it both ways. I'll be back later. In the meantime, you decide how it's going to be."

"Geoff, wait!" Jeannie shouted the words this time as he backed down the driveway and drove away fast. Don't you get it? I have chosen. I chose you.

Next door she saw a curtain move and knew that she had attracted the attention—and no doubt curiosity—of their next-door neighbor. She smiled and waved as she went back inside. To what purpose? Did she really hope the neighbor would simply think that Geoff had forgotten something? Not likely. It seemed to be well known up and down the street that the Messners were having marital problems.

Besides, she had more pressing matters that needed her attention. She ran inside, and for the second time that day, she picked up the telephone to call Emma. This time she was calling her sister to warn her.

~≋≡ *Chapter 38* ≡≋~

Lars

Lars was in his workshop when Emma came rushing in holding the phone. "Jeannie called. Geoff is on his way over here," she said breathlessly. She was still clutching the phone, and when the beeping told Lars she had forgotten to disconnect, he took it from her.

"All right." He lifted his white-blond eyebrows and waited for more information. Jeannie and Emma had not spoken for days, and the stress had begun to wear not only on Emma but on all of them. She walked through her days a lost soul, and he would have thought that a call from Jeannie would be something to lift her spirits.

"They got an enormous bill from the hospital today. Jeannie was going to try to tell him about it after tonight's game, but he found it, and now he's coming here."

"I don't understand."

"Jeannie thinks that he plans to present the bill to Sadie, Lars. To tell her that the charges are her responsibility. She's just come back to us. . ."

"Go back inside, Emma. I'll see to this." He had no idea what he would say. His brother-in-law was so different in both personality and temperament. The two men liked each other, but it had been clear for years that they walked along different paths when it came to what they believed and how best to put those beliefs into action.

Emma hesitated and then did as he asked. A few minutes later, Geoff's car pulled up in front of their house. He sat there a moment, staring straight ahead as if trying to remember why he'd come.

"Geoff?" Lars approached the car. "It's good to see you."

Geoff looked at him and blinked then got out of the car, pausing to pick up an envelope from the seat beside him. "I hear Sadie's home," he said ignoring Lars's greeting. It was apparent that he was struggling to keep his tone conversational, casual.

"Ja." Lars positioned himself between Geoff and the house. He didn't want to appear threatening, but at the same time, he had a duty to protect his family.

"I've got something for her," Geoff said, tapping the envelope against his thigh.

Lars held out his hand. "I can make sure she gets it. She's been spending most of her time in her room. The adjustment has been difficult."

"Really?" The word came as a sneer, but Geoff recovered. "No, I came to deliver this in person. I just need a minute of her time."

It was not in Lars's makeup to play games, and he was uncomfortable with this one. "We heard about the hospital bill, Geoff. Is that it?" He nodded toward the envelope.

Geoff's face went red with fury. "So, she made her choice," he muttered. "Did my wife call to warn you?" This time there was no attempt to disguise his contempt. Lars realized that it was directed not at him but at Jeannie.

"Come on, Geoff. What's to be gained by this? Sadie knows what she did. She's going to have to live with her guilt over Tessa's death for the rest of her days. Our hearts are with you and Jeannie, of course, but surely. . ."

To his surprise, Geoff laughed and looked up at the sky. "Let me get this straight, Lars. Your kid runs my kid over, and you want me to have compassion for her?"

Lars did not flinch. "That's exactly what I'm asking. For her and for Matt as well."

"Let's leave Matt out of this," Geoff said, looking away. "I've made an effort there, and your son. . ."

"We are family, Geoff, and we need to start acting like that again. Tessa's death has—"

"You and your family have no right to breathe my child's name," Geoff growled, his fist tightening around the envelope now, crumpling it.

"We have every right, Geoff, and you know it," Emma said coming forward to stand with Lars. "Tessa was like our own daughter. Sadie and Matt are as much your children as they are ours. If Sadie had been your daughter—if she and Tessa had both been your daughters—would you have turned your back on her? I don't think so. She's family, Geoff. Yours. Ours. It never mattered before, and it shouldn't now."

Emma moved a step closer to Geoff as she continued to talk without giving their brother-in-law a chance to reply. It worked. Slowly but surely, Lars saw Geoff's fingers relax slightly. "Won't you come inside, Geoff," Emma said, "so we can talk about this calmly? This bill has come as an added blow to you and Jeannie at a time when. . ."

It was as if she had reminded him why he'd come. He thrust the envelope toward her. "I want you to give this to Sadie. It's the least you can do for us—me. I want, need for her to see the dollars and cents cost of her actions, actions that cost a fortune and still ended up with Tessa dead." His eyes filled with tears. "Do it," he pleaded as he stumbled blindly back to his car.

"Geoff, I'll drive you," Lars said, following him.

"No," he shouted and slammed the car door behind him.

"Come on, Geoff," Lars pleaded, trying the door and finding it locked.

Geoff was pounding the steering wheel with his palms. After a moment, he stopped and his body sagged as if suddenly and finally all the fight had gone out of him. He opened the window a crack. "I'm okay, Lars," he said, sounding utterly defeated. "Could you just please go on inside and give me a minute?"

Lars did as he asked. Emma watched anxiously from the

kitchen window and reported that Geoff was just sitting there, his forehead resting on the steering wheel. "I'm calling Jeannie," she said. But just as she picked up the phone, Geoff started the car and drove away.

"Was that Uncle Geoff?" Sadie asked coming into the kitchen and glancing out the window.

Lars looked at Emma, and she nodded. "Ja," Lars said and pulled out one of the kitchen chairs. "He brought something that he wants you to see."

He saw that Emma was about to protest, but Geoff was right. There was no point in shielding Sadie from the aftershocks of her actions. "Sit down, Sadie," he said quietly even as he saw Emma signaling him not to do this.

Sadie did as he instructed and accepted the envelope her father handed her. She unfolded the bill and glanced over the figures. Lars knew the exact moment that she realized that the bill was for Tessa's care in the hospital. Her entire face seemed to simply melt. Her mouth sagged as her eyes became little slits, and her hands began to shake until finally he reached over and gently took the bill from her.

"There is a price to our actions, Sadie," he told her. "An emotional and physical cost and often a financial cost as well."

"What have I done?" she said, staring up at him. "Oh Daddy, what have I done? I've hurt so many people and now this. How will Uncle Geoff ever be able to pay such a large amount?"

"He'll have help," Emma told her as she pulled up a chair next to her and wrapped her arm around Sadie's shoulders. "That's what community is about."

"Sadie, this is the one thing we can fix," Lars said, "After everything you've been through—the accident, detention, the court proceedings—paying this bill is not your worry. It's not why I wanted you to see it."

"But, Dad, I have to find a way to help. Will the hospital give us time to pay it off? I could get a job after school and on weekends." Her face went suddenly blank. "Unless. . ."

"Unless?" Emma asked.

"What if the judge sends me away? How can I possibly

contribute anything if I'm locked up somewhere clear across the state?"

Emma and Lars looked at each other. "How about we call Rachel Kaufmann?" Lars suggested. "She might have some ideas."

"Yes, let's do that," Sadie said, getting up to get the phone.

"Sadie, wait, let's talk about this some more," Emma cautioned. "You've got so much on your shoulders right now. Maybe. . ."

"Mom, this is like the first clear sign that God is hearing my prayers to show me some way that I can make this better for those I love—for you and Dad and Aunt Jeannie and Uncle Geoff. This is a way that I can own up to the fact that it was my thoughtless behavior that brought all of this on our family. That it's time to stop feeling sorry for myself and really take a good hard look at how everyone around me is suffering."

"Oh Sadie, please don't take all of this on yourself," Emma pleaded. "There's blame enough to go around. We may not have been in the car, but your father and I could have stopped you from getting in Dan's car that morning. And what about Dan and his responsibility in all of this?"

"No. Rachel told me that how I decide to carry my guilt and remorse is what will matter when my turn comes to face God. Please let's just call and ask her what she thinks."

Lars had never been more impressed with his daughter. He, like others, had always thought of her as a girl more like Jeannie—full of laughter and lightheartedness—even giddiness. But the events of her life these last weeks had changed her, matured her. He felt hopeful again. Perhaps one day they might get past all of this—not forget Tessa, but heal the gaping wounds her death had brought.

"Sadie?" Lars touched her forearm to gain her attention. "Do you understand this program that Rachel has told you about? I mean, do you grasp the extent of it?"

Sadie nodded, but Lars was still not convinced.

"It's a two-way street—offenders and victims—both sides must be willing to participate, to honor the process. Even if you decide to make the effort required, it can't happen unless

Jeannie and Geoff agree."

"And you and Mom and Mattie and Gram and Gramps and probably others I haven't even imagined," Sadie said. "Yes. And I also understand that in spite of everything I may still have to. . .go away for a while."

Emma pressed her fist to her mouth then turned away, no doubt to hide her emotions from Sadie. Lars moved next to his wife and pulled her close. "All right, call Rachel, and then let's all sit down together and think this through." He held up the bill. "But, Sadie, you do understand that even if you worked all day every day for years to come, there is little chance you could ever. . ."

"But I could make a pledge—a promise that whatever I have, a part of it will go to some cause that best honors Tessa's memory."

"She would like that," Emma said, stroking Sadie's hair. "We could ask Jeannie what she thinks of that idea."

Sadie's hopeful smile lit her features. "You think then that Aunt Jeannie and Uncle Geoff will. . . ?"

"One step at a time," Lars told her. "Make your call and then go get your brother. It's time for our evening prayers."

Chapter 39

Matthew

Okay, so once again it was all about Sadie. Matt's parents hadn't even realized that he was right there, in his room with the door open, listening.

He got it that somehow there was this ginormous hospital bill—as Tessa might say. The doctors had charged all that money and still had not been able to save Tessa. What was that about? How could they charge for failing? When Matt failed to do his chores or complete his homework, there were consequences. What were the consequences for the doctors?

There weren't any, which was, Matt had decided, pretty much the way of things out there in the real world. The world outside Pinecraft where he would be living before too long. He carefully gathered up the coins he'd won playing poker with his new friends and put the money back in its safe place—the box that held his favorite T-shirt on the top shelf of his closet. Oh, his mom as well as Sadie knew that he kept that shirt in that box because it was so special to him. It was the T-shirt that Uncle Geoff had given him the night the team won the conference championship. But no one had ever touched the box. He was sure of that, because he had ways of marking it every time he took it down and put it back, and never had it been disturbed. So he felt it was the safest place to put his winnings.

Of course, in the last couple of games he hadn't won anything. In fact he'd lost. In the last game he'd lost everything he'd brought with him. He tried to limit himself, but the temptation to play one more hand had been too great, so he'd borrowed from the kid who had first loaned him money to get into the game and played on. But he'd lost, and when he'd said he would bring the money to the next game, the boy had said that he owed something he called "interest"—a percentage on top of the money owed as a kind of penalty. So now he owed that boy a whole dollar, and so far his winnings only totaled four dollars and fifty-three cents.

He'd set a goal for himself of twenty dollars, but in the past couple of days, he'd begun to rethink that sum. Ten should be enough, he'd decided.

"Matt?"

Sadie was standing in the doorway. Matt quickly shoved the box back from the edge of the shelf and turned around. "Yeah?"

"Evening prayers," she said.

"Coming." He glanced back at the box. He'd have to mark it later, because Sadie was still standing there.

"Mattie?"

He sighed. "Don't call me that, okay? I'm fourteen and that's a kid's name."

Sadie smiled and ducked her head to hide it, but Matt saw and it irritated him. "All right, Matt, I just wanted to say that I really appreciate everything you've done to help Mom and Dad while I've been. . .away."

"In jail," Matt corrected, tired of everybody trying to pretend that Sadie had just stepped out for a while. But the way her face twisted, he felt bad for having said it. "Sorry," he muttered.

"Anyway, I just wanted you to know that."

Matt picked at an imaginary piece of dirt on his shirt.

"Are you coming, then?" Sadie asked. "For evening prayers?"

Do I have a choice? It was something he'd heard one of the boys he played cards with say, and the others had seemed to like it. But it was not something he could say in this house. It would give him away. No Amish or Mennonite kid would ever be so sarcastic. But these days sometimes the ways of his new friends made a lot more sense than the ways of his family. Like this praying thing. God was not going to listen to the prayers of a nobody like him or, for that matter, to his Dad, who was a good man but not like important or anything.

"Matt, are you coming?" Sadie repeated when he made no move to follow her.

"Okay. Give me a minute, will you?"

Sadie hesitated, started to say something, but decided against it and left the room.

Matt centered the box on the shelf and then scooped up a handful of sand from the container where he kept the fossilized seashells he'd found and sprinkled a little around the perimeter. If anyone but him moved it, the sand would be disturbed and he would know. He had never considered what he would do if that happened, but soon it wouldn't matter, because he would be gone and so would the contents of the box.

In the living room, his parents were seated in their usual places. Sadie had taken a position on the floor next to their dad. Like everything else about his sister these days, that choice irritated him. So when his mom held out her hand to him, inviting him to sit next to her on the sofa, Matt accepted, curling into the curve of her arm as he had when he was just a little kid. It felt good—normal and safe.

His father opened his Bible and lifted out the purple ribbon bookmark. "Pray with me," he said, and the four of them bowed their heads. "May the words of my mouth and the meditations of our hearts be acceptable in Thy sight, oh Lord, our strength and our Redeemer. Amen."

The clock on the shelf near his father's chair ticked loudly in the silence that followed. A moment in which Matt knew he was supposed to offer a silent prayer of his own or simply reflect on his actions for the day just passed. But all he could think about was that the boys would have gathered already. That he owed money, and the kid had told him that the debt had to be paid in full with interest before the game started or he was adding another day's interest. They would be waiting for him—one of them impatient to have his money repaid.

He tried to focus on his father's voice, tried to figure out how long it would be before he could slip away.

"And commanded them that they should take nothing for their journey, save a staff only; no scrip, no bread, no money in their purse. . . ."

Matt sat up straighter. No money? Was it possible that he could do this—that he didn't need the money from the card game? He'd begun to feel really guilty about slipping away every night and trying to cover his tracks by saying he was meeting friends for a game, not exactly lying but certainly not telling his folks everything that was going on.

He still thought leaving was the best plan, but as his father continued to read from the Bible, a new plan began to form. The scripture talked about staying with strangers along the way, and he knew for a fact that in Pinecraft people opened their homes all the time to others just passing through—people they barely knew but took in because of their connection to someone who did know them.

What if he paid off the kid by giving him all of his winnings? That would be a way of seeking forgiveness for having fallen into card playing in the first place. If he no longer had any of the ill-gotten gains, as Olive Crowder sometimes called money like that, then surely that would take care of the guilt he'd been feeling.

His father closed the leather-covered Bible and set it on the table by his chair. Matt closed his eyes for the final prayer.

"Matt?"

He opened his eyes to find his dad looking at him. "Yes sir." He felt the flush of shame rush to his cheeks. Somehow his father had found out about his card playing and slipping out and his plan to run away. He was sure of it.

"You remember the program that Sadie's lawyer told us about?"

"Yes sir."

"Well, tomorrow, Mrs. Kaufmann—Rachel—is going to come here to talk to all of us about how we might put that program into action."

Matt looked at his mom. "Will Uncle Geoff and Aunt Jeannie be here?"

"Nein. Just us for now."

"Then what's the point?" He was so tired of having his hopes raised and then thrown back to the ground again.

"The point is that Rachel's program may be a way for your sister to. . ."

Matt stopped listening. It was about Sadie as always. They didn't care anything about fixing things between him and Uncle Geoff. It was pretty clear to him that even if she was sent off to a real jail, everything going on in this house would always be focused on her.

It was time to move on.

Chapter 40

Jeannie

Geoff was home again. Jeannie heard him moving around downstairs. She'd been so nervous after calling Emma and not hearing anything back from her that she'd busied herself once again searching Tessa's room for the lost journal. It comforted her to touch Tessa's things and be in her room, which still held the faint scent of her.

She waited for Geoff to settle somewhere so that she could gauge his mood. If he started fixing himself something to eat, then that would be a good sign. If he went into the den and switched on the television, that would not.

He did neither. Instead she heard him climbing the stairs. Each step he took seemed heavy with the misery that had taken over this once cheerful home they had shared with Tessa. She waited for him to come down the hall to where he could plainly see her standing in Tessa's room. But he didn't even look up as he reached the top of the stairs and turned the opposite way into their room. Curious, she followed him.

He was taking down a suitcase from the top shelf in their walk-in closet. The drawers to his dresser were partially opened. "What are you doing?"

He gave a look that implied Sadie's favorite word, *Duh*, and turned his attention back to his packing.

Speechless, Jeannie watched as he removed stacks of freshly folded T-shirts, underwear, and socks from the drawers and placed them in the suitcase. He couldn't be leaving her. Their faith had no room for divorce. No, there had to be some other explanation.

"Geoff? Talk to me. What happened when you went over to Emma's?"

He swung around and faced her for the first time since she'd entered the room. He laughed, but there was no amusement in the sound. "You mean Emma didn't call to give you a full report? Or more likely you called there and the two of you commiserated about poor, dear Sadie."

"Stop this and talk to me," Jeannie demanded, her voice tight with fury that he was being so rigid. But now his assumption that his way was the only way was wearing on her. How could he even think of deciding that they needed to go through this separately without discussing it? She might agree in the end, but she'd like the opportunity to be heard.

"Geoff, you know that all I want is the same thing you want—for us to find a way through this horror that we did not cause and cannot change." He looked so haggard and exhausted that her heart went out to him in spite of her anger. "Please, we have to get through this somehow. Wouldn't it be better if we did it together?"

"I can't, Jeannie." He sat down on the edge of the bed so hard that the suitcase and its contents tumbled onto the floor.

Jeannie remained by the doorway until she saw his broad muscular shoulders start to heave as he buried his face in his hands. In an instant, she was beside him, holding him as she had held Tessa whenever she was distraught over something. "We're going to get through this, Geoff," she said and realized that the words had become like some kind of Gregorian chant, she had repeated them so many times over these last terrible weeks.

He looked up but not at her. Tears were streaming down his cheeks. "I have to go. It's the only way I can see that either one of us is going to survive. I love you, Jeannie, but. . ."

She placed her finger against his lips, shushing him. "No 'buts'—not where loving each other is concerned."

But instead of holding out his arms to her as he had in the past whenever they had argued, he stood up and set the suitcase on the one chair in the room and began filling it with the clothing that had spilled onto the floor.

"I have to go," he said, and now with his back to her, he sounded so certain.

Jeannie rummaged through her brain, searching for the right words she could say to make him stay, but she found nothing. She shut her eyes and silently prayed for God to intervene, to make him see that this was not a solution. But nothing changed, and she had no words.

"I'll be downstairs," she said softly, hoping that maybe if she left him alone he would see the folly of this solution.

But a few minutes later, he came downstairs carrying the suitcase and a garment bag.

"Where will you stay?"

He shrugged. "I'll stay in my office tonight and then start looking for a room tomorrow." He set down his belongings. "About the bills. . ."

"They've waited this long," she said. "But Geoff, that's something to consider. I mean, paying for the house plus a place for you to live makes no sense. If you really think we need some time apart, then let me be the one to go."

"Go where, Jeannie? To Emma's?"

"I was thinking about my parents' house. They have a spare room," she said quietly.

"That's a good idea. But I'll be the one to go home to Mom. After all, this is my idea."

"You know, this place is big enough that. . ."

"This place is haunted," he said, his voice a raspy whisper. He picked up the suitcase and garment bag, filling his hands with things—instead of with her, Jeannie thought. "I'll call you tomorrow," he said. "We can work out some arrangement so that you'll have use of the car during the day while I'm at school."

"I have Tessa's bike," Jeannie reminded him.

They were talking to each other as if this were any normal day when they needed to work out transportation. Why was she being so nice to him? Why wasn't she ranting at him to come to his senses and see that she loved him and that without him she was completely lost? Why wasn't she begging him not to go?

Chapter 41

Emma

It was Olive Crowder who brought the news the following morning that Geoff had moved out of the house. "Now Jeannine is all alone in that big place," Olive said, clucking her tongue in disapproval. And when Emma said nothing, she added impatiently, "Well, Emma, what are you going to do about this matter?"

She had made herself at home, pulling out one of the kitchen chairs and plopping herself down while Emma prepared lunch for the meeting with Rachel Kaufmann.

"Jeannie is a grown woman, Olive. She has lost her only child. We need to respect the way that she and Geoff may choose to mourn that child whether or not we approve."

"Pshaw! Your sister needs you, Emma. She's not only lost her child. It would seem that she's lost her husband as well."

"Don't even speak of such a thing," Emma scolded. "Jeannie and Geoff may not be of our particular branch of the faith, but they are Mennonite, and if you are for one minute suggesting that they would even consider—" She could not even bring herself to utter the *D* word.

Olive did not lift so much as an eyebrow. "Geoffory converted," she reminded Emma.

"From Catholicism," Emma reminded her, "where I believe

they also believe in the vow of 'until death do us part.'"

"Don't lecture me, Emma." Olive took out an envelope and left it on the table. "I understand that there was quite a substantial hospital bill."

Emma eyed the envelope. "Geoff won't accept that," she said softly. "He thinks of it as charity."

"Well, of course, it's charity. Does he not know the meaning of the word?" Olive tapped the envelope. "I am leaving this in your care. I assume that at some point Jeannine and Geoffory will come to their senses and permit those of us who truly care about them to offer what help we can." She pushed away from the table. "I'm working at the thrift shop today. May I assume that you will not be joining us?"

"No. We have a guest coming for lunch." Emma hoped that would be enough information to satisfy Olive. She could not help but feel relieved when the older woman walked to the back door.

"Emma, you should call Jeannine," she said. "Today."

She did not wait for Emma's response. With a sigh, Emma picked up the envelope to put it away in a safe place. It was quite heavy and fat, and in spite of telling herself that whatever amount Olive had given was no business of hers, she gave in to the temptation to count the bills.

Inside the unsealed envelope was five thousand dollars in cash. Emma was so stunned that she counted the money four times before she hurried out to the workshop to tell Lars.

"Olive is a generous woman," was all that Lars said. He seemed distracted and barely glanced at the envelope.

"But where shall we keep it?" Emma asked.

"Keep it?" He blinked in the sun that was flecked with fine particles of sawdust. "The money was given to Jeannie and Geoff. They will have to decide where best to keep it, Emma."

"They won't take it—at least Geoff won't."

"Then give it to Jeannie." He turned back to his work, measuring a board twice before starting the cut.

"Olive says that Geoff has moved out of the house."

Lars paused in midstroke, but he did not look up. "Do you think that she and Geoff will ever forgive us, Emma?"

She knew what he meant. There was so very much to forgive—certainly they could have taken possession of Sadie's learner's permit until such time as they approved. And in spite of her youth, they had taught Sadie better than to give in to the temptation of impressing a young man when she knew her actions were wrong. And perhaps Emma's greatest failing was the one thing that she had finally confessed to Lars a few days earlier—that she had accused Jeannie of being the cause of all the trouble because she been the one to help Sadie get her permit in the first place.

"I don't know, but I need to do something about that. I'll be back in a bit," Emma said.

"Where are you going?"

"I'm going to take this to Jeannie—and I'm going to try to apologize."

"What about our lunch with Rachel?"

"Ask her to wait—better yet, have Sadie make lunch and get started. I'll join you if I can, but for now. . ."

She had mounted her bicycle and pedaled off before Lars could stop her or she could reconsider. If Jeannie had been guilty of overstepping when she'd taken Sadie for her permit, then how was that any worse than what Emma had been guilty of since their argument at the bay—keeping her distance, refusing to make the first move toward reconciliation?

She pedaled as fast as she could, and by the time she arrived at Jeannie's house, she was breathing hard and intent on her mission. She knocked on the kitchen door even as she peered in through the lace curtain that covered the side glass window. "Jeannie?"

Through the window she could see cardboard cartons, some of them taped shut, others spilling over with contents. The kitchen counters, normally cluttered with the small appliances that Jeannie favored—a coffeemaker, bread machine, blender, and such—were bare.

Unnerved, she tried the handle and found the door unlocked. "Jeannie?" she called out as she entered the kitchen and eased around the boxes on her way to the den where she could hear noise.

Jeannie was on a stepstool taking books down from the built-in shelves that lined two walls of the den. Already half the shelves were empty.

"Jeannie, what are you doing?"

Her sister did not look at her as she flipped through the top book on the stack she was holding. "Do you know how many of these we never got around to reading?" she asked. She was dressed in a plain brown cotton skirt that came to her ankles and a shapeless tan top. Her usual crown of flaming red curls had been tamed into a tight little bun under a white starched prayer covering. "Take these, will you?" she asked, handing Emma the stack before turning to gather more books.

"Are you moving?" Emma asked.

"I am cleansing," Jeannie corrected. "Simplifying. Getting back to basics—and my roots. I am starting over, Emma. It's really the only way I can see. That and surely all of this stuff will bring enough money so that we can at least make a dent in the bills we owe."

"You're going to sell these things?"

"Not just these. I already took a load of my clothes to that consignment shop on Bahia Vista. They only take clothing and maybe a few knickknacks, but there are shops around town that will take all sorts of things—books, cookware, dishes, even furniture." She came down from the step stool and deposited her armload of books into a box. "Of course it will take time, but it will be a start."

"What does Geoff say?"

"He doesn't know." She said this almost as if it had just occurred to her. "I think he might be pleased. He was always fussing about how much stuff we had."

"When did you decide. . . ?"

Her smile was like a beam of sunlight—brilliant and warm. "After Geoff left last night, I was determined to find the journal that we gave Tessa the night of the picnic, but then once I started, it felt as if she was here helping me, encouraging me. It was the most incredible feeling, Emma."

"Did you find the journal?"

"Not yet." Jeannie frowned. "I can't imagine where it might be. I've been through everything in her room several times."

"It's got to be here," Emma said.

Jeannie shrugged. "How about some iced tea?"

"That would be nice." She followed her sister into the kitchen and saw that when Jeannie opened the cabinet where before there had been at least three sets of glasses, there was now only one set of six glasses. While Jeannie took out the pitcher of tea from the refrigerator, Emma moved two boxes from kitchen chairs and sat down. She was still holding the envelope from Olive.

She waited until Jeannie sat down then slid the envelope across the table to her. "Olive stopped by. She asked me to bring you this."

Jeannie fingered the envelope with a half smile. "I'll put it with the rest," she said.

"The rest?"

"Never try to talk a bunch of Mennonites out of wanting to do their part. Charity or not, all morning the money has shown up in a variety of ways—slipped under the door, left in the mailbox, given to Mama." She shrugged.

"And how's Geoff taking that?"

Jeannie stared off into space. "I doubt he knows. Geoff is. . .a little lost right now, but in time. . ."

They each took a drink of their tea then drew patterns in the condensation on the sides of their glasses as they had done as kids.

"I came to ask you to forgive me," Emma said softly.

Jeannie looked up, startled, and then she started to laugh. "Forgive you? Oh Emma, that's too much. I'm the one. Why do you think I've been so all-consumed with this?" She waved her hand around the kitchen. "After Geoff walked out last night, the one person I wanted most to talk to was you, but I was so afraid that. . ."

"We're grown women, so why do we continue to dance around each other as we did when we were young girls?" Emma mused, taking Jeannie's hand between both of hers. "Wasting time when we of all people should realize how very precious every day, every hour, must be."

"I'm so very sorry, Em."

"Oh Jeannie, if you only knew how I have prayed for some way for us to find our way back to each other. I need you so much right now."

Jeannie seemed surprised. "You need me? But, Emmie, you're the strong one. I never was the one—"

Emma couldn't hold back her tears a minute longer. "I don't know how to talk about this with you." She lifted her shoulders and let them drop in utter defeat. "The truth is, I don't know what to say to anyone these days—Lars, Sadie, Matt—but especially to you, Jeannie."

Jeannie pulled her chair closer and placed the flat of her hand on Emma's back. "Talk to me."

"How can I? You have lost a child, your only child. While I still have both of mine—at least for the moment. Yes, it's true that Sadie may yet be sent away, and Matt. . ."

"What about Matt?"

Emma shook her head. "I don't know. Outwardly everything seems all right. I mean, it's understandable that he's a little lost right now with all the attention we're having to focus on Sadie. His grades are fine, but his teacher is worried about subtle changes in his attitude at school. And I have to say that my mother's instinct tells me there's something terribly wrong. I don't know how to talk to him about it, and every time I try, I just have this feeling that I'm only making things worse."

"What if I ask Geoff to talk to him? You know how he's always looked up to Geoff."

"Matt tried going to Geoff to tell him about Rachel Kaufmann's program, but Geoff sent him away. Matt was heartbroken, and yet I understand why Geoff acted as he did."

"Now you just stop that, Emma. We are family, and just because this horror has happened within our circle, that does not mean that we abandon each other." Jeannie got up and began to pace—a pattern Emma recognized as a sure sign that she was concocting some plan to solve everything. Under normal circumstances Emma might have been alarmed, but oddly the idea that Jeannie might come up with some solution—no matter how far-fetched—was comforting.

Suddenly Jeannie turned to her with a smile. "Got it," she said.

"I'm almost afraid to ask," Emma said, but she risked a smile as well.

"We need to prioritize—first we need to do whatever we can to help Sadie's cause with the judge. Surely if the judge heard about this victim offender reconciliation contract, he might go easier on her."

Emma glanced up to where there had once hung an elaborate kitchen clock, but it was gone. "Rachel's probably at the house now. We were going to have lunch and then talk about the program. We thought at least we could work out something with Sadie, even if you and Geoff—"

"Excellent way to start," Jeannie said as she carried their glasses to the sink and then picked up her house key. "Let's go."

"You would. . . ? I mean, I thought that because Geoff. . ."

Jeannie glanced around. "I really don't see Geoff here, Emma, so I would say that it's time for me to make the decisions that seem right to me."

Emma frowned as she followed Jeannie outside. "You can't just give up on your marriage, Jeannie."

"Who said anything about giving up? I spent most of last night praying on this, and God seems to be leading me in certain ways." She held out her plain skirt and curtsied. "Got the clothing down," she said, "and I was up most of the night slowly but surely ridding our lives of superfluous stuff." She made the sign of checking something off a list. "Next, we need to get Sadie in the best position possible for her next court appearance, so come on, and let's pray that Rachel Kaufmann has the right plan for accomplishing that."

Chapter 42

Matthew

Unlike his parents and Sadie, Rachel Kaufmann actually seemed to be aware that Matt was in the room. A couple of times she had turned to him and asked him for his ideas or opinion as if it mattered. Not that her noticing him was in any way going to change his plan to run away. After all, he didn't live with Rachel and her son. He lived with his folks and Sadie. But maybe down the road if he needed a place to stay. . .

"Matt? When I spoke with your folks last night, I suggested that everyone write something that Sadie could read today about how that person felt her actions brought them harm and pain. I wonder if you might want to start?"

He had actually been so wrapped up in figuring out how he was going to come up with enough money to repay his gambling debt and still get out of here that he'd forgotten all about the assignment his dad had mentioned after they finished evening prayers. "No ma'am. I mean, I didn't write anything."

"All right, would you be comfortable just telling her now?"

Matt glanced at Sadie. She had that wide-eyed look that she got when she wanted to impress their folks that she was paying close attention. He was not fooled. "How do I know she'll really listen?"

"I'll listen, Matt, and I'm right here. You can say anything that's bothering you."

Matt swallowed a smile. Sadie sounded more like her old self—a little annoyed with him.

"Your parents have chosen to write down their feelings, Matt," Rachel told him. "But there's no one right choice here. Whatever feels most comfortable."

"You can think it over, son," his dad said.

"I'm ready now." And he realized that he was. He realized that he had been ready to tell Sadie how her stupidity had changed his life for some time now. He saw Rachel exchange a look with his parents. His mom looked worried—no surprise. His dad nodded.

"Okay, Matt," Rachel said. "Talk to Sadie."

"And then I get to leave?"

"Well, not exactly. Talking or writing out how Sadie's actions affected you is the first step of a process."

"Then what?"

"Once Sadie hears from those she harmed, then we start the part where we come up with a contract of reconciliation—specific things that Sadie needs to do in order to gain forgiveness—your forgiveness."

Matt sighed and leaned back in his chair. It seemed to him that there was no way this could end anytime soon—not just the VORP thing. The whole thing. He had never been more certain that his plan to leave and get on with his life was a really good idea.

"So, if you still want to say how you feel. . ."

Matt looked over at Sadie on the edge of her chair. Now her eyes were wary. She was nervous. Matt felt a sense of power like he'd never known before. It was both exciting and a little scary. He had the power to make his sister suffer the way he had had to suffer through all these weeks. He glanced toward the window and then back at Sadie.

She was his sister. The older sister who had read to him when he was just a little kid. The sister who had played games with him—and let him win. The sister who had confided in him, trusted him with her hopes and dreams for a future that they both knew their parents would not approve.

He drew in a breath and said, "It's been hard, Sadie."

She nodded.

"At school everybody looks at me different. My friends whisper about you when they think I'm not listening. A few kids have teased me about my sister being in jail."

"What else, Matt?" Rachel said softly.

"Mom and Dad are sad and worried all the time. They don't know how to make this go away and that scares me. People in the store or that we pass on the street don't look at us the same way. Nobody smiles."

"What's the worst thing, Matt?" Rachel coached.

Matt glanced toward his aunt and then bowed his head. "Uncle Geoff believed in me—in what I might be one day. I could talk to him about anything, and everybody knew that. You knew that. But you cared more about your stupid boyfriend than you did any of us. You chose him."

"I didn't—" Sadie protested.

"Let him finish," Rachel said.

Matt stood up, shaking his head from side to side. He wheeled around to face his parents. "You always told us that we have choices and that if it's a hard choice, we need to pray for God's help. Why didn't you pray that morning, Sadie? You knew it was wrong to drive with Dan."

Sadie swiped at a couple of tears falling onto the backs of her fisted hands. "Do you hate me now, Mattie?" she whispered.

He didn't know how to answer that. On the one hand, he was already regretting what he'd said to her. She had hurt him, but that didn't mean that he had to hurt her back.

Turn the other cheek.

Instead of answering, he looked at Rachel, "That's it. That's all I have to say."

"What about Geoff?" Jeannie asked softly.

Matt looked directly at Sadie instead of his aunt when he answered, "He basically hates me now, and it's all because of you."

Chapter 43

Jeannie

Jeannie had to hand it to Sadie—she took the blows that Matt hurled at her without flinching. She never once tried to make excuses for her behavior. And she never once tried to make any of them feel sorry for her by pleading her case. Her niece had grown up a lot in these last several weeks.

In the end, the five of them came up with a plan that Sadie could reasonably fulfill and still one that would remind her almost daily of the ripple effect of her actions. Sadie herself had started things off with two suggestions.

"I could take a job at one of the restaurants or gift shops and give all of my earnings to Aunt Jeannie and Uncle Geoff."

"We don't need your money, Sadie."

Sadie thought a long moment while everyone else in the room glanced around nervously. "Then it can go to a fund to pay the court costs the judge mentioned. And what if I visit Tessa's grave every week and make sure that there are flowers and no weeds and such?"

Emma glanced at Jeannie.

"We could go there together," Jeannie said softly. "Tessa would like that."

"Thank you," Sadie whispered. She bowed her head to hide

the sobs she could no longer hold at bay.

Rachel gave Sadie a moment to compose herself and then kept prodding. "What else?"

"What if Sadie had to do all my chores as well as hers?" Matt suggested.

"And how would you then practice responsibility?" Lars asked his son, but Jeannie could see that there was a hint of amusement in the way he asked the question.

"Just a thought," Matt grumbled and folded his arms tightly across his chest.

Emma was right, Jeannie thought. Matt was not himself. He'd always been such a cheerful boy, always concerned for others, always eager to help. In the past, that exchange with Lars would have ended with a sheepish smile from Matt and possibly a murmured, "Worth a shot." But now he had the sullen stare of the teenagers she had often seen when she attended functions at the school with Geoff. Young people making it perfectly clear that they would rather be anywhere but with their parents and teachers. Tessa had never been one of them. Nor had Sadie, and certainly Matt had never been that way—until now.

She continued to study Matt's reactions as Rachel led them through the rest of the process. She was barely listening to the terms and conditions that Sadie had agreed to follow—even if the judge sent her away. Geoff would know what to do about Matt's change of behavior, so as soon as they were finished here, she intended to find her husband and ask for his help.

"I want to add one more condition," Sadie said when it seemed that they had formed the required contract.

"Be very careful, Sadie," Rachel warned. "You have agreed to quite a list of things here. You have to keep in mind that right now you want very much to do everything you can to repair and heal what happened as a result of your decision to drive that day, but this contract is a long-term agreement. It will take years for you to fulfill all of the pieces—in some cases, like caring for Tessa's grave, you are agreeing to continue this for the rest of your life."

"I know, but Uncle Geoff isn't here to. . . I haven't heard from him about all the horrible ways I've hurt him, and well, if he can't ever forgive me, then what's the point?"

"We're forgiving you, Sadie," Emma said.

"You love me," Sadie shot back.

Jeannie was stunned. "Geoff loves you, Sadie."

If doubt had a face, Jeannie knew that she was looking at it when Sadie glanced up at her and then back at Rachel. "I just need to leave a place for Uncle Geoff to be able to have his say," she said.

"That could take a long time," Rachel warned. "And it might come at a time when you are finally beginning to feel as if you've achieved reconciliation."

"I don't care. I don't even understand how Aunt Jeannie can be in the same room with me." She turned to face Jeannie. "I killed Tessa," she whispered.

Without a second's hesitation, Jeannie opened her arms to this girl whom she had loved as her own. "Come here," she said, relieved when Sadie willingly came to her, laying her head on Jeannie's shoulder as the two of them stood rocking gently from side to side. "You didn't kill anyone, Sadie. Your reckless behavior caused an accident—a horrific accident that none of us ever could have imagined. And yet it did. We can all find some blame in others—and in our own actions—but none of that will change what happened. We can only move forward, sweetie."

"But Uncle Geoff. . ."

"Shhh, he'll come around." As she looked over Sadie's shoulder, she saw Matt watching her closely. And she realized how very much he wanted to believe what she was saying. But then in an instant, his young hopeful face changed to that of a boy who had seen his world turned inside out by something he had no part in and could not have prevented even if he'd known.

Gently she pushed Sadie back toward Emma. "I have an errand," she said as she turned to Rachel. "Can we get back to this maybe tomorrow? There's something I really need to do."

"Ja. Danke, Jeannie. I am so very aware of the courage it took for you to come here today."

Jeannie stared at her new friend for a moment, thinking about all that Rachel had had to endure over these last months since her husband's sudden death. "I may need to lean on you from time to time, Rachel. You're a lot further down this dark road than I am, than Geoff is."

"I'm here," Rachel promised.

"Me, too," Emma assured Jeannie. Lars nodded.

Jeannie looked at Matt, but the boy just looked down at his shoes and said nothing.

Outside, she mounted Tessa's bike and headed for Geoff's school. She had gotten too used to driving wherever she needed to go and had forgotten the feeling of freedom that came with riding a bike. The ties on her prayer covering playfully tickled her cheeks as she rode, and inside she felt the stirrings of the kind of lightheartedness that had always been her trademark. She knew she had a long and difficult journey ahead of her. She could summon the pain of Tessa's death by simply remembering that moment when she had sat with Geoff on the driveway in the rain holding their child as her very life seeped out of her. But for the first time since that morning, she understood that somehow she would go on.

Geoff was running the football team through a scrimmage when she braked the bike, jumped off, and leaned it against the new storage shed. She couldn't resist fingering the shiny lock— the one they had been searching for keys for that morning. What if they had not found the keys? What if instead of being in the driveway waiting for Sadie and Dan, Tessa had just that moment run to their garden shed to get the keys that Jeannie had hidden there?

And what then? Would the car have struck Geoff? And would her loss have been any less?

She heard Geoff call out a play and knew that whatever happened between them, she loved this man. He was a gifted teacher, a good coach, a loving father, and a tender and devoted husband. Watching him now as he ran onto the field when one of his players went down hard, she understood for the very first time the source of Geoff's anger. He had not been able to save Tessa—he had tried and failed. And just as he took very seriously the fact that the parents of every player on his team had trusted their child to his care, how much more seriously would a man like Geoff take the responsibility of fatherhood?

As the hurt player limped off the field with the help of a manager and another player, Geoff dismissed the team for the day. He checked on the injured boy and was apparently assured by the team doctor—a parent of one of his players who had volunteered to be present whenever possible—that the kid would be okay. Indeed, the boy was almost walking normally by the time he headed for the locker room. Jeannie heard Geoff tease him about faking an injury so they could go home early.

The boy laughed.

And so did Geoff.

She stood on the sideline, savoring the sound of his laughter and relishing the way he took off his battered baseball cap and brushed back his hair.

Then he looked up and spotted her. At first he looked confused. He actually nodded politely and then started across the field, following the others. But suddenly he stopped and turned back, and this time he stared open-mouthed.

Jeannie waved and walked toward him. "It's me," she said, self-consciously fingering the ties on her prayer covering.

He met her halfway, his eyebrows raised in question.

She had come to plead with him to reconsider being a part of the program to reconcile with Sadie. She had come to plead with him to go and find Matt, have a long talk with the boy, and take him for ice cream. She had come hoping that he might see her and beg her to take him back.

But that was before she had seen him run onto the field to tend the injured player. That was before God had shown her what Geoff must have felt when all she could manage to consider was her own pain.

"Why are you. . .is something wrong. . .has something. . ."

She shushed him with a finger to his lips. "I just came to tell you that I'm sorry. Through all of this, I have thought only of my pain, my needs."

He started to protest, but she again silenced him, this time with words.

"Oh, I convinced myself that I was taking care of you, defending you and your pain to those who didn't understand. But the truth is that I didn't understand—not until today. When that boy went down, I saw such fear in your face."

"Can I talk now?" he asked, his voice the husky whisper of a man fighting to keep his emotions in check.

Jeannie nodded.

"What was different about today?"

"I told you—when I saw you with that boy," she said and then shrugged. "Oh Geoff, maybe it wasn't just today. I've had a lot of time to think and pray."

He glanced at the white prayer covering. "You're going back to your family's church?"

"I don't know, maybe. Clothes are just clothes, aren't they? But right now dressing this way reminds me of how I was raised, what I believe, what we taught Tessa to believe. And I just began to think that the best way for me to honor who she was would be to find my way to forgiveness and to accept the kindness of others."

Geoff frowned. "You mean the money for the bills?"

"That and other things. Think of it, Geoff. If this had happened to someone else we know—even if it had happened to a family you knew only because their child was in your class, we would be there. We would make food and take care of chores, and yes, we would give money if that was what was needed. Why? Because that's what we do—that's who we are—that's who we taught Tessa to be."

Geoff looked out toward the setting sun for a minute, his eyes damp. "I miss her so much."

"Me, too." She took his hand and brought it to her lips. "I love you, Geoff, and I'm so very sorry for—"

This time he quieted her. He pulled her into his arms. "Let's go home, Jeannie."

Jeannie had prayed to hear those words, and here they were. She looked up at him, her smile feeling as if it must rival the sun. She wrapped her arms around her husband's neck and kissed him.

"Hey, Coach," one of his players shouted amid a background of whistles and cheers, "get a room."

Chapter 44

Sadie

"It's over, Sadie. You're free."

That's what her father had murmured after the judge accepted the recommendation of the probation team for sentencing.

Earlier that morning, Joseph had explained the procedure. "The probation team has interviewed people and studied the trial transcript. It's up to them to give the judge their recommendation. The judge really has to accept this unless he can make a good argument for doing something else. There's still the matter of him passing sentence, but given this report, that's most likely to be probation and community service."

But Sadie no longer trusted in such promises. So in spite of the relief that she could see on the faces of her parents—both looking suddenly younger and more themselves—and the twinge of relief she felt as well, she knew deep down that for her it would never truly be over. Tessa was dead, and however anybody explained it, the fact was that she was dead because Sadie had thought only in the moment and only of herself—her needs, her desire to impress Dan Kline, her certainty that nothing bad could possibly happen. It never had before, and she'd foolishly assumed that because they were all good people, nothing like this would ever happen to them. How wrong she had been.

She accepted the embrace of her parents and people from the community who were in the courtroom to support her. She looked around for her aunt Jeannie, but she had slipped out of the courtroom as soon as the judge adjourned the case.

"You're free to go, Sadie," Joseph Cotter told her. "Time to start living your life, building your future."

And fulfilling the conditions of the contract I made with my folks, Matt, Aunt Jeannie—and hopefully one day, Uncle Geoff.

"Sadie?" Joseph was looking at her with a worried frown. The lawyer had become a good friend, someone she knew she could rely on to be there if she needed to talk.

"Thank you," she said. "I don't know how to thank. . ."

Joseph waved off her gratitude with an embarrassed but pleased smile. "Just doing my job."

Rachel Kaufmann was waiting at the back of the courtroom, and when Sadie saw her, Rachel gave her a wave. "Let's go," her mother said. "Matt will be home from school soon, and the four of us can have a nice supper and then maybe just. . ." Tears of relief leaked from the corners of her eyes as she stroked Sadie's cheek. "It's over," she whispered.

But Sadie knew that it wasn't over for her mom either. While Jeannie had willingly agreed to participate in the process to craft a reconciliation contract, the fact was that Uncle Geoff had moved back home. No one could say for sure how that would affect things. Once again Jeannie's loyalties had to be split, and that meant that the truce between Jeannie and Sadie's mom was not exactly solid.

Somehow Sadie understood that her aunt still blamed herself. How could that be? It wasn't her fault. Sadie promised herself that now that she could come and go freely, she would go over to Jeannie's house—when Uncle Geoff was at school or football practice, of course—and spend time with Jeannie talking about Tessa, remembering Tessa. Rachel had told her that it was important to remember.

But first she wanted to sit down with Matt. Her brother had remained indifferent to the process, commenting to her the night before that some stupid contract wasn't going to fix anything. She was only now beginning to appreciate how much she had hurt him, how much he had had to pay for her actions by living day in and night out with their parents always worrying about her. He was the one who had seen his life put on hold, who must have sat at many meals where the silence of their parents' worry and fear had made normal conversation impossible. And then when she learned that Uncle Geoff had basically abandoned Matt—all because of her. . .

"Matt, we're home," her mother called out as soon as they were inside the house. "Matt?"

By the time they had finally finished up at the courthouse, it was past time for Matt to be home from school. But the house was the kind of quiet that said nobody was home.

"He must be out in the workshop sweeping up," her dad said and headed for the back door. "Matt?" he called, but Sadie could see that the workshop door was closed, the padlock undisturbed.

A now all too familiar sense of panic gripped her. Something was wrong—terribly wrong. Her dad stepped outside and walked around the yard. "His bike isn't here," he said when he came back inside.

Sadie ran down the hall to Matt's room. She opened his closet and checked on the top shelf. Matt had a special T-shirt that he wore only when he attended one of Uncle Geoff's games.

It was gone. And she knew that there was no game scheduled for that night.

"Mom?"

"What is it?"

"I think Matt's run away."

"No. I'm sure not. Why would he do such a thing? Today of all days?"

Sadie showed her the box that Matt always hid the shirt in. It was the box of an old board game they had played when they were younger.

"Lars," her mom called out. Then she took the box and headed back toward the kitchen. "He's gone," Sadie heard her say.

Her brother had run away, and it was all her fault. Sadie sat down on the side of Matt's bed and wondered if the ripples of her foolish action would ever stop coming.

She heard the muffled sounds of her parents discussing what to do. But she was the one who needed to fix this. She glanced around Matt's room, unsure of what she was looking for but certain that there must be something that would give her a clue. Neither of them was known for neatness, but there was a pattern to the way Matt stored his things. It might look haphazard to their parents. That was the whole idea. But to Matt—and hopefully to Sadie—the placement of his belongings made perfect sense.

Knowing that her brother did nothing without first making detailed plans, she began going through the papers on his small desk. She was mystified when she found several printed sheets from a computer about playing poker. The other side of the paper had material that showed it to have come from the Sarasota library. When had he gone to the library downtown, and how had he gotten this paper? He must be doing a report on the evils of gambling, she decided and put his schoolwork, including the notes on poker, back where she'd found them.

Next, she dumped out his wastebasket and started smoothing out the crumpled papers. On the third paper, she found a rough sketch that looked like a map.

"Dad?" she called out.

Both parents came at once. "What is it? A note?" her father asked hopefully.

"Better," Sadie said. "It's a map."

The three of them gathered around as Sadie spread the wrinkled paper on the desktop then turned it sideways to see if that made more sense.

"It's Payne Park," her dad said. By the way he looked at Sadie's mom, she knew there had to be a connection.

"What?" she asked.

Her mom told her about the night that Matt had gotten lost and had been brought home by the police officers. "We didn't want to worry you."

Sadie glanced at the paper again, realizing it was drawn on the back of a page from the day calendar that Uncle Geoff had given Matt. She read the date aloud.

"It's the same date," her father said, taking the paper from her and studying the map more closely. "He must have sketched this out that night, and the only reason to do that would be so that he could find his way back there again."

When her parents headed for the door, Sadie started to follow them and accidentally knocked Matt's schoolwork to the floor. The papers about poker spilled out from his notebook. Sadie had an idea. "Dad? There was this kid in my class who got in trouble last summer for playing cards. . .for money. He was slipping out to meet some boys from town." She picked up the papers and handed them to her father. "You said something about Matt going out to meet friends after supper, and I found these inside Matt's school folder."

Her father's already ruddy cheeks turned even redder. He passed the papers to her mother and headed down the hall still clutching the map that Matt had drawn.

"Let me go with you, Dad," she pleaded, and to her surprise, he gave her a curt nod.

"Emma, stay here in case the boy comes to his senses and comes home."

Sadie knew that there was not even a question of alerting others and certainly not the authorities in Sarasota. This was a private matter that her parents would try to handle alone. If the time came when they needed help, they would turn first to other family—usually Jeannie and Geoff—and then to Pastor Detlef and other leaders of the congregation. Calling the police would be an absolute last resort.

When Sadie got in on the passenger side, the map was lying on the seat. She picked it up and prepared to navigate for her father. "It looks like you turn left at the corner," she said.

"I know the way, Sadie," her father said, and then he softened his rebuke by patting her hand. "Sorry. I'm just worried."

They rode in silence with Sadie scanning the side streets hoping for a glimpse of Matt or his bike. When they reached the park, her father stopped the car and got out. "Let's see if there's any sign of him or if there's anyone around who might have seen him," her dad said.

"I can search that area," Sadie volunteered as she started off across toward the tennis courts.

"Nein! No Sadie, I nearly lost you once, and now your brother is missing. I need to know where you are. We'll do this together."

It amazed Sadie how these simple words touched her. A knot she'd carried in the center of her chest for weeks—a knot of her own making because she was so sure that no one in her family would ever be able to love her again the way they had before. She slipped her hand into her father's and walked with him.

After they'd searched for several minutes without seeing anyone, Sadie caught a flash of color. "Dad, over there?" she whispered excitedly.

Her father followed her pointing finger then started striding quickly toward the lone figure bent over a picnic table, his back to them. Sadie had to practically run to keep up with him.

"Hello," Lars called out.

The boy turned and quickly gathered whatever had been on the table and stuffed it into his pockets. Then he leaned back against the edge of the table nonchalantly and watched them come. "I'm not doing anything wrong, mister," he said with a sullen frown when they were close enough to see his features.

"I did not accuse you," Sadie's dad replied. "I am looking for my son, and I have reason to believe that he might have come here to this park. Have you been here for some time?"

The boy cocked an eyebrow as he studied their plain dress. "This kid—he's one of your kind?"

"He's my son," her dad repeated. "Have you seen him?"

"Maybe." The boy took a sudden interest in a tree branch hanging over the table. "What's in it for me?"

To Sadie's surprise, her father actually smiled.

"Are you asking to be paid for information that you may or may not have?"

The boy shrugged. "Kid's about my height but younger? He's got hair like yours only not as white but still cut in that dorky way? Rides a bike that's like a bazillion years old? That kid?"

Sadie felt her heart begin to hammer. "Yes," she said, "that kid." Her father squeezed her hand, silencing her.

"All right," her father said, keeping his voice calm as if he and the boy were negotiating a price for a piece of his furniture. "It appears that you know my son. Did you also know that he is missing?"

"He's not missing. I just saw him."

"Ah. So he was here."

The boy let out a sigh of pure exasperation. "Didn't I just say that?"

"Where is he? Where did he go?" Sadie demanded, unable to keep still a minute longer. It pleased her to see the boy sit up a little straighter.

"I don't know to both questions. He owed me some money. He paid up and then took off." He stood up. "I gotta go. I got business."

"Which way was he headed?" Sadie asked and noticed that her father seemed to have accepted that the boy was more likely to answer her questions.

The boy pointed toward the tennis courts.

"How long ago?"

"Do I look like I own a watch?"

"Thank you for your help," Sadie's dad said and then steered her in the direction the boy had indicated. When she glanced back over her shoulder, the boy was gone.

The tennis courts were deserted as was the area around the community auditorium. Her dad checked every nook and cranny of their surroundings. She also noticed how with every passing minute he seemed to lose hope.

"We'll find him, Dad," she said and prayed that she was right.

Chapter 45

Geoff

It was good to be home. Even though he hadn't been moved out for more than one night and the day that followed, it felt like weeks. Of course, he and Jeannie had been heading in different directions ever since Tessa's funeral. But now this house seemed more like the home they had established when he and Jeannie had first married. In his short absence, Jeannie had gone through the house packing up a lot of the things that served only to remind him of all their debt. She continued to dress in the plain clothes of her youth, and he found that somehow comforting.

He was even beginning to consider the wisdom of accepting the money members of their church—and Emma's—had raised to help pay off the hospital bill. Jeannie had made a good argument for that. How many times over the years they'd been married had they done the same for those in need and never once thought about it?

Pride goeth before a fall, he thought. He had allowed his pride to keep him from accepting the kindness of his neighbors and friends. He fingered the large brown envelope where Jeannie had placed all of the cash and checks people had left for them. "I'm going to stop by the hospital and set up a plan for paying that bill off," he called up the stairs where he could hear Jeannie doing more cleaning.

She ran to the head of the stairs and looked down at him. He was still not yet used to seeing her face cleansed of makeup, but he liked it. She looked younger, more like the girl he'd fallen in love with sixteen years earlier. Somehow it made him think that it might actually be possible for them to start over.

He smiled up at her. "Love you," he said, and she grinned. "Me, too."

When they'd been courting, he had teased her about that answer. "I know you love you, too," he'd said, "but what about loving me?"

She had always thrown her arms around his neck and kissed him. He actually considered giving her their trademark banter now, but he wouldn't have her run all the way down the stairs just to kiss him. "How about we go out for supper?" he said.

"We haven't done that since. . ."

"I know. It'll do us both good."

"Okay." She lingered at the top of the stairs. "See you," she said.

"Love you," he replied as he picked up his keys.

By four he had finished his meeting with the billing person at the hospital, turning over the funds to her and setting up a payment plan for the rest. As he drove home, he tried without success to suppress the lingering remnants of his anger at Sadie, the urge to force her to earn the money they owed. From everything that Jeannie had told him, Sadie was going to get off pretty easy, and this whole contract business did not begin to make up for all the harm done by Sadie's reckless behavior.

"You have to know that coming home doesn't mean that I can forgive and forget," he'd warned Jeannie the night before as they lay together.

"I know." She waited a beat and then added, "And you have to understand that they are my family, Geoff, and I can no more turn my back on them than I could on you."

He had been surprised at that. In the past, Jeannie had always been so eager to please him and everyone around her.

Suddenly she was thinking of her needs, and he found that he liked that even if meeting her needs meant going against him.

"So, that's the contract between you and me?"

"No, Geoff, that's us accepting that we have to do some of this alone even as we get through most of it together."

"Sounds like a plan," he'd murmured as he pulled her closer. "And who knows. . .in time. . ." It was, he realized, the first time that he had allowed himself even to consider the idea that there might come a day when he could forgive Sadie.

And then there she was—Sadie. She was standing at the kitchen door, gesturing wildly as she talked to Jeannie. He got out of the car prepared to defend his wife from whatever tirade Sadie was having.

"It's Matt," Jeannie said as soon as she saw him. "He's run away."

Before he knew what hit him, Sadie had rushed forward and was clinging to his arm. "Please, Uncle Geoff," she sobbed. "I know you hate me, and you have every reason to, but this is Mattie—please. . . ."

"How long's he been gone?" Geoff asked Jeannie.

"When they got home from court yesterday afternoon, he was gone. Lars and Sadie talked to a boy in Payne Park who knows him and had seen him, but there was no sign of him."

"Payne Park?"

Sadie was still clutching his sleeve. It seemed the most natural thing in the world to put his hand on hers.

"We think he's been going there to meet some kids from town to play cards," Sadie told him. She talked about papers she'd found about playing poker and then a map they had used to try to find him.

"Why didn't Emma call yesterday?" Jeannie asked. She sounded a little hurt.

"You know Dad. He wanted to try to find him—just us—but now he's been gone all night and all day and there's no sign of him anywhere. It's like he's just disappeared, and it's all my fault."

"Stop that right now," Geoff ordered. "We have to think. Where are your folks?"

"Dad and Pastor Detlef and some men from the church have been out all day searching. Mom's been waiting by the phone in case he calls or something."

Jeannie looked at Geoff. "Maybe Zeke could help. He knows people who hang around that park."

Geoff nodded. "Sadie, I want you and Jeannie to go back to your house and stay with your mom. She needs you both right now. I'll go find Zeke and see if he has any ideas."

"Please find him, Uncle Geoff," Sadie pleaded.

He hesitated, seeing in her uplifted face the child who had been like a sister to Tessa, the child who along with her brother had been in his house almost as much as Tessa had, the child who had in one flash of irresponsibility so typical of young people her age changed all their lives forever.

"Geoff?" Jeannie was next to him, her hand on his shoulder, her face close to his. A worried frown creased her forehead.

He patted Sadie's hand and spoke directly to her, "I'll do my best. You go on home now. Your folks need you."

On the strength of the radiant smile that Jeannie had given him as he got back in his car and drove to the marina, Geoff rid himself of the last of his fury at everything and everyone surrounding Tessa's death. It felt good to focus on someone else's need besides his own for a change.

He found Zeke exactly where he thought he might find him, downtown near the marina talking to friends.

"Alone in a park overnight?" one of Zeke's friends said shaking his head. "Must be one scared boy by now."

"Lars and Sadie searched the park yesterday and talked to a kid that said he'd seen Matt, but then that kid disappeared. They didn't get a name."

"Come on," Zeke said, and when Geoff followed him without question, he noticed that the group of other homeless people were also coming with them. It struck Geoff that they must have made an odd picture walking up Main Street together—Geoff still in the business clothes he'd worn to make a good impression on the hospital billing clerk, and the rest in the scruffy clothing that probably constituted their entire wardrobes.

They reached the library and went inside. There the others spread out, some heading upstairs while others canvassed street people who spent their days there reading. He followed Zeke and was surprised when his friend left by the second doorway and walked quickly across town until he reached the park.

"I like to travel light. The others mean well, but too many people will scare the kid off."

"You know where Matt is?" Geoff couldn't believe that Zeke might actually have an idea where to find his nephew.

"The other kid. His name's Duke—or that's his street name. Hangs out here with a couple of other boys. My guess is that if Matt got caught up in playing cards, these were the guys he was playing with. It's a place to start."

Geoff nodded. "So, what now?"

"We wait," Zeke said as he slid to a sitting position against the side of a building.

The sun was setting when Zeke nudged Geoff and nodded toward a figure sauntering toward them. "Duke," he called out, getting to his feet. "What's happening?"

The kid couldn't be more than thirteen. He was thin and skittish.

"Hey, Zeke," he said even as he eyed Geoff suspiciously.

"I understand you've found a new player."

The kid shrugged. "Found and lost."

"Meaning?"

"He played most every night for a couple of weeks, lost some money and won some, and then yesterday he finds me here and gives me all of it—the whole enchilada—three times what he owed me." Duke shook his head. "I don't get that."

I just bet you don't, Geoff thought and shoved his hands in his pockets to keep from yelling at the kid to tell them where Matt was.

"You see this guy around?" Zeke asked, looking off toward the park entrance as if it didn't matter to him one way or another.

"I told you. He was here yesterday. Oh yeah, and then this man and a girl came looking for him. After they searched everywhere except the right place, I told him he'd best get home."

Geoff thought he might have to beg God's forgiveness for strangling the boy.

"But that didn't happen," Zeke said, still in a tone he'd use to discuss the weather forecast.

"Yeah, I know. He hung around last night with us. Wouldn't get in the game though. Said he was done with card playing. Too bad. He was good."

"And then?" Geoff could no longer hold his tongue.

Duke glanced at him. "He went off with Tony."

"Tony who?"

Duke glanced at Zeke. "You know, the black kid. Tony."

Zeke nodded. "Thanks, little dude." He fumbled in the pocket of his too-small cargo pants and tossed the kid a coin. "All I can spare."

Duke grinned as he took off. "No worries, man. It'll grow."

To Geoff's surprise, Zeke sat back down.

"You know this boy, Tony?"

"Yeah."

"Well? Shouldn't we do something about finding him?"

"We are. We wait right here, and he'll find us."

Sure enough, shortly after the park streetlamps came on, Geoff saw a small African-American boy coming toward them. And with him was Matt. The two of them were deep in conversation and didn't seem to see Zeke or Geoff. Geoff was on his feet at once, but Zeke held him back. "Don't startle him," he warned. "Just let them settle in."

He's not a wild horse, Geoff thought, annoyed with any further delay in getting Matt safely home. But he did as Zeke coached.

Moments later, three other boys appeared, including Duke who glanced their way but said nothing as all the boys took places around a picnic table, some straddling the bench seats, others kneeling on them. Geoff saw that Matt stood quietly at one end of the table, watching the card game intently.

"Now," Zeke whispered. "Follow my lead or you're gonna blow this thing."

"Yeah, like I don't know how to deal with a bunch of junior high. . ."

Zeke ignored him and started across the park.

"Matt Keller, is that you?" Zeke asked, his voice friendly in a surprised-but-glad-to-see-you way.

Matt looked up but didn't take off.

"Hi, Mr. Shepherd," he muttered.

"Mr. Shepherd?" Duke crowed. "I didn't even know you had a last name."

"Just like you, Dwight Buginski."

The other boys howled with laughter and started in on Duke, teasing him about his name. At the same time, Zeke motioned for Geoff to move closer to one side of Matt while he did the same on the other, just in case Matt decided to run.

Geoff placed a gentle hand on Matt's shoulder. "Hello, Matt," he said and felt Matt jerk, so he held on tighter. "How about you and me go get some pizza and talk? It's been awhile—too long."

He watched as Matt struggled with wanting desperately to go with him and at the same time being afraid to be hurt again. "It's over, Matt. If you're willing to forgive me, I'd like to make things right with you."

Matt picked up his backpack and shouldered it the way Tessa had that morning. "I'd like that," he said warily. "You mean it?"

"I mean it." Geoff nodded to Zeke, who took a place at the picnic table with the rest of the boys and dealt the cards. The other boys didn't seem to notice when Matt and Geoff walked away. But then Duke was there. "Here," he said, handing Matt a couple of crumpled dollar bills. "You paid too much."

"I don't want it." Matt pushed the money back at him.

"Too bad, dude. Take it or leave it. I really don't care." He turned his back on Matt and headed back to the game.

Matt stared at the money.

"Hard to know what to do with that, huh?" Geoff said.

"I won it playing cards," Matt told him. "Gambling is a sin. What should I do?"

"Maybe give it to charity?"

"I could do that."

Geoff wrapped his arm around Matt's shoulders. "First, we need to call your folks and let them know you're with me. Then,

I am seriously starving, and I need to run an idea for a new play by you to see if you get it."

Matt walked with renewed confidence. "I'll get it. Question is will the rest of the players get it?"

Geoff laughed and again realized that the weight of all those hours of anger and self-pity had suddenly evaporated. It felt good to laugh again, to be with Matt again, to be living again. It occurred to him that Tessa would be pleased, and that made him realize that he'd spent so much of these last weeks thinking about his feelings, his needs, his pain that he had barely thought about how Tessa might see all of this.

"Seriously, Matt, you need to think about being there for Sadie now. I mean, think about it. She still has to face going back to school, and she's going to need somebody who understands how tough it can be facing those other kids."

"Maybe," Matt said. "Yeah, I guess that's true." The thought clearly lifted his spirits. "But first could we go for that pizza? I am. . ."

". . .seriously starving," Geoff said in unison with him.

Chapter 46

Sadie

Sadie was nervous about actually going back to school. In the weeks that she was home while the judge decided her fate, her parents and teachers had agreed that homeschooling by Matt's teacher was best. Now that she was free, it was time to start getting back into the life she had known before that terrible rainy morning.

But how would everyone react to her being back? How would her teachers treat her? Would her friends still walk with her between classes and want to sit with her and share the news of the day? Most of all, what was it going to be like to see Dan again?

She didn't have to wait long for her answers. As she turned a corner to go to her math class, there he was.

He was not as tall as she had remembered him all those days she'd spent in detention—nor nearly as broad-shouldered. Compared to the huge guards—male and female—at the detention center, he was actually kind of small.

He saw her at the same moment she first spotted him. She looked away. But not before she saw his cheeks glow an embarrassed pink. His discomfort gave her courage.

"Hello, Dan," she said as she eased past him and into her classroom. "Nice to see you."

"Yeah," he muttered as he hurried past her. "You, too."

He was waiting for her when school let out.

"What was that?" he asked, his voice now filled with irritation. "Hello, Dan," he mocked in a high falsetto. "Nice to see you."

"I believe it was a socially acceptable greeting," Sadie replied, fighting her own irritation. "How are you?"

"Fine—better."

"Matt tells me you're back playing football."

They were standing on the steps outside the school. She was clutching her books to her chest, and he was leaning against the wall, his hands jammed into his pockets. In the past, he would have been smiling at her, watching her closely. She would have been looking down but smiling as well, unable to believe that this guy was even talking to her. What a baby she'd been.

"You lied in court," she said. "I forgive you."

He let out a snort of laughter. "Are you for real? I didn't lie, Sadie, and I don't need or want your forgiveness."

"You're not angry with me," she continued, realizing that he was nervous and that being with her made him uncomfortable. Yet he had waited for her. "You're upset with yourself, and you'd really just like for everything to go back to the way things were for you before."

"And you know this because?"

"It's something I've learned over the last several weeks. I've had a lot of time to work through some stuff—and a lot of help doing it. I wish you had someone you could talk to about what happened. Keeping it all bottled up is not good, Dan."

"You sound like my pastor."

Sadie shrugged. "So maybe you should listen to what he has to say."

Dan pushed himself away from the wall. "You've changed," he said, making eye contact with her for the first time.

"We both have."

He ground a toe of his shoe into the concrete. "Do you think about it like all the time?"

"Pretty much."

"Me, too." He drew in a long breath and let it out slowly.

"Coach is devastated, and yet he's never—not once—said anything to me. Do you think he'll ever forgive me?"

"I think he probably already has, but you should talk to him, Dan. It would do you both good."

He went back to staring off into space, lost in thought, and Sadie turned to go. "I'll see you around, okay?"

"Hey," he called when she reached the bottom of the stairs, "how about I walk you home?"

"I'm not sure that's a good idea, but if you want to take a walk around here and talk some, that would be okay."

Dan grinned at her, and a little of his usual self-confidence radiated from that handsome smile. "Good idea. How about down to the creek?"

They had shared their first kiss while walking along the banks of Phillipi Creek, and she understood all too well that need to latch onto something from the past that might just give them the feeling that nothing had changed.

But everything had changed.

"How about to the park? We can sit on the benches in the shade there and watch the play on the shuffleboard courts."

"Gee, why didn't I think of that?" Dan shoved his hands deeper into his pockets and scowled at something in the distance. He wasn't used to not getting his way. He was used to charming others into giving him what he wanted, and right now he apparently wanted to pretend that everything was the same between them.

"We aren't the same people we were before the accident, Dan," Sadie said. "I want to be your friend, and I want you to be mine, but beyond that?" She touched his hand to draw his attention. "You and I both know we can never go back. There's been too much. . ." She was surprised that her eyes had filled suddenly with tears and that her mind had brought forth an image of Tessa. "I miss her so much," she whispered.

"She was a good kid," he agreed. "Smart, funny in that quirky way she had. She always seemed older than she was."

Sadie smiled. "I used to tease her about being an old lady before her time. Of course, to me then an old lady was like my mom—or her mom."

Dan fell into step beside her, and he reached to take her books from her. "Have they forgiven us? Her mom and yours?"

"Us?" She glanced at him.

"Yeah, us," he said biting the words off. "Look, I'm not proud of how I handled myself in court that day. I was scared. And my folks. . ."

Sadie didn't want to hear excuses, so she took his hand. "Come on, I want to go by the cemetery, and it's getting late. My folks get nervous if I'm not home ten minutes before they start to worry, which is about five minutes after they know school is out."

They walked along in silence for a few blocks.

"You said you've forgiven me. I don't get that. I ruined your life."

"It's just the way we do things," she said. "I have to tell you that while I was locked up, I wasn't feeling very forgiving toward you at all."

They had reached the cemetery. Sadie led the way to Tessa's grave. She put her books on the ground and then knelt to clear away some dead leaves and other debris. Dan remained standing.

"How was that? I mean, being locked up." He actually shuddered.

"It was an experience I never want to repeat, and at the same time, I'm beginning to see that it was something that made a big difference in how I am, how I look at my future."

"And your family?"

"My mom and Tessa's mom have always been so close, and when I think about how close they came to never being able to know that closeness again, well, it was scary for me. But they were raised like they raised me—and Tessa and Matt—and that's just who we are. We forgive."

"And forget?"

"I can't imagine ever forgetting Tessa, or that horrible day, Dan."

"Because there were times when Coach—"

"Uncle Geoff has had a really tough time. I never realized this, but he blamed himself because he didn't save Tessa. He thought that his job as her father was to protect her, and when he couldn't, it must have been so awful."

"He told you that?"

"He wrote it." She explained about the VORP program and the contract, telling him about how everyone affected by Tessa's death had taken part in making her see the ripple effects of her careless behavior. "And selfish," she added. "I was so very selfish."

"But he's coming around? Coach, I mean?"

Sadie nodded and continued to pick dried flowers and leaves off her cousin's grave. "Oh, he still looks at me like the very sight of me is a physical wound for him, but Mom tells me that in time. . . The most important thing is that he and Matt have become close again."

Dan smiled and bent to help her. "Yeah, it's good to see the kid back on the sidelines. You know, sometimes he can explain Coach's crazy plays better than Coach can."

"Get me some water, will you?" She nodded toward a spigot, coiled hose, and bucket.

"I'd like to do something," he said when he returned. "Will you ask that lady who did this VORP thing with you if I could meet with her?"

"Sure."

"I've been thinking about asking if I could speak about all this at the next school assembly."

"That's a wonderful idea, Dan."

Her uncle Geoff thought it was a good idea as well, and two weeks later at their weekly assembly where Dan usually presided as president of the student council, he walked to the microphone and cleared his throat. Sadie sat in the front row with Geoff. They both looked up at Dan and nodded.

"I want to talk to you this morning, not as the president of this student body. Not as the quarterback of your football team. I want to talk to you as someone who knowingly broke the rules—rules that seemed pretty dumb to me as rules often do when you're our age. I thought I was above those rules. I thought that those rules did not apply to me because I was too smart, too cool to need them."

Sadie felt as if she could hear people breathing throughou~ the packed auditorium—it was that quiet.

633

"Here's the list of all the rules I violated in just one morning—in less than an hour," Dan continued as he unfurled a scroll-like paper filled with printing. "I was running late but allowed no time for that. It was raining—pouring. I knew the defroster in my car wasn't working properly. I. . ."

He continued reading, cataloging each item on the list, and when he finished, he looked out over the upturned faces and said, "Any one of those things was reason enough not to get behind the wheel of my car that morning, but I'm Dan Kline—senior, co-captain, council president, honor student. I was way too cool to admit that there was anything I couldn't handle. And so I made one more mistake—I encouraged, no, I practically dared Sadie Keller to drive from her house to Coach Messner's house so we could pick up her cousin Tessa, even though I was legally too young to ride with her."

He looked directly at Sadie then.

"And I did that knowing that she would do almost anything I asked of her."

Sadie realized that she was nodding, and she forced herself to be still.

"Then I made another mistake. Instead of coaching Sadie on how to drive, I took out this. . ." He produced his cell phone and held it up for all to see. "And I started texting my friends, making fun of Sadie's driving and laughing at their replies—laughing at her, never for one minute realizing how every snicker only added to her stress."

It was too much. She was as much to blame as he was. He was taking it all on himself. Sadie sat forward, but Dan stopped her with a look and a slight shake of his head.

"And when Sadie pulled into that driveway that rainy morning, she saw her cousin Tessa waiting, and you know who I saw? I saw Coach. I saw the man who has been my inspiration. The man who has spent hours shaping me and many of you as athletes and solid citizens. I saw a man that I love like I love my own father, and we were headed right for him. So I made my final mistake—I tried to make up for all the mistakes I had made that morning by grabbing the wheel away from Sadie."

He paused for a moment, and Sadie heard a couple of girls sniffling behind her. "Only God knows what might have happened if I hadn't done that, if I hadn't done any of this." He shook the long list and then dropped it to the floor. "Maybe Sadie would have swerved the other way. Maybe Coach would have jumped out of the way. Maybe. Maybe. Maybe. But you all know what happened next. A girl who was to start her first day of classes here with us that morning died that day. A girl who a couple of years from now might have been standing where I'm standing now leading this student body died that day. A girl who was everything to Sadie and Coach and their families died that day."

Sadie had thought she could not possibly have any more tears to shed, but she'd been wrong. Tears were leaking down her cheeks unabated. She felt a nudge next to her, and when she looked at her uncle, he was holding out his handkerchief to her.

Chapter 47

Jeannie and Emma

The sisters worked in tandem, going room by room as they cleaned Jeannie's house. She had removed all of the extraneous clothing, furnishings, and—as she called it—just plain stuff. Much of it she had taken to resale shops around town. The profits from her sales were beginning to come in.

"I was in the consignment shop where I took most of my clothes the other day, and the owner told me they were selling like hotcakes," Jeannie told Emma as they scrubbed down walls and washed floors side by side. "We'll have our bills paid off in no time."

"Das ist gut, Jeannie." Emma stood up and stretched her back. "Ready for Tessa's room?" she asked. It was the one room in the house that had remained untouched.

Jeannie looked away toward sunlight streaming through the upstairs hall window. "Yeah. It hasn't had a good cleaning since. . ."

"We don't have to take anything out or pack anything away if you're not ready, Jeannie."

"I know, but we should really move everything so that we can get behind the furniture and into the corners and all. Then we'll put it all back, right?"

"Exactly as it is," Emma assured her.

They worked together, each clearing off the various surfaces in the room—Tessa's dresser, her desk, her bookcase. Emma stripped the bedding and carried it downstairs to put it in the washer. When she came back, Jeannie had moved all of Tessa's clothes into the guest room. Together they rolled up the area rug and slid all of the furniture to one side of the room. Emma started sweeping the hardwood floor.

"Jeannie, when I went down to put the laundry in, I couldn't help noticing that Tessa's backpack is still there by the back door. Do you want me to go through it and have Sadie return any library books?"

"No, I'll do it."

Emma stopped sweeping when she noticed how reluctantly Jeannie moved toward the stairway. "Bring it up here. We'll do it together," she said.

By the time Jeannie returned with the backpack, Emma had finished sweeping one side of the room and was brushing the collected dust into a dustpan.

"So heavy," Jeannie noted, "She was so thin. How did she haul this around?"

Emma leaned the broom against the wall and sat on the side of Tessa's bed. She patted the spot next to her. "Come sit a minute. You know, this could wait."

"No. Geoff and I talked last night about how Tessa would want us to move forward. She would absolutely hate the idea of some sort of shrine, and having the backpack there by the door day after day has been a little like that, I suppose."

Emma resisted the urge to remind her sister that keeping Tessa's room as it was might also be considered a kind of shrine. *One step at a time*, she thought and watched Jeannie unfasten the clasps on the backpack.

There were numerous compartments—pockets on the outside that held pencils and pens and markers, a hairbrush and a tube of pink lip gloss that made Jeannie smile. "I suggested that she might want to carry this with her. She, of course, rolled her eyes as if that was the dumbest idea she'd ever heard. But here it is."

In another zipped compartment they found untouched notebooks and a daily calendar, and from inside the main compartment they removed a heavy dictionary, a thesaurus, Tessa's Bible, and four library books.

"That's it," Jeannie said as she ran her finger down the spines of the stack of books.

"Not quite," Emma replied, lifting the backpack. "There's something in this compartment here inside the main part." She pulled the zipper and took out a handmade journal with a fountain pen clipped to its cover.

"You found them!" Jeannie exclaimed happily as she reached for the book and pen. "Oh Em, I've turned this room upside down half a dozen times looking for this, and all the time it was right there on the chair by the kitchen door." She fingered the leather ties on the journal.

"Are you going to read it?"

"I don't even know if she wrote in it. We only gave it to her that night after the picnic."

"One way to find out," Emma said as she scooted back on the bed and leaned against the pillows stacked against the wall.

Jeannie smiled and loosened the thin, knotted ties. She turned the first page where Jeannie had written, "To Tessa, Love, Mom and Dad," with the date underneath. The next page was filled with Tessa's unique printing.

"Let's read it together," Jeannie said as she pushed herself back on the bed so that she and Emma were side by side.

"Don't you want to wait for Geoff?"

Jeannie took a minute to consider this and then said, "The way I see it is that it was no mistake that we found this together— you were the one who suggested I go through the backpack. I don't think that was an accident. I think we're being led to do this together the way we've always done everything together throughout our lives."

"Maybe we should. . ." Emma was still doubtful.

"Em, it's a prayer answered."

"It is that. Your prayer that you would find this precious link to your daughter and my prayer that you would find it in your heart to forgive mine."

The two sisters looked at each other for a long moment, and then Jeannie moved the journal halfway onto Emma's lap as the sisters bent their heads toward each other and read Tessa's journal.

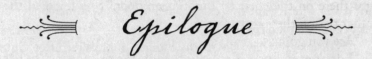

Epilogue

Tessa

Mom and Dad have always given me a small gift to start the school year, but this is so special. Look how beautifully Grandpa's pen writes—so much better than any roller ball or gel pen. I love it—and the journal. I think Mom made this for me. She's been fooling around lately with some art projects, and I thought I saw the paper on the cover of the journal lying in the guest room a few weeks ago.

But it's getting late and tomorrow is a big day—I've tried hard to be cool about it, but the truth is that I'm excited to be finally starting my years at the academy. Sadie has been there a whole year already, and the way she talks about it. . .well, I can't wait. But I am making a promise to myself right now that every single night I will write in my new journal—filling it with all the things that happen over the coming year.

Where to begin?

I have no idea, and I so don't want to look back on this and find it filled with silliness. I know! I'll take a Bible passage, the one from church that Sunday and write about that and how it fits what's happening in my life all that week.

Last week the pastor preached about the Sermon on the Mount—a favorite of mine. I just love the way the words flow, like they have comfort and the promise of better days ahead just pouring out of every syllable.

"Blessed are the poor in spirit: for theirs is the kingdom of heaven." I guess that "poor in spirit" means when someone is sad.

"Blessed are they that mourn: for they shall be comforted." Pastor says that we can mourn many things—not just the death of a loved one but any kind of loss—the loss of a friend or a favorite book or an opportunity to do good.

"Blessed are the meek: for they shall inherit the earth." Well, not really sure I want this earth, but I am meek, so maybe it's all part of God's plan for me.

"Blessed are they which do hunger and thirst after righteousness: for they shall be filled." That's more me, I think—and our good friend Hester and her husband, John—those two are always hungering after some new way to make things right for others.

"Blessed are the merciful: for they shall obtain mercy." Is mercy the same as forgiveness? I'll have to ask about that. It seems like that might be right—like tonight when I could see that Aunt Emma was really upset with Mom for taking Sadie to get her permit, and yet she forgave her. Was that mercy?

"Blessed are the pure in heart: for they shall see God." That's my all-time favorite!

"Blessed are the peacemakers: for they shall be called the children of God." Close second!

"Blessed are they which are persecuted for righteousness' sake: for theirs is the kingdom of heaven." I really hope that one day I'll be brave enough to stand up for others—or for my beliefs—purely because that is the right thing to do.

"Blessed are ye, when men shall revile you, and persecute you, and shall say all manner of evil against you falsely, for my sake. Rejoice, and be exceeding glad: for great is your reward in heaven: for so persecuted they the prophets which were before you."

I think this is maybe the biggest reason that I'm glad we're Mennonite. Pretty much everybody in our faith stays away from the blame shame game. We take care of each other like a ginormous family, and even when we get mad at each other, we always find our way back—like sheep coming into the fold in the darkness.

And speaking of darkness, it is so late and I am so tired and tomorrow is going to be so special. It's starting to rain—good sleeping weather, my dad always says.

DISCUSSION QUESTIONS

1. How does Emma's forgiveness of Jeannie for her impulsive act in the beginning of the book set things in motion?

2. How many instances where characters sought forgiveness throughout the story can you name, and in how many instances was forgiveness granted?

3. How did Geoff's past influence his ability to forgive Sadie?

4. How did the fact that Jeannie and Geoff were already having some problems in their marriage before the accident influence how they handled their grief?

5. What role did blame play in the story?

6. What role did trust—or lack of trust—play?

7. Given the title of the book, in what ways did Emma forgive Jeannie? And vice versa?

8. The story is told from all major characters' points of view—take them one by one and discuss how each was impacted by Tessa's death and how each of them changed.

9. The Mennonite faith is rooted in the teachings of the New Testament. What lessons did Jesus teach his followers about love, forgiveness, and reconciliation?

10. How did the characters in this story apply those teachings (or not)?

11. In your own life (or the lives of those close to you) has there ever been something that threatened to tear your family apart? If so, how was that resolved? If not, how do you think you and your family might weather a situation such as the one the characters in this book had to face?

12. Think about all the ways characters in this story sought comfort. Talk about those that worked—and those that did not.

13. In her journal, Tessa wonders if mercy is the same as forgiveness. What do you think?

A Mother's Promise

Acknowledgments

Writing any story means finding "partners" to guide the process especially in those areas where the author is admittedly no expert. As with other books in this series I am deeply indebted to my Pinecraft/Sarasota friends Rosanna Bontrager, Doris Diener, and Tanya Kurtz Lehman. In addition I could not have brought the medical pieces of the story together without the assistance of Lois Pearson, Suzanne Berg, Barbara Oleksy, Jill Wiench, and Jim Greear. My thanks also go out to editors, Rebecca Germany and Traci DePree, as well as to my agent, Natasha Kern—a dear friend and unwavering cheerleader. Finally not one of the books I have written could ever have come to light without the constant love, support, and encouragement of my husband, best friend, and life partner, Larry.

Prologue

Ohio, Late Autumn, 2010

Rachel Kaufmann stood at the end of the lane that led to the farmhouse and waited for her husband to return from harvesting the last of the winter feed corn. It was coming on darkness and the wind that had come out of the southwest all day had shifted north.

She pulled her shawl over her white prayer covering and wrapped her hands in its folds. She had left her gloves back at the house, so anxious had she been to share her good news with James.

For several years she had helped supplement their farming income with private-duty nursing jobs, but now she'd been offered a full-time job as school nurse for their rural district. The nursing degree that she'd completed just before she and James married would finally be used to its full potential. She knew that her husband would be as pleased by the news as she was.

What could be keeping him?

She shivered a little and stamped her feet to offset the damp and cold as she peered into the lengthening shadows, listening carefully for the sound of the old tractor he would be riding back to the farm. It had rained steadily for days now, and the fields were awash with standing water. Twice that week the tractor had gotten stuck and James had had to abandon the work, but that morning he'd been confident that the strong overnight wind had done its job so he'd headed back to the fields.

She heard a car approach and knew it was a regular vehicle, not the tractor she longed to see coming around the sharp curve in the road. Headlights swept over her as the driver slowed and turned onto the lane.

Her sister-in-law, Rose, rolled down the passenger-side window. "Rachel? Is that you?"

"Of course it's her," James's brother Luke snapped irritably. "Who else would it be?"

"Just waiting for James," Rachel said. She drummed her fingernails on the back window, drawing the attention of the four children crowded on the backseat and waving to them.

"It's freezing," Rose protested as she wrapped a shawl more tightly around her shoulders. "Get in."

"No. I'm all right. I'll wait."

"Better you come on back with us and help Mom get supper on the table." Luke was not making conversation. He was—as usual—giving an order that he fully expected to be obeyed.

"James will be along soon." Rachel met her brother-in-law's eyes.

"Suit yourself," he said as he gunned the motor and sprayed gravel behind him on his way to his parents' farmhouse. Rachel saw Rose's hand waving at her as they sped away.

Perhaps it would have been best to stay in the house even though her mother-in-law, Grace, had smiled when she saw how Rachel kept glancing out the kitchen window watching for James. "Why don't you go on down there? Surprise him."

"Getting colder," James's father, Earl, had announced as he entered the house and hung his broad-brimmed black straw hat on its usual hook by the door. Next to it was the hook where James would hang his hat. "Just going to wash up," he'd added as he passed by his wife's rocker and leaned in to kiss her temple. "Take your shawl, Rachel. That wind is shifting."

Rachel loved her in-laws dearly. She just wished that she and James could have blessed them with more grandchildren. James's brothers all had large families, but James and Rachel had only one son, ten-year-old Justin.

"Can I come with you?" Justin had asked.

"No, finish your homework. We'll eat as soon as Dad gets home."

Now as she turned away from the tail lights of Luke's car and took up her vigil for the sound of James's tractor, she frowned. When she had told Justin that she had applied for the school nurse job, her son had asked a surprising question. "Dad will let you work there, right?"

"Of course. He'll be happy for me—for all of us. Why would you ask that?"

"Because Uncle Luke says that good Mennonite women shouldn't work outside the home," Justin had said. "He says that Aunt Rosie has plenty to keep her busy and then some."

"Aunt Rosie has four children all under the age of seven," Rachel had replied before she could censor herself.

But she knew that Luke would disapprove of her taking the job. In his view, if a woman wanted to take on the occasional cleaning job to earn what he called "pocket money," that was tolerable. But a job like this one, working for the county—outsiders—that would definitely not be to his liking. Even though Luke was the youngest of James's three brothers, he was the most conservative when it came to what he thought Mennonite women should and should not do. He was so strict that Rose always wore solid-colored caped dresses—never the occasional small floral print that other women of their faith wore. And the children—even though they were all well under the age when Mennonite boys and girls would be baptized, join the congregation, and start to follow the dress code and traditions of their elders, Luke insisted they be dressed in the homemade clothing that he and Rose wore.

Just then she heard the familiar sputter of the tractor, and all thoughts of her differences with her brother-in-law flew away on the wind that whipped at her skirt. James was coming. He would be as happy about this as she was. He would pull her up onto the tractor beside him, hold her tight, and kiss her. "That's my girl," he would say, and then he would kiss her again.

She stepped into the road as he came around the curve, the dim headlight of the battered tractor barely visible in the gathering dark. But she could see him waving, so she knew that he had spotted her, and she knew that he was smiling as he began steering the tractor into the left turn he needed to make to reach their lane.

Suddenly she heard another sound, much louder and far too close. Before she could cry out a warning to her husband, she was blinded by headlights that lit James from behind as if he were on a stage.

He motioned for Rachel to step back as he turned the tractor's steering wheel hard to the right.

In the chaos that followed, the screech of brakes applied too late, of metal hitting metal, the blaring of a car horn, Rachel stood frozen to the spot where she had last seen her husband.

And then she heard feet running toward her.

"Call 911, Grace," Earl shouted.

"Stay there, Justin," Luke ordered.

Rachel walked slowly toward the large modern car, its headlights now spotlighting a scene that she could not wholly comprehend. That vehicle showed no signs of damage other than a white airbag lying limply against the driver's seat. A young man was stumbling around next to it, making low keening sounds. On the far side of the car, the tractor lay on its side in the ditch. Pinned underneath it was the very still body of her beloved husband.

"James," she cried as she scrambled into the ditch, uncaring of the muddy water that soaked her skirt and apron. She knelt next to her husband, touching his cheeks and forehead, covering him with her shawl. "Lie still," she instructed. "Help is coming."

But she was a trained nurse. As she searched for a pulse and bent to administer CPR, she knew that the ambulance siren she could hear faintly through the fog of her shock would never arrive in time.

Part One

*I will lift up mine eyes unto the hills,
from whence cometh my help.*

PSALM 121:1

Chapter 1

Summary—Two Years Later

Rachel stood at the end of the lane waiting for the mail to be delivered. It wasn't that she was expecting anything. Her daily walk to the mailbox had become one way that she could find a few minutes respite from the way her life—and Justin's—had changed over the two years that had passed since that horrible night.

At first, as she had faced the hard grief besetting her following James's death, Rachel had asked God for many things—mostly for the strength to go on and for the wisdom to know how best to care for Justin. Certainly her strength to move forward without James's comforting presence had been tested many times and in many ways.

Earl had suffered a mild stroke, and the family had known that there was no way the elderly man could continue to manage the large farm with only some occasional help from his remaining sons. A week after that her brother-in-law Luke and his family had moved into the farmhouse.

Wanting to make them feel as welcome as possible, Rachel had immediately offered them the large upstairs bedroom that she and James had shared. Their boys had moved in with Justin while their girls took over the room once occupied by James's parents. Grace and Earl moved out to the smaller cottage behind the main house.

Rachel had tried blaming their mutual grief for the tenseness that permeated the house. She told herself that everyone was feeling the loss of James in different ways. But as time passed she realized that the discord arose not because everyone was missing James so much but because Luke did not approve of her working.

"Your son needs you," he would tell her.

"Justin is in school during the hours I am at work," she pointed out. "When he is at home so am I."

"And leaving Rose to manage everything," he had continued as if Rachel hadn't spoken. "It's a large house."

Rachel did not point out that whenever she came to the kitchen and offered to help prepare their supper or feed the youngest children, Rose would shoo her away. "You go and rest now," she would chide. "You've been working all day."

Rachel had made the best of the situation and tried to encourage Justin to do so as well, promising that it would just take some time for them to all settle in. But after a year of Luke ordering Justin around and openly criticizing her failure to be the Mennonite woman he thought she should be, Rachel knew that there would be no *settling in*. This was their life.

A life without James.

And then one snowy afternoon just before Christmas break she had been called to her supervisor's office and told that her position as the school nurse was being eliminated due to budget cuts.

Without her job to fill her days, Rachel found herself spending more and more of her time out in the smaller cottage that James had built for his parents. She would sit at the kitchen table with her mother-in-law, rolling out dough or peeling apples for the pies that Grace made and sold at the local store. But after several weeks, she had to admit that there was little room for Justin and her in either house—physically there was, but they didn't fit in other ways. She considered moving down the road to the farm where she'd grown up, but her parents had died and the running of the farm was now shared by her two brothers, both of whom had large families of their own.

As the seasons passed, she watched helplessly as Justin became more withdrawn and somber. Now with no school in the summer he was even more at the mercy of his uncle's demands and criticisms.

"I can't do anything right," he'd muttered one evening as he stormed into the house and up to his room.

"Get back down here, Justin," Luke ordered.

"Let him be," Rachel said. "He's doing the best he can, Luke."

"No he is not and neither are you, Rachel. James was too soft on both of you—taken in by that pretty face and sweet smile of yours from the day you two met. Well, I'm not James, and I expect you and your son to do your part around here."

Rachel had walked away from him without another word. She'd gone up to Justin's room and tried to console him. But her attempts at comfort and reassurance fell on deaf ears—Justin's and her own.

Now as she waited for the mail to come she paced the side of the narrow country road as she tried to think of anything she could do to make things easier for Justin.

"Here you go," the postal worker called out as he leaned out the side of his vehicle and handed her a small stack of envelopes. "Have a good one, now," he added as he pulled away.

"And you," she called after him.

As she slowly walked back up the lane toward the house, she shuffled through the mail and paused when she reached a letter addressed to her—a letter from Florida.

She stopped walking and slid her thumbnail under the flap of the blue envelope. Inside she found a sympathy card and letter from her college friend Hester Steiner—a voice from her past that she found far more comforting than any of the voices surrounding her at the farm.

Dear Rachel,

Greetings from sunny Florida!

I have just heard the news of James's death. I am so sorry that I was not there with you during this terrible time.

ANNA SCHMIDT

*I know we lost touch over the last several years, but I think
of you so often. Oh, how I miss you and our talks so much.*

She wrote of her marriage and her work helping to manage
a nonprofit co-operative that employed homeless people to
distribute fresh fruit and homemade jams to food pantries.
Hester sounded so very happy that Rachel could not help but
feel a twinge of envy.

It took Rachel more than a week to write back. In her letter she
talked of the troubling aspects of her life in the same lighthearted
way the two friends had shared when they were roommates. She
made jokes about being banned from the kitchen, and rightly so,
since Hester would recall that Rachel was not much of a cook.

Hester's reply came within days. She had seen through
Rachel's poor attempts at humor and addressed the deep-seated
unhappiness that lay beneath. And true to form she had a solution.

Come to Florida, she wrote as if it were as simple as that.
Rachel snorted a wry laugh, remembering Hester always seemed
to think everything was possible.

*There's an opening at a local hospital in the spiritual
care department. You'd be perfect for it. I've enclosed an
application form and the name and address of the senior
chaplain. He and his wife volunteer at the co-op, and we've
become friends. I've told him all about you and he's waiting
for your application so don't disappoint him—or me.*

This too, was so like Hester, dishing out orders, expecting
Rachel would do her bidding simply because to her it was the
perfect solution to the problem at hand. Never mind that Rachel's
training was in nursing, not counseling.

Rachel put Hester's letter including the application in a
drawer of her bureau, and for the next three nights just before
she knelt next to her single bed for her nightly prayers, she read
through the form, mentally filling in each blank. Each night she
prayed for guidance, and on the fourth night she sat down and
completed the application. The following morning she waited by

the mailbox and personally handed the completed form to the mail carrier.

"Where is that boy?"

Justin cringed when his uncle Luke stormed into the kitchen. His aunt Rose murmured something. Aunt Rose always kind of whispered when she spoke to Uncle Luke, like she was afraid of him.

He was beginning to understand that fear because Uncle Luke seemed to be mad a lot about one thing or other. He wasn't anything like Justin's dad had been. But then nothing about his life now was like it had been before his dad got killed by a drunk driver.

At first it had seemed like things might get better. His grandpa had been sort of like his dad in those weeks right after the accident. His mom had started her job and his grandma had done what she'd always done—cooking, baking pies for a local store that he delivered with her after school and on weekends. His mom helped his grandma with the cleaning and cooking when she wasn't working. The way things went during that time, it had sometimes been easy to forget his dad was really never coming back. It had been almost normal, like Dad was just out planting a field or something.

But then Grandpa had had his stroke and after that it was like he was suddenly a whole lot older and weaker, and Gramma as well. It wasn't long after Grandpa got home from the hospital that Justin's uncles had this family meeting and decided that Uncle Luke and Aunt Rose should take over running the farm while his grandparents moved back out to the smaller cottage that Justin had helped his dad build for them in back of the main house.

His best buddy Harlan's grandparents lived in a house like theirs while Harlan and his parents and brothers and sisters lived in the main farmhouse. It was the way things were done in their world, although he'd met some kids who were not Mennonite who thought it was pretty weird the way Mennonite families all stayed together in one place. Well, Justin was pretty sure he wouldn't like living the way those kids did with their grandparents in some whole other state. He figured that those kids would be even lonelier than he was if their dad died.

"Justin!"

His uncle stood in the doorway of the small bedroom that Justin now shared with two of his cousins.

"Coming," he said automatically, although he had no idea if that was what his uncle wanted him to do.

"Don't give me that attitude," Luke said, his teeth and fists both clenched. "There's work to be done, boy. Now get to it."

Uncle Luke turned and walked back downstairs.

Justin wondered for a minute what his uncle might do if just this once Justin refused to follow his orders. But he already knew the answer to that one. Luke would take a willow switch to the backs of his bare legs, and his mom wouldn't be able to stop him. His dad could have because he was the eldest and as such Luke would have had to listen to him. But his dad was dead and his mom had no real power—none at all.

In early August, Rachel was hanging laundry on the line outside the kitchen of the main house when her mother-in-law called for her to come answer the telephone in the cottage. "Long distance," she added. Surely a long-distance call in the middle of the day meant bad news.

Rose came out onto the back porch of the main house, her lips pursed with curiosity.

Inside the cottage, where they kept the phone just in case Earl took a turn for the worse, Grace handed her the receiver before quietly returning to the kitchen.

"Hello?"

"Mrs. Kaufmann?"

"Yes?" Rachel's hand was shaking as she gripped the receiver of the old rotary dial telephone.

"This is Pastor Paul Cox, senior chaplain for Gulf Coast Medical Center."

"Oh, hello. How are you?" This was about the job—the Florida job. Her hand began to sweat, and her heart was beating so hard she thought that Pastor Cox must be able to hear it.

"I'm very well, thank you for asking. I have your application here. I am with our hospital administrator, Darcy Meekins, as well as a member of our board of directors, Malcolm Shepherd. Do you have a moment to talk?"

"Yes sir." Her reply was automatic. Her mind was busy trying to quell the hope she felt rising in her chest.

"Excellent. Let me put you on speakerphone." Rachel heard a rustling and crackling, and then Pastor Cox was back on the line, his voice now sounding amplified as if speaking from far away—which of course, he was. "Our time for filling this position is quite short, Mrs. Kaufmann. The hospital is set to open next week, and the truth is we had almost decided on another candidate when we received your application."

Rachel's heart sank. *Then, why call at all?*

As if she had spoken aloud, she heard a different male voice answer. "Mrs. Kaufmann? Malcolm Shepherd here. You see, this is a brand-new medical center. We're located a mile east of the Amish and Mennonite neighborhood here in Sarasota. We hope to serve the residents of that community as well as the growing communities that have sprung up over the years east of downtown Sarasota. One of our goals for the medical center is to offer a diversity of staffing in all departments. With that in mind we were understandably pleased to receive your application."

Malcolm Shepherd's calm explanation of the situation eased her concern that they had only called as a courtesy to say that her application had come too late. In her letters, Hester had mentioned the businessman who was also a large financial supporter of the fruit co-operative Hester and her husband had founded in Sarasota. Hester really admired him and the work he and his wife did in the community. Just hearing him on the phone, Rachel thought she understood why. He had a way of putting people at ease—at least he did that for her.

"Therefore," he continued, "we decided to extend the timeline in order to at least have the opportunity to interview you."

"I appreciate that," she said, her heart sinking once again. "But I cannot come to Florida for an interview."

"Rachel?" a clipped female voice interrupted. "Darcy Meekins, hospital administrator here. Assuming this time works for you, we are interviewing you now."

Rachel could not help being reminded of her brother-in-law when she heard the woman's clipped tone. Like Luke, Darcy Meekins seemed more inclined to giving orders than to being part of a general discussion. Rachel also could not help noticing that the woman had called her by her given name while both men had been more formal in addressing her. What did this mean? Was she supposed to call the woman *Darcy*?

"Is this a good time?" The woman sounded impatient.

"Yes, Miss Meekins. This is fine."

"I prefer *Ms.* Meekins."

Rachel barely heard the correction as Rose and three of her children entered the cottage. Rose shooed the children toward the kitchen. "Gramma has cookies," she promised in a whisper, and then she stood by the front door, her arms folded across the bibbed front of her dress, her eyebrows raised in question. "Is everything all right?" she mouthed.

Rachel nodded and covered the receiver with her palm. "It's. . . I'll tell you all about it after I get off." She met her sister-in-law's stare until Rose finally got the message and headed for the kitchen.

"Mrs. Kaufmann, are you still there?" Pastor Cox asked.

"Yes. I apologize. This is a family telephone and—"

"I see that you attended nursing school," the hospital administrator interrupted. "Please explain why you believe you are qualified to serve in our spiritual care department?"

"Well, I do have my degree in nursing, and as I mentioned on my application, I have additional course work in social work, plus certification in a special counseling program for victims of violent crimes and their offenders. I am a woman of deep faith and I believe I can. . ."

"The counseling needed here is hardly a match," Rachel heard the administrator say in a low voice obviously not intended for her ears. "I see that you are not currently employed. Why did you leave your last position?" Darcy continued.

Rachel's hand began to perspire as she clutched the receiver. All of a sudden she wanted this job and the opportunity it represented for her to start fresh, the possibility that she could provide for Justin. "The position was eliminated due to budget cuts," she replied, fighting to keep her voice calm and professional. "As I noted toward the back of the application, you may certainly contact my former employer for a reference."

One of the two men at the other end of the call cleared his throat, and then she heard Pastor Cox say, "Why don't I tell you a little more about the position?"

"I would appreciate that," Rachel said.

"We have a large children's wing here at Gulf Coast. You would be working primarily with children. Are you comfortable with that?"

Rachel could not control the smile that spread across her face and carried through to her voice. "That would be truly wonderful, Pastor. I love children."

"We are talking about children of all ages," Darcy cautioned. "Infants, toddlers, children in school, children with physical issues that have also, in some cases, exploded into serious emotional problems."

"That was the case when I worked as a school nurse. Well, not the infants and toddlers of course, but children of all ages from kindergarten through high school, and from all backgrounds."

"And faiths?" Darcy asked.

"Yes. All faiths. It was a county school system."

She heard what sounded like a door opening and closing and the rustle of papers as a man's muffled voice apologized for being late.

"Mrs. Kaufmann," Pastor Cox said, "Dr. Ben Booker has just joined us."

"Hello, Mrs. Kaufmann. I read your application. Impressive." The doctor's voice was kind, and she thought that he must've been very good at putting his patients at ease. She pictured a balding gray-haired man wearing a white coat with a stethoscope around his neck. The image made her smile.

"Thank you."

"So, do you think you're interested?"

Rachel hesitated. This doctor had just joined the interview, and this was his first question before he'd even asked one thing about her qualifications?

"I understand that there are other candidates," she said, choosing each word with care. "I certainly appreciate that you would consider my application at all."

There was a moment of such dead air that Rachel thought perhaps somehow they had been disconnected.

"That wasn't the question," the doctor said, breaking the silence.

"Yes. I would be very interested."

"You do understand that you would need to earn your certification as a spiritual counselor per Florida state regulations?" Darcy Meekins asked. "And you would need to do your course work on top of the hours spent at the position, hours that will include some nights and weekends. There's also some fieldwork included in the course."

"Yes. That was clear on the application."

"A formality," Pastor Cox added. "You can do the required field work right here."

"You would need to move here within a matter of a few weeks. Could you manage that should we offer you the position?" Ms. Meekins pressed.

"I could. Yes." Rachel had never felt more certain of anything—other than her decision to marry James—in her life. She wanted this job.

"You don't need time to consider?" the hospital administrator coached. "To speak with your family?" It was as if she was trying to remind Rachel of all the reasons why this was not a good idea.

"There's really just me and my twelve-year-old son, Ms. Meekins. My husband passed away nearly two years ago. My son understands that I make all decisions based on what's best for him."

She heard the woman blow out a puff of air. "Well, *we* need some time," she muttered, and Rachel realized that she had once again covered the receiver and said this to the others.

"Very well, then," Pastor Cox boomed. "We had narrowed the field of candidates to two and now with you we have three. Give us a few days to mull over the pros and cons and we'll be in touch. Is that all right?"

Rachel's heart sank. There was no way they were going to hire someone from over a thousand miles away for the position if they had two other qualified candidates right there. "That would be fine," Rachel said. "Is there anything else you need to know about me?" Now she just sounded desperate.

"As my brother might say, Mrs. Kaufmann," Malcolm Shepherd said in a tone that Rachel could only describe as kind, "no worries. We have already received electronic letters of reference from the superintendent of schools in your district there in Ohio as well as letters from three teachers that worked with you. Hester Steiner has given a verbal recommendation." He chuckled. "She's certainly been persistent in making sure we consider your application."

Rachel smiled. "Hester can be—"

"We'll call you," the hospital administrator interrupted. Rachel couldn't help wondering if the woman was perpetually impatient or maybe she just had a lot on her schedule and was anxious to get this meeting over with.

"Thank you again for considering me at all," Rachel said. "I'll look forward to your call."

"Three or four days," Pastor Cox promised. "We'll call either way. You enjoy your weekend now," he added, and after murmured good-byes all around the line went dead.

But the very next day—Friday—she had once again been called to the telephone.

"Mrs. Kaufmann? Pastor Cox here."

Her heart sank with disappointment. If they had made their choice so quickly then there was no chance that. . .

"How soon can you get here?"

Rachel was speechless. But that didn't seem to faze the chaplain, who continued talking as if the question had been purely rhetorical.

"Assuming you still want the job, we'd like you to get started as soon as possible. Now let me just put Mark from Human Resources on the line and he can give you the details of the offer, okay?"

"Yes, thank you."

The man from Human Resources took the phone and gave her information about salary, hours, benefits such as vacation and personal time, and insurance. "The search committee has approved a certification program for you so you'll work and attend classes, but they're available online so you fit it into your schedule however you like. All right?"

Her mind raced with the logistics of working and going to school even if it was online. And certainly there was the issue of being available for Justin as he got acclimated to his new surroundings. "Yes."

"There will be a probationary period of four months," Mark continued in a voice that told her this was hardly the first time he had delivered this information. "During that time others will be observing and assessing your work. If for any reason at the end of the probationary period, the members of the search committee—or you—decide this isn't working, the appointment can be terminated. Do you understand?"

"Yes."

"So how soon can you get here?" Mark's tone changed from official to casual.

Rachel couldn't help it. She laughed. This was the best news she'd had in months. For the first time since James's death she could actually see the possibility that God had a new plan for her life, one where she and Justin could start again and perhaps recover a measure of the joy they had known before. "I need two weeks if that's all right," she said.

"Suits me," Mark said. "Here's Pastor Cox."

"Let's make that Paul, okay?" the minister said as he took back the phone. "And may I call you Rachel?"

"That's fine. Oh, thank you so very much. You have no idea what this means to me. Please thank the others for me."

Paul laughed. "Happy to have you, Rachel. Now Mark will be

sending you some materials about the hospital, the certification program, and the general area to look over. It'll give you a head start before we see you in a couple of weeks. Until then, as Mark so aptly put it, welcome aboard."

Chapter 2

Just two days after the Kaufmann family celebrated Justin's twelfth birthday his mom gave him the news. Somehow he knew that what he would remember most about this birthday wouldn't be Gramma's spice cake with its caramel frosting—his favorite. Or the new clothes his aunts and uncles and cousins had given him. No, this was the birthday he would remember most because his world had just been turned upside down—again.

"Justin, I've been offered a job," she told him as the two of them sat on the wooden swing that hung from a large horizontal branch of the willow tree just outside the farmhouse kitchen.

He couldn't help but think about another day almost two years before when his mom had made a similar announcement just after Dad's funeral.

"The thing is," she continued as she pushed the swing into motion with her bare foot, "the job is in Florida."

Florida? Justin's mind raced as he tried to take in the idea of moving not just off the farm where his dad had grown up and he'd been born, but halfway across the whole country.

He didn't know a single person in Florida. Mom kept going on about her good friend, Hester. But Hester wasn't family. How could Mom even think of leaving Gramma and Gramps?

"We can start fresh there," he heard her say.

I don't want to start fresh, he thought, feeling a wave of the anger that was pretty much the way he felt most of the time these days. *I want our old life. The one where I helped Dad with the chores. The one where Dad and I fished in the pond in summer and went ice-skating in winter.*

"What do you think?" his mom asked him.

Justin mentally ran down the list of things that he'd learned about Florida from the books he'd read and stuff he'd learned at school.

"I know it's a big change," she continued when he didn't answer right away. She brought the swing to a halt so she could lean forward, her elbows resting on her knees as she stared out at the fields surrounding the farmhouse and its outbuildings. "But just think," Mom said, her voice high and nervous, "you can go swimming in the Gulf of Mexico."

"They have alligators," Justin said, as if that alone illustrated the scope of the change she was asking him to make.

"Alligators don't live in the Gulf," she replied.

"Sharks, then. And snakes—big poisonous ones, and what about how hot it is? Those skinny palm trees I've seen in pictures don't seem like they'd provide much shade." Justin was desperate to find something that would make his mother listen to reason. She didn't like hot weather all that much.

"They have seasons just like we do in Ohio, just no snow or hardly ever. And there are other trees besides palm trees."

"We don't know anybody there," he pointed out.

"I just told you, Justin. When we first get there, we'll stay with my college roommate, Hester, and her husband, John Steiner. When we were in college Hester and I were best friends."

Then why can't you understand that I'm not excited to leave my best friend, Harlan? Justin wondered, but his dad had taught him not to question his elders, especially his mom and grandparents. And now that his uncle Luke was in charge, Justin knew that he'd be risking a paddling if Luke heard him challenge his mother.

It had been a year, nine months and eight days since Justin's dad had died. Justin had heard people say that the force of the car's speed gave his dad no chance at all for survival. He'd died right there next to a stack of rocks that Justin and his cousins had pulled from the field earlier that year and piled by the roadside ditch. He died even though Mom had tried so hard to save him. The driver of the car had been drunk.

At first Justin had been so mad at that man for being drunk and driving his car, but his gramma had reminded him that as Mennonites they believed in forgiveness. He must not harbor hard feelings against the man. So Justin had tried to forgive—he really had. He and his mom had even gone to a kind of school to help people like them get past being so mad.

In the end Justin went along with the program mostly because it came up about the time his mom lost her job, and she was pretty excited about it. Afterward she even took some training so that she could help other people like them and the drunk man.

"It might lead to a paying job," she'd told him.

But it hadn't, and his dad was still dead.

He hated the way people at the funeral had kept clutching his shoulder—the men—or touching his cheek—the women—and saying that Justin was now the "man of this family." He wasn't sure what that meant. Was he supposed to get a job now? Or maybe they were saying that he needed to take on managing the farm like his dad had.

Justin pushed himself off the swing and walked a little ways from his mom, his back to her. He had to think. He had just turned twelve years old, and his world kept getting twisted inside out.

"What about school?" he asked, grasping for anything that might keep this from happening. He stopped short of reminding her that Dad had always talked about how important it was for him to keep up with his studies, especially math. The night his dad died he'd been working on his math assignment and he'd been excited about showing his dad how he'd solved every problem.

"There's a lot you have to figure in running a farm," Dad was always reminding him. "Not just what things might cost but how to know how many fence posts you need to fence in a certain field. Stuff like that."

And what about the fact that his dad had liked to read? Not just the scriptures or about farming but other stuff. Justin also liked to read, and he was good at it. And Dad was always real proud that Mom had gone to college even though as Mennonites, being proud about anything was considered a bad thing. But Dad was always teasing Mom about being the brains of the family. She would get all giggly like the girls at his school did and tell him to stop, but Justin could see that she liked it. Yes, school was important to both of his parents.

"Is there a school—one of *our* schools?" he asked again.

"Hester says that there's an entire Amish and Mennonite community right there with churches and a school and shops and everything." Her voice went all soft and dreamy. He turned around so he could see her face. She looked up at him with a smile and then bit her lower lip before adding, "We'll go to church there and shop and you'll meet people and—"

"Do the Steiners live near there?"

"Well, no. They live some distance away, but they shop there and attend church."

Justin frowned. Ever since his dad died school was his world—the one place where he could escape his uncle's constant criticism.

His mom sat back again. She wasn't looking directly at him—a sure sign that he wasn't going to like whatever she was about to say. "You see, when we first get there, we're going to need to be closer to everything—my work, your school. We won't have a car. There's public transportation of course—a bus line."

Justin's suspicions went on high alert. This was sounding like more change than he was ready to face. "But we'll be close to the school—the Mennonite school?" When his mom didn't answer immediately, he began guessing. "A Christian school? A church school?"

"A public school," she said, and then her words came out in a rush. "It's only for the first semester. Until after the first of the year. By that time we'll know for sure that my job is secure and we'll have had time to explore different neighborhoods and places to live. I'm in hopes that we can rent a little house in

Pinecraft near the church and the Mennonite school, but in the beginning—"

"Pinecraft? You said Sarasota."

"Pinecraft is what people call the Amish and Mennonite community right there in the middle of Sarasota, Justin," she explained. "From what Hester tells me it's more like a neighborhood than a separate town. But the hospital where I'll be working is some distance from there, and the public school is close to the hospital."

Public school. "I'm not dressing the way our people do in a public school," he said defiantly.

"No. I wouldn't ask that of you." She sighed as if she finally got it that he wasn't as excited about this as she was. "I know it's a big move, Justin," she said as she stood up. He was almost as tall as she was—something he wished that his dad could see.

"Justin!" His uncle was standing outside the barn, his hands on his hips. He looked mad. Of course, whenever he talked to Justin at all, he always seemed to be mad about something. "Chores?"

"He's coming," his mom called back. She sounded almost as mad as Uncle Luke did. His mom and uncle had never really gotten along, especially not since his dad had died.

"Justin," his mom said. "I promise you that it's all going to work out—for both of us. We'll come back for visits, and Gramps and Gramma will come see us in Florida. You can take Gramps fishing." She brushed his hair away from his forehead with two fingers the same way she'd done a million times before. "I need you to trust me, okay?"

Justin knew that she wasn't asking his permission. In their world the adults made the rules and the decisions.

"Yes ma'am," he murmured.

As he trudged off, he clung to the promise she had made—a promise he didn't see how she could keep, but one that he intended to hold her to.

As the bus half-filled with passengers sped along the highway connecting the life that Rachel and Justin were leaving behind to the one she prayed would not turn out to be a mistake of catastrophic proportions, she absently fingered the fine silky wisps of her son's hair. He was asleep now, his head on her lap, his lean, long body so like his father's folded into the bus seat beside her. He was tall for his age and looked older than his twelve years.

The growth spurt he had experienced this last year was not all that had changed about Justin. Ever since his father's death, he'd become more introverted. Before that, he had asked questions about everything from the weather to learning about the path the Kaufmann family had taken generations earlier in settling in Ohio. His insatiable curiosity was a source of gentle teasing from everyone in their large extended family. But after the funeral, and especially after Luke's family had moved into the farmhouse, Justin had taken to spending much of his time alone. When he was with family, he barely said two words. It was as if he had buried all of his questions and curiosity about life along with his father, and that worried Rachel.

She felt so uncertain of everything now that James was not with her to make the decisions for their family. It was the way of their people that the man of the house made all the major decisions while the woman cared for the children and managed the household. But James wasn't here. This was a decision she had made completely on her own. Maybe she was making a mistake. Maybe Justin would be better off living close to his cousins and grandparents even if Luke insisted on taking out his dislike of her on her son.

If she challenged him, Luke excused his strictness by telling her that Justin needed the strong hand of a man now that James was no longer around to guide him. He had actually laughed at her the first time she'd worked up the nerve to express her concern. "You and my brother have always been far too easy on the boy. He will not thank you for it when he is grown," he'd warned. "Do not question my authority here, Rachel. You are too much tied to the ways of those outsiders you work with."

As she stared out the tinted window of the bus, she could see little but the reflected lights of passing cars on the highway and the silhouettes of buildings in the distance. She searched the eastern sky for the first signs of the new day and saw only darkness. It was in these blackest hours before dawn that Rachel thought most often of James.

Of course, in the weeks that immediately followed his death, she had thought of little else. How could she possibly go on without him? They had known each other all their lives. Her parents had raised chickens just up the road from where James and his family had their dairy farm. She and her siblings had walked to school with James and his siblings. Her brother had married one of his sisters. The two families had joined forces numerous times to register the hallmarks of their lives—holidays, weddings, births, and deaths.

James had never been sick a day in his nearly forty years. Even the normal childhood illnesses like measles or mumps had passed him by. He had been a tall man with a kind of gauntness to his body and features. After they had married and he had let his beard grow out, more than one person had commented on his resemblance to Abraham Lincoln. It was a comparison that James found flattering in spite of the Mennonite call to avoid such compliments. More than once when he seemed to puff up a bit after someone made the comparison, Rachel had teased him that she might buy him a stovepipe hat like the one that President Lincoln had worn.

Oh, they had laughed together about so many things. And they had cried together as well. After she had miscarried four times, James had held her close, the tears leaking slowly down the burnished plains of his face. "God has a plan for us, darling girl."

And then their prayers had finally been answered with the arrival of Justin. "I'll never ask for anything again," Rachel had vowed.

But James had placed his fingers against her lips, shushing her. "That's a promise you cannot keep. God is with us," he told her. "You can ask."

She had prayed every day since the funeral for God's guidance. Then Hester's letter had arrived, and here they were less than two weeks later on their way to Florida. Of course, Hester was already way ahead of her.

"Malcolm and his wife have a guest cottage on their property that they never use," Hester had told Rachel when she called a week earlier. "They'd be willing to rent it to you. It's small but it's only half a mile from the hospital. As soon as you get here we can take a look at that, and I'll check on other possibilities as well."

"What about a school for Justin?"

"If you decide to rent the Shepherds' guesthouse, he can walk to the public school I told you about. The Shepherds' daughter, Sally, attends classes there, so that will give him someone to know right away. I know public school is not ideal, but the main thing is to get you both down here. Once you get into the routine of work and school and such, we can look at other options— hopefully something closer to Pinecraft."

"I don't know about this, Hester. Mr. Shepherd is on the hospital board and—"

Hester had laughed. "He's on half a dozen boards around Sarasota, including the one here at the co-op, but don't let that intimidate you. Malcolm and his wife, Sharon, are salt-of-the-earth people, Rachel. And as for Sally—I mean, you are going to love her. She'll introduce Justin to a host of friends in no time, so that's a plus."

"It would be nice for him to have a friend right away," Rachel had said.

Hester actually squealed with delight. Her obvious excitement was contagious. "Do you believe this? You are coming to Florida."

Rachel laughed. "You seem to have everything arranged."

"Just get here. We're going to have such fun getting you and Justin settled. Having you near will be like old times when we were back in college."

Except our lives have changed. We have changed, Rachel thought. But she'd been unwilling to dampen Hester's enthusiasm with her doubts. "We'll be there this time a week from tomorrow," Rachel had promised.

"John and I will meet the bus. I can't wait for the two of you to meet."

As the bus rolled on she caught sight of a sign welcoming them to Florida. She glanced down at her sleeping son. He had said little about the move, but she knew him so well. She understood that he was not happy about leaving his friends and the familiar routine of the farm and family—even his uncle—to strike out for the unknown. Truth be told, she had no idea if she had just made the best or worst decision of her life.

She wished James were there to reassure them both.

Chapter 3

D r. Benjamin Booker stood outside the front entrance of Gulf Coast Medical Center, marveling at the twists and turns his life had taken to bring him to this moment. As the son of a small-town preacher, he'd been raised with the idea that he would follow in his father's footsteps into the ministry. But ironically it was his father's example that had made Ben run as far and as fast as he could from that career.

Instead Ben had excelled in the sciences, eventually earning a free ride to one of the best premed programs in the country. His goal had been simple. He would get his medical degree and then go overseas to bring his healing skills to the malnourished and suffering children he'd seen as a boy on the TV news. He was going to go out into the world and not mouth the words his father preached, but do his best to put his faith to the test by offering real solutions.

But then he'd gotten seduced by the opportunities that came his way after he'd completed his training. In those early days when he'd gone to work for Sarasota Memorial, the teaching hospital, he'd told himself that the post was temporary. That he needed to hone his skills, learn everything he could before he tried to save the world. But that year had lengthened into two, then four, then eight. . . .

Then a group of local civic leaders had seen the need for a hospital that placed a major focus on both treatment and research on the illnesses of children. His younger sister, Sharon, and his brother-in-law, Malcolm, had been the driving force behind the movement to get the hospital built. But it had been their freckle-faced daughter, Sally, who had persuaded Ben to make the change. "What if all those poor, sick, and injured children in faraway places could be brought here?" she'd asked. "You could treat them right here where you'd have everything you need."

Now as he watched the construction workers finish mounting the sign at the front of the hospital, he thought about Sally's powers of persuasion and smiled.

"Here's the way I see it, Uncle Ben," she had said one day two summers earlier as they tossed a ball back and forth on the lush front yard of Malcolm and Sharon's large home. "It's pretty clear that you're married to your work so I've given up all hope of helping you find romance. On top of that, Mom and Dad are determined to get this hospital built, and that means that once it's up and running with their name on little brass plates all over the place, they have no choice but to take me there for my medical stuff. You're my pediatrician, so you do the math."

Ben had laughed. "You're the healthiest kid I ever met, not to mention the most precocious." He'd crouched into a catcher's position and pounded his glove. "Now let me see if you've got anything resembling a decent curveball."

A week later Sally had come home complaining of pain in her leg. They'd been tossing the ball back and forth that day as well. When the pain hadn't gone away over the next few days, Ben had suggested that Sharon bring his niece to the hospital. "Routine blood tests," he had assured her. "I want to rule out anything more sinister than a strained muscle or torn ligament."

"I have a game on Tuesday," Sally had reminded him. "I'm pitching."

"Good thing it's not your pitching arm that's causing you trouble, then," Ben had teased. The two of them had bantered back and forth in this way from the time Sally had been six or seven. Ben had been the one Sally had come to when she needed to persuade her mother that playing on an all-boy baseball team was not going to be a problem.

"I'm eleven years old—not exactly a baby." She'd sighed, although at the time she'd been a couple of months shy of that birthday. Still she had a point. As the only child of two well-educated and superactive parents, Sally spent far more time in the company of adults than she did with kids her own age. Being on the baseball team around kids her own age would be good for her.

"Talk to her, please?" she had pleaded.

"I'll talk to your mom," Ben had promised. "But maybe your dad. . ."

Sally had rolled her eyes. "Ever so much more of a problem," she moaned.

The blood tests had come back with the worst possible news. Sally had leukemia and not the *good* kind, if there was such a thing. No, Sally did not have the strain that was 90 percent curable in children her age. Against all the prototypes for the disease, she had been diagnosed with AML—acute myelogenous leukemia. And so their journey had begun with all of its peaks and valleys.

So Sally was no longer the healthiest kid he knew. For more than a year she had spent most of her time in hospitals receiving treatments and living among other children battling childhood illnesses of varying degrees of seriousness. Once the standard treatment regimen of chemotherapy and radiation failed—not once but twice—their only option had been a bone marrow transplant. For the transplant she had gone to a clinic in Tampa that specialized in such procedures. To her credit her spirits had remained high, and she had stayed in touch with friends via Skype and of course, the cell phone that she used incessantly to text back and forth with her friends.

It had been six months now since the transplant and in a few days Sally would head back to school for the first time in over a year.

"I cannot wait to get back to school," she had announced a couple of days earlier when Ben had stopped at his sister's for lunch. "It seems like forever."

"You're sure you're ready for that?" Ben didn't need to remind her that for many transplant patients the recovery time was more like a year than the six months it would be for her by the time the school year started. But even he had to admit that her recovery had been remarkable and unquestionable. Her blood tests consistently came back in the normal range and showed that the graft was helping her to recover the healthy cells and immune system that had been so compromised by the disease.

Sally had rolled her eyes and glanced toward the kitchen where her mom was preparing lunch. "Please do not let Mom hear you asking that. If she had her way I'd be kept in isolation until I'm like twenty-five."

Ben laughed. "She's not that bad, and she worries about you."

"I know. But you cannot imagine how wonderful *normal* sounds to me right about now."

"Just don't push it, okay?"

In many ways Sally's illness had pushed them all to make building the new hospital a reality. Now, standing outside the front doors, Ben shook off the memory of that horrifying journey. The construction team hoisted and attached stainless steel letters that spelled out the new hospital's name. He closed his eyes. If he were a man given to prayer, this would no doubt be a good time to offer a silent one for the skill and wisdom to heal the patients—some of them like Sally—that he would treat here. Certainly his sister would encourage that. Her unwavering faith so like their father's had kept her amazingly calm in the face of Sally's diagnosis and everything that followed. But Ben did not share his sister's brand of blind faith.

As the crew secured the last letter into place, a city bus swung onto the circular drive, forcing Ben to take a step back. The first person off the bus was a woman he would guess to be in her mid-to-late thirties. She wore an ankle-length green print dress with three-quarter-length sleeves, the traditional white-starched prayer covering of the Mennonite faith, and in spite of the heat and humidity, a thin black sweater over her shoulders. She paused for a moment while the other passengers made their way around her and on into the hospital. She closed her eyes and bowed her head.

Assuming that she had come to visit a patient in the hospital, he moved a step closer and waited for her to finish. "May I help you?" he asked.

He saw her take in his white lab coat, his glasses perched on top of his thick black hair, and his stethoscope jammed in a pocket of the lab coat.

"*Nein, danke,*" she said then shook her head and smiled. "Sorry. No thank you, Doctor. It's pretty clear that I have come to the right place." She indicated the stainless steel letters of the sign glimmering in the sunlight. "If you would please excuse me, I don't want to be late for my first day."

He could not help noticing that while her smile was certainly sincere, there was something about the way it didn't quite light up her features that made him reluctant to let her go. He knew that look. He had seen it in the eyes of his sister and brother-in-law and countless others when he'd given them a difficult diagnosis and again over the long months as treatment after treatment had failed. It was a look of deep sadness.

"You work here?" he asked.

"I am to be part of the spiritual care department," she said. "I am Rachel Kaufmann."

Ben grinned, remembering the voice over the telephone, the way her speech had been slightly formal, her tone soft and yet confident. "We've met," he told her. He noted that her eyes were a remarkable shade of violet, like Elizabeth Taylor's. They widened in surprise.

"I believe you are mistaken," she said politely. "I just arrived in Sarasota on Friday."

"Ben Booker." Ben extended his hand and then wondered if her culture would permit her to shake it. He saw her hesitation and instead waved his hand toward the entrance. "I was part of the committee that interviewed you by phone."

"Oh, you were the late one," she blurted and then covered her mouth in embarrassment. "I am so sorry," she murmured.

"Never apologize for being right. I was running late that day as it appears you are today." He glanced at his watch. "How about I show you the way to the chaplain's office? You're going to enjoy working with Paul Cox—the man is quite something."

He started toward the entrance. After a few seconds she caught up to him. "I can ask for directions inside," she said. "You must be busy."

"I'm scheduled to start rounds with the pediatric residents in ten minutes. Come on. Pastor Cox's office is on my way." He waited for her to enter ahead of him and knew the exact moment when she realized that although they had moved inside she was standing in a tropical garden. She took a moment to appreciate the ferns and bromeliads and orchids surrounding the waterfall that cascaded over boulders and then settled into a calm pool featuring several large koi fish.

"Our design team may have gotten a little carried away," he said, aware that for a woman of her faith such opulence might be troubling

"Oh no," she said, her voice barely audible against the noise of the splashing water. "The children will love it. Are those real butterflies?"

"They are," Ben assured her, and this time when she smiled at him, that smile reached her eyes, softening them into violet pools. Flustered to have had such a poetic thought, he pretended interest in the design of the hospital's reception area. "It's pretty neat, isn't it?"

"It's wonderful," she replied. "And such a welcoming place for the children—and other patients—to begin their journey if they must travel this road." She smiled at him. "It's certainly going to be a pleasure coming to work every day."

"My feelings exactly. Now let's get you to Pastor Paul's office."

He led the way down a wide corridor, greeting other members of the staff and nodding to patients and their families along the way. Rachel matched him step for step, her sensible shoes a far cry from the platform heels or wedged sandals his sister wore. He was aware that those they passed were curious about this woman in her plain dress complete with the traditional prayer covering of her faith. But Rachel seemed not to notice, and he wondered if she had simply grown used to being stared at.

"Have you found a place to live yet?" he asked as they turned a corner and started down another long corridor.

"Right now we're staying with my friends Hester and John Steiner. After I finish work today Hester is going to take us to see the guesthouse on Mr. Shepherd's property. It would be convenient—an easy walk or bus ride to the hospital."

"Malcolm is married to my sister," Ben told her. "Want me to put in a good word for you?" He grinned to let her know he was teasing her and was charmed by the way her cheeks turned a shade rosier than their normal pink. But he also saw the shadow of a frown furrow her brow. "Hey, I was kidding."

"I know. It's just. . ." She shook off the thought. "You must have much better things to do than play the role of tour guide for me, Dr. Booker."

"Ben," he corrected. "We're a pretty casual group here. No standing on ceremony, at least behind the scenes."

"So it will be Dr. Booker when we're with patients and Ben when we're with other staff," she said. "Very well. And I am Rachel."

"Before when you mentioned my sister's guesthouse, you said 'we.' It's none of my business of course," he hurried to add.

"Not at all. I have a twelve-year-old son, Justin."

"That's right. You mentioned him on the phone." He recalled that she had also mentioned the death of her husband. "How's your son doing with this big change?"

The sad wariness he'd first noticed in her eyes was back. "He'll be fine. He needs some time." She glanced at the nameplate next to Paul Cox's closed door. "Ah, this must be the place. Thank you, Ben, for making me feel so welcome."

"My pleasure." He reached around to open the door for her. "Hello, Eileen," he said to the woman who looked up from her work as they entered. "Eileen, this is Rachel Kaufmann. Rachel, Eileen Walls."

"Oh, hello, dear," Eileen gushed as she came around the desk and took Rachel's hand between both of hers. She was shorter than Rachel and dressed in an orange knit pantsuit that strained across her ample bosom and hips. She had always reminded Ben of his grandmother. "We have so been looking forward to meeting you in person. Pastor Cox is especially delighted to have you on staff."

"Thank you," Rachel replied.

"Is Paul in?" Ben asked.

Eileen glanced at a large wall clock. "He should be completing his morning rounds." She turned her attention to Rachel. "He likes to see those patients facing surgery or procedures first thing."

She took hold of Rachel's hand and patted it. "Oh, it is going to be so nice having you here with us. You're going to fit in just fine."

Eileen had nothing to base that statement on, and yet Ben could see that Rachel understood that this sweet matronly woman was trying to put her at ease. "I hope so," Rachel replied.

"Well, I'll leave you in Eileen's capable hands," Ben said as he turned to go. "I'm looking forward to working with you, Rachel."

"Danke—I mean, thank you for everything."

Ben smiled. "You're welcome."

He had retraced his steps down the hall when he saw Darcy Meekins coming his way. She was walking fast in spite of her three-inch heels, her cell phone to her ear as she balanced a notebook filled with papers that she was shuffling through.

"Well, I don't have it, Mark," she said curtly. "Never mind." She pulled a single sheet from the stack. "Got it." She ended the call and glanced up. When she saw Ben, her demeanor changed. She smiled and slowed her pace, clutching her binder of papers to her chest. "Are you lost, Dr. Booker?" she teased.

Ben chuckled. "That wouldn't be hard in this place. How about you?"

"Oh, I'm running fifteen minutes behind schedule. Paul wanted me to come down so we could go over everything with the new hire."

"You're in luck. Paul's also running behind. I left Rachel with Eileen."

"So what did you think of her?"

Ben shrugged. "She's nice."

"Well, I mean, no one has actually seen her," Darcy said.

"Oh, you want to know what she *looks* like? Well, let's see, other than the two heads and the single eye in the center of her forehead. . ."

"You know what I mean."

"Not really. I'd say the adage 'what you see'—or in her case, 'heard over the phone'—is pretty much what you get."

Darcy frowned. Of everyone on the search committee she had been the only one to express strong doubts about hiring Rachel Kaufmann. Even when Paul Cox had pointed out that, of all the applicants they were considering, Rachel's background and years working as a nurse and even her limited counseling experience topped the other two candidates who were fresh out of college, Darcy had insisted they offer the position to another person. Only after that candidate had turned it down, citing the fact that he had already accepted another job, did Darcy agree to make the offer to Rachel.

"Hey, give her a chance. It's her first day and frankly—"

"She's different in so many ways. I mean she's not from here, and she's Mennonite—as in *serious* Mennonite. I looked it up—the different groups, and she's from what's called *Old Order*—very conservative and strict. We have to keep in mind that our patients run the gamut of the religious spectrum."

"Well, granted I was only with her a short time, but I have to say she doesn't strike me as someone on a mission to convert anyone." He touched Darcy's arm. "Look, you protected the hospital's interests when you insisted on a four-month probation while she gets her state certification. If she doesn't work out, you can let her go."

This reminder seemed to give Darcy some comfort. She lowered her voice. "Oh, don't mind me. The stress gets to me sometimes. I need to make sure that this place succeeds in a market already crowded with other facilities." She smiled apologetically. "You know what a worrier I am. How about meeting me after work for a pizza? We could decompress."

"I'll take a rain check," Ben said. "I promised Sally that I'd bring over Chinese. The kid is counting the days until she can be out in the world again."

"But until that day, you insist on bringing the world to her, right? You spoil that child shamelessly," Darcy said, but he understood that she was really praising him.

"Don't have kids of my own to spoil, and Sally's the only niece I've got."

"There's a remedy for that," Darcy teased. "You could settle down and get married, and have a house filled with kids."

"Like you, I'm already married to my work." He checked his watch. "Have to run. I'm holding you to that pizza," he called as he turned the corner.

Chapter 4

Darcy Meekins had fallen hard for Ben Booker the first time she met him. He wasn't like many of the other doctors she'd known over the course of her career as she worked her way up the administrative ladder of hospital management. All too often the medical degree seemed to come with an attitude of authority. Darcy thought of it as the I'm-the-doctor-and-you're-not syndrome.

But Ben Booker was different. He wore his medical expertise as a responsibility, not an entitlement. He respected the contributions that others could make. It didn't matter to him if he was dealing with the security guard on duty in the lobby after hours or one of the aides who provided more than half the actual hands-on care a patient received during a hospital stay. He showed them the same consideration as he did any of his professional colleagues. Ben was an equal-opportunity guy when it came to his curiosity about others. That only added to his appeal for Darcy. She wasn't used to being around men who cared what others thought—especially the women in their lives.

Her father had been a bully of the first order, always ordering others around, making fun of their failures, and taking personal credit for their successes.

But Ben was not anything like her father, and Darcy could only imagine how he must have charmed the Mennonite woman. In the course of a walk from the hospital entrance to the chaplain's office, he would have put her completely at ease. To that end, Darcy supposed that she owed him a debt of gratitude. Putting people at ease was not her strong suit.

As Ben had pointed out, they were both workaholics. They spent hours together in meetings when the hospital was being built. Before the hospital food service was up and running, they had shared meals and coffee at a local neighborhood café. They had never had an actual date, but Darcy had high hopes that now that the hospital was open and fully staffed, that would change. Her invitation for pizza had been her first step in a targeted campaign to take her business relationship with Ben to another—more personal—level.

The door to the office for spiritual care services was ajar. She could hear Paul Cox's assistant, Eileen Walls, laughing. She tapped on the door and then entered the reception area. "Hello, Eileen," she said before turning her attention to Rachel. "I'm Darcy Meekins, hospital administrator." She extended her hand to the woman dressed in the garb of her faith. "And you must be the newest member of our team."

"Yes. Rachel. Rachel Kaufmann. I'm so glad to meet you in person," the woman replied, pumping Darcy's hand once and then releasing it.

"I've been filling her in while we wait for Pastor Paul to get here," Eileen explained. "That man needs three clocks to keep him on schedule." She sighed.

"I'm here," a male voice boomed as Paul Cox came huffing his way through the door. He was a large man in both height and weight, and with his bushy gray hair and his pulpit voice, he had a way of filling up whatever space might be left in the small room of the outer office.

Eileen made the introductions, and Darcy saw by Rachel's broad smile that she was not any more immune to the minister's charisma than anyone she'd ever seen him meet had been.

"Now aren't you just a breath of sunshine," he exclaimed as

he smiled down at Rachel. "It's got to be ninety degrees out there and here you are looking fresh as a daisy."

Darcy stifled a groan. Paul Cox was given to clichés. It was part of the aw-shucks folksy persona that had made him so successful in his previous position at Sarasota Memorial Hospital before Ben persuaded him to jump ship and head up the team at Gulf Coast. Paul opened the door to his office and stepped aside to allow Rachel and her to enter ahead of him. "Hold any calls, Eileen," he said, "unless. . ."

"How many years have I been working for you, Pastor Paul?" Eileen said sweetly.

Paul chuckled and gently closed the door. "Have a seat, ladies. Can I get anyone anything? Glass of water? How about a peppermint candy?" He indicated a covered dish on his desk filled with individually wrapped candies.

Darcy was impatient to get down to business. She had another meeting in twenty minutes. She checked her watch and was a little annoyed that Rachel accepted the offer of water. But then Darcy glanced at her and realized the woman was nervous. And why not? Rachel Kaufmann had accepted a job by phone from over a thousand miles away and was only now facing the realities of that decision.

"So, Rachel, how was your flight?" Paul asked as he handed her the water then sat down in the swivel chair behind his desk.

"We did not make the trip on an airplane," Rachel said after swallowing a sip of the water. "We came on the bus."

"My goodness, that must have taken days," Paul exclaimed. "Have you had some time to rest up and get settled into—where are you living now?"

Rachel smiled. "My son and I arrived on Friday. We are staying with friends. We had the weekend to rest."

"That's right. Hester Steiner mentioned you were going to bunk in with her and John when I was there last week for the co-op board meeting. All settled in then?"

"Our stay with the Steiners is temporary. Tonight Hester is taking me to look at a cottage that Mr. Shepherd has for rent."

"Malcolm Shepherd?" Darcy asked, her attention now

riveted on this quiet-spoken woman, surprised that she had already connected with Ben Booker and Malcolm Shepherd. She felt a familiar tingle of alarm. Darcy had worked hard to establish herself in a career where she was in charge, where she reported only to the board of trustees. She was fiercely protective of that position. It had taken her some time to win the respect and support of Malcolm Shepherd, the president of the hospital's board of directors.

Now this woman was possibly going to be living next door to him? On his property?

"You've met Malcolm?" she asked while at the same time assuring herself that Rachel with her prayer cap and her hands now folded piously in her lap was of no possible threat to her.

Rachel smiled. "Only in the way I met both you and Dr. Booker before now. By the telephone interview. It is my friend Hester Steiner who has made the arrangements for me to see the guesthouse on Mr. Shepherd's property."

"Excellent," Paul boomed. "You'll be close to the hospital. We do have emergencies and as the new kid on the block, those will most likely come your way." He arched an eyebrow as if waiting to see how this bit of information would be received.

"That would be fine," Rachel replied and smiled. "What are my other duties?"

"As I mentioned on the phone I want you to focus on the cases that come through our pediatrics wing while I handle the adult cases," he said. "Right now we have more adult patients than children, so you'll have some time to get your bearings. Anyway, I'm taking you at your word."

Obviously confused, Rachel looked up at him and then at Darcy.

"You said on the phone that you liked working with children," Paul reminded her. "And now that I've met you in person I think you might be exactly the right person for the job."

Darcy opened her mouth to object. Paul was getting ahead of himself. He could not possibly know if this woman had the special skills necessary to minister to children and their parents without at least supervising her work initially. He was already handing Rachel a folder and a pager.

"You'll need to wear this pager or have it handy even when you aren't actually here at the hospital. If a kid comes in during the night or on the weekend, this thing will buzz." He pushed a button to demonstrate. "You'll see a number on the screen, and you'll need to call that as soon as possible."

"I believe you mentioned that you had a child, Rachel." Darcy felt the need to remind Paul that he should proceed more slowly here.

"Yes. Justin." Rachel's smile brightened in exactly the same way that practically every mother Darcy had ever met came alive at the mention of her child—every mother that was, except hers.

"And you are a single parent?"

The smile faltered. "*Ja.*"

Darcy could feel Paul's eyes on her. "We are sorry for your loss, Rachel," he said. Then turning his full attention back to the business at hand, he indicated the folder he'd handed her. "I took the liberty of putting together some information I thought might be useful in helping you get up to speed. Well, actually, Eileen put the information together at my request," he admitted with a disarming chuckle. "That woman is my right arm. You need anything and can't find me? Ask Eileen."

Rachel opened the folder and removed the top item—a two-page stapled paper entitled "Role of a Spiritual Care Counselor at Gulf Coast Medical Center."

"Paul, I wonder if I might have a copy of that," Darcy asked, indicating the paper Rachel was scanning.

"Sure." He turned and shouted, "Eileen."

The door opened. "You have an intercom," his assistant reminded him.

"You know me and technical stuff," he said with a boyish grin. "Can you make Darcy a copy of that?"

Rachel quickly scanned the paper before handing it to Eileen and turning her attention back to Paul. "It all looks fine," she said. "I'm certain to have questions as we get started."

"Well, of course you will," Paul agreed. "And either Eileen or I will be right here to answer them. Maybe for the first few days we should plan to have lunch together."

"I'd like that—I would really appreciate it. Clearly I have a lot to learn."

"You'll do fine."

Darcy glanced between them, wondering for a moment if they thought she'd left the room. She stood up. "I have another appointment. It was nice meeting you in person, Rachel. Welcome to Gulf Coast."

Rachel stood as well. "Thank you," she said. "Thank you both so much for giving me this opportunity."

"Now, Rachel, it's you we should be thanking," Paul said. "Isn't that right, Darcy?" He walked her to the door.

Darcy shot him a look of warning. Rachel was a new employee on probation. Statements like that could make it harder down the road if they needed to let her go. "We'll talk later," she said.

But Paul just patted her shoulder in that paternal way he had. "She's going to do fine," he replied as he took the papers Eileen handed him. He gave the copy to Darcy and carried the original back inside his office to hand to Rachel.

Darcy felt dismissed as the office door closed behind him, and yet she had been the one to end the meeting. *No, it wasn't that I felt dismissed,* she thought as she hurried off to her next appointment. *Left out.* That was it. As if once more in her life she had done all the right things and still she did not feel part of the inner circle.

Rachel and Paul had connected almost on sight. Darcy had never in her life known that kind of instant connection—not with school friends, not with her college roommates, not with co-workers, not even with her own family.

Rachel's first day on the job was flying by. After her meeting with Darcy and Paul, Eileen had guided her to the Human Resources department where Mark Boynton had taken her through the details of being an employee at Gulf Coast.

"There's a dress code," he had said at one point, and then he'd looked up at her and his cheeks had turned a fiery red. "You'll be fine," he amended before turning his attention back to the employee handbook that he had insisted on going over page by page.

There were papers to sign followed by a tour of the entire facility that left her head spinning. So many corridors. So many people coming and going in all directions. So much suffering on the cancer wing and then utter joy when they walked through the maternity wing. There she witnessed a man in the midst of a throng of well-wishers in the waiting room as he held up his phone to show pictures of his newborn child. They passed two hospital rooms occupied by mothers nursing their babies.

"Children's wing is across this skywalk," Mark told her. "Patients who come here as well as friends and family have their own separate chapel." He opened the door to a small room that took her breath away.

The chapel he'd shown her in the main part of the hospital had been generic, with stained glass windows in a geometric design that lined the two side walls. The front of the room was furnished with a small lectern and a simple wooden table that held a vase of fresh flowers. The rest of the carpeted room had been furnished with three rows of chairs—four chairs per row to each side of a center aisle. The low-level lighting created an atmosphere of peace and quiet, a haven to escape the noise, bright lights, and fast-paced activity outside the double cypress doors.

But, although it was also a small room, the children's chapel was filled with natural light from a trio of frosted skylights above and windows that looked out onto the manicured grounds of the medical center's campus all around. The floor was tile interrupted by two circles of bright-colored square cushions.

"The children who are able to do so will sit on the cushions," Mark explained. "Those gaps in between are for children in wheelchairs. Those chairs against the walls are for times like Christmas when we might have a special program, or they could be used for a memorial service if necessary. The room will be used for multiple purposes." He pointed to a second door. "In there is a room where family and friends can get away if they need to cry or pray or simply escape the clamor," he explained.

"It's wonderful," Rachel told him. "Thank you so much for taking the time to show me around."

Mark smiled. "Hey, from what I hear this is where you're likely to spend a good amount of your time." He led the way back into the children's area and opened a narrow door concealed as part of the wall. "Locked storage for whatever you might want to keep here," he said, taking out a plastic bag that held a clown's red rubber nose and a chartreuse frizzy wig. "Pastor Paul's," he explained. "He sometimes wears them when he's on his rounds." He placed the items back in the closet and closed and locked the door before handing her the key.

On their way out, Rachel couldn't help but notice a small silver plaque that read CHAPEL OF HOPE: A GIFT OF MALCOLM, SHARON, AND SALLY SHEPHERD.

"There's an activity room across the hall here." Mark pointed to an open door, beyond which Rachel could see an area set up with a quartet of computers, an area for crafts, and some colorful plastic toys geared toward toddlers.

"And that's pretty much the grand tour," Mark said. He glanced at his watch. "Oops. I promised to have you back fifteen minutes ago. Eileen wants to get you set up in your office."

Mark made one more stop at the nurses' station and introduced Rachel to the staff on duty. Then as they retraced their steps back through the corridor lined with patients' rooms, they couldn't help noticing that most were empty. "They'll fill up," Mark said as if she had asked. They rounded a corner, and she glanced into a room where a child was watching cartoons. The boy, who could not have been more than seven, glanced over at her, and Rachel smiled and waved at him.

As they approached the entrance to the skywalk, they passed a room where the window blinds were closed. When she looked closer Rachel saw the silhouette of a small body lying in bed surrounded by a network of tubes. The child was linked to a series of machines blinking their neon signals and wheezing their rhythmic codes. She could barely make out the form of a woman sitting by the bedside, her head resting on her hand.

Rachel's longing to stop and offer the woman some comfort

was huge, but Mark was already several steps ahead of her. The one thing that Rachel had grasped after the two hours she had spent with this young man was that a hospital this large had rules and routines—*protocol*, Mark called it. It would not do to start following her instincts—at least not until she had learned those guidelines.

Back in the spiritual care department, Eileen showed her to a small cubicle next to the reception desk. There was already a nameplate on the cloth wall of the divider that read RACHEL KAUFMANN, CHILD LIFE SPECIALIST.

"That's your new title," Eileen explained when she saw that Rachel had paused to study the sign. "Human Resources seems to have this need to keep reinventing labels for what people do around here. Pay it no mind. When the rubber meets the road, you are a chaplain, just like Paul Cox is."

"But Pastor Cox is an ordained minister and board certified." Rachel remembered the neatly framed degrees and certification documents she'd noticed on the wall of Paul's office.

"Thus his position as senior chaplain. The bottom line is that we all work from the same basic creed—you, Paul, and even me." She pointed to a framed poster on the wall, entitled OUR MISSION.

Rachel stepped closer to read it.

> The spiritual care services of Gulf Coast Medical Center provide support and comfort that respects the full diversity of spiritual values to our patients, the family and friends of those patients, and to members of our staff twenty-four hours a day, 365 days a year.

Eileen reached around her and picked up a laminated bookmark from a clear plastic holder on the counter. She handed the bookmark to Rachel, who saw that it repeated the mission statement and also included information for contacting members of their staff when needed.

"That's impressive," Rachel said.

"And ambitious, especially when it looked like maybe it

would be Paul doing all the work. But you're here now," she added brightly. "Come check out your cubicle and let me know if you need anything in the way of supplies or a different chair or more storage above the desk. Anything at all."

Rachel stepped into the small space and opened the top drawer of a two-drawer file cabinet. It had already been stocked with hanging file folders in a rainbow of colors. She opened one of the overhead bins above her desk. There she found legal pads, pens, a stapler and staple remover, scissors, paper clips, and notepads in a variety of sizes. There was a telephone with an intimidating row of buttons in addition to the usual numerical keypad. And all the while she tried to ignore the computer that dominated the corner where her built-in desk wrapped itself past the window and onto the solid wall. She knew the basics of how to use a computer. In the school system she had been responsible for inserting data, but beyond that she wasn't exactly computer savvy.

"Do not ask me to explain why they would situate your computer and chair so that you are looking out into daylight. Talk about a headache in the making." Eileen frowned, but then she took a step closer to the window and her features softened. "On the other hand, it is a lovely view with the serenity garden and all."

"It's very nice," Rachel assured her.

Eileen pulled her gaze away from the tropical scene outside and glanced around. "Well, I'll leave you to it. Paul wants to meet with you at noon. And then somebody from I.T. will be by at four to finish setting up your phone and computer."

"I.T.?"

"Information Technology. The computer and phone geeks."

"I see."

"There's coffee and tea behind the counter in my space. If you need anything, give me a shout." Her warm brown eyes sparkled with merriment as she indicated the open space above the cloth-covered divider separating them. "I'm right over the fence here."

"Thank you, Eileen. Thank you for everything."

For the next hour Rachel busied herself getting settled in.

She rearranged the supplies to her liking and could not help but wonder if she would ever have enough files to fill up even one, much less both of the file drawers. A volunteer from the hospital gift shop stopped by to deliver a dish garden filled with a variety of living plants. Rachel opened the florist's card and read the typed message: *From everyone at Gulf Coast Medical Center, WELCOME!*

As she worked, she was comforted by the sounds of Eileen attending to her duties. Paul's assistant answered phone calls, dealt with two or three people who came looking for Paul, and in between seemed to be constantly tapping away at the keyboard of her computer.

Rachel had started to read through the materials in the folder that Paul Cox had given her during their first meeting when Eileen said, "Call for you, Rachel. I'll send it over."

Rachel stared at the red light blinking on her phone. "What do I do?" she asked.

"Pick it up," Eileen instructed. "It looks complicated, but it's really just a telephone."

"Hello," Rachel said tentatively.

"Well, hello yourself." Her friend Hester chuckled. "Are you supposed to greet me with something official like 'This is Rachel Kaufmann, Hospital Chaplain' or whatever your title is?"

Rachel couldn't seem to stifle the kind of girlish giggle the two friends had exchanged when they'd been roommates. "My title, I'll have you know, is *child life specialist*," she said, keeping her voice down even though Eileen seemed to be completely occupied with her typing.

"Well, get you," Hester teased, then her tone shifted. "How's it really going?"

"Too fast. I mean the morning has flown by and it's been a whirlwind of meetings and touring the hospital and getting my office space set up." She turned to look out the window. "How's Justin doing? I wanted to call, but I'm not sure if I'm allowed to do that yet." She had lowered her voice to almost a whisper.

"Justin seems fine. John put him to work in the packinghouse getting everything cleaned up and ready for the new season. He's a quiet one, isn't he?"

He didn't used to be, Rachel thought. "He's been through a lot." She glanced at the wall clock and saw that she had only five minutes before her meeting with Paul Cox. "I have to go, Hester."

"Understood. How about I bring Justin and come by to pick you up at the front entrance at five so we can go meet Sharon Shepherd and see the cottage."

"Ja, and Hester?"

"Ja?"

"Thank you so much."

"You don't need to keep thanking me, Rachel," Hester told her. "It's the least I can do after everything you and Justin have been through. See you at five."

The line went dead at the same time that Rachel heard Paul Cox enter the office. "Is she in?" he asked even as he bypassed Eileen's desk and tapped on the metal edge of Rachel's cubicle. "We've got an emergency," he said. "Want to come along and see how this works?"

Paul did not wait for an answer as he headed back out the door and then down the corridor toward the skywalk that led to the children's wing. "I hope you don't get queasy at the sight of blood," he added grimly as he turned down a hallway then strode through a set of double doors that marked the entrance to the emergency room for the children's wing.

Chapter 5

Ben took one look at the boy's arm and knew it was going to take a miracle to save it. At least the arm had not been ripped entirely off. Shark attacks were extremely rare, but when one did strike, the outcome usually always favored the shark. In this case the amazing thing was that the kid still had his arm. Ben was grateful for the team of nurses and specialists surrounding him as he worked to get the boy stabilized so that they could move him on to surgery as soon as possible. Mercifully the kid was pretty much out of it and probably wouldn't remember all the blood loss and pain he was suffering.

A man and woman stood in the doorway as if frozen into a state of disbelief. *The parents.* It was hard to offer reassurance with the better part of his face covered by a surgical mask, but Ben felt the need to make an attempt. He glanced over at the couple, and the father met his look and nodded. Then the man murmured something to his wife. Her wails of panic and fear settled into shuddering sobs.

"Did somebody call for Paul Cox?" he asked the nurse working next to him.

"On his way."

Ben turned his attention back to his work. He gathered

information about vital signs and loss of blood even as he issued orders for what would be needed in surgery. When his colleague and the best orthopedic surgeon in southwest Florida, Jess Wilson, came through the double doors and scanned the chart an aide held for him, Ben let out a breath of relief.

The pneumatic doors swung closed behind Jess but not before Ben saw three other teens still wet, wearing their T-shirts and surfing shorts. They were sitting on the edge of a row of plastic chairs, their hands dangling helplessly between their knees, their gangly bodies seeming too large for the chairs.

"How could this happen?" the mother moaned, drawing Ben's attention back to the job of prepping the kid for surgery. "He was supposed to be at Todd's house," she added, her voice dropping until her tone was that of a lost little girl.

It didn't take much to put the pieces together, Ben thought as he and Jess worked together. Those boys—high school seniors given the age of the kid on the table—had decided to have one last fling before school started in a couple of days. The high, hot west wind that had been building all night would have been all anyone who loved surfing needed to know that the wave action off Lido Key was going to be great. Ben could almost visualize the four of them heading straight for the beach.

"Name?" he murmured to the ER nurse working next to him and nodding toward the boy.

"David Olson," she replied. "Paperwork is done," she added with a glance toward a young woman holding a clipboard out to the father.

Ben pulled down his mask and peeled off his gloves as he approached the parents. "Mr. and Mrs. Olson?"

They lifted dazed glances before Ben went on, "We're going to take David up to surgery," he said even as the medical team unlocked the wheels on the gurney and started rolling it down the corridor. "As soon as there's any news someone will be down to talk with you, okay?"

He really didn't expect an answer. Someone else would take charge of the parents and friends until Paul got there, lead them to the waiting room, offer them coffee, and volunteer to call other family for them. So when Mr. Olson clasped his shoulder, Ben wasn't sure how to react.

"Doc? Can you save his arm?" Olson was a large man, overweight in the way of a former athlete who hadn't kept up with his regimen of exercise. His eyes were full of tears he was fighting to hold at bay, and his voice shook. "See, he's on the basketball team and several colleges have been after him and. . ."

"We're going to do our best, Mr. Olson," Ben said as he gently patted the man's arm. "Just hang in there, okay?"

With relief he saw Paul Cox and the new chaplain enter the waiting area. Paul moved toward the parents, indicating with a nod that his cohort should check on the other teenagers. The gurney was already halfway on the elevator, and the surgeon was holding the door for Ben.

"Got this," Paul said as he stepped between Ben and Mr. Olson. "I'm Paul Cox, hospital chaplain," he said. "Let me show you folks to our family care area. You'll be more comfortable waiting there."

Rachel approached the other boys as Paul led the parents away. She bent down to their level as if she instinctively knew how best to connect with them. As the elevator doors slid shut she glanced up at Ben. For an instant it looked as if she was pleading with him to make things better—not for her but for those boys who had saved their friend. But he would not offer false hope, and he knew she had read the severity of the situation in his expression when she drew in a breath and briefly bowed her head before turning her attention back to the boys.

"I'm sure you did everything you could have done," Rachel said to the boy who had broken down completely and was sobbing into his hands.

"That sucker came out of nowhere," another boy said, shaking his head as if he still couldn't believe it. "I mean one minute we were catching a wave and the next the water was red with Dave's blood and his arm was. . ." He was pacing back and forth.

The third friend remained silent. He was the smallest of the three, and in a way his size made him appear more vulnerable. *Like Justin.* He sat quietly a little apart from his friends and stared at his hands.

"If Todd here hadn't hit that shark with his board," the second boy continued, wheeling around and coming up next to her as he continued his story. "That was amazing, dude. We all froze, but Todd handled it."

Rachel slid onto the empty chair that separated the boy—Todd—from his friends. She placed her hand on his bony shoulder. "You quite possibly saved your friend's life," she told him and silently prayed to God that his life would indeed be saved.

An aide carrying a cardboard tray with cups of orange juice came toward them. "Thank you," Rachel said as she stood up and distributed the juice. All three boys guzzled it down as if they hadn't had liquids in days. All three murmured their thanks as they placed the empty paper cups back on the tray.

"Pastor Paul asked that you bring them to the chapel," the aide told Rachel. "We've called their parents."

"Thank you. Come on, boys." Rachel guided them toward the corridor that led to the chapel and family waiting area. The emergency room was quiet now, and the only sounds were a nurse's rhythmic tapping on a computer keyboard and the squeak of the boys' rubber flip-flops on the polished tile floor.

When they reached the chapel, both Mr. and Mrs. Olson came forward and hugged each boy. Rachel breathed a sigh of relief. She had been afraid that the Olsons might release their own fear by chastising the boys. But when Todd finally broke down and let his tears come, it was Mr. Olson who took him under his wing. "Hey, what's this?" he said. "From what Brent and Jack told us, you saved the day."

"That shark was huge," Todd blubbered.

"You did good, Todd. Whatever happens, you saved our boy," Mr. Olson said as he hugged Todd again.

Over the next couple of hours the family waiting room gradually filled with other family and friends. The parents of the three friends arrived, as did David Olson's coach and the pastor of his church. Paul spoke at length with the minister, and the two men exchanged business cards. Then Paul crossed the room to where Rachel was setting up a makeshift buffet of the snacks, sandwiches, fresh fruit, and soft drinks that Eileen had ordered sent up from the hospital cafeteria.

"Okay," he said, glancing at a young man in scrubs who had come to the room, spoken with the Olsons and Paul and their minister, and was now leaving. "The good news is it looks like the boy's going to make it."

"But?" Rachel said.

"They're working on reattaching his arm and that could take eight to ten hours, assuming they can do it at all." He glanced over to where the Olsons and the boys were seated in the center of a circle of supportive friends and family. "I think things are pretty well in hand here. Why don't we go back to my office and have a late working lunch while we go over your new responsibilities?"

Rachel was reluctant to leave. The truth was she wanted to be there when Ben came from surgery to tell the Olsons how things had gone. Would the surgical team be able to save the boy's arm? Rachel recalled how the floor of the ER had been littered with bloody refuse when David was on his way to the elevator and the operating room. She had never seen so much blood in all her life. "Eight hours more?" she whispered as she looked at the clock in the hall ticking off the seconds.

Paul nodded and thrust his hands into the pockets of his trousers. "We'll check back," he told her. "This is the way it goes sometimes, Rachel. I assure you that the feeling of wanting to do more when there's no more to be done never goes away. But these folks clearly have a strong network of support. They're in good hands."

He waited for her to speak with the Olsons, and then the two of them walked side by side in silence across the skywalk on their way back to the spiritual care department. Rachel could not help noticing how blue the sky was, unmarked by a single cloud. She thought about David and his three friends surfing the waves on this perfect day, never guessing that danger lurked beneath the water's surface.

She thought about Justin. "There are sharks," he had argued when she'd told him about the move to Florida.

"What's a bull shark?" she asked, remembering that one of the nurses had mentioned that species.

"It's a big shark," Paul told her. "Adults average about seven feet long and can weigh close to three hundred pounds. But the real problem is that a bull shark has serrated teeth, and when it bites, it tears. That's what complicates David Olson's chances of coming out with a reattached arm. Hard to put that all back together."

Rachel took a moment to digest the bleak outlook for this boy and his family. "Why would the shark attack?"

Paul shrugged. "It's not done with malice. Usually the problem is that the water is churned up and sharks have poor eyesight. If they see something moving in the water that they can't identify as friend, foe, or food they strike first and ask questions later." He held the door to their offices open for her. "Either way that young man has got a long road ahead of him—physically, emotionally, and spiritually. Good that they are people of strong faith."

Eileen looked up as they entered, her snow-white eyebrows raised in question.

"No news yet," Paul said. "Rachel, call your son. I expect he's on your mind right about now." He walked into his office and closed the door.

"He needs a moment," Eileen explained. "The young ones always hit him hardest." She shook her head and fell silent for a long moment before going on in a quiet voice, "His daughter drowned in a freak swimming accident when she was ten. It's been twenty years, but he still grieves."

"And yet he does this kind of work?"

"Paul feels that it's his calling. In some ways he honors the memory of his daughter by offering comfort to others."

Rachel nodded, understanding all too well how the man felt. "Let me know when he's ready," she said as she sat down at her desk and dialed Hester's number. "Hester? Could I speak to Justin?"

Ben had to give Jess Wilson credit. The man was cocky and abrasive but he was the best surgeon Ben had ever worked with. After six and a half grueling hours, he had secured the final stitch to reattach David Olson's arm. Then he'd snapped off his gloves and pulled down his mask. "He may lose that arm yet, but tell them I've done my best," he said wearily and left the operating room, leaving it to someone else to go and talk with the parents.

The Olsons and their son's friends had been understandably relieved at the news, but it worried Ben that they had also been almost hysterically happy. Ben had tried to caution them that David had months of therapy ahead of him. He doubted that they had grasped what he'd tried to tell them about rehabilitation and the possibility that the boy would never have the full range of motion he had enjoyed before. At least the family's minister seemed to understand that this was only the beginning of a long journey for David and his family.

Due to the length of the surgery, Ben had had to cancel his plans with Sally. Still, he decided to stop by his sister's house. He was bone tired, but even the shower he'd taken in the doctors' locker room had done little to calm him. The intensity of the surgery had left him wired, and he doubted he would be able to settle down to sleep for several hours yet. It was a beautiful night, and sitting around the pool under his sister's screened lanai listening to Sally talk about the upcoming school year would be exactly what he needed.

But when he got to the impressive estate his brother-in-law and sister owned, the bright orange van with the logo for the fruit co-op that Malcolm and Sharon supported and the Steiners managed was parked on the circular drive. Ben wondered if perhaps Malcolm's brother, Zeke, had stopped by.

Zeke worked at the co-op—when he worked at all. He and Malcolm could not have been more different. While Malcolm had taken over the family's multiple business ventures, Zeke had served three tours of duty with the Marines in the Middle East. When he came back the third time, he'd abandoned the comforts of his family's wealth for life on the street. Ben knew that Malcolm had decided to fund the fruit co-op run by Hester and John Steiner in part because it was one way to get Zeke into a situation where he wasn't living hand-to-mouth. Frankly Ben didn't understand Zeke's nonchalance when it came to where he might sleep or get his next meal. Yet Ben couldn't help but admire Zeke—and sometimes he even envied him. After the day he'd had it would be nice to have "no worries," as Zeke was fond of saying.

"Hello?" Ben called as he walked into the front foyer and kicked off his shoes. His sister had white carpeting in the two main downstairs rooms, and she was adamant about the removal of shoes—especially his.

"I don't know what you've been standing in all day," she would say with a shudder. "All those germs."

He had tried pointing out that at the end of the day he always showered and switched to sandals but to no avail. Ever since Sally was first diagnosed with leukemia, his sister had become obsessed with protecting her only child from any danger of infection.

"Hello?" he called out again as he followed the sound of distant conversation through the formal living room with its high ceilings and wall of french doors that opened out onto the expansive deck. For all of Sharon's attempts to make the house and its furnishings formal, there was an open feeling to the place. A lightness that Ben had long ago decided was less about the trappings and more about the people who lived there. Malcolm and Sharon were people who appreciated the many blessings they had received—financially, from Malcolm's father and grandfather as well as his own business astuteness—and they lived by the dedication that with such riches came great responsibility to "share and care," as his sister said so often.

Ben stepped out onto the lanai that screened the large pool area. Across the yard at the end of the path that wound through Sharon's lush gardens stood a cluster of people—his sister, Malcolm, Hester Steiner—who, he decided, must have driven the van over—and the new chaplain. It was little wonder they had not heard his calls. The four of them were standing outside the guesthouse, deep in conversation.

"But that hardly seems fair," he heard Rachel Kaufmann say as he followed the path toward them.

Malcolm shrugged. "Take it or leave it," he said. "It's my final offer."

Hester Steiner sighed. "You may as well stop trying to bargain with him, Rachel. Once Malcolm makes up his mind, there's no changing it."

"Besides," Sharon added, "think of all we stand to gain by having you and your son living here. Justin, is it?"

Rachel nodded. "Ja, *aber*. . .I mean. . ."

"Hester's right," Ben said as he joined the group. "Might as well save yourself some time and give in to whatever they're pushing. My sister and brother-in-law can be two of the most stubborn people I know when it comes to having their way." He grinned at Sharon. "I should know. I grew up with this one and never could win a debate with her once she'd made up her mind."

"But for free? No rent?"

"Just for your probationary period," Malcolm said. "That way if you decide this isn't working out, you and Justin can go back home without obligations tying you down here. And in the meantime, you can check out other possibilities perhaps over in Pinecraft if you think you would be more at home living there. Besides, rules in the neighborhood prohibit us taking in a tenant, so you're saving me some hassle once the neighbors find out you're staying here."

Ben saw Rachel glance back toward the main house where every room was lit up as if to emphasize its sprawling luxury. He thought he saw a hint of a smile play across her lips—a smile that she suppressed as she turned her attention back to Malcolm.

"Very well," she said. "But I insist that Justin and I will tend the gardens."

"Oh Rachel, we have help for that, and you're going to have so much on your plate—work, classes, getting Justin settled." Sharon looked to Hester for support. "You agree, right?"

Now Rachel's smile blossomed in full. "Those are *my* terms," she said.

Malcolm laughed and held out his hand for her to shake, sealing the bargain. "Welcome, Rachel," he said.

"Well, please understand that if things become too difficult, we're right here to help," Sharon added.

"See what I mean?" Ben grinned and wrapped his arm around his sister. "She always has to have the final word."

"Stop that," Sharon said when Ben rubbed her head with his knuckles. "Come on up to the house, Rachel. I have ice cream cake, and I want you to meet our daughter, Sally."

Ben frowned as he followed the others through the garden. He had assumed that his niece was outside with the others, but Sharon's comment made him realize that Sally had been in the house all along. The fact that she had not come running at the sound of his call raised an alarm for him, and he had to wonder if any of them would ever get past that knee-jerk instinct to imagine the worst when it came to Sally's health.

He fell into step with Malcolm as the women went on ahead of them. "How's Sally doing?"

Malcolm glanced toward the house. "Better every day. She's upstairs now—something about needing to get ready for school." He paused for a moment and gazed across the yard at the inviting golden light spilling from the house onto the lawn streaked with the shadows of twilight. "Do you think it's a good idea to send her back to school? I mean, maybe we should wait until second semester—give her a few more months."

Sally's worst fear was that her parents would do exactly what Malcolm was suggesting. "I just want a little normal," she'd moaned one day. "After everything I've been through, is that too much to ask?"

"You can always take her out of school if necessary," Ben reminded Malcolm. "Right now I think it's really important to let her start the school year, be back with her friends and teachers, let others see how well she's doing."

"I know you're right." Malcolm drew in a long breath, and Ben realized that his brother-in-law had been fighting his emotions. "We've operated so long in what Sally calls *sick mode* that it's hard to believe things are better."

"Now that the new hospital is up and running, what are your plans for her medical needs?"

"Well of course, she'll continue to go back to Tampa for anything connected to her bone marrow transplant."

Ben nodded. "I can understand that, but I'll be finishing up at Memorial by the end of the month and well, selfishly I'd like to keep an eye on things where Sally is concerned."

"You mean once you move over to Gulf Coast full-time? Let me talk to Sharon," Malcolm said.

"Ask Sally," Ben added. "It should be her choice."

"We'll go where she can get whatever it takes to keep her healthy, Ben."

"Of course." They had reached the house. The women were already inside. Ben could hear Sharon conducting the grand tour. He noticed that his sister had not asked Rachel or Hester to remove their shoes.

"Uncle Ben!"

Ben turned toward the foyer and saw his niece coming quickly down the stairs. He couldn't help remembering all the weeks and months when merely walking across her hospital room had been exhausting for the child. Now her blue eyes sparkled with delight as she effortlessly descended the curved staircase. She was wearing shorts and a T-shirt with a baseball cap covering her short hair. After the chemo, her hair had grown back in brown tufts highlighted with red instead of the honey blond it had been before she got sick.

"Is it true? Did that boy really get attacked by a shark? It's all over the news. They interviewed Dr. Wilson on national television."

"First, a hug for your weary uncle, then we can talk shark attacks." Ben held out his arms to her.

She threw her arms around his neck and held on. As he released her he fingered the earplugs from her MP3 player dangling around her neck. "So this is why you didn't hear me call out when I first got here. You are going to seriously damage your hearing, turning that stuff you think passes for music up so loud."

"I'll have you know I was listening to a book," she replied, with a quirk in her smile.

Ben tousled her short hair. "Well. . . ," he said, "there may be hope for you yet."

The phone rang, and Malcolm went to answer it. Sally squeezed Ben's hand and lowered her voice, her eyes darting toward the kitchen. "Did you hear? We're taking in boarders," she whispered.

"I heard."

"They're Amish," Sally whispered.

"Mennonite like Mr. and Mrs. Steiner," Ben corrected. "Problem?"

Sally looked doubtful. "I don't know. Do you think Dad's got money problems? I mean my friend down the block? They're selling their house because her dad—"

Ben gave her another hug. "Nothing's wrong. It's your mom and dad doing what they always do—helping others. Ms. Kaufmann started a job at the new hospital today. She needs a place to stay until she can get settled." He released her and added, "She's got a son—Justin. I think he's around your age."

She smiled, her eyes dancing with excitement. "Does he play baseball?"

"I don't know. How about we check with his mom?"

Chapter 6

By the time Rachel returned to Hester's house, she was bone weary. Justin was waiting for her, his blue eyes so like his father's mirroring a dozen unspoken questions. And yet when Rachel had climbed into the paneled orange van after completing her first full day of work, Justin had not been in the backseat as she had expected.

"John took him fishing," Hester explained. Then she sighed. "It was pretty obvious that he didn't want to come see the cottage," she admitted quietly, "and it seemed like maybe. . ."

"It's all right," Rachel assured her. "I've asked a lot of him, and he's still struggling with everything—and there's more he has yet to face."

In two days he would start classes at the public middle school near the hospital, the same school that Sally Shepherd attended. And even though they had talked about all the reasons why this was the best choice at least for the time being, Rachel knew that Justin was extremely nervous. And why not? It was a large school with children he did not know. These children lived in ways that would be so very different for Justin.

"What was it like?" Justin asked when the two of them were alone in the room they were sharing at the Steiners'. Rachel saw his curiosity as the opening she'd been looking for to begin to help him adjust to their new life.

"I think you might like it, Justin," she said as she busied herself turning down the twin beds while he got into his pajamas. "There's a park nearby and the Shepherds have a swimming pool and—"

"Why can't we stay here? I could help John at the packinghouse."

He sat down by the window, his arms folded tightly across his thin chest. He was not looking at her.

"I explained why." She sat on the other bed, across from him. "Until I've had a chance to settle into my new job, this is the best plan. We'll be living close to my work and your school."

Justin said nothing.

"The Shepherds have a daughter about your age. She asked me tonight if you played baseball." She saw a flicker of interest cross his features, but he continued looking out the window. "She goes to the same school you'll be attending. I asked her to look for you."

This, at last, got his attention. "You didn't," he moaned. "Mom, it's bad enough that I'm starting a school where nobody is—you know—like us."

"There will be lots of children who are different from you and from each other. They'll come from all sorts of backgrounds like the people I'll be working with at the hospital do. And besides, you won't be the only new student there."

"You don't know that for sure."

"No, I don't, Justin." She felt so inadequate to calm her son's fears. "I know that tonight it all seems overwhelming," she said. "That's the way I felt last night knowing this morning I would be starting a new job where I knew no one. But I got there and right away someone welcomed me and made sure I got to the right place. And throughout the day I met other people—good, caring people. Some of them needed my help, and before I knew what was happening, all of that nervousness seemed to disappear."

"Kids aren't like grown-ups," he muttered.

Rachel resisted the urge to put her arms around him. "It's

not forever, Justin," she said.

"Promise?"

"Yes, now go brush your teeth."

Later after they'd said their prayers and Rachel had read a passage from the Bible, they lay in their separate beds in the dark. She was aware that Justin was not sleeping. Finally he flipped over onto his side facing her.

"Mom?"

"Ja?"

"Will I have my own room?"

"Ja."

"When are we moving?"

"On Saturday. The cottage is furnished already, but Hester and John will help us move the boxes that Gramma sent from the farm. We'll make the place our own, Justin—just like home."

Her son did not reply, and she thought perhaps he had finally dozed off. But after a moment he said, "Not just like home—we never had a swimming pool." This was followed by a snort of laughter muffled by his pillow.

"That's true," Rachel agreed. "Oh, and I forgot to tell you. In place of paying rent, you and I will be tending the garden."

There was a pause while he digested this news. "How big is this garden?"

"Big."

Justin groaned, and this time it was Rachel who smothered a laugh.

Rachel's second day at work was every bit as busy as her first, and she began to accept that the pace for this job would be double what it had been back in Ohio in her role as school nurse. Thankfully there were no emergencies like the Olson boy's encounter with the shark, but there was plenty to fill the hours, including visiting David and his parents as well as meeting the young mother she'd seen sitting by her child's bedside that first day.

In between she attended a training session on using the computer, accepted Eileen's invitation to join her and other hospital staff members for lunch, and accompanied Pastor Paul on rounds. In the hours she spent at her desk she worked on the assignment that Paul had given her to develop a draft for a training manual for volunteers working in the children's wing.

When she returned to Hester's that evening, she was relieved to see that Justin seemed resigned to the idea that they were in Florida to stay—at least for now. And the following morning—Justin's first day of school—she was not surprised to open her eyes and see Justin already dressed and standing at the window.

Sometime in the night it had started to rain, and it didn't appear that it would let up any time soon. "Well, this rain should cool things off a bit," she said, making conversation as the two of them sat at breakfast with Hester and some of the women who worked at the co-op. She could see by the slight tremor of his hands when he picked up his glass of juice and drained it without pausing for a breath that he was nervous.

"I'd better go help John," he said. "Danke," he added with a nod to Hester as he wiped his mouth on his forearm and bolted out the back door. He was wearing jeans, a solid blue T-shirt, and a pair of running shoes that Hester had insisted on taking him to buy at the thrift store in Pinecraft. Earlier Justin had asked Hester if she thought he looked okay.

"Like any other Sarasota seventh grader," Hester had assured him. Justin had grinned with obvious relief.

Now Rachel stood at the kitchen window of the farmhouse that served as both headquarters for the fruit co-op and home to the Steiner family. Behind her Hester was giving the women their assignments for the day before they too headed off to the packinghouse. Outside Justin ran through the steady rain to where John Steiner was directing a team of men as they unloaded a truckload of empty crates.

"How's Justin doing?" Hester asked, coming to stand next to her.

"He's nervous."

"About school?"

Rachel thought about the way his hands had actually trembled. "About everything," she admitted.

"Well, that's to be expected. He'll be fine, Rachel."

Rachel turned her attention to washing the dishes. "He's changed so much since James died. He's so quiet and reserved when he used to be—"

Hester laughed. "He's twelve. Neither fish nor fowl in the world of boys—too young to count as a teenager but too old to be one of the kids. Give him some time."

"Ja." But in her heart, Rachel wasn't so certain that this was simply a phase. She had asked a lot of Justin since his father died. "Perhaps once we move on Saturday and he's settled in one place, some of the old Justin will return. He'll have his own room there and he seems excited about the swimming pool," she added more to herself than to Hester.

"Did he not have a room of his own in Ohio?"

"He did until James's brother and his family moved into the farmhouse. His uncle was hard on him, far stricter than James ever was. And then I lost my job, and now I've brought him here. Everything is so new for him."

"And for you," Hester reminded her. "You can always go back home if things don't work out here."

"Maybe." But what Hester did not know was that Luke had made it plain that he thought she was making a huge mistake.

"You only think of yourself, Rachel," he had said. "What about my folks? James's folks? Who is supposed to watch over them? Rosie has her hands full with the house and the little ones. I thought with all your nursing training and college at least we might be able to count on you for that. I'm telling you right now that James would be—"

"Do not tell me what James would or would not do," she had told her brother-in-law. Rachel had never come so close to losing her temper with him.

"Suit yourself," Luke had replied. "You always have, but know this—if things don't work out we'll take the boy in, but as for you. . ."

Rachel shook off the unpleasant memory.

"Hey," Hester said as she glanced out the window at the rain now coming down in sheets, "you okay?"

Rachel inhaled, glancing at her friend. "I'm fine," she finally whispered.

"Well, here's a good thing." She motioned toward the window. "At least you aren't moving today in this rain."

Both women laughed, and Hester folded the dish towel and hung it over the edge of the sink. "Tonight we should make a list of things you'll need, and tomorrow we can go shopping."

"Oh, I don't think there's anything," Rachel replied. "I mean every cabinet that Sharon opened was filled—dishes, pots and pans, even the basic foodstuffs like flour and sugar and such. And did you see the refrigerator and freezer?"

Hester nodded. "It's the way she is. Generous almost to a fault."

Rachel accepted the refilled mug of coffee that Hester handed her. She had some time before Justin was due at school and she needed to be at the hospital. Today John would drive them each to their destinations. "Ja. Justin will like having his own room again," she said as if they were still on that topic. "Sharing a room is hard. If James and I had been able to have more—to give him brothers and sisters. . ."

"It'll do you both good to be settled in one place, to know that at least for now, that's home," Hester assured her. "And wait until he meets Sally Shepherd. I know she's a girl but that kid is a guy's girl if ever I met one."

"She seems very nice," Rachel agreed, remembering the effervescent girl they had shared ice cream cake with the evening before. "I didn't want to pry last night, but what kind of cancer does she have?"

"Acute myelogenous leukemia—AML for short."

"We studied that in nursing school, but I thought it affected mostly older people."

"That's right. Less than 10 percent are children. Go figure how a healthy active kid like Sally ends up getting it."

"She's such a lovely child. So that form of leukemia is really fast growing?"

"Ja. It's pretty aggressive."

"When did Sally have her transplant?"

Hester nodded. "Last February. Neither Sharon nor Malcolm was a match and of course, she has no siblings so they had to wait for a donor."

"They must have considered using her own blood cells?"

Hester nodded. "The medical team thought it was too risky in her case."

Rachel was well aware that using the patient's own blood increased the risk of a relapse since that blood could still carry some of the abnormal cells. "But an unrelated donor match is also risky."

"True, but with a lower risk of relapse down the road. The reality is that there are downsides to both options."

The two of them were silent for a moment as they continued to watch the rain.

"Will you listen to us—talking shop like we used to when we were in nursing school?" Hester said, shaking her head at the memory.

Rachel smiled, but she couldn't seem to get Sally Shepherd out of her mind. "She seems to be doing well now," she ventured.

"Remarkably well." Hester started folding clothes from an overflowing basket of laundry. "Can you imagine? One day your child is healthy and whole, and the next. . ." She held on to one of John's shirts, clutching it to her as she stared off into space imagining the impossible.

"She was very sick, then?" Rachel asked.

"Ja."

Rachel thought about Ben and the way he and Sally had laughed together when they shared the ice cream cake. It had been clear that they adored each other. She remembered the watchful way that he studied Sally as the girl gobbled down a large piece of ice cream cake and quizzed Rachel about Justin. She had thought that she understood his concern for his niece. How often over these long months had she watched Justin as he struggled with coming to terms with his father's death? Ben wanting to make sure Sally was truly better was very similar to how Rachel felt whenever she was forced to face the fact that James was gone and there was nothing she could do to change that—for her son or herself.

"Mom? John says it's time," Justin called out to her from the porch. "Bring my backpack, okay?" His voice quavered, and Rachel wasn't sure whether or not that was the result of excitement or nerves or more likely a combination of the two.

"Coming," she called as she picked up her rain slicker and Justin's backpack. She hooked an arm through the straps of the nylon satchel that Hester had bought for her. She'd insisted that Rachel would need something for transporting books and papers for her certification studies from work to class to home and back again. She stepped outside she covered herself as well as Justin with the rain slicker as they ran down the steps to John's truck.

"It's all going to be fine," she told her son as he waited for her to slide in next to John before climbing in beside her and wordlessly closing the door.

Chapter 7

Ben was on his way to Sarasota Memorial Hospital when he heard the ambulances behind him. He pulled to one side of the road to let them weave their way through traffic and across a busy four-lane road. There were two of them—one following less than a minute behind the other. If Ben had to guess he would assume car accident. He just hoped no one was seriously injured and that whatever had happened didn't involve kids on their way to their first day of school.

He was starting his last two weeks at this hospital before moving permanently to Gulf Coast. Selfishly he thought about how difficult it would be for him to leave behind a juvenile patient that he might be able to treat in the short term but not follow up on once he left Memorial for good. And then for one horrible instant as he eased his way back into the flow of traffic, he pictured Sally lying in the back of one of those ambulances.

As hard as it had been for Sharon and Malcolm to come to terms with the idea that their only child had contracted a form of cancer rare in children her age, it had been impossible for Ben to wrap his head around the prospect that he might not be able to find the medical professionals and science it would take to save her life. He was a doctor and dedicated to healing.

Failure was simply not an option.

"Lighten up," Sally had demanded after they had gotten the news that her first round of therapy had not eradicated the disease. "We're only in the bottom of the first inning here," she'd announced with a great deal more certainty than either he or her parents had been able to muster. That was when they had first begun to consider the possibility of a bone marrow transplant.

Sharon and Malcolm had been tested and proved not to be a match, and then everyone in their extended families had been tested with the same results. Understanding that they needed a stranger to be a match for Sally and that finding that perfect stranger could take months, they had launched the search.

Ben's pager buzzed as he pulled into a space reserved for physicians and staff, jarring him back to the present and the reality of the day ahead of him. He glanced at the screen and saw the number for the ER. "And so it begins," he whispered aloud as he dashed through the pouring rain to the hospital's side entrance.

As the morning developed he learned that his concern for the occupants of the ambulances had not been misplaced. A teenage girl on her way to pick up her friend for the first day of school had lost control of the car and struck the other student. Both girls as well as the boy riding with the driver had been brought to the ER.

The girl that had been struck was on her way to surgery so Ben went to check on the other two teens. He was surprised that the nurse indicated a room where a Mennonite couple dressed in traditional garb hovered near the patient. But before he could skim through the chart and enter the room, he was accosted by a man he recognized as a member of the hospital's board of trustees.

"Dr. Booker!"

"Hello, Mr. Kline," Ben replied, glancing into the exam room the man had just left. In an instant he grasped the situation. "Your son was the third victim in this accident?" he asked. He looked at his notes again and saw that of the two, the girl was the more seriously injured. "If you'll give me a moment to check on—"

Kline's eager smile faded. "My son is in pain," he announced, as if this proclamation should be enough for the entire staff to come running.

Ben saw that the hospitalist was already with the Kline boy. "I'll be there as soon as I've tended to the girl."

"Given the fortune I have donated to this institution over the years," Kline said through gritted teeth as he took hold of Ben's arm, "I think I have a right to—"

"—the same quality of care as every other patient we treat here," Ben replied quietly. He met the man's glare directly. "Dr. Thompson is with your son and your wife. I will be with you as soon as I can."

"Thompson is not our son's physician. You are."

"Dr. Thompson is an excellent physician." He looked pointedly at Kline's fingers that were still grasping his sleeve. "Sir, we're wasting time here."

The businessman released him and turned back to the room where his son could be heard anxiously asking the hospitalist if he would be able to play in that week's football game.

Ben turned his attention to the nurse at his side who was quickly filling him in on the girl's injuries. "It's her state of mind that seems to be the worst of it. She just lies there oblivious to everything and everyone around her."

"Well, let's get her lip stitched up and order a psych evaluation. She was the driver?"

The nurse nodded. "The girl in surgery is her cousin."

Ben nodded. "See if there's a bed available in case we want to keep her overnight for observation." He entered the exam room, and the parents glanced up at him with relief. "Hello, Sadie. I'm Dr. Booker. I need to take a look at you and ask you some questions. Would that be all right?"

The girl was sitting on the edge of a chair, her arms locked around her body as if she wore a straitjacket. She had no reaction to his presence as she stared at the wall and rocked slowly back and forth.

Ben took his time pulling on a pair of protective gloves and then walked around the bed to examine her lip. "That's going to need some stitches." The girl was sixteen, but he decided to try addressing her as if she were far younger. Either it would further calm her or it would make her annoyed enough to rouse her from her catatonic state. "I could use my special pink thread—or purple."

No response. The nurse was right. Her state of mind was far more worrisome than the split lip. He tried again as he gently checked for evidence of further injury.

"How about it, Sadie?" he asked, watching her face for any sign of pain as he performed his examination. "What's your favorite color? I'm partial to blue myself—or green. My mom used to say that's because I'm the outdoors type—I like nature—water, trees. . . ." Gradually Sadie's arms and legs started to relax.

As Ben continued his work he addressed his comments to the parents. "I'm going to suggest that Sadie be admitted at least overnight. Right now she's showing all the classic signs of shock, but I'd like to make certain there's nothing else going on."

"The officer. . . ," the father began, lowering his voice and glancing toward the corridor where a police officer was standing at the nurses' station.

"I'd like to get some X-rays—not that I suspect anything, but since she's not really responding to touch or perhaps pain, we want to be sure. And we should probably consider a psych consultation."

Both parents nodded. Ben clipped the thread with a small scissors and then pulled off his gloves. He offered the man a handshake while the nurse assured them that someone would be along soon to transport Sadie to radiology. Not knowing what he could possibly say that might bring this stoic couple a measure of reassurance, Ben simply nodded to the woman and left.

By the time he finished treating Sadie Keller, the Klines had arranged to have their son seen by another doctor—a specialist in sports medicine. They did not even glance at Ben as he passed, for which he was grateful. He stopped at the nurses' station and signed orders for X-rays and a bed for Sadie as well as the psych evaluation, then he headed off to make his rounds.

The rain was still coming down with no sign of letting up.

Ben decided to grab a salad to go from the hospital café before heading to his office in the physicians building across the skywalk where according to his schedule he would have a waiting room filled with patients. On his way out of the hospital he passed by the family waiting room. There he was surprised to see Hester Steiner hovering near a woman with flaming red curls. The woman was sobbing uncontrollably. Hester's husband, John, had his arm around a man who looked as distraught as the woman sounded. Sitting to either side of the woman were the parents of the girl he'd treated that morning.

Ben's heart went out to all three families, including the Klines.

Growing up in his father's house, any sign of emotion had been viewed as weakness. Ben was expected to accept everything that happened as God's will—not to be questioned. And he had quickly learned to bury his feelings and focus all of his energy on achievement—the one thing his father seemed to value. He had excelled in his studies and on the athletic field. He had been elected president of his high school's student council, and eventually he had been accepted into three of the nation's top premed programs. And his father took credit for all of it even as he preached humility on Sundays.

Ben had never understood his father. The man who stood in the pulpit Sunday after Sunday did not mesh with the man who sat at the head of the table in the house where Ben and Sharon had grown up. Somehow Sharon had never struggled with the duality that Ben found so utterly confusing.

Once he became a doctor, Ben had dedicated his life to one purpose—making sure he put his medical skills to work to heal every child that came to him if he could. But once Sally was diagnosed, Ben had found that he was suddenly engaged in a raging tug-of-war between his emotions and his determination not to allow himself to feel—anything.

All afternoon as he attended to his appointments the memory of those Mennonite parents and then the news that the child had died stayed with him. After he finished his last office appointment for the day, he went back to the hospital to check on Sadie Keller. Her father was sitting by her bed, and a boy a year or so younger than Sadie was curled into a chair, sleeping.

Ben checked the notes left by the psychologist.

"She'll be taken into custody as soon as we discharge her," the nurse on duty told him. "These kids today," she added, shaking her head, "they assume nothing like this can happen to them."

The same way Sharon and Malcolm could never imagine that a child as healthy and lively as Sally might be struck down by leukemia, Ben thought. "Let's try to keep her through tomorrow night," he said.

He did not miss the look of skepticism the nurse gave him. The chances that the hospital brass might let the girl stay beyond one night were slim to none, but right then Ben felt he had to bank on slim. If this were Gulf Coast Medical Center he could speak directly to Darcy, but here at Memorial it was common knowledge that he was leaving. Those in charge would hardly be inclined to stretch the rules for him.

On his way home to his condo overlooking Sarasota Bay, Ben suddenly decided to prescribe something for himself—a strong dose of family. His sister's home cooking, his brother-in-law's wry take on the news of the day and most of all, Sally's sunny smile.

Justin's first day of school was a nightmare. The place was an endless maze of hallways lined with lockers and classroom doors that all looked alike to him. At the end of a long assembly where all the students crowded into a large auditorium and paid little attention to the principal as he laid out his plans for the coming year, a jangling bell announced that Justin had less than three minutes to find his locker and get to his class.

So much noise and confusion. The hallways were filled with kids, all talking and laughing and all seeming to be pushing their way toward him. He felt like a fish trying to swim upstream. He saw kids looking at him and in spite of trying not to stand out, he was sure that they knew that he was different from them. They all seemed to know each other, and they all had cell phones that they stared at even as they wove their way through the crowded halls bumping into anyone in their way without so much as glancing up.

Justin found his locker and fumbled with the combination lock.

"Need some help?"

He looked up and saw a chubby-faced girl wearing a pink baseball cap. She was opening the locker next to his.

"No," he mumbled and turned his attention back to the dial.

"The key is to make sure you go a little past the second number before you go back to the third one," the girl said. She was busy storing a bunch of stuff from her backpack. "Are you in Mr. Mortimer's class?"

"Yeah." The lock finally gave, and Justin hurried to hang up the slicker his mom had insisted he take. The minute John had driven off with his mom after dropping him off, Justin had stuffed the slicker into the backpack that was still stiff with newness. He slammed his locker door the way he'd seen a guy do down the way and spun the dial on the lock. Without another glance at the girl, he headed for class.

"Hey," the girl said, catching up to him. "Mortimer's room is this way."

"I know," he lied. "I'll be there, okay?" His voice was practically a growl but at the moment, he would do anything to break this girl's connection. He was all too aware that every move he made in the first few hours would set the way others would look at him for weeks to come. That was the way it was with kids, and the last thing he needed was to be tagged as a guy who hung out with girls. She seemed nice enough, but she was a girl and well, he was pretty sure it would not be a good idea to be seen with her until he could figure out the way things worked around here.

"Well, all righty then," she huffed. "Just trying to help."

Justin kept walking away from her, his head down as he plowed his way through a group of kids.

"Well, will you look who's back? Yo, Fat Sally!" The boy he'd seen slamming his locker yelled, and the two boys standing near him snickered.

From behind him he heard the girl shout, "Shows what you

know about anything, Derek Piper. Maybe if you opened a book once in a while. . ."

The boys around the large muscular guy grinned, and one of them punched him in the arm. But Justin saw the boy roughly shrug him off as he started down the hall after the girl, his eyes ablaze. Then he spotted Justin and paused. "Hey newbie," he said with a grin.

Justin froze and tried to come up with something to say. "Hey," he finally managed as Derek and his friends passed him.

He breathed a sigh of relief, but then Derek turned around and stared at him. "You coming or not?"

And all of a sudden Justin found himself part of a quartet of boys headed for Mr. Mortimer's classroom where the boy called Derek slumped into a seat in the back row and continued to glare at the girl wearing the baseball cap. She ignored him until their teacher decided to rearrange students, and Justin found himself seated across from Derek Piper and just in front of the girl.

"Sally Shepherd," she whispered as if he might not have heard Mr. Mortimer call out each and every name.

"Got it," he muttered, mortified to realize that this was the girl his mom and Hester kept going on and on about. He saw Derek Piper glance his way and roll his eyes. "Sally Shepherd," Derek mimicked with an exaggerated grimace.

Justin couldn't hide his smile. Derek's antics were so over the top. Justin felt flattered that for whatever reason Derek had decided to include him in his group.

"Ah Mr. Piper," the teacher said in a voice that sounded a little like the pastor's voice at church. "So nice to have you back again this year."

Piper sat up to his full height—a good three or four inches taller than any other boy in the class—and grinned at Mr. Mortimer. "It was like I couldn't stay away," he said.

"Do try to move on with the rest of your class this year, won't you, Mr. Piper? I would not want to deny any one of the secondary institutions in the community the pleasure of teaching you next year."

"But Mr. Mortimer, I kind of like it here."

"And I would like to live in Hawaii, sir. Sadly, we cannot always have our way." Mr. Mortimer clapped his hands together, effectively ending the conversation, and instructed the class to open their textbooks.

Halfway through the class, the girl called Sally started to cough.

"Here we go again," Justin heard Derek mutter.

Mr. Mortimer stopped writing on the whiteboard and came down the aisle to stand next to the girl's desk. "Are you all right, Sally?" he asked quietly.

She nodded but continued to cough.

"Perhaps some water," she said.

To Justin's surprise, Derek was immediately on his feet. "I'll get it." He was out the door in a flash. Mr. Mortimer sighed and glanced around, his gaze falling on Justin.

"Mr. Kaufmann, would you be so kind as to take a paper cup from the stack on my desk and get Miss Shepherd some water?"

"But. . ." Justin glanced toward the door.

"Please do as I ask," the teacher said.

In the hallway, Justin saw Derek duck out a side door and take off across the schoolyard. He was actually leaving school in the middle of class.

"Mr. Kaufmann?" his teacher called.

Justin filled the paper cup and returned to the classroom, debating whether or not to tell Mr. Mortimer what he'd seen.

But there was no need. As he entered the room, one of the boys he'd seen hanging out with Derek at his locker glanced out the window. He pointed, and soon the entire class was straining to watch as Derek loped across the ball field. On his way he turned and made rude signs to the students watching him. Mr. Mortimer clapped his hands to get their attention.

"Desks, now, people," he announced and returned to the front of the classroom.

Behind him, Justin heard Sally Shepherd clear her throat. "Thanks for the water," she whispered.

Justin saw one of Derek's friends silently mimic her as he looked straight at Justin. Not knowing what else to do, Justin ignored Sally completely. The boy grinned, and for the second time that morning Justin felt like he might have connected with some of the other boys.

As the day went along, Justin realized that unlike his little Mennonite school in Ohio where he and his friends worked pretty much on their own and at their own speed, here he was going to be expected to deliver assignments daily and actively participate in class. Three times Mr. Mortimer called on him for answers. But that wasn't nearly as embarrassing as when the social studies teacher had him read a passage from their history book aloud and then asked, "And what do you think, Mr. Kaufmann?"

"About what?" Justin replied as he heard a rustle of giggles around him.

"About what you just read."

"I don't know," Justin hedged, trying to come up with the right answer.

"Was it right for America to go to war in this case?"

Justin breathed a sigh of relief. He knew this. He'd learned it from his parents and his pastors. "War is never the answer," he said, quoting them.

But the way the teacher's eyebrows shot up in surprise, Justin knew he'd gotten himself into a deeper hole.

"Why?"

"Because. . ." Justin prayed for deliverance. *Please. It's my first day. Please.*

The bell rang and immediately the other students were clamoring to leave the room. He was saved.

"We'll pick up here tomorrow," the teacher shouted above the noise. "Chapters one and two for tomorrow if you please—and be prepared for a pop quiz."

At the end of the day, Justin headed for his locker to pack his backpack before he went to the hospital where he would meet his mom. Sally Shepherd was waiting for him.

"I realized who you are," she said. "You're Justin Kaufmann—you and your mom are going to live with us in our guesthouse." She actually said this as if it were something that Justin should be really excited about. "Your mom is really nice. I like the way—"

"I gotta go," Justin said as he spotted Derek's friends watching him. He grabbed his backpack and ran down the hall and out the side door that he'd seen Derek use earlier.

Rachel first learned of the car accident involving the teens when she was making her morning rounds, visiting patients on the children's wing at Gulf Coast. Toward the end of her rounds, she stopped by a room where a mother was sitting alone watching the television mounted on one wall. The reporter was standing in front of another hospital.

"The girl died," the woman announced without preamble when Rachel knocked at the door and then entered the room. She must have noticed Rachel's confusion because she gestured toward the television before continuing, "Terrible thing. They were cousins—the girl driving and the one that died. First day of school. Can you imagine? My son goes to school with those kids. Maybe if they'd brought them here instead of to Memorial. . ." She shook her head and turned her attention back to the television.

"How old were they?" Rachel asked, not knowing how else to respond.

"Fifteen and sixteen. Mennonites from Pinecraft, according to the reports. My son's coach is the father of the girl that died."

Rachel couldn't help but wonder if she might have met them when she and Justin went to church with John and Hester that first Sunday. Her heart went out to these families, for she of all people knew at least some of the shock and grief they were facing right now. She closed her eyes and thought of that terrible night when James—

In the corridor behind, her someone slammed a door, and Rachel startled back to the reality of the news of the day. She forced her attention to the television and saw that the reporters had moved on to another more lighthearted story. "Is there anything you need, Mrs. Baker?" she asked the woman.

"No. Thank you for asking." She seemed to focus on Rachel for the first time, taking in her plain dress and prayer covering. "You're Amish?"

"Mennonite," Rachel said.

Mrs. Baker's eyes widened with sympathy. "Then you must know these poor people," she said, indicating the television. It was not unusual for outsiders to assume that people of her faith must all know one another.

"I'm new to this area," Rachel explained, "but we must all pray for them. They have many difficult days ahead."

Mrs. Baker sighed and stood up to straighten the covers on the rumpled hospital bed. "Don't I know it," she murmured. Suddenly her entire body started to shake, and Rachel went to her, placing a comforting hand on the woman's back. "It's so hard," Mrs. Baker sobbed.

"Would you like to talk about it?" Rachel asked.

"I don't want to trouble you. They should be bringing my son back soon."

"There's time. How about a change of scenery? I can let the nurse know where you are so she can send for you the minute he comes back." She gently guided the woman toward the door. "What's your son's name?" she asked.

Mrs. Baker smiled. "Alan—he hates the name—prefers to go by the nickname his friends gave him."

"And what's that?"

Mrs. Baker actually giggled. "Bubba. Can you imagine? He prefers Bubba to Alan."

Rachel smiled and guided the woman toward the chapel. She nodded to the nurse keying in data at the nurses' station and told her where Mrs. Baker would be.

"It'll be awhile yet. They're pretty backed up downstairs," the nurse assured her.

"Thank you," Mrs. Baker said.

They sat together for over an hour as Mrs. Baker poured out the story of her failed marriage, her three other children, her job that was in jeopardy because she was so preoccupied with her son's care, and her worries over the bills.

So engrossed was Rachel in listening to the woman that she barely noticed the time. Eileen had told her that Paul needed her to attend the weekly meeting for department heads—a working lunch, she had called it, her tone laced with sarcasm. "It never fails to amaze me how some folks assume that if there's food involved it can't really be called work."

Rachel was nearly half an hour late when she finally slipped into the single remaining chair surrounding the large conference table. Mark from Human Resources slid a box lunch over to her, and a woman she had not yet met poured her a glass of ice water.

"As I was saying,"—Darcy said even as she pinned Rachel with a look of displeasure—"each department and every individual in that department must understand the mission of that department and its priorities." She waited a beat for this to register and added, "So today I thought we would go around the table and have each department representative state the mission for your area."

There was a rustling of paper as others pulled out folders or notebooks.

"Rachel, why don't you lead the way?" Darcy said with a tight smile. "For those of you who have not had the pleasure—and since she did not arrive in time for our opening introductions— this is Rachel Kaufmann, Pastor Paul's assistant."

"Chaplain," Mark muttered under his breath.

"Did you have something to add, Mark?"

It was a little like being back in school, Rachel thought. She actually felt sorry for Mark as every eye focused on him. But he was undaunted.

"Eileen Walls is Pastor Paul's assistant. Ms. Kaufmann is his associate or child life specialist, to be exact."

"Ooh, my bad," Darcy said sarcastically with that same tight smile. Everyone around the table exchanged nervous glances. "So, specialist Kaufmann, the mission for spiritual care services?"

Rachel had studied the bookmark that Eileen had given her until she had memorized the words, so it wasn't difficult to recall. She said softly, "The spiritual care services of Gulf Coast Medical Center provide comfort and support—"

"If you could speak up for those of us at this end of the table," Darcy interrupted.

"I'm sorry." Rachel stood and delivered the rest of the

statement in a strong clear voice. ". . .comfort and support that respects the full diversity of spiritual values to our patients, the family and friends of those patients and to members of our staff twenty-four hours a day, 365 days a year."

She sat down and took a sip of her water.

"Thank you, Rachel." Darcy turned to a large whiteboard and uncapped a marking pen. "So let's pull out the key words here."

As each department representative stated their mission and Darcy led them in identifying the key words, Rachel saw that she was trying to lead them to come up with a universal mission statement for the entire hospital, one that would incorporate the goals of each department.

"In the end," Darcy said when the last report had been delivered, "we are all individual departments with our roles to play, but we are also a part of the whole." She turned to the whiteboard, covered now with words in many colors. "Where do our missions intersect?"

Over the next half hour the group worked together, and by meeting's end they had constructed a mission statement for the hospital. Rachel was very impressed, and as everyone gathered up their things and headed back to work, she stayed a moment, clearing away the last of the lunch items and wiping the table clean with the leftover unused napkins.

"We have a housekeeping department," Darcy said. She had turned away to take a phone call and seemed surprised to find Rachel still there.

"It's no bother," Rachel replied. "I wanted to apologize for being late. I was with—"

"The work that you and Paul do is very important to the overall work of this institution, Rachel. However, you are going to have to learn to prioritize."

It was the second time she had directed that exact comment to Rachel. "I thought I was—that is, I thought that spending time with Mrs. Baker was—"

"More important than this?" Darcy flung a hand toward the whiteboard. "Well, perhaps you have a point, but a hospital is a business, Rachel, and unless we are all on the same page all the time, then we have no chance if we are to make our mark against the more established hospitals in the area." She began erasing the whiteboard with brisk slashing motions. "I know this may seem trivial to you, but. . ."

"Not at all. I think it's very important. You're right. We must all work together."

But instead of calming Darcy, Rachel's words seemed to only upset her more. "It's more than that," she said. Her tone was argumentative. She set the eraser on the narrow tray at the base of the board and dusted off her hands as if she'd been erasing chalk instead of dry marker. "I don't expect you to appreciate the finer points of running a major business like this one, but make no mistake, our work here goes beyond simply ministering to our patients and their families. The board of trustees will expect results. There is a bottom line, and every department is expected to contribute to it."

Rachel studied the other woman's frown, her failure to look directly at Rachel. "It's obvious that you have been given a great deal of responsibility, but surely the board would not have chosen you as administrator if they did not have complete confidence in you."

Now Darcy looked directly at Rachel for a long moment. She did not smile or in any way acknowledge Rachel's attempt to set her mind at ease. Instead, she picked up the pile of papers and folders she'd brought with her to the meeting and left the room.

Rachel returned to her cubicle and spent the rest of the afternoon in another computer training session and then entering notes about her visits that day in preparation for filing the weekly report that Paul had requested. Meanwhile Eileen kept her up to date on the latest news about the car accident involving the two Mennonite teens.

"They took them to Memorial of course," she announced without preamble when she returned from her midafternoon break. "The younger one was in surgery for some time, but she didn't make it. I wonder if Dr. Booker was there when it happened. He said something yesterday about being over there today."

Just then Rachel saw Justin coming across the hospital grounds toward the entrance. He trudged along under the weight of a bulging backpack, and Rachel felt glad to see him. She was anxious to hear about his first day at school. Paul Cox had agreed that Justin could come to the office and start on his homework while he waited for Rachel to finish her day.

"It will only be until next week," Rachel had assured him. "Once we move into the Shepherds' guesthouse he can go straight home."

"Sally will take him in hand," Paul had told her with a chuckle. "That little girl is going to be president of these United States one of these days right after she retires from playing professional baseball. Never saw a kid more self-confident or capable than that one. She can make your boy feel right at home and before you know it—do you folks play baseball?"

Rachel had smiled. "We do."

But watching Justin now, she wasn't so sure that things would go as smoothly as Paul and Eileen promised. Her hopes for Justin had been so high as she'd watched him jump down from John's truck and head into the school without a backward look. She had prayed that this day would be as good for him as her first day at the hospital had been for her. But now as she watched him cross the parking lot on his way into the hospital, she realized that everything about her son's posture and stride shouted, *Misery.*

Chapter 8

I was thinking," Rachel said later as she and Justin sat waiting for the bus. "Wouldn't you like to see where we're going to live? I already have the key, and the Shepherds said we should not stand on ceremony."

"What does that mean?" Justin mumbled, his eyes still focused on the ground as he sat on the edge of the park bench as if poised for flight.

"Stand on ceremony? Oh, it's an old saying. In this case it means that even though officially we aren't moving to the guesthouse until Saturday, we can go there whenever we like." She held up the key.

Justin showed no interest.

"I thought perhaps you'd like to see your room. I was going to make a list for shopping so that we would have everything we needed on Saturday when we move."

Justin shrugged. "Will they be there? The Shepherds?"

"Maybe, but we are not going for a visit, Justin. If we see them, then of course you must be polite and introduce yourself, but—"

"How far is this house from their house?"

"Not so far. There's the main house and then the swimming

735

pool and the gardens. The guesthouse is at the back of the gardens. Why?"

"No reason."

A city bus made the turn onto the circular driveway. "Do you want to go or not, Justin? If so, this is the bus we need."

Justin picked up his backpack and stood. He wore his unhappiness like a suit of heavy armor. Rachel had prayed for God's guidance to help her see her son through these difficult times and on to the better days she could only hope would be in his future. But in all the time that had passed since James's funeral, it seemed as if nothing she said or did gave her son any comfort. "Justin," she said quietly as she waited alongside him for the exiting passengers to get off the bus, "it will work out."

"You keep saying that," he said and met her eyes for the first time since they'd come out to wait for the bus. Her heart broke as she read in his expression his desperate need to believe her mingled with his doubt that she could ever deliver on her promise.

He turned away and boarded the bus ahead of her, flashing the driver the pass she had bought for him. Several other employees from the hospital stepped around her and boarded so that Rachel was the last to show her pass and look for a seat as the bus pulled away.

Justin was sitting near the back, his backpack between his feet, his head bowed. A man near the front stood and offered Rachel his seat and she accepted.

It was moments like these when she missed James's strength. He would never have allowed their son to show such disrespect for his mother. But what was she going to do? Cause a scene?

She glanced around, and a woman smiled at her over the top of the book she was reading. Next to her sat a young girl, reading a textbook that Rachel recognized as one she had seen Justin studying at the hospital. Perhaps the girl attended the same school, was even in his class. She closed her eyes and prayed silently that in time Justin would find friends at his new school.

As the bus approached the stop for the Shepherd house Rachel sat forward on the edge of her seat and glanced back at

Justin who was not looking at her. Because someone was waiting for the bus, she didn't see the need to signal her desire to get off. Instead when the bus stopped, she got up and moved to the rear exit. "This is our stop," she said when she reached Justin, but she did not wait to see if he would follow her.

Instead she got off the bus and started walking the half block to the Shepherds' driveway. And what if Justin didn't follow her? She had no idea what she would do if the bus continued on its way with Justin still on board.

As she hesitated, she heard Justin running to catch up. "I'm sorry, Mom," he murmured as he fell into step with her. "It's just so. . .hard."

She could point out that it was also hard for her, but she knew that it would be little comfort. "And what did your father teach us about weathering hard times?" she asked, forcing her voice to a lighthearted tone that she did not really feel. She was rewarded by the hint of a grin lifting the corners of Justin's mouth.

"As Thomas Jefferson once said,"—Justin intoned, mimicking his father's deep voice as in unison they chanted the saying that had been a favorite of Justin's father—" 'I'm a great believer in luck and I find the harder I work, the more I have of it.' "

And by the time they started up the service drive that led to the guesthouse, they were both laughing.

Ben was standing at the window in Malcolm's study when he saw the chaplain and her son pass the main house on their way to the guesthouse. They were laughing, and then the boy caught sight of the pool and stopped to take a closer look. Rachel Kaufmann waited on the path and when her son turned back to her, everything about his body language gave voice to his excitement. Rachel smiled, and then she led the way through the garden, gesturing to the plants as they walked.

He remembered how her eyes had finally lost their sadness her first day at the hospital when she had seen the atrium, and he remembered thinking how refreshing it was to see a woman who had no need to rely upon cosmetics or fashion for her loveliness.

There was beauty in the simple serenity of Rachel Kaufmann's smile.

"Oh, is that Rachel?" his sister asked as she set down a tray that held glasses, a pitcher of water, and a decanter of wine along with an assortment of cheese and crackers.

"Yeah." Ben turned away from the window and poured himself a glass of wine. "Have they moved in already?"

"Saturday. But I gave her a key and told her to stop by whenever she liked." She sank into one of two overstuffed chairs and propped her bare feet on an ottoman. "I'll go down there in a minute and invite them to supper, but first tell me about this terrible accident today. Were you at Memorial when they brought those children in?"

Ben nodded and took the chair opposite hers. "I don't know a lot—I heard that the one girl died in surgery."

"Well, it's all over the news, and it's why Malcolm is going to be late. He went out to the co-op after leaving his office today so he could make sure everything was locked up for the night. Hester and John are close friends with the families of both girls, and even if they weren't, you know how everyone in Pinecraft comes together whenever anything like this happens."

"They're going to need all the support they can get," Ben said, and then he realized that Sharon was crying. "Hey, what's this?"

She swiped at her tears. "Oh, don't mind me. Ever since. . . well, you know. . .since Sally. . ."

"This is different," Ben said, moving to sit on the ottoman to be closer to her.

"That girl was their only child," she whispered.

"I know, but she's not Sally." Ben spread cheese on a cracker and handed it to her before preparing another for himself. "Where is Sally, anyway?"

"She had a meeting of the student council—she's the secretary this year and then she and a couple of friends were going to the mall. If she'd known you were going to stop by I'm sure you would have been her first choice."

"Over shopping? I doubt that very much," Ben said.

They turned at the sound of a car on the driveway, followed

by the slam of the front door.

"Mom? I'm home," Sally called, her voice filling the large house with the sheer exuberance of youth. "I got a new hat."

"In here," Sharon called.

They heard the rattle of a plastic shopping bag, and a moment later Sally appeared in the doorway dressed in jeans and a T-shirt and the silliest little hat Ben had ever seen. "What is that thing on your head?" Ben asked, not sure whether to laugh or not. When it came to women's taste in fashion he was often mystified.

"It's called a 'fascinator.' It's all the rage right now ever since the wedding."

Ben must have had a blank expression because Sally placed her hands on her hips and added, "The *royal* wedding—Kate and Will?" Then she rolled her eyes as if he were hopeless. "Of course, it would help if I had a little more hair to anchor it to," she continued.

"How *did* you anchor it?" Sharon asked.

"Chewing gum," Sally said and giggled as she pulled the ridiculous hat away from her scalp, exposing the strings of pink gum with which she'd attached it to her forehead and temples.

"Sally!"

Ben made no attempt to cover his laughter.

"It's not funny," his sister fumed as she leaped up and began examining Sally's head, picking out bits of gum.

"Actually, Mom, it kind of is," Sally said and then grimaced as Sharon worked a blob of the gum free.

"What were you thinking?"

Sally shrugged. "It was a rough day at school. I needed a smile."

Sharon's touch gentled to a tender caress. "What happened?"

"Nothing I can't handle, but it's hard sometimes. Like I'm some kind of freak or something." She picked at the remnants of gum left on the hat then looked up, her eyes bright with excitement. "The new kid started today and guess what? His locker is right next to mine." She pulled away from her mother and flung herself into the chair that Sharon had vacated. "I think he's shy—he's very quiet." Again her eyes widened as an idea occurred to her. "I'll bet he was afraid I would let the other kids know that he's Mennonite. That explains why he took off after school the way he did."

"Wouldn't the other kids know anyway—I mean the dress and all?" Sharon asked.

"Apparently the kids have more freedom when it comes to that," Sally told her. "I looked it up. Kids don't officially get baptized or join the church until they're like practically grown up. That's when they put on the uniform. I'm getting some juice." Sally was up and moving to the kitchen as she continued to talk. "When they move in, we should take them some cookies or something," she called as they heard the slam of the refrigerator door.

"I made some today," Sharon called after her. "The boy and his mother are at the guesthouse now. Your dad is going to be late, so why don't you go invite them to stay for supper?"

"I'll go with you," Ben volunteered. Restless after the long and emotionally draining day he'd had, he too was anxious to be up and moving.

The truth was that in the wake of the accident that morning, he'd realized that he had some regrets about leaving Memorial for good. His time there had shaped the doctor he'd become, and he was grateful for that. In some ways he and Rachel Kaufmann were both starting out fresh at the new hospital. Of course, his was by choice while hers had been the result of a change in her life over which she'd had no control. Perhaps it would do him good to be around someone who might understand that sometimes change—even change by choice—could be hard.

Rachel heard voices from outside. She glanced out the open front door of the guesthouse to see Ben Booker and his niece, Sally, coming through the garden. The girl was carrying a platter of cookies. "We've got company," she called to Justin.

The minute she'd shown him the small bedroom he was to occupy, Justin had busied himself exploring the space, commenting on changes he'd like to make. "Can I take that picture down?" he'd asked, pointing to a painting of three girls looking for seashells at the beach.

"Ja. The Shepherds have given permission for us to arrange things to suit our ways. But you must wrap it carefully and store it in the closet, and when we move it must be put back as it is now."

"I'd like to move the desk over there," Justin said, more to himself than to her. She had left him to think about how best to make the room his while she started making a list of things she would need to purchase and bring with her on Saturday. As she had suspected, her list was short. Sharon Shepherd had truly anticipated their needs.

"It's Dr. Booker and his niece, Sally. Come say hello," she instructed as she nervously adjusted her prayer covering and pressed her hands over her skirt. She wasn't sure why she got so nervous around the doctor. Darcy Meekins was far more intimidating. Like everyone else that Rachel had met at the hospital, Ben Booker was friendly and had made her feel most welcomed.

"I met Sally at school," Justin said. "And Dr. Booker. . ."

"They are our guests," Rachel said firmly.

Justin frowned and then grinned. "Guests in the guesthouse?"

Relieved to see a glimpse of the more easygoing boy her son had been before his father's death, Rachel smiled. "Come," she said at the exact moment that she heard a knock on the screen door.

"Hi, Mrs. Kaufmann."

"Come in, Sally. Dr. Booker."

"It's Ben, remember?" he said as he followed Sally into the tiny living room.

Sally presented her with the cookies.

"Danke," she said. "Did you make these, Sally?"

"Mom did. Does *don-ka* mean 'thank you'?"

"It does, and you must forgive me. Sometimes I forget and slip into the ways of our people."

"I like learning about other people and their ways," Sally said. "Maybe after you and Justin move in I can learn more words?"

Rachel saw Justin hanging back in the shadows of the hallway that led to the two small bedrooms. "Justin can teach you," Rachel offered. She ignored the way her son's body stiffened in protest. "I understand that the two of you met at school today?"

"Yes ma'am. His locker is next to mine. Hi, Justin," she said with a self-conscious wave.

"Hi," he replied, his voice barely audible.

"Please come and sit," Rachel invited, indicating the small couch that dominated the room. "Perhaps a glass of water? It's so warm today."

"We came to say hi, bring the cookies, and invite you to come up to our house for supper," Sally said. "Mom's grilling chicken, and we'll eat as soon as Dad gets home from the co-op."

"Oh, thank you, Sally—and thank your mother for the kind invitation. Justin and I just stopped by to make a shopping list. The Steiners will be expecting us for supper."

Ben looked at her strangely. "I expect Hester and John may have had to make other plans," he said. "There was an accident this morning. Two of the victims were Mennonite. I saw Hester and John at the hospital with the parents."

Of course, Hester would have gone to the hospital to be with the parents—even if she only knew them slightly. In time Rachel knew that she and Justin would be part of the community of those who would gather for events both joyous and tragic in the lives of their neighbors. It was their way, and it was one of the traditions of their faith that Rachel held most dear. There were no strangers in a Mennonite community.

"You have to eat," Sally reasoned. "And my uncle can take you home, right? It's on your way, sort of."

Ben smiled. "Sort of is," he replied, his eyes on Rachel. "Come on—grilled chicken, potato salad, and the best pie you've ever tasted? You can't turn that down."

"All right."

"Don-ka," Sally said. "Hey Justin, want to catch for me? I've got an extra glove, and I need to practice before tomorrow's game."

Justin gave Rachel a pleading look that she decided to take

for him asking her permission to stay for supper and play the game with Sally. "Go ahead," she said.

It was the expression of horror that crossed her son's face that let her know she had said the exact opposite of what he'd wanted. But she'd made her decision. "Go," she said, and Justin reluctantly followed Sally out the door.

"I didn't want to say anything in front of the kids," Ben told her, "but you should know that one of the three teens injured in that accident died earlier today. I treated the other girl—her cousin—and from what I was able to gather, she played a part in causing the accident. It looks like she'll be arrested and charged as soon as she's released from the hospital."

"Oh Ben, no," Rachel said. "Arrested on top of everything those poor families have already suffered?"

"I made arrangements for her to be kept overnight at the hospital, but I'm pretty sure the powers that be will discharge her tomorrow. Poor kid."

"I need to call Hester," Rachel said, picking up her cell phone. "Maybe there's something I can do to help."

"But you'll stay for supper?"

"Ja—yes."

Ben grinned. "*Sehr gut,*" he said as he left her to make her call.

Chapter 9

Saturday dawned sunny and felt far less tropical than it had been over the last several days. "A perfect day for moving," Hester announced as she dished up breakfast. "Are you all packed?" she asked Justin, ignoring his failure to show any excitement at all as she placed three large pancakes on his plate.

"Not much to pack," he replied and reached for the pitcher of maple syrup.

Rachel cleared her throat and bowed her head as Hester sat down and John led them in prayer. She couldn't help but wonder if Justin remembered to say grace before eating his lunch at school. *Probably not,* she thought. Silently she vowed for what seemed like the thousandth time since they'd arrived in Sarasota that she would find them a home in Pinecraft as soon as her probationary period ended. At least in Pinecraft, Justin would be surrounded by others of their faith and tradition.

"Everything's loaded into the van," John said, glancing at Rachel and then Justin. "Zeke should be here soon. He's volunteered to drive you over and help with the heavy lifting."

"I'm sorry we can't help." Hester's eyes filled with tears as they had ever since her friends had lost their daughter in the accident.

"Zeke will be a great help," Rachel assured her, "and besides, there's not that much to be moved."

Malcolm Shepherd's younger brother could not be more different than Ben. The one thing they had in common was that they were both devoted to Sally.

"Yoo-hoo," a raspy female voice called from the back porch.

"Come on in, Margery," John called. "Have some breakfast."

"Already ate," Margery Barker announced. "But I could use a refill on my coffee." She helped herself, filling her travel mug from the pot Hester had left warming on the stove. Like Rachel, Margery was a widow, although she was at least a couple of decades older than Rachel and several more years down the path of her grief. She ran a marina and charter boat business not far from the co-op, and Hester said she stopped by often to visit. She loved to tease John and tell stories of the time when his property had been completely destroyed by a hurricane named Hester.

"And then he came face-to-face with the real deal," she would say as she patted Hester's hand, "and bingo-bongo his life was changed."

Being around Margery gave Rachel hope that one day she and Justin would find their place in a world without James.

"Busy week for you two." Margery pulled a chair closer to the table, next to Justin who was picking at his food. "You gonna eat those pancakes or let them drown in all that syrup?"

Rachel saw Justin flash Margery a hint of a smile as he stuffed a large piece of pancake into his mouth. She could see that he liked Margery, probably because she reminded him of his grandmother. James's mother, like Margery, was a no-nonsense woman with a soft side that she could bring out whenever the occasion seemed to warrant it. But she had little patience for what she called wallowing, and she'd made that clear to Justin the day they'd first met.

"Is Zeke here?" Justin asked, knowing that Zeke often caught a ride with Margery on the boat she used to ferry herself and the homeless people working at the co-op back and forth.

"He's around here somewhere. I saw his guitar leaning up against the porch, and you know Zeke, he and that guitar of his are joined at the hip most times." She took a sip of her coffee and turned her attention to Hester. "I was sorry to hear about the Messner girl." She shook her head. "How's Jeannie holding up?"

Hester shrugged. "It's so very hard, on all of them. Sadie has been arrested and taken to a detention center in Bradenton. Emma and Lars can only visit her for half an hour at a time and only on certain days."

Justin seemed to be following this conversation with interest. "Sadie is the girl who was driving the car that struck the girl who died," she explained.

"She's in jail?"

"Sounds like it," Margery said with a heavy sigh as she stood and headed for the door. "Well, got to go take care of my own business. Got two fishing charters going out today." Margery glanced outside. "Good day for fishing and a good day for moving," she announced. "See you folks later."

"Margery's right," John said, wiping his mouth. "I'll go get Zeke. And, Justin, you help your mother bring out the rest of your things."

"We're staying at the new place tonight?" Justin asked as if the idea had just struck him.

"Of course we are. We're moving there."

Her son glanced around the large kitchen. "But we'll come back here—I mean for visits and stuff?"

John laughed and ruffled Justin's sandy hair. "You're not getting out of working here that easy. I've gotten used to having you around, and soon we'll be getting into the busiest part of the season."

"But how will we get back and forth? It's a long way to the Shepherds' house."

"The boy's right, John," Hester said with a worried frown as she ran water over the dishes. "Wait a minute. What's that Zeke is working on out there?"

John carried his dishes to the sink and looked out the window. "Well, will you look at that? It's a bike," he said. "He's putting a bike together."

"For?" Hester coached as Justin ran to the open door to see for himself.

"For. . .me?" Justin looked from Hester to John and back for confirmation.

"It's a gift from your grandparents," Rachel told him, happy beyond words to see him finally excited about something. "You can ride it to the park and even to the hospital and out here when you come for visits and to help at the packinghouse."

"And to school?"

"You'll take the bus to and from school." She saw his disappointment, but Sharon Shepherd had advised, and she agreed, that riding the bus would provide more opportunities for Justin to make new friends. Besides, he had all those books to carry back and forth.

"Can I go help Zeke finish putting it together?"

Rachel nodded, and Justin bounded out of the kitchen, taking the porch steps in a single leap and running across the yard to where Zeke was working in the shade of the packinghouse.

Hester put her arm around Rachel's waist. "A new bicycle for Justin and a new home for you both."

"Well, good morning," Sharon said when she saw her brother having coffee with Malcolm. "You might as well move in—you're here more than at that mausoleum of a condo you bought. What's all this?"

Ben gathered up the papers spread across the glass-topped table and stuffed them into a manila folder. "And good morning to you, sleepyhead."

But Sharon was not to be pacified. "What's going on?" She indicated the papers.

"I asked Ben to get us copies of Sally's records from Memorial so when we transfer her care to Gulf Coast. . ."

"We haven't decided that for sure yet," Sharon reminded him.

"Just in case," Malcolm replied.

Ben fished a second set of papers out of his briefcase and handed them to her.

Sharon accepted the stack of papers and flipped through it without really pausing to read any of it. "So many medical people," she said.

"It takes a village," Ben said.

She looked at him for a moment then dropped the papers onto the table and sank into a chaise lounge next to them. As she looked out toward the gardens, her eyes welled with tears. "I can't seem to wrap my head around the fact that after everything we went through our Sally has come to a place where she can be in school instead of a hospital. Where she can go to the mall with her friends. That our lives can be normal again."

Malcolm reached over and held her hand. "Believe it, honey," he told her. "All the waiting for a donor, all the fear and sleepless nights, that's all in the past."

Sharon wove her fingers between his. A single tear leaked down her cheek. "I think about that girl killed in the car accident and her parents and what they must be going through. We're so very blessed."

The three of them sat quietly for several long minutes. What more was there to say? Getting Sally to the point where she was finally in remission—a remission that hopefully would last her the rest of her life—had been a journey riddled with medical land mines. Ben understood his sister's hesitancy to put her faith in the idea that Sally might finally be on her way toward a future free of hospitals and medical procedures.

No more false hopes that the second round of chemotherapy would work better than the first induction therapy had. That Sharon or Malcolm would be a match for a transplant. That someone from their extended family would match when Sharon and Malcolm had not. No more if onlys—"If only we had had more children" being Sharon's main regret.

"It's over, sis," Ben said. "Time to start living again."

Sharon brushed her tears away. "You're right. No more living in the past." She stretched her arms over her head and sighed as she looked up at the cloudless sky. "We are so very blessed," she repeated. Ben understood it for the prayer of gratitude that he knew it was.

From the front of the house they heard a vehicle turn onto the property, and a few seconds later the orange van from the co-op made its way past the garage and down the side lane to the guesthouse.

Sharon leaped to her feet. "It's moving day. I almost forgot." She bent and kissed Malcolm's forehead. "I should take them some snacks and lemonade." Then she pushed the papers Ben had shown her back across the table. "We don't need to decide this today. There's plenty of time."

Ben watched his sister walk back into the house. She had aged—Sally's illness had taken years off her life, and she was only in her midthirties.

"Did you and Sharon ever think of trying again, having another child?" he asked and then shook off the question that he couldn't believe he'd spoken aloud. "Don't answer that," he said. "I'm sorry. I just..."

Malcolm's expression was that of a man trying hard to control his temper. "We could never replace Sally, Ben." He stood up abruptly and followed his wife inside.

Having managed to upset his brother-in-law with his stupid question, Ben got up and wandered down the path that wound its way through the gardens. Through an arbor of wisteria vines he saw Justin pedaling a shiny new bike up and down the service road that ran behind the guesthouse. Ben paused to watch him for a moment, recalling the way he'd observed Sally on her bike a mere three months after her transplant, her head thrown back, her eyes closed and an aura of utter joy lighting her entire being in spite of the surgical mask that Sharon insisted she wear anytime she was outside the house. This boy rode with his head down, and his body tensed as if he could not possibly ride fast enough to escape whatever he imagined was chasing him.

Not wanting to startle the kid, Ben waited until he'd pedaled to the end of the drive and turned to come back before stepping out from the foliage of the garden and walking toward him. "Hey there," he called.

The boy looked up, and the bike's front wheel wobbled unsteadily for an instant. He squinted and held his position as if waiting for Ben's next move.

"Remember me? Sally's uncle?" Ben jerked his head in the general direction of the main house.

The boy continued to stare at him, offering nothing more than a slight nod.

"Is your mom here?"

Another nod. "She's inside," Justin said, his pubescent voice vacillating between the tenor of childhood and something deeper.

"I thought maybe I could lend a hand," Ben continued. "With the moving."

The boy shrugged. "It's mostly boxes and stuff."

"Boxes can be heavy," Ben said as he headed toward the open back of the van. "Give me a hand here, will you?"

"Mom wants us to wait. She wants to get things put away as she opens each box. There's not that much."

"So you're kind of on call?"

"Ja." He cleared his throat and tried again. "Yes sir. Mr. Shepherd's with her."

"That would be Zeke Shepherd?"

"Yes sir."

"I'll go see if I can be of any help." He paused as he passed by the boy still balancing his bike ready to take off again. "Maybe later if your mom says it's okay you'd like to come with us to watch Sally's baseball game over in the park?"

Justin stopped short of rolling his eyes, but Ben did not miss the expression of distaste the boy fought to control. Clearly Justin thought he was being asked to watch a girls' game and no self-respecting twelve-year-old boy would be caught dead at such an event. He grinned. "Sally's not playing today, but when she does she's the only girl on the team," he said and walked around the van toward the guesthouse. "I'll check with you later," he called and heard Justin take off on his bike in the opposite direction.

" 'Bout time you showed up." Zeke Shepherd greeted Ben with a grin. "Now that the work's half done." He was sitting at the bistro-style table in the small kitchen, sipping a cup of steaming coffee. The two men bumped fists in greeting.

"Yeah, I can see you're really working hard," Ben said. He

glanced around. The place was small but had an open feeling to it with a high white-beamed ceiling and lots of windows that looked out onto the garden. Sharon had chosen the cast-off furnishings with care—a mishmash of pieces, some of which he recognized from their childhood home, blended with new pieces like the bistro table and chairs that served as dining space.

Sharon regularly visited their father, especially now that their mom had died. Ben always begged off going with her to the family home in Tennessee, but he knew that Sharon saw through his excuse that he had too much work to do.

"You and Dad are the two most stubborn men I have ever known," she would say, but she never pressed him to do more.

Ben fingered the back of a rocking chair that he recognized as the one his mom used to sit in. From the end of the short hallway where he knew there were two small bedrooms and the cottage's only bathroom, he heard drawers opening and closing and the muted sound of singing.

"She's putting stuff away," Zeke reported. "Coffee?" He indicated the half-filled pot on the counter.

Ben filled a mug and took the chair opposite Zeke. He glanced around the kitchen. "How's she going to manage?" he asked. "I mean, electricity and telephone and all? Although the stove is gas. Can her people use gas for cooking?"

"*Her people*, as you so quaintly put it, use electricity, own cell phones, drive cars, even watch television. She's Mennonite—you're thinking Amish. No worries. It's a common mistake."

The two men drank their coffee in silence, each listening to the song coming from down the hall.

"Hester tells me that she's been through a lot, and her boy. . ." Zeke shook his head. "Trying to find his place in all of this. I know how that is."

Ben understood that Zeke was reflecting on his own life and the difficulties he'd had settling back into the routine he'd known before volunteering for the military. After each tour of duty it seemed as if he came back more lost than the time before and the only solution he saw was to sign up for yet another round of service. Ben didn't understand how trying to stay alive in a combat zone could possibly be preferable to the life of comfort he could have enjoyed. But he gave Zeke credit for understanding what Rachel Kaufmann was going through better than he could. "It can't be easy," Ben said.

"You've got no idea," Zeke replied and got up to refill his mug.

Rachel came down the hall and her eyes widened in surprise when she saw Ben, but her smile told him it was a pleasant surprise.

"Looks like we've got an extra pair of hands," Zeke said. Ben gave her a wave. She looked like she'd just stepped out of the shower. Her floral print dress—this one lavender—fell to well below her knees and was covered by a full apron. In place of her usual white starched prayer hat, she had covered her hair with a black scarf. She was wearing white tennis shoes that while still pristine had clearly seen miles of wear.

"How can I help?" Ben asked. "Perhaps with three strong men here you'd like to consider rearranging the furniture to better suit your style?"

"Three?" She blinked.

"Justin?" Ben nodded toward the window where the boy could be seen pedaling up and down the driveway with the same furious intent he'd demonstrated when Ben first arrived.

"Ja." She watched her son until he was once again out of sight, a wistful expression clouding those beautiful violet eyes. "Justin." It came out as a whisper, as if she had not intended to speak it aloud.

"So, what do you think?" Ben asked, moving to stand in the middle of the cottage's main room. "Sofa here or facing the fireplace? How about this chair?"

"I couldn't," Rachel exclaimed, clearly realizing what he was suggesting. "These are not my things."

"No worries," Zeke said. "Sharon said to make yourself at home, and if that means moving a chair or two, then so be it." He set down his mug and moved to the opposite end of the sofa from Ben. "Where do you want this?"

Still Rachel hesitated.

"It's your home," Ben reminded her. "Yours and Justin's, at least for now."

"Justin," Rachel called with a smile. "Come help."

An hour later, after Sharon had shown up with a pitcher of lemonade and a platter of fruit and cookies, they had completely transformed the space. The small flat-screened television that had been the focal point of the room, visible from everywhere including the kitchen, had been relocated to a corner. The sofa had been repositioned to take full advantage of the view of the gardens as well as a cozy fire on cool evenings. A handmade rag rug that Rachel told them had been a wedding present now covered the planks of the floor in front of the sofa.

"But your rug is lovely," Rachel assured Sharon as they rolled up the threadbare Oriental that had been there. Zeke carried it outside.

"This is better," Sharon said, her amateur designer's eye taking in the changes. "Do you have a patchwork quilt or perhaps an afghan you brought along?"

"I do."

"These beige slipcovers are so bland and now with the wonderful muted colors in your rug. . .shall we try it?"

Ben realized that his sister's involvement with the decorating had rekindled a hint of the enthusiasm and high spirits with which she had approached every new day before Sally's diagnosis. It occurred to him that Sharon and Rachel had a lot in common—they both had children they were concerned about. He watched as the two women draped a patchwork quilt first over the sofa and then moved it to the back of his mom's wicker rocking chair.

"You two make a good team," he said when they stood back to consider their handiwork.

"Oh, it's going to be such fun having you here, Rachel," Sharon gushed. "And, Justin," she added, turning to include the boy. "You and Sally are going to have such good times together."

Justin's smile was polite but definitely forced.

"That reminds me," Ben said. "I was telling Justin that Sally's team has a ball game this afternoon, Rachel. I was thinking perhaps Justin could come along with us, meet some of the other kids in the neighborhood. It's only a few blocks away in the park."

"Works for me," Zeke said before Rachel could reply. "Looks like everything's pretty well settled here. Mind if I come along?"

"Sounds like a plan," Ben said. "That is, if it's all right with Rachel."

He watched as Rachel looked first at Justin and then at everyone else. "You are all so kind. Danke. Justin, do you wish to see this ball game?"

Justin shrugged and studied the toe of his shoe. "I guess."

"Ah, the enthusiasm of youth," Zeke said, and all of the adults chuckled. Justin's cheeks flamed red. "Come on, sport," Zeke said as he wrapped his arm around the boy. "Let's you and me return the van and then we can bike back here for the game. Four o'clock, right?"

"See you there," Sharon replied. "Come up to the house before you leave. I have some clothes of your brother's that. . ."

Zeke rolled his eyes and grinned as he hugged Sharon and kissed the top of her head. "She fails to realize that my brother and I are not exactly the same size and that I travel light," he explained to Rachel. "But her heart is in the right place and I love her for it."

Sharon grimaced. "Traveling light for this one means a single change of clothing and his guitar. I will never understand that." She looked up at him and brushed his shoulder-length black hair away from his face. "Do you know how handsome you would be with a simple haircut?"

Zeke laughed. "I'd have to beat the ladies off with a stick, and I really am not up to that in this heat."

Ben heard a snicker and realized it had come from Justin. For the first time all morning the boy looked as if he might actually be enjoying himself. Maybe there was hope for him yet. Ben glanced at Rachel and saw by her smile that she was thinking exactly the same thing.

Chapter 10

Darcy had a plan. She knew that Ben attended his niece Sally's baseball game every Saturday afternoon. Since she lived near the park and often ran there in her off-hours, she had decided to time her run to coincide with the game. Then she would stop by to say hello to Ben and his sister—perfectly normal—and she would remind Ben of that rain check for pizza she'd offered.

Her experience in coming up with plans of action for business projects included making sure she considered all possible outcomes. In this case she believed that one of three things would happen. Ben would have already made plans for the evening. That was the worst outcome and one she could do little to change. Number two was the possibility that Sharon Shepherd would suggest that she join the family for a casual supper after the game. That outcome certainly had appeal. It would give her a chance to become closer to Ben's sister. On more than one occasion she had heard Ben moan that Sharon was a born matchmaker and her current project was finding someone for him. The best outcome of course, was that it would be just the two of them. Ben would be available and offer to pick her up at seven.

With her plan mapped out, she changed into her running clothes then changed again into the red stretch top with black shorts. The outfit flattered her figure, showed off her arms without an ounce of flab on them, and accented her platinum hair. She grabbed her water bottle and sunglasses and set out.

The asphalt track ran around the perimeter of the park's multiple sports fields. She was on her second lap and at the far side of the oval track when she saw Ben arrive with Malcolm and Sharon, their daughter, Sally—who immediately took off to join her teammates—and Malcolm's brother, Zeke. She frowned. Zeke made her uneasy. Not that she had had much contact with the homeless veteran. And it was precisely because seeing Zeke with the family gave her pause that it took a moment and another several yards along the track for her to realize that Rachel Kaufmann was taking a seat in the bleachers next to Ben. Trailing behind Rachel was a boy that looked to be about Sally's age. He sat next to Zeke in the row behind the others.

Darcy stumbled, found her footing, and then paused to take a long drink of her water while she considered the effects of these unexpected developments on her plan. Ben was talking to Rachel, and she was laughing. Darcy capped her water bottle and started to run again, her long, graceful strides bringing her closer and closer to the bleachers.

But Ben never looked up. His focus was on Rachel and then on the players as they took their places on the field. The only one who seemed even vaguely aware of her presence was Zeke Shepherd. He glanced at her as she reached the bleachers and passed behind them.

Say something, she silently coached him. *Ask Ben if that isn't his coworker running the track.*

But Zeke kept watching her, his head turning slowly as he followed her progress. She heard the tinny crack of an aluminum bat and the voices of the fielders calling to each other as the ball sailed high and long. She watched it arc, clear the fence, and land at her feet.

"Hey lady," a kid called out. "Little help?"

She picked up the ball and tossed it back over the fence to the kid and started to run again, but this time as she rounded the curve of the oval and approached the bleachers, she was smiling.

Ben Booker was looking straight at her. As she came closer he got up, eased past Rachel, and jumped down from the bleachers to wait for her.

"Darcy!" he called as she approached.

She waved and turned off the track onto the grass, covering the distance between them with ease. "Hi."

"Nice throw out there," he said.

Darcy tossed her blond ponytail and grinned as she wiped a bead of perspiration from her temple. "I have many talents, Dr. Booker. If you'd care to take me up on that rain check for pizza, perhaps we could talk about it."

Too pushy, she chastised herself silently. She had been determined to let him take the lead, but her need to take control had jinxed that.

"I'm free tonight," he said.

"Great." She smiled. "Seven?"

"I'll pick you up," Ben agreed.

Beside herself with the pure thrill of victory, Darcy took off running again. "I'll look forward to it," she called over her shoulder as she ran behind the bleachers. It was all she could do not to pump her fist in the air. She had a date with Ben Booker. A real honest-to-goodness date. Life was so sweet.

On Sunday, Justin and his mom rode their bicycles to the small church in Pinecraft that John and Hester had taken them to the weekend they arrived. Then, everything was so new that Justin had barely noticed other people filling the church's benches. Now as he parked his bike next to about a dozen others and looked around, it seemed to him that everyone waiting to go in for the service had one thing in common. They were old—as in his mom's age or, more likely, as old as his grandparents were. There was not a kid even close to his age in sight. And if there were no kids, then how could there be a school?

"Let's go in," his mom said, steering him toward the entrance.

He barely heard the sermon. All he knew was that it was hot and his good wool pants made him feel like he was boiling.

Once everyone was inside he did notice a few other kids, but they were either older by at least a year or so or much younger. Not that it mattered while he and his mom were living so far out of Pinecraft.

The way he saw it, this whole move-to-Florida adventure had been a big mistake. And now his mom seemed determined to have him be friends with Sally, but Justin was sure that Derek wouldn't like that—wouldn't like him. After the game the day before—a game where Sally had spent her time sitting on the bench and cheering on her teammates—his mom had urged him to go meet the boys on Sally's team.

Reluctantly he had climbed down from the bleachers and stood at the wire fence that marked the dugout. Sally and the rest of the team were laughing and talking all excited about winning the game and they sure didn't notice him, so he stood there a minute then turned away.

He'd rather spend his time with Zeke anyway. Zeke wasn't like other adults. He didn't talk about rules or manners, and he knew how to do just about everything—work with tools, fix a boat motor or the conveyor belt in the packinghouse, play the guitar. And he lived wherever he felt like living, did whatever he felt like doing when he felt like doing it.

"Hey," he'd heard Sally call out. "Hey Justin."

His mom had been watching him so, even though he had preferred to keep walking, he turned around. "Hey." He retraced his steps until he was once again at the fence. The rest of the team was walking away, and Sally had just picked up her glove and started around the end of the fence.

"Did you like the game?" she asked, like he was some foreigner and had never seen a ball game in his life.

Irritated, Justin frowned at her. "I do know how to play," he grumbled.

"I know. I just. . ." She heaved a heavy sigh. "Okay, let's try this one more time. Would you like to be on the team? I was telling the other guys about you. I saw you tossing the ball with those guys at school. You've got a good arm, and we could use another pitcher while I'm. . .until I can play for real."

"You had another pitcher today," Justin pointed out, still looking at the ground as they walked back toward their parents.

"Mickey? Oh, he was filling in. He plays for another team, the team we play next week. So what do you say? Want me to ask coach to give you a tryout?"

Justin thought then about the two days he'd spent at school—the way Derek Piper and his friends had watched him. The way Derek had asked casually on Friday if Justin wanted to go with them to the mall.

"Can't," Justin had told him.

Derek had smiled. "Oh, I suppose you have to walk your little girlfriend home." He'd nodded toward where Sally was loading her backpack with books.

"I have to be at the hospital."

Derek's eyes had widened. "You sick or something?"

"My mom works there, and we're staying with friends so we have to take a bus."

"Well, maybe next week," Derek had said, apparently satisfied that Justin had a good excuse.

Recalling that moment with Derek, he'd come up with an equally good excuse for turning down Sally's offer. "I can't try out. I have to work in the garden and help my mom," he told her.

"Oh, we can work around that," Sally said with such confidence that Justin got even more annoyed with her.

"Look, I don't want you to work around anything. I don't want to play, okay?" And he'd kept on walking while Sally stopped. He had felt her watching him as he sat down on the first row of the bleachers and waited for his mom to notice. But Mom had been talking to the doctor, laughing and smiling, her voice all high and excited the way it got when she was having fun.

Finally Sally had walked past him, punching her glove with her fist and not even glancing his way. "I'm tired," he'd heard her say to her parents. "Can we go?"

"Sure, honey." Her dad had bent down so he was eye level with her. "You okay?"

Justin remembered now how he had looked at Malcolm Shepherd. He'd seen something in the man's face that he hadn't thought about in a long time. Sally's dad had stopped thinking about the other adults around them. He was giving Sally what Justin's dad used to call his *undivided attention*. The sight of it made his heart ache.

So Sunday during church as he heard the minister droning on and on, Justin thought about those times when he and his dad had spent time together—fishing, working, talking. He could talk to his mom of course. But that was different. He missed his dad so much and there was nothing that would ever make that any better.

He thought about the promise his mom had made that life would be better here in Florida. How could she know that? How could she make that happen? Oh sure, it looked like things were better for her—she loved her job and she talked about friends she was making at the hospital and all. But what about him? Hadn't she promised him that *his* life would be better too?

He looked over at the boy whose sister was in jail. *Matthew*, he remembered Hester telling his mom. The guy looked as miserable as Justin felt. Maybe if his mom would agree to move to Pinecraft so he could attend the school there, he and Matthew could be friends. The hospital wasn't that far away, and there was a bus that went between there and Pinecraft. Hester had said so.

In Pinecraft they would be close to shopping and the church and everything and, most importantly, he could go to school right here with kids like him. It wouldn't be the same as living on the farm back in Ohio or having his friend Harlan close by and it certainly wouldn't make missing his dad any easier, but it would be a start.

He would talk to his mom as soon as they got back to the guesthouse. It was the perfect time. It would be the two of them because the Steiners were going straight to the home of the girl that had died in the car accident. Having made up his mind, Justin stood with everyone else for the singing of the final hymn.

But even after he'd told his mom all the reasons why it made sense for them to move to Pinecraft right away, she still didn't agree.

"I know it's hard right now, Justin. But we've barely been here a week. You have to give this a chance to work."

"I am. I will, but. . ."

"We took a big risk in deciding to move here," his mom told him, and the way she spoke he understood that she was struggling to find the right way to explain why his plan wouldn't work. "I have to prove myself in this job before we can be sure that we have enough of an income to support us."

"But what difference does it make where we live while you do that?"

"This place is free, Justin. If things don't work out we'll at least have some savings from my salary that we can use to live on. . . ."

"And then what?" he asked.

"If I can save most of the earnings I make at the hospital while I'm on probation, then we would be able to rent a little place and maybe I could work as a private nurse like I did before."

"But we'd stay here—in Florida?"

His mom looked at him, her lips moving but no sound coming out. Finally she sighed heavily and got up to get the pie she'd baked the day before. She set the pie on the table and cut a slice for him. "Justin, you're going to have to trust me that I am doing the best I can—for both of us."

After that they ate their dessert in silence; then he took his dishes to the sink and rinsed them. "I have homework."

She looked surprised. "I thought you finished at the hospital on Friday."

"I want to go over it again."

He wasn't exactly mad at his mom, just disappointed. It seemed she was making all the decisions now that they were in Florida. Actually, it had begun even before they'd left for Florida. She sure hadn't asked if he was okay with her taking the job or enrolling him in the public school or taking this place. These were all things he wanted to say to her, but he knew better. His dad would not like it if he questioned her.

"Okay?" he asked when she didn't say anything.

"Ja."

He was already inside the small bedroom when he heard her

call out, "Maybe this evening when it cools off we will go back to the park? I saw an ice cream shop near there."

"Okay." He heard the water running over the dishes and closed the door.

Outside, he heard Sally squealing as she and her dad played some stupid game in the yard. He stood at his window watching them. In spite of the heat she was wearing long pants and a long-sleeved top and a stupid-looking hat. His mom had explained about Sally needing to protect herself from the sun because of the medicine she had to take.

Justin closed his window to shut out the sound of Mr. Shepherd's deep voice. Then he flopped down onto the single bed and stared up at the ceiling. And not once did he move to wipe away the tears that ran down his face and onto the quilt his grandmother had made especially for him. They couldn't go back to the farm. His mom didn't know it, but he'd overheard Uncle Luke saying they would take him back but not her. He'd felt really good when his mom had told Uncle Luke that there was no way that would ever happen. But he knew what that meant— like it or not they would have to find a way to make this place work out.

Part Two

*In the multitude of my thoughts within me
thy comforts delight my soul.*

PSALM 94:19

Chapter 11

Paul Cox had explained to Rachel that in order to qualify for her position in the spiritual care department, she would need to become a certified pastoral counselor. "Here in Florida that means you hold either a license as an LPC—licensed professional counselor or LMFT—licensed marriage and family therapist," he explained.

"Do you have a preference?" Rachel asked.

Paul grinned. "Sure do. The one that gets you certified the quickest." He shuffled through a stack of papers on his desk. "Eileen!"

"You bellowed?" Eileen pushed open his half-closed office door with one hip while she rummaged through a thick folder in her hands. "Is this what you're looking for?"

"The woman is a mind reader." Paul grinned.

Eileen turned to go.

"And I do not bellow," Paul added as he perched reading glasses on the end of his nose and scanned the paper Eileen had given him.

"How about howl or roar or perhaps bark then?"

Paul peered at his assistant over the top of the glasses and grinned. "Bellow it is. Thanks, Eileen."

Rachel could not help smiling. She had come to enjoy the banter that flew back and forth between Paul and Eileen throughout the day.

"Now then," Paul said as he ran his finger down the page. "In your resume you show that you took some credits in social work. Is that right?"

"Ja. Yes."

He turned to another paper. "And in the transcript from the university I see that you completed the required hours of fieldwork."

"Yes, when I was a school nurse."

"Supervised? The fieldwork?"

"Yes."

He leaned back in his chair and grinned at her. "Comparing your transcript and credentials to the checklist of requirements for certification, it would appear that you've already fulfilled several of the requirements. We'll need to submit all of this to the powers that be in Tallahassee. They'll test you and evaluate you for competence to receive certification."

"I would have to go to Tallahassee?" Alarm bells went off as Rachel imagined how Justin might take the news of her having to leave.

"Just for the testing and evaluation." He frowned. "Can you folks ride on an airplane?"

"Yes."

"Then we can make arrangements for you to fly up there, go through the process, and be back the same day."

"And after this evaluation?"

"My guess is that they will require you to perform a certain number of hours of long-term as well as crisis therapy hopefully under my direct supervision, but barring that they will send someone to supervise and observe. There will no doubt be some classes, but I think we can arrange for you to do the course work online. You have a computer?"

"Only the laptop here."

"Fine. You can use that at home on your days off." He made some figures on a scratch pad and then beamed at her. "The way I see it, you will finish your probationary period at about the same time you become fully certified, right after the New Year. How does that sound?"

A little overwhelming, Rachel wanted to admit. "And what if the people in Tallahassee have other ideas? How do you know——?"

Paul chuckled. "Sometimes, Rachel, it's not how you know—it's *who* you know."

Within days Paul had arranged the trip to the state capital. Because she would not get back to Sarasota until well after dark, Justin would spend the night with Hester and John, but she had promised him that she would tell him all about the airplane ride no matter how late she got back.

On the return flight, Rachel could not help feeling hopeful. Her interview with the certification board had gone well. There were courses she would need to complete, but the good news was that she could do most of the work online or attend a class right in Sarasota. The person she had spoken to had indicated that he saw no problem with the state awarding her a provisional license. With that she could work—with supervision—while she completed the other requirements for certification.

"Paul Cox will be an excellent mentor for you during this time," the state employee had said.

Rachel held on to those words as the airplane engines droned and she marveled at the sensation of flying above a field of clouds that looked like marshmallows. Silently, she thanked God for the many blessings He had sent her way over this last month. Then remembering James counseling her that "it never hurts to ask" when she had hesitated to pray for another chance to bring a child to term, she decided to ask for one more blessing.

"Please guide me in the ways that will allow Justin to find his way in this new life we've started," she murmured, and then she closed her eyes as the airplane began its descent.

"Justin can't wait to hear all about your trip," Hester announced after she'd picked Rachel up at the airport. "I've got supper waiting. I'll bet you barely ate all day."

It was true. She'd been too nervous about the plane trip and the meetings in Tallahassee to take more than a couple of bites of toast for her breakfast. Lunch had been a sandwich from a vending machine in the state office building, and supper had been a tiny bag of miniature pretzels and a cup of hot tea on the plane.

"I am a little hungry," she admitted. "But it's not so late. Justin and I can go home after all and—"

"After you have a decent meal," Hester said as she waited for the traffic light to change.

Rachel knew better than to argue and, besides, it would be nice to talk about everything that had happened that day. "It feels like I've been gone for a week," she admitted.

Hester smiled and then focused all of her attention on the road. After they'd gone past the bridge that led to the islands that separated the bay from the Gulf of Mexico, they passed the gigantic statue of the sailor kissing the nurse based on the famous photograph from the victory celebration at the end of World War II.

"Still kissing," Hester murmured.

Rachel smiled. "Do you think the real sailor and nurse ever got together?"

"Oh, you are such a romantic," Hester teased, but then her smile faded. "Do you think you'll ever—I mean it's been what? Nearly two years?"

"Ja." In some ways the time seemed such a brief period, Justin aging from ten years old to twelve. On the other hand the almost two years that had passed since James's death seemed much longer. Rachel supposed that Hester's question was perfectly normal, but she wasn't ready to think about the idea that she might ever love another man the way she had loved James.

"How are your friends doing? The couple that lost their child?" she said instead.

Hester clutched the steering wheel a little tighter and shook her head. "It's a mess. Emma and Jeannie were never just sisters. They've always been best friends as well. But now with one child dead and the other in jail—now when they need each other the most, they barely speak."

"I'm so sorry for them and for you, having to struggle with how best to help them."

"You know me—Little Miss Fix-It, as John sometimes calls me. But this I can't fix. I can't even ease their pain a little bit." Her shoulders sagged with weariness. "I thought I understood grief. I mean, all those years watching my mother get sicker and sicker. . ."

Hester's mother had died of Lou Gehrig's disease a few years before she met John. Hester had been her mother's caregiver for five long years. Rachel could only imagine how awful it had been for her, a trained nurse, standing helplessly by and watching a loved one struggle without being able to offer any help beyond compassion and comfort.

But the car accident that had ripped apart the lives of Hester's friends was a very different kind of grieving. "I imagine that they are all struggling with the suddenness of their loss—and they are fighting their anger as well."

"That's it exactly. It was all so senseless, and yet it has happened and how are they supposed to get through it? Even if Emma's daughter doesn't go to jail, how is she going to live with what happened?" She glanced over at Rachel. "I mean, you must have felt some of that when James died—so sudden and senseless."

"Ja. We all struggled to find forgiveness. I think Justin may be struggling still. It's very hard for the children."

"So how did you get through it?"

"Just after I lost my job with the school system I heard about a program called VORP. It stands for Victim Offender Reconciliation Program. It was all about victims of a crime or accident finding a way to forgive the offender."

"I can't even think how you would begin to do that," Hester said.

"I'll admit that it took me awhile to come to the point where I wanted any part of facing the young man who was driving his car with a blood alcohol content three times the legal limit."

"You had to be so angry."

"I was furious," Rachel admitted. "In a blink of an eye that young man had changed our lives forever and all for what?

Because he didn't think? Because the last person to see him didn't take his car keys and prevent him from driving? It was done, and we had to find our way. Our way has always been forgiveness."

As they made the rest of the drive to Hester's place, Rachel told her about the program—how she and Justin and others from their extended family had met with the young man. How they had learned that he was a husband and father who had recently lost his job. "Something he and I had in common," Rachel said. And most of all she spoke of how with the help of a trained mediator they were able to create a sort of contract so the man could make amends. "Get help with his drinking problem. Go back to school. Speak out to other young people to help them see the consequences of his action."

"VORP," Hester said softly to herself as she turned onto the lane leading to the farmhouse. "Rachel, I hate to ask, but would you be willing to meet my friend Jeannie—she's the one whose daughter was killed—and tell her about this?"

"Of course. Anything I can do that might help." The lights from the farmhouse streaked the yard as Hester drove past the packinghouse and other outbuildings. She parked beside the main house and tooted the horn.

Rachel couldn't stifle a yelp of pure pleasure when she saw Justin come bounding down the porch steps. She got out of the car and held open her arms, and her son came to her.

"How was it?" he asked. "Were you scared? Was it bumpy and stuff?"

"It was like riding on a cloud," she told him as they walked back to the house arm in arm. "Did you miss me?"

Justin ducked his head. "I had school, and you were only gone for the day."

"So you didn't miss me?" she teased.

He looked up at her then and grinned. "Maybe a little," he admitted.

She ruffled his hair. "I don't know about you, but I am starving," she said.

"Zeke's here," Justin said. "He's been playing his guitar and showing me some chords."

Inside, Zeke Shepherd was sitting on the rag rug that lined the hardwood floor in the living room strumming his guitar.

Such a small thing, Rachel thought. *A little music always brings such pleasure.*

"Showtime," Zeke said and handed Justin the instrument.

"Supper time first," Hester instructed, "and then if you guys finish every bite of your vegetables, it will be showtime."

Justin grinned at Zeke, and Rachel couldn't help but think that the prayer she'd said on the plane had been answered. Maybe they were going to be all right—both of them.

It was the music that had attracted Darcy to the room in the first place. She'd been making her weekly tour of the building, checking to be sure that the housekeeping staff was doing their job to the standards she had set for them and that those on the nursing staff were tending to patients and staying on top of their reports.

Oh, she knew how the word of her tour spread from department to department and wing to wing as she made her rounds. Well, if people lived in fear of her visits, then they probably weren't doing their job. She had made it plain from day one that she would accept no excuses and that she expected people to take responsibility if anything was amiss—and fix it.

She had almost completed her tour and had a list of infractions that was disturbingly long when she heard the music. A couple of nursing assistants were standing in the doorway of the activity room. They scurried back to work when they saw Darcy coming.

She sighed. She wasn't a total ogre, after all. Needing a break, Darcy put her phone on vibrate and smiled as she heard the voices of the children raised in the ever-inspiring chorus of "This Land Is My Land."

But when she reached the entrance to the activity room she could not believe what she was seeing. Malcolm Shepherd's homeless brother was sitting in the middle of the floor with a dozen patients gathered around him. He was playing his guitar and appeared to be leading the children in a sing-along.

Beside him Rachel Kaufmann was nodding and smiling as she encouraged the children to clap their hands on cue and join in on the chorus.

He might be the brother of the president of the hospital's board—and technically Darcy's boss—but this was unconscionable. The man lived on the streets. She glanced from Zeke to Rachel and waited for Paul's assistant to meet her gaze.

When finally she did, Darcy motioned that she needed to speak with her right away.

"I'll be right back," Darcy heard Rachel tell Zeke and the children as soon as the song ended. There was a slight pause, and then Zeke started strumming a new tune.

"Who knows this one?" he asked.

Rachel was smiling when she reached the doorway.

Darcy was not.

"Was this your idea?" she demanded in a hushed tone meant for Rachel's ears only.

"You mean Zeke and the music?"

"Of course I mean Zeke. What were you thinking? The man is homeless. Do you have any idea what kind of disease and germs he could be carrying?"

"Zeke?" Rachel blinked as she looked back at Zeke, who caught her glance and raised a questioning eyebrow.

Darcy moved farther away from the doorway. She deliberately positioned herself so that Rachel's back was to Zeke. "Yes, *that* man in there with children, some of whom have compromised immune systems. This is exactly what I feared when we hired you, Rachel. You have never worked in a true hospital setting—oh, I know you were a school nurse in some little rural school system back in Ohio but that is not the same thing, not at all."

Rachel took all of this in her usual pious and serene way. She offered no apology or excuse, just waited there with her hands folded in front of her, her eyes meeting Darcy's without flinching. And that only irritated Darcy more.

"Did Paul Cox authorize this?"

"Pastor Paul and I discussed offering some outside entertainment for the children," Rachel said.

"But did he authorize *this*?" She pointed directly at Zeke.

"No. I invited Mr. Shepherd after observing him playing at a friend's house."

Darcy hesitated. Wondering if the friend had been Sharon and Malcolm Shepherd. "Well, I will be speaking to Paul Cox about this. Clearly he has overestimated your ability to choose appropriate avenues for working with the children." She glanced past Rachel to where Zeke was finishing another song. "Let him finish this song and then send him on his way."

"All right." Rachel turned and started back toward the activity room. Her refusal to debate the point with Darcy made it imperative that Darcy have the final word.

"And, Rachel?" The Mennonite woman turned to face her. "Understand that this incident will be part of your file and probationary review."

"I know." Once again she turned to go and then turned back. "You should know, then, that Zeke was quite adamant about being properly bathed and groomed before coming here. My friends, John and Hester Steiner, lent him their facilities as well as new clean clothes and shoes for him to wear. And at his request both he and the children—as you can see—are wearing masks."

"That's all well and good, but germs travel and germs thrive wherever they remain once the person carrying them leaves the premises," Darcy replied. She was pleased to see that this time Rachel Kaufmann kept walking.

Darcy watched her end the sing-along by asking the children to give Zeke a round of applause, and then the few parents and a couple of nursing assistants that Darcy had not noticed sitting in the back of the room slowly wheeled or walked the patients back to their rooms.

On the one hand, she could see that the escape from their treatment had done wonders for the children. They were talking excitedly and smiling as they left the activity room. But on the other, this was a hospital—*her* hospital in the sense that if anything went wrong she would be the one called upon to answer for it.

"Can I leave or did you want to call security and have me escorted out?"

Darcy wheeled around and found herself face-to-face with Zeke Shepherd. The mask was gone, and he was actually grinning at her. And she couldn't help but notice that it was not a smirk, but an honest-to-goodness and surprisingly good-looking grin at that. His smile made his deep-set dark eyes sparkle. Flustered that it was possible for her to feel any remote semblance of an attraction to this man, Darcy walked past him into the activity room where Rachel was putting away some supplies.

"I'll take that as no security necessary, then," Zeke called out to her after waiting a beat. Then she heard the man actually chuckling as he strolled down the hall, his guitar slung over his back.

Chapter 12

Ben had a problem, and it had nothing to do with his work. In the two weeks that had passed since their pizza date, he and Darcy Meekins had fallen into the habit of grabbing something to eat or reviewing their day with other singles from the hospital over a cold beer at the tiki bar by the bay. Afterward the two of them had twice gone back to his condo to watch a movie. When he'd mentioned that he planned to participate in a charity five-kilometer run, she had laughed and commented that he wasn't exactly prepared for that distance, especially in September when the humidity and temperature could still be real factors.

"I work out regularly," he'd protested.

"But you aren't a runner," she'd pointed out. "If you think you can keep up with me, I could get you ready in the next couple of weeks."

Never one to back down from a challenge, Ben had started meeting her at the park closer to her condo early in the mornings. They would run together and then go back to her place for breakfast. After they ate, he would head for the hospital and the doctors' lounge to shower and change, promising to see her later. On one of those mornings, after his sister had presented him with two tickets to a ball for one of the charities that she and

Malcolm supported, Ben had told Darcy about the tickets.

"Are you going?" Darcy asked as they jogged alongside each other for their cooldown lap.

"Do I have a choice?"

"Well, yeah. You're a big boy."

"I know. It's just that charity balls are not exactly my thing, but this event is very important to Sharon. Agreeing to co-chair was the first real sign that she was ready to start living *her* life instead of living only for Sally. So for no other reason than that it will please Sharon, I'll do it. Wanna come?"

"Gee. I don't know. You make it sound like the world's most boring evening."

"Come on. There'll be great food, dancing, a silent art auction—the usual stuff. If things get too unbearable one of us can fake a headache."

"That would be me, I presume?"

"Well, yeah. What kind of guy would I be if I let you go home alone?"

Darcy had laughed. "All right. I'll come, but you are going to owe me big-time, buster." She'd taken off then, running with those long graceful strides that Ben had come to admire.

"Pick anything you want from the auction," he'd called out as he ran to catch up to her. "My treat."

Darcy had grinned. "Okay, you're on."

She's a good friend, he had thought.

When he told Sharon that he was bringing Darcy, she had beamed her matchmaker smile. "I knew it. This whole 'we're just friends' thing has been a cover."

"We *are* just friends," Ben protested.

"Really? I've never known you to spend this much time with any other friend—drinks by the bay, movies at your place, breakfast at her place." She actually pinched his cheek. "Come on, big brother, admit it. Finally someone has found her way around that science experiment that passes for a heart in you."

Ben did not begin to know how to protest Sharon's multiple assumptions. "First of all, I am all heart and you know it. Did I not turn to absolute mush when Sally was born? And as for Darcy..."

"It's okay, Ben. If you're not ready to go public with this, I get it. But once the two of you show up together at that ball tongues will wag."

Later that night, after he and Darcy had shared a late supper at a restaurant near the hospital, he was walking her back to her car. He had been about to tell her of Sharon's ridiculous assumption when she'd said, "I bought a gown for the ball today."

Half a dozen responses shot through his mind, but what came out was a noncommittal, "Really?"

Apparently that was all the encouragement she needed to provide details. By the time they reached her car in the mostly deserted parking garage, she was twirling around as if modeling the gown for him and laughing like a schoolgirl.

"Oh Ben, this is going to be so much fun," she gushed and pirouetted straight into his arms.

Their faces were inches apart, and her expression turned from girlish exuberance to grown-up serious. She ran her fingers across his lips. In all the time they had spent together these past weeks, they had kissed only twice—a quick peck both times when she left his place after they'd watched the movies.

"Kiss me, Ben," she whispered now, and before he could find words to say. . .whatever he might come up with to explain that he didn't see her that way, she kissed him.

Darcy was one gorgeous woman. And there was no doubt that she was bright and funny and had all the qualities most men would find attractive. But for Ben something was missing. Still, she was a good kisser, and he ignored his feeling of guilt when his natural instincts to return her passionate kiss kicked in. After a moment he was the one to pull away.

And there was the problem. Her kiss told him that she was 100 percent on the same page as his sister was. For Darcy this was no casual friendship—she wanted more. No, she thought it already *was* more.

"Wow," he said for lack of anything else to offer to break the moment.

She grinned. "Yeah, wow indeed." She failed to notice his hesitation. Instead she spun out of his arms and got into her car.

"See you in the morning. I'll have the coffee ready."

The charity run was coming up on Saturday morning, the same day as the ball. He had two more days to train, and certainly he could use every lap he took around the track at the park. But the need to put the brakes on whatever this was with Darcy took priority.

"Can't tomorrow. I have an early meeting at Memorial, and Friday's my last day there before I move over to Gulf Coast full-time, so. . ."

"It's going to be so great working in the same hospital—seeing each other every day." She grinned. "All right, I guess you can miss two days of training. I'll pick you up on Saturday morning."

He'd begun to notice that Darcy spoke in declarative sentences, not questions. She simply assumed he would expect her to stop by his condo and they would go to the run together. And the reality was that there was no way around that. His place was less than a block from the starting line for the run. "Sounds like a plan."

She backed out of her parking space and waved as she drove away.

Wondering what on earth he had gotten himself into and how he was going to fix it, Ben stood rooted to the cement floor of the parking garage. It wasn't as if he could simply sit Darcy down and make it clear that they had a great friendship with lots of interests in common, but that was as far as it went. No, he had to work with this woman, serve on committees to make hospital policy with her, attend the same hospital functions as she did. And the main issue was that he didn't want to hurt her. "How come you've never married?" she'd asked him one night as she prepared a cold supper of sushi at his place before settling in to watch a movie.

He had shrugged. "Medical school took all my time."

"You've been out of med school for years."

"Married to my work, then. How about you?"

She'd been facing away from him when he'd asked it, but there was no question that she had gone very still. "I came close," she said after a moment and then turned to him with a smile. "I actually got left at the altar, or almost. Two days before the wedding the guy sent me a 'Dear Darcy' letter and left town."

Ben hadn't known what to say, but she had saved him by waving off his expression of sympathy. "Not a big deal. I realize now the jerk did me a real favor. The truth is that I think my mother was more upset than I was. She worried for weeks over how this would play with her friends—refused to leave the house for days because she was so mortified."

Again not knowing what to say, Ben had offered the first thing that came to mind. "Well, any guy who would leave you must be a jerk."

Now he realized how a woman who clearly had romantic feelings for him would have interpreted such a statement. He groaned, and the sound echoed in the deserted parking structure as he walked to his car. Saturday was going to be a long day.

Rachel carefully separated the herb seedlings that Hester had given her and knelt to plant them in the flower bed outside the cozy screened porch at the back of the guesthouse. It was hard to believe that they had lived in the cottage for almost a month now. It was even more impossible to believe that she was planting any spring or summer flower in October.

"Rachel?" Sharon Shepherd was knocking on the front screen door of the guesthouse.

"Out here." Rachel wiped her hands on a rag as she went to meet Sharon. The normally cheerful woman's face was lined with worry. "Is Sally all right?" It was the first question anyone asked if Sharon or Malcolm seemed upset.

"She's fine. Thank you for asking. It's this charity ball tonight." She heaved a sigh of pure frustration. "My co-chair called, and it seems that the pastry chef for the catering service we hired just walked off the job and his two helpers left with him."

"That's terrible."

"Fortunately he had already baked the key lime cakes that will form the foundation of our dessert. However, there are five hundred plates that need berries and a chocolate drizzle in the shape of a fiddlehead fern. I suppose we could serve the cake without the decoration, but the fiddlehead is the theme."

Sharon seemed close to tears, and Rachel realized that the woman had come to her not to relieve herself of her frustration but to ask for some concrete help.

"What can I do?" she asked although she could not imagine how she might solve Sharon's problem. Perhaps she could wash the berries?

"I called Hester thinking she might be able to recommend someone from Pinecraft—perhaps a baker from one of the restaurants there—Yoder's or Troyer's. But she's over at her friend Jeannie's and I don't want to bother her when they have far more serious problems than this."

"You could call the restaurants yourself or I could," Rachel offered.

"I already did. It's Saturday—their busiest day." She hesitated. "I really hate to ask, but do you think you might come with me? Perhaps together we could at least see what we could do about the desserts. We might as well forget about the fancy fern design." She sighed. "Although that was the point—it's the Fiddlehead Ball, after all."

"Of course, I can help," Rachel readily agreed. "And Justin can come as well."

Sharon's smile was radiant. "Thank you. Sally's already insisting on going so between the four of us maybe we can save the day. I'll go pack up my gown and shoes. I can change there. We can take my car. Malcolm can come in our other car so he can drive you and Justin and Sally home when we're done." She ticked each item off on her manicured fingernails. "Can you be ready in fifteen minutes?"

"Justin and I will be ready," Rachel assured her. As soon as Sharon left, Rachel called Justin in from his work weeding one of the flower beds and told him to wash up and change his clothes.

As she explained what was happening she changed into a fresh dress and put on a clean apron. She checked her hair, anchoring any stray wisps under her starched prayer covering and then knocked lightly on Justin's door.

"Coming." He had not questioned anything about this strange turn of events, and for that she was grateful since over the last couple of weeks he had become even more reclusive, rarely talking about what had happened at school and never mentioning any new friends.

He emerged from his room dressed in jeans and a short-sleeved shirt. His hair was wet where he had tried to tame the cowlick.

"You look nice," Rachel said.

Outside, a car horn tooted as Sharon pulled up in front of the guesthouse. Rachel saw Justin hesitate when he realized that Sally was seated in the backseat. "You ride up front," Rachel said quietly. "I'll sit in back with Sally." The look of pure relief and gratitude that Justin gave her was worth everything.

The ball was to take place at a large hall on the north end of town. When they entered the building, Rachel saw that the place had been transformed into a tropical garden. While Sharon and Sally went to speak with Sharon's co-chair who was clearly in charge of decorating the hall, Rachel waited patiently with Justin near the entrance.

"There must be a thousand candles," Justin said. "Do you think they plan to light them all?"

"Probably so."

"I could help with that," he offered, and Rachel understood that for a boy the attraction of matches and fire was far more interesting than the idea of working in a kitchen.

"We'll see." Sharon was crossing the room to where they waited. She looked even more stressed than she had when she'd first shown up at the guesthouse. "Is everything all right?"

"When it rains it pours," Sharon grumbled. "The caterer has informed my cochair that his people will not arrive until fifteen minutes before we need them to start circulating with the appetizers, and more to the point, they are *waitstaff*, not *kitchen staff*."

"What's the difference?" Justin asked.

"My point exactly," Sharon said. "But a contract is a contract, and everything was already spelled out there. These people consider themselves specialists. There are separate teams to prepare the appetizers, salad, and entree, a wine steward and bartender, waitstaff, and the pastry chef and his two helpers that walked off the job. The caterer will do what he can, but we really need him overseeing everything and. . ."

Sharon looked as if she might burst into tears. "I'm so sorry, Rachel. I thought that if we could come down here for an hour or so and you could help. . . But I can't possibly ask you and Justin to stay all evening." The lines around her eyes and mouth told Rachel that she was exhausted.

"Perhaps we could see the kitchen. After all, you don't have to replace all of those people you mentioned—just the three who left."

"Right, Mom," Sally said. "We have three people right here, so exactly what is the problem?"

Sharon looked skeptical, but she led the way to the large kitchen. On tables that ran the length of one long wall were stacks of green plates.

"As soon as the salads go out, you can start assembling the desserts here," the caterer told them. Rachel saw several flat trays with the undecorated key lime cakes waiting to be cut. At least the baking was already finished.

Sally peered at a pencil drawing taped to the wall. It was the design for the chocolate fern that the pastry chef had planned to decorate each plate with. She grinned and started rolling back the sleeves of her shirt. "I can do that."

Her mother was skeptical, as was the caterer. "Can't you make an exception and do this part?" she asked him.

"Not if you want everything else to come off smoothly. Have you seen the list of things we have yet to do?"

Sally nudged her mother's side. "Let me try, okay?"

The caterer filled a pastry bag with chocolate and handed it to Sally. Several of the kitchen staff stopped what they were doing and gathered around as she bent over the plate and began drawing the fern.

"Perfecto," one man whispered.

Sally grinned. "I'm going to be a famous artist one day."

"I thought you were going to be a baseball player," Justin said.

"That too," she told him. She glanced at her mother and Rachel. "Well, do you want me to get started on the other four hundred ninety-nine ferns or not?"

Sharon kissed Sally's forehead. "I do love you, kiddo," she murmured before turning her attention to Rachel. "Are you sure this isn't asking too much of you?"

"Not at all. We're happy to help, and one late night is not going to cause us any harm."

"Thank you so much." Sharon clapped her hands together to gain everyone's attention. "So, Rachel and her son, Justin, and my daughter, Sally, will manage the assembly of the desserts."

"If anybody wants to help. . ." Sally left the thought hanging as she grinned at the rest of the kitchen staff. They all chuckled and went back to work preparing trays of appetizers and putting the finishing touches on the other courses. "Guess we're on our own, then." Sally looked at Rachel and Justin. "Just give us the green light when you're ready," she told the caterer.

While Sharon went to change into her ball gown, Rachel, Justin, and Sally did whatever they could to help make sure everything was ready for receiving the guests. They helped prepare the appetizer trays, cleared away used skillets and other cooking utensils, and filled carafes with ice cubes, water, and thin slices of lemon. To Justin's delight, Sharon and her co-chair recruited him to assist with the job of lighting the small votive candles that formed a circle around centerpieces of a single orchid surrounded by ferns on each of the tables set for ten guests.

"Five hundred candles," he said when he came back to the kitchen. "And that doesn't count the ones that are on the stage."

He was excited—more like the boy he'd once been, and Rachel sent up a silent prayer of thanksgiving.

They were so busy that Rachel barely noticed the time passing. It was only after the last large oval tray had been loaded with the final plates of dessert that she accepted the plate of food the caterer handed her.

"Thank you," he said. "I quite literally could not have pulled this off without you and the children. Any time you might want a job. . ."

Rachel smiled. "I have a job, but I do appreciate the offer."

"Mrs. Kaufmann," Sally whispered from her place near the door that led to the ballroom, "come look. It's magical."

Now that the kitchen was quiet, Rachel could hear the music, the clink of flatware on china, and the laughter and conversation of people enjoying themselves.

"Follow me," Sally said with a twinkle in her eyes and a mischievous grin that made it impossible not to want to know what she was up to. Even Justin followed her through the hallway and up a narrow staircase to a balcony that overlooked the ballroom below.

It took a moment for Rachel to adjust her vision from the glaring fluorescent lighting of the kitchen to the shadows and candlelight of the ballroom—a different world where men in tuxedos and women in jewel-toned gowns seemed almost to be a part of the decoration. It was like looking at a painting, a moving painting, as the guests danced or sat enjoying their dessert and talking.

"There's Mom and Dad." Sally pointed toward the center of the dance floor. She sighed happily. "Isn't she beautiful?"

"She is," Rachel agreed.

"I'm glad that she's having a good time," Sally continued. "She's been through a lot, worrying about me and all."

Rachel could not help but marvel at the girl's perceptiveness and her kindness in taking joy from the fact that after all the weeks and months of worry her mother was carefree, at least for the moment.

"Ooh," Sally whispered, "there's Uncle Ben."

Rachel searched the dancers for a glimpse of the handsome doctor.

"He's with that lady from the hospital." For the first time that Rachel could recall, Sally sounded less than her usual upbeat self.

"Ms. Meekins looks lovely," Rachel said.

"Yeah." Sally's tone was grudging.

Darcy Meekins looked very different than she did at the

hospital. She was wearing a beautiful aqua-colored satin gown and her hair—usually caught up into a sophisticated twist at work—cascaded down her back in platinum waves. Rachel turned her attention from Darcy back to Ben. On those occasions when she happened to see him at the hospital, more often than not he was wearing scrubs or an ill-fitting lab coat. Even in such casual clothes, there was no denying how handsome he was. But seeing him in formal wear took her breath away.

Embarrassed and confused by her reaction, Rachel turned her attention back to Darcy who was laughing at something Ben had said. Rachel had to admit that they made a perfect couple. And she wondered why the idea of Ben with Darcy made her feel sad.

Chapter 13

It had not taken long for Justin to realize that the reason Derek Piper had accepted him into his group of friends was that Justin was good at math. So he certainly did not need Sally Shepherd lecturing him on that subject.

"I'm helping him with math. So what?" They were waiting for the school bus together—a situation that Justin had tried his best to avoid without success.

"You are *doing* his math for him," Sally corrected him. As usual she wore clothes that covered her from head to foot and one of her collection of stupid hats. In Justin's view, the way she dressed was one more way she stood out in a crowd. "He won't thank you for it," she continued, "and if Mr. Mortimer catches on, it's for sure that Derek Piper won't take the blame."

"Are you gonna tell?"

The bus arrived at that moment, and without another word Sally mounted the steps, exchanged a cheery greeting with the bus driver—who like everyone else seemed to think the girl was some kind of angel or something—and took a seat next to one of her girlfriends.

Justin walked past her toward the back of the bus where the last two rows were empty and he could hold places for Derek and the other guys. He slouched down in one of the seats and stared at Sally. Like the bus driver and Mr. Mortimer and pretty much everybody else, his mom thought Sally could do no wrong. His mom had gone on and on one day about how very sick Sally had been and how brave she'd been through it all and stuff like that. She sure didn't look sick, and she had an appetite that was enormous.

And besides, what about *his* courage in the way he'd handled himself after his dad died and through this whole business of moving to Florida? What about the way *he* had to smile and act like it didn't matter that his mom had almost no time for him at all now that they were here. She was always studying for some test or course she had to take or she was at work or she got a call in the middle of the night and had to go back to the hospital. What about that?

The bus squealed to its final stop before they reached the school and Derek got on with his best buddies, Max and Connor. Derek was in the lead, and when the bus driver told him to keep his voice down, Derek started speaking in an exaggerated whisper that had everyone on the bus giggling.

Everyone except Sally. She simply ignored him.

Derek paused next to her seat. She was on the aisle, her back to him. She was talking to her friend, but her friend's eyes were on Derek. The bus made a wide turn, and Derek lost his balance and fell heavily against Sally. When he regained his footing, Justin saw that he was grinning and knew that he had lost his balance on purpose.

"Are you all right?" His voice dripped with false concern. "Good thing you've got all that extra padding or I might have really hurt you." He was still grinning as he continued on his way and flung himself into the seat next to Justin. "Hey J-man, got that math homework done?"

Justin saw Sally glance back at them. She was rubbing her shoulder, and she was looking directly at Justin. He felt bad about what Derek had said about her weight, but he also had no doubt that she had heard Derek's question about the math homework. It was all there in the way that she arched her eyebrows, questioning Justin's next move.

With deliberate slowness he pulled his math notebook out of his backpack and handed it over to Derek. He had stayed up late making notes he thought Derek could follow to help him find the answers. He called them *study sheets* and told himself that he was helping Derek understand the problem so that when he had to figure it out on his own on a test he would be able to do it.

So let her tell on him if she dared. He'd take that risk. If the cost of having Derek and the others as his friends—his only friends—was helping them out so they kept up in math, it was worth it. Besides, he was pretty sure Sally wouldn't tell. After all no matter how popular a kid was, nobody trusted a tattler.

When Ben had looked up while dancing with Darcy and seen Rachel peering over the auditorium's balcony, he had actually stumbled a little and narrowly missed stepping on Darcy's exposed toes.

Darcy had laughed. "Easy there. I'm going to need those toes later."

Ben had turned her so that his back was to the balcony. He realized that he was not only surprised to see Rachel standing there, her white prayer covering unmistakable even in the soft candlelight, but he also realized that the novelty of her in this setting had unnerved him. For the rest of that evening—although he did not see Rachel again—he could not seem to get her out of his mind. And in his dreams later that night it wasn't Darcy he was dancing with—he was holding Rachel in his arms.

In the days that followed, on those rare occasions when their paths crossed at the hospital, he tripped over his greeting as he had stumbled on the dance floor that evening. Rachel remained her usual serene self during these brief encounters, her smile warm and open, and, as Paul Cox was given to exclaiming, "a breath of pure fresh air in these sometimes difficult surroundings."

In the monthly meeting of department heads that Ben had just left, Paul had made it crystal clear that in his opinion they could not have chosen a better candidate for the spiritual counselor position. "The woman is a wonder," he declared in that voice that was better suited to the pulpit than the conference room. And Ben had seen Darcy wince as Paul went on to enumerate all the ways that in six short weeks Rachel Kaufmann had established herself as a "pure blessing to this place."

"Ben, wait up."

He turned at the sound of Darcy's heels on the tiled floor. Ever since the run followed by the charity ball he had worked hard at keeping his interactions with Darcy outside the hospital as casual as possible. And to his relief she seemed fine with that, to the point that he'd decided he must have misread their kiss in the parking lot.

"Going my way?" He grinned as he waited for her to catch up to him.

But Darcy was in full business mode—the thin line of her mouth told him as much.

"Hey, what's up?"

"Can we grab a cup of coffee? I need to talk to you about something—something I was reluctant to mention in the meeting."

"Sounds serious." They had reached the entrance to the small coffee bar in the lobby. It was fairly deserted at this time of day, and Ben indicated that Darcy should choose a table while he got their coffee. When he set the cup in front of her and pushed the dish containing packets of sweetener toward her, she was staring out the window.

"Thanks. I needed this." She laughed and added, "Intravenously would be even more helpful."

"Looks like what you need is a break. What's going on?"

She leaned closer, glancing around as if afraid of being overheard. "Houston, we have a problem," she murmured, "and her name is Rachel Kaufmann."

Ben could not have been more surprised if Darcy had suddenly spilled her hot coffee all over him. "Rachel? But Paul said. . ."

Darcy snorted and gave a dismissive wave of her hand. "Paul thinks the woman practically walks on water. That's part of the problem. He believes that her going through certification and getting her license is a mere formality. He can't seem to stop praising her."

"And *your* problem is. . . ?" Ben was surprised to realize that he was feeling a little defensive when the fact was that he knew next to nothing about how she was doing her job.

"I didn't want to mention it before—I mean she is living with your sister and Malcolm."

"But?"

Darcy took a deep breath and dived in. "A few weeks ago I was doing my weekly tour of the various departments. Imagine my shock to see Zeke Shepherd playing his guitar for the children on the children's ward—in the activity room."

"Okay, now you've lost me. What's that got to do with Rachel?"

"She invited him—without Paul's approval apparently. Oh, he approved the idea of musical entertainment for the children, but Zeke? No way would he ever have—"

"Why not?"

Her eyes bugged at this question. Her mouth worked, but no words came out. Finally she managed, "You are joking."

"Not so much." Ben took a sip of his coffee. "What's your problem with Zeke? I've heard him play and sing—he's talented and especially good with children."

"He is a street person, as in he lives on the street, takes his meals out of trash bins, sleeps on park benches or under bushes, and who knows how or where he manages to bathe or shower."

"Whoa!" Ben held up his hands to stop her tirade. "First of all, Zeke has a steady job at the fruit co-op that the Steiners run—and that my brother-in-law funds. Second, I'll grant you that he prefers sleeping out under the stars and I have no idea where he gets his meals or does his personal grooming, but the fact remains that any time I've seen him he is always clean-shaven and dressed in albeit ill-fitting but freshly laundered clothes."

He paused when he saw tears glistening on the rims of Darcy's eyes. "Hey, sorry." He lowered his voice. "Please explain to me why this has you so upset."

"I don't know. It's her. I have this uneasy feeling about her. I know that's totally unprofessional, but I'm usually right about these things. True there was no real harm, but when she goes out on her own and pulls a stunt like this she is not only putting the children in danger of picking up some germ or infection that man might be carrying but she's also endangering the entire hospital. What if a reporter had been here or a TV journalist?"

"You're talking in riddles, Darcy."

She cupped her hand as if holding a microphone. "We're here at the newly opened Gulf Coast Hospital where this reporter was stunned to see Sarasota's own well-known street musician and homeless veteran, Zeke Shepherd, entertaining the children. Given the outbreak of cryptosporidium that spread through the homeless population after last year's hurricane, this reporter had to question—"

"Okay, I get it. So talk to Rachel and help her to understand why—"

"I did."

"And?"

"Oh, you know how she is—all sweetness and light. She told me that Paul had given his permission but that it was her responsibility since Paul did not know that she was going to invite Zeke."

"Okay, so we're back to square one. What's the problem? Seems to me you handled it." Ben took another swallow of his coffee.

"But don't you think—I mean, she placed the hospital in danger."

Ben could see that what Darcy had really wanted was for him to be as incensed by Rachel's action as she was. But he really couldn't see the harm. There had to be more behind Darcy's fury.

"Hey, it's over," he said. "She didn't set the place on fire. There was no reporter or television camera. Zeke didn't infect the children, and you covered the chance for any liability by writing Rachel up for the infraction, right? It wasn't her best choice, but her heart was in the right place. I mean, we want an environment that brings the world to children isolated by their illness, don't we?"

"I suppose. But. . ."

Ben grinned at her, trying to lighten the moment. "Come on, admit it. You hate being wrong about somebody and from day one you were sure that Rachel was the wrong person for this job. Admit that she's good, Meekins, and move on." He reached across the small round table and patted her hand.

She let out a deep shuddering sigh and went so far as to give him a slight nod. "You're right. I worry so much about the hospital and getting our reputation solidly established. Rachel Kaufmann isn't the only one on probation here. I mean, this whole hospital has to shine."

"And that's exactly why the board hired you," Ben assured her. He glanced at his watch and stood up. "I have rounds. You okay?"

"Sure. Thanks for listening."

"What are friends for? Maybe I'll see you later, after work? Some of the other doctors plan to check out that new Italian place in the Rosemary District."

Her demeanor turned on a dime. She smiled up at him. "Why, Dr. Booker, are you asking me out?"

"Actually, maybe the best idea would be to ask Rachel to join us. If the two of you got better acquainted outside the hospital. . ."

Her eyes clouded over and her smile faded. "You know, I completely forgot. I have a previous engagement. Another time maybe."

Without another word she got up and went to refill her coffee mug before heading back to her office.

Rachel's mind was reeling with everything she had going on these days. Her course work was not especially difficult, but it took up a lot of her time. The same was true of her work at the hospital, especially when she had to return after hours to handle some emergency. Then there was the reprimand regarding Zeke that she had received from Darcy Meekins—a reprimand that was now a part of her employment record. Mark Boynton had explained to her that the hospital had a three-strikes-and-you're-out policy when it came to such things.

But uppermost in her thoughts was the feeling that she was not spending enough time with Justin. Not that he had said anything or given any indication that he was upset with her. To her relief he seemed to have connected with a group of boys from his school. One day she'd happened to be coming back to the guest cottage at the same time the school bus pulled up and Justin got off.

He hadn't seen her right away because his attention had been on a boy leaning out one of the windows of the bus, shouting something to Justin. Justin had been smiling and then laughing as the bus pulled away and the boy continued to hang out the window.

"Who was that?" she'd asked.

"Just somebody in my class," Justin replied.

"Does this person have a name?"

"Derek."

"He seems. . ."

Justin had shot her a look that warned her not to say anything derogatory about his friend so she changed tactics.

"Does he live nearby?"

Justin shrugged.

"Because maybe you'd like to invite him over for supper one day, or we could. . ."

"I see him at school. I've got homework," he added. "Math test tomorrow."

On the surface everything with Justin seemed to be going as well as could be expected. His grades were fine. He was making friends given the exchange with the boy on the bus and his occasional comment about a couple of other boys. He did his chores and did not complain when she had to go back to the hospital late at night. But there was something. . . .

"I can call Sally's parents and ask if you could stay with them until I get back, or you could come with me," she'd offered the first time she'd gotten a late-night call.

"I can stay on my own, Mom. I'm not a little kid anymore."

No, he wasn't. In the short time since they'd come to Florida it seemed to Rachel that he had grown taller and his body—always rail thin—had begun to fill out. And his voice was changing as well. It was rougher, and he had developed a tendency toward mumbling. But what worried her most was that his attitude had changed. He was quieter than ever—sometimes bordering on sullen.

She needed to speak to him about that. Sometimes when Sharon or Malcolm Shepherd walked over to the garden when he was out doing the weeding, he was not as polite as Rachel would like him to be. But the fact was that she had little enough time to spend with Justin these days and she was reluctant to use a minute of it to chastise him.

"It's a phase," Hester assured her one day when Rachel and Justin had gone over to the co-op so that Justin could help in the packinghouse and Rachel could help Hester label the jars of marmalade they would sell at the farmers' market.

Rachel wasn't so sure. As she made her way through the labyrinth of corridors that led from the children's wing to her office, she had one more worry on her mind. She simply could not afford to lose this job. She forced herself to take a deep, calming breath and silently sent God a plea to show her how best to earn Darcy's approval.

And then she turned the corner and bumped—quite literally—into Ben Booker.

Chapter 14

"Hey there. I was hoping I might run into you," Ben said with a grin.

Rachel felt her cheeks flush. She lowered her eyelids, protecting herself from the effect that his smile had on her. Ever since seeing him at the charity ball she had been unable to get Ben Booker out of her mind. After Justin had gone to bed, when she would sit alone in the cottage's small kitchen studying, images of Ben dressed up for the ball would return. She was convinced that her thinking of the man at such times was nothing more than loneliness and fatigue.

"Rachel?"

"I wasn't paying attention," she admitted. "I'm so sorry."

"Not at all, and I meant what I said. It's been awhile since I checked up on you." He leaned against the wall, one ankle casually crossed over the other as if he had all the time in the world. "How are things going?"

For one fleeting moment she was tempted to confide in him, to tell him that she often felt overwhelmed by work and her studies for the certification examination and she was worried about Justin. Most of all she was tempted to seek his advice on how best to smooth things over with Darcy.

But then she remembered them dancing. Clearly, they had a relationship that went beyond work. If Rachel could believe Eileen, the two were *an item*.

"I believe that Pastor Paul is pleased with my work. At least..."

"I'm not asking about work, Rachel. How are *you* doing?"

She heard the genuine concern in his words, and she looked up at him. His eyes reflected his sincerity. This was no casual inquiry. He really wanted to know. Still, it was important for her to remember that in spite of the times they had been together when he visited his sister, theirs was a working relationship. "I am well. Thank you for asking," she said, and then with a smile she added, "And you? Have you completed your duties at Memorial yet?"

"I have. From now on I'm full-time here at Gulf Coast, but stop changing the subject. We were talking about you. How's Justin?"

"He is also well." She thought about the note her son had handed her that morning as he rushed off to catch the bus. It was from his teacher asking her to call to set up a meeting. Justin did not answer when she asked him to explain.

"I'm late," was all he'd shouted as he jogged down the lane.

Ben nodded. "Must be tough on a kid his age losing his dad and then moving to a place where he has no friends."

"He seems to have made friends at school—and of course, there is Sally."

"Sally tells me he's some kind of math whiz?"

Rachel fought the swell of pride that came from hearing Justin praised. "He is very good in that subject."

Ben pushed himself away from the wall. "Maybe come tax time I'll get his help. I am terrible at that subject." He hesitated as if not knowing what to say. "It's good to have you here, Rachel."

She did not miss the way his tone had changed from teasing to serious, and she paused, not sure how to answer him. "Danke," she murmured.

Ben seemed about to say something more, but then he cleared his throat. "Well, I have one more patient to see and you've probably got work to do." But he made no move to go. "Sharon tells me that you're always working—studying or cleaning or weeding the garden with Justin. Seems to me you could use a break. How about grabbing a quick bite to eat after work?"

Startled, she said the first thing that came to mind. "With you?"

He smiled and glanced around as if looking for someone else. "Why not? We work together. You live next door to my sister. My niece seems to think you are pretty special—all I hear lately is Rachel this and Rachel that. I thought that maybe we should get to know each other outside of this place."

She had often seen groups of coworkers leaving the hospital together, chatting about plans to share a meal or attend some event. Sometimes they had invited her to join them but she had always begged off, citing the need to go home to Justin.

"Rachel?" Ben was watching her now, waiting for her answer. "It's not a date or anything," he assured her.

She felt her cheeks grow hot with embarrassment. Was that why he thought she'd hesitated? Because she thought he was asking her for a date? Was he right? "Nein," she murmured. "I mean, no, I realize that. It's just that I have Justin and. . ."

"How about I get Sally and you get Justin and the four of us go out tomorrow after work? Do you like boats?"

The way this man's mind leaped from topic to topic was confusing to Rachel. "Boats?"

"I'll rent one from Margery Barker's marina. We could pack a picnic and take a ride around the bay—calm waters and all—and watch the sun set."

"Justin would love a boat ride." It might be the very thing to lift his spirits. He would not be quite as excited that the offer included Sally.

"Then it's a date—not a date—a boat ride with food," he said. "We'll have the kids meet us here after school and as soon as we've both finished for the day, we can go, okay?"

"Okay," she agreed, her head still spinning with the way this casual inquiry about how she was doing had turned into something much more complicated. "I will prepare some—"

"You will not. I'll take care of everything—boat, food, the works, okay?"

It was impossible to refuse him. "Okay."

When Rachel spoke to Hester about the teacher's note, her friend could come up with no ideas about why Mr. Mortimer would ask to meet with Rachel.

"I think it's kind of a normal thing in public schools," Hester had suggested, and that did make sense. After all, in their Mennonite school back in Ohio with its much smaller enrollment it was routine for the teacher to call upon a parent to talk about how a child was progressing—especially a child new to the community.

So Rachel called the school and left a message for Mr. Mortimer to contact her at work after asking Eileen if she thought it would be all right to receive the call there.

"Of course," Paul's assistant assured her. "Heavens, if you only knew how some people abuse the system with their personal calls. It's not like you're going to make a habit of this."

The teacher's call came the next afternoon, right before Justin was due to arrive at her office after school for their boat ride.

"Mrs. Kaufmann? This is Justin's teacher—Ralph Mortimer."

"Yes, hello." Rachel heard the nervousness in her voice and cleared her throat to cover it. "How are you?"

"Very well, thank you. I'm afraid that I have a concern, however, about Justin."

"He has shown me several papers with high marks," she ventured.

"Your son is a bright and industrious student, Mrs. Kaufmann. It is not his work ethic that concerns me. It is his choice in companions."

"I don't understand."

She heard the teacher sigh heavily. "That is why I think it would be good if we could meet in person."

Rachel's mind reeled with everything that she had to accomplish over the coming days. Pastor Paul was out of town attending a conference so she was filling in for him. On top of that she had sole responsibility for any on-call emergencies. In addition she had a paper due for one of her online classes and a supervisor from the certification board in Tallahassee was coming to observe her work.

"Mrs. Kaufmann?"

"I apologize. Is there no way you can simply tell me what the problem is now?"

"Well, I would prefer a face-to-face but it is Friday. Could I meet with you in person on Monday?"

"Of course." Rachel had no idea whether or not she could arrange such a thing, but when it came to Justin, she would move whatever mountain stood in the way of helping her child. "But please tell me exactly what this is about."

"Very well. Has Justin mentioned another student named Derek Piper?"

"Not exactly." Rachel thought about the boy on the bus, the rowdy boy shouting out the window at Justin as the bus pulled away. Was that Derek? She couldn't remember.

"I won't pull punches here, Mrs. Kaufmann. Derek is older—he was held back this year. He's a bright enough student but lazy."

"I don't understand what that has to do with—"

"I have evidence that Justin is providing Derek with answers to the math assignments."

"He wouldn't do that," Rachel protested. "We are a family of strong faith."

"Under normal circumstances I believe that Justin would follow the right path. But Derek can be a very persuasive young man and, as you must know, Justin is quite introverted. Since arriving here, he has struggled in connecting with other students. Derek seems to have taken your son under his wing, so to speak, and I don't think that Justin fully appreciates that there is a price for that friendship."

Rachel's mouth had gone dry, and she had to swallow several times before she could form her next words. "My son is an honest child, Mr. Mortimer. He would not. . ."

"Mrs. Kaufmann, from the brief conversation Justin and I had, I don't believe that he sees himself as breaking any rules. From what I have observed he sincerely believes that he is simply coaching Derek in math."

"I will discuss this matter with him, Mr. Mortimer. Thank you for bringing it to my attention."

"So I will see you on Monday?"

"Ja—yes. I will be there."

As she hung up the phone, she heard Eileen greet Justin. "Going on a little boat ride, I hear," she said in her trademark cheerful voice.

"Yes ma'am."

Not wanting to spoil the outing, Rachel greeted her son with a smile. "I have work to do in the children's wing so why don't you sit at my desk and work on your homework?"

"But you won't have to stay late, will you?" Justin said. "I mean, we'll still be able to go?"

"We certainly will," Rachel assured him. "Dr. Booker told me he might even let you drive the boat."

Justin's smile had none of the hesitation and uncertainty that Rachel had begun to fear was becoming his permanent reaction to anything she might say. "No way."

It was an expression he had picked up at school and she had decided to let it stand without comment. "That's what Dr. Booker told me. He said that Sally takes the helm whenever they go out."

At the mention of Sally, Justin's smile faded. "She's coming, then?"

"Well yes, that was always the plan, Justin."

Without further comment Justin edged past her and sat down at her desk. He bent to unzip his backpack and remove a stack of books.

Eileen's phone rang. "She's on her way." Paul's assistant gave her a sympathetic look and then reached into the small refrigerator by her desk and took out a soft drink. "Hey Justin, how about a soda?"

Justin glanced at Rachel and then swiveled the chair to face away from her. "No thanks. I'm good," he muttered and opened a fat oversized book and started to read.

Later, when they left the hospital, Ben was waiting for them. Rachel did not even hesitate when it came to the seating arrangements. She greeted Sally with a smile and climbed in back with her while Justin deposited his backpack in the trunk and then got into the front seat next to Ben. He was still brooding, but Ben seemed to be very good at finding his way through that.

"What's your mother feeding you, Justin? Looks to me like you've grown a couple of inches since you moved here."

Justin shot Ben a look and gave him a slow grin. "I'm taller than she is."

Ben laughed and glanced at her in the rearview mirror. "That's not saying much. Your mom is a bit of shrimp in the height department."

Justin snorted and Sally giggled.

"I beg your pardon. I will have you know, Dr. Booker, that I am easily the tallest one among my female relatives."

Ben rolled his eyes at her, and both kids exploded into laughter.

It occurred to her that he would make a very good father. But then she thought about him married to Darcy, and somehow she could not picture Darcy as anything other than an overprotective and controlling parent. Embarrassed at such an unkind thought, she turned her attention to Sally.

"I have a message for you from Caroline Royce," she said. "She wanted me to let you know that the group decided to go with lemon yellow."

"Finally," Sally sighed happily.

"Lemon yellow for what?" Ben asked.

"The theme color for our club," Sally said. "A bunch of the kids I got to know last year are forming a club—kind of a survivor support group. They wanted to go with blue—like heaven or something. I said we had made lemonade out of the lemons we'd been handed and therefore, yellow made more sense."

"These are all sick kids?" Justin asked, interested in spite of himself.

"Well, not anymore—or at least not all of us. I'm not sick," she said firmly then turned to Rachel. "When did you see Caroline?"

"Today."

"She's back in the hospital?"

Rachel heard the distress in Sally's voice, and she glanced at the mirror. Ben shot her a sympathetic look and nodded.

"Yes, Sally. She was admitted late last night. She had developed a high fever."

"It's not related to her cancer, honey," Ben assured her. "It's an infection she picked up while she was camping with her parents last week."

"Everything's related to cancer," Sally muttered, folding her arms across her chest and staring out the window. "Why do you think it's called the 'Big C'? Because it's always got to be in charge."

"Hey," Ben said soothingly. "Where's that lemonade spirit?"

Sally's fierce expression softened slightly. "She'll be okay?"

"She'll be okay," Ben assured her.

"I'm going to get her a bright yellow T-shirt. Will you be sure she gets it, Rachel?"

"I will."

Rachel turned her attention back to Justin, his light blond hair visible over the top of the headrest on his seat. How fortunate she was that he was so healthy. And Justin was a good child regardless of his teacher's obvious concern. Surely Mr. Mortimer had misread the situation. Justin would never cheat or help someone else do such a thing. On Monday she would make sure that Mr. Mortimer—and anyone else with questions—understood that.

Chapter 15

Darcy was on her way back to her office but her thoughts were on Ben. Something between them was different, and the shift had come even before she had told him about the incident with Rachel and Zeke. She thought back to the ball and realized that he'd acted differently even before then—at the run.

At first she hadn't noticed. Competitive by nature, she had been totally focused on recording her best time when she and Ben had joined hundreds of other runners at the starting line. And when she had crossed the finish line ahead of Ben she had teased him about how missing those last two days of training had cost him.

He had grinned and invited her to celebrate with breakfast at a popular restaurant on St. Armand's Circle. The restaurant had been full of other runners as well as volunteers from the race. The noisy conversation had made it impossible to share anything more intimate than a smile. Afterward they had walked back across the arching Ringling Bridge with its incredible views of the bay and the Gulf beyond to his condo where she had left her car.

Along the way, Ben had kept the conversation impersonal, talking about his final days at the teaching hospital, the party the staff there had thrown for him, and his relief to be able to concentrate fully on his role at the new hospital. When they reached the entrance to his condo he had walked her to her car, thanking her for helping him train and saying he would see her later.

At the time she had chastised herself for wanting to press for more—lunch by the bay perhaps. But she had sternly reminded herself that men did not like it when a woman was too pushy. If she had learned nothing else from her mother that lesson had been drummed into her head repeatedly. So she had gone home, done her laundry, cleaned her apartment, treated herself to a pedicure, and generally counted the minutes until she would see Ben again in a matter of a few hours.

So engrossed was Darcy with analyzing what might have gone wrong with her relationship with Ben that the very last person that she expected to find waiting for her outside her office was Zeke Shepherd.

"I thought I asked you to stay away from this hospital," she said.

"Actually you never really asked—just sort of implied that I was less than welcome here." He followed her into her office and sat down in one of two blue leather armchairs that faced her desk. "Nice digs," he added, glancing around.

"Thank you. What is it that you want, Mr. Shepherd?" Using his surname reminded her that he was the brother of the president of the hospital's board of directors—her boss. She stepped behind her desk and sat down, folding her hands on the large bare surface.

"I want to make sure that you have no worries about my performance for the children a few weeks ago. It's been eating at me that you might have gotten the wrong idea, so how can I reassure you?"

"Why do you think it's necessary to do this?"

He grinned, and Darcy was unnerved to realize that she found his smile—his white, even teeth, his wide mouth, his entire person now that she was really seeing him for any real length of time—charming.

"Because I upset you that day—rather, my presence here did." He leaned forward to look her in the eye. "Why is that?"

"I am responsible for—"

He got up then and started walking around, his hands locked behind his back as he studied the framed degrees on her wall and the few personal items she'd added to her office. "You see, one thing that I got to be very good at while I was in the service," he continued as if she had not spoken, "was reading other people. I was especially good at reading fear or distrust in others. It made me pretty valuable over in the desert where there are real language and cultural barriers."

"You think I distrust you?"

He shot her a look over his shoulder then continued his tour. "No ma'am. I think I scare the bejeebers out of you."

"Don't be ridiculous."

Zeke grinned, straightened her framed MBA degree, and sat down again. "But here's the thing," he said, leaning forward and pinning her with those deep-set black eyes, "I'm reflecting on my future these days."

He left the comment hanging as he studied his hands. Darcy couldn't help but notice that his nails were clean and neatly trimmed.

"And?" she asked, impatient with herself for being even the slightest bit interested.

"And I was thinking I ought to probably get on with it."

Darcy stood up. "If you're looking for a job, Mr. Shepherd, I'm afraid you've come—"

"It's Zeke, and I've got a good steady job over there at the co-op." He remained seated and continued to study his hands. "What I'm looking for, Darcy, is a mentor."

"A mentor? I'm afraid I don't understand." That was the understatement of the hour. She studied him closely, searching for any sign that he might be putting her on.

"My brother admires you," he continued. "Says you're the kind of self-made business person that he rarely encounters these days—male or female. He and Sharon—among others—have been pushing me to get back into the rat race for some time now." He grinned sheepishly. "But I find that I no longer understand the rules of the game."

Darcy moved to the door, intent on sending him the message that their meeting was over, a message that even he couldn't possibly misinterpret. "Mr. Shepherd—Zeke—if you need mentoring you won't find anyone better than your brother so I suggest—"

"Come on, Darcy. One piece of advice." He ambled toward the door.

"Get a haircut," she said. "Now if you'll excuse me, I have a hospital to run."

He fingered the glossy black ponytail that hung a little past his shoulders. "No worries. Thanks for your time." He walked into the outer office where, thankfully, Darcy's assistant was away from her desk. When he reached the elevators, he turned back. "Just one more—"

"Good day, Mr. Shepherd," Darcy said and closed her office door before he could complete his sentence.

Then, like someone hiding out, she hovered near the door listening for the elevator to arrive. Only after she heard the elevator doors open and close did she return to her desk.

Her hands were actually shaking. That was how much her up close and personal encounter with Zeke Shepherd had unnerved her.

The truth was that he was nothing like the man she had thought him to be—neither in looks nor conversation or attitude. Of course he was very different from Malcolm, and yet the similarities could not be missed. The eyes that probed and questioned. The smile—a little crooked and slow to come. The easy grace and confidence with which both men moved.

Certainly anyone who spent time in Sarasota knew Zeke on sight. He was a regular at the weekly farmers' market and almost as often could be seen on Main Street or near the bay strumming his guitar or sipping a coffee as he enjoyed the passing parade of people. But she had to wonder how many people would be surprised at the way his eyes flashed with curiosity and, yes, intelligence. She wondered how many people would look beyond the ill-fitting clothes and the long hair to see the man himself.

She rocked back in her chair, staring at the place where he had sat across from her, recalling his probing black eyes that had looked at her with amusement yet genuine interest as if he wanted to understand her. The smile that seemed forever lurking behind a mouth that was set at a slightly crooked angle in his sun-toasted face. She found herself imagining what he might look like with a proper haircut. She had never seen him other than clean-shaven and wondered why always if she considered him at all she had assumed he would have at least a scruffy sprout of whiskers.

She opened her eyes and tilted her chair upright, shaking off all thoughts of Zeke and his demeanor and his good looks. What could it possibly matter to her one way or another if the man shaved or not? And yet throughout the afternoon, every time she looked up from her work at the now vacant leather chair she remembered his smile. . .and those eyes. Eyes that challenged and questioned and, she had to admit, eyes that had completely changed the way she thought about Zeke Shepherd.

"You are simply associating him with his brother," she muttered to herself as she gathered the work she needed to carry home with her and prepared to leave for the day. Other than the similarities in looks and intelligence, Zeke was nothing like Malcolm.

She was on her way to the skywalk that led to the parking garage when she looked down and saw Ben with his niece, Sally. He was grinning and waving at someone as he waited by the open door of his car. She was about to continue on her way, assuming he was waiting for his sister when she saw the unmistakable starched white prayer covering the Mennonite woman wore.

Rachel Kaufmann and her son hurried toward Ben's car. The only good news as far as Darcy was concerned was that Rachel took a seat in back with Sally while her son climbed into the passenger seat up front.

So Ben was giving the woman and her son a lift. So what? He was a nice guy, always doing things for others. Still she could not seem to shake the envy that crawled over her like a bunch of pesky no-see-ums, the tiny bugs that attacked those silly enough to linger on the beach past sundown.

It was a perfect night for a boat ride on the bay. The water was calm, reflecting the surroundings like an enormous mirror. Ben set the motor on the small craft that he'd rented to the low speed required in these inland waters and steered along the shoreline of Sarasota. He first headed north, passing under the Ringling Bridge connecting the mainland to the string of barrier islands that gave the city protection from the worst of most hurricanes and tropical storms.

"What's that purple building?" Justin asked.

"It's called the Van Wezel Performing Arts Center," Sally replied before Ben could answer the boy. "They have all kinds of shows there—concerts and plays and everything."

"Why is it purple?" Justin asked and seemed pleased when Sally had no answer for that.

"I don't know. It always has been." Sally brightened. "Remember when we went to see *The Lion King* there, Uncle Ben?"

"Sure do."

"Did you see the movie, Justin?" Sally asked.

Justin's cheeks flushed with embarrassment.

"In our faith we do not go to movies or plays, Sally," Rachel said quietly.

"Oh."

Ben had rarely seen his niece speechless, but he understood that she was wrestling with the idea that she'd always been taught that such cultural events as plays and even some films were part of becoming a well-rounded person.

"Sorry," she murmured after a moment.

Rachel smiled and lightly touched her hand. "No need," she said. "It is our way."

"Do you mind if I ask you a question?" Sally squinted up at Rachel.

"Not at all."

"Well, I know that some Catholic nuns wear a covering

on their head—and Muslim women as well. Is there a special meaning to the little hat you wear all the time?"

Rachel smiled. "It is called a 'prayer covering,' Sally, and we wear it as a symbol of our faith."

"But all the time?"

"Sally," Ben warned.

"You never know when you might need to pray," Rachel said, "and how inconvenient it would be to keep putting the cap on and off throughout the day."

"There's the Ringling Museum," Ben said, taking the opportunity to change the subject by pointing to the lavish mansion that the circus owner had built in the early twentieth century. "There was a time, Justin, when John Ringling owned everything you can see here."

"Even that island over there?" Justin asked, his eyes wide.

"Even that. That's Longboat Key, and if you look back toward the bridge, Ringling owned everything from here to there."

"He must have had a ton of money," Justin said.

"He did, and then he lost most of it when the stock market crashed in the late 1920s."

"But he kept the house and that big building next to it?"

Ben chuckled. "John Ringling was a very smart businessman. He and his wife, Mabel, built the original part of that complex to house the huge art collection they had gathered on their many travels throughout Europe. And when he realized that he might have to sell off his mansion and art collection to pay his creditors, he donated everything to the state of Florida."

Sally turned to Rachel. "There's really a neat tour of the house and the grounds. They've got this cool circus museum and a fabulous miniature circus that has its very own building. Can Mennonites go to museums?"

"We can and do."

Sally grinned and turned to Justin. "Let's go there one day. I'll ask Mom to—"

"Do you ever go fishing out here, Dr. Booker?" Justin asked, interrupting Sally and pointedly turning away from her.

"Justin," Rachel said gently, "Sally was speaking."

"Sorry." But he looked out toward the shore, not at Sally.

"Never mind," Sally said. Ben glanced at Rachel.

"Is anyone hungry?" Rachel asked, her voice a shade too bright, her eyes and worried frown focused on her son.

"I'm not feeling so great," Sally said. She walked unsteadily to the far end of the boat and sat alone on the burgundy plastic seat, her arms locked around her bent knees, her back to all of them.

"Maybe we should go back," Rachel said to Ben.

Maybe you should tell your son that he's being a total jerk, Ben thought, but he could see in the worried way Rachel looked at Justin that she knew her son had upset Sally. So Ben nodded and turned the boat around, heading back toward the marina.

"I don't get it," Sally said later, after they had dropped Rachel and Justin off at the cottage. Sally had suddenly decided she was feeling better and persuaded Ben to take her for a hot fudge sundae at their favorite ice cream shop on Main Street. "What is it with that guy? I try to be nice to him like Mom says I should be. I mean he's living in my backyard—like literally twenty yards from our house. What is his problem?" she fumed as the two of them sat outside the ice cream shop eating their sundaes.

"Well, at least you've recovered your appetite," Ben teased as Sally scooped ice cream into her mouth almost without pausing to breathe between bites.

She grinned sheepishly. "It was either pretend not to be hungry or slug the guy," she admitted. "He's gotten involved with the wrong group at school." She shook her head. "Derek Piper and his crew are not the best influence on him. I think Mr. Mortimer is beginning to catch on, and Justin might be in trouble."

"In what way?"

"Derek is such a total bully."

"So is he bullying Justin?"

"Oh no, that's the thing. He's like best buddies with Justin— as long as Justin is willing to do his math homework for him, that is. Justin thinks he's helping Derek, but that's not what's happening. I mean, how can Derek have all the answers right on his homework but still fail the tests?"

"Maybe you should talk to Justin. . ."

Sally rolled her eyes. "Yeah, that'll work. He already thinks I might tell Mortimer what's going on. That's why he wants to stay clear of me."

"Maybe I should talk to his mom, then."

"Not at all a good idea," Sally protested around a mouth filled with ice cream and fudge sauce. "That would just prove to Justin that I'm the rat he already thinks I am. No, please don't say anything, okay? Not to his mom—or mine. Okay?"

She held up both hands, palms out as if wanting to stop him from even thinking about saying something. And that was when he noticed the white spots on her palms.

Ben dropped his spoon and grabbed his niece's hands, holding them closer to the light to examine them, all the while hoping he wasn't seeing what he most feared was there.

"Hey," Sally protested.

"Sally, when did you first notice these spots on your palms?"

She shrugged. "I don't know. Couple of days ago, I guess." She looked at him, tears filling her eyes. "It's not anything serious, is it? I mean, I've been feeling so good and, yeah, I had that virus last week and I'm still a little knocked out from that but Mom had the blood tests run and everything was normal and. . ."

Her naked fear made Ben repress his own terror. "Let's be sure," he said. "How about we make a quick stop at the hospital on the way home, draw some blood, and see what's going on, okay?"

"You think it's GVHD?"

His smile was forced. This kid had spent way too much time in hospitals. She knew all the lingo. GVHD or Graft-Versus-Host Disease was exactly what he was thinking, but at the moment all he wanted was to calm her fears—and his own. Even though it had been months since Sally's transplant, the possibility that her body might yet reject the donor marrow was still there.

"You know me, kid. I don't make guesses when it comes to medicine. Let's run the tests and see what we find, okay?" He pulled out his cell phone and punched in his sister's number and was relieved when Malcolm answered.

In as few words as possible he gave Malcolm the news.

"We'll meet you at the hospital," Malcolm said tersely and hung up before Ben could say anything more. Of course, what was there to say? The spots were a symptom. Other than the virus that seemed to have passed there were no other signs. Sally's energy level was fairly normal. Oh, she had seemed tired until she'd suggested going for ice cream, and then she had rallied and admitted that she'd been faking on the boat—or had she?

He resisted the urge to quiz Sally as they drove in silence to the hospital. She seemed small and vulnerable sitting in the passenger seat next to him, her arms wrapped tightly around her chest as if to protect herself from whatever the blood tests might reveal. Ben glanced at her, saw her lips moving and realized that she was praying as tears leaked slowly down her cheeks.

He reached over and cupped her head with his palm. "We can fix this, honey," he promised.

But Ben was far from certain that he would be able to deliver on that promise.

By the time the excursion ended Rachel had begun to wonder if Justin had indeed gotten caught up in wanting so much to connect with a group of boys in his class that he had been drawn into questionable activities. His attitude toward Sally while they were on the boat had alarmed Rachel, and his stubborn refusal to apologize only deepened her worry. She decided that before her meeting with Mr. Mortimer on Monday it was imperative that she learn more about this Derek Piper and his relationship with her son.

"I have an idea," she said when they were back home. "Tomorrow is Saturday. Why don't you invite your friend— Derek—is that his name? Why don't you invite him over here? The two of you could study together for that math test you mentioned, and we could have. . ."

The look on Justin's face stopped her in midsentence. "What is it? The boy must live in the neighborhood since he rides the same bus with you and Sally."

"He's probably busy with other stuff."

"How will you know if you don't ask?"

Justin turned away from her. She watched as his shoulders sagged. "Please, Mom."

"I don't understand."

Justin turned to face her, his eyes traveling instantly to her prayer covering and then back to the floor. Suddenly it all made sense. He was embarrassed—by her—by who they were.

"I take it your new friends do not know that you are Mennonite. And what if they did? Would that make so much of a difference?"

His head jerked up, and he looked at her with something she could only describe as pity. "Mom, please let it go. Be glad for me that I've made some friends. That was really hard to do, and I don't want to have to start over."

"Are you saying that Derek and the others would not want to be friends with a Mennonite?"

"They wouldn't understand. They don't like different. Look at the way they treat Sally."

"And how do they treat her? Do they roll their eyes as if her comments are stupid as you did on the boat? Do they ignore her as you did in the car tonight? Is this what you have learned from your new friends, Justin?"

"I'm sorry, Mom. Sorry for how I acted tonight with Sally. She's okay, but. . ." He drew himself up to his full height even with her own. "You're the one who put me in that school with all those outsiders. Now you want to ban the only friends I've been able to make?" His eyes challenged hers. Neither of them blinked.

Rachel was on unfamiliar ground. She wished James were here. She wished she could seek counsel from a man—perhaps Ben would know how best to talk to Justin. But it was just the two of them—and she was the parent.

"Do not speak to me in that tone, Justin," she said quietly. "No one has said anything about banning your friends. I have simply asked to meet them. But I can see that you are ashamed of your heritage—your father's heritage." She knew it was a low blow, but it was the truth. She bit her lower lip to stem her own tide of anger. She sucked in a deep breath and continued, "I had a call from Mr. Mortimer today."

Instantly she knew that Justin understood why his teacher had called her. Instantly she realized that what Mr. Mortimer suspected was not only true but that Justin knew that what he was doing was wrong. It was all right there in his eyes that suddenly could not meet hers, in the way his whole body slouched into a defiant posture, and in the way his lips thinned into a hard unyielding line.

Never had there been a more inconvenient time for her pager to go off than that moment, yet it buzzed insistently on the table where she had laid it when they returned from the boat ride. She picked it up and read the message.

"I have to go," she said. Justin turned toward his room, but she stopped him by placing her hand on his shoulder. "Justin?"

He did not look at her, but stood rooted to the spot as if waiting for something. "We will speak of this in the morning. Now it's too late for a bus so please call a taxi for me while I gather my things." Hester had suggested that she invest in a used car, but Rachel was unwilling to spend any more of their meager savings until she could be certain that they were finally settled. She in her job, Justin in a proper Mennonite school, both of them in a small rental house in Pinecraft where the ways of the outside world could not tempt her only child.

Chapter 16

After rushing Sally to the hospital, trying hard all the way not to alarm her, Ben realized he'd failed. As they waited for Sharon and Malcolm to show up, he saw that Sally was shivering and he knew it was from fear—not the temperature.

"I don't want to be sick again," she whispered as he waited with her in one of the small ER examining rooms. A nurse had drawn blood and hand carried the samples to the lab with Ben's instructions to deliver the results directly to him. He felt sick that he seemed incapable of offering Sally any reassurance.

At her insistence, he had promised not to hold back anything. "I want to know what we're fighting," she'd told him, showing far more maturity than most of the adults surrounding her, who were helplessly wringing their hands.

And through it all, Ben had stuck to his promise. First, after her diagnosis and the failure of the first round of chemotherapy, and then again and again as the search for a donor match failed repeatedly he'd told her the truth. Even over the long months that followed the transplant where Sally endured regular testing to be sure that the transplant was a success he had remained totally honest about what she could be facing. Through all those endless weeks and months it had been as if all of them—except Sally—

were holding their collective breath. Only she seemed certain that the fight had been won. Only she dismissed the caution that her parents insisted upon with a disbelieving shake of her head.

She rubbed her eyes, as if trying to change the picture she feared she might see once she opened them again. "Oh great," she muttered. "Skin lesions *and* dry eyes."

Sally knew the signs for chronic Graft-Versus-Host Disease—or GVHD—as well as any of them. It was a risk of transplant, when the patient's body perceived the transplanted cells as foreign. In which case the body would do what the body always did when a foreign invader threatened—her body would begin to reject the healthy cells from the transplant.

When she had reached the one hundredth day after her transplant with no symptoms of the acute form of the disease, she had framed the results of her blood tests—all showing normal levels—and hung it on the wall of her room.

"Party time," she had crowed. Even Sharon had laughed at that.

"Where is she?" Ben heard his sister's voice as she hurried down the corridor.

"In here," Ben called out.

Sharon went immediately to Sally and cradled her against her shoulder.

"Where's Malcolm?" Ben asked.

"Making arrangements to transport her back to Tampa. Don't you think that's the best plan?"

It was, but Ben did not like it since it would mean that he would not be able to oversee Sally's treatment. Still, the transplant team was in Tampa, and they were the ones best qualified to address any complications. Ben worked up a smile for his sister and niece. "Road trip," he said and was rewarded by Sally's half smile.

"Chopper trip more likely, knowing Dad."

The nurse entered the room and handed Ben the lab results without comment. But he only had to look at her face to know he wasn't going to like what they told him.

"The count is high?" Sharon asked, still holding Sally and

rocking her as if she were a toddler.

"It's high," Sally confirmed.

"It's also early in the game," Ben said. "Let's don't jump to conclusions." The nurse was back with a wheelchair.

With a resigned sigh, Sally pulled free of her mother and trudged over to the chair. "To the roof, driver," she instructed wearily as Ben took hold of the chair's handles.

"Your wish is my command, your ladyship," he replied, but his voice cracked in spite of his determination to match Sally's bravery with courage of his own. He glanced at his sister as the elevator carried them to the rooftop landing pad. Tears slid down her cheeks. When they reached the roof, he gestured that she should take charge of Sally's wheelchair. That way Sally would not see her mother crying.

Malcolm was already there, and in the din of the helicopter's engine there were no words. Malcolm insisted on lifting Sally into the helicopter while Ben hugged Sharon. Then Malcolm helped her in to sit beside Sally and climbed in after her. With a nod from Malcolm the hospital aide shut the door and moved away from the perimeter of the huge rotating blades to stand with Ben. The helicopter lifted off and turned north. Even after the noise that had been deafening softened to only a distant buzz, Ben stood staring at the sky.

"Doc?"

The orderly was holding the elevator door for him. Seeing him, Ben realized that for now there was nothing more he could do.

The calls that Rachel got to return to the hospital in the middle of the night had run the gamut. There had been the gang fight that had ended with three boys and one girl badly injured, their mothers huddled in separate corners of the waiting room, eyeing one another angrily as they sobbed or spoke in whispers to their companions. Somehow Rachel had calmed them, revealing that she, like most of them, was a single parent struggling to do the best she could for her child.

Then there had been the night she had arrived to find a

well-dressed couple sitting dry eyed in the family waiting room while their baby was being treated for hiccups that would not stop. They had been on vacation and, since their own pastor was far away, had requested a hospital chaplain. They wanted Rachel to pray with them for their baby.

In short, in the eight weeks since she'd started work at the hospital, Rachel had had to deal with situations she could never have imagined in her role as school nurse back in Ohio. On this night the person in need was a woman about her age who was suffering from terminal brain cancer. "Is her family here?" Rachel asked the nurse as she prepared to enter the room.

"She doesn't have family—or friends from what we've been able to see. When she first came in she was alert enough to ask us to call a couple of people, but they never showed up. Now. . . well, if she makes it through the next hour it would be a miracle. We'll keep trying to reach the next of kin, a cousin in Virginia."

So Rachel entered the room with its machines marking each labored breath for the emaciated and bald woman lying on the bed. She pulled a chair close to the bed and took one of the woman's hands in hers. "Jennifer?" she said softly.

The woman's fingers twitched and then tightened around Rachel's. It was a little like the first time she had extended her finger to Justin when he was first born. After a moment he too had tightened his little hand around that finger and held on.

"I'm right here, Jennifer," Rachel crooned. Realizing that the sound of her voice might be more soothing than the silence that would only exaggerate the sounds of the medical equipment, Rachel began to quote the twenty-third psalm. Pastor Paul had once told her that if all else failed, Psalm Twenty-three should be her fallback plan.

Slowly she delivered the familiar words of the scripture. "The Lord is my shepherd. The Lord is *our* shepherd," she amended, silently praying that God would forgive her editing. "We shall not want. He maketh us to lie down in green pastures; He leadeth us beside the still waters."

Jennifer's dry lips parted into a soft sigh. Without letting go of the woman's hand, Rachel reached for a washcloth, dipped it in the ice water on the side table, and pressed it to Jennifer's lips.

"He restoreth our souls," she continued. "He leadeth us in the paths of righteousness for His name's sake."

Jennifer sucked on the cool cloth, and some of the tension left her body.

Rachel hesitated, but then knowing that Jennifer surely understood that she was dying, she whispered, "Yea, though we walk through the valley of the shadow of death, we will fear no evil."

She took the cloth away, soaked it in the water that was certainly useless for Jennifer to drink, and pressed the cool cloth to the woman's cheek. Then she noticed that Jennifer's lips were moving. Rachel leaned in close and heard Jennifer whisper, "For thou art with us."

It was her use of the plural that made Rachel certain that she had been listening, that she knew Rachel was there with her. In spite of herself, Rachel smiled and let her tears come. "That's right," she whispered. "Thy rod and thy staff they comfort us. Thou preparest a table before us in the presence of our enemies; thou annointest our heads with oil." She moved the cool cloth over Jennifer's bald head and watched as Jennifer's lips formed the next words.

"Our cup runneth over."

Jennifer smiled then, and her breathing seemed even and steady for a moment. And then her fingers holding on to Rachel slackened as the monitor beeped out its death knell.

Rachel bent next to her and whispered the rest. "Surely goodness and mercy have followed you all the days of your life, and you shall dwell in the house of the Lord forever." She kissed Jennifer's temple as the nurse arrived and clicked off the switch.

"Thank you for coming," the nurse said.

"It's my job," Rachel reminded her.

"Maybe, but you go above and beyond—we've all noticed that."

Uncomfortable with the compliment, Rachel smiled. "I have Pastor Paul as my example." She looked down at Jennifer once more. "You reached her cousin?"

"Finally. But Jennifer had already seen to everything. She even asked Pastor Paul to take charge of her memorial service. I'll leave him a message to let him know she's passed. The funeral home will be here tonight, and the cousin said he would arrive tomorrow."

"*Gut.* I'll go now, or shall I wait with her?"

"Not necessary. We've got some paperwork to finalize for the funeral director, and I'll make sure she's laid out properly by the time they get here."

Rachel saw that the nurse was older—sixty at least—and it made sense that she was used to the old-fashioned terms that came with dealing with a dead body. Jennifer was in good hands. "I'll say good night, then."

And farewell, she thought as she looked back at Jennifer one last time.

So Mortimer had called his mom. Justin wondered if he should call Derek and warn him. But then it was late and what if his dad answered? Derek had made a couple of comments about his dad's temper. The two of them had talked about how everything had to be just so with parents and teachers, with adults in general, or they'd go off.

"I hope I don't get to be that way," Derek had moaned once. "They are either weak cowards like my mom or dictators like Dad and Mortimer."

Actually Justin liked Mr. Mortimer. He was a very good teacher, and he had a way of kidding around that reminded Justin of his father. "Dry humor," his grandmother used to call it. But Mr. Mortimer was his teacher, not his friend. Derek was his friend. Derek and Connor and Max. The four of them had formed a tight circle almost from the first day of school. They rode the bus together. They sat together at lunchtime. They passed notes back and forth in class and snickered. And on weekends they sometimes met at the park for a game of hoops or simply to hang out.

Their weekend gatherings were rare because Justin would

often beg off, saying that he had chores, and Sundays were taken up with church stuff. Mainly he wanted to keep Derek and the others from finding out that he was Mennonite—a secret that would be totally exposed the minute any of them caught sight of his mom. Lucky for him it seemed like Derek was also busy. Justin had noticed that his friend always seemed more tense than usual on Mondays, and more than once he had noticed bruises on Derek's arms. Once he'd even come to school with a black eye.

"Mind your own business," Derek had growled when Justin asked about the injury. And he hadn't spoken to Justin the rest of the day. But by the next morning he'd been waiting for Justin to board the bus, his hand out for Justin's math homework so he could compare Justin's work to his own.

Justin wasn't naive enough to believe that Derek had done more than scribble down some numbers—numbers he would change the minute he got hold of Justin's paper. But lately he wasn't even pretending anymore. He grabbed Justin's homework and then bent over a clean sheet of paper, copying the work as fast as he could as the bus rocked from side to side on its way to school.

Sally had warned him that they would get caught eventually. She had this annoying habit of always being right about everything. Derek couldn't stand her, and Justin was beginning to see why. He was fairly sure that she had been the one to tell Mortimer about the math business. And Derek was not going to like that one bit. Justin shuddered to think of the reaction his friend would have to this news. He actually felt a little sorry for Sally.

He stood at the window and looked up toward the Shepherds' house. As usual, it was all lit up. Those folks wasted electricity like nobody he'd ever known. They were nice enough people, Sally's parents. But like Derek said, they had money—piles of it—and money gave people like that the power to do whatever they liked. Nobody would ever dare question why Sally was treated so special by all the teachers.

Justin had reminded Derek that Sally had been really sick— would have maybe even died without the transplant.

"Yeah, right," Derek had sneered. "And how do you think little Sally went to the head of that list? Her daddy bought that transplant for her. Somebody like me—or you—would have been told, 'So sorry, wait your turn.' But not Sally Shepherd."

Derek's disgust for the girl had bordered on outright hatred, and Justin had wrestled with the teachings of his faith about nobody setting himself—or herself in this case—above others. Not that Sally did that. Even Justin had to admit that she tried really hard to be a regular kid, in spite of her family's money and in spite of her sickness. But when he'd hinted at this to Derek, the boy had sneered, "It's an act, you dope." And he had given Justin a slap on the back of his head.

Justin glanced at the clock. It was past ten. He wondered how long his mom would have to stay at the hospital this time. At first when she'd been called back after hours she had asked John or Hester to come stay with him or take him home with them. If they weren't available, she would call the Shepherds. Twice he had spent several endless hours sitting in that enormous house with its white carpeting that made him nervous to even walk on with bare feet.

The Shepherds had been nice enough. Sharon had made popcorn and suggested they all play a board game. "You can do that, right?" she'd asked him.

"Yes ma'am."

But then halfway through the game Sally had said something about being tired and not able to keep her eyes open, and the game had ended. Then while Sharon and Sally went upstairs he was left alone with Malcolm—the Shepherds had insisted that he call them by their first names and his mom had given in. He liked Malcolm well enough but the man talked to him like a father—how was school? What did he think he might want to do for a career someday? That sort of stuff.

When Malcolm asked if Justin thought he might like to follow in his father's footsteps and farm, Justin had lost it. What did any of these people know about his dad? Or his life before he came to Florida for that matter? Things had changed the day his dad was killed, and the ripples of that just kept coming.

It was right after that second visit that he had presented his case to his mother. He was not a baby who needed someone to sit with him. They lived only yards away from the Shepherds, so if anything happened he could either call them or go to the house. In short, he was old enough to stay in the cottage alone when she had to go back to work.

To his amazement, she had agreed. Of course she had given him a huge lecture about trust and laid down all kinds of rules about safety and stuff. She had called him like every fifteen minutes that first time, but after two more times, the only calls had been to let him know when she might be home and to ask if he had finished his homework.

Although he knew it was wrong, he'd taken some pride in his achievement, especially when Derek let slip that his dad watched him all the time and no way would Mr. Piper ever let Derek stay home alone. Justin was well aware that in persuading his mom to let him stay home alone he had scored major points with Derek.

Of course now with this Mortimer thing, that was all about to change. Somehow he had to warn Derek. He was reaching for the phone when it rang.

His mom sounded different—tired and maybe even a little scared. "Justin?"

Exactly who else did she think would answer?

"Hi."

"Everything okay?"

"Fine. You coming home?"

"Just about to leave. Dr. Booker's giving me a ride."

"Okay. Don't worry, Mom. I looked outside and the lights are on up at the Shepherd house, so if—"

"They aren't home, Justin. Sally had to be taken back to Tampa tonight. Her parents went with her. I think they must have left in such a hurry. . ." Her voice trailed off as if she wasn't talking to him anymore.

"Mom?"

"Right here."

"Is Sally going to die?"

"No. Of course not. She'll be fine." But she didn't sound like

823

she believed what she was saying. Then she cleared her throat. "I'll be home soon, okay?"

Justin hung the phone up and went to stand out on the porch. He looked up at the Shepherds' house, focusing in on the window that Sally had pointed out as her room back a few weeks earlier. He couldn't help noticing that it was the only window in the whole back of the house that was dark.

Rachel had been planning to call a taxi when she stepped out of the elevator into the tropical garden, the waterfall silenced for the night. She was on her way to sign out at the security desk when she saw a lone figure sitting bent, nearly double, his head cradled in his hands. If there were an illustration for someone in deep anguish this man was surely it.

Her innate sense of concern for others would not allow her to simply pass by without offering to help. "Sir?" She touched his shoulder lightly, saw that he was wearing the uniform of a physician, and wondered if perhaps this man had been Jennifer's doctor.

But then he'd looked up at her and she saw that it was Ben. Her heart skipped a beat.

"What's happened?" she asked, sliding onto the bench beside him, her palm still resting on his shoulder.

"It's Sally," he began and his voice broke. "I should have seen it, should have known. The signs were all there."

Having already witnessed death that night, Rachel swallowed back her fear and forced her voice to remain calm. "Tell me what happened, Ben. Is Sally all right?"

He shook his head and once again plowed his fingers through his thick hair. "She's. . .her body is rejecting the transplant."

"After all this time?" Rachel didn't know a lot about bone marrow transplants, but she was fairly certain that the longer a patient went without problems the greater the chances for success.

"It's GVHD—chronic."

"Oh." Rachel knew enough to know that the chronic form

of the disease could be far worse than the acute form that came usually within the first hundred days following a transplant and could in most cases be treated successfully. Chronic GVHD could go on for months—even years.

"Her blood tests were always within the normal range," Ben was saying as if going over the data for the hundredth time. "But there were other signs—lately she's complained of something in her eye but it was always when we were at the park or outside and I thought. . ."

The disease could attack any one or several of the body's systems—skin, eyes, mouth, liver, stomach, or intestines. "You believe it to be ocular, then?"

Ben shrugged. "I'm not going to guess. She's on her way to Tampa. Let the team there make the diagnosis. It's pretty clear that I missed it big-time."

"Sharon and Malcolm must be—"

"They flew up with her." He nodded toward his phone lying next to him. "I was waiting for their call."

"Can I wait with you?"

His gratitude for her offer was reflected in his eyes, but then he shook his head and picked up the phone, perhaps willing the call to come. "That's okay. You should get home. Justin's there alone, right?"

"Yes, but. . ."

"I'll be fine, Rachel. Thanks."

"Is there anything I can do for Sharon and Malcolm? I mean, at the house?"

"I'll ask when they call and let you know." He stood up, and then he did the oddest thing. He lightly fingered one of the ties of her prayer covering. "Get some rest," he said.

"And you as well. Please tell Sharon that I will pray for Sally."

"Yeah. Thanks."

She was outside dialing the number for the taxi dispatcher when Ben called out to her. "Need a ride?"

"I can call a cab."

"I'll drive you. Sharon called and she wants me to check the house, be sure they locked up, and gather some things she'll need while she's in Tampa with Sally."

"Thank you," Rachel said and walked with him to the parking garage where his was the only car still parked in the area reserved for doctors.

He held the door for her then got in and started the engine. That's when she called Justin to let him know she was on her way home.

"They'll know more tomorrow," Ben said as soon as she hung up. "I expect they'll get her started on the steroid cocktail right away. She's going to hate that. She's already sensitive about her weight and that stuff will make her blow up like the Pillsbury Doughboy." He glanced over at Rachel. "You know that reference? Pillsbury Doughboy?"

"I do. We see the commercials when we watch the news." She studied him for a moment. "Are you going to drive up to Tampa tonight?"

"No. I have patients here that need me. We'll know more tomorrow," he repeated, as if that alone gave him some measure of comfort.

The streets were fairly deserted, and the traffic lights were with them. Added to the fact that Ben drove fast and handled turns as if they were no more than a slight curve in the road, it took less time than usual to reach the Shepherd home.

"Go ahead and park at their house," Rachel said as they approached the turn that would take them to the cottage. "I can walk from there."

He did as she suggested, and she did not wait for him to come around to open her car door. "Thank you for the ride, Ben." She started walking on the path that ran through the gardens connecting the main house to the cottage.

"Thanks," he called out. When she glanced back at him, he added, "For. . .just thanks, okay?"

He looked so lost, standing there alone, the light from the empty house washing over him. She almost retraced her steps. Her instinct was to go to him, hold him as she had longed for someone—man or woman—to hold her after James had died. But Sally hadn't died. There was still the possibility that she would be all right. Rachel thought about the woman she had ministered to earlier and understood that the entire night had been too full of emotional valleys.

Ben would be all right once he received an update on Sally's condition and conferred with his colleagues in Tampa about her treatment. The best thing she could do right now was to go home, hug Justin, and thank God for their many blessings.

Chapter 17

It was almost midnight by the time Ben had found the items Sharon had asked him to bring her; then he turned off the lights and made sure the house was secure—alarm set, garage door that Sharon and Malcolm had left open in their rush to get to the hospital closed. Restless and knowing he would get little sleep tonight, Ben walked around to the back of the house and checked the doors that led into the lanai and the pool. They were locked.

The night was still as beautiful as it had been earlier when they had been out on the bay. Had that only been a few hours ago? It seemed ages. There was a full moon—"Harvest moon," Rachel had called it as they cruised into the marina to return the boat to its slip.

The trip had been something of a disaster with Justin sullen and ornery and Sally withdrawn and depressed. And yet Rachel had found the one thing of beauty to focus on—the moon rising, a large golden ball that put the rest of the Sarasota skyline to shame. She was like that, he realized, always focusing on the good in people, the wonder of her surroundings. Whenever Ben was around her he felt such a sense of peace, as if no matter what happened, in the end everything would be all right.

He looked toward the cottage and saw a single light burning

in the kitchen. He was halfway down the path before he realized that he needed a good strong dose of Rachel's composure—the quality that she wore on the inside the way she wore that silly little hat on the outside.

Sitting at the small kitchen table surrounded by books and papers, she was writing something on a yellow legal pad. She was still dressed in her traditional garb, and Ben suddenly found himself wondering what she might look like with her hair down.

Not wanting to startle her, he made noise as he walked, clearing his throat and scuffling his feet along the crushed-shell path. He tapped at the open screen door, calling her name at the same time. "Rachel? Sorry to bother you," he added when she looked up without the slightest hint of alarm.

"Not at all. Come in. I was going to make some tea. Will you have some?" She busied herself preparing the tea while he took the only other chair at the table. "Is everything all right at the house?"

"It's fine. I just saw your light and. . ." He shrugged, unable to form more words as he fought the combination of exhaustion and fear for Sally that threatened to overwhelm him.

"I know. Sometimes as my minister says, 'The world is too much with us.' "

She set mugs and spoons for each of them and brought sugar and sliced lemon to the table while she waited for the kettle to boil.

Ben considered her white prayer covering and remembered how she had explained to Sally that she wore it all the time because she never knew when she might need to turn to God in prayer. "That works for you?" He pointed to her *kapp*. "The religion thing?"

She reached for the whistling kettle at the same time she glanced at him over her shoulder. "It works for everyone who has faith," she said quietly. She filled a china teapot with the boiling water and carried it to the table. "Do you not have faith, Ben?"

It was a fair question, especially coming from her. After all he'd been the one to bring the whole thing up. "I've kind of let things slide in that department," he said with a half smile and realized that it was the truth. There had been a time. . . .

"Sharon relies heavily on the comforts of prayer and scripture," she said. "More than once I have seen her sitting in the garden, her Bible open next to her."

"Our father was a minister, of the fire and brimstone variety. I struggled with that, and he struggled with me. In the end it was pretty much a standoff. Maybe if we had been able to talk calmly about things but it was his way or the highway." He took a sip of the tea she'd poured for him then added, "I chose the highway and went off to med school. I got distracted with studies, and well, it's been a while since I darkened the door of a church."

The confession made him suddenly shy with her. To this woman a strong faith was everything. He turned his attention to the papers and books spread across the table. "What's all this?"

He knew she was watching him over the rim of her mug. If she had wanted to preach to him, she apparently thought better of it and set her tea on the table. "I have a paper due Tuesday for my certification." She reached for the yellow legal pad. "It's nearly finished—except of course, for the typing of it into the computer." She sighed. "I'm afraid I am not very good at that."

"Ah, but I am." Ben took the pad and flipped through the pages. "Ever since medical documentation went electronic I have become one super typist." He grinned at her. "I'd be happy to type it up for you."

"I could not ask such a thing of you, Ben."

"Why not?"

"You are so busy."

"And you aren't? Let's consider busy. You have your work. . . ."

"As do you," she reminded him.

"Noted, although I seem to see you at the hospital almost as often as I'm there, and you have your course work to earn the required certification."

"That will be finished soon."

"You have Justin."

The shadow that dulled her always clear violet eyes was brief but unmistakable. She sighed. "He was sorry to learn of the return of Sally's illness especially after he had behaved so badly on the boat tonight."

"You're worried about him."

"Ja." She drank her tea, lowering her eyes so that all he could see was the thick fan of black lashes that touched her cheeks. And then he realized that her lashes were wet.

"Rachel?" He reached across the table and covered her hand with his.

"May I ask you a question?" She looked up at him.

"Of course."

"When you were a boy and you and your father were having your differences, how did you find your way?"

"It's not the same thing, Rachel. Justin's father died. You moved here. Justin had no choice but to start over. I had choices with my dad. It's not the same thing at all."

"I know, but..." She shook off the thought. "You did not come here to listen to my worries. Will it help to talk about Sally?"

"It will help if you tell me why you are so worried about Justin. At least I might be able to make some small suggestion for that. I certainly have no power to help Sally."

Rachel smiled and pulled her hand free of his to refill their mugs. "And so we are back to our previous discussion on faith, or rather, your lack of it when it comes to God's power to heal Sally."

Ben lifted his mug in a mock toast. "Touché." He took a swallow and let the warm liquid soothe him. "Talk about Justin. I'm a good listener." He grinned. "Part of the job description of being a doctor."

When she described the call from Justin's teacher, Ben was tempted to shrug it off as boys will be boys. But it was clear to him that she was deeply troubled by the very idea that her son might do anything dishonest—even unknowingly, which Ben very much doubted was the case.

"It's times like these when I miss his father so very much," she admitted. "James would know what to say to Justin—and to the teacher. I have no clue how best to handle this with either of them."

Ben leaned back in his chair. "What do you think is really going on here?"

"I don't know. I have not met any of Justin's new friends, and it's evident to me that Sally doesn't care for them. Oh, she hasn't said anything directly, but on the one occasion when I did mention this Derek boy, it was clear that she had serious reservations about him."

"Is this kid Justin's only friend? I mean, what about other boys he's met, perhaps at church?"

"The population of Pinecraft—at least the population of families that are Old Order like us—is aging, Ben. There are only a few young people living here year-round. Hester Steiner assures me that this will change over the winter, but those children who come to vacation with their parents will be temporary. And then there is the problem of distance. Living here means it is not easy for Justin to spend time with those few children who live in Pinecraft."

In many ways his heart went out to Justin. He well remembered the bullying he'd had to endure when he was around the same age—both at school and at home. Ben could hardly blame the boy for doing whatever it took to avoid that, even if it meant doing another kid's math homework.

"Here's my best advice," he said. "Until you know otherwise I would assume that Justin has helped this other boy because he genuinely thought it was the right thing to do for a friend. When you meet with his teacher I would ask the teacher to relieve Justin of the burden he has taken on to tutor this boy by either tutoring the kid himself or finding some older student to do that."

"You think so?" she said.

"Definitely."

Her smile was so radiant that Ben felt as if he had given her a wonderful gift. "But what do I know?" he said. "Going on instinct here."

"It's the perfect solution," she said. "I stand with Justin without either of us abandoning Derek. Thank you, Ben. I was so worried and I had prayed so hard for some solution and then you stopped by—"

"Whoa." Ben laughed. "Way too much credit here, and I've never been accused of being the answer to anyone's prayers."

"Oh, but you are," she insisted without a glimmer of humor. "At the hospital you are always helping others find their way through their illness—that boy in the shark attack? And Hester told me how very kind you were to Sadie Keller, the girl who accidentally killed her cousin? You must not take your gift for healing others physically and emotionally for granted, Ben."

Uncomfortable with her praise, Ben stood and picked up the yellow pad. "If you're done with this, I'll type it up for you over the weekend and e-mail the file to your work computer on Monday."

"I cannot. . ."

Instinctively Ben placed his forefinger over her lips. "Yes, you can," he said. "What are friends for?" Reluctantly he pulled his finger away.

"And what can I do for you?" she asked as she walked with him to the porch.

"Be here for me—for us," he whispered huskily as he looked up toward his sister's house and Sally's upstairs bedroom. "It's possible that Sally is facing another long battle—one we may not know the true outcome of for years."

She touched his shoulder, and it was all he could do to restrain himself from turning to her and finding solace in her embrace. "I'll pray for all of you," she replied. "Good night, Ben. Get some rest."

He did not look back as he retraced his steps along the garden path. But he sat in his car for several moments before driving away. He was thinking about Rachel, and he was not seeing her as a coworker or this nice woman who rented his sister's guesthouse. He was thinking about her as a woman that he could be attracted to, a woman he could see spending time with, a beautiful woman.

"A plain woman," he reminded himself firmly before he could carry that thought to the next level. "Get a grip, Booker."

Rachel awoke the following morning to the memory of Ben's light touch on her lips. She lay in her bed as the late-October sun washed over her as she recalled every detail of the time they had spent together the day before. The boat ride. Seeing him so distraught at the hospital. The ride home. The late-night visit. It was as if in a matter of a few hours they had traveled the path from knowing each other through his sister and people at the hospital to becoming truly connected as friends.

And that brought her thoughts back to Justin and his choice of friends. After several weeks in Sarasota she had made many new friends—Pastor Paul, Eileen, some of the others at the hospital, several of the women at church. She had chosen them all, drawn to them because they accepted her—prayer covering and all. So why was it so hard for her to understand that Justin had found similar acceptance with this Derek boy? What had she expected? She was always tied up with work or her courses. They spent practically every Saturday attending to chores. On Sundays they went to church and then spent the rest of the day at Hester's. They needed to broaden their horizons, she decided, if Justin was going to find the right kind of friends.

"Justin?" she called as she got out of bed, twisted her hair into a knot, and padded barefoot to the kitchen to start breakfast. "Time to get up."

"Did somebody come by last night?" Justin asked as he yawned and rubbed his eyes before setting places for each of them at the table.

"Dr. Booker. He needed to talk some."

"About Sally?"

"Actually we talked about when he was a boy and then also about you."

Justin looked at her, fully awake now.

"You told him about Mr. Mortimer calling?"

"I did. He helped me to understand that you have been trying to help a friend who is struggling. He also helped me see that perhaps you had gotten in over your head in trying to tutor Derek. So on Monday I am going to ask Mr. Mortimer to relieve you of that responsibility."

"But Derek. . ."

Rachel sat across from her son and took hold of both of his hands. "Derek needs help, Justin, his teacher's help. Not yours. If he is truly your friend he will understand and accept that."

"But what am I going to tell him when we take the bus?"

"On Monday you will not take the bus. You will go with me early to school and meet with Mr. Mortimer. I will ask Mr. Mortimer to speak with Derek and explain the situation."

Justin groaned. "You don't understand, Mom."

She squeezed his hands, forcing him to focus on what she was saying. "Justin, I am worried about *you*, not Derek. And what I understand is that Mr. Mortimer believes that you have cheated in his class. Such things—right or wrong—can follow you as you move forward in life. We need to resolve this now."

Justin stared at her for a long moment then pulled his hands free of hers and took his breakfast dishes to the sink. "You promised it would be better here," he said petulantly.

"I know, and I will keep that promise, Justin. But you have to give it time."

Her phone rang, and she glanced at the screen. Hester was calling her. Almost always when Hester called it was good news—an invitation for Rachel and Justin to come out to their place for the day or to come with her to the shops in Pinecraft.

"Hi," Rachel said, trying hard to keep her voice from revealing her stress—but failing.

"What's wrong?" Hester asked immediately.

Rachel cleared her throat and forced a light laugh. "Nothing." She would ask forgiveness for the lie as soon as the call ended. "Frog in my throat. How's that?"

"Better." But Hester's tone told her she was still suspicious. "I'm calling to see if you might have time for coffee today."

"Today? Justin and I were going to go downtown to the farmers' market."

"Perfect. John and I will meet you, then Justin can come back here with him while we go for coffee. I have this friend that I think should meet you."

Rachel noticed that Hester didn't say "that I think you should meet." And now she was the one with suspicions. "Why?"

Hester sighed. "The friend is Jeannie Messner—her daughter was the one killed in that horrible car accident last month. She's really struggling and well, I remembered you telling me about that victim offender program that you and Justin went through after James died—vort or something?"

"VORP."

Justin turned around and looked at her, his eyes curious.

"That's it," Hester was saying. "Well, I mean, when you and Justin went through it, the offender was a stranger. In Jeannie's case it's her niece, Sadie, and that girl is like a second daughter to her and her husband—or at least she was until this happened. Rachel, this thing is ripping these two families apart, and I want to do something to help them."

"It's not a simple solution," Rachel warned. "Everyone has to agree to participate—the offender and in the case of a death, all of the victims impacted by that death including the family of the offender. Are you sure they are ready for this?"

"I don't know," Hester moaned. "But what I do know is that this would be a quadruple tragedy if Jeannie and Emma were never able to get past this—and Sadie. I can't begin to imagine what that poor child is going through. She's in jail, you know, or detention as they so eloquently like to call it when it's a child locked up."

"Hold on a minute." Rachel covered the phone and turned to Justin. "How would you feel about—"

"I heard, Mom. Sure. That'll be okay. Maybe John and I can do some fishing."

Justin's willingness to go along with the change in plans without question or protest gave Rachel enormous relief. "Thank you," she mouthed and put the phone back to her ear. "All right. We will meet you at the market. Where?"

"The coffee bus. You can't miss it. It's a red double-decker bus that serves coffee. Half an hour?"

"Forty-five minutes," Rachel bargained. "We need to dress, and the bike trip will take time."

Hester laughed. "At some point we are going to have to find you a good used car."

"Our bikes are fine and the morning is so beautiful. Red bus—we'll find it."

When she ended the call, Justin was already back in his room making his bed and dressing. Rachel dressed, then finished washing the breakfast dishes while Justin got their bikes from the small shed outside the cottage and checked the air pressure in the tires. She picked up the cloth bag she used for shopping and put some money in her pocket.

"God in heaven, please help me keep the promise I made to Justin of a better life," she whispered as she closed the door to the cottage.

As they pedaled out to the main street, she noticed that Justin was staring at the Shepherds' house. "Are you thinking about Sally?" she asked.

Justin shrugged.

"We must pray for her every day until she is home again and on the mend."

"And what if. . ."

"We will find our way to understanding should that be God's will."

They had stopped to wait for traffic to ease so they could enter the bike lane. Justin looked at her. "Like we did with Dad?"

"Ja. Like we are struggling to do now that your father is not with us," she said. "As every morning and night I ask for God's guidance for both of us. You must do that as well, Justin."

She watched Justin's throat contract as he swallowed. "I miss him so much," he murmured.

"Me too," she admitted. "But sometimes on a morning like this I feel his presence so strongly. Remember how he used to make up those silly songs?"

Justin grinned. "Ja. They were really awful."

"But they made us smile, and the memory of them still does."

Chapter 18

Darcy did a double take as she walked through the farmers' market, intent on finding the ingredients she would need for the fresh vegetable pasta dish she planned to make for Ben that night. He had agreed to come for dinner after she had called to say how sorry she was to hear that Sally was back in the Tampa hospital. She was pretty sure she'd woken him up, poor thing. Of course, that had worked in her favor because he'd been too groggy to refuse her invitation.

Darcy loved to cook. As a teenager she had found refuge from her parents' constant nagging about what they perceived as her lack of ambition and her failure to appreciate the importance of building friendships with "the right people."

"If you're to have any chance at all of getting ahead in this world, then you'd better learn one lesson: It's not so much what you know but who you know," her father had instructed.

She vividly remembered the night she had prepared a five-course gourmet dinner for her parents and six of their friends. That night her parents had glowed with pride as their friends exclaimed over Darcy's cooking. But when she had tested their approval by announcing that she intended to one day open her own restaurant, her parents had smiled tightly.

She had taken their smile for encouragement and gone on to lay out the rest of her plan. "A restaurant where there is nothing on the menu but good healthy food beautifully prepared and served, food that even a truck driver would eat," she exclaimed.

Later that night, her father had come to her room and informed her that if she thought he was going to stand for her throwing her life away as she slung hash in some roadside truck stop she was dead wrong. Her mother had tried to soften the blow by adding that cooking for friends and family was a lovely little hobby. "But it's not a career, dear."

And so cooking had become her way of calming herself from the stresses of achieving the success her parents had expected. Forcing the memory aside, she reached for a bunch of fresh parsley and noticed a man sitting cross-legged on the ground between the herb stand and the next booth. He was strumming a battered guitar.

Since she regularly came to the market, she was well aware that Zeke Shepherd often hung out there, playing for the loose change and occasional dollar bills that people dropped into his open guitar case.

But this man could not be Zeke. In the first place, he was wearing jeans and a freshly laundered plaid shirt—both of which actually fit his lanky frame. Second, the long black hair was a lot shorter. The man strumming the guitar, his face bent low over the instrument, had thick wavy hair that barely covered the tips of his ears. It shone in the sunshine, black as onyx marble. And he was not begging—although Zeke really did not accost people or ask outright for money. The guitar case was nowhere in evidence.

And then as if he felt her staring at him, assessing him the way she might tackle a vexing problem at work, the man looked up and the smile that spread across his burnished face was pure Zeke. "Hey there," he said. "I took your advice." He fingered his hair. "What's next, coach?"

"Very nice," Darcy said primly and turned her attention back to the parsley.

"Ever try this variety?" Zeke asked, moving to his feet and pointing to a curly-leafed parsley. He was standing next to her now, his guitar resting against the support pole of the vendor's stand. He picked up the parsley and sniffed it then sighed. "Heaven," he murmured and held it out to her.

Not knowing what else to do, she leaned in to sniff the fragrance. "Very nice," she said and turned away on the pretense of picking out some other fresh herbs.

"*Very nice* seems to be the slogan you've chosen for today," Zeke teased. "What are you going to make with all these herbs?"

"Spaghetti sauce." Why was she answering him? It would only encourage the man.

"You cook, then?"

Darcy bristled and turned on him in spite of her determination to escape him. "You don't have to sound so shocked."

He grinned. "No worries, Darcy. Simply making conversation."

"Yes, I enjoy cooking. Because of the demands of my work I rarely get to do much of it except on the weekends."

His smiled faded to a frown. "That's the trouble with work, all right—especially working for somebody else. Ever thought about going out on your own?"

She had paid for the herbs and realized that the two of them were moving slowly down the row of vendors—together, him with his guitar slung over his back, her with a cloth bag of fresh produce in her arms. "There isn't a high demand for hospital administrators outside of actual hospitals," she reminded him.

He shrugged. "You could do something else."

As if it were that easy. As if all a person had to do was wish for something and it would be there. "Such as?" She'd meant to deliver the words as a line of dismissal, but the truth was that she was curious about his answer.

"I don't know. You say you love to cook."

This whole conversation was beyond ridiculous. "And speaking of that," Darcy said brightly, "I really do have errands to finish so I can get home. Spaghetti sauce is best simmered slowly."

"No worries." Zeke turned to go but instead of feeling relieved, Darcy felt a tinge of regret. She stood watching him and as if he realized she was still there, he turned. "Hey Darcy, you forgot to give me that second piece of advice," he called out.

Several shoppers turned to look at her—as if they too were waiting. She almost turned and walked away, but then it came to her. Malcolm had worried about Zeke's lifestyle choice for months now. If she could help guide Malcolm's brother to a more traditional lifestyle, then her boss would be in her debt.

"Ditch the flip-flops," she called back.

Zeke grinned and waved as he headed away from her.

The man did have the most engaging smile.

After they all met at the bus, John and Justin loaded the bikes into the van from the co-op, while Hester led the way to her car. "We decided to drive separately. That way the boys can go on back, and then you and I can join them after we meet with Jeannie."

Rachel had to smile at the way Hester lumped Justin and John together as *the boys*. "Tell me about Jeannie," she asked as Hester drove.

"Jeannie is still so fragile and right now that makes her shy away from others, even people she's known all her life. If you wouldn't mind I think it would be best if you didn't know her story. Let's start with three women having coffee and see where things go."

Jeannie was a small woman, dressed in the clothing of the outside world. Her hair was the color of flames that fell in soft curls around her face. She looked as fragile as a porcelain doll.

"Over here," she called when she spotted Hester.

Rachel and Hester dodged traffic as they crossed the busy street to a small café with tables set outside among a garden of potted flowering plants.

"Jeannie Messner, meet another dear friend, Rachel Kaufmann," Hester said.

Over coffee they got better acquainted. Rachel liked Jeannie immediately. But when the conversation came to Rachel's experience with VORP, a shadow of suspicion crossed Jeannie's face. She shot Hester a look.

"Subtle," she murmured as she took a sip of her coffee.

"Okay, tell her," Hester replied with a nod to Rachel.

As Rachel explained the VORP program, Jeannie sat so still and expressionless that Rachel was unsure of how best to proceed. She talked about how James had died and her feelings afterward. When tears welled in Rachel's eyes, Jeannie reached over and squeezed her hand. "I know," she whispered. "I understand."

"Going through the program allowed both Justin and me to talk openly about how much we were hurting to the very person whose action had brought us that pain."

Abruptly, Jeannie stood up. "I'll get refills," she announced. Rachel was relieved to see that she was not leaving—at least not yet. That meant that there was a chance she might consider the idea.

Hester squeezed Rachel's hand. "I think it's working."

But Rachel knew that it would not be that easy. When Jeannie returned, the three of them talked for some time, and finally Rachel offered to act as mediator for the two families.

Jeannie sighed. "Do you really think that you can help us?"

"It depends," Rachel admitted. "Everyone needs to be willing. I'll do my best," she promised. "It will be hard—really hard—for some time, but it will get better." Rachel thought of that same promise that she had given Justin.

Who was she, to go around handing out such assurances as if she had the slightest power to deliver the goods?

Impulsively, Jeannie hugged her, and as Rachel patted the woman's thin shoulders, she squeezed her eyes closed and prayed for the wisdom and guidance to help in whatever way she could.

Driving back from Tampa, Ben's thoughts were consumed with Sally. He'd been reluctant to leave her, but Sharon—upon hearing that Darcy had invited him to a home-cooked meal—had practically pushed him out the door.

"Go. There is not one thing you can do here except sit there looking worried, and frankly that is of no help at all to Sally—or me. So do us a favor and go have dinner. Come back tomorrow full of stories about your evening with Darcy."

But when he thought about who he wanted to talk about his fears for Sally with, it was not Darcy who came to mind. It was Rachel. He glanced at the digital clock on the dashboard. He had time to stop by Sharon's house and check to be sure that everything was okay there. If Rachel was at home he would stop by for a minute to give her the latest update. Plenty of time to do all that and still be at Darcy's by eight.

With his plan in place, he stopped first at his condo where he showered and changed and chose a bottle of wine to take with him to Darcy's. When he arrived at Sharon's house he was disappointed to see no sign of life down at the guesthouse. Instead he found Zeke sitting by the pool, a cup of coffee on the table beside him.

"What's the word?" Zeke asked as if the plan all along had been for Sally's two uncles to meet.

"The diagnosis of ocular GVHD was confirmed."

"In English?"

"She has a chronic condition known as Graft-Versus-Host Disease or GVHD that has settled in her eyes."

Zeke let out a long low whistle. "Is she. . .I mean, tell me she won't go blind on top of everything else."

"No, although there can be some permanent damage. Right now the doctors in Tampa are running a series of tests."

"And you had no pull to speed up getting the results?"

Ben bristled. "It's the weekend, and I'm not on staff there anyway."

"Sorry, man. I just. . ." Zeke shook his head and concentrated on his coffee.

"You got a haircut," Ben said, trying not to sound as shocked as he was.

"Seemed like a good idea. Tell me about the GVHD thing."

Ben pulled a chair closer to Zeke's and sat down heavily. "It comes in two forms—acute or chronic. The acute form usually shows up in the first few months following the transplant. It's usually treatable and short lived. Sally had passed that milestone already."

"And the chronic?"

"Shows up later in various parts of the body—eyes, liver, lungs, skin—can be treated successfully. Or the effects can last a lifetime."

"Treatment?"

"Steroids—prednisone, sometimes with cyclosporine, and a whole cocktail of other drugs."

The two men were silent for a long moment. Then Zeke cleared his throat. "I thought she was being tested. I mean, it seemed like she was always going to have blood drawn and stuff."

"That's the thing. Her blood counts were all within normal range until last night, and then they shot through the roof."

"You know that day we all went to watch her game? She was rubbing her eyes a lot that day."

"Yeah. I missed that. Blamed the wind and the dust blowing off the ball field. I thought it was normal."

"We all missed it—Malcolm usually watches the kid like a hawk, and he missed it too."

"Yeah, well, I'm supposed to be the doctor."

"You are the doctor," Zeke said. "You are also human."

They turned at the sound of an approaching vehicle and saw the co-op's van pull up to the guesthouse. Rachel and Justin got out, along with John Steiner. John and Justin unloaded two bikes from the back of the van.

"I think I'll see if I can catch a ride with John," Zeke said. As he headed back inside to leave his mug, he grasped Ben's shoulder. "She's a fighter, our Sally."

That she is, Ben thought as he watched Zeke head down the path. *But just how many times is a twelve-year-old expected to get back up off the mat and fight again?*

He remembered then that Sally had asked him to get her journal from her room. "Do *not* even think about reading it," she'd ordered. So he walked back through the house—a house that felt so very empty now—and on upstairs to Sally's room.

The journal was lying on her desk, a rainbow of ribbons marking her latest entry. It was a surprisingly thick-bound book easily matching the number of pages in the hardcover mystery on the table next to his own bed. Ben resisted the temptation to read the whole thing. Surely if he read it he would have a far better understanding of what exactly it had cost Sally all these long months to keep up the brave and positive outlook she presented daily to the world. But he had promised.

He picked up the journal and the pen next to it and looked around for something he could wrap them in. On her bed was a heart-shaped pillow. He unzipped the outer covering and stuffed the journal and pen inside.

"Ben?"

He hadn't heard Rachel calling or her movement through the house and up the stairs. She stood inside the door.

"Sally wanted her journal," he said, holding up the heart-shaped bundle.

"Is there anything I can do? For Sally or Sharon—or you?"

A half dozen answers to that question raced through his mind, but he shook his head. "Sally's in good hands. Sharon and Malcolm are surrounded by good friends. As for me. . ." He was embarrassed to hear that last come out in a raspy whisper as evidence of his emotional state.

"Zeke told us the basics," she said, taking another step into the room. "He went back with John to tell Hester. He suggested that I might get a better picture of the situation talking directly to you. But that can wait."

Ben felt her calmness filling the space around him. "No, I want to talk about it. I mean, if you have the time."

She sat on the small bench at the foot of Sally's bed. "I have time."

Once Ben started to talk it was as if the floodgates had opened. As Rachel listened he told her about the transplant, the weeks of worry following that, especially because the donor match had not been as strong as they might have hoped. He told her about the endless round of tests and medications. The fear of infection. The boredom of days and weeks and months cooped up in a hospital room or this very room where they sat now as the shadows of evening stretched across the room.

"Then we were well past the one hundred day mark, and the danger of acute GVHD had all but disappeared. Oh, I know there are no absolutes in medicine, but she was doing so well, breaking all records for recovery. . . ."

Rachel's instinct was to lay her hand on Ben's clenched fist, but he stood up suddenly and began to pace. "How could I have missed it?"

"Was Sally not seeing her doctors in Tampa on a regular basis?"

"Sure. But I saw her every day." He paused by the window and stood there, staring out at the growing darkness.

Rachel went to stand with him. "Ben, sometimes God. . ."

"I place my faith in science," he said flatly.

Rachel closed her eyes and prayed for God to give her the words. "Then you have faith in one of God's creations, and that is a start."

Downstairs a clock chimed and Ben suddenly wheeled around, glancing at his watch and grabbing the bundle with the journal. "I'm late," he said more to himself than to her as he crossed the room.

Rachel followed him down the stairs and out to the lanai. He secured the lock and then started around the house toward his car. He had closed himself off from her—from anything or anyone around.

"Ben?" But there were no words. She could offer little comfort. "I'm here if you ever need to talk."

He placed his hand on her cheek, and she was struck by how smooth his palm was in contrast to James's calloused touch. "That means a great deal to me, Rachel. Thank you." He smiled at her for the first time since she'd come up to Sally's room. "Danke," he murmured then got into his car.

"Give Sally our best," Rachel called out as he drove away. "Tell her. . ."

But he was gone.

Rachel stood on the driveway for a long moment, her hand touching her cheek, her thoughts on Ben Booker. She did not understand these outsiders. They seemed to go from day to day, checking off items on a list. They valued accomplishment and winning, and they seemed to embrace their individual differences as if this were something to be celebrated. Their lives clamored with the noise of their constant chatter and restless activity.

But was she truly that different? Ever since she'd come to Florida her focus had been on making good at her new job, on getting the certification necessary for her to keep that job. How had she gone from the world she'd grown up in—the Mennonite world that was quieter, simpler, and that revolved around community—to this? At what point had she lost that balance so integral to her faith that allowed everyone to live well and in harmony with their neighbors? Had her brother-in-law been right about her? Had she gotten so caught up in achieving success in her work that she had lost sight of what truly mattered—family, friends, community. . .Justin?

She closed her eyes, allowing the warm moist air of the night to caress her cheek—the way Ben had. Oh, how she wished she could help him find his way home to the faith she felt certain he still carried deep inside him. It was evident that he was a man with much to offer but also a man who struggled with the demands and constraints of the world around him.

Rachel understood that. As a girl she had looked longingly at that outside world, imagining that there she would find true happiness.

This belief that there was something more—something better than the life she'd grown up in—was what had driven her to pester her parents until they had finally agreed that she could attend nursing school. This search for happiness and contentment was why she had sought jobs not in her Mennonite or even the local Amish community after her marriage. Instead she had gone into the public schools to offer her skills.

And she suddenly understood that this was why she had been so drawn to Ben Booker from the moment she'd met him. In him she saw the person she had once been—a person searching in a wilderness. In the short time she had known him she had come to care for him in a way that she had not permitted herself to care for any man since James. With a start she opened her eyes and pressed her hands together.

The disloyalty she felt for James in that moment very nearly overwhelmed her. James had been her first love—her only love. Never had she felt for any other man what she had felt for him. Never—until now.

He was late. The sauce was fine, but the appetizers that Darcy had assembled—bruschetta on toast points—were soggy and inedible. She dumped them into the sink and flipped on the disposal. She had tried calling his cell, then his condo, with no response. She had considered calling the hospital in Tampa. Perhaps Sally had taken a turn for the worst, but if that were true then the last thing Ben needed was a woman who did not understand or accept that he was a physician and always on call when it came to his patients—especially Sally.

She sat down and flipped through a magazine then got up and once again checked the table she'd set on the balcony for the two of them. She'd lit the candles way too early, and now they were burned down to pools of paraffin. She straightened a knife but felt that extinguishing the candles would be to extinguish all hope that he would come.

Just then she heard a car enter the parking area below. She leaned over the balcony and, seeing that it was Ben, resisted the urge to call out to him. Instead she watched as he got out of his car and stood for a long moment, staring out at the man-made lake that her building overlooked. His shoulders were slumped and he looked exhausted.

When he turned toward the entrance, Darcy hurried into her galley kitchen and popped the cork on a bottle of wine then splashed a generous amount into two matching crystal goblets. She checked her makeup and hair in the mirror next to the door and then stepped into the hall to wait for the elevator to deliver Ben. All the while her mind raced with how best to orchestrate the conversation.

She would begin with wine and sympathy for the difficult day he'd endured. She would listen with murmurs of concern while he described the details of Sally's condition. And then at the right moment she would suggest that they enjoy their dinner and speak of other things—at least for tonight—so he could relax a bit before he had to face the hardships of Sally's newest complication the following day.

In a perfect world, he would fall asleep on her sofa, lulled by the wine and the food and the rich chocolate cheesecake that she had prepared for their dessert. In a perfect world, she would cradle his head in her lap, comb his thick hair with her manicured nails. And in a perfect world, sometime in the night he would reach for her and find in her kiss the peace of mind he so clearly needed.

When he stepped off the elevator, he gave her a weary smile and held out a bottle of red wine. "I see you're way ahead of me," he said, nodding toward the two goblets of wine that she held.

"The night is young." She handed him one of the goblets, took the bottle of wine, and waited for him to enter her apartment.

"Sorry I'm so late. Sally asked me to go by the house to get something for her, and Zeke was there so I had to fill him in. Then Rachel Kaufmann stopped by and we got to talking and. . ." He shrugged. "Sorry."

Darcy's hand tightened on the stem of her wine glass when he mentioned Zeke and then nearly snapped it in two when he said that Rachel had been there as well. "How's Sally doing?" she asked, determined to get things back on plan.

He actually chuckled. "Not at all happy to find herself back in a hospital being pricked and probed, as she likes to call it. We'll know more come Monday." He took a long swallow of his wine. "But let's talk about the incredible smells coming from such a tiny kitchen," he said as he lifted the cover on the sauce. "You've got enough sauce here to feed a third world country," he teased.

Okay, Darcy thought, *skip the preliminaries of wine and sympathy. Moving on.* "I made enough to freeze some—for myself and for you to have at your place. It makes a wonderful base for chili or sloppy joes."

"Impressive." He replaced the lid and picked up the empty wooden salad bowl. "Want me to chop the salad?"

"Sure. You do that while I boil the pasta. You must be famished."

He seemed to consider this, and then he grinned sheepishly. "Not so much. I have to admit that on my way out of the hospital I picked up a turkey sub sandwich that I ate on the road. That was around five. But never fear, I have plenty of room for homemade spaghetti."

"And chocolate cheesecake?"

"Might have to take a rain check on that one." He patted his stomach. "Have to watch the waistline at least a little."

"Yeah, right." She felt herself relax. Even with a late start the evening held promise. They worked together well in the confines of the small kitchen, and it was easy to imagine them making a habit of this, spending their free time together, living together. *Easy, girl, don't get ahead of yourself.*

"I thought we'd eat out on the balcony. It's such a lovely night."

"Works for me." Ben tossed the salad with the dressing she handed him and then filled two side plates with the mixture. "What else, chief?"

Darcy fought the urge to cringe. She didn't want to be someone he thought of as *chief.* She wanted him to think of her in more romantic terms. "I'll dish up the pasta and sauce and take the bread from the warmer and we'll be all set. Why don't you refill our glasses and take the salads out to the table?"

Once they were seated, Darcy raised her glass to his. "To Sally's speedy recovery," she said.

He clinked his glass to hers and took a sip before starting in on his meal. "Rachel Kaufmann offered to pray for Sally," he said as he focused on buttering his bread.

"Well, that's kind of her area, isn't it?" Was it Darcy's imagination or was her tone a bit critical? "I mean, she is part of the spiritual care team."

"How's she doing with that?"

"As far as I can tell there have been no more incidents since the time she invited Zeke Shepherd to play for the children. The supervisor from the certification board seems quite impressed with her work. And as I mentioned before, Paul Cox thinks she's pretty near perfect."

"And what do you think?" Ben's voice was quiet, and he was watching her closely. "Are you going to back Paul's recommendation to make her position permanent once she's certified?"

"Will I have a choice?" Now she knew she sounded peevish. But Rachel Kaufmann had a way of inserting herself into Darcy's private time with Ben, and she seemed capable of doing that without even being on the premises. "Let's not talk about work, okay?"

"Sorry. This sauce is fabulous. What's your secret?"

"Well, I could tell you but then I'd have to shoot you, so best to leave it a secret. After all, if you really like it and know that this is the only place you can get it, then that's all to my advantage."

"Touché." He smiled, but it was evident as the meal continued that he was distracted.

Darcy tried several conversation openers that went nowhere. "You're still in Tampa, aren't you?" she asked after a long silence had stretched between them.

"Maybe. Probably." He smiled and pushed his plate away as he leaned back and stretched his arms high over his head. He was looking out at the stars. "Do you think there's something out there, Darcy? I mean some higher being that's calling the shots?"

Religion was the very last topic of conversation she would have expected from Ben, but it was clear that this was something weighing on him. "I used to," she admitted.

"What happened?"

"Nothing huge. I went off to the university and everything was about getting top grades so I could get into grad school, and by that time going to church had pretty much fallen by the wayside."

"Do you miss it?"

Darcy did what she always did when she found herself asked a question that made her uncomfortable. She turned the tables. "Do you? I mean, your father was a minister, right?"

"Yeah. Pretty hard core at that."

"Meaning?"

"I don't know. He'd preach about a loving God and then

turn around and assure everyone that this same loving God was going to punish all the sinners in terrible and vicious ways. If there was a hurricane or a tornado, that was God's punishment or God's warning. If a famine struck halfway around the world, that was God's message that those people had sinned. If I thought unclean thoughts, God would know and there would be a price. I have to admit that I never really worked out how my feelings for my father affected my overall faith. I mean, the fact is that I do believe, but. . ."

"What brought all this on, Ben?"

He sighed heavily and stood up, moving to the railing of the balcony and continuing to study the night sky. "I don't know. I keep saying that I don't believe—that I'm a man of science. But there's a part of me that still sometimes wishes maybe there was something greater than us out there. Rachel said. . ."

Rachel. Rachel. Rachel. Darcy thought she might actually scream. "Ben, Rachel Kaufmann is a devout Mennonite, and if she has you questioning what *you* believe, perhaps you can understand why I have such doubts about her as an ecumenical spiritual counselor especially for our younger patients."

She knew that her voice sounded shrill and she was talking far too loudly. Still, she couldn't seem to stop. "I don't trust that woman, Ben. It was a mistake to hire her in the first place, and you may as well know that I plan to do everything I can to see that she is replaced at the end of her probationary period."

Ben was staring at her as if she were someone he'd never seen before. To stop her tirade, she picked up her wine glass and drained the last dregs of wine. "Sorry about that," she murmured. "Now I've gone and spoiled our lovely evening." She started stacking their dishes.

"Hey." Ben took the dishes from her and set them back on the table then led her inside to the sofa. "What's going on here?"

She was so tempted to tell him. To finally admit that she was jealous of Rachel. But how ridiculous was that? There was nothing between Ben and Rachel. The very idea that there could be was ludicrous. He admired the woman as he did any other coworker. So what?

"Don't mind me," she said. "The truth is that from the first time we heard that woman's voice on the phone it seemed as if everyone simply accepted her, embraced her as the perfect candidate for the job and a wonderful addition to the entire team. I've never known that kind of instant acceptance, Ben. All my life I have had to fight for everything I've ever achieved."

"So maybe you should stop fighting."

"Give up?"

"Open up," he corrected. "Have a little trust in others."

"Like Rachel," she said flatly.

"Like anyone you come in contact with. Have a little faith in people."

"I thought you didn't believe in faith," she said petulantly.

He hooked his forefinger under her chin to get her to look at him. "I never said I didn't believe, and this is about having faith in *people*, Darcy." He kissed her forehead then and stood up. "It's late, and I want to get an early start back to Tampa tomorrow."

"I could go with you."

"Thanks, but it would be a waste of your time. Sally can't have visitors right now. Maybe after she gets home." He brought the dishes in from the balcony and set them in the sink. "Hate to leave you with all this. . ."

"Go on. You've had a long day—and my meltdown wasn't exactly what you needed."

"Stop that. You have a lot of pressure on you. The occasional meltdown is an occupational hazard. I'm glad I was here." He walked to the door and then paused. "I would ask you"— he looked her in the eye—"to think about how your personal feelings might be influencing your view of Rachel, Darcy. I think she might be a very good addition to the team we're trying to build at Gulf Coast."

Rachel. Always Rachel. Darcy manufactured a smile. "Promise," she said, holding up the three-fingered Girl Scout sign. "Give Sally my best."

When Ben was gone, Darcy stood for a long time looking down the empty hallway toward the elevator. Not a single thing about this evening had gone according to plan. She had totally embarrassed herself and in the process made the serene Rachel look even more saintly.

With a growl of frustration, Darcy walked back inside her condo, slammed the door, and grabbed a fork. She took the cheesecake from the refrigerator, snapped off the springform pan, and carried the whole thing out to the balcony. There she curled herself into the chaise lounge and attacked the cake, shoveling bite after bite into her mouth until she felt as physically sick as she did emotionally wounded.

Chapter 19

W as that your mom?"

Justin jumped when he heard Derek's low voice behind him after he and his mom had left the meeting with Mortimer and she had gone outside to wait for the bus to the hospital.

"Yeah."

"Fat Sally told on us?"

Justin knew he should defend Sally, especially since she was sick again. "No. Mortimer figured it out."

"Yeah, right." Derek smirked. "What's with your mom and that hat? Is she some kind of nun or something?"

So here it was—the moment Justin had dreaded from the very first day. "We're Mennonite," he muttered. "I have to go."

Derek grabbed him by the shoulder and held on. "Whoa, dude. You mean you wear the dorky suspenders and stuff?"

"My mom dresses in the traditional way. Kids don't have to until. . ."

The bell rang, but Derek didn't budge.

"What did you tell Mortimer?"

"Nothing. Like I said, he'd already figured it out. He knows that you've been copying my homework, and he told me not to let you have it anymore. He's going to give you special

855

tutoring during study period."

Derek let out a howl that passed for a laugh. "Yeah, that'll happen. Now listen up, Kaufmann. You got us into this mess—or your little girlfriend did—so somebody pays. If you don't want to be that somebody, then you need to be sure Fat Sally gets the message loud and clear."

"She's back in the hospital."

"Even better. You live at her house, right?"

"Next door." Justin did not like the way Derek was clutching his shoulder and looking at him. His eyes were wild and scary.

"Get me her glove," he ordered.

"Her glove?"

"Her baseball glove, stupid."

"I can't. . . ."

"Here's the deal, Kaufmann. Either you get me that glove or life as you know it is going to change big-time."

He pinched Justin's shoulder hard and then turned and left school.

Justin had seen what Derek did to those he didn't like. Once he had seen Derek actually shove one of the other boys up against a locker and hold him there until the boy nodded and promised to do anything Derek asked. It occurred to Justin that he wasn't really sure exactly how Derek might carry out his threat to make his life miserable, but he had no doubt that it would happen unless he got Sally's baseball glove.

Unexpectedly, his chance to deliver what Derek had demanded came that very night.

"Justin, I need your help," his mom said as they were finishing up their supper. "I spoke with Mrs. Shepherd today and offered to do what I could to prepare the house for Sally to come home."

"She's well again?"

"No. That will take time, but she's on medication that will help her. If all continues to go well, they hope to be home by the end of the week. Mr. Shepherd will return tomorrow. So after supper Zeke is going to meet us to open the house so we can clean it."

"All of it?" Justin glanced toward the multistoried mansion.

"All of it," his mom confirmed. "Zeke will help us, but it's very important to be sure that everything is as clean as possible. Sally is even more susceptible to germs and infection now that she's on these medicines."

Justin chewed his lower lip. It was always fun being with Zeke. Nothing ever seemed to bother him. In fact, Justin thought he might tell the man about Derek's order, but then he remembered that Zeke was Sally's uncle. Telling him would only make things worse.

It was when his mom gave him the chore of gathering the trash from the wastebaskets in all the upstairs rooms that he saw his chance. There on a hook on the back of Sally's door was the baseball glove. He stood for a long time fingering the smooth leather.

He should have asked Derek why he wanted the glove. Maybe he just wanted to scare Sally. Surely that was it. Taking her glove was a warning and once she'd gotten the message then Derek would give it back.

But Sally hadn't done anything.

On the other hand Derek didn't believe that, and now that he knew about Justin being Mennonite he could make life miserable for him. Justin closed his eyes, shutting out the memory of how Derek picked on kids who were different—torturing a boy who wore thick glasses that kept slipping down his nose and another boy that Derek called a *fairy*.

Life since they'd come to Florida had been hard enough. The last thing he needed was Derek turning on him. He would take the glove, and once Sally had gotten the message he would bring it back.

Justin listened in case his mom or Zeke might be coming upstairs. But he could hear them talking as they worked together cleaning out the refrigerator. Carefully, he lifted the glove off the hook and pushed it into the black garbage bag. Then he dumped the paper from Sally's wastebasket on top of it and did the same with the trash from all the other upstairs rooms.

When he got downstairs Zeke had another bag of trash and held out his hand for the one that Justin was carrying. "I'll take these out to the garage," Zeke told Justin's mom. "Then I can do the vacuuming while you change the beds."

"Thank you, Zeke. Justin, you go on with Zeke and start sweeping out the garage."

Justin followed Zeke out to the garage and stood by helplessly as the man heaved the two bags of garbage into one of the bins. *Now what?* He could hardly admit that he'd hidden the glove in the trash. Panic engulfed him. The garbage pickup was the following day. He could offer to put the bins out by the street so Zeke wouldn't have to come back and do that.

But when he made his offer, Zeke said, "No worries. Malcolm will be home tomorrow. He can put them out."

Justin felt sweat breaking out on his forehead. *Think.* "But the bins are dirty and Mom wanted me to sweep out the garage and Mr. Shepherd—"

"All right, dude," Zeke said, laughing and roughing up Justin's hair. "Take the bins out. You folks just go around looking for work to do." The way he said it, Justin knew it was a compliment.

He waited until Zeke went back inside and he heard the vacuum cleaner running over the white carpeting before he rolled the trash bin down to the end of the long driveway. Carefully he positioned it so that it was blocked from the view of the house by a couple of large hibiscus bushes. He checked to be sure that he couldn't be seen from either the street or the house then pulled out first one bag and then the other. He rummaged through them until he felt the glove. With a sigh of relief he pulled it out, hid it under the foliage of the bushes where he could find it and stuff it into his backpack the following morning, and then replaced the garbage bags in the bin.

As he walked back up the driveway he heard a rumble of thunder. What if it rained? What if the glove got soaked?

"Justin?"

His mom was calling for him. He started back for the glove as a car turned into the driveway. *Dr. Booker.* Had he seen anything?

The doctor beeped the horn of his car and stopped next to Justin. "Need a ride?"

"No sir." Justin studied the man closely. Everything about

him seemed normal except for the way he looked so tired, like he hadn't slept in days. "Just putting out the trash. Tell Mom I'm coming."

"Thanks for doing that," Dr. Booker said and drove on around the curve of the driveway.

Another rumble of thunder. Justin searched the trash bin for something he could lay over the glove to protect it. At the very bottom of the bin was an empty plastic shopping bag. He pulled it out, wrapped the glove in it, and replaced the package under the bushes. His hands were shaking. He knew that what he was doing was wrong. Tomorrow he would not give Derek the glove until he knew what his friend intended to do with it.

Feeling a little more certain that he had not yet crossed the line, he headed back up to the house.

Instead of coming directly home as everyone had hoped, Sally was transferred to Gulf Coast Hospital. Her blood counts had dropped slightly, and Sharon and Malcolm wanted to be very sure that Sally was stabilized within normal levels before they brought her home. This latest setback seemed to be the final straw for Sally.

When Rachel entered Sally's hospital room she was shocked to find the girl curled on her side, refusing to interact with anyone. Sally's obvious fury at the unfairness of this latest blow was—as Ben called it—the elephant in the room that no one talked about. Ben had also told Rachel that everyone was at a loss to know what they might do to coax the Sally they knew and loved out of this shell of a girl.

"She admires you so, Rachel," Sharon said as the two women sat together, waiting for Sally to return from yet another round of tests. In the low lighting of the room—kept that way to protect Sally's eyes—Rachel could not really see Sharon's expression, but she heard the weariness and defeat in her voice, saw the exhaustion in the slump of her shoulders. She had refused to leave Sally's side. She slept on a cot next to Sally's bed, and when she ate at all it was to nibble bits from Sally's leftovers. The trays of food that the staff delivered for her went untouched.

Paul had told Rachel that Malcolm was at his wit's end with worry for both his wife and child. She also knew that Ben had stopped by the spiritual care offices earlier that morning to seek Paul's help. "Maybe you can convince Sharon to take a break."

"I expect Rachel would do a better job of that," Paul had replied after calling for Rachel to join the meeting with Ben. "After all, she's a mother with one child. After losing her husband, she certainly has firsthand knowledge of the kind of fear and anxiety that Sharon is facing, that all of you are."

"I could certainly try talking to Sharon."

The way Ben had looked at her then, with such relief and gratitude, she knew she would do more than try. With God's help she would find some way to help Sharon understand that taking care of herself was as critical to Sally's recovery as any medicine might be. "I need to understand the medical situation," she told Ben. "What have they been told about Sally's prognosis—more to the point, what has Sally been told?"

Ben explained that in Tampa, Sally's condition had been treated symptomatically with antibiotics and steroids to strengthen her immune system. "It's the manifestation of the GVHD that needs to be addressed," he explained.

"And she responded well to the treatment?" Paul asked.

"Yes. The team there was even able to take her off the IV administration of her steroids and give them to her orally. That was the turning point for getting her home."

"Sounds like she has a good chance of coming out of this," Paul said. "I know she's been through a great deal, but surely she understands that in the scheme of things. . ."

"She's a twelve-year-old girl," Rachel reminded him. "She is on the brink of becoming a teenager—a young woman. And to girls her age their physical appearance can mean a great deal. Sally has already had to deal with losing her hair and with the weight gain that comes with taking the steroids. She had just begun to see that such physical manifestations of her treatment could be reversed with time. Then this happens and. . ."

"And every time she looks in a mirror—or actually she

doesn't have to look," Ben said. "She knows the steroids have given her the telltale moon face and chipmunk cheeks she had before. Her skin is splotched red and the weight she worked so hard to control will come back and now, on top of all of that, she has to wear the protective glasses." He looked down at his hands. "When I was with her last night, she kept muttering the word 'freak' over and over again."

He did not look up as he choked out the words.

"Let me try to talk to Sharon," Rachel said.

"And Sally?" Ben looked up at her, his face ravaged by days of worry.

"And Sally," she agreed, glancing at Paul for confirmation of the plan. He nodded and stood up. "I have a meeting," he said, laying his hand on Ben's shoulder, "but I'll check on you and the family later."

"Thanks, Paul. Thanks for everything." He followed Paul to the door.

"Ben, Sharon is a woman of strong faith," Rachel reminded him.

"She was," he corrected. "These days? Who knows?" He held the door open for Rachel. "I wouldn't try praying with her if that's what you've got in mind."

"No. At this point, I will pray *for* all of you."

They stepped into the outer office, and Eileen glanced up at them then immediately went back to her work. Ben seemed at a loss as to what he should do next. Rachel looked at the clock. "Do you have rounds now?" she prompted.

"I do." But still he didn't move.

"Come by Sally's room after you finish your rounds," Rachel quietly instructed him as she led the way into the corridor. "If I'm with Sally and Sharon is not, then you'll know that I had some success." It was a poor attempt at lightening the somber mood that pervaded every fiber of his being. But instead of the smile she had hoped for, he touched the sleeve of her dress. "Please be there," he said and then walked quickly down the hall away from her.

Now she had been sitting with Sharon for nearly half an hour. "Please wait with me," she'd said wearily, indicating the only other chair in the small room. "Sally will want to see you."

Given what she'd been told about the girl's demeanor, Rachel doubted that, but she also understood that Sharon hoped that saying the words would make them true. The two women sat in the shadowy room not speaking for a long moment. Rachel closed her eyes and prayed for words that might help break through the wall that surrounded Sharon.

"I had to meet with my son's teacher the other morning," she found herself saying. "Mr. Mortimer?"

Sharon looked up at her but said nothing.

"It seems that Mr. Mortimer thought that Justin had been giving answers to the math homework to a boy named Derek Piper."

"Derek Piper is a bully," Sharon said. "He picks on Sally all the time. But she's tough. She's always been able to hold her own with him. . . ." Her voice trailed off, and then she looked up as if shaking off further thoughts of how Sally might be able to handle Derek in her current condition. "My guess is that Derek is forcing Justin to share the answers. Justin simply doesn't seem like the kind of boy who would willingly cheat."

"Tell me what you know about this boy."

"His family lives on the next block over, behind us. His father owns a couple of car dealerships. He's always bragging about being a self-made man, especially when Malcolm is around. The implication being that Malcolm was handed his money on a silver platter."

Rachel was surprised at Sharon's vehemence but realized that what she had given Sharon by bringing up Derek was a release from the anger and frustration she must have been carrying inside all these long days and nights.

"So, what did Mortimer say?" Sharon asked when her eyes again met Rachel's in the dark room.

Rachel told her about the meeting and her suggestion that the teacher provide tutoring for Derek. That brought a genuine laugh from Sharon.

"Oh yeah. That'll work. Sally tells me that the boy skips more school than he attends."

"But surely his parents. . ."

Sharon sighed. "From what I've observed, Derek comes by his tendency to bully others honestly. His father is a control freak and his mom is a mouse." She stood and got a glass of water for herself and drank it down. It was the most physical action she had taken since Rachel had entered the room. "You should warn Justin to watch his back," she said. "Because if Derek is in trouble with Mortimer then he's in trouble at home, and if that's the case someone will pay."

"But surely if the boy is struggling with his math, his parents..."

"Derek is as smart as any other kid. He's lazy or maybe it's his way of rebelling against his father's strictness." She glanced toward the hallway and then at the wall clock. "What's taking so long?"

"I'm sure things are just backed up in the lab. She'll be back soon."

Sharon started smoothing the covers on Sally's hospital bed. "When Sally tried out for the ball team, she beat out Derek Piper to become the pitcher. He quit the team that same day and for weeks after that he made her life miserable. Then once she was diagnosed, he let up a bit. Of course, she was being homeschooled for most of the time so it all resolved itself." She clutched Sally's pillow to her chest, and her eyes met Rachel's. "We have to protect our children, Rachel. We have to teach them and..."

Her shoulders started to heave as she muffled her sobs in the pillow. Rachel went to her and wrapped her arms around Sharon's too-thin body. "We have to be there for them," Rachel whispered, "and sometimes that means taking care of ourselves so that we have the strength they need to draw upon. You are running on empty, Sharon, and if you have nothing left to give, then what will Sally do?"

"I'm so very tired," Sharon whispered. "And so very, very scared."

"I know." She patted Sharon's back. "But Ben tells me that Sally has already responded well to the antibiotics she received in Tampa, and the steroids will strengthen her immune system. He says it's only a matter of getting her counts stabilized and then she can go home—you can all go home."

Sharon shook her head vehemently. "She's given up. You haven't seen her this way. It's so awful. My little girl is in such pain and I can't help her."

"Yes you can. When Sally comes back you can let her know that you are going home for a while to shower and nap and take care of things like the mail and phone messages." She rubbed Sharon's back and gently added, "Give her normal, Sharon. Let her see that the routine of daily life continues."

Sharon pulled away and stared at Rachel. "You think that will help bring her out of this? I've never seen her come so close to giving up before."

"It can't hurt to take a couple of hours to restore some of your strength so that you're ready to face whatever comes next. It's possible that in refusing to leave her side you've given her the impression that things are much worse than they really are. She's not going to trust what the doctors tell her—they've been wrong before. For the real story she will always look to you."

"And what if she begs me to stay?"

But Sally didn't. In fact, she barely acknowledged her mother's leave-taking or the fact that Rachel remained seated next to her bed. She merely lay there, her eyes open, her body tensed into a fetal position, her fists clenched against her chest.

At first Rachel said nothing, searching her brain for some possible topic that might bring about a breakthrough.

"Sally, do you remember that terrible car accident last month?"

Sally blinked but did not respond.

Rachel pressed on, telling her about the meeting with the accident victim's mother and the request to help. She described the VORP program and her meeting with the dead girl's parents. As she talked, slowly, Sally's body began to relax. She stretched out her legs and unclenched her fingers to pull the sheet over her shoulders. She lay on her back, staring up at the ceiling. All the while Rachel kept talking. The truth was that she was afraid to stop for fear she would break the web of progress that she was weaving.

"The father is going to be the tough one," she continued with a heavy sigh. "He's so very angry and. . ."

There was a sound from the bed. A croak that sounded like "Duh."

Rachel permitted herself a small smile and kept talking. "Exactly. Who wouldn't be furious at such unfairness? I expect that everyone involved is struggling with anger as well as grief— they go hand in hand. But you see, Sally, in our faith, forgiveness is the cornerstone. And these two families need to find their way back to each other because in each other's love and forgiveness they will find the strength they need to go on without this wonderful girl. I just wish. . ."

Sally rolled onto her side and came up on one elbow. "She would have wanted that for them, don't you think?"

"I do," Rachel agreed as she got up to fill a glass with water and hand it to Sally. *Keep it normal,* she reminded herself. "What makes *you* think that she would have wanted that?"

Sally shrugged and sipped the water. "From what you've told me, she loved them, all of them." She took a little more of the water and then flopped back onto the pillow. "But it's so hard," she whispered.

"Ja. Life can be that way."

They were quiet for a moment. Sally closed her eyes, and Rachel thought perhaps she was asleep. But then she murmured, "Did you ever hear the saying that God doesn't give people more than they can handle?"

"I have heard similar words." Rachel wondered where the girl's thoughts might be headed.

"He must think I'm like the strongest person ever," she murmured and closed her eyes again.

Rachel caught the shadow of movement outside, and then she saw Ben silhouetted in the frosted glass panel of the door. Very quietly he turned the handle and stepped inside.

"I can't speak for God," Rachel continued, "but I do know that you are a very strong girl and that you have a good many equally strong people around you helping you find your way through this." She used one of the sterile pads on the side table to wipe away the single tear that trickled from the corner of Sally's closed eyes. "One of them is here now," Rachel whispered. "So I'll leave you to visit with your uncle."

Sally opened her eyes and gave Ben a crooked smile. " 'Bout time you showed up," she said.

"I do have other patients, you know. People who are actually sick instead of malingering," he bantered as he pulled the chair closer. He took Sally's hand, and his voice cracked a little as he added, "And it's way past time that you came back to us, kiddo."

Rachel moved around the end of the bed. "I'll stop by tomorrow if that's okay."

"Rachel?"

"Ja?"

"Danke," Sally murmured.

"Get some rest," Rachel replied. "Both of you."

"Bossy, isn't she?" Rachel heard Ben tell Sally, and then as she stepped into the hall and the door swung closed behind her she heard Sally giggle.

Chapter 20

After Rachel left, Ben sat with Sally until Sharon and Malcolm returned.

"You and Rachel would make a good pair," Sally announced almost as soon as Rachel had said good-bye, promising to stop by again.

"She's Mennonite," he reminded her.

"And?"

"And I'm not."

"Details," she said with a dismissive wave of her hand.

"All right, let's look at this another way. If Rachel and I were to get together you do realize that Justin would be your stepcousin, then?"

"Fine with me."

"Rachel is my friend, honey. Like she's your friend and—"

"She's a better match for you than Darcy is."

"Darcy and I are only friends as well."

Sally let out a bark of a laugh. "Yeah?" She pointed to her eyes shielded by the tinted glasses. "These are rolling right now. As Dad says, 'If you believe she's just a friend, then there's some real estate in the Everglades that I'd like to sell you.'"

"It's true," Ben protested.

"Maybe *you* think that's the deal, but my money is on the fact that Darcy thinks it's a whole lot more."

"You're a kid. What do you know about such things?"

"Apparently more than you do. Men," she sighed dramatically as if he and the rest of the species were a lost cause.

That was the moment Malcolm and Sharon arrived. Ben made his excuses, wanting to give them time to enjoy Sally, whom he could see was tiring fast and would soon be asleep. Sharon followed him into the hallway.

"Thank you, Ben. I don't know how you did it but. . ."

"I didn't. It's Rachel you have to thank. And apparently that goes double for me. It's good to have both my sister and my niece back among the living." He hugged her and then gave her a little shove back toward Sally's room. "Go enjoy your daughter—and do not listen to anything she has to say about Rachel and me."

His sister's laughter followed him down the hall. He was glad to hear that she found the idea of a romantic attachment between Rachel and him as ludicrous as he did.

Or was it really so farfetched? The truth was that he was far more attracted—romantically speaking—to Rachel than he was to Darcy. And under other circumstances—if she weren't Mennonite—he might have asked her out by now. Certainly between the times they had been together at work and then at his sister's house, they had forged a relationship, a friendship.

He found her easy to be with, and once she'd gotten past her initial nerves at starting a new job in a new city where she basically knew no one, she'd seemed at ease with him as well. So, why not ask her out? Why not suggest that they meet for coffee?

He headed down to the spiritual care offices. Eileen was getting ready to leave for the day when he entered.

"Paul's already left," she said.

"Is Rachel in?"

Eileen nodded toward the cubicle next to hers at the same time that Rachel said, "Right here." She stepped around the barrier. "Has something happened to Sally?" she asked.

"No. Thanks to you, Sally is doing a whole lot better—at least emotionally speaking. And so are her parents and uncle."

Eileen was taking her time collecting her purse, lunch bag, and a dog-eared paperback novel. She cast furtive glances from Ben to Rachel as a small smile played over her lips, a smile that Ben saw her bite back as she turned finally and started for the door. "Well, if there's nothing you need, I'll see you both tomorrow."

"Have a good evening," Ben said, holding the door for her.

"Eileen," Rachel said, "remember I won't be in tomorrow. I have to be in Tallahassee for the day."

"That's right. Good luck with that."

"What's in Tallahassee?" Ben asked once Eileen was gone.

"I'm meeting with my supervisor from the certification board. Thank you for typing my paper. I'd like to repay you."

"You already have."

She lifted her eyebrows. "How?"

"Sally."

"Oh, that is my job. Sometimes I think that I gain as much as the patients and families do when there is a breakthrough. Has Sharon come back already?"

Ben smiled. "Yeah. You did wonders getting her to leave for the little time that she did. She had changed clothes, showered. She looked better, and when she saw Sally sitting up. . ."

"Sally is a fighter. She needed some time to regroup. We all do."

"Even you?"

"Of course I do."

"I don't know. You always seem so composed and calm whatever the situation."

Her cheeks glowed with rising color. "I am not so calm all the time. Ask Justin."

"I'd rather ask you. How about joining me for a cup of coffee before you head home?"

She glanced at the wall clock above Eileen's desk. "Thank you, but I need to be at home. I sent Justin on ahead to start working on the gardens. I want everything to look especially nice when Sally comes home."

"You do know that it won't really matter to her—or any of them. Getting her home is the main thing."

"Ja. But it will matter to me, and it's a way that Justin and I can let them know we are thinking of them."

"Then I'll help." He opened the door and waited. "Ready?"

She didn't move. "I. . .the bus. . ."

"Now, why would anyone stand around on a hot day like this waiting for a bus when she could ride in a convertible?"

"We Mennonites are plain people, Ben. A car is simply a vehicle to get us from one place to another, same as a bus. I would not want others seeing me ride in a convertible car. Something so. . .showy is not our way."

"And yet I seem to recall that you accepted a ride the other night," he reminded her.

She blushed. "That was. . .it was late and Justin was home alone and. . ."

"Got it. Then let's go wait for that bus."

As he paid his fare, Ben realized that he could not remember the last time he'd ridden a city bus. He'd probably been in college at the time. He'd forgotten a lot about the diversity of the riders—each with his or her unique story. In his college days he had enjoyed speculating about each person—who they were, where they were headed, what they were thinking as they stared straight ahead or out the window.

"You know, when I was in med school and used to take the bus between classes and the hospital," he told Rachel as they sat next to each other midway back on the long bus, "I remember having such a deep respect for the people around me. In my mind they were the kind of unsung heroes we barely notice in this country."

"What do you mean?"

"Hardworking folks trying to make it day-to-day. I imagined that in many cases they were coming or going from a job they found unfulfilling but that they worked because they needed the work. I always wondered about their dreams."

"In what way?"

"What did they really want out of this life? What had they once dreamed of achieving?"

She was quiet for a long moment. "And what dreams did

you have in those days, Ben? I mean, why did you wish to be a doctor?"

It had been so long since Ben had thought about those days, those years when his only intent had been to get away from his father's house. The rest had simply fallen into place, and for the first time he realized that he had not chosen medicine at all. "Becoming a doctor was a way out."

"Of what?"

He shrugged and grinned at her as the bus pulled to the curb to discharge and pick up more passengers. "How about you? How did you decide to become a nurse?"

She ducked her head shyly, but he saw that she was smiling. "I'm afraid I was a little rebellious as a girl," she admitted.

"You? I find that impossible to believe."

"It's true. My parents despaired for me, and they could not have been more relieved when James started courting me. They saw him as this steadfast young man who would surely set me on the right path once we married. They didn't even worry that he was older than I was. In their minds that gave him the maturity that I sorely lacked."

"So you married James and then what? How did nursing school fit in?"

"I graduated before James and I married. He thought that having my degree was a good thing because I would be able to serve the community."

Ben stood up as the bus neared their stop. He offered Rachel his hand and noticed that she hesitated a moment before taking it. Once they were off and walking toward his sister's place, he continued the conversation. "So you and James got married and Justin came along. . . ."

A cloud of sadness passed over her features so fleetingly that he thought he must have been seeing things. But she did not look at him as she changed the subject. "You have turned the tables here, Ben. We were talking about you and how you came to be a doctor."

Was she changing the focus back on him because she was still grieving for her late husband so much that the mere mention of his name brought her such sadness? "There was no real plan. I mean, becoming a doctor was never something I consciously thought about. The pieces kind of fell into place and here I am."

"There was a plan," she said. "No one accidentally becomes a doctor." She opened the filigreed wrought iron gate that led to the path next to the driveway then looked back at him. "You may struggle to accept this, but God always has a plan for us."

"What I struggle with, Rachel, is why God's plans seem to include making kids like Sally suffer." He did not wait for her answer but trudged up the path ahead of her, calling out to Justin who was sweeping the flagstone sidewalk.

Rachel went first to the guesthouse to put on an apron and make a pitcher of lemonade. She carried the pitcher and a stack of three glasses out to the gardens and then set to work raking the debris that Ben and Justin had trimmed from some overgrown shrubs into a pile. All the while she was very aware of Ben's nearness. The way he had rolled back his sleeves to expose forearms that were surprisingly tan and muscular for one who worked indoors. The graceful way he moved as he stretched to cut branches that Justin could not reach. The sound of his voice coaching Justin to shape the shrub as he trimmed it.

Not for the first time it struck her that he would be a very good parent, and she wondered again why he had never married. His devotion to Sally was obvious, as was his care and concern for all of his patients. But they were all someone else's children. When a man loved children as much as Ben obviously did, why would he not be anxious to find a wife and raise a family of his own?

She gathered the clippings and deposited them in a rolling cart to be taken to the compost bin hidden behind the shed. She paused to wipe her brow. Justin and Ben were working side by side the way Justin and James had worked back in Ohio.

Ohio. All day she had worried about the meeting with Justin's teacher, knowing that the issue would not even have come up if Justin had been attending the small Mennonite school near their farm. Once again she asked herself if she had made a mistake in coming here. In bringing Justin to this place and exposing him to a world he was unprepared for, had she done what was best for him, or for herself?

It had all seemed so right in the beginning—as if God were leading her to this place, this job, this life. But what if instead she had allowed her grief to rule her decisions, her need to escape the memories of the farm that she and James had shared with his parents? What if instead of facing the future God had set out for her, she had run away and now Justin was paying the price?

"Mom?"

She shielded her eyes from the setting sun. "Ja."

"Are we gonna eat?"

Rachel smiled. Some things did not change, like the appetite of a twelve-year-old boy. "Ja. We will eat."

"Ben too?"

"Ben too."

Darcy was mystified. Ben's car was still parked in its usual spot, and yet he was nowhere to be found in the hospital. She had lingered as long as she could, keeping an eye on the parking garage exit from her office window while she worked on reports for the upcoming board meeting.

The last she'd seen of Ben he'd been on his way to see Sally. She'd actually gone to the children's wing on some excuse but with the sole purpose of running into Ben at the end of the workday, hoping he might suggest they grab a bite to eat together. But that had been well over an hour ago. She picked up the phone and punched in the number for the nurses' station outside Sally's room.

"Is Dr. Booker still with his niece?" she asked.

"He left a while ago. It's just the parents in there now," the voice on the other end assured her. "Do you want me to page him?"

"No, thanks." She hung up and drummed her manicured nails on her desk as she stared out the window at the parking garage. Maybe she'd missed him after all.

With a heavy sigh, she packed her briefcase with the files and reports she still needed to review and hooked the bulging bag over one shoulder. She retrieved her handbag from the drawer of her desk and headed for the parking garage.

Ben's car was still there, so she retraced her steps to the hospital lobby. "Have you seen Dr. Booker tonight?" she asked the security guard sitting at the information desk.

"Yes ma'am. He left a little while ago."

"But his car. . ."

"He took the bus."

The bus?

"He and the new chaplain lady."

"I see." But Darcy didn't see at all. Why would Ben take a bus unless his car had a problem and even then, why not call for a mechanic? And why on earth would he get on a bus with that woman?

"I expect he'll be back directly," the guard continued, clearly wanting to be of help. "His car's here, after all, and Doc Booker does take pride in that car of his."

He grinned at Darcy, and she tried hard to find a smile to offer in return. "Thank you," she murmured and headed outside.

"I'll let him know you were looking for him," the guard called after her.

Darcy walked blindly past the valet parking booth where two employees were busy helping visitors. Without any true destination in mind she walked out to the street and waited for the light to change. She saw the OPEN sign flashing in the family-owned café where she and Ben had shared a few late-night meals of scrambled eggs, toast, and coffee. From the window she would be able to see him return to get his car. It would be the most natural thing in the world for her to call out to him. After all, how many times had he teased her about keeping doctor's hours?

It was after seven, and the café was nearly deserted. She waved to Millie, the owner's wife, who was wiping the counter. "Sit anywhere," the woman said.

Darcy chose a booth near the door with a view of the entrance to the hospital. She took out her laptop and one of the folders.

"Just coffee," she said when Millie offered her a menu.

Only when she heard a bus slow to turn onto the circular drive did she glance up from her work. A few more customers came and went, but Darcy barely noticed them. She was on her third cup of coffee and well aware that she should probably switch to decaffeinated when someone entered the café, started toward a stool at the counter, and then came over to her booth.

"Working pretty late, aren't you?"

The very last person Darcy had expected to see that night was Zeke Shepherd.

Chapter 21

Justin liked the doctor. He reminded him of his dad. Not in the way he looked of course. Except for both having dark hair, the two men didn't look at all alike. His dad's eyes had been so blue that his mom always said it was like looking at the sky on a clear summer day. Ben's eyes were kind of a mix of green and gold. Eyes that looked at you like he was really interested in anything you might have to say. Dad used to look at Justin that way.

Justin missed the talks he and his dad used to have. Talks about how things were going, what Justin thought about stuff, things like that. But that evening working together in the gardens, Ben had seemed really interested in what Justin had to say about school and then about how he was feeling about living in Florida now that he'd been here a couple of months.

"You and your mom are pretty extraordinary people," he'd told Justin. "I mean, picking up and leaving behind everything you've ever known and starting fresh here? That's pretty unusual."

"Starting fresh" was the phrase his mom had used when she was explaining about taking the job in Florida. She hadn't exactly told him that she'd not only have to work but also would have to go to school to get some kind of license. She hadn't exactly mentioned the late nights when she had to return to the hospital.

"It's kind of lonely," Justin had admitted to Ben.

"I'll bet. You making any friends?"

"A couple." Justin didn't really want to talk about Derek Piper. Ever since the thing with Mr. Mortimer and taking Sally's baseball glove, Justin had his doubts about whether or not Derek was really even interested in being his friend. It seemed these days he was only interested in how Sally was doing and when she might get home. And when Justin had asked Derek why he wanted the glove all he would say was that he needed it for a surprise for Sally.

"Sally mentioned a boy called Derek?"

"Yeah." Justin turned away, looking for his mom. "Hey Mom. Are we gonna eat?"

After that Ben had stopped trying to make conversation. Together they cleaned and put away the garden tools and finished adding the clippings to the compost bin. Then they walked back to the guesthouse to wash up and sit down in the little kitchen for supper.

Justin's mom was the best cook he knew, and it looked like Ben thought so too, the way he went back for seconds on almost everything. "You'd better save room for pie," Justin warned him with a shy grin.

"There's pie?"

"There's always pie, right, Mom?"

"Your favorite—banana cream."

"See?" Justin said, nudging Ben's elbow. "Told you."

It was nice having three people at the table, like it used to be when they lived on the farm. He wished they could go back to those times, but all that had changed.

"You should have told me sooner," Ben teased. "I wouldn't have stuffed myself."

Justin got up and helped clear the table while his mom cut pieces of pie for the three of them. To his surprise Ben helped as well. His dad had never done that. In fact, none of the men in his family had done that. Justin had kind of assumed that once he was married with his own place he would no longer help with those kinds of chores either. He glanced at his mom, who looked like she was as surprised as he was to see Ben scraping the food remains off plates into the garbage.

"I'll take care of that, Ben. You come have your pie and some coffee."

She refilled Justin's milk glass before pouring coffee for Ben and herself.

Ben sat down and put his napkin on his lap then waited.

"We only pray at the start of the meal," Justin advised in a low tone, remembering how Ben had started to pass the rolls to him before the blessing had been said earlier.

"Got it," Ben whispered back. "I was waiting for your mom to sit down."

Justin set his glass of milk aside and waited as well. Ben winked at him.

"Don't you like it—the pie?" Mom said. It seemed pretty important to his mom that Ben like her pie.

"Haven't tried it yet," he replied. "Justin and I were waiting for you."

It had been a long time since Justin had seen his mom smile the way she did just then. It was the kind of smile she used to have whenever his dad teased her about something or paid her a compliment. It was a smile that made her look really pretty, and Justin realized that he wasn't the only one who liked having the doctor around.

After supper, Rachel washed the dishes while Ben helped Justin with a science assignment he'd been struggling to understand. Watching the two of them, their heads bent low over the work, Rachel felt the pangs of the loneliness that had become her constant companion ever since James's death.

In the two years that had passed there had been some healing of the gaping wound his absence had left in her life. After the first anniversary, she had finally begun to accept that her life—and Justin's—must go forward. James would want that for both of them. And she found that she could see a clear path for Justin. In time—God willing—he would find his true calling; he would meet a girl who would turn his thoughts to marriage and family, and the cycle of life would continue.

For Rachel, finding her way into a future that would not include James had been far more difficult. Lately Hester had implied that there were one or two men in Pinecraft that Rachel might enjoy meeting. Rachel had not been fooled by her friend's transparent hints at matchmaking. But she had protested that between work and school and Justin she had as much as she could handle. "Perhaps once I get my certificate and know that the job is secure," she'd told her friend.

She folded the dish towel and wandered out to the screened porch where she stared up at a sky filled with stars. Sometimes at night after Justin was asleep she would stand at the windows and wonder what God's plan might be for her. In taking James so suddenly there had to have been a lesson. She had thought that God's plan had led her here to Florida, but things did not seem to be falling into place the way she had hoped. Not for Justin—and not for her.

Earlier that week she had received her second warning from Darcy via Mark Boynton. Mark had called her to his office in Human Resources and closed the door. When he took his seat behind his desk, he did not look at her but focused instead on a file—her file.

"Is there a problem, Mark?"

He cleared his throat. "Earlier this week you were working with a family, a boy about your son's age whose father had just died."

"The Wilson family. Yes, such a sad case."

"You were speaking with the boy in the hallway outside his father's room, and you were overheard to tell him that with the passing of his father he was now the man of the family." All of this Mark delivered in a flat, impersonal tone without once looking up from the file.

"That was not. . ." Rachel bit her lip to stop herself from saying more. In her faith, a person did not try to argue or defend when accused. Doing so was seen as arrogant, as putting one's self before the good of the community. But surely this was different.

These were outsiders who did not practice such things.

"Did you say this to that boy, Rachel?" Mark had looked at her then, his eyes pleading with her to deny the charge.

"What I said was that when my son's father died, several well-meaning people had said such words to him, but they were not true. Justin was not the man of the family, and neither is the Wilson boy. They are both still children, to be protected and comforted and—"

"I thought it must be something like that, but it may be too late. It's already part of your file. There's really nothing I can do about it. You can appeal it to the powers that be, but frankly I would just leave it alone." Mark had stood and offered her a handshake then, indicating that the meeting was over. "Look, you didn't hear this from me, but be careful, okay? Darcy seems to be trying to build a case for letting you go at the end of your probation."

"Why would anyone go to such lengths to. . ."

Mark shrugged. "Welcome to the ways of corporate America, honey. I'll try explaining things, but don't hold your breath. Now, I really have said too much already. Just be careful, okay?"

Later that day when Rachel had offered to drop off some mail for Eileen on her way home for the night, she had passed by Mark's office. Inside Darcy Meekins was standing, her hands braced on Mark's desk as she leaned toward him and made her point. She couldn't hear what they were saying, but Mark had glanced up and seen Rachel. Their eyes had locked for an instant, and she was positive that his look held pity.

Strike two, she thought with a sigh.

She was so lost in her thoughts and worries that she was unaware that Ben had come out onto the porch, leaving Justin to finish his homework at the kitchen table. "You're very quiet," he said.

"A little tired," she admitted. "You must be exhausted. Seeing patients all day long and worrying about Sally."

Ben shrugged.

"I will pray for her."

A silence stretched between them. "You really believe that

prayer can make a difference, don't you?" Ben asked.

"Ja."

"Even though your husband. . ."

"God did not kill my husband, Ben." The two of them were standing side by side, neither looking at the other, and yet she felt a connection that could not be ignored. "Your father was a minister?"

"He was."

"And yet you question the very idea of faith in things unseen, in a higher power?"

Ben sighed. "When I was growing up, my father painted a picture of God as angry and vengeful. His sermons dwelled on the punishment awaiting those who did not follow the precise teachings of the scriptures. I remember one time I had read a news article about children starving in Africa because of a terrible famine."

"Did you ask him about that?"

"I did. He told me that clearly the people in that land had sinned and turned away from God. To him this was another version of the plague God had sent to the firstborn of every household in the time of Moses."

Rachel had no words to respond to such an idea.

"Once I decided to be a doctor, my plan was to go wherever children were suffering and do what I could to make their lives better."

"And you have done that."

Ben laughed. "Not so much. It's true that I treat sick and injured children, but I do it right here in the safety of America, in the luxury of a medical center where I have everything I need to succeed at my fingertips. I go home at night in my fancy sports car to my high-rise condo overlooking a bay filled with yachts. I open a bottle of wine that costs more than some of those people in Africa make in a year. I am—in short—a fraud, Rachel."

"It's not too late for you to follow your dream, Ben. Perhaps God. . ."

"What about your dreams, Rachel?"

She knew that she should take a step away from him, and

yet she stayed where she was. "We are a simple people, Ben. We accept the path God has chosen for us. I went to nursing school, I married James, we had Justin, and then James was killed, and I brought Justin here."

"Why?"

"Because I needed to provide for our son. I needed to find a place where he could find his way without his father. And my husband's brother took over as head of household and made it clear that if we left, we would not be welcomed back."

"Have you ever considered that maybe you are running from the memories of the life you thought you would have with your husband?"

Was she?

"No. I know people sometimes think that moving away will make a difference, but grief dwells inside you. It cannot be healed by something as simple as a change of location."

"Then how is it healed?"

"Time. Prayer. Watching Justin grow. Making sure he is safe and well." The conversation was disturbing on a number of levels. They were standing too close. His voice was too soft. It was too dark, and far too intimate. Finally, she stepped away. "Perhaps you should think about going to church again...," she said, grasping at anything that might break the mood that held them in its web. Then she covered her mouth with her fingers. "I'm sorry. That was..."

"I do pray sometimes," he said and smiled. "Most times it surprises me to realize that's what I'm doing, but it comes mostly when I've run out of solutions. See. Maybe we aren't as different as you think."

Gently, he tugged her hand away from her lips and kissed the tips of her fingers. "Good night, Rachel. Thank you—for everything you've done today."

Darcy and Zeke had been sitting across from each other in the worn vinyl booth of the diner for nearly two hours. They had talked about everything from the fact that the current owners of the diner were ready to retire to whether or not Darcy's downing three cups of coffee in less than an hour could be labeled an addiction.

She had no idea how it had happened. She certainly had had no intention of inviting Zeke to join her or of spending the time she should have been concentrating on her work trying to follow his casual leap from one subject to another. But here she was—all thoughts of Ben Booker gone—as she tried not to give in to her growing attraction to this impossibly charming man.

Only when she heard the definitive roar of Ben's sports car speeding out of the hospital parking garage and on down the street did she glance out the window.

"He's a good guy—Ben Booker, but he's not for you," Zeke said as he too watched the flash of the blue convertible pass by.

"And you are the authority on this because. . . ?" Darcy challenged.

Zeke shrugged. "You're both wound too tight. You both think you've climbed the mountain, but now that you're at the top, you're not all that thrilled with the view."

"Interesting theory coming from a man who has pretty much laid down at the bottom of the mountain. How's that plan to get back into life coming along?" Darcy meant for her sarcasm to sting him, but Zeke simply grinned.

"No worries. Got the haircut, updated the wardrobe. . . ." He pointed to the freshly pressed cotton shirt he was wearing. "I'd say I'm on a roll."

"Job? Career? Future?"

"Got a job at the packinghouse that gives me enough to live on while I do what I really love—play guitar and write my songs. And as for the future? Who knows? The one thing I know for sure is that anybody thinking she has the least bit of control is fooling herself."

His dark eyes met hers and held them.

"You don't want a family?" she challenged.

"I do indeed but first I have to find me a wife."

She laughed in spite of herself. "You've got everything mapped out, don't you?"

"That would be the way you operate. You like to have a step-by-step plan, and that's probably a good thing in business, but in life. . .in love? Not so much."

"For a man who—"

"You're tired, Darcy. Tired of the fight. That's something I know about. When I got back from my first tour of duty it seemed like everything had changed. I wasn't the same person. I'd seen too much of the way things really were over there. I came back and went to work for Malcolm, but more than a couple of months before, I had signed on for another tour."

"And the second time you came back?" Darcy was fascinated in spite of her determination not to be.

"I didn't. I took some time off and hung out in Europe, then signed up for number three."

The expression that crossed his face in that moment was so filled with pain and sadness that Darcy found she could not look away. Instead she reached across the table and covered his hand with hers. "It must have been. . ." Her words trailed off.

"Nothing had changed," he said, as his dark eyes clouded over with memories. "Nothing. In all that time. I had joined up after 9/11 because I thought I could make a difference. But it was the wrong fight, Darcy, for all the wrong reasons, and in that situation all you can do is tread water until you can pull yourself out."

"So you came home and surrendered?"

His smile was one of pity. "You might think that. I prefer to think of these last years as a kind of strategic retreat, a time to regroup. As the Paul Simon song goes, 'Make a new plan, Stan.'"

"And that plan is. . .?"

He glanced around the café. "I'm thinking of buying this place."

She couldn't help herself. She burst out laughing. "With what?" An image of the loose change accumulating in his guitar case at the farmers' market flashed through her mind.

He grinned. "I'm a Shepherd, remember? There's this little trust fund my dad left me. Wanna come be the chef when I get this place up and running?"

"Yeah. Right."

"Think about it." He got up then and laid some bills on the table to cover the cost of her coffee.

"You don't have to—"

"Ah Darcy, let a guy do the right thing, okay?" He cupped her cheek gently, waved to Millie, and sauntered out.

Darcy watched out the window, and as he passed by, he grinned and blew her a kiss. She put a hand to her cheek and realized she was blushing.

Chapter 22

Justin had begun to dread school. He'd made a huge mistake taking up with Derek and his group. Now that Derek had turned on him, he had no friends and whenever he approached Derek and the others they would turn around and walk away. He'd begun to live for Fridays when he knew he would have at least the weekend to stop trying to figure out what Derek planned to do with Sally's baseball glove.

He never should have taken it. If his mom knew—if she ever found out. . . Every night he prayed hard for a miracle, for some way that he could get the glove and return it to Sally's room before she got home from the hospital. He'd seen it hanging in Derek's locker where Derek had put it when Justin delivered it to him. If he could just get it back.

Oh, how he wished his mom had never taken this job, had never decided to move onto the Shepherds' property, had never left their little community in Ohio. No, that part wasn't true. He didn't miss Ohio all that much, especially living with his uncle. The truth was that there was lots about Florida that he liked— the weather and the beach and the fishing with John and Zeke. The weekends were great when he and his mom spent their time in Pinecraft shopping and visiting and going to church. A couple of times they'd attended programs at the bigger church on the edge of Pinecraft, and he'd even met some kids his age there—Mennonite kids like him. Being in Pinecraft was like being in a whole other world. He wished they could live there all the time.

Whatever came of this business with Derek and the baseball glove, it was up to him to fix it. He decided to talk to Derek and try to convince him once again that Sally had had nothing to do with Mortimer catching them cheating. What he knew for sure was that the conversation needed to take place when Max and Connor weren't around. With Derek it was all about looking good in front of the others.

So when Justin's mom got a call from the hospital right after breakfast that Saturday, Justin saw his chance. He assured her that he would take care of his chores, and then he asked her permission to take his bike and ride over to the park. What he left out was that Derek's house was on the way to the park.

As soon as his mom had boarded the bus, Justin mounted his bike and took off. He would have plenty of time to handle his chores later, but right now the important thing was to catch Derek at home.

He'd never actually been to Derek's house, just ridden by the long driveway guarded by an impressive pair of black metal gates that opened only when Derek—or his parents—entered some secret code. It occurred to him now that his first problem was going to be getting past those gates. He decided the best thing to do would be to wait across the street and hope that Derek would come out.

He leaned his bike on a patch of grass and then sat down on the curb to wait. No more than five minutes later the gates slowly swung open. A minute later a car came toward him, a woman driving. She saw him waiting there and frowned. "Are you lost?" she asked, her voice high and tight when she rolled the window down.

"No ma'am. I'm a friend of Derek's. Is he home?"

She glanced at the rearview mirror and then back at Justin. "Do we know you?"

"Well, no—I mean you never met me exactly. I'm Justin

Kaufmann. My mom and I live. . ."

Her smile was one of pure relief. "Oh, you're the boy who has helped Derek with his math assignments."

"Yes ma'am." Justin was confused. His mom didn't know what had happened? He knew that Mr. Mortimer had met with Derek. Surely he'd also asked to see his parents like he had asked to see Justin's mom.

"Go on through," she said with a wave toward the gates. "Derek is having his breakfast on the terrace. Tell our cook that I said to prepare anything you want—pancakes, eggs—she makes wonderful waffles." She glanced both ways and then turned onto the street. The car window glided silently closed, and Derek's mom waved as she drove away. Justin mounted his bike and got through the gates as they started to swing shut.

It was pretty clear that Justin was the last person Derek expected to see that morning.

"How did you get in here?" he snarled.

"Your mom. . ."

Derek rolled his eyes and attacked the stack of pancakes in front of him. "So what do you want?"

Suddenly Justin had no words. He should have thought this through more thoroughly, practiced what he would say, how he would make his case. "It's about Sally Shepherd," he blurted.

A slow smile spread across Derek's face as he leaned back and fixed his gaze on Justin. "What about her?" He pinned Justin with a glare. "Is she home? Why didn't you tell me she was coming home today?"

"She was supposed to come home a few days ago, but now she's in the hospital where my mom works. Something about her blood counts not being right." He was hoping that Derek might feel some tiny bit of sympathy "She's coming home for Thanksgiving if everything goes okay and I was thinking maybe. . ."

"You were thinking about letting her off the hook for what she did to us?"

"No. Yes. I mean. . ."

"Spit it out, Kaufmann. I haven't got all day."

"I want you to give me back the glove."

Derek made a show of looking around as if searching for something. "Gee, now let me think. Her glove?"

"It's in your locker. I want you to give it back to me Monday so I can return it."

"And I would do this because?"

"It's me you should be blaming for getting in trouble with Mortimer. Sally had nothing to do with it."

"Right." Derek stood up and moved around the glass-topped table to tower over Justin. "Let's get something straight here, freak. What I do or don't do to Sally Shepherd or her precious glove is no longer any of your business. You need to think about what I'm going to do to you."

He walked past Justin, picked up Justin's bike, and casually tossed it into the deep end of the swimming pool that took up most of the backyard. Then he turned and walked into the house without another word.

Now that Rachel had entertained the first hint of a romantic thought about Ben Booker, she could not seem to get the man out of her mind. Of course, the more time that passed without James the more the idea that someday she might love again lingered there. In addition to Hester pointing out the eligible men Rachel's age living in Pinecraft, John had teased her about one older man in their congregation who seemed to have his eye on her.

But how shocked would her friends be to discover that the man she felt drawn to was Ben Booker?

It was impossible of course, and the sheer impossibility of the match made it all the more difficult to turn her thoughts elsewhere. He was not of her faith. He was not of *any* faith, really, although she had been touched to hear him admit that he did pray.

She had seen him with his patients and their parents. She could never forget the hours he'd spent checking up on the boy whose arm had been nearly severed by the shark, sitting with him in the days following the surgery and stopping by to encourage the teen as he struggled through weeks of rehabilitation. And that was only one example of his devotion to his work. Surely, in spite of the fact that he did not seem to be a churchgoing man, he was ministering to their emotional and spiritual needs as much as she or anyone else was.

But daydreaming about a future with Ben Booker was pure folly. Even taking the issue of religion out of the discussion altogether, a man of the world like that in love with a plain woman like her? It was—as she'd once heard Sally say—beyond ridiculous.

Determined to put aside any fantasy of what it might be like to love Ben, Rachel turned her attention to other matters. She spent hours working to finish the course work for her state certification. She identified and then tried to avoid those places at the hospital where she was most likely to see Ben. She timed her visits to Sally and her parents when she knew he was otherwise occupied. Twice when she saw his car parked in his sister's driveway, she had suggested to Justin that they take a bike ride down to Pinecraft for ice cream and see if any new rental listings had been posted on the bulletin board outside the post office.

Out of sight, out of mind became her guidepost.

She certainly had plenty to keep her busy. The pressure she placed on herself to excel increased as she neared the completion of the requirements for earning her certification. Pastor Paul had given her high praise for the work she had done, and Eileen talked as if it was a foregone conclusion that by Christmas Rachel would be a permanent member of the staff. The supervisor sent by the certification board in Tallahassee to observe her work had been equally reassuring.

But getting her license was only one step in the process. There was still the job review, and Mark Boynton had told her that although he had tried explaining her side of things to Darcy, the second perceived offense was still included in her record. "Unfortunately, no one but the boy heard the entire conversation," he told her. The review was set for the Monday following the Thanksgiving holiday.

Because Hester and John were planning to be away for that weekend visiting relatives near Orlando, Rachel was planning a quiet day with Justin. But Sharon Shepherd wouldn't hear of it.

"If you have no other plans," Sharon said, "Sally comes home that Wednesday and she's so looking forward to the day. I know that she would be so happy if you and Justin could come." Sharon smiled and squeezed Rachel's hand. "Surely you know by now that our Sally considers you one of the people she is most thankful for meeting this last year."

It was difficult to refuse after that. Rachel admitted that she and Justin had no special plans for the day, and Sharon clapped her hands together with delight. "Then you'll come. It's going to be such a wonderful celebration—a celebration of true thanksgiving." She sighed.

"You will allow me to bake the pies?" Rachel asked.

"Absolutely. Malcolm loves your pies, and so does Ben."

Of course, Ben would be there. And Zeke. Suddenly Rachel was having second thoughts about the whole idea. But it had been so long since Rachel had seen Sharon looking so happy. How could she disappoint her?

"Malcolm's mom makes a wonderful sweet potato casserole," she gushed. "Our dad—mine and Ben's—won't be able to come, but I have all my mom's best recipes. Sage and pecan stuffing, acorn squash soup, and the most wonderful molded cranberry salad." She ticked off each item on her manicured fingernails. "I thought I would invite Darcy Meekins as well. Ben's been seeing her and well. . ." She smiled mischievously. "Malcolm tells me not to interfere, but I so want my big brother to be happy."

So Darcy would be invited. Rachel felt her stomach lurch.

"We dine at four but don't stand on ceremony," Sharon continued. "Come anytime after one and don't make the pies ahead of time. It's all such fun with the women together in the kitchen cooking and the men watching their football games and the house is alive with. . .well, life." She sighed happily, and then her eyes welled with tears. "Oh Rachel, was it only a few weeks ago that everything looked so bleak?"

Apparently the question was a rhetorical one because Sharon

gave Rachel a quick hug and then hurried away. Rachel remained standing outside the children's chapel, her mind cluttered with everything she needed to accomplish in the next few days. Surely God was taking a hand in making sure that she was kept so busy that she would have little time to think about Ben. And yet somehow thoughts of him were never far from her mind.

Darcy was nervous, and excited. If Sharon Shepherd had invited her for Thanksgiving dinner then surely Ben had approved. Things between them had gotten pretty awkward over the last couple of weeks. Understandably he'd been preoccupied with Sally's recovery, and the few times they had run into each other at the hospital there had been little time for more than a few words. Sitting down together for a family dinner would be the perfect solution for easing them back into the kind of relationship Darcy had imagined them building.

Imagined.

That was the crux of it. She had to admit that she had fantasized about a future with Ben, envisioning the two of them doing everything together. But she could not get past the reality that some of those encounters at work could have turned into a quick lunch or cup of coffee. There had been time for Ben to ask if she wanted to go for a pizza after work. There had been time to suggest a light supper by the bay or watching an old movie to give him some distance from worrying about his niece and his sister. But it had not happened.

So when Darcy parked her car on the circular drive in front of the Shepherds' home and saw Ben's sports car, she had to wonder what the next several hours might hold for her—for them. She opened her trunk to retrieve the bags of fresh herbs and vegetables that she'd brought at Sharon's urging.

"You must be quite the gourmet cook," Sharon had gushed when she'd called to invite Darcy for the day.

Darcy's heart had raced with pleasure at the very idea that Ben might have mentioned the meal she'd prepared for him.

"Zeke says that you're a regular at the market. I love going there, but I never know quite what to do with all those beautiful herbs and veggies," Sharon continued. "Come early and prepare your veggie casserole here. It's a huge kitchen. Maybe you can give me some pointers."

So it had been Zeke who had mentioned her flair for cooking—not Ben. Well, she would simply have to try harder to impress Ben with her culinary skills. Zeke was wrong about her being wound too tight. She knew how to relax and have fun. The man needed to stop playing the amateur shrink and open his eyes to the idea that she had ever so much more to bring to a relationship than he imagined.

She frowned. Not that she gave two cents for what Zeke Shepherd might think of her. It was Ben she was out to impress. She rang the bell even though the front door was open.

"Come on in," Malcolm called as he came toward her. "Need some help?" He held open the screen door to let her pass then took the shopping bags from her. He smiled and tilted his head for her to follow. "Sharon? Reinforcements," he called as he led the way toward the kitchen.

In the background Darcy could hear the sounds of a college football game, and then Ben's shout as his team scored a touchdown.

"Who's playing?" she asked Malcolm, suddenly much preferring to be in the family room with its big-screen television—and Ben.

"Florida State and Florida." Malcolm set the bags on the island counter and grinned at her as another roar—this one more like a groan—erupted from the family room. "Oops, sounds like somebody's team messed up. Glad you could make it, Darcy," he said as he left.

Darcy smiled and turned to greet Sharon and Sally as well as Malcolm's mother, Angie. And one person it had never occurred to her would be there—Rachel Kaufmann.

Rachel couldn't help but notice that Justin had seemed more than a little nervous about sharing Thanksgiving dinner with the Shepherds. When they were still at the guest cottage, he kept glancing outside, up toward the Shepherds' house. "It's just dinner," she told him, assuming that was the cause of his jitters.

"I know," he mumbled. "So Sally came home yesterday?"

"That's right. She was discharged right after lunch."

"She'll be there, then?"

"Well of course she will, Justin. She lives there. What is going on in that head of yours?" She playfully ruffled his hair hoping for a smile.

But none came. Thankfully the moment they arrived at the Shepherds', Zeke took Justin in hand. "You like football?"

Justin shrugged and Zeke grinned. "Me neither, but it's part of the script for today."

For the first time all morning Justin showed some real interest in what the day might bring. "I don't understand."

" 'Tis a day of rituals dating back decades," Zeke announced. "No worries. I'll help you through it. For starters, your mom and all other females are banished to the kitchen while we men. . ." He actually puffed out his chest and pounded it so that Justin laughed. "We men take up our places in the man cave with the ginormous television and watch a bunch of college kids run up and down a field trying their best to give each other concussions."

Rachel frowned. "I don't know if—"

"It's a show," Zeke assured her. "Now from time to time you ladies in the kitchen are going to hear the men do any or all of the following—cheer, shout, groan, possibly cry out as if in pain. You must ignore all of it because it's part—"

"—of the script," Justin said, grinning from ear to ear.

"That's right. So, Rachel, you run along and bake those pies while Justin and I. . ."

Just then Sally came down the stairs. She was much thinner than she'd been a few weeks earlier, but her blood levels had been normal for more than a week now and the special eyedrops, tinted glasses, and regimen of medications prescribed to treat her GVHD and rebuild her immune system seemed to be working. Still, she was frowning.

"Mom," she called out and then seemed to notice that Rachel,

Justin, and Zeke were standing in the hall next to the stairway. "I can't find my glove."

"You don't need your glove today," Sharon called back. "Come here. I need some help."

"That's right," Zeke said as he relieved Justin of the basket of supplies he was carrying and passed them along to Sally. "Women in the kitchen and men. . ." He wrapped his arm around Justin's shoulder.

"Got it," Sally said with a roll of her eyes. "But if Florida State gets ready to score. . ."

"No worries. I'll send my minion here to fetch you. Now scoot."

Rachel liked Zeke so much. Hester had confided to her that lately Zeke's interest in settling into a more orthodox lifestyle had been on the rise. "I think he might be falling in love," she'd whispered. "Why else would he have this sudden interest in how he looks and what he wears?"

It was true. The Zeke that Rachel had met when she first came to Florida was far different—at least in appearance—from the man leading Justin off to watch the game. This current Zeke was dressed in jeans that fit him without the benefit of the piece of rope that doubled as a belt he'd worn when she'd first met him. He was also wearing a solid blue shirt, sleeves rolled back to his elbows, and what looked to Rachel like new sandals.

"I'm really glad you came today, Rachel," Sally was saying as she led the way to the kitchen. "Mom wasn't sure you could do this—I mean, that maybe it wouldn't be right, you know, because of your religion."

"Thanksgiving is a lovely tradition, Sally. Dinner with friends and family all pausing to consider the many blessings God has given them," Rachel assured her. "How could there be anything wrong with that?"

Sally grinned. "Can I help you make the pies?"

"I'd love it."

By the time Darcy Meekins arrived, Rachel was up to her wrists in flour and dough, a wisp of her hair having worked its way loose from her tight bun and tickling her nose as she showed Sally how to roll out the crusts for the pies. By contrast

Darcy looked like a magazine cover model. She was wearing a sleeveless print sundress, her hair pulled back but loose around her shoulders, and her makeup so perfect that it was like she wasn't wearing any at all.

"Darcy, why don't you set up over here?" Sharon directed, pointing to a clear area of the large granite-topped island that dominated the room.

From the family room came a rising chant of, "Food! Food! Food!" Rachel blushed when she realized Justin's voice was a part of the chant.

Malcolm carried several empty soda cans into the kitchen. "Halftime," he commented as he took the cans out to the recycle bin and then headed back to the family room with a fresh supply of soda.

Sharon removed two large platters—one loaded with fresh vegetables and a container of dip and the other piled high with a variety of cheeses and deli meats—from the double-door refrigerator and handed one to her mother-in-law, Angie. "Come on, Mom, let's go feed the animals. Sally, bring those crackers and napkins."

Suddenly Rachel and Darcy were alone. The kitchen was so quiet that Rachel could hear the pan of water that Angie had set to boil for cooking the yams bubbling away. At the same moment she and Darcy reached to turn down the flame. Rachel smiled and stepped away. Darcy set the flame and turned back to chopping the herbs for her casserole.

"It seems you've become quite close to the Shepherds," Darcy said after a moment. "Almost like family."

"They have been very kind to Justin and me. Everyone has been so very kind, and patient."

"Everyone meaning Ben?"

Rachel paused in mixing the apples with cinnamon, dried cherries, nuts, and brown sugar. "Ben is also our friend, yes."

Darcy did not look at her, but Rachel could not miss the way her chopping knife seemed to come down on the bunch of chives with extra force. "Do you think this is a good idea, Rachel? I mean, your close association with the president of the hospital board and his family? Well, it could be seen as something of a conflict of interest in terms of your position at the hospital."

She was as surprised as Darcy apparently was by the comment given the expression on her face. Rachel closed her eyes for a moment, sending up a prayer for guidance. Then Rachel's next words were, "And yet you also work at the hospital and are also very close with the Shepherds—and with Dr. Booker."

Blessedly that was the moment when Sharon, Angie, and Sally returned. They were laughing, bringing with them all the joy that had filled the house earlier. Rachel turned her attention back to Sally. "Shall we do plain pecan for the second pie or perhaps chocolate pecan?"

"Oh, definitely chocolate," Sally said.

Darcy picked up a tray filled with chopped vegetables and turned to Sharon. "Did you say there was a grill outside? I have more than we'll need for the casserole, so why don't I grill the rest?"

"Lovely," Sharon said. "Let me turn it on for you."

"You know after we eat dinner and clean everything up," Sally said, "then we make Christmas cookies, right, Grams?"

Rachel saw Angie frown slightly before changing her expression to a loving smile. "Well, perhaps tonight—since you've only been home. . ."

"Oh Grammie, I've been lying in bed for like an eon. We always make cookies. And I'll bet Rachel has a bazillion recipes for cookies, don't you?"

"Your grandmother is right to worry, Sally. You mustn't overdo it," Rachel said. "Perhaps you could come to the guesthouse on another day and we could bake some together."

"One batch tonight," Sally bartered.

Angie and Rachel exchanged a look. "One batch," Angie agreed. "One batch of sugar cookie dough that we will freeze and decorate when you are stronger."

Sally sighed. "Grams drives a hard bargain," she admitted, and all three of them were laughing when Sharon and Darcy returned from grilling the vegetables.

"I'll take these into the family room." Darcy held up the tray of grilled vegetables.

Rachel had gotten so accustomed to Darcy's disapproval that when the woman glanced at her with something that Rachel could only label as envy, she was stunned. Surely Darcy with all of her success and beauty could not possibly be jealous of Rachel. Her heart went out to Darcy. Seeing her here out of the hospital where she was so clearly in charge made Rachel realize that there was far more to Darcy Meekins than she had thought. Was there any reason why she and Darcy could not find something in common beyond their roles at the hospital?

Until now, Rachel had followed Eileen's advice and simply ignored Darcy's evident concerns when it came to whether or not Rachel was up to the job. That had been a mistake, she decided. Starting here and now she intended to take the first step toward changing that.

So when they were all at dinner and Angie raised the topic of the Keller and Messner families and how difficult the coming holidays would be for them, it was Justin who gave her the opening she'd been seeking.

"Mom's counseling them," Justin blurted, and Darcy's head shot up, her eyes pinning Rachel. "It's a program that Mom and I went through after Dad died. It helps," he added, seemingly oblivious to the adult dynamics surrounding him.

Darcy was staring hard at Rachel while Malcolm's eyebrows had lifted with interest. Everyone seemed to be waiting for her to say something.

"After my husband died, Justin and I were fortunate enough to take part in a counseling program that allowed us to face the man responsible for his death, work through our grief—and anger—and begin to move on."

"I remember seeing something about that on your résumé," Malcolm said. "You got some kind of license to counsel?"

Darcy was focusing all of her attention on her food, but Rachel was determined not to give up on finding some way to connect with this woman. "That's right. I've been thinking about seeing if you and I might talk about possibly bringing some form of the VORP program to Gulf Coast, Darcy." She could have just as easily made the statement to Malcolm as head of the board, but she focused on Darcy as she continued to explain the concept.

"It has some potential," Malcolm jumped in.

"It would certainly be unique to Gulf Coast—Memorial has nothing like that," Ben added, glancing at Darcy. "It could be a positive marketing tool."

"You've been trained as a mediator for this program?" Darcy asked Rachel.

Rachel nodded, her heart hammering. Darcy actually seemed interested. "If you have some time on Monday, I could. . ."

The front doorbell chimed.

"Got it," Malcolm said, placing his napkin on his chair as he went to answer the door. Conversation around the table turned to speculation about who the visitor might be. He returned a moment later with a large gift-wrapped package that he handed to Sally. "Seems you have a secret admirer, kiddo."

"Dad," she groaned, but she took the package and eagerly tore off the gold foil bow and ribbon.

"Who brought it?" Sharon asked.

Malcolm shrugged. "It was sitting there—nobody in sight."

"No card?" Angie asked, examining the wrapping paper that Sally had now cast aside.

Sally pried open what looked like a large hatbox and fished through the layers of tissue paper.

Suddenly her face twisted into a grimace of such pain and shock that both her parents as well as Ben and Zeke were immediately on their feet.

"Give me that," Ben ordered when Sally withdrew a shaking hand from the box.

He dumped the contents onto the floor, and there was a collective gasp as everyone saw Sally's baseball glove, the leather scorched black from a fire and sliced into strips.

Sally was shaking as she stood and stared at her ruined glove. "How. . .who. . . ? It was in my room. It's always in my room."

Justin made a noise as if he might be choking and squirmed uncomfortably in the chair next to Rachel. She glanced at him and so did Sally.

"It was you, wasn't it? Uncle Zeke told me that you and your mom helped him clean the house. You took my glove."

Justin seemed incapable of meeting her glare, and now everyone around the table was looking at him.

"Why?" Sally demanded, her fists clenched at her sides. "What did I ever do to you but try to be your friend?"

And then she ran from the room, Sharon and Malcolm and her grandmother following her up the stairs. Those left behind heard the slam of a door and then silence.

Part Three

But it is good for me to draw near to God...

PSALM 73:28

Chapter 23

All through the long hours that followed the dinner at the Shepherds' Justin tried to figure out some way—any way—that he might explain himself. He had not denied Sally's accusation. How could he? It was the truth.

Instead while Sally and her parents and grandmother were upstairs, Zeke and Darcy began clearing the table and then stayed in the kitchen leaving him, his mom, and Ben at the table.

"Please give me a moment with my son," his mom had said, her voice so soft it was not much more than a whisper.

Ben had folded his arms across his chest and leaned back in his chair. "I'm not going anywhere until you explain what's going on here, Justin."

That was when his mom stood up. "Then I think it's best if we leave. Please thank Sharon and Malcolm for the dinner."

"Don't you want to know. . ."

"What I know is that Justin was sitting right here next to me when that box was delivered. If there is more to it, then I trust my son to tell me himself, but right now it is best for everyone if we leave."

Justin had followed her through the kitchen where Zeke and Darcy were busy loading the dishwasher and covering leftovers.

Neither of them had looked at him as his mom retrieved the basket she'd used to bring the pie ingredients and then left without a word through the back door.

The minute they were inside the guesthouse, she set down the basket and turned to him. "Did you steal that glove, Justin?"

"Not exactly," he hedged.

"Did you take it with Sally's permission?"

"No, but..."

"Then you stole it." She sighed as if she needed to get rid of all the air inside her lungs and start fresh. "Why?"

Guilt welled up in him, but instead of feeling ashamed all he felt was angry. "It's your fault," he told her. "If you hadn't gone to that meeting with Mr. Mortimer..."

"Do not speak to me in that way, Justin." He had never seen his mother look at him the way she had in that moment. Her mouth had tightened so much that her lips had almost disappeared. "What does our meeting with your teacher have anything to do with—"

"Derek saw you, okay? He saw the way you dress and he put it together. He was already mad because he'd been caught cheating and then he was mad all over again because he'd been hanging around somebody like me without even knowing it."

"What's wrong with someone like you?"

"We're different...weird."

"We are different. And if living our lives according to centuries of the faith is weird, then so be it." The heavy silence that fell between them was worse than if his mom had started to shout at him. All he could hear was the ticking of the clock on the fireplace mantel.

"Justin, I am trying to understand this. Tell me why you took Sally's glove."

"Derek threatened me."

"How?"

The question stumped Justin completely. There had been nothing specific. "He said he would make my life miserable."

"How?"

Justin's shoulders slumped. "I don't know," he admitted. "It's what he does. Everybody knows it. I was afraid."

"Oh Justin, why did you not come to me?"

The full force of his anger and disappointment hit him like a fist. He stared at her. "Right. When exactly was I supposed to do that, Mom? You are always gone or busy or thinking about somebody else—Sally, the Keller girl, some kid at the hospital." His voice was shaking and his fists were clenched. "You promised," he shouted, and then stormed off to his room and slammed the door.

Almost immediately he regretted his actions. Never in his life had he spoken to either of his parents that way. If his dad had still been alive Justin had no doubt that he would be in for a paddling. He waited for the door to open, for his mom to confront him—to punish him as he deserved.

Instead after a long while he heard the murmur of her voice and realized she was talking to someone on the telephone. A few minutes later he saw her walking back up to the Shepherds' house, her pace slow like it had been the day they buried his dad.

Ben had helped Zeke and Darcy finish clearing the table, and still there had been no sign of Sally or Sharon or Malcolm. Angie had come downstairs to report that Sally was resting and it was probably best if everyone else left. She had picked up Sally's glove with two fingers and handed it to Zeke. "Get rid of this thing, son, and then please take me home. I'm suddenly too exhausted to drive myself."

To Ben's surprise Darcy had offered to follow Angie and Zeke in her car so that she could give Zeke a ride back. Once they all left, Ben was alone in the spacious downstairs of his sister's house.

He wandered from room to room, window to window, pausing to look out toward the guesthouse. He wondered what Rachel was saying to her son. Would she punish the boy or, like so many parents that Ben had encountered in his practice, insist that her child had done no wrong? That he was in fact the victim of the bully Derek Piper. For Ben had no doubt that it was the

Piper kid who was behind this whole business.

From the day that Sally had beaten him for the position of pitcher on the team, he had set out to get his revenge. He was a first-class bully. Of course, he had learned from the best. Ben recalled Malcolm's tales of Derek's father terrorizing weaker students—including Zeke—when the two of them had been in high school together.

He considered going over to the Piper house and confronting Derek. But what good would that do? He glanced out the window. It was dusk now, and he saw Rachel coming through the gardens on her way up to the house. He thought about how he'd wanted this day to go—how he had planned to find some time when the two of them could talk, how he had wanted to tell her that his feelings for her were complicated but undeniable.

Moving out to the lanai, he stood in the shadows and waited for her. The last rays of the sun cast her features in shadow, but he did not need to see her face to know that she was as filled with misery as he was. His anger had dissipated. Now in its place he felt only sadness and regret for what the day might have been.

He opened the side door for her. "Rachel," he said.

"Is Darcy still here?" she asked.

It was the very last thing he had expected. "No. She went with Zeke to drive Angie home."

Rachel nodded, her eyes downcast. "Then I would like to speak with Sharon and Malcolm if they are available."

"They are with Sally. If you've come to apologize for what Justin—"

"My son will seek their forgiveness," she said.

"Then what? You certainly have nothing to apologize for, and right now the last thing they need—"

"I have come to let your sister know that Justin and I will be moving out on Saturday, and I wanted to offer my resignation to Darcy and Malcolm."

"You're giving up and going back to Ohio?"

"If we need to, Justin and I can stay with Hester and John until I can determine what is best. In the meantime I will enroll Justin in the Mennonite school in Pinecraft."

"You've decided all of this in the last hour?"

She looked at him then. A half smile played across her lips. "I have made many mistakes since coming here. Most of all I have placed my only child in a position where he was so afraid—and felt so alone—that he has lost his way. We both have."

Suddenly the understanding that she planned to simply walk out of his life—out of all their lives—hit him. And as angry as he was with Justin for whatever part he'd played in the horrid prank, the idea that he might never have contact with Rachel again was unthinkable.

"Don't you think you're overreacting here?" He seemed incapable of keeping the anger from his voice.

Her eyes flashed, but she did not raise her voice in response. "I am doing what is best for my son."

"And what about you? What about us? Rachel, I have feelings for you that go beyond. . .that could grow into. . ."

She placed her fingers on his lips, silencing him. "It has been an emotional day for everyone, Ben. Please don't speak of things that are impossible. It only makes this more difficult." She turned then and started back down the path. "If you would please tell Sharon and Malcolm why I stopped by," she said as she walked away. "Thank you, Ben." She stopped and looked back at him. "For everything."

It took him less than a second to realize that somehow he had to stop her. As she walked away he ran to catch up with her, caught her arm, and spun her so that she was close enough to kiss. "Don't you realize that I am falling in love with you, Rachel?"

She did not try to pull away from him. Instead she pushed a lock of his hair back from his forehead. "I know that feeling as well, but we are the adults here, Ben. It is not our wants and needs that are at stake here. Justin. . ."

"Justin is twelve. He'll get over this."

"When I moved him from the only home he's ever known to here, I made a promise to my son, and I will honor that promise. As for you and. . .as for us. . ." Her fingers lingered, curled around the lock of his hair. He pulled her closer.

"Tell me why this has to be impossible," he said.

"You know why as well as I do, Ben. You place most of your faith in facts—what you can see and prove. I am a woman whose whole life is rooted in faith. Tell me how that can work?" She pulled away then. "The mistake I made in taking the position at the hospital was to put my need to escape a life that I hardly recognized anymore ahead of everything else. I thrust Justin into a world that was so very different from the one he knows. I only pray that I can remedy that so that in a couple of years when his time comes to be baptized and take his place as a member of the church, he will have found his way again."

Ben was fresh out of arguments. The light from Sally's bedroom window spilled across the lawn. Rachel was right of course. In fact, she had proven her case so well that he could find no fault with it. "For a woman who makes decisions on faith, you sure can come up with a convincing argument."

He had hoped to make her smile. Instead she looked up at the stars. "I wish you happiness, Ben, or if not happiness at least peace—contentment."

The light in Sally's room went out, and a moment later Ben heard Sharon and Malcolm talking quietly as they came downstairs. Rachel had also heard them, and in her hesitation he saw that she was considering going back inside the house to meet with them.

"Let me tell them," Ben said. "It'll be best that way."

Rachel nodded and stood on her toes to kiss his cheek. Without another word, she walked back toward the guesthouse, the thorns of the rosebushes tugging at her ankle-length skirt as she went.

A thin stream of light shone from under Justin's door. Rachel knocked and then entered the small bedroom. Justin was sitting against the headboard of the single bed, still wearing his best clothes.

"Are you hungry?"

He shook his head, watching her closely, no doubt trying to figure out what might be coming next. She sat on the side of the bed and took his hand between both of hers.

"Pray with me, Justin." She closed her eyes and poured all of her energy into entreating God to help them both find their way. On her way up to the Shepherds' house she had been so certain of her plan. She had called Hester and told her the whole story, and her friend had agreed that if necessary she and Justin could come stay with them until they could rent a cottage in Pinecraft.

"But leaving your job when you're so close to getting your license?" Hester had protested.

"I'll finish the work I need for certification, Hester. But my job and studies are the two things that have taken me away from Justin when he needed me most. I can find work, and I've saved enough to cover our other needs until then."

Together they had come up with a plan that would work for getting Justin to and from the Mennonite school while Rachel looked for steady work and a house to rent in Pinecraft. After she hung up, Rachel had stood for a long moment, the phone still in her hand. How she would miss the hospital and Eileen and Pastor Paul and especially the children and their parents.

She had fallen into the trap of thinking of her needs and ambitions, and it was time to remedy that. The temptation to feel sorry for herself in having to give up all she had worked so hard to achieve was all the impetus she needed to head for the Shepherds' house immediately and make sure they knew that she and Justin would vacate the guesthouse by Saturday.

But when she had run into Ben she had come so very close to changing her mind. The very suggestion that he might have feelings for her that went beyond mere friendship had almost been her undoing. But surely his declaration had arisen from his desperation to stop her from leaving the hospital. Ben could not love her—he barely knew her. She had no doubt that he truly believed that his feelings for her went beyond simple friendship, but what he felt for her was not love. And what she felt for him— what had been growing inside her these last weeks—that was only more evidence of how she had gotten so caught up in the ways of these outsiders that she had lost her way. With God's forgiveness and guidance there was still time to put such feelings to rest and concentrate on building the life she'd promised Justin they would find in Florida. The simple life that did not stray beyond the teachings of their faith.

So she bowed her head and closed her eyes and thanked God for pulling her back from the precipice of her selfishness. Oh, she had told herself that the hours she had given to work and study had been for Justin. But the truth was that she had enjoyed the work, the camaraderie with her coworkers, the knowledge that she could make a difference in the lives of patients and their families.

"Pride goeth before destruction, and an haughty spirit before a fall," she thought. But it was Justin who had suffered the fall. She opened her eyes and looked up at Justin, cupping his cheek tenderly. She realized that she was crying and that his eyes were filled with tears that he was fighting hard to hold back.

"I'm so sorry, Mom," he said, his voice husky with emotion. "For the way I talked to you before. For what I did to Sally, for. . ."

"I forgive you and, knowing Sally, in time she will as well. But you must think of how best to seek her forgiveness, Justin. Whatever part you had in this business, you wronged her."

"I know." His voice choked and he looked away. "Dad would be so ashamed of me," he whispered.

"He would be disappointed in both of us, but he would know that in the end we will make this right."

Justin looked at her with such trust and hope that her heart overflowed with love for him. "Justin, I have thought about what you said, and you are right. When we left Ohio I made you a promise, a promise I have not kept."

"You've really tried," Justin protested. "I know you have."

"Tried and failed. I got all caught up in their world, Justin, never pausing to consider what really mattered—you. I have come to understand that the path I chose is not the path that God had for us."

"I don't want to go back to Ohio."

Rachel smiled. "Good. Neither do I. So for now here is what we will do. . . ."

As she explained her plan, Justin's eyes cleared and she saw in the place of his tears a look of hope that was a welcome relief from the furtive glances filled with doubt that he'd given her these last weeks. Seeing that gave her the courage to believe that she was finally making the right decision. And it was at that moment that she heard the familiar roar of Ben's sports car driving away.

"Well, that was certainly an interesting day," Darcy said after she and Zeke had taken his mom home. She was driving Zeke back to his sister's so he could pick up the van from the fruit co-op that he'd driven there earlier. Ever since they'd said good night to Zeke's mom he'd not said a word. "I'm sure Sally will rally, but I don't know.... It's just so hard."

"It's hard to fathom the damage a bully can do," Zeke said as he stared out the side window.

"Well, I certainly would never have thought that Rachel's son..."

"He's not the bully," Zeke defended. "He's collateral damage. That other kid—Derek—he's the bully."

"And yet Justin took Sally's glove and gave it to him, making it possible for him to..."

"He was afraid."

Darcy glanced at him. "Of what? The guy was after Sally, not him. Besides, Justin looks like he could hold his own."

"That's how bullies work. They find a person's weak spot and then they work that angle. In Justin's case my guess is that Derek discovered that he was Mennonite."

"So?"

"Different—especially *that* different—doesn't play all that well when you're twelve. And if Derek knew that Justin would never fight back—that in his religion..."

"You're going pretty light on the kid."

There was a moment's pause, and then very quietly she heard Zeke say, "Maybe it's because at that age I *was* that kid."

"You? That's pretty hard to believe. From what Malcolm tells me you earned pretty much every medal for bravery that exists in the military."

"I wasn't twelve then, and I was proving a point." He stretched and yawned and then turned his full attention on her, that lazy grin that she was coming to like spreading across his face. "Let's talk about you. I mean, talk about somebody who goes through life trying to prove herself."

"I do not," she protested. "If holding myself and others to high standards qualifies me as a bully. . ."

"Whoa, who said anything about you being a bully?"

"That was the topic," she shot back, her hands tightening around the steering wheel.

Zeke reached over and pulled one hand free and held it, weaving his fingers through hers. "Hey, it's been a strange and upsetting day. I don't know about you, but on Thanksgiving I want dessert. How about we stop at the café for some of Millie's pie?"

"It's Thanksgiving," she pointed out. "The café's probably closed."

"Is the hospital open?"

"Of course, but. . ."

"Then Millie and Al are open. Let's go."

She glanced at him. He was still holding her hand, and she realized she had no desire to pull away.

Chapter 24

Ben did what he always did when he was at a loss to make sense of his personal life—he buried himself in work. If he could only get through the last two weeks that Rachel would be at the hospital then maybe he could move forward. To that end he arranged his schedule so that he was making rounds well before she arrived in the morning and checking in on patients that he needed to see more than once during the day later in the evening, after he knew she had gone home.

With Hester's help it had taken her only two days after they moved out of the guesthouse to rent a small cottage on the banks of Phillippi Creek in Pinecraft and move there with Justin. He had actually driven through the small Amish/Mennonite community one night after Eileen had, unsolicited, offered this bit of news. There had been any number of people out on the main and side streets that made up the neighborhood, but he had not seen Rachel.

"Oh good," he muttered to himself as he turned around and headed back to his condo, "you're very close to becoming a stalker, Booker."

Sharon had reported that Rachel and Justin had moved out without a word, although there had been notes of apology and appreciation from both of them left on the guesthouse's kitchen table. In the envelope that Justin had left for Sally there had been two crisp twenty-dollar bills and a note that read:

Sally,

I made a big mistake that first day at school. I chose the wrong friend and I'm sorry for that. I know a new glove can't replace your other one but in case you decide to buy a new one, I want you to have this money I earned helping out at the co-op. If it's not enough, let me know. Mom says that if I ask for forgiveness and you give it then this is all behind us, but she doesn't understand that that's our way and might not be yours. I don't expect you to forgive me, but please know that I am very, very sorry for hurting you and if I could have a do-over, I would choose you to be my friend.

Justin

Typical for her, Sharon seemed inclined to forgive Justin, as did Sally. In fact it was Sally who had instructed Ben to "let it go."

"Derek Piper is a creep," she'd told him. "That's not exactly news, and if you want to know the truth I feel really bad that Justin and his mom moved out. He took a stupid baseball glove, not a kidney."

Ben had smiled at that. Leave it to Sally to find the pony in a barn filled with manure. He wished he could be as pragmatic in facing the fact that Rachel was leaving the hospital to find her place once again with her own people. It was impossible not to admire the strength it had taken her to put her son's happiness ahead of her own.

A week to the day after the Thanksgiving debacle, Ben rounded a corner on his way to the physicians' locker room to change for the night and saw her coming toward him. She moved with the unselfconscious grace of a dancer and, as always, her loveliness emanated from the inner calm with which she seemed to face whatever life might throw at her. Once she left her position in the spiritual care unit, she was going to be hard to replace.

She was talking to someone on her cell phone, her smile evidence of the good news she was hearing. She had not yet noticed him, and Ben savored the moment that he had to observe her. Then she glanced up and their gazes connected. Her features softened into a smile as she ended the call.

"Hello," she said, and he was reminded of that very first day when she'd stepped off that bus and into his life.

"Good news?" he asked, nodding toward the phone she held.

Her smile widened and her eyes sparkled. "Amazing news. My friend Hester tells me that Zeke Shepherd has bought the café across the street from the hospital."

It was such an unexpected bit of news that Ben laughed. "Zeke?"

"Apparently he has this trust fund left to him by his father and, well, he has decided to put it to use."

"Good for him."

She studied him closely for a moment. "You look tired, Ben."

"Just finishing up for the day. How about you? You're here later than usual."

"Paul and his wife are celebrating their anniversary so I offered to be on call in his place."

"Eileen told me you moved to Pinecraft. How's Justin doing in his new school?"

"He is settling in—we both are."

"Seems to be a lot of that going around these days—you, now Zeke making these big life changes." He was incapable of keeping a note of bitterness from creeping into his voice.

"And you, Ben? Are you. . .well?"

Instinctively he knew that she'd deliberately avoided asking if he was happy. He met her eyes directly. "I miss you."

"Me too," she admitted. "And Sharon and Sally. It's been. . . harder than I thought it would be."

"Then stay—at least in the job. In time we can find our way. I mean, if we're just to be friends so be it, but to give up everything?"

She glanced at her pager as if willing it to interrupt this conversation she clearly did not want to have. Ben pressed his point by taking her hand. "Stay," he pleaded.

"I have promised Justin. . ."

"You promised Justin that you would make a life for him that was better than life without his father back on the farm. Why can't you give him that and have a life for yourself as well?"

Slowly she withdrew her hand. "I have to go," she said and hurried away down the corridor to the elevator, where the door was about to close.

By the time the elevator had come to a stop and the doors slid open to reveal the tropical gardens of the atrium in the lobby, Rachel had managed to get her breathing back to normal. The encounter with Ben had been unexpected, and at first—because of the news she'd been able to share about Zeke—she had thought she could keep the encounter light and unemotional.

Over the last several days she had seen him only twice, and neither time had he been aware of her presence. The first time, he'd been sitting with a family, talking quietly to them, reassuring them that their child—the victim of a terrible fall—would be all right. The second was when she had been waiting for the bus to take her home to Pinecraft and she'd seen him drive out of the parking lot, Darcy Meekins at his side.

In the first instance her admiration and respect for the way he cared for his patients and their families had almost overwhelmed her. In the second she had felt the cruel and relentless undertow of pure unadulterated jealousy.

What was the matter with her? Didn't she want Ben to be happy? If she cared for him, wasn't that what she should wish for him? But when he'd asked her to stay on, promised her that if friendship was all there could be, then that would be enough, she had known in her heart that it would never be enough for her. She was in love with him.

"Rachel?"

She looked up to find Darcy Meekins standing before her.

"Hello, Darcy. You're here late."

"The board meets tonight. Do you have a minute to talk?"

"Of course." Darcy had taken the news of Rachel's resignation in stride, showing neither surprise nor regret. Rather she had turned the entire matter over to Mark Boynton, instructing him to post an ad for Rachel's replacement and to work with Paul Cox to set Rachel's schedule for the time she had left. Rachel could not help but be surprised that Darcy would have any reason—or inclination—to speak with her now.

She followed the hospital administrator to a bench near the atrium's waterfall.

"I heard you were still in the hospital. I was about to have you paged."

"Is there a problem?"

"We are having some difficulty attracting appropriate candidates for your position. I need to report our progress to the board tonight and, given Mark's report, they are not going to be pleased with what I have to tell them. I was wondering if you might consider staying on."

The very last thing Rachel could ever have imagined was that Darcy Meekins—the woman who had seemed to dedicate her days to getting Rachel out of the hospital—would be asking her to reconsider.

"It seems to me," Darcy continued, "that your reasons for leaving had to do with being overwhelmed with the combination of work and the prep for the certification."

"I would not say that I was overwhelmed," Rachel replied. "There were other concerns, but the main reason that I am leaving is because my son needs me."

"Yes, and that includes needing you to have some way of supporting the two of you. What better care could you possibly offer the boy than to have a secure job with benefits?"

Rachel fought a smile. For Darcy such matters were so clear. "Justin needs my time, my presence. If I take a position where I can build my schedule around his, then I can meet all of his needs."

Darcy frowned. "I really don't understand you, Rachel." She seemed genuinely mystified.

"My needs are simple enough," Rachel explained. "It was when I allowed those needs to become more complicated that I lost my way."

"And what about the children here? Paul cannot do this alone. As the hospital gets busier, he will have to divide his time..."

Rachel understood that Darcy was less concerned about the children—or even Paul—than she was about making a good impression to the board. Admittedly the offer was tempting. Now that she had earned her certification she found that she had a lot more time to call her own—hers and Justin's. There would be no more trips to Tallahassee and no more long nights of study.

And with Paul's approval, Eileen and Mark had worked out a schedule for her that made sure she was home when Justin finished school for the day. And she could not deny that a few more weeks of the wages she received at the hospital would go a long way toward establishing a nest egg that she and Justin might need down the road. But it was too late. She had made her choice, and she was certain that it was the right one.

"I am sorry for your difficulties, Darcy."

"Stay until the end of the year, then."

"That's really not possible. My son and I have the opportunity to travel to Central America in two weeks. Our church is sponsoring a relief mission to help rebuild a remote village that was destroyed by last Tuesday's earthquake."

She stood up and offered Darcy a handshake. Shuffling her stack of files from one arm to the other, Darcy stood as well. She clutched her files to her chest instead of accepting Rachel's offer to shake hands. "As I said before, I don't understand you," she said.

Rachel smiled. "Then at last we have something in common, for I don't understand you either, but I know that you are a good person, dedicated to your work. I genuinely admire you and I thank you for the opportunity you and the others have given me here. But I need to focus on my son for now. It really is that simple. So I'll say good night, Darcy."

Outside, she stood for a moment enjoying the cool dry night. The sky was filled with stars, the fronds of the tall, thin palm trees silhouetted by the light of a half moon. As she walked to the bus stop she checked her pager to be sure there were no more emergencies she needed to address before she left for the night. Justin was on an overnight camping trip with the youth group from the church, part of the preparation for the mission trip. Once there he and the other young people would help rebuild housing and a school while she helped out in the mobile medical unit that the Mennonite Disaster Service had set up in the village.

Her heart welled with pleasure when she thought about how excited Justin had been when she'd agreed that joining the mission trip was the perfect way for them to celebrate Christmas. Hester and John were going as well as several other adults and young people from the congregation. They would leave two days after she completed her work at the hospital and return on New Year's Eve.

Across the street, Rachel saw the lights on in the café. She decided to treat herself to a cup of coffee before heading home. Inside the café, she was mildly surprised to see Zeke sitting at the counter. She congratulated him on buying the business, and then she had an idea.

"Have you got a minute to talk?"

"For you? Anytime." He patted the stool beside him then reached across the counter to retrieve a clean mug and the pot of coffee brewing there. "Regular or decaf?"

"Decaf."

He filled her mug and refilled his own and then swiveled on his stool to face her. "So, what's up?"

She knew that he was aware of the missions trip, so she told him that she and Justin were going. Hester and John had asked him to manage the co-op while they were gone. "But once we return I'm going to need a job."

"Go on."

"Well, I don't know what you have in mind for this place, but I was thinking that maybe if you needed somebody to wait tables. . ."

Zeke frowned. "Wait tables? You? Why would you give up nursing to wait tables here?"

"Right now I need uncomplicated, Zeke. You of all people must understand that."

"But when Darcy was in here earlier she said she was going to ask you to stay."

"She did. I turned her down."

Zeke grinned. "Bet that blew her mind."

"She'll find somebody."

Zeke covered her hand with his. "I get it, Rachel. Sometimes you simply need to sit on the sidelines awhile. It's just that I'll be keeping the waitstaff that's here now."

"Oh." Rachel sipped her coffee to hide her disappointment.

Zeke also focused on drinking his coffee. The silence that stretched between them threatened to ruin the good mood Rachel had brought with her into the café. Zeke drummed his fingers on the counter. "Now if you'd be interested in handling the baking—pies, cakes, breads—that position is wide open. And I could probably use a busboy—evenings and weekends—if you think Justin might be interested."

Rachel smiled. "I'll ask him."

"And the baking?"

"Count me in."

After Rachel turned down her offer, Darcy remained seated in the atrium for several long minutes. What was it with that woman? Who in their right mind walked away from a sure thing—with benefits, not to mention the opportunity to someday take charge of the entire spiritual care department? Maybe if Darcy had offered her the two weeks for the mission trip. . .

She sighed heavily and went to wait for the elevator. The board meeting was scheduled to begin in ten minutes and she still had to figure out how to put the best possible spin on her report. Rachel Kaufmann's leaving wasn't the only bad news she had to deliver tonight. Of even more concern would be the fact that the patient census for the quarter had not lived up to projections.

She wished Zeke Shepherd was going to be at this meeting rather than his brother Malcolm. Zeke had a way of looking at things that helped calm her. Admittedly at first his "no worries" philosophy had driven her to distraction. But ever since

Thanksgiving when they'd shared pie at the café and stayed there talking well into the morning, she had realized that Zeke Shepherd was the one person she didn't have to impress or prove herself to. He liked her. He'd said as much when he kissed her lightly on the lips as she'd dropped him off to pick up the co-op's van early that Friday morning. And she had carried the memory of that kiss with her now for an entire week.

The elevator doors slid open, and Ben stepped out. "Hi." He held the door for her. "You look like you're running off to something. Don't you ever take a break from this place?"

"Board meeting," she replied as she stepped onto the elevator.

"How about I meet you, say, in an hour at the café?"

"Can't. I promised. . .I have another. . ." The elevator doors slid shut. Now why hadn't she simply said that she was meeting Zeke at the café once the board meeting ended? And why not invite Ben to join them?

Because it's not Ben you want to be with. It's Zeke.

Chapter 25

"This is going to be the best Christmas ever," Justin exclaimed as he pressed close to the window of the plane that was carrying the relief team to Costa Rica.

Rachel could not disagree. For the first time since leaving the farm in Ohio she finally felt some certainty that she was traveling the path that God had set for her and Justin. In only a matter of days after they moved to Pinecraft and he had enrolled in the Mennonite school there, Justin's whole outlook had changed.

She could actually see signs of the talkative, inquisitive boy he'd been before his father died. Suddenly he was interested in everything about life in Florida. And the few other boys and girls living in the community seemed to accept him into their circle without question.

Going on the trip had been Justin's idea. He'd argued that the ten days of relief that they would provide for the devastated inhabitants of the mountain village of Kingstown was the perfect way to spend Christmas.

And Rachel had agreed. This trip was more than a chance for her to spend time with Justin. It was also exactly what she had needed to let go of any regrets she had held about leaving her job at the hospital.

Once they arrived at the main airport in San Jose they transferred to a much smaller plane for the last leg of their journey to reach the devastated village.

"Mom, look," Justin said in an awed whisper. Everyone on the plane grew silent as they all looked out the tiny windows and saw for the first time the havoc left in the wake of the earthquake. Whole villages were underwater. Piles of rubble that had once been buildings dotted the landscape. Here and there a decapitated palm tree stood sentry over the devastation. A couple of small boats moved slowly over the water that probably had not been there before.

"Search parties from the government," Pastor Detlef—Hester's father—guessed. "Hopefully they've found everyone by now."

There was more dry land but no less destruction as their plane approached a short runway surrounded on all sides by trucks and a couple of other small planes. The tower that had served the airport was tilted at an odd angle, and if there had been a terminal, it was gone.

As the plane landed and taxied, every member of the team prayed silently, and once it stopped the band of rescue workers gathered their belongings and filed off in silence. They were ready to get to work.

After a short but harrowing ride in the canvas-covered back of a military truck to what was left of the village they had come to help, Rachel was pressed into service almost immediately in the large tent that served as a hospital for the area. She soon learned that there were no doctors, only Mary Palmer, a nurse practitioner from the area who had taken charge.

"Where do you need me?" Rachel asked, sliding the straps of her backpack from her shoulders and glancing around at the cots filled with patients.

"Everywhere," Mary said wearily. "You're both trained nurses?" she asked, including Hester in her question.

"Yes," they said as one.

"Good. Why don't the two of you start triaging those folks waiting out there?" She nodded toward a small gathering of children and adults huddled together as if it were below freezing instead of almost eighty degrees outside.

"We don't speak Spanish," Hester admitted.

"Fortunately, most of them speak enough English to understand and be understood. If you need help, there's an interpreter—Juan Carlos. Just shout out for him if you need him."

John and the other men took charge of the teen volunteers and headed off to assess the damage to the school that had once been the largest and most stable building in the village. An engineer had told them that if they could repair the roof on the school, they would be able to provide better shelter for the wounded and displaced. Once that was accomplished they could go to work repairing other buildings that could be used to shelter the earthquake victims. Hester's father, Pastor Detlef, had assured the engineer that there was much that could be accomplished in the ten days they had. The engineer had looked skeptical but then he'd apparently never seen what a group of Mennonite relief workers could accomplish in short order.

As Rachel and Hester checked each person for injuries, they tried to gather each person's medical information. With the help of Juan Carlos they came to understand that these people were not all from this village. Many of them had found their way here from the surrounding area after the initial earthquake had hit. Some of the children had no idea where their parents or siblings were. Others pointed toward the filled beds of the hospital tent when asked about their parents. It was all so very heartbreaking.

After several long hours, someone brought them prepackaged food rations and bottles of fresh water. "Water's going to be the main problem," Hester mused as she held a plastic water bottle for a little girl who was too traumatized to hold the bottle herself.

"Why do you say that?"

"If they run out of clean water then they'll use what's available. Contaminated water means disease—likely cholera. Those trucks at the airport were loaded with cases of water. Why aren't they distributing it?" She directed this question to Mary.

"Because," Mary said, as she joined them, "the local government is in a turf war with the powers that be in another, less damaged village down the road as to which of them gets the water and other supplies. It's an oft-told tale—supplies pour in from all over the place and then they sit." She shook her head and then turned her attention to Rachel. "If you think you can handle things here I could use some help from Hester on the ward." She indicated the larger hospital tent.

"Yes. I can manage," Rachel assured her.

The setting sun brought little relief from the humidity. Rachel wiped sweat from her forehead and looked around to face a woman of indeterminate age dressed only in a thin shift, her hair matted and tangled, her face a mask of dirt marked with scrapes and cuts.

"*Hola,*" Rachel said, using one of the few words she'd picked up from listening to Juan.

"My son is still there," the woman said, pointing toward a pile of rubble several yards down the road where Rachel could see men in uniform working alongside some of the locals. Her English was perfect.

"The men are searching," Rachel said. "They will find him."

Vehemently the woman shook her head. "They are not looking where he is. They sent me away. They believe he is dead, but I know he is not."

"How do you know?"

"God has already taken the boy's father. He would not take my son as well and leave me alone."

In the gathering darkness, Rachel saw that the men were returning to the tents where the volunteers would stay while they were here.

"They are giving up," the woman said angrily. "We must do something!"

Rachel had no idea why this woman had chosen her to champion her cause, but she understood that she could offer her no comfort unless she at least tried. She followed the woman toward the men.

They were filthy with caked dust, streaked with rivulets of sweat, and so weary that they stumbled over the rubble that passed for a road. They carried their tools over their bent shoulders or hanging from limp fingers. When Rachel told them the woman's story, they looked at her with sympathy but offered no hope.

"We'll start again at daybreak," the soldier in charge told the mother.

"You are looking in the wrong place," the woman argued.

The man—Hispanic in features but American by his accent—met her gaze. Rachel saw him struggle to hold his temper. "It may seem that way from where you're standing but trust me, we need to get to him in a way that doesn't risk having the whole hillside cave in on top of him." He nodded to Rachel and then walked on toward the kerosene light coming from the hospital tent. Meanwhile the woman walked on down the road in the direction of the rubble.

Justin had come alongside Rachel, and he placed his hand on hers. "Mom?"

She looked at him and knew in an instant why the woman had come to her. Perhaps she had seen Rachel sending Justin off with the others to start work on the school. Perhaps not. But somehow she had known that Rachel was a mother and that only a mother would understand that she could not—would not—abandon her son until he was found.

It was tradition that Ben spent the Sunday before Christmas with his sister and her family. But this year, as a marker of how well Sally's recovery was going, they decided to drive north to spend Christmas Day with Sally's grandfather.

"You should come," Sharon said as they sat by the pool early one morning watching Sally swim laps before the sun could become a factor.

The last time Ben had seen his father had been when his mom had died. On that occasion, his father had greeted him with, "Her last wish was to see you. You should have come sooner." It did not matter to him that Ben had been halfway around the world attending a medical conference when the call came—not from his father, but from Sharon. It did not matter that his mom had slipped into a coma as soon as she was brought to the hospital after the stroke and never regained consciousness.

Ben glanced at Sharon, but her eyes were hidden behind large black sunglasses. "You're never going to stop trying to mend that particular fence, are you?" Ben said.

She lifted her sunglasses for a moment and pinned him with her startling blue eyes. "All I'm saying is that it would do you good to get away. I gave up on trying to get you and Dad to play nice a long time ago." She let the sunglasses drop back into place and returned to watching Sally. "But I will say this," she added, this time without looking at him. "I will say that you have allowed this feud with Dad to impact everything about your life—and not in a good way."

Ben could have protested her logic, but Sharon was on a roll and it was evident that she did not expect him to debate with her. She needed to say her piece.

"Here's the thing, Ben. I get it that you and Dad have always been on different pages when it comes to religion, but you're as guilty as he ever was of wanting things your own way."

"Dad is—"

"A man, Ben. Just like you. He figured out how to make this life work for him and Mom. He did what he thought was best for you and me and everyone in his congregation. But he can be wrong. There can be another way. Grow up already, and stop blaming him for your restlessness and failure to find your true calling."

"I'm a doctor," he reminded her. "It's what I set out to be and I got there."

"I seem to recall that your original plan was to go to med school and then use your skills to minister—yes, *minister*—to those less fortunate, those who could not afford to pay or get insurance. What happened to that?"

"Why are you suddenly so mad at me?"

Sharon sighed and stared out toward the pool where Sally was swimming laps. "Because the one lesson I have learned in everything we've been through with Sally is that life is short and we don't get too many do-overs."

Ben reached over and took his sister's hand. "Hey, Sally's going to make it."

She turned to him and covered his hand with hers. "I know that. We're not talking about Sally here, Ben. We're talking about you."

"I am fine."

"Right. And I'm Lady Gaga." She stood up and laid her sunglasses on the chaise then walked toward the pool's deep end. "Clock's ticking, big brother." Then she pinched her fingers to her nose and bellowed, "Cannonball!" as she jumped into the water.

As the spray from the pool splashed over him, Ben's phone began vibrating on the small round table next to him. He checked caller identification and saw that it was the hospital calling. "Gotta go," he shouted over the noise of Sharon and Sally laughing and splashing each other. "Hospital emergency. I'll be back later."

When he got to the hospital and walked through the atrium, waving to the security guard and then taking the elevator to the children's wing, he realized he was hoping to see Rachel.

But Rachel wasn't there. If a counselor had been called, it would be Paul Cox waiting with the family—or the new guy they had shifted over from social services to fill in. Ben couldn't remember his name—only that he wasn't Rachel.

At her farewell party, Rachel had told him about the trip that she and Justin would be taking over the holidays. "Our church is sponsoring a youth mission to help victims of the earthquake in Central America."

"You're leaving again?" He had blurted out the words, and

he'd made no attempt to censor his assumption that she was running away.

The flash of anger that passed over her face was gone in an instant, and she'd smiled at him. "It's only for ten days, Ben. It was Justin's idea for us to go."

But after the party—after she had boarded the bus for Pinecraft, refusing his offer of a ride home—it had struck him why the idea of Rachel at the site of an earthquake was so unsettling for him. It wasn't safe there. Some of the aftershocks had been pretty powerful, and there had been widespread flooding. The feeling that had washed over him as he'd watched the bus leave the hospital had been similar to the helpless not-again feeling he'd had when he'd first spotted Sally's GVHD symptoms.

"Dr. Booker?" Ben turned at the sound of the nurse's voice. Somehow he had left the elevator, made his way to the station, and this nurse had handed him the patient's chart.

"Sorry." He focused all of his attention on the facts laid out before him—a girl of seven had been stung by a jellyfish and had had an allergic reaction to the venom. Ben gave the nurse a series of orders and then went in to examine the child and reassure the parents.

By the time he had gotten the child stabilized and out of danger, it was well past dinnertime. He was bone weary. He called Sharon and made his apologies, spoke with Sally and teased her about the gift he had for her, that she would have to wait until she returned from her trip to open it, and then he headed for home.

Home. Who was he kidding? This sterile place with its rooms filled with furniture picked out by some designer had no more feeling of being a home than a hotel room. There was not a single personal item in the place—artsy glass vases where there should have been framed family photos. And an impressive set of leather-bound books chosen for their ability to accent the décor instead of the dog-eared oft-read novels that had once lined the bookshelves of his room when he was a boy.

Twinkling Christmas lights from a neighbor's balcony were

reflected in the floor-to-ceiling windows. They were the closest thing he had to having any decorations for the season. He flipped through the mail and found two Christmas cards from college friends. Each featured a photo of the family dressed for the season and smiling at the camera.

He didn't send cards. He didn't have a family. He was a doctor, and it dawned on him that this had become his entire identity. Suddenly the need for human contact was overwhelming. He called the only person he could think of that was unlikely to be busy with family or the festivities. He called Darcy.

"Ben?" She was definitely surprised to hear from him.

"Yeah. Look, I just finished up a tough case and I thought maybe if you're up for it, we could grab a late supper."

There was a long pause, and he became aware of background noises—music, laughter. "But it sounds like you've got something going, so. . ."

"No, wait. I'm at the café—with Zeke and some people. We're helping Zeke paint the place. Come help us. There's plenty of food. . . ."

"Another time. I'm pretty beat." *And the last thing I want right now is a party.* "Give Zeke my best."

"Sure. Merry Christmas, Ben."

"Yeah. Merry Christmas."

He hung up and paced the rooms of his condo—the spacious, mostly unused rooms. Then he picked up his keys and left. Outside, he walked along the bay then up Main Street to Pineapple on his way to Burns Court. He was thinking maybe a movie would clear his mind, and the theater there always offered something of interest. But as he walked past one of the large old churches that dotted the streets of downtown Sarasota, he heard music—not the usual organ/choir music he might have expected but the sounds of the season's carols rendered by a jazz group.

He stood on the sidewalk for a moment listening then stepped inside. A woman smiled at him and handed him a program then pointed out a seat on the very end of the last pew in the church's chapel. The place was lit by candlelight, and a trio of jazz musicians were seated on a small platform at the front of the room. It took less than a minute for Ben to be drawn into the unique beauty of their rendition of "O Come All Ye Faithful."

How long had it been since he'd sung the familiar words? And yet he found himself thinking them as he closed his eyes and listened. The carol took him back to the Christmases of his youth. The services at his father's church. The nativity story acted out by the children—he had played Joseph to Sharon's Mary for three years running. The packed house for his father's annual midnight service on Christmas Eve—the one sermon, Ben realized, he had always looked forward to hearing.

This service was when his father spoke only of God's love for all humankind, where he exhorted those blessed with more to share their blessings with those less fortunate. And always after that service ended and the last member of the congregation had gone, Ben and Sharon and their parents had not gone home—they had gone instead to a local shelter where they had personally delivered the congregation's generous donations of coats and sweaters and blankets and food to those in need.

Ben opened his eyes and tried to swallow around the lump that had formed in his throat. He hadn't thought about those days in a very long time, not since the day he'd left home for college, left home for good. He thought about what Sharon had said to him earlier that day. Their father wasn't any more perfect than any other human being. But he had done what he thought was best for his family—and his congregation.

After the concert, instead of heading for the theater, Ben walked down the mostly deserted streets until he reached the bay. There he sat on a park bench and took out his phone.

It rang for some time, and he was about to hang up when he heard his father's sleep-filled, raspy voice. "Pastor Booker here."

"Dad?"

The silence that stretched across the miles separating them was a fragile thread, one that Ben was suddenly afraid might snap if he didn't say something. "I was thinking—if it's okay with you—that I might drive up with Sharon and Malcolm and Sally. Maybe stay with you for a few days."

Silence—the silence that screamed with all the hurt that had never been spoken between Ben and his father. Then finally, "That would be fine, son. Really fine."

Chapter 26

On their second day in the village, much-needed supplies of water and food and medical supplies were delivered. Cooking over open fires, the earthquake victims prepared the food while the teams of soldiers and volunteers continued their work. By sundown the Mennonites had made a good start on repairing the school so that at least part of it was again roofed, and plans were made to move the most seriously injured there.

"We just got word that there's a medical team on the way," Mary told Hester and Rachel as the three of them sat on toppled stone walls eating their supper. "Let's hope there's a doctor in the mix."

"Too late for her," Hester said with a nod toward the woman whose son had been buried in the rubble.

"It wasn't the original quake that buried her son," Mary told them. "It was an aftershock yesterday before you got here. The boy was out there helping in the search. The ground shifted and. . ." She shrugged.

"So he's been buried how long?" Rachel asked, her eyes on the mother whose vigil for her son was unceasing even as the woman halfheartedly picked at her supper.

"A day and a half now." Mary scraped the last of her food onto her fork. "Going without food or water for that long? You do the math," she said somberly as she headed back to work.

"You okay?" Hester asked Rachel once they were alone.

"I feel so sad for her." Rachel watched the woman who was now fingering the beads of her rosary, her eyes closed, her lips moving.

"Well, clearly she has not yet given up hope."

Rachel looked over to where Justin was part of a lively group of nationals and volunteers kicking a soccer ball around in a circle. She was so very blessed to have him in her life. Her heart went out to the woman praying for her child. "I'll be back," she told Hester, and taking two cookies from a package, she picked her way across the rubble.

"My name is Rachel," she said after waiting respectfully for the woman to finish her prayers.

"Isabel," the woman replied, accepting the cookie that Rachel handed her and taking a bite.

"My son's name is Justin." Rachel nodded toward the group of young people.

"Raoul," the woman replied with a glance toward the pile of rocks and stones.

"I'm so sorry for your loss—your husband..." The two women ate their cookies while Rachel tried to come up with some topic that might offer the woman a reprieve. "Your English is perfect."

Isabel shrugged. "My husband is...*was* American. I met him when I was in graduate school. He was a professor in California. Raoul was born there, but every year over the Christmas holidays we come here to see my family. He died in the aftershock that followed the original quake."

Rachel was almost afraid to ask the next question. "And the rest of your family?"

"Safe. They had gone to San Jose for the day. But Raoul had a stomachache—it takes him some time to adjust to the change in diet—so we stayed here. I had left for church when the earthquake struck. I turned back and saw my son running toward me yelling for me to go back to the church."

"And your husband?"

"Stayed behind to check on the neighbors to make sure everyone was out." She fingered her rosary and murmured, "Everyone got out except for him."

Rachel let the silence and the darkness wrap around them until she heard Isabel release a shuddering sigh. "When I awoke, Raoul had gone with the soldiers and men of the village the next day to search. He was there when they brought out my husband's body. It was so very hard for him."

"How old is he?"

"Ten." She stared at the rock pile that had killed her husband and now held her son. "He kept going back there as if it might not be true. Then yesterday there was a strong aftershock and the shifting. . ." She buried her face in her hands, the rosary dangling from her fingers.

Rachel wrapped her arm around Isabel's shoulders. "You need to rest."

Isabel pulled away with a vehemence that was surprising. "No. I will not leave him. As long as there is a chance, I will not leave him out here alone."

"Then I will watch with you—we can spell each other."

"Your son. . ."

". . .has the comfort of friends. He knows where I am. He understands."

"*Gracias.*"

Hester sent John to deliver blankets for them to rest on as well as several small bottles of water. He also handed Rachel her Bible and a flashlight. "Justin asked me to bring you these."

The two women settled in for the night's vigil. "One of the other women in your group told me that your husband died suddenly too," Isabel said.

"It was two years ago, but I well remember the immediate shock of not having him there—of having to come to grips with the idea that he would not be there again."

They sat in silence for a long moment, Isabel resting her chin on her bent knees. "And after two years is it. . .better?"

Rachel had to think about that. "I still miss him—I expect that a part of me always will. I especially miss what we shared together in raising our son."

Isabel glanced at her. "But?"

"But I am a woman of faith as you are. So I know that God has a plan for our lives, Isabel."

"I only hope. . ." Isabel's voice broke and she shook her head vehemently then surrendered to the tears.

Rachel held her until her sobs finally dwindled to shuddering sighs. "You will make it, Isabel. If you hold fast to your faith, you can get through this. But you need to get some rest."

Promising Isabel that she would wake her in two hours—sooner if anything happened—Rachel settled against a tree and opened her Bible. But she did not turn on the flashlight. Instead she ran her fingers lightly over the pages, praying silently for Raoul and Isabel and thanking God for giving her and Justin this opportunity to serve others.

The two hours passed, but Isabel was sleeping so soundly that Rachel could not bring herself to wake her. Instead she focused her attention on the blackness of the night sky, the sheer vastness of it like the boundless sea. How could anyone doubt God's existence?

It did not surprise her in the least that her query brought thoughts of Ben to mind. She couldn't help but think that somehow if he could find his way back to God he would be a happier man. She tried to imagine Ben in this place, and she smiled as she envisioned the way his lighthearted teasing would comfort the children. He was so very good with children. Not for the first time she thought about what a good father he would make. And perhaps it was the quietness of the night, the starless sky, or her own weariness, but she found herself envisioning him as Justin's father, as the father of children that he and she might have together.

"I love him, heavenly Father," she whispered. "I love him as I first loved James. He fills my thoughts and my dreams, and I don't know what to do."

Beside her, Isabel stirred. "What time is it?"

"Almost four," Rachel confessed. "You were sleeping so soundly."

"Well, I am awake now, and it is you who must rest." She stretched and sat up.

She was right of course. Rachel had come here as part of a relief team, and what relief could she offer if she were exhausted? She curled onto her side and closed her eyes. The last thing she remembered hearing was the rhythmic clicking of Isabel's rosary beads.

It had been two long years since Justin had felt so sure that everything was going to work out for him and his mom after all. Coming on the youth mission had been exactly what he needed to get past the disaster of Sally's ruined glove and his part in it. Being in a place where he could do things that actually helped other people gave Justin a sense of purpose. Somehow every time he made an injured kid laugh or brought water to another patient he felt like he was making amends for hurting Sally. He knew that he wasn't supposed to take pride in things he did, but he and the others were making a real difference for these people—and doing that made him feel closer to his dad.

They had already managed to repair the school building as well as a few of the less damaged homes and shops in the village. The youth volunteers spent their free time in the evenings with kids their age from the village, learning a few Spanish words, singing songs, and trading stories. Justin was telling one of the older kids about moving to Florida when he heard a cry go up from the rock pile where they all knew a boy was still buried. Just about everybody took off running to see what was happening.

As everyone crowded together at the base of the pile of rubble, Justin saw one of the soldiers carefully roll back a boulder. The heavy rock tumbled down toward them, causing everything in its path to shift and resettle. The onlookers jumped out of its way. It was almost like they were all holding their breath until the boulder came to a stop.

"There," he heard the boy's mother say, her voice high pitched and excited. "Can you see him?" She switched to Spanish, edging closer to the opening that the soldier had exposed. "Raoul!" she cried out. The sound echoed in the silence of the crowd.

Justin edged closer to his mom. "What's going on?"

"The soldier came this morning with a dog specially trained to search for any signs of someone still buried beneath the rocks," Hester told him. "We think the dog may have located Raoul."

"Is he alive?"

His mom wrapped her arm around Justin's shoulder. "We don't know yet. Pray that he is."

"I see him," the soldier yelled.

"Can you reach him?" another man shouted in Spanish, gesturing as he made his way across the rubble, trying hard not to disturb the loose rock.

The soldier shook his head.

The crowd groaned.

The boy's mother lay on her stomach as she edged closer and closer to the small opening. "Raoul," she said, her voice husky now, like she might cry.

The men worked together through the long, hot afternoon, but it seemed everything that they tried only caused the ground to shift and the opening they had made to get smaller.

Around suppertime, a truck rolled into the village and most of the people went to unload the supplies. "Go help the others," Justin's mom said, urging him away from the scene playing out on the rock pile. "Go on," she said, turning him toward the truck and giving him a little push.

"Mom? Is Raoul going to make it?"

"We must pray that he will," she said.

But Justin wasn't sure prayer was going to work in this case.

Rachel found herself wishing Ben was with them. He would know what to do, she was certain of it. Somehow he would find

a way to reach the boy, treat him, and bring him to the surface. But Ben was not there.

Instead, Mary introduced Rachel and Hester to the new arrivals—three medical students. "I was filling them in on the situation out there." Mary jerked her head in the general direction of the rubble pile.

"The mother has great faith even now," Rachel said. She saw how the medical students followed her gaze up to the place where the boy had been buried now for almost two days. The mother still lay on her stomach staring down at her son.

"What's keeping them from bringing the boy up?" one student asked.

"The opening is very narrow, and the terrain surrounding it is still so unstable," Rachel told him. "They do not want to try anything until they are certain that they will not cause another cave-in. Soon it will be dark and they will stop for the night—but his mother will stay with him."

"We have lights," another of the students said, more to himself than to Rachel.

"Let's go," the third added as he took the knapsack that held his medical supplies and a large LED lantern from the truck. "If they can't get him out, then maybe we can figure out how to get a man down there. If by some miracle he is still alive, then he's got to be badly dehydrated."

Rachel followed the group to where the rescuers stood helplessly off to the side as the woman repeated her son's name over and over again, her voice now no more than a whisper.

After consulting with the rescue team, using Juan Carlos as their interpreter, one of the medical students edged his way carefully toward the opening. "You're the nurse?"

Rachel nodded.

"Come with me."

With every step, a trickle of pebbles tumbled down the slope. The young man would freeze waiting for everything to settle before pressing on. At the base of the pile, Rachel saw the workers setting up more lights and focusing the beams on the path that she and the medical student must take to reach the opening. Isabel sat up, watching them come.

"I cannot see him," she said. "It's so dark."

At last, Rachel and the young doctor made it to the opening and sat down. "Then let's throw a little light down there, okay?" He tied a rope to a thin but powerful flashlight and slowly lowered it into the crevice. The rescuers had not been kidding when they said the opening was impossibly narrow. There was no way that any of the men could make it down there.

"Raoul?" Isabel called. "The doctor is here now. Just hang on a little longer. The doctor will save you."

"I can't see anything," the doctor admitted. He scooted to one side. "You try."

Rachel settled herself between him and Isabel then lay prone as she edged her way over the lip of the crevice. The light swung like a pendulum as the med student lowered it as far as the rope allowed. She could see the boy. He was on his back, one leg straight and the other at an angle. His hands, white with the dust of the rubble that surrounded him, were resting against his chest. He wore a dark T-shirt and shorts.

Rubbing sweat from her own eyes, Rachel studied the boy, searching for signs of life that she prayed she might find. And then she thought she saw the slightest twitch of the boy's eyelids and lips. Surely it was a mirage, a longing for the boy to have made it when there was almost no possibility that he could have. *Please.*

She waited, forcing her breathing to steady. Then, seeing no more signs of life, she considered how best to break the news to Isabel. Suddenly one of the boy's hands moved toward his face— less than an inch—but this was no mirage. *He's alive,* she thought incredulously. Never in her life had she witnessed a miracle. Yet this child had been lying at the bottom of this pit with no food or water for two days now, the extent of his injuries—especially the internal ones—unknown and still he was alive. She shouted the news to those gathered above her.

She sat up, felt Isabel grasp her shoulder, and then carefully lowered as much of her upper body as possible into the opening for a closer look. Now the boy's hand was thrown across his eyes, so there was no doubt that he was alive.

"Raoul, lie still. We're going to get you out," she promised and closed her eyes tight for a moment as she sent up a prayer of thanksgiving. The odds against getting this child to the surface in time were still astronomical. It would take hours—perhaps days. *Please. He's made it this far. Don't let us fail him now.*

She felt a hand on her back and turned her head to find Isabel and the med student both leaning in close. "He's really alive?"

Rachel nodded as she pulled herself back to the edge and faced Isabel. "Your son is alive," she told her, "but he is very weak. We need to get him medical attention and fluids as soon as possible."

Isabel nodded, her tears flowing freely now, her smile radiant even in the darkness that surrounded them. She leaned closer to the opening, her hand extended as if to touch her son so many feet below her. "We are coming, Raoul. I promise you. . .we will come."

"Do you think we can get to him in time?" the medical student asked Rachel.

"We must. Isabel has given her son her promise, and we mothers do not make promises we cannot keep."

By morning the trio of medical students had rigged up tubing by which they could send down a trickle of water for Raoul, but even in the rare moments when he was conscious the boy was too weak and disoriented to follow their instructions. An engineer was studying the area, trying to decide the best way to get to the boy without causing the rubble around him to collapse. And at the base of the earthquake-created hill, everyone else gathered to pray and sing, hoping to keep up the spirits of the rescuers as well as provide comfort for Raoul and Isabel.

Rachel could not stop thinking about the boy. The place where he lay was not so very deep. There was a jagged piece of concrete jutting out from a wall of rubble that prevented them from getting all the way down to where he lay. One of the medical students had actually climbed down to the thin ledge, but his report was not good. He had been unable to reach Raoul, and unless they could get past the barrier. . .

Rachel closed her eyes. *There has got to be an answer,* she prayed. *Show us the way.*

Two rescuers walked past her on their way back to their trucks to gather more supplies. "If we had a kid—a skinny kid. . ."

"You can't ask any kid to go down there," his companion argued. "What if the whole thing caves in? Then we've lost two kids, devastated two families."

Rachel opened her eyes, pressing her palms down the front of her apron. Suddenly she stared down at her hands, stilling them on her body—her thin-as-a-boy's body. Could she make it past the barrier? And if she could, wasn't she the next best person to reach Raoul first? To administer the emergency care he so badly needed? To check him for injuries not readily evident from their vantage point at the top of the hole that held him?

"Justin!" She beckoned for her son to join her in the tent the staff used as their sleeping quarters. Inside the tent she pulled out a pair of her son's jeans and a shirt. "Sit there," she said, indicating the cot next to his. "I need to talk to you while I change." She pulled closed the curtain that hung between cots to give herself a little privacy and began laying out her plan while she changed into Justin's clothes.

"But Mom, it's dangerous. Let me go."

Rachel's heart swelled with love for him. She pulled back the curtain, her change of dress causing his eyes to widen in surprise. "You are such a brave young man."

"You look—different." He glanced toward the top of her head and then to the starched white prayer covering lying on the cot.

"Ja." She knelt next to him and took his hands in hers. "I have asked a great deal of you since your father died, Justin."

"But. . ."

She pulled him close and stroked his hair as she continued,

"And if you had not asked to come—to be a part of this youth mission, then just think... We would not have been here."

"And you would not be doing this," Justin argued.

"Time is wasting, Justin. Tell me you understand why I need to try."

He sighed. "Because like Raoul's mom or Sally's, you can't stand seeing any kid in trouble. It's a mom thing." His voice dripped with resignation. He straightened and faced her squarely. "But I'm going to be there and if there's any chance at all that..."

"I'll be tethered to a rope—they'll pull me out if anything starts to go wrong," she said.

"Promise?"

"Promise." She waited. If he begged her not to go she wouldn't. Justin had already lost one parent, and he was right to be concerned about the possible danger. "If you don't want..."

"Maybe this is why we came here, Mom. Do you think maybe this is why God sent us here?"

She had never loved her child more than she did in that moment. "I don't know. What does your heart tell you?"

"Go," he said as he wrapped his arms around her and held on. "Please come back safe, okay?"

To Rachel's relief, Hester and the others from their church had gone to get their lunches in the mess tent when she made her way up to the opening on the rock pile. It was going to be a lot easier to convince the rescue team that she was the perfect candidate to go and get the boy than it would ever be to convince her friends.

And sure enough, they had already rigged her to the necessary climbing apparatus and begun to lower her into the hole when she heard Pastor Detlef's stern voice. "Bring her out of there—now."

She found her footing on the cleft of concrete and looked up. "It's okay, Pastor. I'm here. Now what?"

On a separate rope, the medical team lowered down a canvas bag that they had packed with emergency medical supplies and water. Lying flat on her stomach, she lowered the bag past the jagged edges of her fragile platform and down to where Raoul lay. He was so still, and there had been almost no sign that he was still alive for hours now.

"Okay," she reported, feeling the dust fill her lungs. "Going now." She paused for a moment to gather her wits and heard the faint strains of a favorite Christmas carol sung in harmony. She smiled. It was Christmas Eve. Surely God would be with them on this of all days.

She was halfway between Raoul below her and the ledge above when the rope caught on one of the jagged edges. For an instant she was left dangling, swinging back and forth the way the flashlight had the night before. She was surrounded by the ominous sound of rock coming loose. Instinctively she covered her head with her arms as a trickle of stones and dust pelted her from above.

"That's it," she heard one of the medical students say. "This is too dangerous."

Rachel swung her body over toward the place where the rope was caught, freed it, and landed with a thud inches from Raoul's inert body. "I'm here," she called up and immediately opened her bag and took out what she needed to check the boy's vitals.

In an instant she was lost in her work, oblivious to her surroundings, focused only on calling out her findings, checking Raoul for injuries, and assessing his status. Using one of the clips from her climbing apparatus, she was able to hang a bag of fluids and get an IV started. He groaned a little when she poked him with the needle. She thought it was the most wonderful sound she had ever heard.

He was alive and with God's help, he was going to make it. She pulled out a thin but strong nylon sheet the engineer had given her. "Once he's got that first bag of fluids in him, then we can move him. Wrap him in this and then hitch the ropes to him like so," he'd instructed her as they'd lowered her into the hole. "Hopefully we can get him through the crevice and past the concrete barrier. Once we accomplish that he'll be home free, and we'll send down the rope for you, okay?"

Rachel set the drip on the IV and then squatted against the rough wall to wait. Above her, she could hear Isabel praying the beads of her rosary.

She sat for a long moment, watching the fluid slowly drip down the tubing. And she thought about Ben. Where was he spending this Christmas Eve? Would anything about the season touch him, bring back memories of what his faith must have meant to him once? Sharon had told her how as a teenager Ben had been a real leader—at school and in the summer camp they had attended. "But not in our father's church," she had admitted sadly. "He and Dad never seemed to be on the same page."

Finally, the IV bag was empty. Rachel pushed herself to her feet and unhooked the tubing, leaving the port so that once Raoul was brought to the surface he could continue to receive the vital fluids.

"Call the others. I'm getting him ready for the ascent," she said.

It took the rescuers nearly half an hour to maneuver Raoul's wrapped and upright body to safety. Then a shout of victory echoed around the opening and funneled down into the hole where she waited her turn to be brought up. She smiled and thanked God for this blessing. Then she heard another sound, nothing so soothing or consoling as the hymn singing or the shouts of celebration. No, this sound was a sharp crack followed by silence followed by a scattering of stones and dust falling from above.

Rachel turned to face the wall and covered her head with her arms when she heard a loud thundering noise that seemed to be coming directly at her. Seconds later she felt the scrape of something sharp and hard brush her shoulder and then land with a heavy thud inches from where she crouched. She waited an instant, aware that above her the celebration had gone silent, and now there were voices calling out for her as the hole around and above her filled with dust and falling debris.

In the sudden shadowy confines, she realized that if she hadn't moved to where she now was, the heavy concrete slab that had broken loose and fallen would have landed right on her.

"Mom!" she heard Justin shriek.

"Rachel!" Hester sounded every bit as panicked.

Her throat was filled with dust and her bag with its bottled water and other supplies was buried beneath the huge piece of concrete. She coughed and tugged on the dangling rope. "Right here," she croaked.

"Get her out of there *now*," she heard Pastor Detlef order for the second time.

This time she hoped the others would listen to him.

Chapter 27

Justin had never in his life prayed as hard as he did that afternoon. He squeezed his eyes closed and kept them that way, allowing his ears to tell him what was happening with the rescue. A shout of joy from the rescue workers told him that the boy was alive.

"Thank you, God," he murmured aloud. "Now please please please bring them both out of there alive."

Was he asking for too much?

He felt Hester's comforting hand on his shoulder, and then he heard another cry of relief from those gathered on the hillside. Opening his eyes, he saw rescue workers grab hold of the boy as he reached the opening. They carefully put him on a stretcher they'd had waiting, and two workers carried the stretcher down the hillside toward the medical tent.

But where was his mom?

Justin broke free of Hester's grasp and started up the hill. "Mom?"

He heard a distant rumble like thunder, but it wasn't coming from the sky. It was coming from the ground. Around him small avalanches of stones trickled down the hillside. "Mom!" he shouted and ran for the place where Pastor Detlef and others were leaning over the opening.

"Get back, Justin," John Steiner ordered.

He looked worried and scared. "Is Mom. . ."

"She's okay," John said. "We have to figure out how to get her out of there."

A thousand thoughts raced through Justin's mind. What if they couldn't get her out? What if she was trapped like the boy had been? What if they were too late?

"Mom?" he shouted and was grateful when everybody else stopped talking for a minute.

"I'm okay, Justin. Do what John tells you, okay? John and Hester will take care of you, okay?"

He tried to make sense of her words. Why would she say something like that? "Mom? You promised," he shouted, and then he broke down in the tears he'd forced back ever since he'd watched her head up that hillside.

"You promised," he sobbed as Hester wrapped him in her embrace.

Rachel thought her heart might actually break when she heard Justin calling out to her. It was hard not to cry out to God to stop her son's suffering. But instead she closed her eyes and prayed the prayer she had known from childhood on. *Thy will be done.*

And after a moment she felt such a sense of peace wash over her. In spite of the fact that she was pretty certain that she had a broken arm and perhaps other injuries, she felt sure that whatever her fate might be, it was what would be best for Justin. She would keep her promise of giving him a better life.

Hester and John would take Justin if she didn't make it out of here. Hester had told her as much once when they'd been talking about how hard things were for Justin without James.

"Thank You, God, for bringing Hester back into my life," she murmured and then coughed because her throat and mouth were filled with the dust that continued to fall all around her. If this was to be her death then she was at peace because Justin would have a good life with Hester and John.

Suddenly she felt the rope she was holding grow taut, and

her will to survive and care for Justin herself kicked into high gear. "I can climb the wall if you pull," she called up to the men above her. It would be difficult with only one working arm, but she was determined to do it.

She planted her feet against the wall and squeezed her body past the barrier above. She felt the sharp rock rip her clothing and into her skin, but she was not going to let that stop her.

"Pull," she called, and then she closed her eyes against the sudden brightness of the sun as she realized that she had finally reached the top.

She held out her good arm to John, wincing as pain shot through her other arm. "Thank you," she whispered as John and another man pulled her the rest of the way out and helped her to a stretcher,

"Mom!"

Never in all her life had she heard a sound more sweet than Justin's voice.

"Right here," she answered, and as he buried his face against her chest, she cradled his head. "Right here as long as you need me," she said.

On Christmas Day everyone stopped working to celebrate. Together they all sang carols and Pastor Detlef along with the local priest led services.

A few days later Justin and his mom and the others were at the San Jose airport. It all seemed like a world away from the little village as they waited for the plane that would take them back to Sarasota.

"Mom?"

"Right here," she said, and patted his knee.

"I've been thinking. I mean, do you really want to bake pies and stuff for Zeke's café?"

"I like to bake and he needs help."

"I know but, well, I mean lots of people can bake and lots of people need jobs."

"I need a job, Justin. We have rent to pay and food to buy and—"

"But what about the kids at the hospital?"

"They have Pastor Paul."

"They need you, Mom."

Her eyes flickered away as if she wasn't quite sure how to answer him. He decided to press his case. "And that's not all. They need you—not just those sick kids but Pastor Paul—and Dr. Booker."

Now she was staring hard at him. "Why would you say that—about Dr. Booker?"

Justin sighed. "Come on, Mom. I may be twelve, but it's pretty clear even to a kid like me that he likes you—a lot. And you like him. I mean, he makes you happy—the way Dad used to."

"Dr. Booker is a good friend. . . ."

"He's more than that. I overheard Hester saying that he's in love with you." Instantly he realized that he might have gone too far. Hester—who was seated on the aisle across from them—rolled her eyes and then shrugged when Justin's mom looked at her.

"Well, he is," she said and turned back to her knitting.

"So, I mean. . .people get married again after someone dies, don't they?"

"Yes, but. . ."

"So if you went back to work at the hospital and you and Dr. Booker spent time together, maybe. . ." For the first time since his father's death Justin found himself excited about the future—more than excited, he felt certain about the future. "It could work," he said hopefully.

"I'll think about it."

It had been a long time since Ben had spent any real time with his father. When he'd gone home for his mom's funeral, there had always been people around and he hadn't stayed long. But being back in his childhood home with Sharon and her family made things easier somehow. For one thing, his father doted on Sally, and from all evidence the feeling was mutual.

The man he watched with Sally was not at all the man he remembered parenting him.

"You doing okay with the change in hospitals, son?" his dad asked one day as the two of them sat at the kitchen table eating lunch. Sharon and Malcolm had taken Sally shopping, and for the first time Ben found himself alone with his father.

"Yeah. It's good."

"Maybe now you'll think about settling down—raising a family?"

"I think about it."

"Good, because you'd make a good parent—not like me. You've got more patience than I did—and you're not as scared."

It was an odd thing for him to say, and for a minute Ben was at a loss for words. Uncomfortable with the situation, he laughed. "You? Scared?"

His father pinned him with those ice-blue eyes that so often had seemed to expect more than Ben could give. "Scared," he repeated, and Ben realized that those eyes weren't nearly as cold and penetrating as he'd remembered them.

"Of what?"

"Failing."

"You were the senior minister of one of the largest churches in the state," Ben reminded him.

His father waved his hand impatiently. "Not at my work. At home—right here. With you and your sister."

Ben was speechless. "I never knew," he said. "I mean, Dad, you were always so. . ."

"I know." He turned away and stared out the window. "I'm sorry, son. I really thought that I needed to be that way if you were going to be stronger than I was. But I see now that in many ways I still failed you."

"How can you say that? I have a successful practice, friends—a good life."

"And I'm proud of you, but I want more for you than a career. I want you to have faith. I want you to have a wife and family. I want so much for you, son." His father stood up and took his dishes to the sink. "Those things are the keys, son. I was never able to make you see that." He stood at the sink with his back to Ben, letting the water run.

When Ben saw the older man's shoulders start to shake, he went to him and placed his hand on his father's back, noticing for the first time how old and frail he'd grown in these last years. "You didn't fail me, Dad. If anything, I failed you."

"I wanted so much for you kids. . . ."

"We have it, Dad. Look around you. Sally alone is reason enough for you to believe that you and Mom did everything. . ."

"I miss her so much," he blubbered. "She was the rock in this house."

Ben was desperate to say anything that might give his father some comfort. "I was thinking maybe, if you feel up to it, we might all go for midnight services tonight. Remember how much Mom loved that?"

His father sniffed back the last of his tears and nodded. "I haven't been able to go since she passed."

"We'll go together—all of us—exactly like we did when you were in the pulpit."

And to his astonishment his father turned and gripped him in a bear hug. "I love you, son. Sally tells me I don't say that enough so I'll say it twice. I love you, and I couldn't be more proud of the way you've turned out."

Out of the mouths of babes, Ben thought as he returned his father's embrace. "Love you too, Dad."

And he realized that he truly did.

On New Year's Eve Rachel got a call from the hospital. It was so good to be back. She thanked God every day for the blessing of her work. She finished counseling the couple whose son was going into surgery and was escorting them to the waiting room when she saw Ben waiting for her.

"Do you have a minute?" he asked.

She nodded and said a few last words to the couple then returned to the chapel. Ben closed the door and leaned against it. "Hi. You're back."

"I am."

"To stay?"

"It was Justin's idea." She moved around the room, straightening the cushions and putting away some materials in the small closet. "Eileen tells me that you went to visit your father over the holidays."

"I did."

"How did that go?"

"We made our peace—found our way."

"I'm glad for you—and your father."

"I told him about you. He'd like to meet you, and Justin of course."

"You should invite him here for a visit."

She felt shy with him and was well aware that their conversation was stiff and uncomfortable.

"How's your arm?"

She glanced down at the cast. "It'll heal." She had run out of things to do and started to open the door.

But he took her hand between his to stop her from going. She did not pull away—or look up. "I missed you."

"I'm happy to be back here with everyone."

"Not working with you—although I missed that. I missed *you*, Rachel."

She pulled her hand free of his and placed her palm against his cheek. "I missed you as well."

He smiled. "Ever hear of the song lyrics, 'What are you doing New Year's Eve?'"

"Is that a question?"

"It's an invitation—to spend some time with me—to welcome in the New Year together."

"I promised Justin...," she murmured then shook her head.

"What? You promised Justin what?"

"Oh Ben, he misses his father and he has built up this idea—this fantasy—about you and me."

Ben covered her hand still resting lightly against his cheek and pulled it away so that he could kiss her palm. "Then it would seem that Justin and I are on the same page. I love you, Rachel. The one thing I realized when I saw my father was that I had allowed too much time to pass—lost too many chances to build memories with him—to know the man he is and the man he helped me become in spite of what I once thought. And then when I heard about you in that hole and realized that I might have lost you forever. . ."

Her eyes glistened with tears, but she was smiling. It was a little like seeing a rainbow through the clouds. "So?" he pressed. "You—me—Justin? A New Year and a new beginning?"

"Yes," she whispered as she stood on tiptoe and kissed him gently.

Ben drew her closer and deepened their kiss. "I love you, Rachel," he said. "I don't know how we're going to work things out, but that's a fact."

She pulled a little away and stroked his hair away from his forehead. "And we both know that facts are very important to you, Dr. Booker. But I'm curious. Facts must be provable. How do you intend to prove this one?"

He smiled. "I've learned that there are some things it seems even a doctor has to accept—on faith."

Epilogue

A lot of stuff changed after Justin and his mom got home from Costa Rica. She went back to work at the hospital and seemed happier than he'd seen her in a long time. Dr. Booker—Ben—started coming around just about every day. He even started attending services at the bigger Mennonite church where Justin had joined the youth group and made several new friends.

Then one day his mom asked him how he would feel if they both started going to that church regularly. She had made some friends there, the couple whose daughter had been killed in the car accident, for one. Next thing Justin knew, it was him, his mom, and Ben going there together just about every Sunday—unless Ben had to be at the hospital or his mom got a call.

After church, they would head over to Hester and John's place for a big lunch. Then one day Ben suggested they stop by his sister's house—Sally's house. That was pretty awkward at first, but then they were all sitting around the swimming pool and all of a sudden Sally pushed him in.

He came up sputtering and saw that everybody was laughing—even his mom had a smile on her face.

"That's for not trusting me to be your one true friend when you first got here," Sally said.

Justin had made his way to the side of the pool where she was standing, hands on her hips, looking pretty healthy for a kid that had been through everything she'd been through. He squinted up at her. "Hey, I apologized for that," he reminded her. "I put it in writing."

She grinned and squatted down to offer him a hand so he could get out of the pool. "Okay, so now we're friends?"

"Not quite," Justin said, taking her hand and pulling her into the water. He waited until she came to the surface, sputtering the way he had, with all the adults laughing at them. "*Now* we're friends."

But the most amazing change of all was the day that Ben asked him to go fishing with him.

"You mean just you and me?"

"Yeah. I've got something I want to talk over with you."

Justin wasn't sure where this conversation was headed so he simply shrugged. "Okay."

On the way to the park at the south end of Lido Key Ben asked him all about the trip to Costa Rica. While they staked out a spot on the pass that led from the bay to the Gulf and set up their equipment, Ben continued to praise Justin for the courage he had shown in deciding to join the mission.

"I'd do it again," Justin told him.

"Maybe next time I could go with you," Ben said.

"Sure."

They fished for a while in silence. A great blue heron stood a few feet to Justin's right, keeping an eye out for any possibility of snaring a baitfish. A motorboat came by, and the people on it waved like they were in a parade or something. And Justin was aware that Ben kept glancing over at him—like he had something to say but wasn't sure how to say it. Finally, he cleared his throat and slowly reeled in his line.

"Justin? What would you think about the idea that maybe your mom and I—I mean one day—might get married?"

Justin felt a grin start to spread across his face. "For real? Like we'd be a real family and everything?"

He liked the way Ben laughed. It was a sound that came

from somewhere deep inside him. He liked it even better when Ben reached over and ruffled his hair, the way his dad used to do when he was pleased with something Justin had done or said.

Justin thought about the promise his mom had made him when they'd left Ohio—the promise he had thrown back at her on a couple of occasions. If his mom and Ben got married they'd be a family again. "Did you ask her yet?"

"Sort of. But not officially. First I wanted to ask you how you'd feel about it."

Justin was suddenly cautious about saying too much before he had a chance to talk to his mom about how she felt. "I'm pretty sure she'll say yes."

"What do *you* say?"

"I guess it could work."

Ben offered him a handshake—an actual grown-up handshake—and Justin accepted. "We're going to be okay," Ben said as he cast his line far out into the water. He was smiling.

Justin couldn't seem to control the grin of pure joy that spread across his face. "Yeah."

Just like his mom had promised.

DISCUSSION QUESTIONS

1. What is Rachel's promise to Justin?

2. Why does she feel such a promise is needed?

3. How does she try to keep her promise in the early days after she and Justin arrive in Florida?

4. Twelve-year-old Justin and twelve-year-old Sally are struggling with different challenges—how does each face those challenges and deal with them as the story progresses?

5. What are your impressions of Darcy Meekins and how her story develops?

6. What role does faith play in the romance between Rachel and Ben—how does it keep them apart and how does it bring them together?

7. How does Rachel's daring rescue of the boy trapped underground change her relationship with Justin?

8. Almost all of the main adult characters are struggling with the choices they are making for themselves in terms of their careers and their personal lives—how do each of them (Rachel, Ben, Darcy and Zeke) meet those challenges?

9. One of the underlying themes of the book is the impact bullying can have. Other than Derek, who else in the story might be identified as a bully in certain situations and what are those situations?

10. Does Rachel truly live up to the promise she made to Justin after his father died and she decided to move them to Florida? If so, how, and if not, why not?

ANNA SCHMIDT is the author of over twenty works of fiction. Among her many honors, Anna is the recipient of *Romantic Times'* Reviewer's Choice Award and a finalist for the RITA award for romantic fiction. She enjoys gardening and collecting seashells at her winter home in Florida.